THE COLLECTED SHORT STORIES

OF BHARATI MUKHERJEE

In the series *Asian American History and Culture*, edited by Cathy Schlund-Vials, Shelley Sang-Hee Lee, and Rick Bonus. Founding editor, Sucheng Chan; editors emeriti, David Palumbo-Liu, Michael Omi, K. Scott Wong, and Linda Trinh Võ.

ALSO IN THIS SERIES:

Y-Dang Troeung, *Refugee Lifeworlds: The Afterlife of the Cold War in Cambodia*

George Uba, *Water Thicker Than Blood: A Memoir of a Post-Internment Childhood*

Long T. Bui, *Model Machines: A History of the Asian as Automaton*

erin Khuê Ninh, *Passing for Perfect: College Impostors and Other Model Minorities*

Martin F. Manalansan IV, Alice Y. Hom, and Kale Bantigue Fajardo, eds., *Q & A: Voices from Queer Asian North America*

Heidi Kim, *Illegal Immigrants/Model Minorities: The Cold War of Chinese American Narrative*

Chia Youyee Vang with Pao Yang, Retired Captain, U.S. Secret War in Laos, *Prisoner of Wars: A Hmong Fighter Pilot's Story of Escaping Death and Confronting Life*

Kavita Daiya, *Graphic Migrations: Precarity and Gender in India and the Diaspora*

Timothy K. August, *The Refugee Aesthetic: Reimagining Southeast Asian America*

L. Joyce Zapanta Mariano, *Giving Back: Filipino America and the Politics of Diaspora Giving*

Manan Desai, *The United States of India: Anticolonial Literature and Transnational Refraction*

Cathy J. Schlund-Vials, Guy Beauregard, and Hsiu-chuan Lee, eds., *The Subject(s) of Human Rights: Crises, Violations, and Asian/American Critique*

Malini Johar Schueller, *Campaigns of Knowledge: U.S. Pedagogies of Colonialism and Occupation in the Philippines and Japan*

Crystal Mun-hye Baik, *Reencounters: On the Korean War and Diasporic Memory Critique*

Michael Omi, Dana Y. Nakano, and Jeffrey T. Yamashita, eds., *Japanese American Millennials: Rethinking Generation, Community, and Diversity*

Masumi Izumi, *The Rise and Fall of America's Concentration Camp Law: Civil Liberties Debates from the Internment to McCarthyism and the Radical 1960s*

Shirley Jennifer Lim, *Anna May Wong: Performing the Modern*

Edward Tang, *From Confinement to Containment: Japanese/American Arts during the Early Cold War*

Patricia P. Chu, *Where I Have Never Been: Migration, Melancholia, and Memory in Asian American Narratives of Return*

Cynthia Wu, *Sticky Rice: A Politics of Intraracial Desire*

A list of additional titles in this series appears at the back of this book.

THE COLLECTED SHORT STORIES OF

BHARATI MUKHERJEE

Edited by Ruth Maxey

With a Foreword by Nalini Iyer
and an Afterword by Lysley Tenorio

TEMPLE UNIVERSITY PRESS   *Philadelphia • Rome • Tokyo*

TEMPLE UNIVERSITY PRESS
Philadelphia, Pennsylvania 19122
tupress.temple.edu

Copyright © 2023 by Temple University—Of The Commonwealth System
   of Higher Education
All rights reserved
Published 2023

Stories from *Darkness* are copyright © 1985 by Bharati Mukherjee. Used with the
permission of The Permissions Company, LLC on behalf of Nonpareil Books, an imprint
of David R. Godine, Publisher, Inc., godine.com. All rights reserved.

Permission to reprint the stories from *Darkness* in territories outside North America
granted by Clark Blaise on behalf of the estate of Bharati Mukherjee. All rights reserved.

All other stories are copyright © by Bharati Mukherjee. Used with the permission of Clark
Blaise on behalf of the estate of Bharati Mukherjee. All rights reserved.

Library of Congress Cataloging-in-Publication Data

Names: Mukherjee, Bharati, author. | Maxey, Ruth, editor. | Iyer, Nalini,
   writer of foreword. | Tenorio, Lysley A., 1972– writer of afterword.
Title: The collected short stories of Bharati Mukherjee / edited by Ruth
   Maxey ; with a foreword by Nalini Iyer and an afterword by Lysley
   Tenorio.
Other titles: Short stories | Asian American history and culture.
Description: Philadelphia : Temple University Press, 2023. | Series: Asian
   American history and culture | Includes bibliographical references. |
   Summary: "This volume is the first work of its kind to collect the
   complete short fiction of acclaimed author Bharati Mukherjee"— Provided
   by publisher.
Identifiers: LCCN 2022060143 | ISBN 9781439924457 (cloth) | ISBN
   9781439924464 (paperback)
Subjects: LCSH: East Indian Americans—Fiction. | LCGFT: Short stories.
Classification: LCC PR9499.3 .M77 2023 | DDC 813/.54—dc23/eng/20230320
LC record available at https://lccn.loc.gov/2022060143

♾ The paper used in this publication meets the requirements of the American National
Standard for Information Sciences—Permanence of Paper for Printed Library Materials,
ANSI Z39.48-1992

Printed in the United States of America

9 8 7 6 5 4 3 2 1

CONTENTS

Foreword • NALINI IYER	vii
Editor's Acknowledgments • RUTH MAXEY	xi
Introduction: Positioning Bharati Mukherjee's Short Stories • RUTH MAXEY	xiii

EARLY STORIES (1963-1966)

The Shattered Mirror (1963)

A Weekend	3
The Transplanted	15
The End of the Road	24
A Twilight World	36
Bless This Day	49

Debate on a Rainy Afternoon (1966)	58

MIDCAREER STORIES (1985-1988)

Darkness (1985)

Angela	71
The Lady from Lucknow	79
The World According to Hsü	87

vi | CONTENTS

A Father	99
Isolated Incidents	108
Nostalgia	118
Tamurlane	128
Hindus	133
Saints	141
Visitors	150
The Imaginary Assassin	160
Courtly Vision	167

The Middleman and Other Stories (1988)

The Middleman	171
A Wife's Story	185
Loose Ends	197
Orbiting	206
Fighting for the Rebound	220
The Tenant	231
Fathering	244
Jasmine	250
Danny's Girls	258
Buried Lives	264
The Management of Grief	281

LATE STORIES (1997–2012)

Happiness (1997)	299
Homes (2008)	305
A Summer Story (c. 2008)	312
The House on Circular Street (c. 2008)	326
The Laws of Chance (2011)	347
The Going-Back Party (2012)	355

Afterword • LYSLEY TENORIO	365

FOREWORD

NALINI IYER

I FIRST ENCOUNTERED Bharati Mukherjee as a short story writer when I picked up her award-winning *Middleman and Other Stories* soon after it won the National Book Critics Circle Award. I was a young graduate student from India just beginning her Ph.D. in English at a midwestern university. Mukherjee's stories and her biography resonated deeply with me and ignited a scholarly interest in South Asian American writing. I eagerly read all her works as they were published and, as a newly minted assistant professor, went to hear her read from her novel *The Holder of the World* (1993) when she came to Seattle on a book tour. By then I was aware of how controversial Mukherjee was among postcolonial scholars of Indian descent because of her political pronouncements about immigration and assimilation. Although I did not identify with her political perspective or her critiques of life in India, I also felt deeply that she was an important chronicler and critic of the Indian immigrant experience in Canada and in the United States. Although many postcolonial South Asian scholars rejected Bharati Mukherjee's writing, so many of my non–South Asian colleagues were including her works, especially *Jasmine* (1989), in their courses on feminist writing, immigrant fiction, and Asian American writing. Another equally popular text by Mukherjee in classrooms is "The Management of Grief," which has been anthologized and is thus easily accessible.

When I first read that short story, it was as a graduate student who had discovered a new writer. I still recall the shock of recognition and the simultaneous unfamiliarity that the story evoked in me. I was a college student in India when the crash of the Air India flight Kanishka made front-page news, and many publicly expressed their collective horror at the loss of 329 lives. In

viii | FOREWORD

an India still reeling from the government's raid of the Golden Temple in Amritsar and the assassination of Indira Gandhi in 1984, the bombing of that flight was one more horrific chapter in the history of postcolonial India. When I read Mukherjee's story, I discovered another perspective on the events—the experiences of Indo-Canadians dealing with a racist and pseudo-multicultural government and the heterogeneity of the Indo-Canadian immigrant experience. I also discovered the power of Mukherjee's writing. She captured grief, loss, and a history of alienation, while displaying remarkable narrative control of a short story. Although Mukherjee published two short story collections in her lifetime, her short stories remain underexplored by scholars.

Mukherjee's role in the formation of South Asian American writing as a distinct body of writing should not be overlooked. Mukherjee came from upper-middle-class India, born into an educated Bengali Brahmin family. She arrived as a graduate student in Iowa a few years before the passage of the Immigration and Nationality Act of 1965, which opened the doors for educated Indian immigrants who had been previously excluded or limited in their numbers by U.S. immigration laws. Although Indian students had been coming to American universities since the beginning of the twentieth century, most of them were men. Some of these male students, such as Dhan Gopal Mukerji and Taraknath Das, were also writers. These men wrote fiery political tracts and autobiographical works and Mukerji won a Newberry Medal in 1928 for his children's novel *Gay Neck: The Story of a Pigeon* (1927). A woman writer, Santha Rama Rau, had graduated from Wellesley in 1944 but traveled around the world before joining the faculty at Sarah Lawrence College in 1971. Dhan Gopal Mukerji saw himself as a spiritual ambassador for Hinduism, Taraknath Das fought against restrictive immigration laws, and Santha Rama Rau wrote extensively about cosmopolitan life. It was Bharati Mukherjee who wrote about the material and psychological challenges of Indian immigration to the United States. She explored such topics as racism, nostalgia, alienation, gendered violence, interethnic relationships, and the evolution of postcolonial India from the Nehruvian era to the age of neoliberal globalization. Her early novels, like *Wife* and *Jasmine*, examine the rage and violence that shapes the lives of Indian women immigrants. Her writing highlighted the messiness of being an immigrant and the constant search for home and belonging. Importantly, she fought for immigrant writers like herself to be recognized as American and challenged the equation of "American" with whiteness by rejecting hyphenated identities. Her writing paved the way for other women writers, such as Chitra Banerjee Divakaruni and Jhumpa Lahiri and many others, who are now publishing across many genres of fiction from literary novel to romance, mystery, young adult, and speculative fiction.

This collection, brilliantly edited by Ruth Maxey, whose scholarship on Mukherjee is well known, is an important contribution to South Asian American studies. Literary scholars focus on Mukherjee's novels, and a few works of scholarship have addressed some of her short stories. However, we need more scholarship on Mukherjee as a short story writer, and this volume paves the way for a systematic study of Mukherjee's craft and evolution as a short story writer and the relationship between her short fiction and her novels. Not only does this book bring together stories from previously published collections, it also offers us Mukherjee's unpublished M.F.A. thesis collection, *The Shattered Mirror* (1963), from the Iowa Writers' Workshop, and works from the end of her literary career. In bringing the whole collection together, Ruth Maxey offers scholars an opportunity to study Mukherjee's evolution as a writer in terms of themes, craft, and ideas through her short stories. Maxey's introduction provides a balanced and thoughtful assessment of Mukherjee's stories, including helpful connections between the stories and her novels.

This collection is also valuable for teachers gathering material for undergraduate or graduate courses on Asian American writing, immigrant writing, the short story, women's writing, and creative writing. In editing this volume, Ruth Maxey makes Mukherjee's writing easy to access and paves the way for a substantive reassessment of Mukherjee's contributions to ethnic American literature.

EDITOR'S ACKNOWLEDGMENTS

RUTH MAXEY

THIS BOOK HAS BEEN YEARS in the making, and I have many people to thank for its existence. First and foremost, I am enormously grateful to Clark Blaise for granting permission to reprint Bharati Mukherjee's short stories, kindly sharing her unpublished late stories with me, and willingly answering my questions about this material. I am very thankful indeed to Shaun Vigil and the team at Temple University Press for their belief in the project and their commitment to it throughout the publication process. Sincere thanks go to Nalini Iyer and Lysley Tenorio for their involvement in this book, thereby strengthening and enriching it. I also thank Celia Johnson, editor at Godine, for her enthusiasm, generosity, and open-mindedness in collaborating with me, and I thank Mukherjee's literary agent Lynn Nesbit and her colleague Mina Hamedi for their readiness to help with publication of this volume.

At the University of Nottingham, Judie Newman eagerly offered advice about the project at an early stage, while Peter Ling enabled me to pursue my research on Mukherjee at a crucial point. I am very grateful to them both. Bethany Davis, Digital Processing Coordinator Librarian at the University of Iowa, was extremely helpful in making Mukherjee's M.F.A thesis available to me. Allison Wagner, Senior Rare Books and Manuscripts Advisor, Archives and Special Collections, University of Calgary, readily afforded me access to unpublished documents from the Bharati Mukherjee archive during my research for this critical edition, part of my bigger project to uncover and do justice to the little-known writing of this pioneering, courageous author and make it available to a wider audience.

xii | EDITOR'S ACKNOWLEDGMENTS

A number of Mukherjee's stories first appeared in the following journals and magazines: "Debate on a Rainy Afternoon" in *The Massachusetts Review*; "Angela" and "A Wife's Story" in *Mother Jones*; "The Lady from Lucknow" in *The Missouri Review*; "The World According to Hsü" in *Chatelaine*; "Isolated Incidents" in *Saturday Night*; "Tamurlane" in *Canadian Forum*; "Saints" in *The Threepenny Review*; "The Middleman" in *Playboy*; "The Tenant" in the *Literary Review*; "Fathering" in *Chelsea*; "Happiness" in *DoubleTake*; "Homes" in *South Asian Review*; "The Laws of Chance" in *The Southampton Review*; and "The Going-Back Party" in *The Drum Literary Magazine*. I thank the editorial staff at many of these publications—Emily Smith Gilbert, Jordyn Kamil, Henriette Laziridis, Wendy Lesser, Jamie Maloney, Lou Ann Walker, and Emily Wojcik—for their patient assistance and heartfelt encouragement of this project.

I am thankful for the warm support of my friends, especially Caitlin, Logan, Maria, Penny, and Steph. And finally, I am extremely grateful to my family— my husband Olly; my parents, Robert and Carole; and my sister Margaret— for their consistent faith in Mukherjee's *Collected Short Stories* and for their unwavering support and firm guidance at some of the most challenging moments in this process. I close with deep gratitude to my very special children, Rebecca and Joe, for all their love and affection and for the many things I have learned from them both.

INTRODUCTION

Positioning Bharati Mukherjee's Short Stories

RUTH MAXEY

Mukherjee's Early Short Fiction

IN A CAREER SPANNING more than fifty years, Bharati Mukherjee (1940–2017), a pioneering Indian American writer, published an *œuvre* that included eight novels, two long works of nonfiction, and many essays and reviews. Born in Kolkata into a privileged Bengali Brahmin family, Mukherjee emigrated to the United States as a graduate student at the prestigious Iowa Writers' Workshop before moving to Canada to take up an academic position at McGill University in Montreal in 1966. After painful experiences of white racism in Canada, she returned to the United States with her husband, the white Canadian writer Clark Blaise, and their two sons in 1980.

The first South Asian American writer to receive real critical and popular acclaim, her fiction invited younger writers, especially Asian American women, to see themselves reflected on the page (Jacob 2019) and inspired them to produce their own novels (Hajratwala 2017). Particularly influential in this regard was *Jasmine*, a coming-to-America novel published in 1989 that has since been widely taught and researched. Mukherjee's long teaching career at a host of North American colleges and universities—including her distinguished professorship at the University of California, Berkeley, from 1989 to 2013—also empowered later generations of writers from diverse ethnic backgrounds (Kamali 2019; McCormick 2020; Tenorio 2020). Her work was driven by her thematic preoccupation with the browning of America via new Americans from untraditional regions—Asia, Africa, the Middle East, and South Amer-

xiv | INTRODUCTION

ica and the Caribbean—who arrived after the Immigration and Nationality Act was passed in 1965. When Mukherjee died, her life's work was celebrated by such leading U.S. and Canadian writers as Joyce Carol Oates, Margaret Atwood, Michael Ondaatje, Ann Beattie, and Amy Tan (McMurtrie 2017; Leith 2017).

Despite this undoubted success and influence, Mukherjee occupied a vexed position vis-à-vis Asian American literary studies, especially in relation to issues of assimilation, for much of her career. Her views on India and the United States—often expressed in impassioned, even opinionated, fashion—sometimes proved unpopular and contentious, especially among other Indian American critics and scholars who perceived her fiction and nonfiction as politically reactionary. An exemplary text in this regard is *Jasmine*, which, as a kind of love letter to American possibility, must apparently reject a benighted India in order to celebrate its protagonist's exceptionalism as a new American. Mukherjee's ideas about South Asia shifted in her later writing, however, and she set her final novel, *Miss New India* (2011), solely within this excitingly fast-paced, rapidly globalizing region.

In her long and prolific working life, Mukherjee wrote many short stories. Yet scholars have often overlooked this rich area of her literary production. To gain entry to the M.F.A. program at Iowa in the early 1960s, she sent in "six handwritten stories" (Mukherjee 2005)[1] and, as a new student there, short fiction was the form through which she learned her craft. The five stories that compose her M.F.A. thesis, *The Shattered Mirror*, submitted in 1963 and published here for the first time,[2] draw on the sense of place and epiphanies to be found within James Joyce's 1914 *Dubliners* stories (see Mukherjee n.d., 50). Each tale focuses on Indian and other Asian immigrants in the American Midwest and New York. As Mukherjee later recalled,

I became increasingly fascinated by foreign-student life around me. I soon found myself writing rapidly, feverishly, of the world of Indians, Chinese, Taiwanese, Singaporeans, Indonesians, Bulgarians, Sudanese. . . . We were graduate students, post-docs, student wives, refugees adrift in the U.S. Anecdotes overheard fused with imagined lives. Stories of uprooted lives became the focus of my M.F.A. thesis. From those years I evolved a credo: make the familiar exotic (Americans won't recognize their country when I get finished with it) and make the exotic—the India of elephants and arranged marriages—familiar (Mukherjee 2005).

Four of the five *Shattered Mirror* stories—"A Weekend," "The Transplanted," "The End of the Road," and "A Twilight World"—form a kind of short story cycle, since each is narrated through the same, usually third-person perspective: that of Tara, a world-weary Bengali graduate student navigating existential questions and states of ennui and depression as she finds her way at a midwestern university—most likely the University of Iowa—in the early 1960s. Protagonists called Tara reappear in Mukherjee's novels, *The Tiger's Daughter* (1971), *Desirable Daughters* (2002), and *The Tree Bride* (2004), and often operate as an authorial alter ego; the Tara of these early stories establishes that precedent.

"A Weekend" and "The Transplanted" recount Tara's ambivalence toward white Americans, who routinely fail to show any nuanced knowledge of India, and toward her fellow South Asian Americans. "The End of the Road" relates her ill-fated romantic relationship with Andrew Wong, a staid and much older Chinese academic at her university, a relationship that seems particularly doomed during the story's long restaurant scene in which, in a moment of double consciousness, Tara sees the couple through the eyes of the white waiting staff and other diners. In "A Twilight World," Tara reads to Al, a blind Latvian student, in a story about different forms of vision. "Bless This Day," the final story in Mukherjee's M.F.A. collection, is a more ambitious and experimental text in which the vexations of Naren—a young married Indian student, also resident in the Midwest, and father to a small son—are told through a shifting narrative voice of unspoken thoughts and interior monologue versus the conventions and niceties of spoken conversation. As Mukherjee later put it, "the writing rule that I was exposed to as an M.F.A. student and which I love to break is constancy to a consistent point-of-view. I want to capture the whole world in any novel or short story I might write, and the world speaks in many (delightfully confusing) voices" (quoted in "Writing Rules" 2011, 83). Beyond the protean voice of "Bless This Day," Mukherjee punctuates the story with many run-on words: "starkstaring," "failurewhipped" and "browfurrowing" (Mukherjee 1963, 111, 112) are just a few examples. They continue in the tradition of such earlier American writers as John Dos Passos and E. E. Cummings, while anticipating the neologisms of Cormac McCarthy's much later novel *The Road* (2006). In defamiliarizing such words, Mukherjee invites her reader to understand the fresh, confused reality of Naren's life in the United States. Mukherjee's next short story, "Debate on a Rainy Afternoon," became her first American publication, appearing in *The Massachusetts Review* in 1966. It takes place entirely in Kolkata and focuses on the frustrations and loneliness of Miss Ghose, a spinsterly schoolteacher.

xvi | INTRODUCTION

Darkness and the Evolution
of Mukherjee's Short Fiction

"Debate" and the *Shattered Mirror* stories reveal a young, inexperienced writer honing her literary techniques. It was not until Mukherjee returned to short fiction in the late 1970s that her stories took on a new level of Chekhovian sophistication and assurance. Although she did not then consider herself as a short story writer (Hertz and Martin 2018, 304), this was the period in which she wrote such tightly constructed, compelling, and haunting tales as "The World According to Hsü" and "Isolated Incidents," the semiautobiographical story "Hindus," and the ekphrastic thought experiment "Courtly Vision," her bid to capture a Mughal miniature painting in fictional prose. "Hsü" and "Isolated Incidents" appeared in North American literary journals and magazines, as did four other stories in the 1980s: "Angela," "The Lady from Lucknow," "Tamurlane," and "Saints." Yet Mukherjee initially struggled to publish these tales in book form. The same was true of a further four works of short fiction: "A Father," "Nostalgia," "Visitors," and "The Imaginary Assassin." Eventually all twelve stories were anthologized in her first collection, *Darkness*, published by Penguin Canada in 1985 and then for many years out of print. They remain underresearched by Mukherjee scholars, who have generally focused on *Jasmine* at the expense of much of her other writing.

The *Darkness* stories can be divided into tales of white racism toward South Asian Canadians—"Isolated Incidents," "Hsü," and "Tamurlane," three of Mukherjee's most visceral and painful short stories—and U.S.-based tales about new immigrants from India, Pakistan, and Bangladesh—"Angela," "The Lady from Lucknow," "A Father," "Nostalgia," "Hindus," and "Visitors"—and their children: "The Imaginary Assassin" and "Saints." For reasons of space, I will focus specifically on three *Darkness* stories here—"Saints," "Visitors," and "The Imaginary Assassin"—tales whose complex vision of twentieth-century U.S. life warrants further critical attention and analysis.

"Saints" takes up the point of view of Shawn Patel, the fifteen-year-old son of Manny, a successful Indian immigrant psychiatrist, whom we first met in the earlier *Darkness* story "Nostalgia." Told through the intimate, first-person voice of Shawn's thoughts, "Saints" uses a religious language that straddles India and the United States. Its title is taken from an Indian book sent to Shawn by his father "about a Hindu saint who had visions" (Mukherjee 1985, 153). By contrast, America is depicted as a predominantly Christian country with the protagonist speaking of his "state of grace" (146, 156). That sense of freedom links to Shawn's intermediate status: as an adolescent, he is "too old to be a pawn" between his separated parents yet "too young to get caught in problems of my own" (146). At the story's conclusion, his liminal status relates to his cross-dressing as he wanders after nightfall in his upstate New York college town, heavily made up and dressed in his mother's clothes, becoming "somebody else's son . . . a potentate in battledress" (156, 158). This semimedieval image recalls "Tamurlane," one of the Canadian-themed stories in *Darkness*, and Manny's own impulse to reinvent himself and perform an alternative identity in "Nostalgia."

Shawn's sense of self is also indeterminate because he is biracial, the son of an Indian father and a white American mother. He occupies a position alternative to either of them, although Mukherjee chooses not to explore this racialized identity in the story. Instead it is cross-dressing that becomes Shawn's means of self-expression: simultaneously covert, since he does it after dark, and attention-seeking, because he revels in the special sense that he is a "visionary" whom his mother is "really looking at. . . . Finally" (158). In this way, the story also thematizes the acts of seeing and looking. The question of Shawn's sexuality is left unspoken, although his most significant relationship in the story is with Tran, a Vietnamese American boy in his class, and just before Tran asks Shawn whether he can "sleep over in my room" (155), same-sex love is explicitly raised in relation to the Hindu saint from the book Manny sent Shawn. But unlike a later character, Rabi, who comes out as gay in Mukherjee's novel, *Desirable Daughters*, the idea of sexual difference is not properly developed.

Rather, Shawn is navigating his life as one of "the children of 1965" (Song 2013). Through an image of the school chess club, whose members have "names like Sato, Chin, Duoc, Cho and Prasad" (Mukherjee 1985, 151), and echoing the earlier "pawn" image, Mukherjee demonstrates the intellectual dominance of young, so-called model-minority Asian North Americans.[3] This idea is repeated when Shawn spies on a "junior high kid," the son of Dr. Batliwalla, who, "wanting good grades . . . studies into the night" (156–157). What is notable here is how Mukherjee also unsettles the notion of Asian American ascendancy. In part, she suggests this idea through Shawn's transgressive status and his embarrassed response to what he perceives as the vulgarity of his father's flashy, ostentatious immigrant success. The story also questions the power of young Asian Americans through Shawn's bald statement that Farelli, presumably an Italian American, is "the only *real American* in the [chess] club" (151; emphasis added). In historical terms, this claim is of course debatable, since some Americans of Japanese, Chinese, and Korean descent (possibly with names like the story's Sato, Chin, Cho) can trace their U.S. roots as far back as the early twentieth and even nineteenth century. But in a sociocultural sense, Mukherjee's message is clear: Asian American teenagers in the 1980s are—like Nafeesa and Iqbal, a wealthy and glamorous Pakistani couple based in Atlanta, in *xviii* | INTRODUCTION

another *Darkness* story, "The Lady from Lucknow"—"not-quite[s]" (25, 30; and compare Dlaska 1999, 86): provisional Americans who must employ their academic excellence as cultural and economic capital to secure their place in the nation.

"Visitors" also explores the differences between Indian immigrants and a post-1965, American-raised generation. Narrated in a present-tense, third-person singular voice, it reflects the idea that the protagonist Vinita's life in the United States is an unfolding story with an uncertain outcome.[4] Her ancestral India is not so easily forgotten, however. As with Angela in her eponymous story in *Darkness*, the South Asian homeland is remembered through terrifying flashbacks, this time to the Naxalite era, which saw the violent aftermath of a peasant uprising in spring 1967 in Naxalbari in the northern part of West Bengal. Thus, Vinita recalls the moment when she witnessed "a fresh, male corpse in a monsoon muddy gutter" and "undernourished child-rebels" with guns making their way onto her parents' lawn in Kolkata (Mukherjee 1985, 164). Mukherjee is on accustomed territory that—like her early novel *The Tiger's Daughter*, her memoir *Days and Nights in Calcutta* (1977, cowritten with Blaise), and "Hindus," another *Darkness* story—recalls her own life and those of her Bengali friends: Vinita even attended Loreto College in Kolkata, the author's alma mater. As several critics have observed, the story also echoes Mukherjee's second novel, *Wife* (1975), in its concern with the life of a young Bengali woman who has moved to America after an arranged marriage (see Nazareth 1986, 188, and Dlaska 1999, 78). Unlike Dimple Basu in *Wife*, however, Vinita is beautiful and privileged; she has married an affluent Indian executive, Sailen Kumar, a glittering example of the model-minority South Asian American; and she is living in an expensive condominium in Guttenberg, New Jersey, rather than being reduced to the transience of housesitting in New York City, as Dimple is.

As so often happens in Mukherjee's 1980s fiction, "Visitors" dramatizes the perils and excitements of "a new country with no rules" (Mukherjee 1985, 167), where the future threat of "betrayal" (163) and "disaster" (168, 176) haunt the present and Vinita must reconcile an American belief in "causality" (163) with her traditionally Indian sense of fate. She views with suspicion the idea that one can shape one's destiny because of the hubris this implies. When she encounters Rajiv Khanna, a handsome young graduate student at Columbia, who left Kolkata as an infant, her old-world "*deshi*" (168) customs clash with an unknown American social system. But this disjuncture only leads to misunderstanding as Rajiv, infatuated with Vinita, interprets her willingness to entertain a man she barely knows as proof that she reciprocates his feelings. Vinita's response is surprise because "she had assumed [Rajiv] . . . was the looter of American culture, not hers. And she had envied the looting. Her own transition was slow and wheezing. . . . This is America, she insists. . . . We are both a new breed, testing new feelings in new battlegrounds" (172). Her language is reminiscent of other *Darkness* stories: that is, the imagery of medieval and early modern battle and conquest implicit in "Tamurlane" and "Saints," imagery that is also figured through the leitmotif of Mughal painting in the collection, as seen in "The Lady from Lucknow," "Hindus," "Saints," and "Courtly Vision" (compare Gabriel 2005). This imagery also recalls another Indian-born protagonist—Leela in "Hindus"—who sees herself as a "blind and groping conquistador" in the United States (Mukherjee 1985, 141), since Vinita's metaphor of "looting" indicates the bold claiming of a nonancestral culture. But that dynamism is undermined by an overwhelming sense of confusion, and even illness, as suggested by a "transition . . . slow and wheezing" (172). "Visitors" ends with the clear message that Vinita's socially impeccable marriage is dull to its core and that the realization of this fact will lead her into untold dangers. Like Dimple, she questions the match when her husband is asleep, picturing his "fleshy lips [that] . . . flap like rubber tires" (176): an image that recalls, in a recursive sense, her confrontation with Rajiv and the "high-pitched angry words undulating from his fleshy lips" (172). The repetition of this pejoratively physical image suggests that neither man can provide Vinita with the excitement or sense of purpose she requires from her new American life. Mukherjee implies—in feminist terms reminiscent of *Wife* and the failed affair between Dimple and Milt Glasser, a young Jewish American man—that sexual attention is not the basis for an immigrant woman's self-realization.

In "The Imaginary Assassin," Mukherjee returns to second-generation Indian Americans and their feelings of pressure to succeed, but—reflecting South Asian American heterogeneity—she does so through a rather different ethnoreligious and U.S. regional lens than in "Saints." Like much of Mukherjee's later fiction, this is a California story. What distinguishes it from the later fiction and from the rest of *Darkness* is that it is about working-class Sikhs, the oldest South Asian community in America. Set in the late 1960s, the environment of "The Imaginary Assassin" is far removed from that of the Bengali Brahmin "new Americans" of "Visitors" or "Hindus." Indeed, as in "Tamurlane" and a later, *Middleman* story, "Jasmine," it reflects Mukherjee's bid to represent working-class subjects and subjectivity.

Assuming a first-person male voice as she does in "Tamurlane" and "Saints," Mukherjee depicts Gurcharan, the story's U.S.-born protagonist, as a backward-looking figure adrift in America. Rather than embracing contemporary realities, he clings to his grandfather's stories of India—especially a mythologized, counterhistorical account of assassinating Mahatma Gandhi—as pro-

xx | INTRODUCTION

tection against a mainstream culture of "rock stars and . . . movie stars" (190). Despite the decades-long history of Sikh settlement on the West Coast, Gurcharan does not feel connected to the world around him.

To an even greater extent than Shawn in "Saints," the protagonist rejects model-minority expectations and "the shabby diligence of [his parents'] . . . immigrant lives in Yuba City" (180). Specifically, Gurcharan has no interest in his father's dream for him to win a scholarship to study aerospace engineering at Caltech, following the success of a string of Asian American laureates: "Yee, Wang, Yamamota" (181). In line with his grandfather's bold, subversive story-within-a-story, Gurcharan is more comfortable with imagined violence, harboring "a secret fascination with a different kind of immigrant, Sirhan B. Sirhan" (181). This reference offers a revealing link to a fellow non-European immigrant, one who never became a U.S. citizen and was famously convicted of Robert F. Kennedy's assassination. It bridges the acts of political murder in the United States and India while gesturing more broadly toward those individuals who seek to overthrow regimes and must then face the consequences: specifically, Gurcharan's grandfather, whose anti-imperialism led to his imprisonment in 1926 after spitting at a British captain.

Formed by his boyhood experience of listening to his grandfather's tales, Gurcharan remains more connected to this inner life than to the outside world, appearing either unwilling or unable to disentangle the real from the imagined. When the story concludes with the ironic revelation that his family's unnamed houseguest is later arrested by Yuba City police on suspicion of being an actual assassin, Gurcharan has no interest in finding out the details. In a metafictional sense, "The Imaginary Assassin" is about the power of stories to confer a greater emotional truth than the banalities of everyday life. For Carole Stone, it even exposes "the poverty of imagination in American culture . . . and the loss of the old culture's storytelling as an impoverishment" (1993, 223). I would argue that the "truth" the story reveals is the desire to shape Indian history felt by Gurcharan's grandfather and the wish of his grandson to feel connected to his Indian heritage through the weight of that history. Mukherjee meanwhile asserts her own right to reimagine one of the most crucial moments—and figures—in modern Indian history (see Nyman 1999; and Maxey 2019b, 114n63).

Mukherjee's Critical Breakthrough:
The Middleman and Other Stories

After her struggles to publish the *Darkness* collection, Mukherjee believed that there was little appetite for her tales of new Canadians and Americans. Just three years later, in 1988, her second short fiction collection, *The Middle-*

man and Other Stories, was released in the United States by Grove Press. It was later published in Britain by Virago, but—like *Darkness*—remained out of print for many years and was only reprinted by Grove in late 2020. In contrast to *Darkness*, however, *The Middleman* won the National Book Critics' Circle Award for Fiction, with Mukherjee becoming the first naturalized U.S. citizen ever to achieve this accolade. Such recognition put her writing on the international literary map in unprecedented ways. And it is worth noting that she garnered this acclaim through a short fiction collection rather than a novel.

The eleven *Middleman* stories explore the experiences of new Americans of multiple ethnicities: Filipina ("Fighting for the Rebound"); Iraqi Jewish ("The Middleman"); Vietnamese ("Fathering"); Afghan ("Orbiting"); Indo-Caribbean ("Jasmine"); Bengali ("The Tenant"); Gujarati ("A Wife's Story," "Loose Ends," "Danny's Girls"); Nepali ("Danny's Girls"); and Maharashtrian ("The Management of Grief"). The narrative perspective in "Fathering," "Fighting for the Rebound," "Orbiting," and "Loose Ends" is white American. In a further story, "Buried Lives," Mukherjee imagines the misadventures of Mr. Venkatesan, a prim Sri Lankan Tamil high school teacher trying to get to Canada and ending up in Hamburg. Here I will discuss two stories in more detail, "Fighting for the Rebound" and "Fathering," because in these works Mukherjee assumes a hegemonic white male voice. Thus, she raises intriguing questions about white U.S. nativism through a kind of ethnic and gender ventriloquizing (compare McGurl 2009, 382).

In "Fighting for the Rebound," Mukherjee explores an Asian-white relationship through the eyes of Griff, a "low-level money manager" (Mukherjee 1989b, 80), who describes himself as "a solid, decent guy" (80) and feels both bewildered and blasé about Blanquita, his beautiful Filipina immigrant girlfriend. Her existence proved to be a landmark for some readers, even inspiring later literary depictions of Filipino Americans. Thus, Lysley Tenorio, an American writer of Filipino descent, Mukherjee's former student at Berkeley, and author of the afterword to this volume, recalls:

> it was . . . the first time that I encountered a Filipino character in contemporary fiction . . . and seeing her made me realize what I'd been missing in my own reading: the presence of Filipino characters . . . there weren't nearly enough, and though I didn't think of myself as someone who might actually contribute to that literary conversation, the stories in *The Middleman* made me want to try (2020, n.p.).

Returning to the story's white narrator, Griff's reliability is clearly at stake—as ever with first-person voices in fiction—and it is also difficult to warm to this *xxii* | INTRODUCTION

narcissistic character and to accept his apparently self-deprecating, yet actually self-valorizing, descriptions. As Susan Koshy (2004) has argued, Mukherjee problematizes certain U.S. interracial unions to a greater extent than others, often betraying more ambivalence toward alliances between white men and women of color than those involving a white woman and, for instance, a South Asian man (141). For Griff, Blanquita's physical perfection inspires poetic imagery, but his interior monologue also reveals his cynicism and emotional detachment from their relationship. His blend of desire and condescension aptly illustrates the interracial dynamic anatomized by Koshy. Yet it also replicates the fraught and contradictory position of Rindy, the white American female protagonist of "Orbiting," another *Middleman* story, toward her Afghan immigrant boyfriend, Ro. Just like Ro, Blanquita is spoken for in narrative terms, suggesting the enduring strength of white privilege and a neocolonial, infantilizing attitude toward people of color.

As with "Loose Ends," another white-focalizing story in *The Middleman*, there is a tension in "Fighting for the Rebound" between white male dominance and Mukherjee's implication that Asian immigrants are superior to native-born Americans. Hence, Blanquita is described as a "Third World aristocrat, a hothouse orchid you worship but don't dare touch" (Mukherjee 1989b, 83). Like Panna in "A Wife's Story," another *Middleman* tale, she speaks with an "eerily well-bred, Asian convent-schooled voice" (85). Dazzlingly multilingual, Blanquita grew up enjoying the benefits of her influential family in Manila. That past remains vague, however, and Griff takes her reluctance to discuss it with him as proof of her need to feel "less foreign" (81). Of course, she may also sense that her white Atlantan boyfriend would simply not grasp the complicated cultural context of her earlier life. She may resent her family's downward mobility in America, too: another recurring idea about new immigrants across Mukherjee's short fiction and one that challenges model-minority myths. The currently debased status of Blanquita's parents is in fact a bone of contention when Griff openly gloats about it. At the same time, the story reveals nothing at all about his own ethnic or family history, as though to make him a generic representative of white American manhood, a status with apparently no need to explain itself in cultural terms. But this withholding of information may also suggest that he has something to hide.

Like his fellow white southerner Jeb in "Loose Ends," Griff dislikes the feeling of mediocrity that new immigrants evoke in him and he tries to play down any cultural ascendancy Blanquita might enjoy. Thus, he focuses on the failures of her parents and on his girlfriend's flamboyance and glamor at the expense of her intellect, portraying her as manipulative, ill-informed, and emotionally dependent. He is quite capable of using language that recalls Jeb's:

"aliens" to refer to foreign medical staff in Atlanta (92) and the statement that "it's okay for a nation of pioneers to bully the rest of the world as long as the cause is just" (85). Yet Griff shows a subtlety beyond anything that Jeb, a brutish figure, can muster. In Griff's hands, the word "pioneer" is subject to semantic variation, as he celebrates the ethnic diversity of the Atlanta Farmers' Market: "just wheel your shopping cart through aisles of bok choy and . . . Jamaican spices . . . and you'll see that the US of A is still a pioneer country" (81). As distinct from Jeb's sexual violence toward Asian American women, Griff sees Blanquita as his sparring partner. The story even ends with what appears to be his choice of her over a series of white American women. Like "Orbiting"—and such other *Middleman* stories as "Fathering," "Jasmine," and "Danny's Girls"—his response suggests the preeminence of "new" over "old" Americans.

The couple's verbal jousting also relates to sporting metaphors. Griff and Blanquita are playing a game with one another, as they have with previous lovers, but Mukherjee is also rightly recognizing the centrality of sport within American life. "Fighting for the Rebound"—like "Orbiting"—is full of references to U.S. teams: football, baseball, and basketball. Mukherjee uses such shorthand as "Dolphins" (70) for the Miami Dolphins football team to display her knowledge of U.S. culture and to prove her American authenticity. Indeed, she asserts the right of an insider—historically a white male nativist like Griff—to produce fiction about national obsessions. Sport is also a distancing device as Griff bemoans Blanquita's complete lack of interest in watching U.S. sport on television, just as Rindy experiences awkwardness in "Orbiting" when Ro fails to follow the sporting references of her white brother-in-law Brent or her Italian American father Mr. deMarco.

In "Fathering," Mukherjee adopts a very different white male voice to explore an alternative kind of Asian-white encounter by examining the attempt by Jason, a white Vietnam veteran, to raise Eng, the young Amerasian daughter he has successfully traced and brought to the United States.[5] The story is exophoric, reflecting the American Homecoming Act that enabled the immigration of Vietnamese children of U.S. fathers: the act was passed in 1988, the year in which Mukherjee's *Middleman* collection was published. Jason is a very different kind of Vietnam vet than Jeb in "Loose Ends." Whereas Jeb boasts that, during his tour of duty, he was "the Pit Bull—even the Marines backed off. I was Jesse James hunched tight in the gunship" (45), Jason is deeply traumatized by the experiences he has tried to repress and cannot fully name. Thus, he states simply that "Vietnam didn't happen . . . Until Eng popped up in my life, I really believed it didn't happen" (117–118). Yet "it" has ruined his subsequent life and Eng did not exactly "pop up." Jason reveals that "I was track-

xxiv | INTRODUCTION

ing my kid" (118), although the presentist focus of the story—typical of much of Mukherjee's 1980s short fiction—elides the circumstances of this search and recovery. Like the traumatic flashbacks Eng experiences in her delirium or the actual details of Jason's combat duty, these circumstances may not bear too much remembering. Eng is nonetheless a physical reminder of the U.S. war in Vietnam, the "return of the repressed" for Jason (see Drake 1999, 78). Indeed, the young girl embodies the need for the United States to face up to the aftermath of its military conflicts overseas. As Mukherjee later put it in a 1997 interview, "the national mythology . . . my imagination is driven to create, through fiction, is that of the post-Vietnam United States" (quoted in Chen and Goudie 1997).

Whereas Jeb refuses the responsibilities of fatherhood in "Loose Ends," Jason welcomes them. But this position is complicated by the presence of twins by his ex-wife, whom he claims to have "brought up" in their early years (Mukherjee 1989b, 117) yet now feels little love for. The sex of Jason's other children is not even specified and they remain unnamed in the story. By contrast, Mukherjee's spotlight is resolutely Asian American with Eng and her right to a new life in the United States dominating the story. For Jason, Eng is "my baby . . . my kid" (118, 124): a point made repeatedly, as though he needs to remind himself of this new reality as he atones for his wartime guilt. His need to remember that Eng is his biological daughter may also arise from their many differences. Jason's knowledge of Eng's cultural and personal history appears almost as patchy and limited as the sporadic glimpses of it afforded the reader. And at an obvious racial level, she is—like Shawn with his parents in "Saints"— quite physically distinct from her biological father. He even observes that "I can't help wondering if maybe Asian skin bruises differently from ours, even though I want to say skin is skin; especially hers is skin like mine" (121). At the same time, her skin is clearly *not* like his, with Mukherjee exploring an issue that directly shaped her own life: being the parent of mixed-race children (compare Maxey 2012, 146–147). The language that Jason employs to discuss Eng suggests that he is actually much more disoriented by their differences than he cares to admit. Hence, she is described unattractively as having a "wild, grieving pygmy face" (123), she is a "frightened, foreign kid" (119), and the double meaning of "alien" is used. Having read a science fiction novel to his feverish daughter about "aliens [who] have taken over small towns all over the country. Idaho, Nebraska: no state is safe from aliens" (121), Jason later admits that "I can't pull my alien child down, I can't comfort her" (123). It is not clear that he is even aware of this slippage. "Alien," which legally means "a person who is not a [U.S.] citizen"—and is often regarded as a derogatory term (Maxey 2019a, 44n44)—is being used by a white American character

INTRODUCTION | *xxv*

troubled and baffled by the foreignness of a new immigrant, even when she is his own flesh and blood.[6] That said, the story ends in a spirit of hopefulness as Jason leaves home with Eng. Thus, his Asian American child triumphs over Jason's white partner, Sharon—now rendered a "wicked stepmother" figure— through this "dissolution of heterosexual coupling" (Drake 1999, 77).

Conclusion

After *The Middleman*, Mukherjee went on to produce some six stories at intervals from the late 1990s until a few years before her death. Her published stories from this period are "Happiness" (1997), "Homes" (2008)—which reappeared in a slightly different form as "The Laws of Chance" in 2011—and "The Going-Back Party" (2012); her unpublished later tales are "A Summer Story" (c. 2008, most likely unfinished) and "The House on Circular Street" (c. 2008). These tales have yet to be anthologized. Indeed, Mukherjee told interviewers in 2010 that her agent was "uninterested in floating a book of stories" (quoted in Field and Ticen 2010, 250).

In her late-career short fiction, Mukherjee returned quite explicitly to her ethnocultural roots, focusing on Bengali American lives and particularly those of women, sometimes left unnamed, as in "Happiness," "Homes," and "The Laws of Chance." Recalling her early novel *Wife*, these late stories imagine unfulfilling relationships in which a Bengali woman travels to the United States to marry a successful Bengali American man, only for the marriage to end in abandonment or death. But unlike the detached, third-person narrator of *Wife*, Mukherjee uses the immediacy of a first-person voice in stories of immigrant women boldly asserting their right to be in the new nation.

In "A Summer Story," "The House on Circular Street," and "The Going-Back Party," Mukherjee reveals the marital and familial tensions that lurk just beneath the surface of apparently comfortable and affluent Bengali American lives. Like "Saints" and *Desirable Daughters*, they show Mukherjee's interest in a younger U.S.-born generation achieving its place in America free from inherited cultural expectations. This terrain is familiar to readers of Jhumpa Lahiri's fiction, for instance, her Pulitzer Prize–winning first collection *Interpreter of Maladies* (1999) and her 2003 novel, *The Namesake*. But Mukherjee—the older Bengali American writer—puts her own distinctive mark on this material through well-paced, sometimes ethnographic stories, largely told in the present tense, that sometimes conclude with a twist—especially "The House on Circular Street" and "The Going-Back Party"—in otherwise open endings.

The Collected Short Stories of Bharati Mukherjee finally brings together in one place her thirty-five short stories, introducing readers to her lesser-known

xxvi | INTRODUCTION

short fiction and, for the first time, to her seven unpublished tales. There is a political need for anthologies of this kind, since short story collections in English are still too often the preserve of white male writers. It is therefore all the more important, necessary, and overdue that writers of color—especially women writers of color—should be recognized for their short fiction. And, after her tumultuous move back to the United States from Canada in 1980, Mukherjee was empowered to continue writing fiction by a book of collected stories. Clark Blaise has recalled that in 1983 "our friend and mentor Bernard Malamud sent his new book of *Collected Stories*. Bharati sat down to read it and suddenly saw that his characters were hers, his themes were hers" (Blaise 1999, 163). This pivotal encounter, anticipating her own impact on a younger literary generation, inspired her to produce eight new stories that later formed the bulk of *Darkness*.

Charles E. May (2017) has hailed Mukherjee as a "Writer of Perfectly Constructed Short Stories," and it is no surprise that many of her stories have been anthologized across a wide range of collections (see Maxey 2019a, 35). It is also no accident that, in his tribute to the writer after her death, May chose to discuss her most reprinted story, "The Management of Grief." This tale, which concludes the *Middleman* collection, is Mukherjee's best-known story: a beautifully constructed narrative of an Indian Canadian woman struggling with unimaginable loss. It has reappeared in at least sixteen anthologies since the late 1980s, touching readers and provoking them to learn about a real-life tragedy that, according to Mukherjee, was hidden for many years under the weight of white Canadian racism: the terrorist attack on an Air India flight from Canada to India in June 1985 in which 329 people, mainly Indian Canadians, lost their lives. Throughout her fiction, Mukherjee often gave voice to the voiceless, challenging readers to learn about the lives of others and, for a U.S.-born audience, to discard any nativist complacency they might harbor toward new immigrants: hence the implicit critique of mainstream America contained within her white-focalizing tales. This urgent need to speak for so-called "shadow" people or undocumented migrants (Mukherjee 1989a, 100) also confirms the ongoing political relevance of Mukherjee's short fiction in a world of rising ethnonationalism and xenophobia (compare Hebbar 2021, 269). "The Management of Grief," an unnerving and unforgettable story, fully achieves her educative, heuristic mission. On the basis of this work alone, she deserves to be honored for her vital contribution to the short story. But readers will find themselves provoked and moved by many other stories in this volume.

For instructors, *The Collected Short Stories of Bharati Mukherjee* can be productively used in a wide range of university courses from introductory to a more advanced level. Such courses might include contemporary fiction; postcolonial literature; world Anglophone writing; twentieth- and twenty-first-century American literature; Asian American literature and culture; the U.S. short story; immigrant, ethnic, and multicultural literature; and creative writing. The sheer multiplicity of these courses demonstrates the contemporary significance and reach of Mukherjee's short fiction and the many pedagogical opportunities it allows.

The formal complexity and sophisticated intertextuality of her stories will offer students abundant possibilities for interpretive comparison and close textual analysis. They will present instructors with exciting opportunities to pursue many theoretical and discursive approaches. The thematic richness of Mukherjee's short fiction and the provocative, often prescient, political questions it raises—about migration, gender, sexuality, race, ethnicity, nationhood, language, class, religious belief, coming of age, the workplace, and multiple histories and legacies (U.S., South Asian, colonial, postimperial, postconflict, terrorist)—will invite critical thinking through wide-ranging classroom discussions. As an invaluable literary resource, then, Mukherjee's *Collected Short Stories* should elicit lively interest from readers, writers, instructors, students, and scholars.

NOTES

1. Unfortunately, these stories have not turned up in any of my searches, including the Bharati Mukherjee archive in the Special Collections at the University of Calgary.

2. The final story in this collection, "Bless This Day," was—according to Mukherjee—"published in Kolkata's leading avant-garde magazine" (Mukherjee 2005). But the story has never reached a wider audience, and the provenance of its original publication is now unclear. The reasons that Mukherjee's other *Shattered Mirror* stories have never been published before now, either together or individually, are also uncertain.

3. Compare Blaise and Mukherjee 1987, 108; and for discussions of chess in Asian American writing, see Fickle 2014, 71–72, 80, and Ninh 2015, 123. On more recent Asian American dominance of the game, see Guillermo 2015.

4. Compare the use of the present tense in "Angela" and "Saints," and see Stone 1993, 217: "the present tense . . . suggest[s] the desire of [Mukherjee's] . . . characters to eradicate past lives and adopt new ones."

5. For a critique of artistic representations of this particular white-savior fantasy, see Houston 1997.

6. Da Zheng questions whether Eng is actually Jason's biological child; see Zheng 2000, 101–102.

REFERENCES

Blaise, Clark. 1999. Untitled introduction to "Bharati Mukherjee, 'Saints.'" In *The Workshop: Seven Decades of the Iowa Writers' Workshop*, edited by Tom Grimes, 163–164. New York: Hyperion.

Blaise, Clark, and Bharati Mukherjee. 1987. *The Sorrow and the Terror: The Haunting Legacy of the Air India Tragedy*. Markham, ON: Penguin.

Chen, Tina, and S. X. Goudie. 1997. "Holders of the World: An Interview with Bharati Mukherjee." *Jouvert* 1, no. 1, https://legacy.chass.ncsu.edu/jouvert/v1i1/BHARAT.HTM.

Dlaska, Andrea. 1999. *Ways of Belonging: The Making of New Americans in the Fiction of Bharati Mukherjee*. Vienna: Braumüller.

Drake, Jennifer. 1999. "Looting American Culture: Bharati Mukherjee's Immigrant Narratives." *Contemporary Literature* 40, no. 1: 60–84.

Fickle, Tara. 2014. "American Rules and Chinese Faces: The Games of Amy Tan's *The Joy Luck Club*." *MELUS* 39, no. 3 (Fall): 68–88.

Field, Robin C., and Pennie Ticen. 2010. "'We're Not Adversaries': An Interview with Bharati Mukherjee." *South Asian Review* 31, no. 1: 247–261.

Gabriel, Sharmani Patricia. 2005. "'Between Mosaic and Melting Pot': Negotiating Multiculturalism and Cultural Citizenship in Bharati Mukherjee's Narratives of Diaspora." *Postcolonial Text* 1, no. 2. http://postcolonial.org/index.php/pct/article/view/420/827.

Guillermo, Emil. 2015. "Drama and Intrigue as Asian Americans Sweep Chess Championship." *NBC News*, April 17. http://www.nbcnews.com/news/asian-america/asian-americans-sweep-top-three-national-chess-championship-n340571.

Hajratwala, Minal. 2017. "J Is for Juxtaposition: The Legacy of Bharati Mukherjee's *Jasmine*." *Los Angeles Review of Books*, February 6. http://blog.lareviewofbooks.org/essays/j-juxtaposition-legacy-bharati-mukherjees-jasmine/.

Hebbar, Reshmi. 2021. "Bharati Mukherjee's *Jasmine*: Unsettling Nation and Narration." In *Teaching Anglophone South Asian Women Writers*, edited by Deepika Bahri and Filippo Menozzi, 269–275. New York: Modern Language Association.

Hertz, Judith Scherer, and Robert K. Martin, eds. 2018. *E. M. Forster: Centenary Revaluations*. Toronto: University of Toronto Press.

Houston, Velina Hasu. 1997. "To the Colonizer Goes the Spoils: Amerasian Progeny in Vietnam War Films and Owning Up to the Gaze." *Amerasia* 23, no. 1: 69–84.

Jacob, Mira. 2019. "Finding Nuance and Much-Needed Relief in the Writing of Bharati Mukherjee." *Literary Hub*, December 17. https://lithub.com/finding-nuance-and-much-needed-relief-in-the-writing-of-bharati-mukherjee/.

Kamali, Marjan. 2019. *The Stationery Shop of Tehran*. London: Simon and Schuster.

Koshy, Susan. 2004. *Sexual Naturalization: Asian Americans and Miscegenation*. Stanford, CA: Stanford University Press.

Leith, Linda. 2017. "Author Bharati Mukherjee Wrote of Immigrant Lives." *Toronto Globe and Mail*, February 10. https://www.theglobeandmail.com/arts/books-and-media/author-bharati-mukherjee-wrote-of-immigrant-lives/article33990951/.

Maxey, Ruth. 2012. *South Asian Atlantic Literature, 1970–2010*. Edinburgh: Edinburgh University Press.

———. 2019a. "Bharati Mukherjee and the Politics of the Anthology." *Cambridge Quarterly* 48, no.1: 33–49.

———. 2019b. *Understanding Bharati Mukherjee*. Columbia: University of South Carolina Press.

May, Charles E. 2017. "A Tribute to Bharati Mukherjee." *Reading the Short Story*, February 8. http://may-on-the-short-story.blogspot.com/2017/02/a-tribute-to-bharati-mukherjee.html.

McCormick, Chris. 2020. "On Mentorship: Chris McCormick Remembers Bharati Mukherjee." *PowellBooks.Blog*, January 13. https://www.powells.com/post/original-essays/on-mentorship-chris-mccormick-remembers-bharati-mukherjee.

McGurl, Mark. 2009. *The Program Era: Postwar Fiction and the Rise of Creative Writing.* Cambridge, MA: Harvard University Press.

McMurtrie, John. 2017. "Bharati Mukherjee, Chronicler of Indian American Life, Dies at 76." *San Francisco Chronicle*, February 1. https://www.sfchronicle.com/books/article/Bharati-Mukherjee-who-wrote-of-Indian-American-10900596.php.

Mukherjee, Bharati. n.d. "On Being an American Writer." In *Writers on America*, edited by George Clack and Paul Malamud, 50–53. Washington, DC: U.S. Department of State, Bureau of International Information Programs.

———. 1963. *The Shattered Mirror.* M.F.A. thesis, University of Iowa.

———. 1985. *Darkness.* Markham, ON: Penguin.

———. 1989a. *Jasmine.* London: Virago.

———. 1989b. *The Middleman and Other Stories.* London: Virago.

———. 2005. "Autobiographical Essay." *Encyclopedia.com.* https://www.encyclopedia.com/arts/educational-magazines/mukherjee-bharati-1940-0.

Nazareth, Peter. 1986. "Total Vision." *Canadian Literature* 110 (Fall): 184–190.

Ninh, Erin. 2015. "Model Minority Narratives and the Asian American Family." In *The Cambridge Companion to Asian American Literature*, edited by Crystal Parikh and Daniel Y. Kim, 114–128. Cambridge: Cambridge University Press.

Nyman, Jopi. 1999. "Resisting the Resistor: Bharati Mukherjee, Memory, and the Murder of Gandhi." In *Postcolonialism and Cultural Resistance*, edited by Jopi Nyman and John A. Stotesbury, 158–167. Joensuu, Finland: Faculty of Humanities, University of Joensuu.

Song, Min Hyoung. 2013. *The Children of 1965: On Writing, and Not Writing, as an Asian American.* Durham, NC: Duke University Press.

Stone, Carole. 1993. "The Short Fictions of Bernard Malamud and Bharati Mukherjee." In *Bharati Mukherjee: Critical Perspectives*, edited by Emmanuel Nelson, 213–226. New York: Garland.

Tenorio, Lysley. 2020. "Lysley Tenorio: Bharati Mukherjee as Catalyst and Inspiration." *Library of America.* https://www.loa.org/news-and-views/1725-lysley-tenorio-bharati-mukherjee-as-catalyst-and-inspiration.

"Writing Rules I Break." 2011. *The Southampton Review* 5, no. 1 (Spring): 83.

Zheng, Da. 2000. "Ambiguity in Bharati Mukherjee's 'Fathering.'" In *Asian American Studies: Identity, Images, Issues Past and Present*, edited by Esther Mikyung Ghymn, 101–111. New York: Peter Lang.

THE COLLECTED SHORT STORIES

OF BHARATI MUKHERJEE

EARLY STORIES

(1963-1966)

The Shattered Mirror (1963)

Debate on a Rainy Afternoon (1966)

The Shattered Mirror (1963)

A Weekend

I KEEP TELLING MYSELF that really nothing in my life has changed. I am here. I told my parents I had to go away for a while. That's why I am here. Weatherington looks just the way it did in the college catalog I used to read in my room at home. The pictures always set me dreaming in those days. Funny how the campus doesn't seem more real than the pictures. It's all translated into stone and bricks now, into dark arches and ivy. But it's no more real than my old dreams.

Yes, I am here. I am sitting at my desk in my room in the dorm. The *French for Beginners* is open at a page of irregular verbs.

J'irai	nous irons
tu iras	vous irez
il ira	ils iront

I shall go, you will go, but how shall I go? In the dreamshapes of childhood, I read I will go, I will go, when will I go? But no, nothing has changed in my life.

I must learn the French verbs for Mademoiselle Dubois' class tomorrow morning. Tomorrow will be Tuesday. I know it will be like any other Tuesday. Weatherington has not changed, Turner Hall is still the same, my room is still the same. The apple I saved from dinner a whole week ago is squatting like a paperweight on a couple of unanswered letters. Well, maybe the apple *has* changed a little. Its skin seems to have darkened in patches, and I think it is beginning to smell faintly. But, at least, the drapes I am staring at have not changed. They are the same ones I have been staring at every evening since last fall. I cannot stand dirty burlap drapes. I really ought to change them. I just have to go down to the Foreign Students' Exchange and pick out new ones. I guess I shall one of these days.

Honestly, I don't think I've changed either. I'm feeling a bit restless, that's all. Usually, when I get kind of jumpy like this, I stack half a dozen records on the hi-fi, switch off all the lights, and sprawl on the bed. I love soft jazz and Johnny Mathis. But it doesn't seem to work tonight. I have run through both my albums and Angie's, too. Angie is a plump blond and lives in a double across the hall. She has been pestering me all day to tell her what happened during the weekend. There is nothing to tell, nothing happened. A weekend can't matter that much, I'm sure. It must be something more deep-rooted than that; or do I mean more rootless?

"What's the matter, Tara?" she keeps asking. "I bet something happened in New York. Something traumatic." Life doesn't happen to me in traumas. Maybe that's the trouble. It creeps up to me in mean little wrinkles and crow's-feet.

No, nothing happened this weekend, but Angie won't believe me. She came into my room again about half an hour ago, wearing her hideous pink bathrobe, the one with the big green flower running up her back.

She sat on the bed, and said, "I can't figure you out anymore, Tara. You used to be so peppy beginning of this semester. And now . . . you act so . . . so sort of indifferent to everything. Like you wanted to build a wall around you or something."

Angie's a good friend of mine. I had half a mind to tell her about dreams and giants. It was on the tip of my tongue, ready to roll off. I wanted to explain it all to someone so that I might understand it myself. She kept staring at me, her eyes curiously taut. She smelt of cold cream and ink and stale deodorant. That depressed me suddenly. I knew she wouldn't understand. I had quite a time getting rid of her.

I am not sure when I had my first suspicion that I had to get away from everything I knew for a while. I remember looking into the gilt-framed mirror in the hall at home and thinking something is wrong, something is dreadfully wrong with this quick image on the glass. Or whenever I caught my own reflection on someone else's spectacles, I used to pause in the middle of a sentence and wonder, Is that me? Is that really me? Lying on my stomach in the long hot Calcutta nights, I dreamed of being a hero. I entered rooms, and people paused to stare, freezing their rhythm of action and talk. No, I don't think Angie would have understood those gigantic dreams.

What could I have told Angie about the weekend except that, after I left her, I rode the subway, had lunch, went to the museum and to a crazy party? And that I was lonely, and vaguely defeated. I was lonely even then in those dreams I loved, lonely and proud and sad. I looked into the faces of men and women, and they were the faces of dwarfs, grained with age and mediocrity.

Sitting in the walled garden at home that summer afternoon last year, with Father on one side and Mother on the other and the dog panting at my feet, I thought how secure the garden is, how beautiful and soft and green. And I knew, in that knifeblade moment of recognition, my everyday world was like the garden, beautifully arranged, and soft, and green. As I turned first to my parents, then to the dog, and then objectively to myself, I thought what a pretty picture we made, so peaceful and affectionate and safe. So I told them I must go away, not for long, just a few years probably, I told them I must go away before it is too late.

I remember Mother leaning over the teacups, beautiful, all roses and pearls and expensive perfume, wanting to know why, why, why. Because I want to. And Father had slipped a dead curling leaf into the pages of his business journal and blinked like the ghost of a giant. It's strange how I remember that leaf. I wanted them to understand. I said it was something like running off to the sea, like signing up with the ship's captain and getting caught in typhoons and being shipwrecked. He wanted to know what I was running away from. And I was shocked and hurt, he had got it all wrong. I wasn't running away. On the contrary, I wanted, desperately, to discover new green islands. He said, once I start running, I'll never be able to stop. But he was wrong. There are walls everywhere. I cannot run away.

Well, Angie and I went to New York last weekend. We usually do every other weekend. We took the school coach in the morning, and in less than two hours we were on the doorstep of the Lexington Hotel.

"Hey, look who's here!" Angie whispered to me the moment we walked in through the doors. "Your old faithful as faithful as ever."

She has a nasty habit of whispering in my ear, though most of the time I can't make out what she says.

I checked in at the school club and left my overnight case upstairs. Then Ashoke and I went out into the street. Oh, I suppose I should have explained that Ashoke is the old faithful. He isn't good-looking; he's pretty ugly, really, I guess. He is tall and thin and owl-eyed. I've gotten sort of used to his face now, so it doesn't bother me. But he certainly does not look like a giant. That's because he does not think like a giant. Ashoke is twenty-three, and a grad student at NYU. In fact, he was twenty-three last week, but I forgot to send him a birthday card. I just can't seem to remember people's birthdays and anniversaries. Angie says it's because I don't try to. She thinks I am horribly unfeeling, that I don't care for people. But that's not true. I'm sure it's not true. I do care. Sometimes I even remember an anniversary. But I don't do anything about it. It's almost as if some ancient enthusiasm, some vintage faith has gone away forever; as if I've suddenly discovered, or perhaps at last acknowledged, that there are no giants in this age. So now I wear this dwarfish armor of aloofness, and I say I do not care.

I met Ashoke two summers ago when he came to India for the vacation after four semesters of school abroad. His father owns a textile mill in Ahmadabad, bigger and better than anyone else's, he used to brag. He told me he was home to bag his first tiger. Of course, I knew he was bluffing to impress me, he's the kind of chap who wouldn't set up mousetraps, let alone kill tigers. I thought he was a pretty good sport except for the bluffing. That was pathetic. But in a way it was wonderful, too, because I could tell it was his way of showing he was outside the humdrum shabbiness of life.

Angie calls Ashoke my old faithful because he comes to meet me whenever I decide to come to New York. I just have to call him long distance (I usually call collect), and he comes rushing to the Lexington Hotel to wait for the bus. I suppose I should have been happy to see him, but I can't honestly say I was; though I wasn't unhappy to see him either. We went out through the revolving doors of the hotel, and Ashoke raised his arm as if to call a cab. Then he felt in his billfold and asked me if I minded taking the subway. I said I didn't.

So we ambled down the sidewalk, Ashoke shortening his stride to match mine, and he asked me what I would like to do.

"Anything you like," I answered.

He seemed rather put out by this, as if I wasn't being very obliging. He stood for two full minutes on the sidewalk. He has a way of stopping short and twisting the top button of his coat when he is trying to think. Then he suddenly looked very bright and said, "Let's go sightseeing."

"Okay," I agreed.

I couldn't see why we should go sightseeing when this was my umpteenth weekend in New York (and I had already seen most of the places one is supposed to, anyway). I had known somewhere in the dark whorls of my brain Ashoke wouldn't be able to think of something new and exciting. But then I couldn't see why we shouldn't either. So I shrugged my shoulders inside my coat and we raced down the steps of the subway station.

When we had sat down in the lurching car, Ashoke started cross-examining me about my midterm grades. He considers himself my unofficial self-appointed guardian.

"How did you do in the test on Chaucer?" he asked me.

"Oh, all right," I replied. I don't like talking about school during weekends, especially in a noisy subway.

"What do you mean, all right?" he asked, mimicking me. "Did you get a C or a B?"

"A," I told him.

Ashoke scratched his ear in exasperation. I could tell from the way his mouth was set he thought I was horribly unambitious, that I got things rather easily. He himself is always going for bigger and better things. To him that's a value in itself. The old dreamer in me sympathizes with him. I quicken at his need to soar above the pettiness and the feebleness of our mediocre lives. And the poor fellow thinks I'm not ambitious, I want to curl cozily in the rut, I want to relish the flat taste of ordinary lives! I had to laugh at that, it was so absurd. Ashoke has no sense of humor. He doesn't like people giggling next to him when he hasn't caught the joke himself. So he sat in a huff, ignoring my existence, and read all the ads on the wall opposite. But it wasn't so funny really. I could have told him his dreams were useless. There was nothing grand or majestic about him. He was not shaped for extremes. One day, at the height of his dreams, he would discover walls. And then, only then, he would know the new green islands are not for him to discover. Then his dreams would peter out into middle-aged respectability. But sometimes, sitting at a club started by the British, or while dictating a letter to his secretary, he would meet a dream-shred of long ago, and it would tease him, torture him with its promise of escape. For a moment, I was sorry for him, because he, too, was condemned to be a giant in his visions.

I turned to Ashoke in pity. He had a pleased, sleek look on his face, the look of a man who has forgiven great wrongs done him. It annoyed me. Then Ashoke launched into a long tale about his thesis. He is majoring in electronics, and he talks about the subject with an almost religious fervor. I have forgotten the title of his thesis though I've been told it many times. I couldn't hear very well what Ashoke was saying, so I amused myself by sneaking stares at an old woman sitting across the aisle, casually sucking her gums. She had a huge Gimbels sack propped between her legs. Her legs were sort of funny, long spindly sticks ending in massive furlined boots. Unfortunately, she left two stations after I had discovered her. I began to get bored with the ride after that.

"Let's get off at the next stop," I whispered to Ashoke. I must have spoken in the middle of one of his sentences. He pushed his glasses well up the bridge of his nose with that hurt look he has.

Then he said, "All right, if you want to."

I swayed and clutched my way to the sliding doors, waiting for them to open. It felt good to be up in the cold daylight again.

We were strolling aimlessly down the sidewalk, just drifting with the Saturday morning crowd, when Ashoke spotted a newsstand. He immediately halted and started to go through the papers. He has an irritating habit of scanning each of the separate piles and then buying only one newspaper. While he was fumbling with dimes and nickels, a long-haired man sidled up to him and touched him on the shoulder. Ashoke introduced the fellow to me right away, but I could not quite catch his name. I never do when I am introduced. Angie says it's because I don't want to hear it. The man was, apparently, an old neighbor of Ashoke's during his Washington Square days. The two of them started talking, and I watched, in despair, the mild stooping man snatch greedily at atoms of sympathy. It was tragic, this man, this greed, this preying on affection. He seemed beaten from the start, not daring to dream big dreams. And I thought he would never find an escape, not even in rare moments after all dreams have been found wanting, no catastrophes, no romance. I did not want to listen to him anymore, it made me so sort of sad.

I started to edge away toward the bookstand. Ashoke noticed I was drifting off, and, from the way he looked at me, I knew he wanted me to stay and be polite to his friend. But I just couldn't bear the man's miserable orgy of self-pity, and so I pretended I had a book to buy and concentrated on the paperbacks.

The revolving rack was stacked with flashy covers. I twirled it around to amuse myself. There was quite an intriguing one in the top row. It showed a pouting sexy woman in a pink negligee, sitting at a littered dressing table. A man in blue shorts stood behind her, a towel slung across his muscular shoulders. They both looked angry as if they had been fighting with each other. I flipped through the first few pages, but they were a bore. I picked out some more books. Then I grew tired of the whole thing. So I slipped all the paperbacks back in their places and joined Ashoke again. His friend had vanished by that time.

Ashoke was peering at me shyly from behind the thick lenses of his specs. He held something awkwardly behind his back. It turned out to be a small box of candies with an Italian name on the lid that he must have bought while I was pretending to look at books. He likes to give me surprise gifts. I should have been flattered at his thoughtfulness. But I am afraid I wasn't. In fact, I could hardly bring myself to say an enthusiastic thank you. And that's funny in a way, because I love candies, I really do. And I thought, with sudden pain, there's something wrong with me, something dislocated, or perhaps missing. I wanted to be happy at receiving the gift.

Well, Ashoke must have been hungry by then. He kept looking at me like he wanted me to open the box of chocolates. But I wouldn't. Maybe, if he had come right out and asked me to, I would have. But I guess he wanted me to offer him one without being told to, like I really wanted to share the candies with him. I don't much like to give or take anything from anyone. I suppose I must like being sort of cut off from the rest. But, to tell you the truth, that depresses me, too.

I just kept walking with my head hunched sideways, making out like I was really interested in the shop windows all done up for Christmas. Finally Ashoke asked me if I would like to go to Toffinetti's for lunch, or would I rather grab a hamburger at a drugstore and visit the Guggenheim?

"Anything you like," I replied.

And I really meant it, too. He seemed sort of annoyed at this, like couldn't I please take sufficient interest to help him decide one way or another. He is the kind of chap who wants to plan every moment of his life and then stick rigidly to the plan. He is disgustingly well-organized most of the time. Of course, in the end, he made both our minds up, and in another quarter of an hour, I found myself perched on a high stool upholstered in blue plastic, munching hot dogs.

Then we took the bus to the Guggenheim. Ashoke thinks it's a great place. I think it's all right myself, but I just can't understand his pilgrimage attitude at all. He stood reverently in front of colossal blotches of blues and greens. I glanced around at the people on our sloping floor. There were only three elderly ladies near us, the white-gloved, sternly-hatted, hushed-voice kind.

"What's the matter?" Ashoke wanted to know. "Don't you like it?"

He gave me a tremendous poke in the ribs, embarrassed at my unaesthetic response. Naturally I yelped. The three ladies looked up in our direction and then quickly looked away again. Ashoke blushed a purplish brown—he looks terrible when he is embarrassed—and tried to cover up his awkwardness by explaining the painting to me. He has a thin, tinny voice. It made my mind awfully sore. Then he got all carried away by the sound of his own explanation. It made me feel a bit sad, he was so enthusiastic about it all. I couldn't see how one could get so worked up about a few colors. I wished I could so that I wouldn't feel so left out like I do in front of a canvas. I just stood there, depressed and self-conscious, turning my head from the colored squiggles to Ashoke's mouth sloping fast in different angles as he talked, and back to the squiggles and blobs again.

We spiraled our way down to the main floor. I stopped in front of a sculpted woman. There was something about it I liked. I tried to figure out what kind of a woman the sculptor had had in mind; she must have been a very womanly woman. I felt, instinctively, it was a dream captured in stone. It was a gigantic dream. There was something truthful and direct about it, something that stood apart from the smallness and meanness of the everyday. And I thought how lucky the man who had made it was, his dream would be his forever.

"Very moving, isn't it?" Ashoke remarked.

I wish he wouldn't say things like that. It spoils it all for me.

"It's sort of all right," I said.

I ran an exploratory finger up the massive female leg of polished stone. The commissionaire[1] directed what he must have thought was a forbidding stare

---

1. British word for "guard" or "attendant."—Ed.

at me. So, as a matter of honor, I returned his stare. The fellow turned a funny color and drifted away. You could tell he didn't know a thing about art and that he didn't really care about it either, at least not in any aesthetic sense. But he just didn't want anyone messing up the art pieces in his charge. That made me giggle. But then, I thought, he was at least serious about his job. He was all, oh, all involved, if you know what I mean, in keeping people away from his precious sculpture. That sort of depressed me.

"Let's get out of here," I said to Ashoke.

"Don't tell me you're bored already," he said. But he followed me out of the building all the same.

We walked through Central Park for a while. It must have snowed while we were inside, because there was a soft white dusting of flakes on the branches and on the ground. It wasn't too cold yet, just right for a walk, and I thought how nice it would be just to keep walking for a long, long time, without going anywhere or even wanting to go anywhere. I felt Ashoke surreptitiously take hold of my hand. It spoiled the lovely feeling somehow. I don't mean I was revolted by it; but I wasn't thrilled either. I merely wanted to stroll through the park without anyone getting all emotional about it, and now I didn't want to walk anymore.

Suddenly Ashoke looked at the black dial of his watch and exclaimed, "Hell! We'll have to hurry to the apartment. I'd forgotten all about that goddam party." I am sure he thinks it's smart to swear.

We took a cab to Fifty-eighth Street, and Ashoke almost forgot to tip the cabbie in his hurry. I helped him and his roommates (and their current girlfriends) to convert the dining table into a bar and arrange the plates of hors d'oeuvre on the sideboards. In fact, I was quite enjoying myself fussing around in the kitchen. There were no mirrors here to make me stop and wonder, is that me, is that really me, no intense talk to mark the distance between individuals. We worked with our hands, rhythmically, efficiently, happily.

But Ashoke came and spoiled it all.

"What's the matter?" he teased. "You're being strangely helpful this evening."

Of course, I immediately turned off the gas and retired to the living room in a huff. The rhythm had stopped. I couldn't be an unthinking part of the group again. Besides, I don't like to feel I'm being consciously useful to anyone. That's just one of those things about me. I mean, after all, we are all useless, aren't we? I mean to ourselves and to everyone else. Very often I feel kind of superfluous. Sure, I sometimes pretend I'm absolutely indispensable to the world, but that's all rot and I know I'm only making believe. Well, most of the time

I figure the only way out is to take nothing and give nothing. And I say that's fine, that that's all I want.

It was a pretty wild party really when I come to think of it. I kept a sharp watch over my glass of orange juice. Is it against your religion, the kids wanted to know; they were all delightfully high. No, I told them, it was just a matter of habit. Stop being a party pooper, they laughed, you've got to take risks, baby, *c'est la vie, la vie.* And I hugged my orange juice, knowing I could never take big enough risks, knowing I had the strength to dream but not the drive to make them real. I sat in my corner defending myself; I said I liked champagne and stuff like that; I said, to myself, they are drunk, they don't know what they are talking about. But, you know, when you're the only sober person in a party, it can make you feel very lonely.

In the middle of the evening, a Princeton junior came and sat next to me in the chair actually meant for one. He had dead-fish-on-marble-slab eyes.

"Hey, do you speak Hindu?" he drawled.

"Hindi," I corrected automatically.

"I think your country's great, just great. By the way, do you know any maharajahs?" No, I told him, I did not know any maharajahs.

"What made you come so far for school?" he asked me, playing with the end of my sari, the part that falls over the left shoulder.

I thought of explaining it all to him, the need to discover new gardens that I myself would landscape, which would be soft and green and beautifully arranged. I thought I'd tell him even though he was a stranger. Sometimes it is easier to confide in strangers, for you can tell them things without feeling self-conscious, safe in the thought you'll never see them again. I looked him in the face. I wanted to tell.

"Can I get you a drink?" he asked. He wasn't really interested in answers.

"No, thank you," I replied. And I knew I could not even try to tell him.

Then he asked me what I thought of the Common European Market, and his voice was all sort of italicized. I told him I didn't know too much about it. And that's the truth. I haven't read the papers for almost nine months now. He blinked at that and said I was a funny kid. I supposed I was.

We didn't seem to have anything more to say to each other. I just sat there, staring out the dirty windowpane that overlooks a clock tower, seeing the minute and the second hands and yet not quite seeing them, and suddenly a seductive voice called my name from somewhere near my elbow.

Renée belonged to that voice. She is steady-dating one of Ashoke's roommates. Renée is French, wide-hipped, divorced, and very arty. She led me into the bedroom and asked me to show her how to wear a sari. She didn't have one with her, so I took mine off and draped it over her, tucking it sloppily into the thick belt around her waist. She preened herself before the mirror, wriggling her hips in drunk delight under the six yards of silk. Then she ran out of the room, shouting, "*Regardez-moi, mon petit, regardez-moi.*" And I was left standing on the rug in my long white slip.

I suppose I could have made a fuss and gotten her to return my sari immediately. But I didn't really care about rejoining the party. I had begun to feel sick all of a sudden. A shadowy twilight indifference of the world hurt me deep down somewhere I couldn't reach. An old fear crawled through my tissues and gripped me till I shook with fear at the fear. And I thought all these people, so bright, so gay, had nothing to discover, nothing to dream about perhaps. Perhaps it was better not to be able to see beyond the wall, better not to know there was a wall at all. But I knew I didn't believe it, no matter what I said. Instead, I picked up a book at random from the shelf and sat yoga-legged on the bed, reading, till Renée decided to return the sari of her own accord.

At about one o'clock there were only a dozen of us left in the apartment. We got into our coats and decided to go on to Old Nick's for a final round. It was cold outside. As we walked, I saw the tiny snowflakes gather on the brims of the boys' hats, and Ashoke's nose turned a deep pink.

Old Nick is a fat, bald Greek, and his bar is about the dirtiest in the Village. But it has what you can call atmosphere. We ordered a round of beers. I drank beer, too, because there never is any orange juice at Old Nick's. Two men were Indian wrestling in front of us.

"C'mon. Let's try it," the Princeton junior said. He sounded mildly belligerent after all that liquor. Nobody paid any attention to him.

"C'mon, Ashoke. You must be good at it. You're from India, darn it," the chap went on.

I didn't want Ashoke to try his skill. I didn't want him to try because I was dead sure he'd lose. I didn't want to see him lose.

"This Indian wrestling must be American Indian," I said, "not Indian from India."

Nobody paid any attention to me, either.

"What about a bit of arm wrestling instead?" Ashoke asked.

The two boys placed their elbows on the table. I hated them. Each grasped the other's right hand firmly. I hated them both. I knew Ashoke was going to lose, and that would make him feel all humiliated and small and useless. I knew I'd despise him then, for not being bigger and better, for not being big enough to fight the world; I'd hate him for not being a giant.

They arched their necks like spitting tomcats. I just kept hoping, hoping Ashoke'd win, he had to win, it was so absolutely important to me. The whole world was centered on that barroom game. All my hopes, my dreams, my need to order the confusion of life were in one hand; and in the other were fear, destiny and weakness, and the shame of ultimate failure.

A vein stood out on Ashoke's temple. I watched it writhe, blue and tubular against the pale brown of his skin, and I wondered if there was any point in struggling. I began to panic then. I mean, it's awful to realize you're always going to get the bad end of a bargain and there's nothing you can do about it except grin and bear it. Well, I'd have to bear it, I guess, but I refused to grin, too.

Ashoke's grip went slack. Both the palms came down on the tabletop.

"Great!" someone shouted. "Some show all right." I hated them all, each and every stinking, fighting one of them. And I hated myself, too, for dreaming so big, for wanting to find new green islands and stuff like that when I didn't have it in me to find anything.

We ordered another round of beer. I felt a pair of knees bumping insistently against mine. I suppose I should have objected. I didn't, though. Something had gone dead inside me. I just couldn't get worked up about anything. I didn't even bother to find out whose knees they were, at least not till they knocked a bit too hard and I gave an involuntary start. Ashoke picked a fight with the offender at once. I just sat there chasing the bitter bubbles of froth on my lips with the tip of my tongue, feeling the yellow liquid warm the linings of my throat, till someone said the two boys were getting too excited and that it was time for everyone to go home anyway.

We stepped out into the narrow street again. This time, Ashoke took me firmly by the elbow. He has a hard kind of a grip, and I could feel the bony fingers right through the sleeve of my coat. We walked without talking for some time. Then suddenly he stopped short right in the middle of the sidewalk and began to fiddle with the button on his sleeve. I knew he was thinking of something. He shifted his weight from one galoshed foot to the other. I could almost see the question forming in his brain, his throat, his tongue, I swear I could, but I couldn't share his agony. That was what was so terrible. I was all dead inside, all the blue veins had stopped twitching. He blurted it out all of a sudden. He asked me to marry him. I didn't laugh. I didn't cry. I just couldn't. I don't know if I even wanted to. I shrugged my shoulders and said, "I don't mind."

He stared at me a full minute and then looked down at his gloves. First he pulled the right one off, and then the left one; then he began to pick the lumpy wool on the fingers. He looked pretty funny playing with his gloves like that, he's not that kind at all really. After a bit, he fixed his gaze at something just beyond the top of my right shoulder blade and said that "I don't mind" was not enough for him. Didn't I *love* him? I turned up the collar of my coat because the wind was rising and told him, no, I didn't. I didn't want to pretend anymore. There was no point in pretending now that I had seen the corpses of dreams. But Ashoke seemed rather mad at me. He asked me whether I disliked him. I was getting pretty bored and cold, standing there telling little truths in the middle of a street in the Village at four o'clock in the morning. But I answered his question civilly all the same. I said, no, I didn't. And honestly, I didn't dislike him at all.

Ashoke tried to say something after that. But he decided the better of it and whistled for a cab instead. We sat stiff and silent on the two extreme ends of the back seat all the way to the Lexington. He saw me to the door of the elevator and patted me on the shoulder.

"Goodbye, Tara," he said. "I shan't be in New York next weekend."

"Goodbye," I called back, and slid the doors shut on his face.

Ashoke did not call me on Sunday. I sat around in my room all morning, half expecting the phone to ring. I said to myself I couldn't care less, I said I don't want him to call, I won't pick up the phone even if it does ring. It sat there on the table, the phone I mean, white and serene and godlike, and I knew I was drifting away into a tight little, cold little world of my own where dreams and giants have no place. I heard one of the seniors say she was driving back to Weatherington around noon. I asked her for a ride; I knew I couldn't wait till five for the bus.

This girl was a soc. major. She talked about sociology part of the way. She told me all about the term paper she was writing on the "street corner society." I was very polite. I faked a lot of interest. Then I translated Sanskrit hymns to her part of the way. This time she was very polite. She pretended to be enthusiastic about the hymns. She asked a few questions about them, too, and nearly stumped me. The rest of the way we were silent.

When we were nearing school, I clicked my purse open to take out a lipstick. My purse is one of those enormous leather things that were in fashion last year. I always have to hunt frantically in it for what I want. I groped around and felt the crumpled edge of an aerogram under my fingers. It was last week's letter from home. Suddenly I remembered my mother, and my father, and the curving spine of the nurse who had looked after me long ago. For an instant, I saw again the dark corner between the bed and the wall in my room at home where I hide when I am fed up with everyone and everything. Home seemed far away just then. I tried to reach it in my imagination, directing my will with all the power and intensity I could. But home seemed merely an unrelated series of images floating in a blue-gray haze. And I felt a desperate need for I don't know what or whom, and I knew I couldn't go on like this, I didn't even want to, but, oh, it is so difficult to have to ask for something, almost as difficult as giving someone something without being asked to, and I knew sooner or later I'd come to another wall to scale.

I guess I must have started crying, because the senior smiled at me rather lamely. I could feel my nose begin to run. How could I tell her about the islands and walls, about the discoveries I'd never make; how could I explain about the weekend?

So, instead, I sniffed furtively and asked, in what I hoped was a nonchalant voice, "Could you give me a Kleenex, please?" but it didn't sound very convincing even to my ears.

The Transplanted

SHE WANTED TO SCREAM, I am sick, I am sick and shriveling, yes, rotting to the roots, can't you see? But all she said was, "Could you pass the salt, please?"

And they went right on with their twittering and chirping, these bright-eyed bird-women, Janice relishing the feel of her Woolworth drop earrings against her cheeks, Mary pinning peas with her fork, Miss Lambeth arguing about religion, her mouth full of shredded chicken.

She repeated her request, and now her voice was thin, with frayed ends. "The salt, please."

Janice smiled and pushed the half-filled saltshaker toward her. It came sliding over the vinyl surface of the table, knocked against the rim of her tray, and fell on its side.

"Thank you," she mumbled, straightening the shaker. But no one had heard her.

And at once a profound dissatisfaction—with herself, with these people sitting so innocently at table, with the whole world—came wave-surging over her. It was an ancient misery she could not quite beat off. Sometimes, as now eating in a crowd, or sitting at desk in a smoky classroom, or even in bed in the mornings waiting for the alarm to go off, she would think something is not right, no, something is dreadfully wrong, and cover her face with her hands. She knew, even as she put her hands up to her face, it was a horror not so much of the world as of herself, of her own shoddy inadequacy and the little acts of cowardice.

"What's the matter, dear?" Miss Lambeth asked, spewing bread, masticated and soggy, out of the corners of her mouth. "Aren't you feeling well?"

"I'm fine, thank you," Tara answered.

EARLY STORIES (1963–1966)

"Well, you looked so pale just now, hugging your forehead like that. I just hope you don't catch that nasty Asian flu going around the dorm."

Tara rearranged the dishes on her tray, stacking the plate of nibbled-at salad on top of the soup bowl. Then she dug her spoon, ferociously, into the melting scoop of ice cream, longing, longing all the while, for a tablecloth, and starched napkins in silver rings, and perhaps flowers in a vase.

Someone shouted, cupping her hands around her mouth, from the other end of the table, "Janice, how was your date last night?"

"What was he like?" Miss Lambeth asked. She looked old and gray and twitchy.

"I heard you come in very late last night."

"C'mon, kid," the girl from Boston said. "Cut out the giggling and tell us, willya?"

Janice moved her head from side to side, coyly, making the earrings swing like bells.

"Well . . . ," she began, at first only pecking at words. A yellow incisor was speckled with "Strike Me Pink" lipstick.

"Well . . . he was sort of . . . *wild*, you know. We went to this movie downtown . . . and then to that little Italian place for pizzas. Then we drove back to the dorm. Well, he parked his Chevy right near the front door. And here comes the juicy bit, girls, well, he slid across the seat, all smooth and Casanova-like, an' he said to me, 'shall we neck?'"

"Well, I'll be darned!"

"Holy cow!"

"That's really the limit!"

Tara thought, Mother, I think I should come home for a while. And she knew, in the deep convolutions of the brain, that she had not meant home really. No, it was something far more fundamental, something more deep-rooted, like misery, something that was an admission of defeat.

Miss Lambeth turned her kind, bulging eyes on Tara and said, "You don't do things like that in your country, do you? Do our customs seem strange to you?"

And she thought, I'm a stranger to my own ways, having no principles, no convictions, all, all dissolved in the vacillations of weak blood, lost in the school-day transitions in four countries. So now I sit here and am ashamed, belonging nowhere, incapable of believing in anything.

"Why? Don't people date in your country?" It was simple curiosity.

"No," Tara said. "At least, we're not supposed to." She lifted the saucer off the rim of the steaming coffee cup and watched the beads of moisture drip into each other.

"Gosh!" Janice exclaimed, making a funny face, her lips droopy, one eyebrow arched. "I'd go crazy if I weren't allowed to."

"But how do you people get married then? Your parents don't arrange it *still*, do they?"

And she wanted to scream again, please leave me alone, I am sick, sick in the roots of my being.

Lambeth the Crusader rested her hairy arms on the table and said, "Just think of all the changes you can make in your village when you go back. You'll have been well educated, so you can help others."

Her nostrils became pink and cavernous.

"Aren't you excited?" she asked. "It must be such a challenge!"

"I don't live in a village," Tara said.

No, she knew she was not of the kind who reshaped worlds. One had to be a giant to do that. She was too small and limp to house a giant. She looked around in panic, and thought, yes, a giant would suffocate and die, in gasps, in my cage.

Mary peered at her thickly through her glasses. "Don't you feel terribly confused or anything? I mean, you being an Indian and going to school here? I mean," she paused, wanting someone to help her out, "it must be quite a cultural conflict."

Tara stared at her for a moment and then shrugged her shoulders. She thought, you can't sit at table and play with words like "conflict." No, conflict was something you didn't bother to think about, you were too busy living it out. Conflict was a defensive taste of adrenalin in the blood; a compulsive stuttering for systems you had known, and still knew, to be true; it was a moment of humiliation in the corners of conversation.

The talk had drifted to the midterm exams. Tara sat back in the shadows of a pillar and sipped her coffee, now cold and scummy. It tasted like soapsuds on her tongue and against the insides of her cheeks. From overhead came a metallic, jazzy version of "Pretend you're happy when you're blue."

Tara saw Janice pursing her lips, and she was sure the girl wanted to say something to her. Now they were all looking at her, with wonder, with pity, the way one looks at a friend who has just received bad news from home. So she knew she must get up and leave before Janice uttered any words. One word of kindness, or even of affection, and Tara would have to suffer tortures of reality. She pushed her chair back, lifted her tray, it felt so light and unreal in her heavy hands, and walked toward the conveyor belt.

She walked past the glass doors of the dining room, and in the corridor, half-lit and shadowy on the way to the elevator, were rows of mailboxes. She stooped to squint into her box, though she knew it was not the day for mail from home. And she thought, as she twisted the knob of the combination lock first to D, then to G, and finally to A, how greedy I am, how greedy and feeble-minded to have to vulture the moment like this for something hard, something real. There were two sweatshirted girls on either side of her, one blue and one gray.

"Oh, darn!" the girl in blue said, making a mock tragic face at her empty mailbox.

The other girl grinned. "Jim's forgotten me for ten whole days."

Tara's box was empty as she had known it would be, yes, as she had expected it to be. She straightened up, pretending she was not disappointed. The two girls smiled at her in quick, shared sympathy and ran toward the elevator. And she thought, these two backs, one blue and one gray, each solitary and inward-turning, are running their rings of pleasure and disappointment. And she saw with pity, with love, the mean little circles of baubles and tears that one calls endurance. Tara smiled at the girls, though by now they had gone; she smiled back at the moment, now past, of bluegray solidarity.

And it was good to let oneself into one's room at last, and pull the drapes together, and sit, quiet, unmoving, on the bed.

"It's no use," Tara said.

It was as it had always been. Just as it had been way back in the Sloane Square school days in London, dressed in navy gym tunic and red blazer, listening inarticulate and hot-eyed to childish voices that were eager and full of curiosity.

"Do you have lions and tigers running around in your backyard?"

"Do you go around naked at home?"

"Do you live on treetops?"

But she knew it was no use crying. She had to stay it out and study. And she thought, Mother, I think I'd like to come home for a while, though, even as she said it, she knew it was a convenient tag she clung to because she did not know what it was she wanted. It was frightening not to know what one wanted, to be angry and not know why. For home was an eleven-cent aerogram every week, and snapshots of a brick house behind a palm-tree-lined drive. Home was summer vacations in India, visiting unfamiliar people who were one's relatives, listening to eddies of "Do you recognize me? I'm your aunt on your father's side. Praised be Lord Shiva! She actually does speak Bengali!"

Then she heard the brisk tread of size-four oxfords in the hall. She remembered a bluegray moment, and suddenly she wanted to talk and smile. She leaped off the bed and splashed cold water on her face, peering anxiously at the swollen eyelids, the angry blotches, in the mirror above the washbasin.

THE TRANSPLANTED | *19*

Her roommate sidled in. Foong-Kow had a sneaky way of entering rooms, even this room they had shared for a whole semester.

In the mirror, Tara saw a brown spot, and in a corner near the top edge was a yellow spot, and she thought, good gracious, all this agony and passion is contained in tiny colored spots like this. And they were all detached from each other, each moving up and down, leaning, gesticulating, together and solitary, in a big silver mirror.

"I had a funny dream last night," Tara said. Foong-Kow took off her coat and hung it in the closet, rattling the coat hanger against the metal rod.

"What did you dream about?" the girl asked.

"I dreamed I was home," Tara said.

Foong-Kow flung her arms wide into the air and struck a familiar ad pose.

"I dreamed I was home in my Maidenform bra," she chirped.

Then she collapsed in spasmodic rings of laughter.

Tara looked into the mirror again, and now the brown spot was absurdly tragic. She looked, and the face was condemning, condemned.

"Gosh, Tara," Foong-Kow added, "you don't have a sense of humor."

She envied people who could laugh things off, who did not have to store the misery piece by piece till it became strong and overwhelming, too strong even for giants and dreams to battle. Her own laugh was always a miserable offering, suspicious, half-hearted.

Then the Chinese girl took a step toward her, her voice crawling with excitement.

"Guess who gave me a ride back to the dorm?" she asked.

And Tara knew she should put in a word, say something polite, show some interest.

"I said, guess who gave me a ride back from class this morning," Foong-Kow repeated.

"I haven't the foggiest notion," Tara answered, knowing it was a mean thing to say, but feeling too tired and weak-kneed to play the game.

"Well, it was Robert Peterson! You know the chap I told you about last week. He's in my abnormal psych class."

"Oh."

"He asked me if I were going back across the river. So I said, yes, of course. And he said, I'll drive you back. And we walked to his sports car parked in the back lot, a blue Porsche just like my cousin Hsin-Pao's . . ."

"I thought you said it was green," Tara interrupted.

"What was green?"

"Your cousin's car."

"Did I? No, it's blue."

"Really? And the last time you told me about this wonderful cousin of yours he was racing around in a Lancia."

"Look, Tara! Are you suggesting I'm a liar?"

Only the Mongolian tongue stumbled over the r in "liar," and Tara laughed, despising the nasty streak in her nature that forced her to laugh at moments like this.

Foong-Kow swung tersely on her heels and left the room. Tara heard the door slam heavily behind the girl. She heard the angry heels in the corridor outside. And she heard the hardness of her own laugh like sunglint on cut glass.

And then it was time to go to class. Tara smoothed the folds of her sari and fixed her chignon in place, and the image she saw in the mirror this time was not a speck of agony and passion, but an ordinary face on an ordinary girl. Standing on the soft mattress of her bed, she pulled the heavy *Complete Works of Shakespeare* off the bookshelf high up on the wall. It was twenty-two past two already. She grabbed her trench coat and hurried out of the room.

She was late for class. The instructor had started to read aloud from *King Lear*. Tara closed the door. The faces turned to look at her; eyes, faces, curious, staring. They saw; they saw behind her, a rabbit cornered, a rabbit with wild pink eyes and twitching nose. The instructor paused a moment, looked up from his book, and then continued with *Lear*. He raved, he screamed, he hurled himself into the role of the madman. The faces turned back. And Tara was grateful, for the rabbit was free, the rabbit could sneak back into its burrow.

Tara reared her head. She was free. She scurried toward an empty desk. But then she tripped. The books, her heavy volume of Shakespeare, her purse, all clattered to the floor. And she stood there, pinned to the ground, flushing, quivering, twitching, hating herself for her clumsiness, hating the others for turning to stare, hating the eyes, the faces.

A boy near the door got up to help her. He knelt on the floor and picked the books up, a lean, kind boy with blond hair.

"There you are," he said.

He handed Tara her notebooks, her Shakespeare, her purse, and he smiled at her reassuringly. She snatched the books from the boy, the boy with the blond hair and kind eyes, and she swung on her heels. She slipped into the last row of chairs and hated him for his kindness, hated him for drawing attention to her.

Tara sat in the last row and doodled with the blunt end of her pencil. She filled the margin of her notebook with birds and horses' heads. Once she heard the instructor read

> "Blow, blow, thou winter wind.
> Thou art not so unkind
> As man's ingratitude."

And she thought, Mother, I know you've done your best by me and I'm grateful, I really am. But it's turned out all wrong. I've failed. Okay, I've failed. Not in any grand catastrophic way, no, just in one small insignificant detail after another. And she knew now that she was not talking to her mother, but to something or someone who fitted into a larger pattern of things. Everything's gone flat and stale, she thought. Romance has become a dried-up twig. I can't dream anymore, she thought.

She picked up her pencil again with a hopeless gesture and drew a freckle-faced boy without a nose. You don't understand, she sighed, because the phrase came easy to her lips, and it was a good way of putting off things she herself did not understand.

But the fifty minutes was over and it was time to trudge back to the dorm again, to read over the next day's assignment and to wait till it was time to stand in the cafeteria line and pick up trays and watch Miss Lambeth covertly pick her teeth before dessert.

Tara climbed the road up the hill, taking small clumsy steps in her sari. She heard a voice at her elbow. It said,

"Hey, Tara, do you have time for a cup of coffee with me?"

It was one of the fellows from her Shakespeare class, one of those to whom she said "Hi! Nice day, isn't it?" on Mondays, Wednesdays, and Fridays. She stared at the boy's face intently for a second, and then looked away, pretending to search for something in her purse, not sure whether she should say yes or no. Then she heard herself say "Okay," and she knew it was because she wanted to put off going back to the dorm for as long as possible.

They went into the "Ye Olde Inn," a tiny restaurant for people who liked to be different. The only old-world thing about it was the swinging tinplate signboard outside. Inside the Dutch doors it was like any other coffee shop, complete with plastic-topped tables, student waitresses, and an overworked jukebox. They sat at a table near the window, and Tara nervously took in the boy's tattered sneakers, scruffy beard, and cast-off hunting jacket.

"How do you like Iowa City?" he asked her.

"Very much," she replied automatically, because it was the thing to say, and she did not dislike the town at all.

Tara remembered asking and answering other questions, all of them polite, all of them banal. She did not know how or when the talk became more personal. It was only after she heard him ask, "Do you have a guy back home?

I mean some guy with whom you're going to raise lots of little Indian kids?" that she stopped playing with the sugar cubes in the bowl and concentrated for a full minute.

"I could hardly raise anything else," she retorted. The sugar cubes had crumbled in her palms, and the grains lay, hot, white, sticky, against her skin.

The boy began again.

"You know, when I was a kid, my old man, he said, 'Son, going unconscious is one of the nicest feelings a man can have,' and then he beat me up. And boy! He was right. It feels great."

She was horrified. She wanted to get up and run away.

"Hey, don't look so goddamn scared," he laughed. Then he leaned eagerly across the pile of books on the seat.

"You know something," he said. "I'm writing a novel. It's about an Indian girl in a midwestern city, like Iowa City maybe. Well, she meets this American writer, you see. He buys her a cup of coffee, and they talk about life and death and sort of stuff like that. Got any ideas for what happens after that?"

"End of the chapter," she answered, reaching for her notebook and the heavy volume of Shakespeare.

"Hey, wait a minute," he whispered.

He looked self-conscious, and a little sad, like a child who has just been scolded.

"I'm sorry if I acted obnoxious just now, Tara. I always say the wrong things, tell the wrong jokes. That's the story of my life."

He was smiling nervously at the table. Now with the cockiness drained out of it, his face was white and beautifully boned.

"You know something," he added, "you scare me a bit. Don't ask me why you do, but you do. I guess that's why I talked so smart."

She was sure he dreamed of being a giant, of challenging the world and conquering the shabbiness and the dinginess in his life. So she smiled in sympathy.

"Let's start from the beginning again," he said. "I'll ask you how you like Iowa City and all that." He cleared his throat.

"How do you like Iowa City, Tara?" he asked.

"No," she said. "No, you can't ever. I mean you can't ever begin all over again. You have to go on from wherever you left off, always."

You can't cancel your past, she thought, no, you can't jerk yourself out of the circle.

"Goodbye," she said.

Tara walked down the street, slowly, mechanically, stopping in front of store windows to gaze at the spring coats and hats and Easter bunnies. Sometimes, on a dark patch of plate-glass window, between clothes that meant color, that meant cut, that meant style, she caught sight of a face that was not angry. The face was hard and serene, and she thought how amazing that these moments of hardness, of serenity, should come at unexpected moments like this.

She strolled down Clinton Street, slowly, remembering other enchanted moments, sudden, isolated, tiny islands in the stream of time, past the Old Capitol building, slowly, slowly, feeling bold and firm and lithe, on her way to the dorm. The traffic lights in front of her said DON'T WALK. But she knew she must keep walking to hold this precious moment. It was so rare, so divine, and in a way so irrational, suddenly creeping into her while writing a letter, or doing the laundry, or opening a novel. Tara changed her direction and turned into Jefferson Street.

It was eight-thirty when she let herself into her room again. Foong-Kow was standing in front of the mirror, rolling snitches of her stiff black hair on pink sponge curlers.

"Hi!" Tara called, still riding the crest of the wave. She hung up her trench coat in her section of the closet they shared. Foong-Kow was silent, her mouth bristling with bobby pins. She did not even nod her head in greeting.

"It was so beautiful out today," Tara offered. "I went for a long walk." She wanted to share the crystal of hardness and serenity that was wedged in her. She wanted to share it with this girl before it was lost in the dark folds of consciousness.

"After that, I went to the library," Tara continued. She had taken her shoes off, and her toes rested damp and curling on the floor. Watching the toes, quite detached, then shifting her gaze to the pink curlers, she knew that each was solitary, each self-centered, whirling, whirling in a myriad of orbits.

The skin on two of her fingers was ridged with ink. She walked to the sink.

"Excuse me," she said, making her roommate move from near the mirror in order to turn on the faucet.

"Oh darn!" Foong-Kow exploded. She had jabbed a pin too hard in her scalp without the mirror.

"It was a lovely afternoon," Tara tried again. This time the roommate turned around, took all the bobby pins from between her tightly pressed lips.

"So what?" she asked.

"So nothing."

And all the while in the bath, and even while reading *L'Étranger* for Professor Heidman's class, she kept thinking, Mother, can't you see I don't know how to be happy, even in razor-bright moments of happiness I wobble, I fall. When the small type began to swim before her eyes, Tara took a dime from her purse to get herself a bar of milk chocolate. She shuffled all the way down to the slot machine in the recreation room. She stopped in front of the machine, gaudy and full of promise. She pressed a button. A packet of mint candies slid into her waiting hand. And standing there, feeling absurd and slightly wronged, clutching the candies she had not wanted, she noticed the old misery, damp and dark and smelling of moss, crawl into her veins, her arms, her thighs, her head. It was the deep-rooted force that, in spite of her dreams, in spite of the giant in her, made her go wrong in little ways, in small details, till she knew she could not rid herself of the meanness and drabness of daily existence, till she thought it was futile even to try.

Tara dreamed that night. She dreamed she was eating at a Chinese restaurant with a very fat man in madras cloth bermudas. He tried to poke her with a pair of chopsticks, and she ran and jumped into the sea. She swam and swam till she was home again, and she stood in front of her mother, dripping salt-water. She said, Mother, I had to come home.

She woke up at that point because Foong-Kow was sitting up in bed, a ridiculously hunched figure in the dark. The girl yelled to her, "For Pete's sake, shut up! Do you have to talk in your sleep, too? I've a seven-thirty class tomorrow morning."

"I'm sorry," Tara murmured, and turned her face to the wall.

There was a moving angular shadow of a denuded tree on the wall. She watched it till it deepened and grew, and it was her mother standing against the yellow plaster. She heard her mother say, Come, my child. She looked over her shoulder. I'm not licked yet, she said, I'll come back, I bet I'll come back and be a giant one day. Then she turned to go home.

The End of the Road

TARA WAS NOT SURE when she had her first suspicion that something was not quite right. It was so vague, this feeling of hers, and triggered by such little things. Just little things, like waiting in the lobby of the Swallow while Andrew went in to hang up her coat, or like the look on the hostess' face before she led them to a corner table; just stupid things she had not noted before. A look and it cuts into my flesh, she thought; a look and suddenly I am self-conscious.

"I love this place," Tara said, summoning all her charm, all her girlishness. "It's so old and quaint." She looked around at the mirrored walls, at the plush seats and the chandeliers.

"It's all right," Andrew answered.

No, Tara thought, no, that was the whole trouble, it wasn't all right anymore. Once, in the early spring, that was only three months ago, those chandeliers had meant style, meant glamor, meant an evening out with Andrew. Now they were just chandeliers, bits of glass strung in circles, a little dusty, a little sad; now they were grotesque light arrangements that made her shudder.

In the mirror, an old man in a gray suit stared at her. He whispered something to the woman beside him; she could only be his wife, she was so plain, so dowdy; and they both stared.

At once an old dissatisfaction crept into Tara. She began to chatter, idly, emphatically, without an idea in her head. But the dissatisfaction grew like a river, bearing her down, bearing memories, old shames, old blushes, old humiliations, till she wanted to scream, "stop me, please stop me before I run into the sea!"

"I hate this kind of weather," Andrew Wong said. "I wish it would rain soon."

She bristled. She grated. She did not want to talk about the weather.

Now the mirror was full of eyes that teased her, tore her, made her suffer. They sent covert side glances, those eyes, under baku hats and over shoulders. And suddenly, without warning, she saw herself and Andrew as the eyes saw them, as the eyes fell on them and sized them up. She saw a girl in a sari, not more than twenty-one, not ugly, not beautiful, and a man of, oh, fortyish, wouldn't you say, decidedly Mongolian, scholarly, stooping, I'd never have thought . . . well, uh hmm. It made her feel naked, and soft, and horrible, like a peeled grape. She thought she had seen the truth at last.

"That's a new sari, isn't it?" Andrew Wong asked. "It's beautiful. And very becoming."

Tara dared not look in the mirror again. She could not face the whole horror, the eyes, the simpers, the two dummies, an old man paying nice little compliments, a girl in a new sari that was beautiful, that was becoming.

"Thank you," she said. "Actually, I hate it. Blue looks awful on me."

She regretted the words as soon as she had uttered them, they sounded so mean and undeserved. He had probably been polite and quite sincere. He always meant what he said. She told herself they were not what the eyes in the mirror saw. She told herself they were Tara and Andrew, two intelligent, sensible adults, good friends, who were even a bit in love perhaps. She thought, this is the truth, the real picture; the other is false, just shapes in a mirror, a fantasy of my mind.

"The chicken's just right this evening," Tara remarked, and she smiled to show her renewal of faith.

But, by the time she reached the last forkful of dessert, the small nasty doubts were back, creeping like flies over the edge of her mind. She had nothing to say to Andrew, nothing she thought she would like to share. The whole thing was becoming a bore. It jolted her. She had not dared to give it body before, this thought, this dread; she had just sensed it during pauses in conversation, sensed it and dismissed it peremptorily, because it was so absurd and tragic. Because it meant she had reached the end of another dream.

"I'd like more coffee," Tara said. She would put up a show of fight at least. She could not let the dream die without any resistance. That is the trouble with dreaming, she thought. For a dream always makes things seem much more real, or much less so. She wished she could freeze the dream into stone, then chip a piece here, knock a piece there, sculpt it and keep it forever.

Andrew blinked around, trying to spot the waitress in his half-blind, muddled way. The girl was circling the room, coffeepot in hand, attending to other guests. He coughed. He raised a feeble finger in the air. And, irritated, Tara remembered he was one of those men who cannot catch the eye of waiters in restaurants. It's perfectly petty of me, she said, to pick on mean details like this; I didn't want any coffee anyway. But it was important, too, for it meant more than an inability to impress waiters. It meant he had no force, no strength, no compulsion. It meant he was not a giant.

But Andrew is a giant in his own field, she told herself, wanting to be fair to him. Why, he was quite an authority on the Ming dynasty, and were people not always asking him to read papers at conferences, or write essays and book reviews?

"When is your book on the opium war coming out?" she asked.

"I don't know." Andrew Wong shrugged his shoulders. "Maybe this winter. Maybe next year. Who knows? Nobody's interested in an obscure thing like the opium war, except people like me who have to teach it."

He was being horrid, she thought. He was helping to feed her cormorant doubts. Tara wanted reassurance for the dream. She wanted to be told the dream was real, that he was a giant at least in his own small area of history. It was not such a big demand, she felt. And instead, he insisted on being modest; or worse, he always cut himself down to pygmy size in her eyes.

"This book," he began, "is very important to you, isn't it?" He paused uncertainly. "That makes me happy. . . . But I don't quite understand why it's so important. Perhaps it'll never be published."

Tara stirred the ice cubes in her glass.

"Will it make," and now he looked very shy, "will it make any difference to our relationship?"

"But your book *will* be published," she said. And when he did not answer, when he did not soothe the tickling doubts in her throat, she added in a panic, "Won't it?"

"I don't know," he answered.

And, in a flash, she saw to the bottom of his heart. He was truthful and modest and sincere. He did not have to intensify reality, he did not have to dream. She wanted to share her dreams with him. Or better still, to confide her need to dream, because it was this need that was so important, this overwhelming need to build up people she liked into giants who could conquer the world. She needed giants to shatter mirrors in restaurants so no eyes could tease her, torture her, reduce her to a thousand doubting fragments.

Andrew Wong cleared his throat deliberately.

"You like being bigger and better than most people, don't you, Tara?"

"I suppose so," she answered. "Everyone does, I'm sure." She hated him. He had destroyed her dreams. They seemed flat and silly and childish now.

"That's the difference between us," he said. "I was brought up on old Confucian principles. The average man is the ideal man."

"You mean, you really *aim* at being average? You want to be like everyone else?"

"I can't help it," he laughed. "I am a good Chinese, remember?"

But you must be joking, she wanted to say, you can't mean that, it's too weak-blooded, too dwarfish. She had always suspected Andrew was not a giant, and that had been bad enough. But now she had discovered something worse. He did not *want* to be a giant.

She faced him straight across the table. He looked the way he always did, a thin, scholarly Chinese in American clothes, sitting, slightly hunched, in a booth in a midwestern restaurant. His jacket was wrinkled, enough to make Tara wish he took more pains over dressing, but not enough to pass for a flaunting rebellion against conventions. His tie was bluish, quite expensive, quite conservative; but you felt at once it was not quite right; it was not the thing you would have chosen yourself. You could tell from his clothes he had tried. He had tried to be all that was proper and acceptable, and he had failed.

Tara wondered how anyone could see himself as one of the other dwarfs in the world and still be satisfied; how anyone could crawl so close to the surface of the earth, and not be tortured with pain, with longing, with dreams, at the sight of blue-black skies so far, far away. She knew what it was that made her want to leap to the stars, what it was that made her treasure daydreams that seemed paltry and tinny when seen through others' eyes. It was shame. It was humiliation.

"It's horrible," Tara said, looking at the chandelier.

She meant, or tried to make herself think she meant, the chandelier was grotesque. If Andrew had said, yes it's horrible, I understand, I hate it, too, I'd like to smash it, it would have made all the difference to her. They could have laughed over it together, and started from the beginning again, without any doubts or misgivings. But, instead, he looked at her with pity, with affection, with a shadow of sadness even, as if he knew it was not the chandelier she hated, but her life, the scanty, sordid, miserable littleness of her life, and he remained silent.

Tara thought, Andrew's life must be smooth and secure and painless. He had no extremes in his nature. He had no desire, nor need, for romance. All Andrew wanted was to be like everyone else, a settled man, with a house, a wife, two children, a car, and a bigger TV set. It was all so petty, so ordinary, this equating one's aims with other people's convictions. She herself needed gigantic dreams. She soared to heights where only giants dared to tread. When she fell, and you fell sooner or later, it was to depths of humiliation no dwarf could plumb. They were moments of madness, these dreams of hers. They were exalting and tragic and absurd. I am capable of madness, she said, it's the only thing that keeps me sane.

"Do you think I'm crazy?" Tara asked, burning with color and heat, a bird of the tropics, strange and out of place in the Swallow, where people pecked at the grains of life and tried to look very conventional, very proper.

"More coffee, ma'am?" the waitress asked, bending over her shoulder.

Andrew looked uncomfortable, afraid the waitress might have overheard Tara's question. Madness did not belong to his circle of feelings. It was a word one did not associate with oneself. To him, it was something unfamiliar and ugly and embarrassing. He laughed perfunctorily, perhaps to show the waitress it was only a joke, this crazy question, all part of the charm of a very young woman.

He began to speak quickly. "I met François at the Faculty Club last Thursday. He told me he'd just finished reading *La Condition Humaine* with your class." He was trying to cover up his own sense of uneasiness in front of the waitress. Tara watched the hard-knuckled hand pour coffee into her cup and was embarrassed for him. She thought, this man, with whom I'm tossing words back and forth, was once a part of a dream. He was part of my dream, and I built him into a giant to suit my own needs. Now we have seen through the dream, and we must part.

"Yes," she said. "It was rather a frightening book. I hated all that violence and terrorism."

"Do you believe in nonviolence, too?" he asked. "In Gandhi and his . . . what is that word? *Satyagraha*?"

"Yes," she said.

"I do, too, in a way," he answered, running a hand through his coarse Mongolian hair. "But I don't understand it. It's not for ordinary people like you and me."

She remembered she had been fond of him once, even thought of calling him Andy.

"I don't understand it completely," she said. "But I believe in it all the same." There was an awkward pause. She recognized a dead end.

And they sat there, two ordinary people, one talking, gesticulating, the other listening, dreaming. Each sat quite alone, aware of the other's fears, but not aware enough to help him out. So they sat there and pretended everything was going well.

"It had a scrambled background of Chinese history," Tara began. "Tell me about the Kuomintang." Andrew looked puzzled for a moment.

"Oh, you're talking of Malraux's book," he exclaimed. "I can't keep up with you. You always jump from one thing to another."

"You're getting old, Andrew," she teased. "But tell me all about it. Wasn't there a revolution in your country around 1927?"

He took another gulp of coffee and began very deliberately: "The Kuomintang was a political . . ." There was a faint note of gratitude in his voice.

The two waitresses were standing in a corner, near a potted rubber plant—it was that kind of a place, full of rubber plants and chandeliers. They whispered among themselves and stared at Tara and Andrew from time to time. Tara heard the quiet Chinese modulation of the voice and did not listen to the individual words. Ah, she thought, to these two farm girls, Andrew and I are a touch of the exotic, perhaps, a smell of the unknown, we are lands beyond mountains and oceans, we are veiled women and hookah-smoking men, we are serpents and beggars and disease. To them, we are a myth, we are a thousand and one enchanted nights, we are not real.

And that was the way Andrew had appeared to her once, not quite real, an escape, a hope, a giant. But he was real, that was what was wrong. He had colds and blew his nose on Kleenex. He had dust under his furniture. He cooked his meals and washed dishes. He had sordid academic tragedies, like not getting a lecture prepared in time or being heckled by a student in class.

She listened to the voice again. It had changed imperceptibly. It had changed the man, too. He had been transformed from a Chinese refugee in the States, an uncertain and self-conscious middle-aged man who snatched at conventions in his greed for security, to Dr. A. Wong, M.A. (Columbia), Ph.D. (Harvard), a confident name in a college prospectus. His voice was all around her in pleading waves, touching old dreams she had learned to see through. She hoped he would go on forever. The eyes lost their sting, the spears lost their sharpness while he talked.

But it stopped, as she knew it would sooner or later.

"Have I made it any clearer, Tara?" he asked. There was an anxious look on his square face.

"Of course," she answered.

He had made it all too clear. He had destroyed a myth. He had exploded it under the chandeliers.

Tara got up from the red plush seat, because there was a cold, dead weight on her mind. She had thought she had sighted a giant at last, and she had been wrong. Andrew was a dwarf like all the others, he was even happy with his size. He strove to be the perfect little dwarf. Oh, she knew it was foolish to live one's dream so intensely; but what could one do when one was given the strength to dream without the will to act? What could one do, Tara asked herself, except dream and suffer walls of reality?

She heard the legs of his chair scrape the floor. The waitress said, "thank you sir," the manager rang the cash register, and Andrew picked up a chocolate-coated mint drop for her on the way out. Then they were out in the open, in the dark, outside the big bay windows of the restaurant.

Andrew helped her absent-mindedly into the car. He banged the door shut too soon, in his usual muddled way, before she could pull the flowing end of the sari out of the way. Tara jerked it to free it, and the silk tore. He was full of apologies at once. She assured him it did not matter, she would get a new one, he was not to worry, her mother mailed them to her every two months. But it did matter. Andrew was always bungling things, always making mistakes, not big ones so you could admire the audacity of the man, but insignificant ones which irritated you and embarrassed him.

He swung out of the parking lot, hitting a car in his hurry. ("That's what bumpers are for," he apologized.) Tara listened to the sound of the engine in the half dark. It rounded out the sharp edges in her mind.

"Did you enjoy the evening?" Andrew Wong asked her suddenly, raising his voice above the noise of changing gears in his '57 Plymouth.

She summoned a quick, gay air. "Yes. Very much, thank you."

"It used to be a lot of fun, didn't it?"

"It still is," she reassured him, because he was weak and wobbly like her.

He needed the reassurance of words. He could not make a fool of himself and laugh it off. He wanted his friends to think well of him. That was his refuge.

He turned his head toward her and asked, without warning, "Tara, what's wrong with us?"

She could have told him it was all because her refuge was not words, nor approval of society, but dreams. She could have told him it was because he was small and muddling, and not a giant. But now that the dream was dead, all the fight had left her, leaving her heavy with emptiness.

"I beg your pardon?" she asked, pretending not to understand.

Tara was sure she could never explain it to him. He would think her crazy if she did. It would break up the lines of his smooth life, and he would become more uncertain.

"What's wrong with us?" he repeated. His voice was frantic.

"Nothing," she replied, snuggling deeper into the dark hollow of her deadness.

"Okay," he agreed.

He was a man defeated.

"We could listen to the Minneapolis Symphony Orchestra this Saturday," Andrew Wong said when they were about two blocks from her apartment building.

"I'm sorry," she answered. "I can't go this Saturday."

"I've already bought the tickets."

"You should have asked me first," she snapped. "I'm sorry, but it's absolutely impossible."

"Why?" he asked, sounding hurt.

"Because I can't."

Tara resented his taking things for granted. He liked falling into grooves. He was quite a stickler for cultural entertainments. He would go faithfully once a year to the Minneapolis Symphony Orchestra's performance when it stopped for a day in town, Tara was sure of that. He would go down to the desk with his two dollar bills, pick up his ticket, and be moderately pleased at the end of the evening. He was not of the kind who could be moved by music, passionately, and admit it. If it touched him a little more than the man in the chair beside his, if it left him longing for star-domed skies, he would hide his emotion in shame and smile self-consciously.

Tara pressed one of the buttons for the radio. Ella Fitzgerald shouted the blues into the car. Andrew Wong retreated in front of the naked voice.

"I see," he said.

He pressed another knob, and a commercial came over the radio, sleek, suburban, and quite persuasive.

"Is it because I didn't ask you before getting the tickets?"

Oh, it was dreadful, the way he sounded so amused and tolerant. It made her furious to be treated like a child in a sulky mood.

"I thought you'd be pleased," he said. "That's the way we've been doing things for the last three months."

She was sorry for him for a moment. Andrew had wanted to please her and bungled it as usual. They saw each other in distorting mirrors, that was their trouble. If they both came out of hiding and faced each other directly, they might still be saved. Well, she had tried, had she not, she had asked him if he thought her crazy, and he had changed the subject. Andrew did not want to take risks. He evaded the sanity of moments of madness. And, in his own way, he had tried, too; he had asked her quite plainly what was wrong between them. She should have told him the truth then. She should have said, we belong to two different races of men; one to the dwarfs, men who get on in life, not fantastically, but fairly well, who in time acquire a wife, a TV, and two children; the other to the giants, men who have opium in their brains and water in their blood, men who change the shabbiness of their daily existence either by bursting the circle or by going mad. But they both had missed their cues. She could not tell him now.

The car halted at the door of her house. Tara decided to tell him the truth, but not the real truth. She was afraid to crack the mirror between them.

"I can't go," she said, "because I'm going camping with Mary and her friends this weekend."

"In a sari?"

"Yes. Why not?"

"You didn't tell me about your . . . about this camping trip."

"I guess I forgot. Mary's in my art metal class." She laughed at a sudden vision of Andrew meeting her long-haired, sandal-shod friends.

"You'd probably find them too silly and childish," she said.

The last remark had hurt him. She could tell that from the way he turned away abruptly. The hair above his ears was graying. Once Tara had found it charming. She had told Andrew the gray hair made him look sophisticated. But now she would have to say he looked old, just a tired old man with a headache.

"Yes," he said. "Yes, I suppose forty-two does seem pretty old to you."

"Tara," Andrew said suddenly. "Could we go for a drive? Just a short one. Please?"

She waited a full moment before answering. The green door of her house, rather complacent, quite above reproach, beckoned her. It was a refuge. She could go through that door, up the staircase, and shut herself out from truth, from ugliness. Or she could say yes; she could take risks and perhaps find new green doors to open, new dark steps to climb.

"All right," Tara agreed. "But it must be a short one."

They left her apartment building behind and raced quietly on the road along the river that divided the campus in two.

"Where are we going?" she asked.

"To a place where I go only when I want to think things out," Andrew smiled.

They swung off into a dirt track, and a couple of low-hanging branches brushed against the rolled-up windows of the car.

"Road's end, Tara," he called softly, and shut off the engine.

Tara saw microscopic lights winking on the other side of the windshield. For the moment, all seemed transparent to her, as if looking through the windshield she could see the very source of the night. She could look into the heart of Andrew, her own, and the heart of their relationship.

"Oh, look! Glowworms," she said brightly, sensing a showdown.

"No. They're only fireflies."

And again that familiar, uneasy silence.

Andrew Wong groped for her arm in the dark. Oh dear, she thought, Andrew has emerged from his refuge of words. His fingers were moist, scurrying, nervous, against her palm. Oh god! she said, this really is the road's end. Then his arm was around her shoulder, his fingers moving up and down feverishly over the sleeve of her blouse. She sat limp and unresisting in the curve of the leather seat, and an emptiness, heavy and intense, crept like fog into her veins. Now he was kissing the cold skin of her temples. She wanted to laugh, oh god! A Chinese trying to make love to an Indian! Why, it's as grotesque as that chandelier!

And all around them was the same uneasy silence.

Behind Andrew's head was the sharp rectangle of the window, gray with the summer evening, brilliant with fireflies, and soft with the promise of truth.

"Andrew," she said in a panic, "talk to me. Please say something."

"Why?" he asked.

"It's so quiet. I can't stand it."

"Speech," he answered, "is for those who do not know. Those who know, keep silent."

"Zen Buddhism?"

He did not reply. He moved closer.

Another moment of silence, it seemed to Tara, and the truth would emerge from the rectangle of the evening. Another moment of silence and she would blaze white like a star.

"No!" she shouted, suddenly afraid.

"I'm sorry," Andrew Wong mumbled, pushing his glasses up the broad bridge of his nose.

"Could I have a cigarette, please?" she asked, her voice on edge.

"Yes. Yes, of course." He was still very apologetic. "I didn't know you smoked," he added.

"I don't usually."

He lit her cigarette.

"Andrew," she said, "tell me about your schooldays on the mainland, or about your mother, your book, anything you like. Talk to me, please."

"Tara!" he called her name quietly in the dark. "Look, I've been thinking." There were vague fears in his voice. "Couldn't we . . . get . . . married?"

"No," she replied, pressing her cheek against the window of the car. "No," she added, and the monosyllable fell dead, and emphatic, on her own ears.

"Is it because I'm a Chinese?"

She looked at the smooth-skinned round face, the narrow eyes, the straight black hair.

"No," she said.

"Because I'm much older than you?"

"No."

"Then why? Is it because you don't. . . ." he hesitated for a moment, and she waited for him to finish the question in his heavy Mongolian accent. "Because you don't love me?"

"No," she said, watching the fireflies outside.

She saw Andrew trace patterns on the window with his little finger.

"I think we should go back now. I have a paper due next week. I haven't started writing it yet."

"Yes." His voice was apathetically polite. "This must be a busy time for you. End of the semester."

But, suddenly, his voice quickened. "What will you do at the end of the school year, Tara? I mean, when there are no more exams and no more papers?"

"Well," she hesitated, "I was thinking of applying for a scholarship someplace in the East. I haven't made up my mind where exactly though."

"And what will you do after that? Go home?"

"Yes, naturally. If not next year, then the year after."

"Yes," he said bleakly. "You'll go home. You've a home to go to."

In the angle of his head, in the very humping of his shoulders, she read agony and a quaint old-world restraint.

"I need you," he whispered. "I need you all to myself."

"I'm sorry. I'm terribly sorry." She was miserable at his wretchedness, he looked so puny and embarrassed by it.

"You and I are both strangers in this country. You're an alien, and I'm an alien. That should give us a common bond."

"Andrew," she said, "you haven't stopped running yet, have you? The war and China are over for you. They were over fifteen years ago. That's an awfully long time." She laid a quiet hand on the sleeve of his jacket. "You don't need me. Only someone like me. Someone or something to belong to."

"Yes," he smiled ruefully. "I suppose it's the old refugee mentality."

He was framed against the rectangular window, a hunched, compact figure, and Tara thought, he will travel toward his frugal goal, opening his purse each time to count the small risks, measure the small gains, and he will never know of giants.

Andrew tried again. "But if it makes both of us happy?" His voice was higher than usual and shy and tentative. "We could buy a house just outside town. I'd teach school here."

She felt tired then, tired and small and inadequate.

"Our kids would speak American, Chinese, Hindi . . ."

"Please stop it!" she screamed.

He was startled.

"No, Andrew. I'm sorry. It's not that. It's . . . you won't understand. You see . . . we're two different kinds of people. Andrew, I don't think I understand either."

"What do you mean, two different kinds of people?" he asked, puzzled.

The knob of the car door was in her hand now. She would explain it to him, or try to explain at least. She opened her mouth to speak. But even as the lips parted, and the tongue poised itself for the attack, she knew she would refuse to tell. She knew she would frown, and be angry with herself later, angry and then immensely relieved.

"It's getting late," Tara remarked. "I'd like to go home."

Andrew Wong drove right up to the door of her house. Yes, Tara smiled, watching him walk around the front of the car to open the door for her. Yes, Andrew would endure forever. He would be patient. He would give and take pleasures with little clutches of the hand. She was sure he would remain safe. But she, who saw the promise of green doors in mirrors, on windows, and in the sky, who adored it passionately and would give anything to possess it, would blaze for the space of seconds and then die.

For the moment, her heart went out to him in envy and pity, he needed so little to be happy. Softly she enclosed his hand in hers.

"Goodbye," she said.

A Twilight World

IT IS MONDAY EVENING, Tara's evening to read to Al. She reads to him thrice a week, every Monday, Wednesday, and Friday, from 8 to 9:30 P.M. Most evenings, she does not care. For Al is a habit, a part-time job, a cold beer and leather smell, a sip of water between Proust and Taine. But this evening she is tired. She fixes her coat and scarf before the mirror in the hall and looks at her watch. That, too, is a habit. This evening she will be late. She pulls the door shut and sighs, because it will be an evening like all the others, just another gray, flat, barren evening. She sighs again. She looks around her. The twilight seems very still, very unchanging. It promises no discovery. She shakes her head, for she has found nothing; she has nothing to tell the world.

Sitting in the closeness of Al's apartment, Tara flips through pages to find the sentence where she had left off the Friday before. Stereo sounds of Dizzy Gillespie seep through the walls from next door. The trumpet triggers something inside her. It releases half lights in her mind, vague emotions and voices she cannot identify. And she wonders, beginning to read aloud from the 631st page, what it will be like to go home to Calcutta at the end of the semester. Four years of school abroad is a long time. She smells damp sheets on narrow beds, gravy congealing on mashed potatoes in the cafeteria, the rough pages of books from the university library. She smells the four years. And now they are almost over. She sighs again, softly, and she reads on.

Tara reads the black print on white. It twists; it stretches; it falls into patterns of consonants and vowels, black on white, white on black. They are patterns she does not understand. She does not try to either. She hurries through the paragraphs, wanting to get the hour and a half over with quickly. In the building opposite, a window lights up on a direct level with her, and she sees the hatted shadow of a man through the Venetian shutters. It is a debonair shadow, holding what looks like a bottle in a paper sack in one hand and a cane in the other. Four years is a long time, she thinks. The shadow comes to the window and raises the blinds. The man is wearing a brown jacket too tight for him and a yellow speckled tie. She pauses. She wonders what sort of life he leads, this man with the bottle, this shadow wearing the jaunty yellow tie. She says to herself, now he will uncork the bottle, he will pour himself a drink and lie on the sofa and he will think back over his day and he will laugh to himself and light a cigarette and he will laugh some more. She sighs another time. She thinks his life must be full and unkempt and abrupt. The man fusses with a cord at the window. He pulls it and blots out the rectangular frame of light from Tara.

She is tired. She can feel the fatigue mounting like a fog in her bones. The trumpet and saxophone, the flute and drums and bass have ceased to play. And now there are only tinkly piano sounds from behind some closed door. She hears time running away pianissimo, and still she has made no discovery. She has found nothing so will have nothing to tell the world.

Al flexes his legs under the dining table.

"I think we better stop here for this evening, Tara," he says. It is a low, modulated voice.

"But the time isn't up yet," she answers, darting a guilty eye at her watch.

"It doesn't matter. I bet you're tired."

She looks at the Latvian face across the table, fingers bunched tightly under a heavy cheek, the head bent slightly to one side, the blind eyeballs blue and turning inward.

"But we should finish your reading assignment for Wednesday's class."

"Don't worry. I'll get it done somehow."

"I'm awfully sorry. I can carry on if you'd like me to."

She is apologetic. She knows her voice must have given her away.

The blind man pushes his chair back and gets up to fetch his billfold. Tara watches him pick his deft way in and around the furniture and disappear into the bedroom where he does not switch on the light. She clasps her arms around her knees and hopes the man in the brown suit and yellow tie will open his shutters again. He had had some quality she envied. But the window remains dark on the wall opposite. She sighs. She remembers a woman she had seen long ago, a thin, gaunt woman pressing against the railings of her house, peering in. She shudders. She is afraid the man really might come to the window again. She hopes he will. But he does not. She sinks back in her chair in relief.

Al comes back into the room, a bulging wallet with a rubber band around it in his hand. For the first time, she realizes with a shock that the lights in the living room do not mean a thing to him. She wonders if he bothers to turn them on when he is alone in that room.

"I'll be back home in India this summer," Tara says idly.

She does not know why she says it.

"Really? Do you mean for good?"

Al feels for coins in his wallet, passing his square-tipped fingers over their rims and faces.

"Yes, I suppose so. I should finish school in June." Four years, she thinks. Four years of talking late into the night, of trying out vodka in ladylike orange juice, of sharing lavatories with other boarders.

"Four years is a long time," she says.

Al takes out two dollar bills and two quarters and places them on the table with a soft click.

"Do you ever get homesick?" he asks her. "It's such a long way to come to school."

"Sometimes. Sort of awfully blue and depressed, if you know what I mean."

"Yes," he answers. "Yes, I think I know what you mean."

Tara slips the money into her purse. She stretches a hand toward her coat hanging on the back of the chair beside her. A button scrapes against the wood of the chair.

"Would you like to stay for a cup of coffee?" Al invites her suddenly.

"I'd love to," she replies, lifting her arm out of the sleeve of her coat.

She looks out of the window and sees a rectangle of darkness on the wall opposite. She remembers vaguely there had been a shadow in that patch of darkness, a shadow that had teased her and torn her and left her in shreds. But now it becomes a phantom in her mind, pale and very unreal.

Al steps into the kitchen and lights the gas under the coffee percolator. Tara watches him curiously while he takes out, with great care, two cups and two saucers and spoons from the cupboard. He opens the door of the refrigerator, and his fingers glide over the cold sides of bottles, searching for the carton of cream. One fingernail looks bitten. He finds the cream and sets it on the table.

"How do you like the pretty pink flowers on the china?" he asks.

Tara discovers with a shock that colors must be just words to Al, just a group of sounds.

"Pink's my favorite color," he adds and laughs at his own joke.

And Tara joins in the laugh, reading into it a secret chuckle, hands scraping walls, the click of a door. She smiles. She knows it is going to be all right.

They talk about home, and Al describes his house in Latvia where he lived as a child before he escaped. He shows her snapshots of his mother and sister, heavy bovine women, slipping them out of the billfold with the rubber band round it.

"What is your home like?" Al asks her. "Do the houses in Calcutta look anything like ours?"

Tara sees a house that is big and ornate. She says to herself she will be home in another two months; she will become part of that house, big and ornate; she says she will endure like the house and its tradition. Then she pauses. She pulls a thread, she straightens a spoon, she is afraid. Gazelle-footed doubts run through her mind. No, she admits sadly, she will not endure like the house or the tradition.

"We live in brick houses," Tara answers. "Brick and cement houses with flat roofs. D'you know the kind I mean? Very big and ornate."

They talk about school, about the Irish nuns who taught her, and the Perkins Institute, and she discovers with surprise she can ask questions about braille without feeling self-conscious.

"What'll you do when you go home?" Al asks her. She stops. She gropes. She has no words to specify the void in her heart. Nothing, she wants to shout at him, nothing at all. She has not found anything in the richness of evenings, so she must sit inert. For all her dreams, she knows she will do nothing spectacular, nothing catastrophic. She will run through her little graph of triumphs and failures, economically counting the points. She will marry a man picked out for her by her parents, a fairly bright, fairly well off young man, and lead a pleasant suburban life. And feeling something, a horror perhaps, or distaste, or shame, rise within her and choke her, Tara laughs, an unpleasant laugh, at herself and the world.

The blind man glances up at her face. She sees strips of shadow run across his forehead, his eyes, his nose, and over his mouth, half rebellious and half resigned. She tastes darkness in the light of that blind stare. He has seen more than her, she is sure. He has seen and felt and lived more deeply.

"I don't know," Tara replies. Her voice is sad and quiet. She leans her head against the wall.

"I don't know," she repeats, knowing she will never do a tenth part of all she would like to do, or has dreamed of doing as a child.

"You don't know?"

She senses the shock in Al's voice.

"But you must have some idea surely. Otherwise . . ." and here he hesitates. "Otherwise . . . these four years . . . ," now he shrugs his shoulders in disbelief, "these four years are . . . a total loss."

Tara stops. She kindles. She burns with a renewal of hope.

"No," she says urgently, "they aren't wasted. These four years of school, I mean."

He is a stranger; he does not know the promises she once made to herself, gigantic promises she is too small to keep. She thinks she can tell him new lies and he will accept them as truth.

"Well," she tells him, "I suppose I'll teach school when I go home."

"Really?" Al laughs. "I hadn't quite pictured you as a high school teacher."

Tara hears a hall of mirrors break in his laughter.

"It sounds too dreary," Al remarks. "I'd expected something like the rope trick or walking on nails!"

But it isn't dreary, she argues, it isn't dreary at all.

The really dreary thing is that she does not want to teach. She is not sure what she wants and, till she has made her discovery, she must keep scratching walls, keep running into blind alleys.

And suddenly words tumble out of her, pushing, elbowing, bruising each other; words thrilled with the light after long damp years in the prison of her mind. No, she tells him, for now she is past caring, no, she will not teach school. She confides her dreams, she glows, she becomes a hard core of light against the wall.

"I see," he whispers.

But black fear nets her again. For she knows he does not see, he cannot see they are only her dreams, they are only words showing off weak muscles. She repeats, in despair, she will do nothing, she has no courage, no energy. She tells him in future years she will see dark faces against a canvas and she will turn away because she will not have discovered what she had hoped to find.

"I see," Al whispers, "you want to be a giant."

Their eyes meet. Their stares collide. He has seen her dream, given it the shape of words. She stands in the cold hard light of the moment while all emotion drains out of her mind, leaving it thin and rigid and sealed, like her body.

Then the phone rings. Al gets up. An arch voice pours out of the earpiece. Al answers.

"Yes, yes," he says. "I read your gossip column in the *Collegiate*. . . . Yes, it was pretty good. But you deserve to be cut dead after what you had to say about me. . . ." The precision melts. Blurred bits of darkness float back. The spell is broken. And Tara grows limp in her leather chair.

Al returns to the chair beside her.

"Aren't you going to ask me what *I'm* going to do when I graduate?" he asks impatiently.

She wonders what the future seems like to a blind man. She has an image of a small, closed room, which needs to be aired but which has only one window, narrow and barred.

"I'm going to write," Al says proudly. "For real classy magazines."

She notes his simple smile, the intensity of his sightless gaze, the confidence in his voice, and she knows it is a picture she will long remember. The past throws up snapshot images of ugly oozy-eyed boys, squatting on mats on the floor, weaving fancy shopping baskets of cane. And now she is not sorry for them. She is proud of them instead. She remembers a blind beggar from the days of her childhood. He used to sit all day under a tree near her house and scrape away on a fiddle. And every evening, when the sun went down, he gathered up the *annas*[1] and the handfuls of rice people left him and tap-tapped down the road past her gate, tapped with a long white stick.

"Do you have a white stick?" she asks him.

He stiffens at once. He draws up his head. She realizes her mistake and is ashamed, it was so foolish to ask a question like that, so thoughtless, when all the while she had meant to be kind and understanding.

"No," Al replies. "Not anymore. I use my brains for a cane. You don't think I'm feebleminded as well as blind, do you?"

"Of course not."

"They gave me one when I was in school," he continues almost to himself. "It was long and thin and tipped with a spring. Didn't make a noise or anything. But I hated it. Gee, how I hated it!"

Al pours more coffee into his cup, this time spilling some of it on the saucer and on the table. Tara lifts her hand to pick up a paper napkin and wipe the coffee from the vinyl top. Hearing the soft swish of her arm in the air, he stares at her to guess her movement. In the stare Tara hears moans of resistance, a whimper of pride, and she drops her arm on her lap.

"I broke it . . . in half . . . one day. What a silly thing to do!"

Tara sees lonely caverns in his smile.

"You know how touchy fifteen-year-olds are. It sort of seemed like a, well, like a symbol or something to me. Made me feel I was different. You know, not like the rest of you."

The spilt coffee dries in ugly brown patches. And now she feels no desire to wipe it up.

Then it is time for her to leave. She puts her cup down with a click of finality. He hears the cup on the saucer and asks:

"Does that mean you've had all the coffee you want?" He helps Tara into her tan coat.

"I rarely get to know my readers," he says, standing just inside the door of his apartment. "In fact, I rarely get to know anyone."

On the third evening of their adventures with Leopold Bloom in Dublin, Al takes Tara for supper to an Italian restaurant close to his apartment.

The air in the restaurant smells of meatballs and spaghetti and red wine.

"I see lots of people," Al remarks.

He is right, the place is crowded, and Tara has almost forgotten he is blind.

---

1. *Anna* refers to a fractional unit of Indian currency used during the British Raj.—Ed.

"Table for two, sir?" the waitress asks, and, glancing up at Al's face, her eyes pop slightly.

And now, rising above the sour smell of food and chianti and the sweat of patrons is the smell of surprise. Al takes hold of her elbow, and together they follow the waitress to a booth, skirting scattered islands of diners who look up curiously at the blind man with a girl in a sari.

The waitress places two menus in front of Tara and Al and waits on three greasy boys in leather jackets at the next table. Tara sits with her head bent low, chipping pink nail polish from her fingers, still feeling questions in eyes she does not know.

"What would you like to eat?" Al asks.

She looks at the card in front of her and has to laugh.

"It's all in Italian. I can't make out a thing."

"Read them out to me," he says.

And she remembers, but this time not with surprise, that Al has to be read to.

When they have ordered their meal, and the strangers' eyes have lost their questions, Tara fixes her gaze on the wall behind Al.

"I wish you could see that painting," she says suddenly.

"Which one?"

"The one on this wall, right behind you."

"What does it show?"

She wonders if Al hates words like museums and art galleries.

"Well, aren't you going to tell me?"

She pauses a moment, not knowing how to explain the quickening of color to a blind man.

"Yes, of course," she says. "It's supposed to be a violin, I think. But not the ordinary kind. It's all in bits and pieces. Sort of broken up and distributed all over the canvas."

"Uhh! Nice composition," he grins.

"The violin itself is a vivid yellow."

"That means an awful lot to me!" Al retorts.

She feels again fingers scraping walls, she feels the cold dead air of a blind alley.

"It's the color of daffodils in summer, Al. It's daffodils and liquid gold and the heart of a fire. It's so bright and alive and so happy. Honestly, Al, the whole thing looks so, oh, I don't know how to say it, so terribly full of promise. It's as if . . . as if the little bits and pieces know someone's coming to put them together. And when that someone comes, he'll play the violin . . . without any score . . . just straight out of his head."

Tara realizes suddenly her voice has risen with the pulse of the moment. The boys in leather jackets stare at her. She is embarrassed. She takes a gulp of water and taps a nervous finger against her fork.

They are horrible, Tara cries, they have spoiled my white-gold moment of happiness. Now the violin is receding into spools of color on a canvas (nice composition, Al had joked), and she knows now no one will put it together and play it in pure naked waves. It is all their fault, she sobs, they will not let me escape; each time I spread my wings poised for flight, someone speaks, someone laughs, someone stares, and I am nailed by my wings to the earth; I flutter; I die.

"That's the first time anyone's explained a painting to me. Thank you."

Tara looks at him. She stares at his blind blue gaze, and she is satisfied. The enemy has disappeared. The battlefield has vanished. Now she can turn to the leather jackets without a tremor or twitch.

After dinner, they walk the five blocks to her home. It has begun to drizzle. The damp on Al's hair glints in the electric pool of the porch light.

"You're getting wet," she says.

"I like getting wet," he says.

"I love the monsoons in Calcutta."

"Are you really going home in June?"

"Yes."

"Back to your Calcutta?"

"Yes."

"Have you enjoyed your stay here, Tara? Four years's a pretty long time."

"Yes, I have. Yes, very much. It's been wonderful," she says, discovering evenings are a hall of doors waiting to be opened.

They smile as friends, say their good nights, and part.

One balmy day late that spring, passing in front of a small shop window on a downtown street in San Francisco, Tara catches sight of a jar of spices she has not seen in four years.

She stops short, unbelieving, in front of the squat little jar. Through the plate glass of the window she reads the label with its fancy lettering in blue: "Maharajah's authentic Indian condiments." And she sees shadows of her father reading the hometown daily, her mother drying her hair in the sun, the servants' children stealing mangoes on slow, hot afternoons. She hurries inside to buy the spices.

Back home again, she takes off her coat and scarf and flings them down on a chair. Her eyes tense to read the small print on the label. (She decides it says "made in Bombay.") She leans against the table by the phone and calls Joe and Ginny, Tom Davies, and the Buckley sisters, to invite them all for rice and curry that evening. Only after she has cut short Iris Buckley's giggles with a "see you this evening" does Tara remember it is Wednesday, her evening to read to Al.

Still holding the jar, she flexes her wrist in absentminded lines, making the red, yellow, and brown grains break up and resettle in new patterns against the sides of the glass. She thinks of the small, close apartment on Melrose Avenue, winces at the sound of her dry, Carlyle-teased voice mingling with the drums in some room down the hall, and she lifts the receiver off the hook again. When Al promises to join her friends for the evening, she is happy.

It is seven minutes to seven, and the guests, all except Al, have long since arrived, and Tom has fixed them scotch and sodas. Tara delays supper, running in and out of the kitchen, stirring the shrimp curry still on the stove. And, every now and then, from behind crisp white curtains, she steals a look at the street below. At fourteen minutes after, only the ice is left in their glasses.

Iris Buckley, the cheekier and more popular of the Buckley sisters, complains she is hungry and says, "Tara, couldn't we sit down for supper? The shrimps smell so delicious."

And then, interrupting Tara's hedging, the phone rings in the hall.

"Look, Tara, I'm terribly sorry. I can't come this evening."

She senses Al's fear, senses his white wooden fence around a core of darkness and solitude.

"I got held up in the library. There's a book on reserve I must finish," the voice continues.

She thinks a blind man is like an empty house, with all its doors and windows locked, the furniture swathed in dust sheets, where children have stopped running, and tumbling, and laughing.

"I'm sorry, Tara, I really am. But this book's important. I just have to finish it tonight. . . . You aren't angry, are you? . . . You don't think I'm nervous or anything like that? . . ."

She wonders what it is like to feel people are nudging each other and pointing at one without ever being really sure. Tara finds words of reassurance that she does not remember ever having learned.

"Okay, Tara," the voice yields. "I'll be there after dinner."

When the doorbell rings later in the evening, Tara puts her cards down, she had had a good hand this time, and walks to the door, pausing a brief minute on the edge of the carpet to say, very casually:

"By the way, Al's blind."

She returns with Al to the living room, and the marks of surprise are still on their faces, five mature faces with parted lips and shaded eyes, each trying to hide the knowledge from the other.

Tom is the first to recover. He grasps the blind man's hand and greets him with unnatural heartiness.

"Here's a chair to your left, about five steps from where you are standing," Iris says, fluffing up her pale yellow hair with an instinctive palm.

"Let me help you. Here, hold my hand. I'll lead you to it." Joe offers the newcomer his arm.

"Give me your coat. I'll hang it up in the closet." Maud smiles at Al uncertainly.

They're being kind to you, Tara would like to tell him, they're not nudging or staring or pointing, they want to help. She sees his face, pinched and blue, and is embarrassed for him, for her friends, for herself. And she keeps silent.

The blind man feels his way toward the sofa. He bumps against its broad arm and blushes.

"Are you a senior?" Ginny asks him kindly.

His back rigid against the blue cretonne of the upholstery, Al twists his head in the direction of the voice.

"Yes," he answers.

And Tara, gathering up the cards from the floor, thinks it would be almost unbearable to be caught in a thick fog without a flashlight or at least a packet of matches.

She stands with Ginny in front of the sink, feeling the hot, soapy surface of dishes under her fingers. And Ginny, a damp dishcloth in her hand, says the baby is due in October and wouldn't it be dandy if it turned out to be a boy, little boys are such darlings. Tara thinks maybe inviting Al was not such a good idea after all.

In the next room, Iris says brightly, "Let's all go to a show."

"Yes, let's. A Terry-Thomas movie[2] is playing downtown." Tara follows Ginny back to the living room.

"Shut up, idiot," Maud whispers. "He can't go to the movies!"

Tara shudders. She looks into the rough, thick stillness of the moment and she sees, not the gardens green and beautiful and tender she had hoped to discover as a child, but walls, high brick walls that graze her forehead.

But Al breaks up the uncomfortable silence. He laughs. He says, "I'd love to go to the movies."

Joe winks in relief, and now it is all noise of people deciding which one to see.

---

2. Terry-Thomas (1911–1990) was a popular British comic actor who came to prominence in international cinema in the 1950s and '60s.—Ed.

46 | EARLY STORIES (1963–1966)

Someone asks, "What's showing at the Strand? It's only a few blocks from here."

"I bet it's that Indian movie," Maud exclaims. "Don't ask me to pronounce the name.[3] But a lot of the kids were talking about it in the cafeteria."

"Oh, yeah, I remember. Isn't it a trilogy or something?"

They begin to move, emptying the closet of their coats and hats, tripping down the steps, bursting into the lavender of the evening outside.

The sidewalks are crowded. They walk in twos and threes, Tom, Ginny, and Iris in front, then Maud and Tara, with Joe and Al bringing up the rear. Scraps of Joe's voice float up to Tara, "Look out, Al, a hydrant in your way," "better walk on the inside, the cars swing so close to the sidewalk!" She keeps her eyes on the ground. She cannot help either of the two men.

They come to a stop at the intersection because the lights are still red. Tara glances up at Al, now beside her, and sees him sneak his elbow out of Joe's light hold. The lights change to amber, and Al rears his head, sharing the expectancy of the pedestrians. They turn green, and he dashes forward into the street.

A couple of cars trickle into the stream of people, waiting to take a right turn. Joe towers beside Tara, separated from the others by lines of strangers. She sees him eyeing the cars and, before she can stop him, he shouts in his boyish voice, "Look out, Al! A car!"

Through a gap in the shoulders, Tara spots the blind man panic to an abrupt halt. Then he must have tripped, for she hears shouts. She sees hands helping Al up. There's a bruise, faintly pink, on his left cheek, just under the eye. And standing again on the sidewalk, she keeps repeating, sick with anxiety, tasting his humiliation in the darkening of the bruise, "why did you run off like that? Why didn't you wait for us?"

They reach the movie theater, a silent uneasy group. The auditorium is empty, except for a few old women smelling of cats and TV dinners. They file into the last row, disturbing a little lady enjoying a private weep in the dark.

On the screen, a small boy chases butterflies among flowers. This is Bengal, she remembers, sharing the boy's wonder, adding to it leaves and trees of a forgotten childhood.

Again she tastes the mud of rivers where children sometimes bathe and the faint clover smell of her grandmother's lap as she tells tales of princesses at dusk.

---

3. It is most likely that the unnamed film here is Satyajit Ray's *Pather Panchali* (1955), the first installment of his internationally acclaimed, Bengali-language Apu Trilogy.—Ed.

"Oh, look!" Maud exclaims. "How beautiful!"

It is beautiful, this lotus on the water, its petals opening slowly, till the heart, the yellow heart rich and tender, is open to the world waiting to be loved and caressed and crushed and thrown away.

"Oh, look, Al," Tara whispers. "It's a lotus. It's big and beautiful on the water."

"What's a lotus?" Al asks.

Tara has no time to explain, for the flower has faded into the countryside, into long grass and children running along railway tracks.

"Why are those kids running?" Joe asks Tara.

"To the peepshow. The peepshow's come to the village."

"Who's running? What children? What're they up to, Tara?"

Al sounds impatient.

Iris leans toward her in the dark. "What's that big box on the man's shoulders?"

"That's the box that has all the pictures," Tara answers. "You know, all sorts of fairy tales. Giants and princesses galore. You pay your *anna* and you get to squint through the hole in the box."

"Look at the little boy's face!" Maud whispers. "Just look at him. He's so cute."

"Is that what little boys wear in Bengal?"

"What do they wear?" Al asks her fiercely.

But the picture changes and there are new questions to be answered, new images to remember.

"Hey, what's that old woman yelling for?"

"She sure does look angry!"

Tara sees two women, one old, one young, both tired, both poor, shouting, screaming, flailing their arms.

"The old woman is an aunt by marriage," Tara explains, pausing to listen to the dialogue. "She has stolen some mangoes from the neighbor's garden. The niece is furious. She says she'll never be able to face the village again. Now the old woman's threatening to leave. She says she'll pack her saris and go off to the jungle."

"Oh, there's that little girl again! Isn't she a darling!"

"What's she saying?"

"What! Are there three women on the screen now? Tara, please tell me what's happening?"

Al's voice is raw with wounds.

"Yes, Al, there are three people together now. Two women and a child."

"What did the kid say just now?"

"The little girl does not want the great-aunt to leave. She is begging the old woman to stay with them."

"Oh, my gosh!" Iris screams suddenly. "Oh, that's terrible."

"What's happened? What's terrible?"

Al clutches her arm impatiently.

"That was a bit brutal, wasn't it?"

"What is it, Tara? What's going on?"

"Say, that's beautiful countryside."

"Do you live in a village like that? It's beautiful. Like a picture book. And so quaint."

"No," Tara says. "But my father did as a child. And his father before that. And I suppose his father before that."

"Tara, please explain what's going on."

She thinks, yes, they lived in villages that were beautiful but not quaint (no, certainly not quaint, that was such an odd word to use for something that was alive and part of a tradition); yes, they lived in villages that were beautiful and they were content, dreaming no dreams and so not breaking their hearts.

"My people came from a village called Mahimpur," she says.

"Tara," Al whispers. "The music sounds weird now. Is it a very dramatic moment?"

She sighs softly. For a moment, her dream has opened to her, petal by petal, softly, revealing, though only for the moment, its big yellow heart. But now it withers; it dies; it falls.

"The music is sad, Al. A little girl is dying."

And long before the music dies down, Tara has acknowledged she can never be a giant.

She shrivels and blushes and is silent. An infinite pain rises like a wave over her head. And then it leaves her to crash over other shores, leaves her floating among the flotsam knowledge of her own smallness and inadequacy.

And now, standing outside the Strand again, they talk, they laugh and argue. She asks Al how he liked the movie so he will not feel left out.

"I liked the music," he replies harshly. "Now let's go home. It's chilly here."

Then she looks at him and thinks she could cry. Not to understand the dialogue would be bad enough; but just darkness and strange music would be unbearable. She smiles at him to show she understands. But he senses her inadequacy. He turns his face toward the street, a stone image of a man who has rejected all sympathy. People dribble in twos and threes around them and in between them. She thinks, with acute pain, how good it is to see the crowd, to see gray, black, and tan coats, shoes and hats. She thinks she hears a door open and close in the evening.

The silence is full of sharp points, this silence between Al and Tara. She wants to tell him she is sorry she spoiled his evening, she had meant so well, her friends had meant so well, too, they had tried in their own ways to be nice to him so he would not feel any different. But she cannot open her mouth. She holds out a hesitant hand like a social worker, which he cannot see. And she is ashamed.

"I should have kept the cane," Al says abruptly. She is startled.

"But you don't need it!"

"Not to help me walk. I didn't mean that." There are tiny clots of blood on his bruised cheek.

"It's no use," he says. "You can't expect to break a thing like that."

He smiles down at her, a quiet, wise little smile.

"You know something," he says gently. "There are no giants in the world. No giants at all."

And she is helpless before the truth. She hears a door shut on their twilight worlds. Of all things, Tara thinks, nothing is so dead as a dead dream. For how else can one define the numbing pain, the heavy emptiness, the withdrawing of light from the dark of her brain?

"I have a long day ahead of me," Al remarks. "I'll have to get back to my term paper. Goodnight, Tara. Goodbye, everybody. Nice meeting all of you."

Tara pauses a moment to stare at the rigid back walking away. On Friday evening, she will read again to Al. Al is a part-time job found her by the Student Employment Office; an hour-and-a-half stopover on the way to the library; a sip of water between printed words. And now, the shutting of doors in the night; and the new, damp smell of a dreamcorpse.

Bless This Day

NAREN WALKED into class exactly six and a half minutes late. I sneakthief into the room, a guilty thing surprised. Just look at these heads turning to stare at me. Nerveless muscle and skin glances. One, two, three, four. It isn't easy to get up at six in the morning, at least not in Columbus, Ohio. Back home's different, Father. There's another one to the far left, that fellow with the padded football player shoulders. One stareful of eyes, empty shapes, gold flecked

50 | EARLY STORIES (1963–1966)

with brown, gray shadowed with blue. You had big dreams, Father, that was your trouble. Numb-frozen morning mammal, I sit in my simple horror. Must get a Ph.D. from Belait[1] or America, my son. Daydreams. You poor old man. D.Litt. (Oxon.). Ha! I must go to Oxford, you said. But the ivy choked the walls and you and me and Prometheus, too.

Shifty-attentive people, they have turned back to their books. The core of our being has become mutable. But *I* am the seed that is changeless in all that is changing. I sit and breathe down their pink necks. That fat piggy neck is fascinating. The light brown hair springs stiffly out of the pores and curls upward. There is a dusting of dandruff on his coat collar. Use Dermatol shampoo and lather the embarrassment away, yours at low, low prices. I stare and do not turn away, for I am no guiltbent creature. I am a man of honor. And Brutus was an honorable man. No, Father, you didn't need Dale Carnegie to teach you public speaking. Dreams and words. But maybe I'm wrong. Maybe you believed what you said. If only I.

Naren set his briefcase down on the empty seat next to him, opened his notebook at the page where he had left off the day before, and balanced his volume of Chaucer on his knees. Still rooted to the "Knight's Tale." The Middle English *gh* is pronounced like the German *ch* sound. *Ichhhh*, let the air out slowly. *Ichhh bin*, I am, and that's God's crossword puzzle for man to worry over on idle Sunday mornings. Now, Mr. Jacobson, will you read out the next line, please? I peep unobtrusively over the shoulder of the man in front. Which line, which page? He bares his teeth, long, yellow, separated, and words come torrenttumbling in mangled Middle English. And I sit here in the fourth row of seats, isolated and vulnerable, running my finger, the one that has the ring on it, yes, the ruby her family gave me, over the lines, knowing I shall not find it, and knowing I don't care about it either. Now Old Saunders reads a verse, gulping air, and his voice is like a tire crunching a gravel driveway. Like Father's secondhand Buick braking sharply under the porch. Only I always came on a bicycle. A serious, bespectacled young man, pedaling furiously.

He uncapped his pen to start taking notes. Saunders had not drawn any of his strange diagrams on the blackboard yet.

BLACKBOARD (discreetly holding out an undertaker's card): After the beginning, gentlemen, comes the end. Speak, Sir Palamon.
PALAMON (clutching a bleeding heart in a proud hand): I die for love!
BLACKBOARD: Your turn, Sir Arcite.

---

1. Also known as *Bilayat* or *Vilayat*, Belait is an Indian term for Britain dating from the imperial era.—Ed.

ARCITE (dressed for the City, complete with bowler hat, umbrella, and stiff upper lip): I, sir, die for honor.

BLACKBOARD: And you there! What about you?

NAREN (with a start): Eh? Me? What are you talking about?

EMILIA (in the shrewd, confident voice of the intuitive woman): He dies for nothing.

NAREN (frantic): Don't believe her, sir. I don't die at all. Not for anything. I am unborn and undying.

BLACKBOARD (hastily pulling out a chalky white wig and placing it on his bald head): Guilty, guilty. You are blind and mutable. I condemn you to death. Guilty.

I catch Saunders' sharp, multicapillaried look, and wear my contrite face. A little overdone, was it? A matter of habit, I am afraid. They made us say the Act of Perfect Contrition at school, and the wooden floor pressed geometric designs on our chubby infantile knees. I screwed my eyes into tight slits to watch Father Bernard fold his hands over his paunch and mouth the words I understood better then.

But all Professor Saunders said was "Mr. Ghose, would you mind moving up to the front row, please? I have two more lectures this morning and it would be disastrous if my voice were to break down [a phlegmatic laugh, which I echo]. I'm sure you'll cooperate with me."

Naren picked up his pen and briefcase and stood up. His sneakers fell with soft ignominious glockplucks on the stone floor. The exiled and the wandering. The guilt of the species weights our feet, and the dust of the old land is in our eyes. Through all changes *I* alone remain unchanged. Sure, there's a divinity that shapes our ends, rough-hew them how we will. Even now I feel the prenatal kicks of my tragic destiny. But to you it will seem like a tragicomedy.

He found an empty seat, and slid in clumsily, rearranging his *Complete Works of Chaucer* (the Robinson edition), and his notebook. Only this time, more people stared. It haunts me, this vapid trail of eyes. I strike an aggressive, stickchinout pose, but I am afraid. Father, you have shrunk knee-high, freshfaced, ball under arm, while I must stand guard, in my white stage-prop beard, a cane in my hand. You talked so big, remember? Palamon and Arcite. We bandy the words around. Boccaccio and Teseida. They were fantastic, those people, and escaped into the dignity of courtly love. We flounder in the modality of the flesh. A man, and woman, tears. I plunge my fist into the borrowed bag of your savings. You and I, Father, are proud progenitors. But hungry, moving lips hem me in. The kitchen and the crowded desk at the office

52 | EARLY STORIES (1963–1966)

are all shifting points in the flux. *Ich bin* will only be a whirlpool, and perhaps the seed of immutability will dry up and eddy and drown when my back is turned.

At the end of the hour, Professor Saunders reminded his class to pick up their papers on the structure of *The Canterbury Tales* from his desk. Naren searched with frantic fingers through the neatly stacked pile and did not find his own. Just as he was beginning to feel disturbed enough to ask Saunders about it, a bermuda-clad coed said, giggling shyly, "Excuse me. I think I picked up yours by mistake."

And I am excited and catarchbacked as I snatch the paper, for I know I wrote it well. Don't work so hard, she said, setting the teapot on the kitchen table and curling up on the chair to keep the vigil with me. I wrote and scratch-wrote, canceling, blotting, only vaguely aware of her ministrations. He has not graded it. Just a few scrawled lines. Just some starkstaring words that my eyes form into two sentences. "Your generalities are pretty good and your style excellent. All you have missed is the point." Typically Saunderian, that. That's why the girl was. Spends his time inventing acidic comments. The eagle has found its Prometheus. A stupid, snickering undergraduate. I was a fool who overreached himself. The point. The immutable in the modality of existence. That was your lifelong quest. The I within me. You failed. Yes. Failurewhipped little man. Saunders is a fool if he thinks he has found the point. But in a little boy's eyes. No. A gigantic dreamswelling perfection. I shall arise and go now. Drown it all in a cup of tea. All that tradition, son, all that tea-drinking at four won them empires. I saw. Then the library. Saw through it all. Impress the form of the printed word on the flux. That's mental yogi for you.

It was almost six o'clock in the evening when Naren returned home. He stamped in through the front door, flung his books on the sofa, and called, "Where's everybody?" His wife came running from the kitchen to greet him. His son, four years and eight months old, crawled out from underneath the table where he had been drawing blue and yellow squiggles on a piece of paper. Genuflection before the monarch? He holds his handiwork out to me, waiting to be admired. You fussed over me. I hug his precious body. Till I found you out. I kiss away the serious frowns. The eagle tore at the liver. The dear little browfurrowing of an effort that does not know it is wasted. A serious, bespectacled young man, pedaling furiously. Alas! I am no Prometheus. She smiles at me, now stop pestering your father, and drags the child away, hot from bending over the stove, her hair smelling of curry, while I stare at their retreating backs. I, the mute lord and master.

Naren followed the rest of his family into the kitchen. His fingers working to undo the top button of his shirt, he asked, "Could you make me some tea?" She nods her head and stretches her arm way above her head to reach the tin marked "Tea." This, then, the spine of a tradition. A bare inch of flesh that widens and tautens with the stretching of the arm. You passive progenitor of the changeable. The child is hungry and clamors for attention. That the incarnation of sinful mutability?

"I'm sorry," she said, pulling the lid off the tin and squinting inside. "There aren't any teabags left."

She looks up at me with round, apologetic eyes. My throat is suddenly dry. You, too. I wrench open the door of the refrigerator. You tormenting eagle-woman. Two cans of beer rattle against the white enameled sides. There's escape for one in a glass of bitter. But they won't do.

No, thank you, no canned elysium for me. I routineslip into the role of the tyrant. That deliberately contrite look. Father Bernard, were you sincere? I rant. I rave. The strength of the martyr is in her, and I a puny persecutor. I hurl words against that passive impassivity. Bruised and hurt. And I am the tearful little boy who has lost a belief. Now it's not about teabags anymore. I could never build an empire, you know. I'm just a changing point in the circle. But about assistantships and budgets and any word I find handy. Appearing and reappearing. They hit the wall and fall at her feet, crushed and broken-backed. But it must all cease one day and disappear. I raise my arm threateningly. Must disappear and become one with the I. The child whimpers suddenly, sensing an unequal pitting of strength. But when, oh when, if ever? He hides behind his mother, tugging at the loose end of her crumpled cotton sari (a faded green that I've always hated) and twists it around his bony fingers. And I am ashamed. And therefore angrier.

"Go and play with the Murphy children," Naren ordered his son.

A whimper.

"Go outside and play with Fred and Johnny." The boy wiped his nose with the thin back of his hand.

"Do as I tell you. At once."

He came menacingly toward the mother and child.

"But I don't want to," the boy pleaded. "I don't understand what they say."

"Go and play."

The voice was unrelenting. He knew how hard it was for the child to obey, and knowing, he was ashamed, not for the child, but for himself.

"Darling, do as your father tells you," she said. But it was not an alliance.

You look up at me, hot-eyed and violated. A child on the brink of an adult discovery. I'm trying to protect you. You slink away, hating my power and my authority. Listen. He kicks the door and walks away. Listen, my father. She is furyrepressed, tightlipping the protest at her son's first humiliation. He was

54 | EARLY STORIES (1963–1966)

a dream addict. These, then, are the birth pangs of change, my child. I found him out. This mutability the curse of our species. Your father is a dreamless fool.

A fool who missed the point. Your style is excellent. At least that. Oh, where is the immutable in the modality of my illusion?

Now he was ready for a showdown. But she turned her back on him and stirred something that was cooking in a large pan on the stove. And all at once he lost the words he had fumbled for and found in the dark recesses of his hate. He swung sharply on his heel and went back to the living room. He stood in front of the print of Amrita Shergil's "Sisters" (cut carefully out of *The Illustrated Weekly of India* and tacked on the wall of their quonset hut apartment), transferring his hate to the cheap frame around the print, to the carpet with a charred hole in it where some tenant before them must have dropped a cigarette, to the uneven-legged tables stacked with gaudy paperbacks.

Naren heard his wife's bare feet softly cross the linoleum floor, and then she was beside him.

She smiles. Now I am a leaf falling, falling from a branch high, high up in the tree. She smiles. The ground will be soft and damp, smelling of yesterday's flowers. I come, still falling, falling. She shifts her weight to one foot and leans a shoulder against the wall. On her marble cornea I think I see a point. I am not sure. Is it all a mirage? Must it always be a mirage? I want the damp dusty softness of the ground. Oh, how I want. I want. I. Help me, please help me, help me.

The woman laid a hand on Naren's wrist. Ah, now the marble moment is crumbling as I knew it would. There is no ground, no tree, no leaf. I see through her. Schemer. She is trying to make up with me. You lied to me, you. Soon she will open her mouth. You and I are both dwarfs, Father. Don't speak to me, I beg of you. Her lips quiver with the weight of half-born thoughts. Gigantic midgets. The words will slither off the edge and ruinembrace us. Don't speak. Weep, instead, for this protean leaf flesh.

"Did Mr. Saunders return your paper on Chaucer?" She wants to make me happy. It is important to her because she thinks it matters to me. And she is right. Only she is wrong, too. Schemer. Just a few white sheets with black symbols that now have lost their meaning to me, their creator. That is my fate. Eagleflower. I say nothing. She is content, she is triumphant, yes, she smiles. But now it is just a smile. I grin in return because she is a fool and does not know.

Naren's wife went over to the sofa and flipped through his notebook.

Your generalities are good. You taught me to lust this changing form, all of you. A stupid, giggling coed. They laugh because it is their birthright. And I, even I, am a schemer. All you've missed is the point. But she does not laugh. No, no, you have noticed nothing, you have not seen or heard or suffered. I am grieving, woman, speak to me. Those shirking eyes send me curling, spiraling, with exquisite pain, into the ground. That's the worst of dreams, my dear, these silly dreams. It's your fault after all. The tongue wanted to clap, how lovely, how splendid, oh, my big hero, my god. But it came to something gray instead, something furtive and muddy and altogether embarrassing. You found me out. All right. You found me out. So the mutable changed its shape once more. So you were sorry for me and slunk away. So I was angry and left.

Without a word, he walked out through the front door, not banging it shut behind him because he hated anything dramatic. He saw his son standing quietly on the fringe of the group of neighbors' children playing ball. His son waved to him, a sad little wave, and he turned his face away, and under his palm the steering wheel of the car throbbed to life.

They were sitting together in one corner of the crowded bar, Naren, Benny Friedman, and Jim Wilson. All three were drunk, and happily conscious of the fact.

Jim Wilson banged his fist on the table.

"What we have to go for in this world," he said, "is happiness. Yeah, go for it in a shrewd, determined sort of way."

"I am not unhappy," Naren said. No, only mutable. But I do not. Dream, dreamer, dream and think it's reality. He thought, I like to dance, laugh, feel the river between my toes and my son's damp tendrils around my thumb. Know what it is to be happy. Father, the marble pillars looked so firm holding up our gigantic roof. You left me to perish in your doom, you wept among the ruins of shakable marble and crumbling cement. She knows now. So she, too, must fall back in the muting shade of this flesh. The boy, too, with his teeth in the cookies and the catapult[2] in his hand. But at least you believed. Oh, for the strength to dream! Oh, for the strength to know there is a point after all!

"Another round of the same, please," Benny Friedman called to the passing waiter. Then he leaned forward, elbows on the table, and asked, earnest, sincere, drunk, "Do you think men are potentially good, Naren?"

I am suddenly sick, sick to the pit of my stomach. A little boy looks up at me with a wet hurt in his bosom. I am sick. I feel fingers against my face in the dark, fire-tipped fingers that chill me, chill my bones, my blood. These walls, these tables with bright steel legs, these booths so cozy, so vapid, these people scurrying, garrulous, the glasses empty, emptying, the talk, the men, the heart, all empty, emptying. I know I shall be sick.

Naren raised his arm, holding aloft the glass of beer, and stared at it intently. I. The arm, the glass, the beer. I. The I? There are smaller boxes within

---

2. British word for "slingshot."—Ed.

smaller boxes within smaller boxes. The arm stiffens, the glass is held rigid, and I concentrate my total consciousness. On the arm, the glass, the beer. I drink. The glass, now empty, stands on a wet ring on the dark wooden table. The arm is limp and relaxed and on my lap. Again the modality. And I am a changeling who has not yet discovered the immutable. I am also very drunk.

"We better get a move on, Jim," Benny Friedman said. "This fella is lucky. I bet Oriental wives don't kick up a row when their hubbies come home late stinking of liquor. I bet they get out the icebags instead."

"That's right," Naren answered. "They know who's the boss all right."

Benny Friedman and Jim Wilson began to struggle into the sleeves of their coats. He watched their faces, shadowed and guilty, like painted faces on a gray canvas. They slapped him on the back in a show of jocularity and they left. He saw the door swing closed behind their stooping backs and he ordered another beer. He could not hurry home after what he had just said.

And now that he was home at last, he felt alone and water-veined. His wife was dozing in the living room, a shirt she must have been darning folded clumsily on her lap. He did not dare wake her. Now, this moment, he said, I am a dowdy, slimy-eyed, decrepit old woman. Very deliberately, he lurched against the Kashmiri lampstand, the one they had brought from home because she liked it so much (it was a wedding present from a favorite aunt of hers). It would have crashed to the floor if she had not started suddenly out of her sleep and flung out an unsteady arm against it.

She is a butterfly, warm and browngold and beautiful. If only she could reassure me somehow, tell me she has seen nothing, heard nothing, has not been disillusioned. If only she would say something to me, something foolish and womanly, so that I could go on being a hero, and even a god perhaps. A word, a smile, and I can look at myself in the mirror again and scribble verses that are charming and witty and so clever.

The woman came toward him. Lies! He knew instantly. Lies! Schemes! Pretences! He turned his back on her. I am nasty, half-consciously, half-drunkenly nasty. She has seen the truth. She sees this self, she has seen myriad others. She sees this gray-green mass of horror and agony. But I want to be good and tender and true. And even as I say it, I feel I am making an idiot of myself. She weeps. I ignore her.

The faucet is running in the sink. The water feels cool, sharp, and thin as it trickles down the skin of my neck and down the rims of my ears. Now the hair is wet and sticky under my palm. The water runs from the back of the head to the forehead and the points of the cheeks, and then it drips back on the white porcelain of the sink. My day is over. All you've missed is the point. The silly girl snickered. I am and am not unhappy. She is already in bed. I run to her. Sita, help me find the immutable in the modality of this my illusion. Make me your Ram. She lies there, quiet, still, like a sacrificial victim. I cannot touch her. No.

Naren climbed into his side of the bed and lay on his back, now staring at the ceiling, now watching darkness fade into pleasant recognizable gray shapes. When he grew tired of that, he turned on his side and slowly, carefully, he said, "Lord, bless this day."

58 | EARLY STORIES (1963–1966)

Debate on a Rainy Afternoon (1966)

SATURDAYS WERE HALF HOLIDAYS in Lady Banalata Mitter (English) High School. Miss Ghose, the school's Geography teacher, hated Saturdays. It always drizzled on Saturdays, she said, and even when it didn't it threatened to. The monsoons were still three weeks away. Miss Ghose looked forward to the monsoons. The rain was virile then, she said.

In a very neat, very proper hand, she wrote on the blackboard: CANBERRA IS THE CAPITAL OF AUSTRAILIA. It had already started to rain. She had left both windows open at home, she remembered. She thought of home: a tartar-coated tea kettle, a moist, moldy plant, a pungent view of Bhowanipur from the wooden *chowki*,[1] which was her sofa during the day and her narrow bed at night.

A girl giggled in the second last row. She was sure it was the fat Banerjee girl. Miss Ghose could feel her left eye twitch nervously.

"See me after class," she snapped.

The giggle now yielded to a smirk, and the smirks multiplied, and Miss Ghose felt them lurking behind atlases and open textbooks. She readjusted her glasses to give herself time to think. She coughed, slow and full-throated. She sneaked a quick look at the writing on the board. Of course. She had spelt the name wrong.

"Please, Miss," a round-shouldered front-bencher said, "the textbook spells Australia another way."

Miss Ghose corrected her mistake, and prayed for the end of the hour.

The bell rang about eighteen minutes later, and Miss Ghose was left alone with the offender in a huge, dusty classroom. It was a pleasant sensation. She liked the smell and feel of the empty school. In fact, she often thought she was more at home here than in her own flat. She rubbed a palm against the scratched desk top and eyed the bent head with benevolent sternness. Then the Banerjee girl blew her adenoidal nose, and Miss Ghose squirmed.

With great determination the schoolteacher plucked the glasses off her nose; she took a deep breath to prepare herself for a harangue on discipline; she licked her lips and even opened her mouth. And remembered, quite suddenly, the Saturday staff meeting. The scolding would have to wait till the girl came for her private lesson in the afternoon. Miss Ghose was rather relieved.

"You will learn," she began, opening her desk to get her purse and grade book. "You will learn . . ." Her eyes fell on a faded leather bound copy of Shel-

---

1. A short bench.—Ed.

ley near the lunch box. Miss Ghose loved poetry. "You'll learn *The Skylark*[2] by heart for Monday."

And feeling blithe and aerial all of a sudden, Miss Ghose flew toward the Teachers' Common Room.

Her colleagues had already begun to fill the chairs round the mahogany table that was a recent gift from the school's wealthiest benefactor, Mr. Amarnath Banerjee. They came in twos and threes, wiping chalk-stained fingers on the ends of their saris. Soon the air became thick with schoolroom anecdotes, friendly back-slappings and a cheerful feeling of Emancipated Womanhood. Miss Ghose took her place in front of a huge white cup, and the maid who reflected, though more dimly, the general air of emancipation, filled it with hot tea. Miss Ghose slipped the sandals off her feet and sipped the tea noisily. She wanted to edge her way into the puddles of conversation around her. But she could not think of a way of doing this without appearing pushy or left out.

She was glad when the headmistress' steps sounded in the corridor outside. The Head was the only staff member to wear heels. And to pin her sari to her blouse to keep it in place. The Head was a Christian.

Miss Naskar entered the room briskly and rapped the table for attention. Miss Ghose looked across at Miss Naskar with myopic admiration. There was something commanding in the very set of Miss Naskar's bosom. She was neat, efficient, respected. Then, catching herself admiring and drinking tea with a low-caste Naskar, Miss Ghose felt rather pleased with herself. This was proof positive of her free-thinking nature. This was what she often called Calcutta's "progress syndrome." She realized what an important part she was playing in this progress and beamed at Miss Naskar.

The principal, quite unprepared for this sudden onslaught of smiles, asked, "Did you wish to bring anything to our notice?"

There was an embarrassing pause. Should she explain to Miss Naskar her thoughts about "Free-thinking Womanhood" and "Progress Syndromes"? Miss Ghose made an important decision.

"I was just thinking of what you said last week," she said quickly.

As Miss Naskar's face appeared rather blank, she continued, "I mean what you said about Useful Punishments and all that." She thought the Sita of legends was darned lucky when the earth opened up and swallowed her from further embarrassment in Ram's court. "Well so this afternoon . . . *arré* excuse me, I meant morning . . ." She decided a smile would improve matters considerably at this point. But the horror on the Christian features of Miss Naskar at the sight of two rows of betelnut-stained teeth made her snap her smile shut.

---

2. Mukherjee is referring to Percy Bysshe Shelley's 1820 poem, "To a Skylark."—Ed.

60 | EARLY STORIES (1963–1966)

"I made a girl in my class learn *The Skylark* as a punishment this morning," she said through clenched lips. "That's so much better than writing lines, don't you think?"

The English teacher bristled. "You mean 'Hail to thee blithe spirit bird thou never wert'?"

It was still drizzling, Miss Ghose noticed. It always did on Saturdays. "Yes," she answered, trapped and fluttering. "I . . . I love poetry."

"Shouldn't you have stuck to geography?" The English teacher waved a militant cup.

"But . . . well, you know Shelley . . . I mean it's different."

It was a regular Saturday morning drizzle all right, nagging, constant, like a guilty conscience sheltered from worthwhile guilt. She knew she couldn't finish the sentence without becoming emotional. *Arré Ram!* she exclaimed to herself. At moments like this her spirited western thoughts broke down completely. But Miss Naskar disapproved of any display of emotion, for she modeled her codes of behavior after the missionary lady from Lancashire who had founded this school in a moment of spiritual frustration.

Miss Ghose wiped her perspiring hands on her hips. The rain was doubly irritating, because the British Council's debate had been scheduled for the afternoon, she remembered. She had hoped to wear her new slippers to the debate.

"Let me remind you girls the old-fashioned method of writing lines still has its efficacy," the Head arbitrated. She heaved her commanding bosom and continued, "Now we shall discuss and formulate a policy relating to attendance."

So they discussed the new policy, and should parents be invited to prize distribution, and what was one to do with the dumb Banerjee girl's grades when her father gave so generously to the school fund (they all agreed the child must on no account be flunked, the poor dear).

Miss Ghose sat quietly through it, and watched the drizzle ruin her plans for the debate in the afternoon. It was the kind of drizzle that always spread a nasty wetness between her sandaled toes, and even tried to dampen the general tenderness she felt for the school. *Arré Ram!* was all she could say to herself.

"Well, have a good weekend girls. I'll see you on Monday, at nine sharp." With another shrug of the majestic bosom Miss Naskar dismissed her brood for two whole days of freedom.

When Miss Ghose got outside, the streets were milling with a rained-on, noon-hour crowd. She was glad to lose herself in it. Crowds fascinated her; she so rarely found herself in one. It gave her an exhilarating sense of adventure.

The tram was full, and she had to stand most of the way home, clutching her purse for fear of pickpockets. Each time the tram braked to a stop she bumped into the man strap-hanging beside her, and she blushed to the tips of her spreading ears. But the man was very nice, and offered to hold her straw basket of geography themes, because it looked so heavy, he said.

When she sat down the man managed to find an empty seat very close to her. At first, she went out of her way to ignore him and opened her new copy of the *Reader's Digest*. "Urban Renewal in Pennsylvania" the open *Digest* disgorged to her. She felt the texture of the article. It was smooth, expensive paper. The phrase "Urban Renewal" quite excited her. It became one of *her* words, like "syndrome." Next week she would tell her class about the possibilities of urban renewal in Bhowanipur, she decided.

But the gentleman was inclined to talk. He peered over her shoulder and pointed to the article. Since he *did* appear to be a gentleman, and had a dashing little mustache in the bargain, Miss Ghose allowed him to draw her into conversation.

He told her amusing stories about the *Jatra*, the newspaper for which he worked (Miss Ghose did not subscribe to it), his official pseudonym (Chameleon), the smart captions he had written up that day (Come into My Parlor Said the Spider to the Fly under a picture of refugee tenements), till Miss Ghose could distinctly feel the blithe and birdlike sensation return. She, in turn, told him her hopes of one day leaving the job, leaving the flat, leaving Calcutta, just plain leaving this spectacled-Miss-Ghose-life in a filing cabinet, and taking a Fulbright to the States—maybe to the Pennsylvania of the *Reader's Digest*.

The man smiled at her. It suddenly occurred to the spinster schoolteacher she was being bold—wonderfully, commendably bold. Here she was in a public vehicle in the rush hour, talking to a man, a stranger. Her gaunt frame burnt with the quiet pride of the free-thinking Feminist. She wanted to be gay and amusing. So she told him about the symbolism in *The Skylark*.

All too soon they pulled up at her home stop, and she had to get off after thanking the man profusely for carrying her basket. She stood on the muddy green boulevard, adjusting her books, bag, basket, and discovered she had forgotten her coin purse in the tram: she only carried about eight *annas*[3] in small change at a time. She spent agonized moments hoping the gentleman and the lost purse were not in any way connected.

Her room felt damp and greenish when she entered the flat at last. She turned the light on to cheer things up a bit, and set the kettle on the hot-plate,

---

3. The *anna* was a fractional unit of currency dating back to the British Raj.—Ed.

and finally looked out the window. There was Calcutta, her hometown, waiting out the rain a little sadly, a little courageously, under her second-floor gaze. She felt left out of it somehow; she was alone in spite of the dampness, the greenness and the pot of water warming slowly on the hot-plate.

Miss Ghose turned her back on the view and began to comb her hair in front of the bathroom mirror. The mirror was a cheap one she had picked up long ago from a roadside hawker; it gave her face a clownish twist. But it didn't really matter. She wasn't expecting anyone except the Banerjee girl for an hour of private tutoring. The beautiful waist-long black hair seemed to irritate her, for she knotted it roughly, then watered the *aparajita* plant in the bathroom. The plant was soggy and half dead. Miss Ghose returned to the main room of the flat, crossed her hands on her lap, and waited impatiently for the kettle to whistle.

Promptly at two the doorbell rang. She opened the door to let Nanda Banerjee in, and was startled to find a boy of about twenty standing behind the girl in the dark of the hall.

"This is my brother, Miss Ghose," the girl explained through her adenoids. "The servant was busy this afternoon, so Ashok *dada* had to bring me over."

Miss Ghose was so flustered at the sight of an unexpected visitor she forgot to be irritated with Nanda's adenoids.

"Come inside, come inside," she said. "I've just made a huge pot of tea."

"Oh no! Please don't bother," the boy mumbled. "I have to go right now. Some things to do in town."

He was rather gangly and awkward, but Miss Ghose could tell he would cut a stylish figure in a couple of years.

"It's raining," she protested. "The tea's ready."

"No, excuse me, I must go. At once. I'm in a hurry. Nanda, I'll pick you up in about an hour."

Miss Ghose's hospitality grew belligerent. "Stay for a little while," she commanded. "You can't refuse my humble refreshments. I'll be offended if you do."

The boy stayed; but only for a short while.

After he left, the teacher and pupil took out their prescribed texts on the geography of the southern hemisphere.

"I'm sorry he acted so impatient," the girl said. Miss Ghose was fussing with the rain charts of Australia. "He *was* in an awful hurry . . . to see . . . a friend of his." The teacher seemed quite unimpressed, so she added, "A very close friend. . . . It's a girl!"

Miss Ghose looked up sharply from the chart she had been studying. Even that skinny fellow had romance in his life. He was in love. A boy in love had walked in her room, and sat down on that chair, and drunk tea. No wonder her poor heart had warmed instinctively toward him. She felt a headache coming on.

"Excuse me," she said, walking to the medicine shelf in the bathroom. Headaches had to be nursed carefully, like children. She frowned at the bottle of aspirin, and a clownish mirrored face frowned back at her.

"Of course, nobody knows at home," the girl went on, savoring her rôle of conspirator. "Nobody except me, and even I found out accidentally." Nanda had a whole-hearted hatred of geography, especially after school hours. "If they did, I bet father would turn Ashok *dada* out of the house."

"But what's wrong with it?" Miss Ghose asked, blushing violently as she sensed her own rising excitement. She often thought about love. The books were full of it; and the records, too; even the little ditties she sang to herself sometimes in the evenings after all private tutoring was over. But she had never discussed love with another person. "It's a natural human emotion. It's a part of growing up, my dear. Anyway, the psychology books say so. All these famous men in America and England, they know what they're talking about."

And it was true, she thought fiercely, as if her whole emancipation was at stake. One had to make decisions, one had to commit oneself; but how could anyone discuss it all with this stupid girl whose father gave generously to the school fund?

The girl eyed her sharply, making Miss Ghose break out into a nervous twitch, her second for the day. Miss Ghose decided she really did dislike the girl after all; for being a gossip and rich and adenoidal. She decided she hated the brother in love even more. Miss Ghose preferred her long and companionable monologues on love.

"But it *is* wrong," the girl insisted. "This . . . this woman of *dada's* . . ."

"Well?"

"*She's of a lower caste!*"

That was a bit of a surprise, the schoolteacher had to admit. But just in time she reminded herself she was a free-thinking career woman. In fact, she often thought, only in the privacy of her room of course, she was the epitome of The New Indian Woman.

"There's no caste system in India," she said sententiously. "All that's been abolished by legislation." She felt very superior to the rich Mr. Banerjee. She hoped the word "legislation" would squelch Nanda with its ring of officialdom.

"You just try telling my parents that," the girl retorted. "Anyway, my mother's arranging his marriage with Cotton Mill Mukherjee's eldest daughter."

Miss Ghose took refuge in the economic map of New South Wales. It was a dismal hour.

EARLY STORIES (1963–1966)

A little after three (late, but not late enough so Miss Ghose could enjoy a sense of resentment at being inconvenienced), the brother came for the sister. The schoolteacher would not look the boy in the face. She hoped she had not acted too forward earlier in the afternoon. The two backs, one tall and one short, descended into the dark of the stairway while she stood with her hand on the door. She wondered if he had had a good time, and the twitch came on again, quite suddenly.

She shut the door, and saw three dirty tea cups on the table, a pile of themes to be graded, and the rain outside. That's all it took to make up a weekend. She could have sat down and cried outright, she was so upset.

The debate was scheduled for four, and it was already twenty-seven after three. They were bound to start late, she reasoned with herself, powdering her face, one didn't have to worry about being on time in India, and most of the speakers were Indians (but with such crisp British accents). But, on the other hand, it *was* a British Council affair; it'd probably start on time. Miss Ghose could not find the new pair of sandals she particularly wanted to wear. It would take her at least twenty minutes to walk there. They *had* to be under the bed. Miss Ghose was in a terrible dither. She shouldn't really waste time looking for sandals; in fact she shouldn't go at all at this late hour. But her intellectual and free-thinking prestige needed boosting. She picked up her umbrella, tucked it under her arm, and marched out the door—in her new pale pink slippers.

The hall was very full when she arrived at the British Council. A young man on the rostrum was fluttering his artistic fingers in the direction of his opponents.

"Mr. Chairman," he was saying, "Mr. Chairman, sir, the argument we've just heard is *so* preposterous . . ."

Miss Ghose busied herself with the task of finding a seat. She spotted an elderly gentleman in the last chair of the fifth row. He was the kind of old man, she decided, who went to Sunday morning showings of vintage Shakespeare films and could recite all the *Hamlet* speeches by heart. Miss Ghose sent him an imperative stare. He glanced back at her with a good deal of annoyance, then offered her his seat.

". . . it's so absurd . . ." What a charming lisp the young man had! " . . . as to be *amusing.*"

She settled down comfortably for an afternoon's entertainment, taking off her slippers and hooking her heels on the bars between the chair legs, but knocked her umbrella down in the process. The old man, now standing beside her, gave her a nasty look.

"Why on earth would the rational soldier fight? He has *reason.* He *is* a man of reason. . . ." The young man smiled irresistibly at his audience.

"What's the topic this afternoon?" Miss Ghose asked the old man. He remained in outraged silence for three full minutes. Then he bent down, opening his mouth like a whale, and whispered, "The rational soldier will never fight, and the rational lover will never marry."

She thought how ugly the inside of one's mouth was.

"What about the fate of the conscript in war?" a young man from the opposite team interrupted. He had long hair and a short beard. Miss Ghose couldn't help admiring his romantic looks. Some undergraduate girls up front applauded his insight. Silly women, the schoolteacher said to herself in disgust. "What about Owen and his famous sonnet?"

"Ah, you're mistaken, sir," retorted the first young man. "They don't *have* to fight. They can lay down their arms and hide in trenches."

This drew a laugh from the audience, and the speaker acknowledged it with a caressing wave of the hand. Miss Ghose propped her umbrella against the chair in front. She was glad she had decided to come. The very impulsiveness of her decision, together with the sensation of being in hallowed, academic precincts, delighted her.

"And as for the rational lover. . . ." The young man put on his Don Juan face. The effect was slightly marred by the weak line of his chin, but he was such a dear that Miss Ghose decided to overlook the chin. "The Opposition has failed to establish any good reason why the lover should marry. The rational lover is *reasonable*. He's *guided* by Reason."

The Beard sprang up once again. "Whoever heard of a reasonable lover?" he quipped. It went down well with the audience.

"The rational lover, sir," explained Weak Chin, "is a special lover. When we went up to Cambridge, the first thing we were taught, unofficially of course. . . ."

To Miss Ghose, Cambridge was a magic word. She had always been partial to men from Cambridge, even when she read of the annual boat race in the local papers. An uncle of hers had, long ago, studied at King's College; he had told her about Girton and Newenham.[4] In her damp and moldering imagination the Ideal Woman was generally a gowned, bird-like Cambridge female.

"Why on earth should a sensible chap marry? What's a certificate anyway? Just words, my dear sir. *Meaningless* words on a paper."

Miss Ghose twitched uneasily. His rhetoric had begun to disturb her.

"Words that *fetter* you to one woman, that impose *responsibility*. . . ."

---

4. From the 1870s until the early 1950s, Girton and Newnham were the two women's colleges in Cambridge.—Ed.

She felt gypped. It was peculiar, this fetal sense of loss, sharper, keener than when she had discovered the loss of the coin purse after the tram ride home.

"Today's womanhood is intelligent; it is educated. The women themselves want free love."

The headache was back. It gnawed her neck and temples with sharp little teeth of irritation. It told her, quite simply, the young man was wrong, very wrong; that he was dangerous even; that men like him were responsible for her hay-fever from chalk dust, for Australia being spelt wrong on the blackboard, for the snubs and mild humiliations in the Teachers' Common Room. He was to blame for the intrigue and the love and the adenoids of a Saturday afternoon.

"No!" she shouted, standing boldly in her corner of the room. And suddenly, all restraint snapped, the control of seven years of teaching the same textbooks gave way, and she was bounding over rocks, villages, men, like a river in flood, brandishing her umbrella in a thin hand.

"No! The lover must marry! He must be *made* to marry. It's not fair! Don't talk to me about education and free love. That's bilge. Don't let him hoax you! He's a liar! He's a swine!" She stopped abruptly. She had uttered the word "swine." She hung her head in shame. "Swine!" when she had always considered herself so refined, so circumspect.

The chairman must have been ringing his tiny bell throughout her harangue. She knew him by sight, a pale Englishman with quiet debate-hall humor.

"Will all floor speakers please reserve their contributions till the debate is thrown open to the house?"

But I can't wait for the proper time to speak, she wanted to tell him. The heart won't wait for rules and turns. This is my moment. Now I must soar, with passion, with truth. Or I shall die. But how could she explain about the heart to the blond young man with the bell? She sat down, cowering, in her place. Outside, beyond the British Council windows, it rained.

The old man was very deliberately avoiding her gaze, afraid someone might think they had come together. She could tell what he was thinking from the way he arched his back; that she was a freak, a spinster lady who had studied too much. She had to smile at that. She hadn't studied much; just the B.A. without a major and nine months of B.T. hack work. She didn't try to show the old man his mistake.

While the last speaker was still having his say, Miss Ghose quietly picked up her umbrella and slipped out the door. On the broad sidewalks of Chowringhee, beggars, bums, pariahs stood in wet, shapeless groups. She walked carefully in the rain, feeling alone, feeling foolish.

"*Paan,*[5] sister? Sweet betel-nut? All varieties, all prices." There were dry voices from the vendors' stalls.

"Shut up!" Miss Ghose snapped. But self-pity was only for the weak: she decided to be cheerful. She would go home and make herself a nice cup of hot tea, put her feet up on the chair, and forget the whole stupid thing. What did she care about the debate or the young man with the beard or the Banerjee girl's family? She would go home and treat herself to a couple of imported English crackers she saved for special occasions.

"Peanuts? Roasted peanuts? Only four *annas,* four-four *annas.*" One final gesture, and then she would go back to her room. She walked into a store that had a yellow and blue sign saying: TELEPHONE. The directory was chained to the shelf, and she had trouble looking up the number she wanted to call.

"Hello?" Her voice was just a hoarse whisper. "*Jatra* editorial offices?"

"*Jatra Daily,* circulation two and three quarter million, at your service ma'am."

"Good. This is urgent. I want. . . ."

"Urgent news item, ma'am? I must get the right department, you see. Is it national, international, criminal, society column. . . ."

"Oh, please! This is *important!* I want to speak to Chameleon."

"Chameleon? Did you say you have a speaking Chameleon?"

"Oh for goodness' sake! Your *reporter* Chameleon. I want to speak to him. He's a friend of mine."

"No such name in *Jatra Daily* office."

"Oh! I see. My mistake. Sorry I bothered you."

The man had hung up. She supposed it was only right that Chameleon had changed his name. She hurried through the thick gamey smell of rain, sweat and despair. Half a block from home, the corner *paan*-shop owner stopped her.

"What's the hurry, big sister?" he shouted. "Try one of my Delhi *paans.* Excellent-*sabas,* but free of charge for you. I know you'll bring me good luck."

The rogue, with all his good luck talk. A face like hers, pinched and schoolteacherish, could never bring luck to anyone. Besides the betel-nut would stain her teeth red.

"Only the best for you, big sister."

She held out her hand to receive his gift. The *paan* lay against the dark lines of her hand: a tiny, wilted, decaying thing.

---

5. *Paan* is a popular Indian digestive and mouth freshener, which also acts as an addictive stimulant. It is made from betel leaves, chopped betel (or areca) nuts and a range of different fillings, including red *katha* paste.—Ed.

Back in her flat once more, Miss Ghose plugged in the hot-plate. All the cups were dirty. Her headache was growing worse, her slippers were soaked, and her toes muddy. She carried a cup and saucer to the bathroom sink to wash. She would have to buy a new mirror one of these days, she thought. A corner was flecked with dry toothpaste. With finicky nails she scratched at the spots. And as she scratched a gaunt clownish face stared at her.

"Fool," Miss Ghose said to herself sadly, and bared her red-stained teeth in a ferocious grin.

Outside it still rained.

MIDCAREER STORIES

(1985-1988)

Darkness (1985)

The Middleman and Other Stories (1988)

Darkness (1985)

Angela

ORRIN AND I ARE IN Delia's hospital room. There's no place to sit because we've thrown our parkas, caps and scarves on the only chair. The sides of Delia's bed have metal railings so we can't sit on her bed as we did on Edith's when Edith was here to have her baby last November. The baby, if a girl, was supposed to be named Darlene after Mother, but Edith changed her mind at the last minute. She changed her mind while she was being shaved by the nurse. She picked "Ramona" out of a novel.

My sisters are hopeless romantics.

Orrin loves Delia and brings her little gifts. Yesterday he brought her potted red flowers from Hy-Vee and jangly Mexican earrings I can't quite see Delia wearing; the day before he tied a pair of big, puffy dice to the bedrails. Today he's carrying *One Hundred Years of Solitude*. Delia can't read. She's in a coma, but any day she might come out of it.

He's so innocent! I want to hold his head in my hands, I want to stop up his ears with my fingers so he can't hear Dr. Menezies speak. The doctor is a heavy, gloomy man from Goa, India. Hard work got him where he is. He dismisses Orrin's optimism as frivolous and childish.

"We could read twenty or thirty pages a day to her." Orrin pokes me through my sweater. "You want to start reading?" It's a family joke that I hate to read—my English isn't good enough yet—and Orrin's almost family. "It's like 'Dynasty,' only more weird."

"You read. I'll get us some coffee."

"A Diet Coke for me."

DR. VINNY MENEZIES LIES in wait for me by the vending machines. "Hullo, hullo." He jerks his body into bows as I get myself coffee. "You brighten my day." He's an old-fashioned suitor, an unmarried immigrant nearing forty. He has put himself through medical school in Bombay and Edinburgh, and now he's ready to take a wife, preferably a younger woman who's both affectionate and needy. We come from the same subcontinent of hunger and misery: that's a bonus, he told me.

I feel in the pockets of my blue jeans for quarters, and the coffee slops out of a paper cup.

"I'm making you nervous, Angie?" Dr. Menezies extracts a large, crisp handkerchief from his doctor's white jacket, and blots my burning fingertips. "You're so shy, so sensitive."

He pronounces the "s" in sensitive as a "z."

"Do you have a nickel for five pennies? I need to get a Coke for poor Orrin."

"Of course." He holds a shiny nickel out to me. He strokes my palm as I count out the pennies. "That boyfriend of Delia's, he's quite mental with grief, no?"

"He loves her," I mumble.

"And I you."

But Dr. Menezies lightens the gravity of his confession by choosing that moment to kick the stuck candy machine.

A WEEK BEFORE the accident Orrin asked Delia to marry him. Delia told me this. I've been her sister for less than two years, but we tell each other things. Bad and good. I told her about the cook at the orphanage, how he'd chop wings off crows with his cleaver so I could sew myself a sturdy pair of angel wings. He said I was as good as an angel and the wings would be my guarantee. He'd sit with me on the kitchen floor and feed me curried mutton and rice, creamy custards meant for Bishop Pymm. Delia told me about her black moods. Nobody knows about the black moods; they don't show, she's always so sweet tempered. She's afraid she's going crazy. Most of the time she loves Orrin, but she doesn't want him to marry a nut.

Orrin calls me by my name, his special name for me. "Angel," he says. "Tell me, was she going to say yes?"

I pull open the flip-top of his Diet Coke. He needs looking after, especially now.

"You've come to know her better than any of us." He sits on the windowsill, his feet on the chair. His shoes squash our winter things. "Please, I can handle the truth."

"Of course, she loves you, Orrin." In the dry heat of Delia's hospital room, even my smile is charged with static.

Delia's eyes are open. We can't tell what she sees or hears. It would have been easier on us if she'd looked as though she were sleeping. Orrin chats to her and holds her hand. He makes plans. He'll quit his job with the Presbyterian Youth Outreach Council. He'll move back from Des Moines. When

Delia gets out, they'll fly to Nicaragua and work on a farm side by side with Sandinistas. Orrin's an idealist.

I believe in miracles, not chivalry.

Grace makes my life spin. How else does a girl left for dead in Dhaka get to the Brandons' farmhouse in Van Buren County?

When I was six, soldiers with bayonets cut off my nipples. "They left you babies for dead," Sister Stella at the orphanage would tell me, the way I might tell Ramona bedtime stories. "They left you for dead, but the Lord saved you. Now it's your turn to do Him credit."

We are girls with special missions. Some day soon, the mysteries will be revealed. When Sister Stella was my age, she was a Muslim, the daughter of a man who owned jute mills. Then she fell in love with a tourist from Marseilles, and when he went home she saw him for what he was: the Lord's instrument for calling her to Christianity. Reading portents requires a special kind of literacy.

MRS. GRIMLUND, the nurse, steals into the room in her laced, rubber-soled shoes. Dr. Menezies is with her. "Hullo, again." At the end of a long afternoon, his white doctor's jacket looks limp, but his voice is eager. "Don't look so glum. Delia isn't dying." He doesn't actually ignore Orrin, but it's me he wants to talk to.

Orrin backs off to the window. "We aren't looking glum," he mutters.

Dr. Menezies fusses with Delia's chart. "We're giving her our best. Not to worry, please."

Mrs. Grimlund, deferential, helps out Dr. Menezies. "My, my," she says in a loud, throaty voice, "we're looking a lot livelier today, aren't we?" She turns her blue, watchful eyes on Orrin. As a nurse and a good Christian she wants to irradiate the room with positive thinking. She marches to the window and straightens a bent shutter. Then she eases the empty Coke can out of Orrin's hand and drops it in the wastebasket. She can always find things that need doing. When I first got to Iowa, she taught me to skate on the frozen lake behind our church.

Dr. Menezies plucks Delia's left hand from under the blanket and times her pulse. His watch is flat, a gold wafer on a thick, hairy wrist. It looks expensive. His silk tie, the band of shirt that shows between the lapels of his jacket, even the fountain pen with gold clip, look very expensive. He's a spender. Last Christmas he gave me a choker of freshwater pearls he'd sent for from Macy's catalog.

"Splendid," he agrees. But it's me he's looking at. "Very satisfactory indeed." In spite of my bony, scarred body and plain face.

MIDCAREER STORIES (1985–1988)

Sometimes I visualize grace as a black, tropical bat, cutting through dusk on blunt, ugly wings.

"You wonder why a thing like this happens," Mrs. Grimlund whispers. She lacks only imagination. She tucks Delia's hand back under the blanket and tidies up Orrin's gifts on the night table. I brought a bag of apples. For Orrin, not Delia. Someone has to make him keep up his energies. "She's such a sweet, loving Christian person."

Orrin turns on her. "Don't look for the hand of Providence in this! It was an accident. Delia hit an icy patch and lost control of the wheel." He twists and twists the shutter control.

"Let me get you another Coke," I beg.

"Stop mothering me!"

Orrin needs to move around. He walks from the window to the bed, where Dr. Menezies is holding his flashlight like a lorgnette, then back to the window. He sits on the chair, on top of our parkas. I hate to see him this lost.

"Delia always carries her witness," Mrs. Grimlund goes on. "I never once saw her upset or angry." She's known Delia all of Delia's life. She told me that it was Delia who asked specifically for a sister from Bangladesh. She was dropping me off after choir practice last week and she said, "Delia said, 'I have everything, so I want a sister who has nothing. I want a sister I can really share my things with.'"

I never once saw her angry either. I did see her upset. The moods came on her very suddenly. She'd read the papers, a story about bad stuff in a daycare center maybe, about little kids being fondled and photographed, then she'd begin to cry. The world's sins weighed on her.

Orrin can't seem to stay in the chair. He stumbles toward the door. He isn't trying to leave Delia's room, he's just trying to get hold of himself.

Once Orrin goes out of the room, Mrs. Grimlund lets go a little of her professional cheeriness. "It just pulls the rug from under you, doesn't it? You wonder why?"

I was in the backseat, that's how I got off with a stiff neck. I have been blessed. The Lord keeps saving me.

Delia was driving and little Kim was in the bucket seat, telling a funny story on Miss Wendt, his homeroom teacher. Mother says that when Kim first got here, he didn't speak a word of anything, not even Korean. He was four. She had to teach him to eat lunch slowly. Kim was afraid the kids at school might snatch it if he didn't eat real fast.

He braced himself when we went into that spin. He broke his wrist and sprained his ankle, and the attendant said probably nothing would have happened if he'd just relaxed and sort of collapsed, when he saw it coming.

"THERE'S NO TELLING, is there?" The world's mysteries have ravaged Mrs. Grimlund. Her cap has slipped slightly off-center. "Who'll be taken and who'll be saved, I mean."

Dr. Menezies gives her a long, stern look. "Our job is not to wonder, but to help." He reaches across Delia to touch my arm.

Mrs. Grimlund reddens. What was meant as rebuke comes off as a brisk, passionate outburst. The dingy thicknesses of coat and shirt envelop a wild, raw heart. In the hospital he seems a man of circumspect feelings, but on Sunday afternoons when we drive around and around in his Scirocco, his manner changes. He seems raw, aimless, lost.

"I didn't mean anything wicked," Mrs. Grimlund whispers. "I wasn't questioning the Lord's ways."

I calm her with my smile. My winning smile, that's what the Brandons call it. "Of course you didn't." I am Angela the Angel. Angela was Sister Stella's name for me. The name I was born with is lost to me, the past is lost to me. I must have seen a lot of wickedness when I was six, but I can't remember any of it. The rapes, the dogs chewing on dead bodies, the soldiers. Nothing.

Orrin rushes us from the hall. Dr. Menezies, his passion ebbed, guides Orrin to the chair and I grab the parkas so Orrin will have more room to sit. He needs looking after. I imagine him among Sandinista farmers. He tells slight, swarthy men carrying machetes about rootworms and cutworms. His eyes develop a savior's glittery stare.

"We shouldn't be just standing around and chattering," he shouts. "We're chattering in front of her as though she's dead."

He's all wired up with grief. He was up most of last night, but he doesn't look tired. He looks angry, crazy, stunned, but not tired. He can be with Delia two more days, then he has to go back to Des Moines.

"Take him home." Dr. Menezies is at his best now. He takes charge. He helps Orrin into his jacket and hands him his scarf, cap, mittens. "He isn't doing Delia any good in this state. We have our hands full as it is."

Mrs. Grimlund watches me pull a glove on with my teeth. "I didn't mean it should have been you, Angie." Her lower lip's chewed so deep that there's blood.

Then Dr. Menezies' heavy arm rests on my shoulder. If his watch were any closer to my ear, I'd hear it hum. "Give my regards to your dear parents," he says. He makes a courtly, comical bow. "I shall be seeing you on Sunday? Yes, please?"

ON SUNDAY, after church, we sit down to a huge pork roast—pigs aren't filthy creatures as they are back home—and applesauce, mashed potatoes and gravy, candied carrots, hot rolls. My older sister Edith, and Mary Wellman, the widow from two farms over, have brought dessert: two fruit pies, a chocolate cake and a small jar of macaroons. My brother Bill's wife, Judy, is studying for her Master's in Library Science, so she usually brings something simple, like tossed salad.

I love these Sunday dinners. Company isn't formal and wearying as it was in the orphanage. The days that the trustees in their silk saris and high heels sat at our tables were headachy and endless. The Brandons talk about everything: what Reverend Gertz said about Salvadoran refugees, the blizzard we've just gone through, the tardy Farm Bureau officials who still haven't authorized the loan for this season's plantings. Dad's afraid that if the money doesn't come through by the end of March, he and a whole lot of farmers in the county will be in trouble.

"It'll come through." Mother's the Rock of Gibraltar in our house. She forks carrot slivers delicately and leans her head a wee bit toward Judy who is telling us about her first husband. "I wouldn't let him near the children, I don't care what the judge says." Bill just melts away from conversations about Judy's first husband. Mother wanted to be a school teacher, Delia told me. She wanted to help kids with learning difficulties. Delia wants to be a physical therapist.

"I shouldn't be so sanguine," Ron says. Ron is Edith's husband. He worked for John Deere until the big lay-off, but he's not waiting for recall. He's training himself for computers at the Community College, and during the day he sits in a cubicle in a hall full of cubicles and makes phone calls for a mail-order firm. The firm sells diet pills and offers promotional gifts. Ron thinks the whole thing's a scam to misuse credit cards.

"Oh, you always look on the negative side," Edith scolds. She eats at the small table—to the left of the dining table—with Kim and Fred and Ramona. Fred is Judy's six-year-old. She's expecting a baby with Bill in the spring. Ramona is propped up and strapped into her white plastic feeding seat. Edith lifts teaspoonfuls of mashed potatoes to Ramona's full, baby lips. "She really goes for your gravy, Mom. Don't you, darling?"

Ron reaches into the basket of rolls. "Well, life hasn't been too upscale lately for any of us!"

Dr. Menezies bobs and weaves in his chair, passing the plate of butter curls and the gravy boat. He's clearly the most educated, the most traveled man at the table, but he talks the least. He is polite, too polite, passing platters and tureens, anticipating and satisfying. This Sunday his hair springs in two big, glossy waves from a thin parting, and his mustache has a neat droop. He tries to catch my eye as he passes the butter.

"I don't know what we'd have done without you, Vinny," Dad says. Dad looks away at the yard, and beyond it at the fields that may not get planted this season.

We have deep feelings, but we aren't a demonstrative family. Fellowship is what we aim for. A parent's grieving would be a spectacle in Bangladesh.

Dr. Menezies tugs at his mustache. It could be a pompous gesture, but somehow he manages to make it seem gracious. "It was my duty only, sir."

I can tell he is thrilled with Dad's praise.

AROUND THREE-THIRTY, after Edith and her family and Bill and his family have driven away, and Mary Wellman, Mother and I have washed and dried the dishes, I play Mozart on the piano for Dr. Menezies. He likes to watch me play, he says. He's tone-deaf, but he says he likes the way the nuns taught me to sit, straight and elegant, on the piano bench. A little civility is how he thinks of this Sunday afternoon ritual. It's one more civility that makes the immense, snowy Midwest less alarming, less ambiguous. I throw myself into the "Fantasy in C Minor," the "Exultation." The music, gliding on scarred fingers, transports me to the assembly hall of the orphanage. The Bishop sits in the front row, flanked by the trustees in their flowered saris, and a row or two behind, blissful Sister Stella, my teacher. The air in the hall is sweet and lustrous. Together, pianist and audience, we have triumphed over sin, rapacity, war, all that's shameful in human nature.

"Bravo!" the doctor shouts, forgetting himself, forgetting we're in a farmhouse parlor in the middle of America, only Mary Wellman, my parents, and himself to listen. He claps his soft fists, and his gold watch reflects, a pure white flame, on a window pane. "Bravo, bravo!"

When I've lowered the lid, Mary Wellman gathers up her coat and cake pan. I've wrapped what was left of the chocolate cake in tinfoil and she carries the small, shiny package breast-high as if it is a treasure. Then Mother excuses herself and goes up to her room to crochet an afghan for Christmas. She doesn't know whom she's making it for, yet. She knits, she crochets. On Sundays, she doesn't read, not even the Des Moines *Register*.

Dad joins Kim in the basement for basketball. Dr. Menezies doesn't care for basketball. Or football or baseball. He came to America as a professional, too old to pick up on some things. The trivia, the madness, elude him. He approaches the New World with his stethoscope drawn; he listens to its scary gurgles. He leaves the frolicking to natives. Kim and I are forced to assimilate. A girl with braids who used to race through wet, leechy paddy-fields now skates on frozen water: that surely is a marvel. And the marvels replicate. The coach has put me on the varsity cheerleading squad. To make me feel wanted. I'm grateful. I am wanted. Love is waving big, fluffy pom-poms in school colors; it's wearing new Nikes and leaping into the air. I'd never owned shoes in Bangladesh. All last winter, when Delia played—they said, she was tough on the boards, she was intimidating, awesome, second team All-State, from a school of only two hundred—I shook my pom-poms fiercely from the court's edge, I screamed my sisterly love. Delia sent for me from Dhaka. She knew what her special mission was when she was just in tenth grade. I could die not knowing, not being able even to guess.

"We're alone. At last."

DR. MENEZIES FLOATS TOWARD ME on squeaky new leather shoes. He's the acquisitor. His voice is hoarse, but his face is radiant. He should not alarm me now. After three-thirty on Sunday afternoons, the Brandons leave the front room to us, and nothing untoward ever happens.

I retreat to the upright piano. Shockingly, my body trembles. "Where did everyone go? We seem to be the only idle ones around here."

The doctor laughs. "Idleness is the devil's workshop, no?"

I suggest a walk. But my suitor does not want to walk or go for a drive. He wants to sit beside me on the piano bench and whimper from the fullness of love.

I hold my shoulders pressed back, my spine taut and straight, so straight, the way Sister Stella taught me. Civilities to see us through minor crises.

"You must be worrying all the time about your future, no?" He strokes my hair, my neck. His inflection is ardent. "Your school will be over in May."

"In June."

"May, June, okay. But then what?" He rubs the lumpy scars between my shoulder blades.

There's a new embarrassing twitchiness to my body. My thighs, squeezed tight, begin to hurt.

"In America, grown-up children are expected to fly the coop," my suitor explains. "You will have to fly, Angie. Make your own life. No shilly-shally, no depending on other people here."

"I thought I'd go to Iowa City. Study physical therapy, like Delia."

"Delia will never study physical therapy, Angie." His voice is deep, but quiet, though we are alone. "You are the strong one. I can tell you."

Mrs. Grimlund dances a sad, savage dance on weightless feet. There's no telling who'll be taken and who'll be saved. I wait for some sign. I've been saved for a purpose.

"Anyway, you're going to make the Brandons shell out three-four thousand dollars? I don't think you're so selfish." He gives a shy giggle, but his face is intense. "I think when school is over, you'll be wanting to find a full-time job. Yes. You'll want to find a job. Or a husband. If it is the latter, I'm a candidate putting in an early word."

He slips a trembling arm around my waist and pulls me close. A wet, shy kiss falls like a blow on the side of my head.

Tomorrow when I visit Delia, I'll stop by the Personnel Department. They know me, my family. I'll work well with handicapped children. With burn-center children. I'll not waste my life.

But that night, in the room with two beds, Dr. Menezies lies on Delia's pink chenille bedspread. His dark, ghostly face rests on pillowshams trimmed with pink lace. He offers me intimacy, fellowship. He tempts with domesticity. Phantom duplexes, babies tucked tight into cribs, dogs running playfully off with the barbecued steak.

What am I to do?

Only a doctor could love this body.

Then it is the lavender dusk of tropics. Delinquents and destitutes rush me. Legless kids try to squirm out of ditches. Packs of pariah dogs who have learned to gorge on dying infant flesh, soldiers with silvery bayonets, they keep coming at me, plunging their knives through my arms and shoulders. I dig my face into the muddy walls of a trough too steep to climb. Leeches, I can feel leeches gorging on the blood of my breasts.

The Lady from Lucknow

WHEN I WAS FOUR, one of the girls next door fell in love with a Hindu. Her father intercepted a love note from the boy, and beat her with his leather sandals. She died soon after. I was in the room when my mother said to our neighbor, "The Nawab-*sahib* had no choice, but Husseina's heart just broke, poor dear." I was an army doctor's daughter, and I pictured the dead girl's heart— a rubbery squeezable organ with auricles and ventricles—first swelling, then bursting and coating the floor with thick, slippery blood.

We lived in Lucknow at the time, where the Muslim community was large. This was just before the British took the fat, diamond-shaped subcontinent and created two nations, a big one for Hindus and a littler one for us. My father moved us to Rawalpindi in Pakistan two months after Husseina died. We were a family of soft, voluptuous children, and my father wanted to protect us from the Hindus' shameful lust.

I have fancied myself in love many times since, but never enough for the emotions to break through tissue and muscle. Husseina's torn heart remains the standard of perfect love.

At seventeen I married a good man, the fourth son of a famous poet-cum-lawyer in Islamabad. We have a daughter, seven, and a son, four. In the Muslim communities we have lived in, we are admired. Iqbal works for IBM, and because of his work we have made homes in Lebanon, Brazil, Zambia and France. Now we live in Atlanta, Georgia, in a wide, new house with a deck and a backyard that runs into a golf course. IBM has been generous to us. We expect to pass on this good, decent life to our children. Our children are ashamed of the dingy cities where we got our start.

Some Sunday afternoons when Iqbal isn't at a conference halfway across the world, we sit together on the deck and drink gin and tonics as we have done on Sunday afternoons in a dozen exotic cities. But here, the light is different somehow. A gold haze comes off the golf course and settles on our bodies, our new house. When the light shines right in my eyes, I pull myself out of the canvas deck chair and lean against the railing that still smells of forests. Everything in Atlanta is so new!

"Sit," Iqbal tells me. "You'll distract the golfers. Americans are crazy for sex, you know that."

He half rises out of his deck chair. He lunges for my breasts in mock passion. I slip out of his reach.

At the bottom of the backyard, the golfers, caddies and carts are too minute to be bloated with lust.

But, who knows? One false thwock! of their golfing irons, and my little heart, like a golf ball, could slice through the warm air and vanish into the jonquil-yellow beyond.

It isn't trouble that I want, though I do have a lover. He's an older man, an immunologist with the Center for Disease Control right here in town. He comes to see me when Iqbal is away at high-tech conferences in sunny, remote resorts. Just think, Beirut was once such a resort! Lately my lover comes to me on Wednesdays even if Iqbal's in town.

"I don't expect to live till ninety-five," James teases on the phone. His father died at ninety-three in Savannah. "But I don't want a bullet in the brain from a jealous husband right now."

Iqbal owns no firearms. Jealousy would inflame him.

Besides, Iqbal would never come home in the middle of the day. Not even for his blood pressure pills. The two times he forgot them last month, I had to take the bottle downtown. One does not rise through the multinational hierarchy coming home in midday, arriving late, or leaving early. Especially, he says, if you're a "not-quite" as we are. It is up to us to set the standards.

Wives who want to be found out will be found out. Indiscretions are deliberate. The woman caught in mid-shame is a woman who wants to get out. The rest of us carry on.

James flatters me indefatigably; he makes me feel beautiful, exotic, responsive. I am a creature he has immunized of contamination. When he is with me, the world seems a happy enough place.

Then he leaves. He slips back into his tweed suit and backs out of my driveway.

I MET JAMES BEAMISH at a reception for foreign students on the Emory University campus. Iqbal avoids these international receptions because he thinks of them as excuses for looking back when we should be looking forward. These evenings are almost always tedious, but I like to go; just in case there's someone new and fascinating. The last two years, I've volunteered as host in the "hospitality program." At Thanksgiving and Christmas, two lonely foreign students are sent to our table.

That first evening at Emory we stood with name tags on lapels, white ones for students and blue ones for hosts. James was by a long table, pouring Chablis into a plastic glass. I noticed him right off. He was dressed much like the other resolute, decent men in the room. But whereas the other men wore white or blue shirts under their dark wool suits, James' shirt was bright red.

His wife was with him that evening, a stoutish woman with slender ankles and expensive shoes.

"Darling," she said to James. "See if you can locate our Palestinian." Then she turned to me, and smiling, peered into my name tag.

"I'm Nafeesa Hafeez," I helped out.

"Na-fee-sa," she read out. "Did I get that right?"

"Yes, perfect," I said.

"What a musical name," she said. "I hope you'll be very happy here. Is this your first time abroad?"

James came over with a glass of Chablis in each hand. "Did we draw this lovely lady? Oops, I'm sorry, you're a *host*, of course." A mocking blue light was in his eyes. "Just when I thought we were getting lucky, dear."

82 | MIDCAREER STORIES (1985–1988)

"Darling, ours is a Palestinian. I told you that in the car. This one is obviously not Palestinian, are you, dear?" She took a bright orange notebook out of her purse and showed me a name.

I had to read it upside-down. Something Waheed. School of Dentistry.

"What are you drinking?" James asked. He kept a glass for himself and gave me the other one.

Maybe James Beamish said nothing fascinating that night, but he was attentive, even after the Beamishes' Palestinian joined us. Mrs. Beamish was brave, she asked the dentist about his family and hometown. The dentist described West Beirut in detail. The shortage of bread and vegetables, the mortar poundings, the babies bleeding. I wonder when aphasia sets in. When does a dentist, even a Palestinian dentist, decide it's time to cut losses.

Then my own foreign student arrived. She was an Indian Muslim from Lucknow, a large, bold woman who this far from our common hometown claimed me as a countrywoman. India, Pakistan, she said, not letting go of my hand, what does it matter?

I'd rather have listened to James Beamish but I couldn't shut out the woman's voice. She gave us her opinions on Thanksgiving rituals. She said, "It is very odd that the pumpkin vegetable should be used for dessert, no? We are using it as vegetable only. Chhi! Pumpkin as a sweet. The very idea is horrid."

I promised that when she came to our house for Thanksgiving, I'd make sweetmeats out of ricotta cheese and syrup. When you live in as many countries as Iqbal has made me, you can't tell if you pity, or if you envy, the women who stayed back.

I DIDN'T HEAR from James Beamish for two weeks. I thought about him. In fact I couldn't get him out of my mind. I went over the phrases and gestures, the mocking light in the eyes, but they didn't add up to much. After the first week, I called Amina and asked her to lunch. I didn't know her well but her husband worked at the Center for Disease Control. Just talking to someone connected with the Center made me feel good. I slipped his name into the small talk with Amina and her eyes popped open, "Oh, he's famous!" she exclaimed, and I shrugged modestly. I stayed home in case he should call. I sat on the deck and in spite of the cold, pretended to read Barbara Pym novels. Lines from Donne and Urdu verses about love floated in my skull.

I wasn't sure Dr. Beamish would call me. Not directly, that is. Perhaps he would play a subtler game, get his wife to invite Iqbal and me for drinks. Maybe she'd even include their Palestinian and my Indian and make an international evening out of it. It sounded plausible.

THE LADY FROM LUCKNOW | *83*

FINALLY JAMES BEAMISH CALLED ME on a Tuesday afternoon, around four. The children were in the kitchen, and a batch of my special chocolate sludge cookies was in the oven.

"Hi," he said, then nothing for a bit. Then he said, "This is James Beamish from the CDC. I've been thinking of you."

He was between meetings, he explained. Wednesday was the only flexible day in his week, his day for paperwork. Could we have lunch on Wednesday?

The cookies smelled gooey hot, not burned. My daughter had taken the cookie sheet out and put in a new one. She'd turned the cold water faucet on so she could let the water drip on a tiny rosebud burn on her arm.

I felt all the warm, familiar signs of lust and remorse. I dabbed the burn with an ice cube wrapped in paper towel and wondered if I'd have time to buy a new front-closing bra after Iqbal got home.

James and I had lunch in a Dekalb County motel lounge.

He would be sixty-five in July, but not retire till sixty-eight. Then he would live in Tonga, in Fiji, see the world, travel across Europe and North America in a Winnebago. He wouldn't be tied down. He had five daughters and two grandsons, the younger one aged four, a month older than my son. He had been in the navy during the war (*his* war), and he had liked that.

I said, "'Goodbye, Mama, I'm off to Yokohama.'" It was silly, but it was the only war footage I could come up with, and it made him laugh.

"You're special," he said. He touched my knee under the table. "You've been everywhere."

"Not because I've wanted to."

He squeezed my knee again, then paid with his MasterCard.

As we were walking through the parking lot to his car (it was a Cougar or a Buick, and not German or British as I'd expected), James put his arm around my shoulders. I may have seen the world but I haven't gone through the American teenage rites of making out in parked cars and picnic grounds, so I walked briskly out of his embrace. He let his hand slide off my shoulder. The hand slid down my back. I counted three deft little pats to my bottom before he let his hand fall away.

Iqbal and I are sensual people, but secretive. The openness of James Beamish's advance surprised me.

I got in the car, wary, expectant.

"Do up the seatbelt," he said.

He leaned into his seatbelt and kissed me lightly on the lips. I kissed him back, hard. "You don't panic easily, do you?" he said. The mocking blue light was in his eyes again. His tongue made darting little thrusts and probes past my lips.

84 | MIDCAREER STORIES (1985–1988)

Yes, I do, I would have said if he'd let me.

We held hands on the drive to my house. In the driveway he parked behind my Honda. "Shall I come in?"

I said nothing. Love and freedom drop into our lives. When we have to beg or even agree, it's already too late.

"Let's go in." He said it very softly.

I didn't worry about the neighbors. In his gray wool slacks and tweed jacket, he looked too old, too respectable, for any sordid dalliance with a not-quite's wife.

Our house is not that different in size and shape from the ones on either side. Only the inside smells of heavy incense, and the walls are hung with rows of miniature paintings from the reign of Emperor Akbar. I took James' big wrinkled hand in mine. Adultery in my house is probably no different, no quieter, than in other houses in this neighborhood.

Afterwards it wasn't guilt I felt (guilt comes with desire not acted), but wonder that while I'd dashed out Tuesday night and bought myself silky new underwear, James Beamish had worn an old T-shirt and lemon-pale boxer shorts. Perhaps he hadn't planned on seducing a Lucknow lady that afternoon. Adventure and freedom had come to him out of the blue, too. Or perhaps only younger men like Iqbal make a fetish of doing sit-ups and dieting and renewing their membership at the racquet club when they're on the prowl.

October through February our passion held. When we were together, I felt cherished. I only played at being helpless, hysterical, cruel. When James left, I'd spend the rest of the afternoon with a Barbara Pym novel. I kept the novels open at pages in which excellent British women recite lines from Marvell to themselves. I didn't read. I watched the golfers trudging over brown fairways instead. I let the tiny golfers—clumsy mummers—tell me stories of ambitions unfulfilled. Golf carts lurched into the golden vista. I felt safe.

In the first week of March we met in James' house for a change. His wife was in Madison to babysit a grandson while his parents flew to China for a three-week tour. It was a thrill to be in his house. I fingered the book spines, checked the color of sheets and towels, the brand names of cereals and detergents. Jane Fonda's Workout record was on the VCR. He was a man who took exceptional care of himself, this immunologist. Real intimacy, at last. The lust of the winter months had been merely foreplay. I felt at home in his house, in spite of the albums of family photographs on the coffee table and the brutish metal vulvas sculpted by a daughter in art school and stashed in the den. James was more talkative in his own house. He showed me the photos he wanted me to see, named real lakes and mountains. His family was real, and not quite real. The daughters were hardy, outdoor types. I saw them hiking in Zermatt and bicycling through Europe. They had red cheeks and backpacks. Their faces were honest and marvelously ordinary. What would they say if they knew their father, at sixty-five, was in bed with a married woman from Lucknow? I feared and envied their jealousy more than any violence in my husband's heart.

Love on the decline is hard to tell from love on the rise. I have lived a life perched on the edge of ripeness and decay. The traveler feels at home everywhere, because she is never at home anywhere. I felt the hot red glow of blood rushing through capillaries.

HIS WIFE CAME BACK EARLY, didn't call, caught a ride from Hartsfield International with a friend. She had been raised in Saskatchewan, and she'd remained thrifty.

We heard the car pull into the driveway, the loud "thank yous" and "no, I couldn'ts" and then her surprised shout, "James? Are you ill? What're you doing home?" as she shut the front door.

We were in bed, sluggish cozy and still moist under the goosedown quilt that the daughter in Madison had sent them as a fortieth anniversary gift some years before. His clothes were on top of a long dresser; mine were on the floor, the stockings wrinkled and looking legless.

James didn't go to pieces. I had to admire that. He said, "Get in the bathroom. Get dressed. I'll take care of this."

I am submissive by training. To survive, the Asian wife will usually do as she is told. But this time I stayed in bed.

"How are you going to explain me away, James? Tell her I'm the new cleaning woman?" I laughed, and my laugh tinkled flirtatiously, at least to me.

"Get in the bathroom." This was the fiercest I'd ever heard him.

"I don't think so," I said. I jerked the quilt off my body and didn't move my legs.

So I was in bed with the quilt at my feet, and James was by the dresser buttoning his shirt when Kate Beamish stood at the door.

She didn't scream. She didn't leap for James' throat—or mine. I'd wanted passion, but Kate didn't come through. I pulled the quilt over me.

I tried insolence. "Is your wife not the jealous kind?" I asked.

"Let's just get over this as quietly and quickly as we can, shall we?" she said. She walked to the window in her brown Wallabies. "I don't see any unfamiliar cars, so I suppose you'll expect James to drive you home."

MIDCAREER STORIES (1985–1988)

"She's the jealous type," James said. He moved toward his wife and tried to guide her out of the bedroom.

"I'm definitely the jealous kind," Kate Beamish said. "I might have stabbed you if I could take you seriously. But you are quite ludicrous lounging like a Goya nude on my bed." She gave a funny little snort. I noticed straggly hairs in her nostrils and looked away.

James was running water in the bathroom sink. Only the panicky ones fall apart and call their lawyers from the bedroom.

She sat on my side of the bed. She stared at me. If that stare had made me feel secretive and loathsome, I might not have wept, later. She plucked the quilt from my breasts as an internist might, and snorted again. "Yes," she said, "I don't deny a certain interest he might have had," but she looked through my face to the pillow behind, and dropped the quilt as she stood. I was a shadow without depth or color, a shadow-temptress who would float back to a city of teeming millions when the affair with James had ended.

I had thought myself provocative and fascinating. What had begun as an adventure had become shabby and complex. I was just another involvement of a white man in a pokey little outpost, something that "men do" and then come to their senses while the *memsahibs* drink gin and tonic and fan their faces. I didn't merit a stab wound through the heart.

It wasn't the end of the world. It was humorous, really. Still. I let James call me a cab. That half hour wait for the cab, as Kate recalled tales of the grandson to her distracted husband was the most painful. It came closest to what Husseina must have felt. At least her father, the Nawab-*sahib*, had beaten her.

I HAVE KNOWN all along that perfect love has to be fatal. I have survived on four of the five continents. I get by because I am at least moderately charming and open-minded. From time to time, James Beamish calls me. "She's promised to file for divorce." Or "Let's go away for a weekend. Let's go to Bermuda. Have lunch with me this Wednesday." Why do I hear a second voice? She has laughed at me. She has mocked my passion.

I want to say yes. I want to beg him to take me away to Hilton Head in his new, retirement Winnebago. The golden light from the vista is too yellow. Yes, *please*, let's run away, keep this new and simple.

I can hear the golf balls being thwocked home by clumsy mummers far away where my land dips. My arms are numb, my breathing loud and ugly from pressing hard against the cedar railing. The pain in my chest will not go away. I should be tasting blood in my throat by now.

The World According to Hsü

THEY HAD COME to this island off the coast of Africa for simple reasons: he to see the Southern Cross and she to take stock of a life that had until recently seemed to her manageably capricious. Their travel agent, a refugee from Beirut, morbidly sensitive to political and epidemical tremors, had not warned them of the latest crisis in the capital. Coups and curfews visited with seasonal regularity, but like nearly everything else about the island, went unreported in the press. The most recent, involving melancholy students and ungenerous bureaucrats, had been especially ferocious; people had died and shops had been sacked but nothing had stained the island's reputation for languor or spices.

The Claytons did not blame Camille Lioon, the travel agent. No one could have told them about the revolution, this thing called, alternatively (in the island's morning daily), *les événements de soixante-dix-huit*, and *l'aventure des forces contre-revolutionnaires, impérialistes, et capitalistes*. Continents slide, no surface is permanent. Today's ballooning teenager is tomorrow's anorexic. The island should have been a paradise.

They wanted an old-fashioned vacation on the shores of a vast new ocean. They had planned to pick shells, feed lemurs on the balcony of a hotel managed by a paunchy Indian, visit a colonial museum or two, where, under glass, the new guardians of the nation enshrined the whips and chains of their unnatural past. They had readied themselves for small misadventures—lost bags, canceled hotel reservations—the kind that Graeme Clayton could tell with some charm on their return to Canada.

But Ratna Clayton, groping for the wisdom that should have descended on her in her thirty-third year, hoped for something more from this journey to the island below the equator. Surely simple tourist pleasures, for instance, watching the big pink sun fall nightly into calm pink waters, would lighten the shadows of the past six months? She imagined herself in her daring new bikini on a shoreline tangled with branches and cattle skulls. The landscape was always narcotically beautiful. But always, Graeme was just behind her, training his Nikon on that chaotic greenery to extract from it some definitive order.

In Montreal, each Ektachrome transparency of the island, she knew, would command a commentary, every slide a mini-lecture. Lecturing was Graeme's business. For his friends he would shape and reshape the tropical confusion. Ratna would serve her cashew-lamb pilaf and begin hesitant anecdotes about pickpockets and beggars. The friends would listen with civil, industrious faces until Graeme, having set up the projector, was free to entertain and instruct. The burned-out buses, they would learn, were Hungarian; the plump young paratroopers with flat African faces were coastal people, a reminder of the island's proximity to the Dark Continent. The ducks in the rice paddies did not yet answer to genus and species; Graeme would have to look it up. And bitter, terrified, politicized Freddie McLaren, Graeme's colleague at McGill, would find an opportune moment to pipe up, "I don't know why you two went to Africa. If you wanted trouble you could've found it right here in Canada." Freddie with his talk of Belfast and Beirut, and what the future held for Montreal. "It's not going to matter one damn bit to them that you speak French and hate Ontario as much as they do," he'd say, and Graeme would answer, "But Freddie—I don't hate Ontario." Ratna Clayton would add, quietly, "And I don't hate Quebec." And soon the McLarens would lead the Claytons back from Africa and its riots to the safe disasters of letter-bombs and budget cuts.

Camille Lioon had prepared them for lesser dangers. "No, m'sieur, you should not make the *escale* in Zanzibar, where I have heard there is much cholera." Camille had contacts in World Health, in banks, in subministries around the world. Ratna pictured a small army of sallow Lioons frenziedly sending telegrams to all parts of the French-speaking world: *disaster imminent. Don't come. Hide.* And to Ratna he'd whispered, "No, madame, if I were Hindu I would cancel the *escale* in Jiddah. Those Saudis, they're so insensible." Ratna smiled, suspecting that Camille had slipped on a tangled cognate.

"Insensitive?" she'd asked.

"Yes, yes, insensitive."

"Unfeeling?" Ratna pursued.

"That's it! *Un peu brutale.*"

In Riyadh, chopped-off hands were lying on the street. The street was black with flies, feasting on hands, according to Camille. "I am no less an Arab than they, but if I land in Mecca—phfft—they slit my throat, no questions asked. Not even in anger. No, I would definitely not stop in Jiddah." The trouble with Saudis, Graeme had thought, was not with their quaint notions of punishment. It was that they had lost some of their wayward mystery. In spite of their genial floggings and stoical dismemberments, petro-dollars had opened them up, made them accessible to Rotarians and the covers of *Time*. And so the Claytons had given up their earlier itinerary, not because Camille's caution was infectious, but because they yearned for once to be simple-minded travelers yielding to every expensive and off-beat prompting. This island of spices, this misplaced Tahiti, this gorgeous anachronism, would serve them beautifully, they'd thought.

Graeme had reserved his strength, which came to him in paroxysms much like panic, for this voyage of a lifetime to what everyone called *la grande île au bout du monde*. Islands and endings were Graeme's business too, and he demanded, in his leisure, a certain consonance with his discipline. He was thirty-five, the youngest full professor of psychology at McGill, an authority on a whole rainbow of dysfunctions, and he had a need for something which he in his old-fashioned way called romance. It was not the opposite of reality; it was more a sharpening of line and color, possible only in the labs or on a carefully researched, fully cooperative, tropical island. In the place of a heart he should have had a Nikon.

Besides, he hoped the vacation would be the right setting for persuading Ratna to move to Toronto, where he'd been offered—quite surprisingly in a year when English Montrealers would leap at just about anything—the chair in Personality Development. So far, she'd been obdurate. She claimed to be happy enough in Montreal, less perturbed by the impersonal revenges of Quebec politicians than personal attacks by Toronto racists. In Montreal she was merely "English," a grim joke on generations of British segregationists. It was thought charming that her French was just slightly short of fluent. In Toronto, she was not Canadian, not even Indian. She was something called, after the imported idiom of London, a Paki. And for Pakis, Toronto was hell.

She had only a secondhand interest in the English language and a decided aversion to British institutions; English had been a mutually agreed upon second language in her home, in her first city, in her first country, in her career and it had remained so, even in her marriage. Frenchification was quaint, not threatening. She'd even voted for the separatists. She had claimed reluctance to chop off what tentative roots she had in Montreal. *La grande île* was to be a refuge from just such fruitless debates.

So, having picked their archipelago to get away to, the Claytons had flown in on schedule one wintry June morning (it was cool; sweater weather, though many of the islanders at the airport had been wearing overcoats, gloves and caps with tied-down earflaps) and immediately found themselves prisoners of an unreported revolution.

Their prison, a twenty-five-dollar-a-day double room with a bath and bidet at the Hotel Papillon, was not uncomfortable. In a time of lesser crisis they might have complained, among themselves, of the lumps in the mattress or the pale stains on the towel. They might have wondered at the new gray wall-to-wall carpeting, the Simenon novels on the window ledge, the Cinzano ashtrays ("This is Africa? This is a People's Republic?"). But now, on their first day in the capital, still convalescing from thirty hours' flying and the teetering ride in the airport taxi, the Papillon appeared a triumph of French obstinacy in the face of antipodean distraction.

The entrance to the hotel, whose walls were ochre deepening to brown where the water pipes had rusted, was off a sidewalk choked with stalls. Around the entrance were pyramids of tomatoes, green peppers, dried fish, fried grasshoppers, safety pins and chipped buttons. The sidewalk directly in front of it was gouged and fissured, as though islanders walking by had wrenched up the paving stones and put them to more urgent, if unrecorded, use. The gouges were coated with the pulp of chewed rotting food spat out by stallkeepers. An opaque glass door behind a sidewalk tangle of metal tables and chairs had announced in neat black lettering:

HOTEL PAPILLON
Prop: M J-P Papillon

Monsieur Jean-Paul Papillon, the Claytons learned from Justin, the taxi-driver, had died thirteen years before. The hotel had been declining with his health. Why hadn't they chosen the new Hilton? The Hilton was a touch of Paris.

"In the old days," Justin said, "this place was better than anything in Marseilles. The French called it the pearl of the Indian Ocean. The restaurant of the Papillon had two stars from Michelin." Then, turning to Ratna Clayton, he'd asked, "Do you want me to drive you to the Hilton?"

They had gotten off at the Papillon to spite the driver. To Justin, the Claytons had seemed American or German, part of the natural Hilton crowd. The Hilton had four dining rooms and a rooftop casino. From late October through to the beginning of autumn, in April, it maintained an outdoor pool. Graeme understood the typecasting and decided not to forgive him.

"Papillon," Graeme had ordered, having studied all the guidebooks on the flight from Paris. "L'avenue d'Albert Camus."

"M'sieur-dame, you don't understand," Justin had pleaded, placing a pink restraining palm on their luggage. "The Papillon is in the center of the marketplace."

"*Tant mieux*," Ratna had said, nudging a suitcase out of his grip.

"But madame, *les manifesteurs*. . . . there might be trouble again tonight."

"We'll manage," Graeme had said. Other people's revolutions could not shock or dismay. He wondered if tourists in Montreal, those few who still came, counted themselves equally bold.

"But m'sieur," Justin begged, now flushed from his coyness, "all the Indians, they stay at the Hilton. In times like these, it's the safest place."

"I am a Canadian," Ratna said arrogantly. "I am a Canadian tourist and I want to stay at the Papillon in the marketplace, okay?"

The truth was, she knew, that even on this island she could not escape the consequences of being half—the dominant half—Indian. Her mother, a Czech nurse, had found love or perhaps only escape in a young Indian medical student on holiday in Europe in 1936, and she had sailed with him to Calcutta. She'd died there last year, a shrunken widow in a white sari, allegedly a happy woman. The European strain had appeared and disappeared, leaving no genetic souvenir (for her first two years, family legend had it, Ratna had been a pale, scrawny blond, shunned by her father's family as a "white rat"). Ratna's Europeanness lay submerged like an ancient city waiting to be revealed by shallow-water archaeology. Her show of unaccustomed fervor apparently satisfied Justin.

"*Alors, madame, vous n'êtes pas indienne?*" He had then swung the bag out of her hand and carried it to the hotel entrance.

"Are the nights cloudy in June?" Graeme had asked, paying him off. "I've come a long way to see the Southern Cross."

That's when they'd learned the cruncher. Justin pointed to a hastily scrawled sign, pasted to the door. COUVRE-FEU 17h.

"All-night curfew, m'sieur. *Tout est fermé.* . . . No stars, no nothing."

"God!" muttered Graeme Clayton.

"That explains those paratroopers tramping around the paddy-fields," Ratna remarked. She was a freelance journalist grateful for good copy. There had been paratroopers everywhere, black faces from the coast, ubiquitous sentinels among the copper-skinned, straw-hatted natives of the capital. Descending on the adobe villages like Van Gogh's crows, they had squatted in the clean greenness of banana groves, kicked the muddy flanks of water buffalo and sped down the airport road in their frail Renaults. They had even stopped Justin's taxi a few miles outside the city and ordered a half-hearted search of the Claytons' baggage. She'd not realized, until seeing the curfew sign, that she and Graeme might have been in danger, that the soldiers' comments in a different language, obviously directed to Justin about her, could have led to untraceable tragedy in a paddy-field.

Justin seemed reluctant to leave them. "You want me to come back for you this afternoon? I'll make you a cheap excursion."

"How much?"

"Ten thousand francs. I'll give you the two-hour tour, bring you back before the curfew."

Ratna had not yet calibrated the local currency. Ten thousand was, roughly, thirty dollars. At the sound of ten thousand she had snapped instinctively, "Too much."

"Eight thousand."

"Come for us at three."

Still Justin hung around. He had become transformed from taxi-driver to gracious host. She wondered if they owed him their lives; that if they'd not been cheerful and approving and engaging in that brief ride from the airport to the informal roadblock, and if he had not said something preventive to the troops, she and Graeme would have been slaughtered, their travelers' checks and local currency and Canadian dollars and gold chains and Nikon apportioned as the usual supplemental wages.

The lobby was narrow, dark, no more than a corridor partitioned off the hotel's former dining room. Three islanders were still breakfasting on *café au lait*, croissants and a Gauloise: each at his table replicating France. Compared to them, Ratna thought, the Montrealers they had left behind at Charles de Gaulle Airport—those for whom Paris and not the end of the world had been the destination—were nothing but wonderstruck Americans, accidental French speakers with fleurs-de-lis sewn on their bulging hip pockets. Far less Gallic than these Peruvian-looking Africans waiting out another bizarre crisis at the Papillon.

The proprietress sat at the end of the dark corridor, behind an uneven counter and under a cardboard arrow that said: Caisse. She was obese, with densely powdered, flour-white skin.

Justin preceded the Canadians. He asked first after Madame Papillon's daughter, who had apparently been sent back to France for *traitements*. Treatments for what? Graeme was about to ask, then suppressed it. Madame Papillon asked Justin about *les événements*: had there been much looting? He reassured her. Nothing new. Only two blocks burned. The epicenter of the looting was only a block away; Madame Papillon was evidently reclusive. The shops of the Indians in la Place de l'Indépendance and along the Faubourg. *Les indiens*, they had fled as usual to the Hilton, to lock up their gold and money in the hotel's safe. *"Ah, toujours les indiens,"* wheezed Madame, *"les juifs de l'Afrique."* Students were gathering again in front of the Secretariat building. Possibly, another outbreak might occur that night. (Later, during the sightseeing trip, Justin explained that Madame Papillon, a model of Vichy rectitude, had not stepped from the hotel since her husband's death thirteen years before. "I bring her news like infusions," he said.)

After the bellboy had left, cautioning them that the tap water was not potable and that mineral water could be secured through him more cheaply than through room service, they forced open the window shutters for their first private view of the city.

"Don't worry about the smoke," Graeme said. "The fires are out."

"I'm not worrying about this island," Ratna said from the closet where she was checking the wallpaper seams for roaches. "I'm worrying about Toronto." A week before their flight, a Bengali woman was beaten and nearly blinded on the street. And the week before that an eight-year-old Punjabi boy was struck by a car announcing on its bumper: KEEP CANADA GREEN. PAINT A PAKI.

He knew from the deadness of her voice what was to come. "It won't happen to you," he said quickly. He resented this habit she had of injecting bitterness into every new scene. He had paid five thousand dollars in airfare so they could hold hands on a beach under the Southern Cross, but already she was accusing him of selfishness and bigotry.

"That's not the point."

"Look—violence is everywhere. Toronto's the safest city on the continent."

"Sure," she said, "for you." She hung a cotton dress in the closet. She had married him for a trivial reason—his blue eyes—and then discovered in him tenderness, affection, decency. Once not long ago she had believed in the capacity of these virtues to restore symmetry to lives mangled by larger, blunter antipathies. "An Indian professor's wife was jumped at a red light, right in her car. They threw her groceries on the street. They said Pakis shouldn't drive big cars."

"If you don't want to go to Toronto, we won't go."

"But you want to go. It's the best place for you. You said Montreal's finished."

"Can we just relax and enjoy the vacation?"

Ratna nodded. He deserved a truce.

Justin returned for them at 3:05. He had borrowed his brother's Peugeot. His brother sold polished stones; he could give them a good price. He drove them to a lookout point near an old French fort. The city lay spilled over the greenish-red hills like bushels of stone eggs, clinging to ledges and piling up in colorful heaps in the valleys. In the afternoon light, the oranges and yellows of the buildings were brilliant. They counted thirty-seven churches, Lutheran predominating. "Swedish missionaries in the 19th century," Justin explained. "Very successful, before the massacre." Graeme asked if all the islanders were Christian, and Justin said they were; religion was called *la troisième force.* They were reluctant to inquire about the first two. *"Mais les peuples de côte nord, ils sont un peu musulman au même temps."*

The heat of the June sun was gentle. The people wore their winter clothes capriciously, as though experimenting with other nations' castoffs. It was hard to think of them as revolutionaries, but in that morning's paper, the riots of the night before had been termed counter-revolutionary, the work of enemies of the revolution, fueled by agents of international capitalism. The only foreign country with influence besides France, according to Justin, was North Korea.

He showed them the legitimate sights: the President's house, the squares where various presidents had been assassinated or executed, a housing project, an artificial lake and the Hilton Hotel which was the tallest building in the city.

The zoo was closed to the public because of the disturbances. The museum, too, was closed indefinitely. The mission school, run by Quebec fathers, was closed. At the Monday market they walked around two burned trucks and bought mangoes.

Finally, Justin said, "If you like, we can drive past the Indian shops."

They drove behind a truckload of jeering paratroopers who pointed their rifles and fired mock salvos into their taxi. Justin appeared worried and Graeme cringed, but Ratna felt safer than she had in the subway stations of Toronto. They swung onto a wide boulevard, la Place de l'Indépendance, lined with gutted shops. In one ruined shop, a mannequin in lavender silk stuck an intact head out of a jagged hole in the display case. The signboard was splashed with tomatoes:

LUI ET ELLE
Importeurs
Props. K. Mourardji Desai et Fils

A paratrooper, daubed in garish greens and browns, waved them on.

"Drive slowly," Graeme whispered. He hid his Nikon half in his shirt and snapped the paratrooper beside the mannequin.

Justin had promised them a two-hour trip but he had shown them the city in forty-five minutes. Too many things were closed, too many sections of town under guard. So they asked him to drive out into the country.

For miles the road was nothing more than an untidy gash, an aid-project miscalculation, on the side of an endless red hill. They feared the road might strand them among wet rice fields and blood-red adobes. Then, without warning, the flaccid gash acquired a scab of gray; it became an oddly formal *grande allée* wider than a runway, lined with jacaranda and light standards. The boulevard terminated at the iron gate of a wooden house with painted columns.

"*Et voilà*," Justin announced. "*Le palais de roi.*"

"Where's the King?" Ratna asked.

"The French threw him out in 1767. He was seven feet tall and used to kill missionaries by biting their heads off—phfft."

"Where's that music coming from?" Graeme asked. Faint, almost familiar, it seemed to be coming from the royal grounds.

"Oh, that? It is a recital by the King's band."

"But you have no king."

"We still have his band. Only the best musicians are allowed to play."

"It is open to the public?"

"No, no," said Justin, throwing up his hands. "The public is not allowed. No photography is allowed."

"Then who the hell are they playing for? Are they practicing for a special occasion?"

"Yes, they are rehearsing," said Justin.

"For a holiday?"

"No, no, the revolution outlawed all the old holidays. Now they give recitals here every day."

"For themselves?" asked Ratna.

"Yes, yes, only for themselves. They rehearse for when the holidays come back and they give recitals every day for themselves."

The Claytons walked up the shallow steps that led to the iron gate. Heavy chains and an ornamental lock were looped around its rusty trelliswork. It was hard to think of that entrance or of that wooden house as royal. There were no guards, not even the gaudy paratroopers in open-topped boots. The Claytons searched the wooden structure—the wood turned out to be just a façade for another large adobe box—for clues to its forgotten history, but all the plaques had been taken down. The walls showed no flags, no heraldic signs, not even the mysterious wounds of battle. Over to one side, under the shade of jacaranda trees, sat the King's band. Their uniforms were splendidly gallant, red satin with gold braid. It was a brass band; the bandmaster wore a yachting cap and a bright red tunic. His white beard was neatly trimmed. The band knew the piece well, whatever it was; this was a recital, not a practice. The notes meandered in the wintry twilight, refusing to coalesce into anything familiar. The music revealed no hurt, no quiet suffering—it was intended for pomp and public celebration, it was music of the plazas and reviewing stands. The moment held no pathos, only dust and gallantry. When the visitors had to leave because it was too perilously close to the curfew deadline, the man playing the tuba tipped his instrument in Ratna's direction.

At 5:30, Madame Papillon taped down the windows of the dining hall so that even if stones were thrown later that night, the glass would not shatter. At 6:30,

96 | MIDCAREER STORIES (1985–1988)

she locked the glass-fronted entrance to the hotel. At seven, the Claytons came down for dinner.

Graeme brought his copy of *Scientific American* that he had begun to read on the plane. This was his light reading; he had brought no psych or medical journals with him.

"Did you know that it's always irritated me, I mean your reading at the table?"

"I'm not reading," he said, meaning *you're free to interrupt me, I'm not advancing my career; I'm being open and conversational, this is just the sports page to me.* "Did you know, according to . . ."

She couldn't catch the name, but it sounded like a dry sneeze. Hsü? Could it be Hsü?

". . . that six million years ago the Mediterranean basin was a desert? And it took the Atlantic a million years to break through and fill it again? Gibraltar for a million years was the most spectacular waterfall the world will ever see. The old sea was called Tethys and it connected the Atlantic with the Indian Ocean."

At the table to her right a German communications expert was teaching an English folksong to three Ismaili-Indian children.

"Row, row, row your boat," the children shouted, before collapsing in giggles.

"In the last Ice Age the Black Sea was a freshwater lake. They have fossil crustaceans to prove it."

The children's father, a small handsome man, scraped his chair back and said, "Watch me. Here is Bob Hope playing golf." The children giggled again. How, Ratna wondered, how in the world had they seen or heard of Bob Hope? Or golf? Or had they, or did it matter? It struck her as unspeakably heroic, gallant.

Graeme asked her if she was crying.

An American at the next table looked up at her from the paperback he was pretending to read and winked at her. He was tanned like a marine biologist.

Graeme slid the magazine across to her. She read the title: "When the Black Sea Was Drained," by Kenneth J. Hsü.

"He writes very well," said Graeme. This, she realized, was a concession to her; he was appreciating something remotely journalistic, though still respectably scientific.

An African chef, in a flowered shirt, carried a casserole to their table. Ratna had ordered "the National Dish." She found it a concoction of astonishing crudity.

A waiter turned on the television set for the World Cup scores, relayed from Dar es Salaam, *en provenance de* Buenos Aires, on another cold night under the Southern Cross. The Claytons had not expected color television on such an island. The German (East or West, Ratna wondered), overhearing the Canadians, informed them that it was cheaper to install the latest color system than an obsolete black-and-white one. It had to do with the island's profound underdevelopment. They could not even manufacture their own spare parts, and the industrialized countries no longer turned out components for black-and-white. That's why he was on the island, he said; to install a complete microwave transmitting system. Given her mood, it struck Ratna as one of the most brutal stories she had ever heard.

"What about India?" she asked.

"Oh, India is technologically sophisticated," he said. And she was faintly, absurdly, assured. India would keep its sophisticated black-and-white system for the foreseeable future and leave color to the basket-cases.

A woman news announcer said in carefully articulated French that there had been a coup on a nearby archipelago. Counter-revolutionary forces led by neocolonialist intriguers had killed the popular, progressive prime minister and placed the islands under martial law. Progressive people everywhere expressed their concern, and from Pyongyang, Kim Il Sung spoke for the whole world in denouncing this act of capitalist desperation. Demonstrations in support of the true revolutionaries would be held tomorrow in the capital, at the municipal football stadium. No mention was made of the riots on the island, which led Graeme to speculate that things were getting worse.

"According to Hsü," he said, "the last time the world was one must have been about six million years ago. Now Africa and Asia are colliding. India got smashed into Asia—that's why the Himalayas got wrinkled up. This island is just part of the debris."

Ratna played with forkfuls of the national dish. Why did the Black Sea have to drain? Why did continents have to collide? Why did they have to move to Toronto?

On that small island, in that besieged dining hall, she felt that with effort she might become an expert on the plate tectonics of emotion. As long as she could sit and listen to the other guests converse in a mutually agreed-upon second language, she would be all right. Like her, they were non-islanders, refugees.

She heard Graeme ask Madame Papillon, "Is it safe to go outside for a moment? I've spent a fortune to see the Southern Cross."

At nine, while they were lingering over a local red wine, a waiter burst in with news. Snipers had shot the Bulgarian ambassador's wife. She had been watching the riot from her balcony and phfft—a sniper had got her in the chest. Now the paratroopers would probably go on a rampage.

"It's always the same," Madame Papillon sighed. "The students want to overthrow the government. You can't carry on an honest business on this island." She left, to sit again at her desk.

Graeme poured more wine, draining the bottle. "An acceptable red wine— surprising, eh, from such a place?"

"It used to be French," Ratna said. At least the French left palpable legacies, despite the profound underdevelopment.

"By the way," Graeme said. "I wrote to Toronto before we left. I've accepted the Chair. And don't worry, if anything happens to you there I promise we'll leave. Immediately, okay?"

"What can I say?"

"Will you come see the stars with me?"

"Not tonight."

He signaled for the waiter and ordered another half-bottle of red wine. He poured her a glass, then called the waiter back. She heard the waiter mention *La Voie lactée* and *les sacs de charbon*, and Graeme's eyes lit up. "The Coalsack! I didn't think I'd ever see it." And just below the coal sacks in that luminous tropical Milky Way, low on the horizon, the waiter told him he'd see the Southern Cross.

They went out, through the kitchen and the service entrance.

He'd be all right, she thought. Wherever he went.

The American leaned toward her from his table. "What's this," he asked, "this *champignons farcis*?" He looked drunk, but courteous. She had to look where he was pointing.

"Mushrooms," she said, smiling. From that odd opening on that odd island a conversation could go anywhere. Not all North Americans were forced to fear the passionate consequences of their unilingualism.

For the first time she saw that the label on the bottle read: Côte de Cassandre. A superior red table wine that no one had ever heard of; perhaps the lone competent industry on the island. Better, she thought, than the Quebec cider she and Graeme made such a patriotic point of always serving.

She poured herself another glass, feeling for the moment at home in that collection of Indians and Europeans babbling in English and remembered dialects. No matter where she lived, she would never feel so at home again.

A Father

ONE WEDNESDAY MORNING in mid-May Mr. Bhowmick woke up as he usually did at 5:43 A.M., checked his Rolex against the alarm clock's digital readout, punched down the alarm (set for 5:45), then nudged his wife awake. She worked as a claims investigator for an insurance company that had an office in a nearby shopping mall. She didn't really have to leave the house until 8:30, but she liked to get up early and cook him a big breakfast. Mr. Bhowmick had to drive a long way to work. He was a naturally dutiful, cautious man, and he set his alarm clock early enough to accommodate a margin for accidents.

While his wife, in a pink nylon negligee she had paid for with her own MasterCard, made him a new version of French toast from a clipping ("Eggscellent Recipes!") Scotchtaped to the inside of a kitchen cupboard, Mr. Bhowmick brushed his teeth. He brushed, he gurgled with the loud, hawking noises that he and his brother had been taught as children to make in order to flush clean not merely teeth but also tongue and palate.

After that he showered, then, back in the bedroom again, he recited prayers in Sanskrit to Kali, the patron goddess of his family, the goddess of wrath and vengeance. In the pokey flat of his childhood in Ranchi, Bihar, his mother had given over a whole bedroom to her collection of gods and goddesses. Mr. Bhowmick couldn't be that extravagant in Detroit. His daughter, twenty-six and an electrical engineer, slept in the other of the two bedrooms in his apartment. But he had done his best. He had taken Woodworking I and II at a nearby recreation center and built a grotto for the goddess. Kali-Mata was eight inches tall, made of metal and painted a glistening black so that the metal glowed like the oiled, black skin of a peasant woman. And though Kali-Mata was totally nude except for a tiny gilt crown and a garland strung together from sinners' chopped off heads, she looked warm, cozy, *pleased*, in her makeshift wooden shrine in Detroit. Mr. Bhowmick had gathered quite a crowd of admiring fellow woodworkers in those final weeks of decoration.

"Hurry it up with the prayers," his wife shouted from the kitchen. She was an agnostic, a believer in ambition, not grace. She frequently complained that his prayers had gotten so long that soon he wouldn't have time to go to work, play duplicate bridge with the Ghosals, or play the tabla in the Bengali Association's one Sunday per month musical soirees. Lately she'd begun to drain him in a wholly new way. He wasn't praying, she nagged; he was shutting her out of his life. There'd be no peace in the house until she hid Kali-Mata in a suitcase.

She nagged, and he threatened to beat her with his shoe as his father had threatened his mother: it was the thrust and volley of marriage. There was no

MIDCAREER STORIES (1985–1988)

question of actually taking off a shoe or applying it to his wife's body. She was bigger than he was. And, secretly, he admired her for having the nerve, the agnosticism, which as a college boy in backward Bihar he, too, had claimed.

"I have time," he shot back at her. He was still wrapped in a damp terry towel.

"You have time for everything but domestic life."

It was the fault of the shopping mall that his wife had started to buy pop psychology paperbacks. These paperbacks preached that for couples who could sit down and talk about their "relationship," life would be sweet again. His engineer daughter was on his wife's side. She accused him of holding things in.

"Face it, Dad," she said. "You have an affect deficit."

But surely everyone had feelings they didn't want to talk about or talk over. He definitely did not want to blurt out anything about the sick-in-the-guts sensations that came over him most mornings and that he couldn't bubble down with Alka-Seltzer or smother with Gas-X. The women in his family were smarter than him. They were cheerful, outgoing, more American somehow.

How could he tell these bright, mocking women that in the 5:43 A.M. darkness, he sensed invisible presences: gods and snakes frolicked in the master bedroom, little white sparks of cosmic static crackled up the legs of his pajamas. Something was out there in the dark, something that could invent accidents and coincidences to remind mortals that even in Detroit they were no more than mortal. His wife would label this paranoia and dismiss it. Paranoia, premonition: whatever it was, it had begun to undermine his composure.

Take this morning. Mr. Bhowmick had woken up from a pleasant dream about a man taking a Club Med vacation, and the postdream satisfaction had lasted through the shower, but when he'd come back to the shrine in the bedroom, he'd noticed all at once how scarlet and saucy was the tongue that Kali-Mata stuck out at the world. Surely he had not lavished such alarming detail, such admonitory colors on that flap of flesh.

Watch out, ambulatory sinners. Be careful out there, the goddess warned him, and not with the affection of Sergeant Esterhaus,[1] either.

"French toast must be eaten hot-hot," his wife nagged. "Otherwise they'll taste like rubber."

Mr. Bhowmick laid the trousers of a two-trouser suit he had bought on sale that winter against his favorite tweed jacket. The navy stripes in the trou-

---

1. The name of a character played by Michael Conrad in *Hill Street Blues*, a long-running 1980s U.S. police drama.—Ed.

sers and the small, navy tweed flecks in the jacket looked quite good together. So what if the Chief Engineer had already started wearing summer cottons?

"I am coming, I am coming," he shouted back. "You want me to eat hothot, you start frying only when I am sitting down. You didn't learn anything from Mother in Ranchi?"

"Mother cooked French toast from fancy recipes? I mean French Sandwich Toast with complicated filling?"

He came into the room to give her his testiest look. "You don't know the meaning of complicated cookery. And Mother had to get the coal fire of the *chula* going first."

His daughter was already at the table. "Why don't you break down and buy her a microwave oven? That's what I mean about sitting down and talking things out." She had finished her orange juice. She took a plastic measure of Slim-Fast out of its can and poured the powder into a glass of skim milk. "It's ridiculous."

Babli was not the child he would have chosen as his only heir. She was brighter certainly than the sons and daughters of the other Bengalis he knew in Detroit, and she had been the only female student in most of her classes at Georgia Tech, but as she sat there in her beige linen business suit, her thick chin dropping into a polka-dotted cravat, he regretted again that she was not the child of his dreams. Babli would be able to help him out moneywise if something happened to him, something so bad that even his pension plans and his insurance policies and his money market schemes wouldn't be enough. But Babli could never comfort him. She wasn't womanly or tender the way that unmarried girls had been in the wistful days of his adolescence. She could sing Hindi film songs, mimicking exactly the high, artificial voice of Lata Mangeshkar, and she had taken two years of dance lessons at Sona Devi's Dance Academy in Southfield, but these accomplishments didn't add up to real femininity. Not the kind that had given him palpitations in Ranchi.

MR. BHOWMICK DID HIS BEST with his wife's French toast. In spite of its filling of marshmallows, apricot jam and maple syrup, it tasted rubbery. He drank two cups of Darjeeling tea, said, "Well, I'm off," and took off.

All might have gone well if Mr. Bhowmick hadn't fussed longer than usual about putting his briefcase and his trenchcoat in the backseat. He got in behind the wheel of his Oldsmobile, fixed his seatbelt and was just about to turn the key in the ignition when his neighbor, Al Stazniak, who was starting up his Buick Skylark, sneezed. A sneeze at the start of a journey brings bad luck. Al Stazniak's sneeze was fierce, made up of five short bursts, too loud to be ignored.

102 | MIDCAREER STORIES (1985–1988)

Be careful out there! Mr. Bhowmick could see the goddess' scarlet little tongue tip wagging at him.

He was a modern man, an intelligent man. Otherwise he couldn't have had the options in life that he did have. He couldn't have given up a good job with perks in Bombay and found a better job with General Motors in Detroit. But Mr. Bhowmick was also a prudent enough man to know that some abiding truth lies bunkered within each wanton Hindu superstition. A sneeze was more than a sneeze. The heedless are carried off in ambulances. He had choices to make. He could ignore the sneeze, and so challenge the world unseen by men. Perhaps Al Stazniak had hayfever. For a sneeze to be a potent omen, surely it had to be unprovoked and terrifying, a thunderclap cleaving the summer skies. Or he could admit the smallness of mortals, undo the fate of the universe by starting over, and go back inside the apartment, sit for a second on the sofa, then re-start his trip.

Al Stazniak rolled down his window. "Everything okay?"

Mr. Bhowmick nodded shyly. They weren't really friends in the way neighbors can sometimes be. They talked as they parked or pulled out of their adjacent parking stalls. For all Mr. Bhowmick knew, Al Stazniak had no legs. He had never seen the man out of his Skylark.

He let the Buick back out first. Everything was okay, yes, please. All the same he undid his seatbelt. Compromise, adaptability, call it what you will. A dozen times a day he made these small trade-offs between new-world reasonableness and old-world beliefs.

While he was sitting in his parked car, his wife's ride came by. For fifty dollars a month, she was picked up and dropped off by a hard up, newly divorced woman who worked at a florist's shop in the same mall. His wife came out the front door in brown K-Mart pants and a burgundy windbreaker. She waved to him, then slipped into the passenger seat of the florist's rusty Japanese car.

He was a metallurgist. He knew about rust and ways of preventing it, secret ways, thus far unknown to the Japanese.

Babli's fiery red Mitsubishi was still in the lot. She wouldn't leave for work for another eight minutes. He didn't want her to know he'd been undone by a sneeze. Babli wasn't tolerant of superstitions. She played New Wave music in her tapedeck. If asked about Hinduism, all she'd ever said to her American friends was that "it's neat." Mr. Bhowmick had heard her on the phone years before. The cosmos balanced on the head of a snake was like a beachball balanced on the snout of a circus seal. "This Hindu myth stuff," he'd heard her say, "is like a series of super graphics."

He'd forgiven her. He could probably forgive her anything. It was her way of surviving high school in a city that was both native to her, and alien.

There was no question of going back where he'd come from. He hated Ranchi. Ranchi was no place for dreamers. All through his teenage years, Mr. Bhowmick had dreamed of success abroad. What form that success would take he had left vague. Success had meant to him escape from the constant plotting and bitterness that wore out India's middle class.

Babli should have come out of the apartment and driven off to work by now. Mr. Bhowmick decided to take a risk, to dash inside and pretend he'd left his briefcase on the coffee table.

When he entered the living room, he noticed Babli's spring coat and large vinyl pocketbook on the sofa. She was probably sorting through the junk jewelry on her dresser to give her business suit a lift. She read hints about dressing in women's magazines and applied them to her person with seriousness. If his luck held, he could sit on the sofa, say a quick prayer and get back to the car without her catching on.

It surprised him that she didn't shout from her bedroom, "Who's there?" What if he had been a rapist?

Then he heard Babli in the bathroom. He heard unladylike squawking noises. She was throwing up. A squawk, a spitting, then the horrible gurgle of a waterfall.

A revelation came to Mr. Bhowmick. A woman vomiting in the privacy of the bathroom could mean many things. She was coming down with the flu. She was nervous about a meeting. But Mr. Bhowmick knew at once that his daughter, his untender, unloving daughter whom he couldn't love and hadn't tried to love, was not, in the larger world of Detroit, unloved. Sinners are everywhere, even in the bosom of an upright, unambitious family like the Bhowmicks. It was the goddess sticking her tongue at him.

The father sat heavily on the sofa, shrinking from contact with her coat and pocketbook. His brisk, bright engineer daughter was pregnant. Someone had taken time to make love to her. Someone had thought her tender, feminine. Someone even now was perhaps mooning over her. The idea excited him. It was so grotesque and wondrous. At twenty-six Babli had found the man of her dreams; whereas at twenty-six Mr. Bhowmick had given up on truth, beauty and poetry and exchanged them for two years at Carnegie Tech.

Mr. Bhowmick's tweed-jacketed body sagged against the sofa cushions. Babli would abort, of course. He knew his Babli. It was the only possible option if she didn't want to bring shame to the Bhowmick family. All the same, he could see a chubby baby boy on the rug, crawling to his granddaddy. Shame like that was easier to hide in Ranchi. There was always a barren womb sanctified by marriage that could claim sudden fructifying by the goddess Parvati. Babli would do what she wanted. She was headstrong and independent and he was afraid of her.

Babli staggered out of the bathroom. Damp stains ruined her linen suit. It was the first time he had seen his daughter look ridiculous, quite unprofessional. She didn't come into the living room to investigate the noises he'd made. He glimpsed her shoeless stockinged feet flip-flop on collapsed arches down the hall to her bedroom.

"Are you all right?" Mr. Bhowmick asked, standing in the hall. "Do you need Sinutab?"

She wheeled around. "What're you doing here?"

He was the one who should be angry. "I'm feeling poorly, too," he said. "I'm taking the day off."

"I feel fine," Babli said.

Within fifteen minutes Babli had changed her clothes and left. Mr. Bhowmick had the apartment to himself all day. All day for praising or cursing the life that had brought him along with its other surprises an illegitimate grandchild.

It was his wife that he blamed. Coming to America to live had been his wife's idea. After the wedding, the young Bhowmicks had spent two years in Pittsburgh on his student visa, then gone back home to Ranchi for nine years. Nine crushing years. Then the job in Bombay had come through. All during those nine years his wife had screamed and wept. She was a woman of wild, progressive ideas—she'd called them her "American" ideas—and she'd been martyred by her neighbors for them. American *memsahib. Markin mem, Markin mem.* In bazaars the beggar boys had trailed her and hooted. She'd done provocative things. She'd hired a *chamar* woman who by caste rules was forbidden to cook for higher caste families, especially for widowed mothers of decent men. This had caused a blowup in the neighborhood. She'd made other, lesser errors. While other wives shopped and cooked every day, his wife had cooked the whole week's menu on weekends.

"What's the point of having a refrigerator, then?" She'd been scornful of the Ranchi women.

His mother, an old-fashioned widow, had accused her of trying to kill her by poisoning. "You are in such a hurry? You want to get rid of me quick-quick so you can go back to the States?"

Family life had been turbulent.

He had kept aloof, inwardly siding with his mother. He did not love his wife now, and he had not loved her then. In any case, he had not defended her.

A FATHER | *105*

He felt some affection, and he felt guilty for having shunned her during those unhappy years. But he had thought of it then as revenge. He had wanted to marry a beautiful woman. Not being a young man of means, only a young man with prospects, he had had no right to yearn for pure beauty. He cursed his fate and after a while settled for a barrister's daughter,[2] a plain girl with a wide, flat plank of a body and myopic eyes. The barrister had sweetened the deal by throwing in an all-expenses-paid two years' study at Carnegie Tech to which Mr. Bhowmick had been admitted. Those two years had changed his wife from pliant girl to ambitious woman. She wanted America, nothing less.

It was his wife who had forced him to apply for permanent resident status in the U.S. even though he had a good job in Ranchi as a government engineer. The putting together of documents for the immigrant visa had been a long and humbling process. He had had to explain to a chilly clerk in the Embassy that, like most Indians of his generation, he had no birth certificate. He had to swear out affidavits, suffer through police checks, bribe orderlies whose job it was to move his dossier from desk to desk. The decision, the clerk had advised him, would take months, maybe years. He hadn't dared hope that merit might be rewarded. Merit could collapse under bad luck. It was for grace that he prayed.

While the immigration papers were being processed, he had found the job in Bombay. So he'd moved his mother in with his younger brother's family, and left his hometown for good. Life in Bombay had been lighthearted, almost fulfilling. His wife had thrown herself into charity work with the same energy that had offended the Ranchi women. He was happy to be in a big city at last. Bombay was the Rio de Janeiro of the East; he'd read that in a travel brochure. He drove out to Nariman Point at least once a week to admire the necklace of municipal lights, toss coconut shells into the dark ocean, drink beer at the Oberoi-Sheraton where overseas Indian girls in designer jeans beckoned him in sly ways. His nights were full. He played duplicate bridge, went to the movies, took his wife to Bingo nights at his club. In Detroit he was a lonelier man.

Then the green card had come through. For him, for his wife, and the daughter who had been born to them in Bombay. He sold what he could sell, and put in his brother's informal trust what he couldn't save on taxes. Then he had left for America, and one more start.

ALL THROUGH THE WEEK, Mr. Bhowmick watched his daughter. He kept furtive notes on how many times she rushed to the bathroom and made hawking,

---

2. "Barrister" is a British word for a particular type of lawyer.—Ed.

106 | MIDCAREER STORIES (1985–1988)

wrenching noises, how many times she stayed late at the office, calling her mother to say she'd be taking in a movie and pizza afterwards with friends.

He had to tell her that he knew. And he probably didn't have much time. She shouldn't be on Slim-Fast in her condition. He had to talk things over with her. But what would he say to her? What position could he take? He had to choose between public shame for the family, and murder.

For three more weeks he watched her and kept his silence. Babli wore shifts to the office instead of business suits, and he liked her better in those garments. Perhaps she was dressing for her young man, not from necessity. Her skin was pale and blotchy by turn. At breakfast her fingers looked stiff, and she had trouble with silverware.

Two Saturdays running, he lost badly at duplicate bridge. His wife scolded him. He had made silly mistakes. When was Babli meeting this man? Where? He must be American; Mr. Bhowmick prayed only that he was white. He pictured his grandson crawling to him, and the grandson was always fat and brown and buttery-skinned, like the infant Krishna. An American son-in-law was a terrifying notion. Why was she not mentioning men, at least, preparing the way for the major announcement? He listened sharply for men's names, rehearsed little lines like, "Hello, Bob, I'm Babli's old man," with a cracked little laugh. Bob, Jack, Jimmy, Tom. But no names surfaced. When she went out for pizza and a movie it was with the familiar set of Indian girls and their strange, unpopular, American friends, all without men. Mr. Bhowmick tried to be reasonable. Maybe she had already gotten married and was keeping it secret. "Well, Bob, you and Babli sure had Mrs. Bhowmick and me going there, heh-heh," he mumbled one night with the Sahas and Ghosals, over cards. "Pardon?" asked Pronob Saha. Mr. Bhowmick dropped two tricks, and his wife glared. "Such stupid blunders," she fumed on the drive back. A new truth was dawning; there would be no marriage for Babli. Her young man probably was not so young and not so available. He must be already married. She must have yielded to passion or been raped in the office. His wife seemed to have noticed nothing. Was he a murderer, or a conspirator? He kept his secret from his wife; his daughter kept her decision to herself.

Nights, Mr. Bhowmick pretended to sleep, but as soon as his wife began her snoring—not real snores so much as loud, gaspy gulpings for breath—he turned on his side and prayed to Kali-Mata.

IN JULY, when Babli's belly had begun to push against the waistless dresses she'd bought herself, Mr. Bhowmick came out of the shower one weekday morning and found the two women screaming at each other. His wife had a rolling pin in one hand. His daughter held up a *National Geographic* as a shield for her head. The crazy look that had been in his wife's eyes when she'd shooed away beggar kids was in her eyes again.

"Stop it!" His own boldness overwhelmed him. "Shut up! Babli's pregnant, so what? It's your fault, you made us come to the States."

Girls like Babli were caught between rules, that's the point he wished to make. They were too smart, too impulsive for a backward place like Ranchi, but not tough nor smart enough for sex-crazy places like Detroit.

"My fault?" his wife cried. "I told her to do hanky-panky with boys? I told her to shame us like this?"

She got in one blow with the rolling pin. The second glanced off Babli's shoulder and fell on his arm which he had stuck out for his grandson's sake.

"I'm calling the police," Babli shouted. She was out of the rolling pin's range. "This is brutality. You can't do this to me."

"Shut up! Shut your mouth, foolish woman." He wrenched the weapon from his wife's fist. He made a show of taking off his shoe to beat his wife on the face.

"What do you know? You don't know anything." She let herself down slowly on a dining chair. Her hair, curled overnight, stood in wild whorls around her head. "Nothing."

"And you do!" He laughed. He remembered her tormentors, and laughed again. He had begun to enjoy himself. Now *he* was the one with the crazy, progressive ideas.

"Your daughter is pregnant, yes," she said, "any fool knows that. But ask her the name of the father. Go, ask."

He stared at his daughter who gazed straight ahead, eyes burning with hate, jaw clenched with fury.

"Babli?"

"Who needs a man?" she hissed. "The father of my baby is a bottle and a syringe. Men louse up your lives. I just want a baby. Oh, don't worry—he's a certified fit donor. No diseases, college graduate, above average, and he made the easiest twenty-five dollars of his life—"

"Like animals," his wife said. For the first time he heard horror in her voice. His daughter grinned at him. He saw her tongue, thick and red, squirming behind her row of perfect teeth.

"Yes, yes, yes," she screamed, "like livestock. Just like animals. You should be happy—that's what marriage is all about, isn't it? Matching bloodlines, matching horoscopes, matching castes, matching, matching, matching . . ." and it was difficult to know if she was laughing or singing, or mocking and like a madwoman.

MIDCAREER STORIES (1985–1988)

Mr. Bhowmick lifted the rolling pin high above his head and brought it down hard on the dome of Babli's stomach. In the end, it was his wife who called the police.

Isolated Incidents

SEVEN YEARS BEFORE, on a cool afternoon in May, the two girls had come out of the musty warmth of Miss Edgar's and Miss Cramp's and straggled down a leafy Westmount street to their separate futures. Poppy had done better than Ann. She called herself Peppi now—Peppi Paluka and the Pistolettes—and wore leather muscle-shirts and fearless disco pants. Through the listless years at McGill, Ann had kept a scrapbook: of Poppy stroking a cat in the lobby of the Beverly Hilton, of Poppy kissing Mike Douglas, of Poppy driving something sleek and low on the mad freeways of Los Angeles. "You can take the girl out of Canada," said Peppi Paluka in a promotional for her first CBC Special, "but you can't take Canada out of the girl, no way!"

Poppy had been wearing her "Fuddle Duddle" T-shirt. "Fuddle Duddle" had been her first hit single. Around that time Ann had inherited a little money from her Aunt Nellie, moved to Toronto (ahead of the rush) and had her heart broken by a feckless condo promoter. Now Ann and Poppy were in the same city again. Ann had seen a picture of the Pistolettes in the *Star*. "I miss Canada," Peppi had said, "I really do. I miss everything about Canada, you know. I miss the good manners, the plodding, the uncrowdedness." You'll love her, too, the *Star* predicted, you'll love her gutsy, grungy performance. Poppy had called Ann—"Let's have a quick salad at least"—and Ann had agreed to meet her for lunch at her hotel.

All morning Ann sat at her corner desk in a large office, trying to hide her nervousness. Definitely, she told herself, she would not ask silly questions. It would just be two old friends, two professional women, two Westmount girls who'd been brought up to handle any social situation. But, my God, Poppy was a celebrity now. She had limos and a house in some dangerous Los Angeles canyon. She had a swimming pool laid out to resemble something ornate or disgusting, she couldn't remember which. She'd spent eight thousand dollars at the Eaton Center the night before. "Mostly presents. I don't need anything for myself."

Ann's supervisor, Gladys Wakamatsu, had to ask twice for the file on recent incidents in the subway, and Bella Herzog went on for longer than usual about her husband's chest pains before Ann could pull together her practiced look of demure commiseration. She'd been gathering data on the Supariwala case. Doctor (Miss) Supariwala was a stern, stocky woman of forty-three, with doctorates from Western Ontario and Bombay, who claimed to have been passed over at job interviews in favor of lesser candidates. She was a Canadian citizen, she'd published numerous articles, she'd won a few research grants. No one could fault her promptness, her discipline, her preparedness. Against these accomplishments were arrayed certain half-articulated, coded objections. Students could not relate easily to her, some might complain of her accent, her methodological stiffness, her lack of humor. *My social poise and my good humor might be enhanced*, Dr. Supariwala had written, *if I had a position commensurate with my training.* "She belongs to the world of research, not of the classroom," wrote one chairman, adding shyly, "like many of her countrywomen." "She should apply to StatsCan," said another. "Sing-song accent." "The university year is a six-month voyage in a first-class stateroom," wrote another, choosing the higher road. "Surely we have a right to choose our companions carefully." And in spite of everything, the Supariwalas wanted to stay on. That was what amazed Ann. They came to her, cowering, crying, thundering, insulting—rehearsed or spontaneous—and still they found reasons for staying where Ann herself, on bad days, found few.

A little before eleven Bella brought over a small, mustached man in white shirt and bright blue suit, gold cuff-links, gold tie-bar, gold rings and a gold tooth. He'd recently lit a cigarette; he took two frenzied puffs before crushing it out.

"Annie, this is Mr. Hernandez. He has a problem but I told him I don't think we can help him."

He did not take a seat.

"Is it a Human Rights problem, Mr. Hernandez?"

He waved away the question. "I would not be here for anything less than Human Rights," he said.

She rolled paper into the typewriter, typed in the date, the time, and in the appropriate box, HERNANDEZ.

"Your first name, please."

"It is not for me. It is for my sister. You see, she came to Canada to join her new husband, but he's the big shot, see. He runs off to P.E.I. with another girl. What can she do? Her visitor's visa runs out in three days."

"Her husband now refuses to sponsor her?"

"Yes, yes, he wants now to marry that other girl."

"If she has no spouse to sponsor her, then she is in a difficult situation."

"That is what Immigration says. But I will sponsor her. I make good money. I sell houses all day. At night I am cosmetic salesman. What do they think? She is going to become a welfare mother with a dozen kids?"

She watched his thin body stiffen. It crossed her mind that Mr. Hernandez was a proud man, that the gold was in some way intended to publicize his importance, and that it might have succeeded in a different country. Such men were hard to deal with, they took Human Rights too literally. She would probably have to take a taxi to the Windsor Arms, instead of walking.

"Mr. Hernandez"—she flashed her most sympathetic smile as she unrolled the sheet of paper—"what you describe, I'm afraid, really is not a problem for Human Rights." She looked beyond him at the lobby where two more complainants sat alertly, one of them bandaged and clearly a candidate for her time. What to tell Mr. Hernandez? Buy a T-shirt and proclaim something defiant? Hire a caustic lawyer? The cuffs—too wide—were dingy; the collar wrinkled; it was a sign, Ann felt, that she'd been too long in the job. A long time ago, she had come early to work and stayed late and been greedy for piles of complaints to process. Each form, somehow, improving things just a little. She'd listened to other people's catastrophes and been drawn to their garish wardrobes, their inappropriate flatteries, their occasional threats, their faith in her power. At Miss Edgar's and Miss Cramp's she had been thought of as a selfless person because she talked of joining CUSO[1] eventually. But she had not gone to New Guinea or Malawi. She had gone to McGill, then moved to Toronto. Her job had worn her down. She had tried too earnestly to correct the nation's wrongs. Now she saw problems only as a bureaucrat. Deal only with the sure things. Pass the others off. Get documentation. Promise nothing.

"Her name is Isabella," Mr. Hernandez said. "I can bring her in."

"That won't be necessary, Mr. Hernandez. Please. You must understand: Human Rights refers to a specific set of grievances. You must understand—"

She was thinking of the picture of Poppy in that morning's *Globe and Mail*. Poppy looked vulnerable in spite of all her sexiness. She remembered the leafy playgrounds of Westmount and Poppy leaning against her bicycle, peeling back kneesocks to show off what she called "kiss-wounds," where boys with teeth like penknives had paid their homage.

"What? Understand what?"

Now it's your turn, Annie. Come on, show me, don't be a spoilsport. But Ann had nothing to show, then or now; at twenty-six her skin was still spongy white, impervious to damage.

---

1. A Canadian international development charity.—Ed.

Mr. Hernandez reached for her wrist across the cluttered desk and knocked aside a stack of dossiers. Ann was well brought up; she could not draw back her hand from the distasteful pressure of Mr. Hernandez's fingers. She let her wrist go limp in the warm funnel of his clutch. She knew she was safe; she could refer his case to a different department. She could afford to pat his hand, to smile, to assure him that Immigration would listen to his case. She sealed off the promise with another sympathetic smile.

After Mr. Hernandez left, she excused herself and took refuge in the staff-only toilet. She wore little make-up, and her face always looked edgy, only the bright red lipstick made people think the effect was contrived rather than accidental. She leaned against the wet, scarred counter and touched up the faded red, trying not to feel guilty about the men still waiting to be interviewed. Her wrist was warm and throbbing, as though wrapped in a tight, moist bandage. Mr. Hernandez, for a frail man, had left his mark.

WITH TWENTY MINUTES to go, she found herself typing PERSAWD, JOHN MOHAN. A subway assault. Queen Street Station this time: chipped teeth, cut lips, broken nose, blackened eyes. Cuts, abrasions. Persawd had brought a lawyer, or a law student, perhaps a relative, to press his grievance. Three months in Toronto, the lawyer was saying, and *this*. What kind of people are you? What kind of city is this?

"You have reported this to the police?" she asked.

"Of course, of course. But what good are the police? The assailants fled. We have no witnesses. The police suggest my client got drunk and started a fight, Miss Vane. They make this boy feel like a complainer. The victims are made to feel guilty."

I know, thought Ann. But what, exactly, could Human Rights do? What specific recommendation follows from this incident? She took down documentation, ages of the assailants, fodder for another Royal Commission. The Queen Street file was already thick, justification for permanent patrols? But no thicker than a dozen others. And Torontonians were proud of their subway, their politeness, proud of their moral spotlessness. This after all was not New York. Assaults on John Mohan Persawd and dozens like him would always be considered isolated incidents, and who's to say they were racial in nature? Police treated it as simple assault, rowdiness, and drew no necessary inferences regarding race. No witnesses, no case, and police involvement ended. And so she typed, entering facts, censoring opinions, absorbing a small human drama that had lost its power to touch her. What of my client's dignity? the lawyer

112 | MIDCAREER STORIES (1985–1988)

asked. What of the boy who dreamed of coming to Canada? Who waited five years for immigration? Who trained as an electrician in Guyana but now washed windows?

"I have no answers for such questions," said Ann.

"It's time that you did, Miss Vane."

The snowy gleam of fluorescence helped; it stamped out feelings and faces, it miniaturized passions, like a television screen. Hand in hand with January, it helped her accept imperfections in the world, her own limitation. She had wanted to be a poet, and at one time she seemed closer to success in poetry than Poppy had in music. Poppy had sung, not badly, in a schoolgirl performance of *Brigadoon* and, like dozens of other Westmount girls, had sung in little clubs on Dorchester, then Stanley and Mountain. No one thought too much of her; just another aspiring Joni Mitchell, looking better than she sounded. But Ann had gone to McGill and won some prizes; she'd fantasized about expiring exquisitely like Sylvia Plath, leaving behind a poignant lyric or two. Then suddenly Poppy was in New York and they wrote her up in the *Gazette* as a hot new property. By the time Ann graduated, Poppy had become Peppi, folk had yielded to disco, and she'd dumped the Montreal boy who'd been guiding her career and had taken on a genius agent and business manager who ran her life like Prussian generals, according to *People*. And Aunt Nellie had died and Ann had bought herself a small, sturdy house on Tranby.

"Canadians are mean as hell," said John Mohan Persawd. "Life is hopeless, man, no justice, no redress."

"I don't know about that," said Ann. "If this had happened in New York, you'd have been left for dead."

"Correction, Miss Vane," said the lawyer. "If this had happened in New York, he'd have been mugged for his money, not racially assaulted."

On good days it would have seemed an academic distinction. Statistically, where would you rather be? Aesthetically, which subway would you prefer to ride? But on bad days, judgments curled up at her from a thousand scraps of paper and she could only tell herself that if all these recommendations, all this paperwork, all this good sense and reason were not influencing *something*, she would quit.

———

SHE HAD A HARD TIME getting a cab. A young taxi-driver delivering a dozen giant, obscenely inscribed chocolate-chip cookies took pity on her, there in the cold without benefit of her trusty boots, and dropped her at the corner of St. Thomas and Bloor.

The hotel lobby was full of stout, tanned men in denim suits, and of tall, tanned women glowing like oranges from too much California. All the faces seemed anonymously familiar: from soap operas, perhaps, or supporting roles in long-running series. They were here to star (she'd read somewhere) in some Canadian pornographic film. Ann had hoped Poppy would meet her in the lobby so she wouldn't have to pick her way through the thicket of self-possessed guests, but Poppy was still in her suite, just recently risen, sipping champagne, watching a game show and painting her nails.

Her public would not have recognized her. She was almost a tired-looking Poppy Pennington of Anwoth Drive. Ann thought of herself always looking the same: sensible, efficient, vaguely sporty. Poppy-Peppi had settled into at least two selves: one a ravishing seventeen (latest album, *Cream in Your Jeans*), the other a wispy thirty. Her voice was breathless, as though it now required amplification simply to be audible, as if it wouldn't be heard at all if she weren't belting it out. She didn't move from her chair—she indicated the wet, green nails—and her feet were up on the bed. But she radiated her oldest and warmest smile and said to Ann, "Have some champagne?"

A sideboard was stocked with liquor, with stacks of plastic glasses and bottles of mix. Ann poured herself a Dubonnet and topped it with ginger ale.

"You look wonderful," Ann said. "Different, of course, but wonderful."

The throaty laugh, the long cough, "You're as nice as ever. You don't have to say things like that, you know. I look like I belong on the Main—no, I look like the morning after a night on the Main. It's a punishment, Annie, getting up this early. It's this life—another album and I split. But you're the one who's looking wonderful. So *healthy*, Christ! So . . . *centered*, you know? How do you do it—men? Exercise, pills, a shrink, what?"

"Poppy, come on."

"They'd eat you alive in California, Annie. They haven't seen fresh meat in years out there—my God, you're actually blushing! A girl who can blush is worth her weight in gold or other substances, believe me. When I get off the road this time, you'll come and visit me, promise, okay?"

Ann sipped the Dubonnet; with the ginger ale it looked as if she'd been too greedy. She gulped it quickly, then poured another, smaller, without the mix. She was unsure if lunch was to be sent up or eaten below in the Courtyard. Poppy looked at least an hour away from any public appearance, and Ann would have to be back, filing complaints by then. California! All the questions that Ann had prepared—anything she could say to such a wildly successful friend from her childhood—seemed suddenly giddy, or vaguely insulting, as though she were trying to whittle Poppy down to the level from which they'd both started.

114 | MIDCAREER STORIES (1985–1988)

"Tell me about Los Angeles," she begged. "Is it really . . . crazy?"

"Every place is crazy," Poppy teased. She slid a freshly-painted nail into her glass of Perrier and flicked pulp off the twist of lemon. "L.A.'s just crazier than most."

She began to sketch, with relish, her life of apparent immorality. She described circular waterbeds, the mirrored ceilings ("They're glued like tiles, and I know one day a tile's going to fall and slice some guy's ass to pieces!"), the amyls given her by her last boyfriend, the parties she gave, the parties she had to go to to please her agent. She named some names, denied some others. Her kimono fell away, baring her sloping, blue-veined thighs. "I'm sick of sex, frankly," she said.

"I think I know what you mean," Ann ventured.

"I'm sure you do, I was admiring those marks on your wrist. Bondage? Oh Annie, you've got that blush down *pat*. It's great!"

Ann was on her third Dubonnet; she'd forgotten the forceful entreaties of Mr. Hernandez, bless him. Poppy continued with the anecdotes. With bold, crude gestures she relived the saga of the resisting heart. Ann could still detect that old charm, the vulnerabilities of the prepubescent Westmount girl who had inflicted flesh wounds on her shins and calves to set herself apart from the comforting staidness of her surroundings. It should have been entirely predictable even then: she would leave in order to be able to return, again and again. The dour reasonableness of Canada would see to that. Who knew how flamboyant and crude Ann herself might have become if she had escaped on a Greyhound carrying a sleeping bag and *Beautiful Losers*? From the window, which was gritty with cold, she could make out the diners at the Courtyard. Poppy made no move to get dressed. There was little hope of eating now and being seen and still getting back to the office on time.

Every anecdote brought Ann down to the deep spongy core of her own failure. "You were a bit of a writer in school, weren't you, Annie?" Poppy said suddenly. She turned the TV off, snapping shut a middle-aged nurse who had won $876 worth of rattan furniture. "Tom Packer and you would get on famously. He's an old Montrealer with connections. He can throw script-writing jobs your way. He fixes scripts that get botched. Very important work, if you don't mind not getting credit."

"I wouldn't mind." She drifted in a speculative haze: still a poet, her poems remembered, but a freelancer, too. She watched hours of television, she still read and went to movies; she probably wouldn't be bad. Every day at work she saw men and women who had sold their savings in tropical villages to make new beginnings in icy Canada. Not everyone had done well, but they had taken a chance. Sometimes you had to leave the safe and sober places of this world.

She could learn to write scripts instead of poems, which she didn't write anymore anyway. Jokes and brilliant one-liners could punctuate improbable car chases. She wouldn't be responsible for the action scenes anyway, she thought. Poppy had shown her that you could come home again and again.

The Dubonnets were getting to her. Her face, she expected, was already flushed (a hereditary flaw), though her deportment would remain respectable for another couple of hours. Poppy had taken over the bathroom. Her voice rose and fell over the splash of water and the whine of electrical gadgetry. She was telling Ann about Tom, how she absolutely adored him. He was building a yacht. He had worshiped Baba Ram Dass. He had played with Herb Alpert. He had once barbecued a rattler.

It was not Poppy, but Peppi Paluka who came out of the bathroom. She wore a leather vest without shirt or bra; even her forearms were sullenly sensuous. She was nearly the girl on the jacket of *Cream in Your Jeans*.

"I've got to get back to work," Ann said. She was a little frightened of this manifestation.

"I wish you could stay longer, but some people are coming up." Poppy sat on the coffee table and pulled on her boots. They were cowboy boots of bright baby blue, with purple, hand-tooled leaves and flowers.

"I thought of you all morning," Ann confessed. "I could hardly get any work done."

"Me too, Annie-poo. You've gotta come out and visit."

Ann promised, all too readily. In the spring, before Poppy's London opening, definitely. Poppy would arrange for her to meet everyone: Donald Sutherland, if he wasn't filming on an ice floe somewhere, would she like that? Margot Kidder, Tom Packer, anyone. They would gossip about home. They would careen down the canyons. They would cruise the beaches with Tom, once he worked out his sexual identity. The future would be even better than the past. In order to get her ready, Poppy rooted through the closet, opening sacks and boxes, taking out bright summertime T-shirts and open-toed, pastel shoes with high acrylic heels. "All the rage, Annie. Here, take what you want. I'll make you into a disco-mama. We'll have fun." She pressed Ann against her hard, slithery breasts, they brushed cheeks, and Ann—flushing and shivering—gathered her presents and left.

Ann stopped at a Colonel Sanders spot on Bloor for a quick snack-pack. The only other time she had eaten there had been with a girl from the office—Marie something—who had taken out half a dozen girls on the day she'd quit. She'd married an engineer and gone off to Zambia. "I'm afraid," she'd told Ann. "Toronto's the farthest I've been from Jonquière." But Ann had thought her fear a form of vanity, a way of showing off that her life was not closing in

116 | MIDCAREER STORIES (1985–1988)

on her, as was the life of the more circumspect Ann Vane. Anyway, when you're from Jonquière, what fears can Africa hold? Coming to Toronto had been her training in foreign travel.

"What's there to be afraid of?" Ann had deflated her. "Guy'll be working for a Canadian company, won't he? You'll be living in a Canadian compound. You'll probably even have a Canadian PX."

"The seasons come at the wrong time," Marie had said. "They don't have electricity all day. My things won't work there."

Ann had no idea how it had turned out for the girl in Zambia. There had been no letters to anyone at the office, not even a Christmas card, though Ann had hunted up a *Joyeux Noël* and sent it to the engineering company in Lusaka. Africa had swallowed her. Now, as she sat at a table not far from teenagers wearing roller skates, the old irritations at Marie's confession returned. She, too, could leave if she wanted to. It wasn't fear or frugality that kept her back. She lacked ferocity of desire. That was her failing. She would think of going to L.A. to visit Poppy Pennington. Who knew, she might even try writing for Tom Packer. Home was a territory of mind; it was altogether possible she would call up one of the dozens of real estate agents who dropped cards in her mailbox and put the house on Tranby up for sale. She'd make a killing.

"Miss Vane, excuse me, please, may I bother you? You have one minute?"

She cringed. The man—it was Mr. Hernandez, this time in an overcoat that muted his dingy flamboyance—had been sitting a few tables away and must have been studying her, waiting for the moment (her thoughts of California? of selling her house? had she been moving her lips?) to pounce. But why would he drag over his tray and briefcase?

"It's my lunch hour," she said stiffly. She had not meant to humiliate him. She had not meant to stop at a fast-food place. She had meant to be dining in the famous Courtyard Café with Peppi Paluka.

"You have a moment for someone in pain?" He stood before her, accusatory, penitential, the briefcase wedged upright between his tireless legs.

"You see that lady there." He didn't point, and she did not lift her head, or smile. "She wants to meet you, Miss Vane. That is my sister. She says you understand melancholia. She talks to you, woman to woman—I am going away. She says you know the pain in her heart, you will help. You will let her stay."

Please, thought Ann, *enough*. She wasn't good with melodrama, with passionate delivery that sounded like bad translation. "I told you," she said, "it is not my department. I have nothing to do with visas." She would not permit him to wheedle away her resistance. She knew nothing about love, though she had been betrayed once. Her man in condo development, who had brought her pale, pretty bottles of wine, who'd flown her once to Florida, who'd pinned her indiscriminately against refrigerator doors, in closets, on sofas and guest beds, in a burlesque of uncontainable passion. It had been a mistake, and after he had wounded her vanity she had returned to work as usual, slowed just a little by Bella's Valium. She thought Mr. Hernandez, who'd left his marks on her wrist, who sold houses and cosmetics, capable of the same behavior. She had not done what she had wanted to—put her head in an oven like Sylvia Plath—and she would not do whatever Mr. Hernandez wanted now. She had been, and would be, sensible and brave.

"You will not let her be deported. Please." He reached for her arm, which she skillfully withdrew. "You see how crazy she is with devotion. She *will* find her husband. I will go and talk reason. Then she will take the bus to P.E.I."

"*Mi*ster Hernandez, please. Kindly leave me alone, have I made myself clear? I'm going on vacation soon. You could try talking to Mrs. Herzog. She'll take over my cases. But I hold out little hope for your sister. The law is quite inflexible on that point."

"It's not fair," Mr. Hernandez shouted. "You cannot leave us like . . . like dogs on the street."

To keep him from shouting, from making a scene in a room full of roller skaters, she was forced to look up. He was a madman. He pushed his briefcase toward her with angry, shuffling steps. His breathing was unsteady, full of clucking and rattling noises. He thrust his ungloved hands at her in a petition so savage that she was afraid he might kill her. His fingers were flat and bony under the too-short sleeves of his coat. They came at her, like knife blades, to gouge and slice her face.

"Go away," she cried. "Tell your sister to go back. They'll find her and arrest her if she overstays."

He withdrew. "You promised to work something out," he said, plaintively. "My poor sister, now she goes mad, she kills herself, who knows? She has too much pain. But don't worry. I don't want you to worry, Miss Vane. You're free to finish your food and look at all the nice clothes you bought from all the nice shops. I don't want to give you stomach ache or worse. You people cannot feel, that is the problem."

She hated him. If only she could think of something wounding enough to say. "That's preposterous. Absolutely preposterous." But he was already walking away, his back sternly discouraging of second thoughts, second chances. "Nothing is fair!" she shouted, ashamed at letting go like that, in a public place. "You think I have it good?"

She watched him fade into the wintry crowd. The woman he'd pointed to did not jump up, did not even take notice. Wherever the sister was, she would not go mad or jump out of a window and splatter herself on downtown traf-

MIDCAREER STORIES (1985–1988)

fic as Ann had dreamed of, often. Mr. Hernandez's sister would hide in back rooms with drapes pulled tight, crouch behind the sofa at each ring of the doorbell, stare at game shows till glassy-eyed. She would not get caught. She would not be deported. She wasn't ambitious enough to get deeply hurt.

"Nothing is fair!" she shouted. "There isn't any justice. And your sister was never married! It's a trick to cheat Immigration." Her voice sagged with grief, and she sat, a small figure at the end of a long, busy dining hall. She would not stand in line with Donald Sutherland, not Ann; she would remain in Toronto surrounded by Chinese and Indians and Jamaicans, bent over their snack-packs of Kentucky Fried Chicken.

After a while, they stopped staring. Ann gathered up her presents and walked back to the office.

Nostalgia

ON A COLD, snowless evening in December, Dr. Manny Patel, a psychiatric resident at a state hospital in Queens, New York, looked through the store-front window of the "New Taj Mahal" and for the first time in thirteen years felt the papercut-sharp pain of desire. The woman behind the counter was about twenty, twenty-one, with the buttery-gold skin and the round voluptuous bosom of a Bombay film star.

Dr. Patel had driven into Manhattan on an impulse. He had put in one of those afternoons at the hospital that made him realize it was only the mysteries of metabolism that kept him from unprofessional outbursts. Mr. Horowitz, a 319-pound readmitted schizophrenic, had convinced himself that he was Noel Coward and demanded respect from the staff. In less than half an hour, Mr. Horowitz had sung twenty songs, battered a therapy aide's head against a wall, unbuttoned another patient's blouse in order to bite off her nipples, struck a Jamaican nurse across the face and lunged at Dr. Patel, calling him in exquisite English, "Paki scum." The nurse asked that Mr. Horowitz be placed in the seclusion room, and Dr. Patel had agreed. The seclusion order had to be reviewed by a doctor every two hours, and Mr. Horowitz's order was renewed by Dr. Chuong who had come in two hours late for work.

Dr. Patel did not like to lock grown men and women in a seven-by-nine room, especially one without padding on the walls. Mr. Horowitz had screamed and sung for almost six hours. Dr. Patel had increased his dosage of Haldol. Mr. Horowitz was at war with himself and there was no truce except through psychopharmacology and Dr. Patel was suspicious of the side effects of such cures. The Haldol had calmed the prisoner. Perhaps it was unrealistic to want more.

He was grateful that there were so many helpless, mentally disabled people (crazies, his wife called them) in New York State, and that they afforded him and Dr. Chuong and even the Jamaican nurse a nice living. But he resented being called "Paki scum." Not even a sick man like Mr. Horowitz had the right to do that.

He had chosen to settle in the U.S. He was not one for nostalgia; he was not an expatriate but a patriot. His wife, Camille, who had grown up in Camden, New Jersey, did not share his enthusiasm for America, and had made fun of him when he voted for President Reagan. Camille was not a hypocrite; she was a predictable paradox. She could cut him down for wanting to move to a three-hundred-thousand-dollar house with an atrium in the dining hall, and for blowing sixty-two thousand on a red Porsche, while she boycotted South African wines and non-union lettuce. She spent guiltless money at Balducci's and on fitness equipment. So he enjoyed his house, his car, so what? He wanted things. He wanted things for Camille and for their son. He loved his family, and his acquisitiveness was entwined with love.

His son was at Andover, costing nearly twelve thousand dollars a year. When Manny converted the twelve thousand from dollars to rupees, which he often did as he sat in his small, dreary office listening for screams in the hall, the staggering rupee figure reassured him that he had done well in the New World. His son had recently taken to wearing a safety pin through his left earlobe, but nothing the boy could do would diminish his father love.

He had come to America because of the boy. Well, not exactly *come*, but stayed when his student visa expired. He had met Camille, a nurse, at a teaching hospital and the boy had come along, all eight pounds and ten ounces of him, one balmy summer midnight. He could always go back to Delhi if he wanted to. He had made enough money to retire to India (the conversion into rupees had made him a millionaire several times over). He had bought a condominium in one of the better development "colonies" of New Delhi, just in case.

America had been very good to him, no question; but there were things that he had given up. There were some boyhood emotions, for instance, that he could no longer retrieve. He lived with the fear that his father would die before he could free himself from the crazies of New York and go home. He missed his parents, especially his father, but he couldn't explain this loss to Camille. She hated her mother who had worked long hours at Korvette's and brought her up alone. Camille's mother now worked at a K-Mart, even though she didn't need the money desperately. Camille's mother was an obsessive-compulsive but that was no reason to hate her. In fact, Manny got along with her very well and often had to carry notes between her and her daughter.

His father was now in his seventies, a loud, brash man with blackened teeth. He still operated the moviehouse he owned. The old man didn't trust the manager he kept on the payroll. He didn't trust anyone except his blood relatives. All the ushers in the moviehouse were poor cousins. Manny was an only child. His mother had been deemed barren, but at age forty-three, goddess Parvati had worked a miracle and Manny had been born. He should go back to India. He should look after his parents. Out of a sense of duty to the goddess, if not out of love for his father. Money, luxuries: he could have both in India, too. When he had wanted to go to Johns Hopkins for medical training, his parents had loved him enough to let him go. They loved him the same intense, unexamined way he loved his own boy. He had let them down. Perhaps he hadn't really let them down in that he had done well at medical school, and had a job in the State set-up in Queens, and played the money market aggressively with a bit of inside information from Suresh Khanna who had been a year ahead of him in Delhi's Modern School and was now with Merrill-Lynch, but he hadn't reciprocated their devotion.

It was in this mood of regret filtered through longing that Manny had driven into Manhattan and parked his Porsche on a sidestreet outside the Sari Palace which was a block up from the New Taj Mahal, where behind the counter he had spied the girl of his dreams.

The girl—the woman, Manny corrected himself instantly, for Camille didn't tolerate what she called "masculists"—moved out from behind the counter to show a customer where in the crowded store the ten-pound bags of Basmati rice were stacked. She wore a "Police" T-shirt and navy cords. The cords voluted up her small, rounded thighs and creased around her crotch in a delicate burst, like a Japanese fan. He would have dressed her in a sari of peacock blue silk. He wanted to wrap her narrow wrists in bracelets of 24-carat gold. He wanted to decorate her bosom and throat with necklaces of pearls, rubies, emeralds. She was as lovely and as removed from him as a goddess. He breathed warm, worshipful stains on the dingy store window.

She stooped to pick up a sack of rice by its rough jute handles while the customer flitted across the floor to a bin of eggplants. He discerned a touch of indolence in the way she paused before slipping her snake-slim fingers through the sack's hemp loops. She paused again. She tested the strength of the loops. She bent her knees, ready to heave the brutish sack of rice. He found himself running into the store. He couldn't let her do it. He couldn't let a goddess do menial chores, then ride home on a subway with a backache.

"Oh, thank you," she said. She flashed him an indolent glance under heavily shadowed eyelids, without seeming to turn away from the customer who had expected her to lift the ten-pound sack.

"Where are the fresh eggplants? These are all dried out."

Manny Patel watched the customer flick the pleats of her Japanese georgette sari irritably over the sturdy tops of her winter boots.

"These things look as if they've been here all week!" the woman continued to complain.

Manny couldn't bear her beauty. Perfect crimson nails raked the top layer of eggplant. "They came in just two days ago."

If there had been room for a third pair of hands, he would have come up with plump, seedless, perfect eggplants.

"Ring up the rice, *dal* and spices," the customer instructed. "I'll get my vegetables next door."

"I'll take four eggplants," Manny Patel said defiantly. "And two pounds of *bhindi*." He sorted through wilted piles of okra which Camille wouldn't know how to cook.

"I'll be with you in a minute, sir," the goddess answered.

When she looked up again, he asked her out for dinner. She said only, "You really don't have to buy anything, you know."

SHE SUGGESTED they meet outside the Sari Palace at six-thirty. Her readiness overwhelmed him. Dr. Patel had been out of the business of dating for almost thirteen years. At conferences, on trips and on the occasional night out in the city when an older self possessed him, he would hire women for the evening, much as he had done in India. They were never precisely the answer, not even to his desire.

Camille had taken charge as soon as she had spotted him in the hospital cafeteria; she had done the pursuing. While he did occasionally flirt with a Filipino nutritionist at the hospital where he now worked, he assumed he did not possess the dexterity to perform the two-step dance of assertiveness and humility required of serious adultery. He left the store flattered, but wary. A goddess had found him attractive, but he didn't know her name. He didn't know what kind of family fury she might unleash on him. Still, for the first time in years he felt a kind of agitated discovery, as though if he let up for a minute, his reconstituted, instant American life would not let him back.

His other self, the sober, greedy, scholarly Dr. Patel, knew that life didn't change that easily. He had seen enough Horowitzes to know that no matter how astute his own methods might be and no matter how miraculous the dis-

MIDCAREER STORIES (1985–1988)

coveries of psychopharmacologists, fate could not be derailed. How did it come about that Mr. Horowitz, the son of a successful slacks manufacturer, a good student at the Bronx High School of Science, had ended up obese, disturbed and assaultive, while he, the son of a Gujarati farmer turned entrepreneur, an indifferent student at Modern School and then at St. Stephen's in Delhi, was ambitious and acquisitive? All his learning and experience could not answer the simplest questions. He had about an hour and twenty minutes to kill before perfection was to revisit him, this time (he guessed) in full glory.

Dr. Patel wandered through "little India"—the busy, colorful blocks of Indian shops and restaurants off Lexington in the upper twenties. Men lugged heavy crates out of double parked pickup trucks, swearing in Punjabi and Hindi. Women with tired, frightened eyes stepped into restaurants, careful not to drop their shopping sacks from Bloomingdale's and Macy's. The Manhattan air here was fragrant with spices. He followed an attractive mother with two preschoolers into Chadni Chowk, a tea and snacks stall, to call Camille about the emergency that had come up. Thank God for Mr. Horowitz's recidivism. Camille was familiar with the more outrageous doings of Mr. Horowitz.

"Why does that man always act up when I have plans?" Camille demanded. "*Amarcord* is at the rep tonight only."

But Camille seemed in as agreeable a mood as his goddess. She thought she might ask Susan Kwan, the wife of an orthodontist who lived four houses up the block and who had a son by a former marriage also at Andover. Her credulousness depressed Manny. A woman who had lived with a man for almost thirteen years should be able to catch his little lies.

"Mr. Horowitz is a dangerous person," he continued. He could have hung up, but he didn't. He didn't want permission; he wanted sympathy. "He rushed into my office. He tried to kill me."

"Maybe psychiatrists at state institutions ought to carry firearms. Have you thought of that, Manny?" She laughed.

Manny Patel flushed. Camille didn't understand how the job was draining him. Mr. Horowitz had, for a fact, flopped like a walrus on Dr. Patel's desk, demanding a press conference so that the world would know that his civil liberties were being infringed. The moneyless schizos of New York state, Mr. Horowitz had screamed, were being held hostage by a bunch of foreign doctors who couldn't speak English. If it hadn't been for the two six-foot orderlies (Dr. Patel felt an awakening of respect for big blacks), Mr. Horowitz would probably have grabbed him by the throat.

"I could have died today," he repeated. The realization dazed him. "The man tried to strangle me."

He hung up and ordered a cup of *masala* tea. The sweet, sticky brew calmed him, and the perfumed steam cleared his sinuses. Another man in his position would probably have ordered a double scotch. In crises, he seemed to regress, to reach automatically for the miracle cures of his Delhi youth, though normally he had no patience with nostalgia. When he had married, he burned his India Society membership card. He was professionally cordial, nothing more, with Indian doctors at the hospital. But he knew he would forever shuttle between the old world and the new. He couldn't pretend he had been reborn when he became an American citizen in a Manhattan courthouse. Rebirth was the privilege of the dead, and of gods and goddesses, and they could leap into your life in myriad, mysterious ways, as a shopgirl, for instance, or as a withered eggplant, just to test you.

At three minutes after six, Dr. Patel positioned himself inside his Porsche and watched the front doors of the Sari Palace for his date's arrival. He didn't want to be late, but more than that he didn't want to give the appearance of having been early, or of having waited nervously. There was a slight tremor in both his hands. He was suffering a small attack of anxiety. At thirty-three minutes after six, she appeared in the doorway of the sari store. She came out of the Sari Palace, not up the street from the New Taj Mahal as he had expected. He slammed shut and locked his car door. Did it mean that she, too, had come to the rendezvous too early and had spied on him, crouched, anxious, strapped in the bucket seat of his Porsche? When he caught up with her by the store window, she was the most beautiful woman he had ever talked to.

Her name was Padma. She told him that as he fought for a cab to take them uptown. He didn't ask for, and she didn't reveal, her last name. Both were aware of the illicit nature of their meeting. An Indian man his age had to be married, though he wore no wedding ring. An immigrant girl from a decent Hindu family—it didn't matter how long she had lived in America and what rock groups she was crazy about—would not have said yes to dinner with a man she didn't know. It was this inarticulated unsanctionedness of the dinner date that made him feel reckless, a hedonist, a man who might trample tired ladies carrying shopping bags in order to steal a taxi crawling uptown. He wanted to take Padma to an Indian restaurant so that he could feel he knew what he was ordering and could bully the maitre d' a bit, but not to an Indian restaurant in her neighborhood. He wanted a nice Indian restaurant, an upscale one, with tablecloths, sitar music and air ducts sprayed with the essence of rose petals. He chose a new one, Shajahan, on Park Avenue.

"It's nice. I was going to recommend it," she said.

PADMA. LOTUS. The goddess had come to him as a flower. He wanted to lunge for her hands as soon as they had been seated at a corner booth, but he knew better than to frighten her off. He was mortal, he was humble.

The maitre d' himself took Dr. Patel's order. And with the hors d'oeuvres of samosas and poppadoms he sent a bottle of Entre Deux Mers on the house. Dr. Patel had dined at the Shajahan four or five times already, and each time had brought in a group of six or eight. He had been a little afraid that the maitre d' might disapprove of his bringing a youngish woman, an Indian and quite obviously not his wife, but the bottle of wine reassured him that the management was not judgmental.

He broke off a sliver of poppadom and held it to her lips. She snatched it with an exaggerated flurry of lips and teeth.

"Feeding the performing seal, are you?" She was coy. And amused.

"I didn't mean it that way," he murmured. Her lips, he noticed, had left a glistening crescent of lipstick on a fingertip. He wiped the finger with his napkin surreptitiously under the table.

She didn't help herself to the samosas, and he didn't dare lift a forkful to her mouth. Perhaps she didn't care for samosas. Perhaps she wasn't much of an eater. He himself was timid and clumsy, half afraid that if he tried anything playful he might drip mint chutney on her tiger-print chiffon sari.

"Do you mind if I smoke?"

He busied himself with food while she took out a packet of Sobranie and a book of matches. Camille had given up smoking four years before, and now handwritten instructions THANK YOU FOR NOT SMOKING IN THIS HOUSE decorated bureau tops and coffee tables. He had never gotten started because of an allergy.

"Well?" she said. It wasn't quite a question, and it wasn't quite a demand. "Aren't you going to light it?" And she offered Manny Patel an exquisite profile, cheek sucked tight and lips squeezed around the filter tip.

The most banal gesture of a goddess can destroy a decent-living mortal. He lit her cigarette, then blew the match out with a gust of unreasonable hope.

The maitre d' hung around Manny's table almost to the point of neglecting other early diners. He had sad eyes and a bushy mustache. He wore a dark suit, a silvery wide tie kept in place with an elephant-headed god stick pin, and on his feet which were remarkably large for a short, slight man, scuffed and pointed black shoes.

"I wouldn't recommend the pork vindaloo tonight." The man's voice was confidential, low. "We have a substitute cook. But the fish Bengal curry is very good. The lady, I think, is Bengali, no?"

She did not seem surprised. "How very observant of you," she smiled.

It was flattering to have the maitre d' linger and advise. Manny Patel ended up ordering one each of the curries listed under beef, lamb and fowl. He was a guiltlessly meat-eating Gujarati, at least in America. He filled in the rest of the order with two vegetable dishes, one spiced lentil and a vegetable pillau. The raita salad was free, as were the two small jars of mango and lemon pickle.

When the food started coming, Padma reluctantly stubbed out her Sobranie. The maitre d' served them himself, making clucking noises with his tongue against uneven, oversize teeth, and Dr. Patel felt obliged to make loud, appreciative moans.

"Is everything fine, doctor-*sahib*? Fish is first class, no? It is not on the regular menu."

He stayed and made small talk about Americans. He dispatched waiters to other tables, directing them with claps of pinkish palms from the edge of Manny's booth. Padma made an initial show of picking at her vegetable pillau. Then she gave up and took out another slim black Sobranie from a tin packet and held her face, uplifted and radiant, close to Manny's so he could light it again for her.

The maitre d' said, "I am having a small problem, doctor-*sahib*. Actually the problem is my wife's. She has been in America three years and she is very lonely still. I'm saying to her, you have nice apartment in Rego Park, you have nice furnitures and fridge and stove, I'm driving you here and there in a blue Buick, you're having home-style Indian food, what then is wrong? But I am knowing and you are knowing, doctor-*sahib*, that no Indian lady is happy without having children to bring up. That is why, in my desperation, I brought over my sister's child last June. We want to adopt him, he is very bright and talented and already he is loving this country. But the U.S. government is telling me no. The boy came on a visitor's visa, and now the government is giving me big trouble. They are calling me bad names. Jealous peoples are telling them bad stories. They are saying I'm in the business of moving illegal aliens, can you believe? In the meantime, my wife is crying all day and pulling out her hair. Doctor-*sahib*, you can write that she needs to have the boy here for her peace of mind and mental stability, no? On official stationery of your hospital, doctor-*sahib*?"

"My hands are tied," Manny Patel said. "The U.S. government wouldn't listen to me."

Padma said nothing. Manny ignored the maitre d'. A reality was dawning on Manny Patel. It was too beautiful, too exciting to contemplate. He didn't want this night to fall under the pressure of other immigrants' woes.

"But you will write a letter about my wife's mental problems, doctor-*sahib*?" The maitre d' had summoned up tears. A man in a dark suit weeping in an upscale ethnic restaurant. Manny felt slightly disgraced, he wished the man would go away. "Official stationery is very necessary to impress the immigration people."

"Please leave us alone," snapped Manny Patel. "If you persist I will never come back."

The old assurance, the authority of a millionaire in his native culture, was returning. He was sure of himself.

"What do you want to do after dinner?" Padma asked when the maitre d' scurried away from their booth. Manny could sense him, wounded and scowling, from behind the kitchen door.

"What would you like to do?" He thought of his wife and Mrs. Kwan at the Fellini movie. They would probably have a drink at a bar before coming home. Susan Kwan had delightful legs. He had trouble understanding her husband, but Manny Patel had spent enjoyable hours at the Kwans', watching Mrs. Kwan's legs. Padma's legs remained a mystery; he had seen her only in pants or a sari.

"If you are thinking of fucking me," she said very suddenly, "I should warn you that I never have an orgasm. You don't have to worry about pleasing me."

Yes, he thought, it *is* so, just as he had suspected. It was a night in which he could do no wrong. He waved his Visa card at the surly maitre d' and paid the bill. After that Padma let him take her elbow and guide her to the expensive hotel above the restaurant.

An oriental man at the desk asked him, "Cash or credit card, sir?" He paid for a double occupancy room with cash and signed himself in as Dr. Mohan Vakil & wife, 18 Ridgewood Drive, Columbus, Ohio.

He had laid claim to America.

In a dark seventh-floor room off a back corridor, the goddess bared her flesh to a dazed, daunted mortal. She was small. She was perfect. She had saucy breasts, fluted thighs and tiny, taut big toes.

"Hey, you can suck but don't bite, okay?" Padma may have been slow to come, but he was not. He fell on her with a devotee's frenzy.

"Does it bother you?" she said later, smoking the second Sobranie. She was on her side. Her tummy had a hint of convex opulence. "About my not getting off?"

He couldn't answer. It was a small price to pay, and anyway, he wasn't paying it. Nothing could diminish the thrill he felt in taking a chance. It wasn't the hotel and this bed; it was having stepped inside the New Taj Mahal and asking her out.

He should probably call home, in case Camille hadn't stopped off for a drink. He should probably get dressed, offer her something generous—as discreetly as possible, for this one had class, real class—then drive home. The Indian food, an Indian woman in bed, made him nostalgic. He wished he were in his kitchen, and that his parents were visiting him and that his mother was making him a mug of hot Horlick's and that his son was not so far removed from him in a boarding school.

He wished he had married an Indian woman. One that his father had selected. He wished he had any life but the one he had chosen.

As Dr. Patel sat on the edge of the double bed and slid his feet through the legs of his trousers, someone rapped softly on the hotel door, then without waiting for an answer unlocked it with a passkey.

Padma pulled the sheet up to her chin, but did not seem to have been startled.

"She's underage, of course," the maitre d' said. "She is my sister's youngest daughter. I accuse you of rape, doctor-*sahib*. You are of course ruined in this country. You have everything and think you must have more. You are highly immoral."

He sat on the one chair that wasn't littered with urgently cast-off clothes, and lit a cigarette. It was rapidly becoming stuffy in the room, and Manny's eyes were running. The man's eyes were malevolent, but the rest of his face remained practiced and relaxed. An uncle should have been angrier, Dr. Patel thought automatically. He himself should have seen it coming. He had mistaken her independence as a bold sign of honest assimilation. But it was his son who was the traveler over shifting sands, not her.

There was no point in hurrying. Meticulously he put on his trousers, double-checked the zipper, buttoned his shirt, knotted his tie and slipped on his Gucci shoes. *The lady is Bengali, no?* Yes, they knew one another, perhaps even as uncle and niece. Or pimp and hooker. The air here was polluted with criminality. He wondered if his slacks had been made by immigrant women in Mr. Horowitz's father's sweatshop.

"She's got to be at least twenty-three, twenty-four," Dr. Patel said. He stared at her, deliberately insolent. Through the sheets he could make out the upward thrust of her taut big toes. He had kissed those toes only half an hour before. He must have been mad.

"I'm telling you she is a minor. I'm intending to make a citizen's arrest. I have her passport in my pocket."

It took an hour of bickering and threats to settle. He made out a check for seven hundred dollars. He would write a letter on hospital stationery. The uncle made assurances that there were no hidden tapes. Padma went into the bathroom to wash up and dress.

"Why?" Manny shouted, but he knew Padma couldn't hear him over the noise of the gushing faucet.

AFTER THE TEAM LEFT HIM, Manny Patel took off his clothes and went into the bathroom so recently used by the best-looking woman he had ever talked to (or slept with, he could now add). Her perfume, he thought of it as essence of lotus, made him choke.

He pulled himself up, using the edge of the bathtub as a step ladder, until his feet were on the wide edges of the old-fashioned sink. Then, squatting like a villager, squatting the way he had done in his father's home, he defecated into the sink, and with handfuls of his own shit—it felt hot, light, porous, an artist's medium—he wrote WHORE on the mirror and floor.

He spent the night in the hotel room. Just before dawn he took a cab to the parking lot of the Sari Palace. Miraculously, no vandals had touched his Porsche. Feeling lucky, spared somehow in spite of his brush with the deities, he drove home.

Camille had left the porch light on and it glowed pale in the brightening light of the morning. In a few hours Mr. Horowitz would start to respond to the increased dosage of Haldol and be let out of the seclusion chamber. At the end of the term, Shawn Patel would come home from Andover and spend all day in the house with earphones tuned to a happier world. And in August, he would take his wife on a cruise through the Caribbean and make up for this night with a second honeymoon.

Tamurlane

WE SLEEP in shifts in my apartment, three illegals on guard playing cards and three bedded down on mats on the floor. One man next door broke his leg jumping out the window. I'd been whistling in the bathroom and he'd mistaken it for our warning tune. The walls are flimsy. Nights I hear collective misery.

Was this what I left Ludhiana for?

It was below freezing and icy outside but inside the Mumtaz Bar B-Q it was hot and crackly with static. Mohan the busboy was gobbling the mints by the cash register. The cook was asleep on the bar's counter in his undershirt and shorts. He's a little guy and he can squeeze into the skinniest space, come three o'clock, or during a raid. The door is locked and the drapes are pulled. We have a "CLOSED" sign in English and Hindi on the door, courtesy of Cinema Sahni, next door. Mr. Aziz doesn't mind our spreading out of the kitchen and into the dining room as long as we spray air freshener before the dinner crowd comes in. These days Mr. A. is dividing his time between the Mumtaz in Toronto and a 67-unit motel on the Gulf coast of Florida. Canadians don't want us, it's like Uganda all over again, says Mr. A. He says he can feel it in his bones.

So there we were, the regulars. The new tandoor chef, Gupta, was at a table with a huffing and puffing gentleman I didn't know. He had the crafty eyes of a Sindhi, but his graying hair was dyed reddish so he could have been a Muslim. I've been too long here; there was a time when I could tell them apart, not just Hindu and Muslim, but where, what caste and what they were hiding. Now all I care about is legal or illegal? This man has called himself Muslim, a Ugandan, a victim of Idi Amin. These sad rehearsals, heaping indignity on top of being poor. As if poverty and opportunity weren't enough, like it was for the Italians and Greeks and Portuguese. How did this vast country suddenly get so filled? But Mr. A. and this chap probably have their British passports and their tales of mistreatment, and the rest of us have a lifetime debt to a shifty agent in Delhi who got us here, with no hint of how to keep us. The new chef and his friend made Mohan and me watchful.

He didn't have an old man's harassed face. His skin was oily still, and supple. He didn't look old enough to need to dye his hair. Vanity we're all guilty of; even the cook dropped a hundred and fifty dollars this December on hand-tooled, baby blue antelope boots. This man didn't look vain. He just seemed troubled. He held his cigarette Indian-style, high up near the glowing tip and in between the thumb and index finger, like a pencil.

I hadn't made up my mind about the new chef. He was a good chef, but an improviser. We didn't have an authentic tandoor oven because Mr. A. thinks people get bored of watching their meat cooking in a clay oven in front of them and if you aren't going to do the tandoor in public you might as well go down to Buffalo and buy one of the small, sturdy brick things from Khanna & Sons. We don't have one of the brick things either, not yet, but the new chef was doing wonders with chicken breasts and lamb chops under the broiler of our old gas stove. He didn't complain when he saw the Mumtaz's kitchen. He didn't say anything about the stove. He just limped into the freezer and took out two trays of lamb and chicken. Then he asked me where the cleaver was. But he wasn't friendly. He didn't want to talk. He walked like a man on unbending but fragile stilts. His knees didn't bend and when he sat his legs fell straight out. When he worked in the kitchen, he propped his stomach against the sink in order to keep his balance. Severe damage like that is difficult to watch, you want to pull away, as from a beggar.

Now he was doing the listening, and the man with the dyed hair was doing the talking.

The man said, "Maharaj, I don't know why you stay in Toronto, I really don't. I can find you a place in Atlanta, no immigration problems. Have you seen Atlanta in January? It's like a hill station, my friend. Like Simla, healthy. Or Dallas, here, let me check—" he took out a long list of names written on the back of a supermarket stub. "Ft. Worth, you are knowing?"

"Hey, man," Mohan called from the cash register, "you got a place for me on that list? I want New York City. Or Miami, hot-hot like Bombay."

"Pah, in Miami and New York they are finding thousands of boys like you. Big mouth and no skill. Don't bother me, I am talking to an artist with fish and fowl. Such a man is worth gold."

The man put a hand on the new chef's hands which were folded and still, and red with tandoori *masala* in the knuckles and under the nails. The new chef didn't move. He looked dead, or very relaxed. I couldn't make up my mind about him. He was odd.

"If you stay here, trouble's going to find you. I can guarantee you that, my friend. Aziz-*sahib* has the right idea. Get out while you can. You're one of the lucky ones."

Mohan rang the cash register. The drawer shot open and he took out a couple of quarters and fed them into a juke box. A noisy little number by a British group, and a duet by Chitra and Ajit Kumar.

The agent said nothing during the singles. When the music stopped, he said in the same hectoring tone he had used before, "You don't have to go looking, friend. Because trouble's coming. If you stay in Toronto, it's coming to your door. You know what happened to me when I was coming to see you? Right here on Gerrard Street, a block and a half from your fancy Bar B-Q?"

Mohan didn't like the man. I could tell that from the way he kept trying to disrupt his story. He thought the man was giving the chef a hard time when all he wanted was a rest and smoke before his next shift. Mohan said, not loud but loud enough for me to hear and I was farther from him than the man was, "This place isn't fancy. Mr. A. is a tightwad. Mr. A. couldn't run a fancy place."

The recruiter didn't even look Mohan's way. He said, "I was walking as fast as I could so we'd have time together before you had to cook again. You know how fast I can walk. You remember the time I was running to catch that train from Grand Central and I was stopped by a cop? He thought I was Puerto Rican, remember, because he had never seen an Indian run before. Well, I wasn't walking that fast, but fast, after getting off the trolley at the wrong stop. It was like the time we got off in the middle of Harlem—remember? I could see all the Indian shops up ahead, but I was still two blocks away. I started running, when out pop three young chaps from an arcade . . ."

"That must be Sinbad's," Mohan said. "The other arcade's four blocks the other side."

"One boy knocked me down. Actually he tripped me, so it looked like an accident. Then the other two spat on me, called me names you wouldn't believe. I'm a Gandhian of the old school. I just lay there with my face against a parking meter, to protect my eyes, you know. The eyes are delicate, the rest is reparable. And all the time the hooligans were belaboring me, my friend, I was thinking of you. Why did Gupta come back to Toronto, I kept asking. You were out once—I can get you back. I would be proud to sponsor a hero like you. I am proud to call you brother or cousin. You can pay me back a little every month—you'll be free in a year. Why, after what happened to you?" He turned now to Mohan, and there was scorn in his voice. "This man is a hero to us all. Six years ago when you were naked in Bombay, he was thrown on the subway tracks in this city. He would never walk, they said. Now look. Like a true Gandhian, he forgave them. Good men left Canada for less cause. Dr. Choudhury, he left his seventy-thousand-dollar-plus practice. On a matter of principle, you remember, when the courts let go of those boys who beat up the worshipers at the Durga Puja festival."

"Poor Dr. Choudhury," Mohan said to me. Principles are easy to have when you're rich and have a skill like Dr. Choudhury and Dallas is waiting. The problem is for Mohan and me and the little cook asleep on the bar. Hooligans and everyone else can do what they want and they know we don't dare complain.

"Why, my friend?" The man put out his cigarette. "What kind of a life is this if your dignity is on the line every time you step out the door?" Ah, dignity. *Dignity*! That beautiful word that has never fed an empty stomach.

The chef just shrugged, but Mohan wasn't finished. He shouted, "It's worse in British Columbia, except the Sikhs can look after themselves better than we can. They do head-to-head with everyone. Thick skulls can be very useful."

AT FOUR-THIRTY, the cook woke up and put away his pillow. The tandoor chef said goodbye to his friend, and walked back to his pans of marinating breasts and chops. The man said he was going back to Buffalo that night. Mohan was busier than the rest of us at any given hour. As a waiter I had it easiest. But it was lonely when the others went about their chores in the kitchen and I'd already folded the napkins into fancy shapes and laid the blue overcloths on the wobbly tables. Mr. A. had been gone so long to the Gulf Coast that he didn't know the cook stole supplies and that I had become very bored. The Indian patrons came only on nights Sahni-*sahib* screened a Bombay blockbuster in the cinema next door. The white Canadians barely came at all. Maybe some old English types, or Indian boys with Canadian girlfriends, trying to show off. I don't know why our food never caught on with Canadians the way Chinese food did. We kept waiting for a notice in the papers, something like that. Mr. A. has a bigger place than this in Ft. Myers. Light of India or Star of India, something like that. He said he wanted to get into the take-out roti kabab business. "They'll be eating roti kababs the way they do hamburgers by the time I'm through," he used to brag. "I want to be the McDonald's of Indian food." Maybe he will, in Miami or the Gulf Coast. He had a British passport and he could always claim mistreatment at the hands of crazy blacks. His heart wasn't in Toronto. Mohan is right; those who can run, do.

At five minutes after five came the call we always listened for. Two rings, then nothing. We had a drill. The little cook dove under the sink and piled the biggest aluminum platters around him. I locked the door. Gupta looked unconcerned, and he couldn't move anyway. Right then I knew he must have his papers. He just flipped the lamb chops over, then slid the broiler pan back under the flames. Mohan and I headed for the basement and since I was taller, I unscrewed the lightbulb on the way down.

THAT WASN'T THE FIRST TIME. We knew where to hide, Mohan and I. We even had bedrolls on the shelves behind the sacks of rice. We could hear the Mounties up in the kitchen, and we didn't know how Gupta would handle himself. Sometimes they'll let one of us off, if he can turn in three or four.

I knew it was all over when they opened the door to the basement. "Light?" one of them called out. They sounded like they were right on top of us. One carried a torch,[1] brighter than a searchlight.

"What have we here, eh?" He was a big fellow, blond with a rusty-colored mustache, and he knew exactly where to look. The other was in plain clothes, an immigration officer. They traveled in twos, acting on tips.

They took us up to the kitchen. "There's another one," said the immigration man. Aziz-*sahib* has enemies, and jealous friends. Someone else bought a little time for himself. We are all pawns.

"You, too," said the Mountie, pointing to Gupta. "We're all going down to the station."

"This is a business establishment," said Gupta. "I am responsible here while the owner is away."

"We're closing you down. When the owner comes back we'll get him, too."

---

1. British word for "flashlight."—Ed.

Mohan was crying. For all his Bombay smart-talk, I could see he was very young, maybe only twenty. Gupta the chef was propped up in his strange way against the sink and the small cabinet underneath it where the assistant cook was hiding. I had a silly thought just then: if they find him, what will they do with his hundred-and-fifty-dollar boots?

"Get out of my kitchen," said Gupta. "Get out immediately."

"It's cold. Get your coats," said the Mountie. "That goes for you, too." It had become a personal thing between them.

"He is a lame man, sir," I said, "he cannot move without his crutches."

"I don't care if I have to sling him over my shoulder—he's coming with us now."

The plainclothesman stepped between them. "It will only go harder if you resist," he said.

"I am not resisting. I am ordering you away from here." His voice was very quiet, but I could see the color rising in his neck.

"Very well," said the Mountie, and he was suddenly in motion, two quick steps toward the chef, one arm out to grab his neck, the other to club him if necessary. But the chef was quicker. All he had to do was slide his hand along the rim of the sink. The Mountie saw it the same time I did—the cleaver— but he didn't have time to react. Gupta whirled, falling as he took a step, with the cleaver high over his head. He brought it down in a wild, practiced chop on the Mountie's outstretched arm, and I could tell from the way it stuck, the way Gupta couldn't extract it easily for a second swing, that it had sunk well below the overcoat and service jacket. The Mountie and Gupta fell simultaneously, and now Gupta was reaching into his back pocket while the screaming Mountie rolled on one side.

Gupta managed to sit straight. He held his Canadian passport in front of his face. That way, he never saw the drawn gun, nor did he try to dodge the single bullet.

Hindus

I RAN INTO PAT at Sotheby's on a Friday morning two years ago. Derek and I had gone to view the Fraser Collection of Islamic miniatures at the York Avenue galleries. It bothered Derek that I knew so little about my heritage. Islam is nothing more than a marauder's faith to me, but the Moghul emperors stayed a long time in the green delta of the Ganges, flattening and reflattening a fort in the village where I was born, and forcing my priestly ancestors to prove themselves brave. Evidence on that score is still inconclusive. That village is now in Bangladesh.

Derek was a filmmaker, lightly employed at that time. We had been married three hundred and thirty-one days.

"So," Pat said, in his flashy, plummy, drawn-out intonation, "you finally made it to the States!"

It was one of those early November mornings when the woodsy smell of overheated bodies in cloth coats clogged the public stairwells. Everywhere around me I detected the plaintive signs of over-preparedness.

"Whatever are you doing here?" He engulfed me in a swirl of Liberty scarf and cashmere lapels.

"Trying to get the woman there to sell me the right catalog," I said.

The woman, a very young thing with slippery skin, ate a lusty Granny Smith apple and ignored the dark, hesitant miniature-lovers hanging about like bats in daytime.

"They have more class in London," Pat said.

"I wouldn't know. I haven't been back since that unfortunate year at Roedean."[1]

"It was always New York you wanted," Pat laughed. "Don't say I didn't warn you. The world is full of empty promises."

I didn't remember his having warned me about life and the inevitability of grief. It was entirely possible that he had—he had always been given to clowning pronouncements—but I had not seen him in nine years and in Calcutta he had never really broken through the fortifications of my shyness.

"Come have a drink with me," Pat said.

It was my turn to laugh. "You must meet Derek," I said.

Derek had learned a great deal about India. He could reel off statistics of Panchayati Raj and the electrification of villages and the introduction of mass media, though he reserved his love for birds migrating through the wintry deserts of Jaisalmer. Knowledge of India made Derek more sympathetic than bitter, a common trait of decent outsiders. He was charmed by Pat's heedless, old-world insularity.

"Is this the lucky man?" he said to Derek. He did not hold out his hand. He waved us outside; a taxi magically appeared. "Come have a drink with me tomorrow. At my place."

He gave Derek his card. It was big and would not fit into a wallet made to hold Visa and American Express. Derek read it with his usual curiosity.

---

1. Exclusive girls' boarding school in the south of England.—Ed.

H.R.H. Maharajah Patwant Singh

of

Gotlah

Purveyor and Exporter

He tucked the card in the pocket of his raincoat. "I'll be shooting in Toronto tomorrow," he said, "but I'm sure Leela would like to keep it."

There was in the retention of those final "h's"—even Indian maps and newspapers now referred to Gotla and to maharajas, and I had dropped the old "Leelah" in my first month in America—something of the reclusive mountebank. "I'm going to the Patels for dinner tomorrow," I said, afraid that Pat would misread the signs of healthy unpossessiveness in our marriage.

"Come for a drink before. What's the matter, Leela? Turning into a prude in your old age?" To Derek he explained, "I used to rock her on my knee when she was four. She was gorgeous then, but I am no lecher."

It is true that I was very pretty at four and that Pat spent a lot of time in our house fondling us children. He brought us imported chocolates in beautiful tins and made a show of giving me the biggest. In my family, in every generation, one infant seems destined to be the repository of the family's comeliness. In my generation, I inherited the looks, like an heirloom, to keep in good condition and pass on to the next. Beauty teaches humility and responsibility in the culture I came from. By marrying well, I could have seen to the education of my poorer cousins.

———

Pat was in a third-floor sublet in Gramercy Park South. A West Indian doorman with pendulous cheeks and an unbuttoned jacket let me into the building. He didn't give me a chance to say where I was going as I moved toward the elevator.

"The Maharaja is third floor, to the right. All the way down."

I had misunderstood the invitation. It was not to be an hour of wit and nostalgia among exotic knick-knacks squirreled into New York from the Gotla Palace. I counted thirty guests in the first quarter hour of my short stay. Plump young men in tight-fitting suits scuttled from living room to kitchen, balancing overfull glasses of gin and tonic. The women were mostly blonds, with luridly mascaraed, brooding eyes, blond the way South Americans are blond, with deep residual shading. I tried to edge into a group of three women. One of them said, "I thought India was spellbinding. Naresh's partner managed to get us into the Lake Palace Hotel."

"I don't think I could take the poverty," said her friend, as I retreated.

The living room walls were hung with prints of British East India Company officials at work and play, the vestibule with mirror-images of Hindu gods and goddesses.

"Take my advice," a Gujarati man said to Pat in the dim and plantless kitchen. "Get out of diamonds—emeralds *won't* bottom out. These days it *has* to be rubies and emeralds."

In my six years in Manhattan I had not entered a kitchen without plants. There was not even a straggly avocado pushing its nervous way out of a shriveling seed.

I moved back into the living room where the smell of stale turmeric hung like yellow fog from the ceiling. A man rose from the brocade-covered cushions of a banquette near me and plumped them, smiling, to make room for me.

"You're Pat's niece, no?" The man was francophone, a Lebanese. "Pat has such pretty nieces. You have just come from Bombay? I love Bombay. Personally, Bombay to me is like a jewel. Like Paris, like Beirut before, now like Bombay. You agree?"

I disclaimed all kinship to H.R.H. I was a Bengali Brahmin; maharajas—not to put too sharp a point on it—were frankly beneath me, at least by one caste, though most of them, like Pat, would dispute it. Before my marriage to Derek no one in my family since our initial eruption from Vishnu's knee had broken caste etiquette. I disclaimed any recent connection with India. "I haven't been home in ages," I told the Lebanese. "I am an American citizen."

"I, too, am. I am American," he practically squealed. He raised his glass with a bit of gin still left in the bottom, as though he were trying to dislodge lemon pulp stuck and drying on its sides. "You want to have dinner with me tonight, yes? I know Lebanese places, secret and intimate. Food and ambiance very romantic."

"She's going to the Patels." It was Pat. The Gujarati with advice on emeralds was still lodged in the kitchen, huddling with a stocky blond in a fuchsia silk sari.

"Oh, the Patels," said the Lebanese. "You did not say. Super guy, no? He's doing all right for himself. Not as well as me, of course. I own ten stores and he only has four."

Why, I often asked myself, was Derek never around to share these intimacies? Derek would have drawn out the suave, French-speaking, soulful side of this Seventh Avenue *shmattiste*.

It shouldn't have surprised me that the Lebanese man in the ruffled shirt should have known Mohan and Motibehn Patel. For immigrants in similar trades, Manhattan is still a village. Mohan had been in the States for eighteen years and last year had become a citizen. They'd been fortunate in having only sons, now at Cal Tech and Cornell; with daughters there would have been pressure on them to return to India for a proper, arranged marriage.

"Is he still in Queens?"

"No," I told him. "They've moved to a biggish old place on Central Park West."

"Very foolish move," said the Lebanese. "They will only spend their money now." He seemed genuinely appalled.

Pat looked at me surprised. "I can't believe it," he exclaimed. "Leela Lahiri actually going crosstown at night by herself. I remember when your daddy wouldn't let you walk the two blocks from school to the house without that armed Nepali, what was his name, dogging your steps."

"Gulseng," I said. "He was run over by a lorry[2] three years ago. I think his name was really something-or-other-Rana, but he never corrected us."

"Short, nasty and brutal," said Pat. "They don't come that polite and loyal these days. Just as likely to slit your throat as anyone else, these days."

The Lebanese, sensing the end of brave New World overtures, the gathering of the darknesses we shared, drifted away.

"The country's changed totally, you know," Pat continued. "Crude rustic types have taken over. The *dhoti-wallahs*,[3] you know what I mean, they would wrap themselves in loincloths if it got them more votes. No integrity, no finesse. The country's gone to the dogs, I tell you."

"That whole life's outmoded, Pat. Obsolete. All over the world."

"They tried to put me in jail," he said. His face was small with bitterness and alarm. "They didn't like my politics, I tell you. Those Communists back home arrested me and threw me in jail. Me. Like a common criminal."

"On what charges?"

"Smuggling. For selling family heirlooms to Americans who understand them. No one at home understands their value. Here, I can sell off a little Pahari painting for ten thousand dollars. Americans understand our things better than we do ourselves. India wants me to starve in my overgrown palace."

"Did you really spend a night in jail?" I couldn't believe that modernization had finally come to India and that even there, no one was immune from consequences.

"Three nights!" he fumed. "Like a common *dacoit*.[4] The country has no respect anymore. The country has nothing. It has driven us abroad with whatever assets we could salvage."

---

2. British word for "truck."—Ed.

3. Alluding to the *dhoti*, a kind of everyday Indian-style sarong, Pat is dismissing left-wing politicians and what he regards as their cynically populist tactics.—Ed.

4. Hindi word for "armed robber."—Ed.

138 | MIDCAREER STORIES (1985–1988)

"You did well, I take it." I did not share his perspective; I did not feel my country owed me anything. Comfort, perhaps, when I was there; a different comfort when I left it. India teaches her children: you have seen the worst. Now go out and don't be afraid.

"I have nothing," he spat. "They've stripped me of everything. At night I hear the jackals singing in the courtyard of my palace."

But he had recovered by the time I left for the crosstown cab ride to the Patels. I saw him sitting on the banquette where not too long before the Lebanese had invited me to share an evening of unwholesomeness. On his knee he balanced a tall, silver-haired woman who looked like Candice Bergen. She wore a pink cashmere sweater which she must have put through the washing machine. Creases, like worms, curled around her sweatered bosom.

———————

I DIDN'T SEE Pat for another two years. In those two years I did see a man who claimed to have bounced the real Candice Bergen on his knee. He had been a juggler at one time, had worked with Edgar Bergen on some vaudeville act and could still pull off card tricks and walk on his hands up and down my dining table. I kept the dining table when Derek and I split last May. He went back to Canada which we both realized too late he should never have left and the table was too massive to move out of our West 11th Street place and into his downtown Toronto, chic renovated apartment. The ex-juggler is my boss at a publishing house. My job is menial but I have a soothing title. I am called an Administrative Assistant.

In the two years I have tried to treat the city not as an island of dark immigrants but as a vast sea in which new Americans like myself could disappear and resurface at will. I did not avoid Indians, but without Derek's urging for me to be proud of my heritage, I did not seek them out. The Patels did invite me to large dinners where all the guests seemed to know with the first flick of their eyes in my direction that I had married a white man and was now separated, and there our friendships hit rock. I was a curiosity, a novel and daring element in the community; everyone knew my name. After a while I began to say I was busy to Motibehn Patel.

———————

PAT CAME TO THE OFFICE with my boss, Bill Haines, the other day. "I wanted you to meet one of our new authors, Leela," Bill said.

"Leela, *dar-ling!*" Pat cried. His voice was shrill with enthusiasm, and he pressed me histrionically against his Burberry raincoat. I could feel a button tap my collarbone. "It's been years! Where have you been hiding your gorgeous self?"

"I didn't realize you two knew each other," Bill said.

All Indians in America, I could have told him, constitute a village.

"Her father bailed me out when the Indian government sought to persecute me," he said with a pout. "If it hadn't been for courageous friends like her daddy, I and my poor subjects might just as well have kicked the bucket."

"She's told me nothing about India," said Bill Haines. "No accent, Western clothes—"

"Yes, a shame, that. By the way, Leela, I just found a picture of Lahiri-*sahib* on an elephant when I was going through my official papers for Bill. If you come over for drinks—after getting out of those ridiculous clothes, I must insist—I can give it to you. Lahiri-*sahib* looks like Ernest Hemingway in that photo. You tell him I said he looks like Hemingway."

"Daddy's in Ranikhet this month," I said. "He's been bedridden for a while. Arthritis. He's just beginning to move around a bit again."

"I have hundreds of good anecdotes, Bill, about her daddy and me doing *shikar* in the Sundarban forest. Absolutely *huge* Bengal tigers. I want to balance the politics—which as you rightly say are central—with some stirring bits about what it was like in the good old days."

"What are you writing?" I asked.

"I thought you'd never ask, my dear. My memoirs. At night I leave a Sony by my bed. Night is the best time for remembering. I hear the old sounds and voices. You remember, Leela, how the palace ballroom used to hum with dancing feet on my birthdays?"

"*Memoirs of a Modern Maharajah*," Bill Haines said.

"I seem to remember the singing of jackals," I said, not unkindly, though he chose to ignore it.

"Writing is what keeps me from going through death's gate. There are nights . . ." He didn't finish. His posture had stiffened with self-regard; he communicated great oceans of anguish. He'd probably do well. It was what people wanted to hear.

"The indignities," he said suddenly. "The atrocities." He stared straight ahead, at a water cooler. "The nights in jail, the hyenas sniffing outside your barred window. I will never forget their smell, never! It is the smell of death, Leela. The new powers-that-be are peasants. Peasants! They cannot know, they cannot suspect how they have made me suffer. The country is in the hands of tyrannical peasants!"

140 | MIDCAREER STORIES (1985–1988)

"Look, Pat," Bill Haines said, leading the writer toward his office, "I have to see Bob Savage, the sub-rights man one floor down. Make yourself at home. Just pull down any book you want to read. I'll be back in a minute."

"Don't worry about me. I shall be all right, Bill. I have my Sony in my pocket. I shall just sit in a corner beside the daughter of my oldest friend, this child I used to bounce on my knee, and I shall let my mind skip into the nooks and crannies of Gotlah Palace. Did I tell you, when I was a young lad my mother kept pet crocs? Big, huge gents and ladies with ugly jaws full of nasty teeth. They were her pets. She gave them names and fed them chickens every day. Come to me, Padma. Come to me, Prem."

"It'll be dynamite," Bill Haines said. "The whole project's dynamite." He pressed my hand as he eased his stubby, muscular body past the stack of dossiers on my desk. "And *you'll* be a godsend in developing this project."

"And what's with you?" Pat asked me. I could tell he already knew the essentials.

"Nothing much." But he wasn't listening anyway.

"You remember the thief my security men caught in the early days of your father's setting up a factory in my hills? You remember how the mob got excited and poured acid on his face?"

I remembered. Was the Sony recording it? Was the memory an illustration of swift and righteous justice in a collapsed Himalayan princely state, or was it the savage and disproportionate fury of a people resisting change?

"Yes, certainly I do. Can I get you a cup of coffee? Or tea?" That, of course, was an important part of my job.

"No thanks," he said with a flutter of his wrinkled hands. "I have given up all stimulants. I've even given up bed-tea. It interferes with my writing. Writing is everything to me nowadays. It has been my nirvana."

"The book sounds dynamite," I assured him. An Indian woman is brought up to please. No matter how passionately we link bodies with our new countries, we never escape the early days.

Pat dropped his voice, and, stooping conspiratorially, said to me in Hindi, "There's one big favor you can do for me, though. Bill has spoken of a chap I should be knowing. Who is this Edgar Bergen?"

"I think he was the father of a movie actress," I said. I, too, had gone through the same contortion of recognition with Bill Haines. Fortunately, like most Americans, he could not conceive of a world in which Edgar Bergen had no currency. Again in Hindi, Pat asked me for directions to the facilities, and this time I could give a full response. He left his rolled-slim umbrella propped against my desk and walked toward the fountain.

"Is he really a maharaja?" Lisa leaned over from her desk to ask me. She is from Rhode Island. Brown hasn't cured her of responding too enthusiastically to each call or visit from a literary personage. "He's terrific. So suave and distinguished! Have you known him from way back when?"

"Yes," I said, all the way from when.

"I had no idea you spoke Hindu. It's eerie to think you can speak such a hard language. I'm having trouble enough with French. I keep forgetting that you haven't lived here always."

I keep forgetting it, too. I was about to correct her silly mistake—I'd learned from Derek to be easily incensed over ignorant confusions between Hindi and Hindu—but then I thought, why bother? Maybe she's right. That slight undetectable error, call it an accent, isn't part of language at all. I speak Hindu. No matter what language I speak it will come out slightly foreign, no matter how perfectly I mouth it. There's a whole world of us now, speaking Hindu.

THE MANUSCRIPT OF *MEMOIRS* was not dynamite, but I stayed up all night to finish it. In spite of the arch locutions and the aggrieved posture that Pat had stubbornly clung to, I knew I was reading about myself, blind and groping conquistador who had come to the New World too late.

Saints

"AND ONE MORE THING," Mom says. "Your father can't take you this August."

I can tell from the way she fusses with the placemats that she is interested in my reaction. The placemats are made of pinkish linen and I can see a couple of ironing marks, like shiny little arches. Wayne is coming for dinner. Wayne Latta is her new friend. It's the first time she's having him over with others, but that's not why she's nervous.

"That's okay," I tell her. "Tran and I have plans for the summer."

Mom rolls up the spray-starched napkins and knots them until they look like nesting birds on each dinner plate. "It isn't that he's really busy," she says. She gives me one of her I-know-you're-hurting, son, looks. "I don't see why he can't take you. He says he has a conference to go to in Hong Kong at the end of July, so he might as well do China in August."

142 | MIDCAREER STORIES (1985–1988)

"It's okay. Really," I say. It's true, I am okay. At fifteen I'm too old to be a pawn between them, and too young to get caught in problems of my own. I'm in a state of grace. I want to get to my room in this state of grace before it disintegrates, and start a new game of "Geopolitique 1990" on the Apple II-Plus Dad gave me last Christmas.

"Can you get the flower holders, Shawn?" Mom asks.

I take a wide, flat cardboard box out of the buffet.

She lifts eight tiny glass holders out of the box, and lines them up in the center of the table. She hasn't used them since things started going bad between Dad and her. When things blew up, they sold the big house in New Jersey and Mom and I moved to this college town in upstate New York. Mom works in the Admissions Office. Wayne calls it a college for rich bitches who were too dumb to get into Bennington or Barnard.

"Get me a pitcher of water and the flowers," Mom says.

In a dented aluminum pot in the kitchen sink, eight yellow rosebuds are soaking up water. Granules of sugar are whitish and still sludgy in the bottom of the pot. Mom's a believer; she's read somewhere that sugar in lukewarm water keeps cut flowers fresh. I move the pot to one side and fill a quart-sized measuring cup with lukewarm water. I know her routines.

It's going to be an anxious evening for Mom. She's set out extra goblets for spritzers on a tray lined with paper towels. Index cards typed up with recipes for dips and sauces are stacked on the windowsill. She shouldn't do sauces, nothing that requires last-minute frying and stirring. She's the flustery type, and she's only setting herself up for failure.

"What's happened to the water, Shawn?"

It's a Pizza Hut night for me, definitely. I know what she's going through with Wayne. He's not at all like Dad, the good Dr. Manny Patel, who soothes crazies at Creedmoor all day. Nights he's a playboy and slum landlord, Mom says.

Mom says, "Your father will call you tomorrow, he said. He wants to talk to you himself. He wants to know what you want this Christmas."

This is only the first Thursday in November. Dad's planning ahead is a joke with us. Foresight is what got him out of Delhi to New York. "Could I have become a psychiatrist and a near-millionaire if I hadn't planned well ahead?" Dad used to tell Mom in the medium-bad days.

Mom thinks making a million is a vicious, selfish aim. But Dad's really very generous. He sends money to relatives and to Indian orphanages. He's generous but practical. He says he doesn't want to send me stuff—cashmere sweaters and Ultrasuede jackets, the stuff he likes—that'll end up in basement cedar closets.

"I'll be late tomorrow," I remind Mom. "Fridays I have my chess club."

Actually, Tran and I and a bunch of other guys from the chess club play four afternoons a week. Thursdays we don't play because Tran has Debate Workshop.

"You know what I want, Mom. You can tell him."

I ask for computer games, video cassettes, nothing major. So twice a year Dad sends big checks. Dad's real generous with me. It makes him feel the big benefactor, Mom says, whenever a check comes in the mail. But that's only because things went really bad two years ago. They sent me away to boarding school, but they still couldn't work things out between them.

At five, Wayne comes into our driveway in his blue Toyota pickup. The wheels squeal and rock in the deep, snowy ruts. Wayne has a cord of firewood in the back of the truck. Mom paid him for the firewood yesterday and for the time he put in picking up the cord from some French guy in Ballston Spa. Wayne's a writer; meantime he works as a janitor in the college. A "mopologist" is what he calls himself. It's so corny, but every time Wayne uses that word, Mom gives him a tinkly, supportive laugh. Janitors are more caring than shrinks, the laugh seems to say.

We hear Wayne on the back porch, cursing as he drops an armload of logs. For all his muscles, he's a clumsy man. But then Mom could never have gotten Dad to carry the logs himself. Dad would have had them delivered or done without them.

Mom takes five-dollar bills out of the buffet drawer and counts out thirty dollars. "For the wine, would you give it to him? I couldn't do a production all by myself on a weeknight."

"Why do a production at all?"

She stiffens. "I'm not ashamed of Wayne," she says. "Wayne is who he is."

Wayne finally comes into the dining room. I slip him the money; it's more than he expected. "I got some beer, too, Mila." Mom's name is Camille but he calls her Mila. That's a hard thing to get used to. He drops my rucksack on the floor, turns the chair around and straddles it. There are five other chairs around the table and two folding chairs brought up from the basement for tonight. Under Wayne's muscular thighs, the dining room chair looks rickety, absurdly elegant. Red long johns show through the knee rips of his blue jeans. He keeps his red knit cap on. But he's not as tough as he looks. He keeps the cap on because he's sensitive about his bald, baby-pink head.

"Hey, Shawn," he says to me. "Still baking the competition?"

It's Wayne's usual joke about my playing competitive chess. Our school team has T-shirts that we paid for by working the concession stands on basketball nights last winter. Tran plays varsity first board, I play third. Now we need chess cheerleaders, Wayne kids me. *"Hey, hey, push that pawn! Dee-fense, dee-fense, King's Indian dee-fense!"* Wayne isn't a bad sort, not for around here. Last year we went for trout out on the Battenkill. The day with Wayne wasn't bad, given our complicated situation. I went back to the creek with Tran a week later, but it was different. Tran's idea of fishing is throwing a net across the river, tossing in a stick of dynamite, then pulling it up.

"You'll like Milos and Verna," Mom tells Wayne. "They're both painters in the Art Department. From Yugoslavia, but I think they're hoping to stay in the States."

From the soft, nervous look she's giving Wayne, I know it isn't the Yugoslavs she's thinking of right at the moment. Wayne grabs her throat in his thick hairy hands. She lifts her face. Then she glances at me in a quick guilty way as if she's already given away too much.

I know about feelings. I've got a secret life, too.

"D'you have enough for a pizza?" Mom asks me. She's moved away from Wayne.

Yeah, I have enough.

FROM THE PIZZA HUT, Tran and I go back to Tran's place. Tran's sixteen and he owns a noisy used Plymouth. It's two-tone, white and aquamarine. I like the colors. Tran's a genuine boat person. When he was younger, the English teacher made him tell the class about having to hide from pirates and having to chew on raw fish just to stay alive. Women on his boat hid any valuable stuff they had in their vaginas. "That's enough, Tran, thank you," the teacher said. Now he never mentions his cruise to America.

We skid to a stop inside the Indian Lookout Point Trailer Park where he lives with his mother in a flash of aqua. The lights are on in Tran's mobile home. Tran's mother's muddy Chevy and his stepfather's Dodge Ram are angle-parked. Tran's real father got left behind in Saigon.

"I don't know," Tran says. He doesn't cut the engine. We sit in the warm, dark car. "Maybe we ought to go on to your place. He never gets home this early."

It's minus ten outside, maybe worse with the wind chill factor. I open the car door softly. The carlight on Tran's face makes his face look ochre-dingy, mottled with pimples.

"Mom's entertaining tonight," I warn him. The snow is slippery cold under my Adidas. I pick my way through icy patches to the trailer, and look in a little front window.

Tran's mom is at the kitchen sink, washing a glass. She's still wearing her wool coat and plaid scarf. Her face has an odd puffy quiver. There are no signs of physical violence, but someone's sure been hurt. Tran's stepfather (he didn't, and can't, adopt Tran until some agency can locate Tran's real father and get his consent) is sitting hunched forward in a rocker, and drinking Miller Lite.

Like Tran, I've learned to discount homey scenes.

"That's okay," Tran says. He's calling out from the car. His sad face is in the opened window. "Your place is bigger."

It makes sense, but I can't move away from his little window.

"I can show you a move that'll bake Sato," he says. "I mean really bake his ass."

We both hate Sato but Sato isn't smart enough to wince under our hate or even smart enough to know when his ass has really been baked.

"Okay." There's that new killer chess move, and a new Peter Gabriel for us to listen to. Tran's chess rating is just under 1900. Farelli's is higher, but Farelli is more than arrogant. He's so arrogant he dropped off the team. He goes down to Manhattan instead and hustles games in Times Square or in the chess clubs. Tran's a little guilty about playing first board; he knows he owes it to Farelli's vanity. The difference between Farelli and Tran is about the same as between Tran and me. Farelli wants to charge the club four-fifty an hour for tutoring. He's the only real American in the club. The rest of us have names like Sato, Chin, Duoc, Cho and Prasad. My name's Patel, Shawn Patel. Mom took back her maiden name, Belliveau, when we moved out of Upper Montclair. We're supposed to be out of Dad's reach here, except for checks.

A WEEK AFTER Mom's dinner party, Tran and I are coming out of an arcade on Upper Broadway Street when we see Wayne walking our way. Upper Broadway's short and squat. The storefronts have shallow doorways you can't hide in. Wayne is with the Yugoslav woman, the painter who doesn't intend to go back to her country. They aren't holding hands or anything, they aren't even touching shoulders, but I can tell they want to do things. The Yugoslav has both her hands in the pockets of her duffle coat. A toggle at her throat is missing and the loop has nothing to weigh it down. The Yugoslav has red cheeks. With her red cheeks, her button nose and her long, loose hair, she looks very young. Maybe it's a trick of afternoon light or of European make-up, but she looks too young to be a friend of Mom's.

Wayne wants to hug her. I can tell from the way he arches his upper body inside his coat. He wants to sneak his hand into her pocket, pull out her fist, swing hands on Upper Broadway and be stared at by everyone.

I pull Tran back inside the arcade.

"I got to get to Houston," Tran says. We're playing "Joust," his favorite game, but his slight body is twisted in misery.

"It'll work out," I tell him. Wanting to go to Houston has to do with his mother and stepfather. Things always go bad between parents. "You can't leave in the middle of the semester. It doesn't make sense."

"What does?"

Tran has an older brother in Houston, in engineering school. Tran thinks his mother will come up with the bus fare south. She works at Grand Union, and weekends she waitresses. "My luck's got to change," he says.

Luck has nothing to do with anything, I want to say. You're out of the clutch of pirates now. No safe hiding places.

Wayne and his painter make us spend too many tokens on this Joust machine.

MOM'S IN THE EATING NOOK of the kitchen, reading a book on English gardens when I come in the back door. She's wearing a long skirt made of quilted fabric and a matching jacket. The quilting makes her look fat, and ridiculous.

She catches my grin. "It's warm, don't knock it," she says of her skirt. These upstate houses are drafty. Then she pulls her feet up under her and wriggles her raised knees gracelessly under the long skirt. "And I love the color on me."

I bleed. Mom should have had a daughter. Two women could have consoled each other. I can only think of Wayne, how even now he's slipping the loops over Serbian toggles. It's a complicated feeling. I bleed because I'm disloyal.

"Your father's sent a present by UPS," she says. She doesn't look up from the illustration of a formal garden of a lord. A garden with a stiff, bristly hedged maze to excite desire and contain it. "I put the package on your desk upstairs. It looks like a book."

She means to say, Dad's presents are always impersonal.

Actually it's two books that Dad has sent me this time. The thick, heavy one is an art book, reproductions of Moghul paintings that Dad loves. Even India was once an empire-building nation. The other is a thin book with bad binding put out by a religious printing house in Madras. The little book is about a Hindu saint who had visions. Dad has sent me a book about visions.

"May this book bring you as much happiness as it did me when I was your age," Dad's inscription reads. Then a p.s. "The saint died of throat cancer and was briefly treated by your great-uncle, the cancer specialist in Calcutta."

Forty pages into the book, the saint describes a vision. "I see the Divine Mother in all things." He sees Her in ants, dogs, flowers, the latrine bowls in the temple. He keeps falling into trances as he goes for walks or as he says his prayers. In this perfect state, sometimes the saint kicks his disciples. He eats garbage thrown out by temple cooks for cows and pariah dogs.

"Did I kick you?" the saint asks when he comes out of his trance. "Kick, kick," beg the disciples as they push each other to get near enough for a saintly touch.

My father, healer of derangements, slum landlord with income properties on two continents, believer of visions, pleasure-taker where none seems present, is a mystery.

Downstairs Mom is dialing Wayne's number. In the whir of the telephone dial, I read the new rhythms of her agony. Wayne will not answer his phone tonight. Wayne is in bed with his naked Yugoslav.

It's my turn to call. I slip my bony finger into the dial's fingerholes. "Want to ball?" I whisper into the mouthpiece. My throat is raspy from the fullness of desire.

"What?" It's a girlish voice at the other end. "What did you say?"

The girl giggles. "You dumb pervert." She leaves it to me to hang up first.

THE NEXT NIGHT, a Friday night, Tran and I come down from my room to get Mountain Dew out of the fridge. Mom and Wayne are making out in the kitchen. He has her jammed up against the eating nook's wall. There are Indian paintings on that wall. She kept the paintings and gave Dad the statues and framed batiks. Wayne holds Mom's head against dusty glass, behind which an emperor in Moghul battledress is leading his army out of the capital. Wayne's got his knee high up Mom's quilted skirt. The knee presses in, hard. I see love's monstrous force bloat her face. Wayne has her head in his grasp. Her orange hair tufts out between his knuckles, and its orange mist covers the bygone emperor and his soldiers.

Tran's used to living in small, usurped spaces. He drops a shy, civil little cough, and right away Wayne lets go of Mom's hair. But his knee is still raised, still pressing into her skirt.

"Get outta here, guys," he says. He looks pleased, he sounds good-natured. "You got better things to do. Go push your pawns."

"Tell her about the painter," I say. My voice is even, not emotional.

"What're you talking about? What's the matter with you?"

Tran says, "Let's get the soda, Shawn." He picks up the six-pack and two glasses and pushes me toward the stairwell.

Upstairs, Tran and I take turns dialing the town's other insomniacs. "Do you have soft breasts?" I ask. I really want to know. "Yes," one of them con-

MIDCAREER STORIES (1985–1988)

fesses. "Very soft and very white and I'm so lonely tonight. Do you want to touch?"

Tran reads aloud an episode from the life of the Hindu saint. Reaching the state of perfection while strolling along the Ganges one day, the saint fell and broke his arm. The saint had been thinking of his love for the young boy followers who lived in the temples. He had been thinking of his love for them—love as for a sweetheart, he says—when he slipped into a trance and stumbled. Love and pain: in the saint's mind there is no separation.

Tran makes the last of our calls for the night. "You bitch," he says as he shakes his thin body in a parody of undulation. To me he says, "Mother won't come through with the bus fare to Houston."

Tonight Tran wants to sleep over in my room. Tomorrow we'll find a way to raise the bus fare.

I want to tell him things, to console him. Bad luck and good luck even out over a lifetime. Cancer can ravage an ecstatic saint. Things pass. I don't remember Dad in any intimate way except that he embarrassed me when he came to pick me up from my old boarding school. The overstated black Mercedes, the hugging and kissing in such a foreign way.

A LITTLE BEFORE MIDNIGHT, Tran's moan startles me awake. He must be dreaming of fathers, pirates, saints and Houston. For me the worst isn't dreams. It's having to get out of the house at night and walk around. At midnight I float like a ghost through other people's gardens.[1] I peer into other boys' bedrooms, I become somebody else's son.

Tonight I'm more restless than other nights. I look for an Indian name in the phone book. The directory in our upstate town is thin; it caves against my eager arms. The first name I spot is Batliwalla. Meaning perhaps bottle-walla, a dealer in bottles in the ancestral long-ago. Batliwalla, Jamshed S., M.D.

I dress in the dark for a night of cold roaming. It'll be a night of walking in a state of perfect grace. For disguise, I choose Mom's red cloth coat from the hall cupboard and her large red wool beret into which she has stuck a pheasant feather. She keeps five more feathers, like a bouquet, in a candy jar. The feathers are from Wayne the hunter. Wayne's promised to put a pheasant on our table for Thanksgiving dinner. I can taste its hard, stringy birdflesh and pellets of buckshot.

Like the Hindu saint, I walk my world in boots and a trance. But in this upstate town the only body of water is an icy creek, not the Ganges.

---

1. "Garden" is the British word for "yard."—Ed.

The Batliwallas have no curtains on their back windows. I look into a back bedroom that glows from a bedside lamp. A kid in pajamas is sitting up in bed, a book in his hands. He's a little kid, a junior high kid, or maybe a studious dwarf. The dwarfkid rocks back and forth under his bedclothes. He seems to be learning something, maybe a poem, by heart. He's the conqueror of alien syllables. His fleshy, brown lips purse and pout ferociously. His tiny head in its helmet of glossy black hair bumps, bumps, bumps the bed's white vinyl headboard. The dwarfkid's eyes are screwed tightly shut, and his long eyelashes look like tiny troughs for ghosts to drink out of. Wanting good grades, the dwarfkid studies into the night. He rocks, he shouts, he bumps his head. I can't hear the words, but I want to reach out to a fellow saint.

When I get home, the back porch is dark but the kitchen light is on. I sit on the stack of firewood and look in. I'm not cold, or sleepy. Wayne and Mom are fighting in the kitchen, literally slugging each other. I had Wayne figured wrong. He isn't the sly operator after all. He's opened up my Mom's upper lip. It's blood Mom is washing off.

"Get out," Mom screams at him. This time I can make out all the words. I feel like a god, overseeing lives.

The faucet is running as it had done the day there were yellow rosebuds in a kitchen pot. Steam from the hot, running water frizzes Mom's hair. She looks old. "Get out of my house."

"I'm getting out," Wayne says. But he doesn't leave. First he lights a cigarette, something Mom doesn't permit. Then he flops down on one of the two kitchen stools, props his workboots on the other and starts to adjust the laces. "I wouldn't stay if you begged me."

"Get out, out!" Mom's still screaming as I turn my house key in the lock. She might as well know it all. "Do me a favor, get out. Lace your goddamn boots in your goddamn truck. Please get out."

I move through the bright kitchen into the dark dining room, and wait for the lovers to finish.

In a while Wayne leaves. He doesn't slam the door. He doesn't toss the key on the floor. The pickup's low beams dance on frozen bushes.

"My god, Shawn!" Mom has switched on a wall light in the dining room. She's staring at me, she's really looking at me. Finally. "My god, what have you done to your face, poor baby."

Her fingers scrape at the muck on my face, the cheek-blush, lipstick, eyeshadow. Her bruised mouth is on my hair. I can feel her warm, wet sobs, but I don't hurt, I am in a trance in the middle of a November night. I can't hurt for me, for Dad, I can't hurt for anyone in the world. I feel so strong, so much a potentate in battledress.

150 | MIDCAREER STORIES (1985–1988)

How wondrous to be a visionary. If I were to touch someone now, I'd be touching god.

Visitors

WHEN VINITA LIVED in Calcutta, she had many admirers. Every morning at ten minutes after nine o'clock when she left home for Loreto College where she majored in French literature, young men with surreptitious hands slipped love notes through the half-open windows of her father's car and were sternly rebuked by the chauffeur. The notes were almost always anonymous; when she read them in class, tucked between the pages of Rimbaud and Baudelaire, the ferocity of passion never failed to thrill and alarm her.

For a time after college she worked as a receptionist in the fancy downtown Chowringhee office of a multinational corporation. She had style, she had charm, and everyone genuinely liked her. Especially two junior executives from the fifth floor which was occupied by a company that exported iron manhole covers. If it hadn't been for Vinita's tact, and her ability to make each of the suitors feel that he was the one who made her happier, the two men might have become embittered rivals. She was quietly convivial and on weekdays went, usually in a group of six or eight, for Chinese lunches to the Calcutta Club. Even the club waiters brightened up when they saw Vinita, though she had never actually been heard to say anything more personal to them than "A lime soda, please, no ice," or "I'll have the Chou En Lai carp."

She had known all along that after marriage she would have to leave Calcutta. Her parents wanted to marry her off to a doctor or engineer of the right caste and class but resident abroad, preferably in America. The groom they finally selected for her was a thirty-five-year-old accountant, Sailen Kumar, a well-mannered and amiable-looking man, a St. Stephen's graduate who had gone on to London University and Harvard and who now worked for a respectable investment house in Manhattan and lived in a two-bedroom condominium with access to gym, pool and sauna across the river. He was successful—and well off, Vinita's parents decided—by anyone's standards. Six days after the wedding, Vinita took an Air India flight to citizenship in the New World.

MARRIAGE SUITS VINITA. In the months she has been a wife in Guttenberg, New Jersey, she has become even prettier. Her long black hair has a gloss that owes as much to a new sense of well-being as to the new shampoos she tries out and that leave her head smelling of herbs, fruits and flowers. Her surroundings—the sleek Bloomingdale furniture Sailen had bought just before flying out to find a bride in India, the coordinated linen for bed and bath, and the wide, gleaming appliances in the kitchenette—please her. She finds it hard to believe that she has been gifted the life of grace and ease that she and her Loreto College friends had coveted from reading old copies of *Better Homes and Gardens* in Calcutta. This life of grace and ease has less to do with modern conveniences such as the microwave oven built into a narrow wall which is covered with designer wallpaper, and more to do with moods and traits she recognizes as new in herself. Happiness, expressiveness, bad temper: all these states seem valuable and exciting to her. But she is not sure she deserves this life. She has done nothing exceptional. She has made no brave choices. The decision to start over on a new continent where hard work is more often than not rewarded with comfort has been her parents', not hers. If her father had brought her a proposal and photograph from an upright hydraulics engineer living in a government project site in the wilds of Durgapur or from a rich radiologist with a clinic on a quiet boulevard in South Calcutta, she would have accepted the proposal with the same cheerfulness she has shown Sailen Kumar. She's a little taken aback by the idea of just deserts. Back home good fortune had been exactly that: a matter of luck and fortune, a deity's decision to humor and indulge. She remembered the fables she read as a child in which a silly peasant might find a pitcher of gold *mohurs*[1] on his way to the village tank for his bath. But in America, at least in New Jersey, everyone Vinita meets seems to acknowledge a connection between merit and reward. Everyone looks busy, distraught from overwork. Even the building's doorman; she worries about Castro, the doorman. Such faith in causality can only lead to betrayal.

Vinita expected married life, especially married life in a new country and with no relatives around, to change her. Overnight she would become mature, complex, fascinating: a wife, instead of a daughter. Thoughts of change did not frighten her. Discreet, dutiful, comfortable with her upper-class status, she had been trained by her mother to stay flexible, to roll with whatever punches the Communist government of Calcutta might deliver. In Vinita's childhood, the city had convulsed through at least two small revolutions. Some nights in Guttenberg, New Jersey, even with her eyes closed, she can see a fresh, male corpse in a monsoon muddy gutter. Her parents still talk of the two boys who had invaded their lawn one heady afternoon of class struggle and pointed pipe-

---

1. The name for a type of Indian coin first introduced in the mid-sixteenth century.—Ed.

152 | MIDCAREER STORIES (1985–1988)

guns[2] at the trembling gardener. Sometimes the designer wallpaper seems to ripple like leaves in a breeze, and she feels herself being watched.

But it's not the corpse, not the undernourished child-rebels, who feed her nightmares. It's nothing specific. She considers fear of newness a self-indulgence, quite unworthy of someone who has wanted all along to exchange her native world for an alien one. The slightest possibility of disruption pleases her. But if change has come into her life as Mrs. Sailen Kumar, it has seeped in so gradually that she can't fix it with one admiring stare when she Windexes toothpaste flecks off the bathroom mirror.

———

THIS AFTERNOON Vinita has three visitors. Two of them are women, Mrs. Leela Mehra and Mrs. Kamila Thapar, wives of civil engineers. They stay just long enough to have spiced tea with onion pakoras and to advise her on which Indian grocers carry the freshest tropical produce in the "Little India" block on Lexington. Vinita is convinced the real reason they have come to visit is to check out what changes she, the bride, has made to Sailen's condominium. They have known her husband for almost ten years. Mr. Thapar and Sailen roomed together when both were new to America (she has trouble visualizing the dark-suited, discreetly groomed men as callow foreign students forty pounds lighter with little money and too much ambition). Sailen, while sketching in his bachelor life—all those years when she had not known that the man of dreams would have only nine fingers!—had told her how the Thapars and the Mehras made themselves his substitute family in the new world, how they fed him curries most weekends, made him sleep on their lumpy front room sofas instead of letting him take a late-night bus back to Manhattan, and how the two women hummed bits of old Hindi film songs to tease him into nostalgia. Otherwise, they said, he'd become bad-tempered and self-centered, too American. In Mrs. Mehra's and Mrs. Thapar's presence, Vinita is the intruder.

After they leave, Vinita takes out a rubber-banded roll of aerograms from a desk built into the wall system. She makes a list of the people she must write today:

1. her parents (a short but vivacious note)
2. her closest Loreto College friend who now works for Air India
3. her married sister in Bombay (it can wait till the weekend)
4. Mother Stella, the Mauritian nun who'd taught her French.

———

2. A type of homemade firearm.—Ed.

VISITORS | *153*

Writing letters on the pale blue aerogram paper makes her feel cheerful and just a little noble. Writing to Mother Stella puts her in a special mood, a world tinged slightly with poetic, even rhapsodic passion. Even lines of Rimbaud's deemed unsuitable for maidenly Calcutta teenagers were somehow tamed by Mother Stella's exquisite elocution. How preposterous was a passion—*le dos de ces Mains est la place qu'en baisa tout Révolté fier!*—parsed by a half-Indian, French-speaking, Mauritian nun.

She writes her mother, converting each small episode—buying half a dozen cheese Danishes, spraying herself with expensive fragrances from tester atomizers—into grand adventures. When she licks and seals each envelope, she is grateful Sailen agreed to her father's proposal of marriage and that she is now cut off from her moorings. Her letters are intended to please and comfort. She knows that when the postman rings his bicycle bell and keels into the driveway twice a day, the servants, her mother, her sister, her friend and even the nun who has taught her all she knows about literature and good manners run to the front door hoping for a new instalment of her idylls in America. But before Vinita can decide what vivacious clichés to end her last letter with, a third visitor arrives at the door and holds out a bright, amateurish poster announcing an Odissi dance recital on the Columbia campus.

"Mrs. Kumar, I thought you might be interested in dance performances," the visitor says. He smiles, but does not step into the tiny hall which is crowded with a pair of Vishnupuri clay horses and a tall, cylindrical Chinese vase that holds umbrellas. "I was afraid that you and Mr. Kumar might not have heard about Rooma Devi coming to Columbia."

"Odissi style?" She knows it is up to her to invite him in or send him away. She has met him, yes, she has talked to him at three, maybe four, cultural evenings organized by one of the Indian Associations in Manhattan. He is a graduate student in history at Columbia.

"Mrs. Kumar, if you don't mind my saying so, the first time I saw you I could tell that you yourself were a dancer. Right?"

She glances at him shyly, and steps back, her slippers grazing the rough clay foot of one of the giant horses. Still she doesn't ask him in. Let him make that decision. In India, she would feel uncomfortable—she knows she would!— if she found herself in an apartment alone with a man not related to her, but the rules are different in Guttenberg. Here one has to size up the situation and make up one's own rules. Or is it, here, that one has to seize the situation?

"You have the grace of a *danseuse*," he says.

Vinita has not heard anyone use the word *danseuse*. She likes the word; it makes her feel elegant and lissom. "I'll have to confess I am. I've danced a bit. But not in years."

154 | MIDCAREER STORIES (1985–1988)

She blushes, hoping to pass off for modesty the guilt she feels at having lied. She is not a dancer, not a real dancer. She has studied Rabindra-style dancing for about six years. Her mother, who regarded dancing as necessary a feminine accomplishment as singing and gourmet cooking, had forced the two sisters to take weekly lessons at a fine arts academy in Ballygunge. She looks down at the floor, at his two-tone New Balance running shoes. The shoes deepen her blush. She is in a new country with no rules. No grown man in India she knows wears gym shoes except for cricket or squash. But there's mud on his New Balances, a half-moon of mud around each toe part. He has taken the bus to Guttenberg, New Jersey, just to make sure that she'll know about the recital. Because he has guessed—he had divined—that she is a *danseuse*.

She takes two hesitant steps back, her left hand entwined with the elongated clay neck of the larger horse. Here, as in India, friends stop by without calling, and she is foolish to worry over why the graduate student in his running shoes has come with a poster in the early afternoon. ("All that formality of may-I-come? or hope-we're-not-disturbing-you is for Westerners," the immigrants joke among themselves. She has heard it once already this afternoon from Mrs. Thapar. "We may have minted a bit of money in this country, but that doesn't mean we've let ourselves become Americans. You can see we've remained one hundred percent simple and *deshi*[3] in our customs.") Vinita wants to remain *deshi*, too, but being *deshi* and letting in this good-looking young man (a line darts across an imaginary page, enunciated in rotund Mauritian French and Vinita almost giggles: *Le jeune homme dont l'oeil est brillant, la peau brune, Le beau corps de vingt ans qui devrait aller nu* . . . and Vinita blushes again, more deeply), a young man who told her the first time they met, after a movie, that he'd been born in Calcutta but immigrated with his parents when he was just a toddler—letting him in might lead to disproportionate disaster.

"It is very kind of you, Mr. Khanna, to bring over Rooma Devi's poster," she says miserably. She has never heard of Rooma Devi. Rooma Devi cannot possibly be a ranking Odissi dancer. Yet Rooma Devi has succeeded in pounding thin whatever tranquility the promise of letter-writing had produced in Vinita.

"You remember my name, Mrs. Kumar?" It is not so much a question as an ecstatic exhalation. "But please call me Rajiv. Unless you want to call me Billoo, which was my pet name in India. Just don't call me Bill."

She is relieved that Rajiv Khanna is inside the condominium and that the period of indecision is over. He has somehow shut the front door behind him and has suspended his baseball cap on the smaller horse's ear.

---

3. Adjective deriving from the Hindi word *desh* or "country" and used, like *desi*, to mean Indian, Pakistani, or Bangladeshi.—Ed.

"Would you like some authentic India-style tea?" she asks. It is the correct thing for an Indian hostess to do, even in New Jersey; to offer the guest something to drink, even if it's just a glass of water. "I am making it exactly like the *chai-wallahs*. I am boiling tea leaves in a mixture of milk, water and sugar, and throwing in pinches of cardamom, cloves, cinnamon, etcetera."

"I don't want you stuck in the kitchen," he laughs. "I want you to tell me stories about Calcutta. I was only three when Baba took the postdoctoral fellowship at Madison but I still remember what our alley smelled like in July and August." He laughs again, hyper and nervous. "Let's use teabags. You must take advantage of American shortcuts."

Rajiv Khanna stalks her into the living room, forcing her to take quicker steps than usual so his New Balances won't catch the thin, stiff leather edges of her Sholapuri slippers.[4] She begins to see Sailen's Bloomingdale decor—the pastel conversation pit made up of modular sofas, the patio-atrium corner defined by white wicker—the way a hard-up graduate student might, as opulent, tasteful. When Rajiv compliments her artistic touch, she swings back to smile at him, bashful but flattered.

An issue of *Technology Review* on an obviously new coffee table catches his eye, and he lingers in the conversation pit, one knee resting deeply on an ottoman. In that pose, he reminds her of marsh birds she had seen on vacations in rural Bengal. The image automatically makes her pitch her voice low. Her gestures now softly wary, so the bird will not fly off.

She slips off to the kitchenette to make tea. The work counter of butcher's block is a barrier against the unseemly jokes that fate might decide to try out on her. In fact, in the bluish-white fluorescent light that threatens to never burn out, her earlier fears now seem absurd.

"I miss the cultural events of Calcutta," she says chattily. "It's such a lively city. Always some theatrical program, some crafts exhibit, something that touches the heart." From the asylum of the kitchenette, she watches him flip through the pages of Sailen's magazine without actually reading. There's an archness to her posture, she knows. She can feel her body tauten the way it often had in college while Mother Stella sanitized the occasional salacious verse. *On n'est pas sérieux, quand on a dix-sept ans*, Rimbaud said, but now she thinks twenty-five is not a matronly age. Mrs. Mehra and Mrs. Thapar are at least ten years older than her. Sailen had specified to his parents that he wanted a youngish bride, one who could speak fluent English and who could—once he felt he could afford it—bear him two or three children. He has spoken to her of his dream of having a son play in Little League games. Hearing him dream aloud,

---

4. Possibly a reference to a type of traditional Indian women's sandal.—Ed.

she assumed that it wasn't so much a son that he wanted as to assimilate, to be a *pukka*[5] American.

Rajiv Khanna ignores the comment. He sits astride the new coffee table (she's distracted with worry that if the glass top breaks, it cannot be replaced; or more accurately, that if the table falls apart she'll have to confess, but confess to what?) and drums his thighs with his fingertips. The fingers are long, the fingers of a poet. No wonder he had not been absorbed by Sailen's *Technology Review*. She waits for him to make small talk, to keep up his part as charming guest.

"I can't believe I went through with it!" It's an outburst, and it confuses her. She busies herself with cups and saucers.

"I can't believe I had the courage!"

She steals a look at him, thankful for the cumulous clouds of steam from the boiling water. Courage for what? Instinctively, she smooths down the hair on her crown which she knows from experience turns frizzy in hot, humid weather. Girls should make the best of their looks. She's been taught this by the nuns at school and by her relatives for so long that prettying herself has become a habit, not a vanity. Rajiv approaches her, his gait uneven, nervous; he is a potential invader of her kitchenette-fortress.

"I knew you were special the very first time I saw you. At the India Republic Day celebrations at the Khoranas'. I told myself this is it, this is the goddess of my dreams. I couldn't get you out of my mind."

Vinita finishes steeping two Twinings teabags in a teapot before responding to the young suitor's outburst. She is not as shocked as she had expected to be. Yes, she has rehearsed moments like this; she has put herself on the television screen, in the roles of afternoon wives taken in passion. Not as shocked as she *should* have been, she worries. A warmth (from Rajiv's compliment? from anxiety? the kettle's steam?) swirls just under her glycerine-and-rose-watered skin. She concentrates on making tea; the brew must be just the right amber color. But tea-making in New Jersey is no challenge. She plucks and dunks each bag repeatedly by its frail string. You give up a little taste, but you grab a little convenience cleaning up. The new world forces you to know what you really want.

He barks again. "You haven't discouraged me."

She shrinks behind the counter. He shakes an accusatory index finger. She draws the loose end of her sari over her right shoulder so that her arms, her

---

5. Originating from the Hindi word *pakka* or "ripe, mature, cooked," according to Henry Yule and Arthur Coke Burnell in their historical dictionary *Hobson-Jobson* (1886), *pukka* here means "real" or "genuine."—Ed.

silk-bloused breasts and bare midriff are swathed. But the sari was bought at the Sari Palace on Lexington, and her breasts seem to her to loom and soar through the Japanese chiffon. The young man has turned her into a siren.

"I don't know what you mean." She wants to sound stuffy, but it comes out, she knows, innocent, simpering.

"You should have thrown me out minutes ago. You could have refused to let me in. I know you Indian girls. You could have taken the poster and slammed the door in my face. But you didn't!"

He is a madman. It's true; he *is* a madman, but she is no siren. She repeats this to herself, a litany against calamity. Because of his windbreaker and his running shoes she had assumed he was just another American, no one to convert her into a crazy emblem. She had assumed that he was the looter of American culture, not hers, and she had envied the looting. Her own transition was slow and wheezing.

"You offered to make tea instead." He sounds triumphant.

"It was the least I could offer a guest," she retorts. "I haven't lost all my manners because I've moved to a new country. I know some Americans won't even give you a glass of water when you drop in."

He is not listening. He blabs, high-pitched angry words undulating from his fleshy lips. Love, it would appear, torments Rajiv. The face, which she had initially considered symmetrical, now devastates her from across the butcher's block counter, the features harsh, moody. His New Balance shoes are anachronistic; he is a lover from the turn-of-the-century novels of Sarat Chandra, the poems of Rimbaud—*Oh! quel Rêve les a saisies . . . un rêve inouï des Asies, Des Khengavars ou des Sions?*—unmoored by passion. One long-lashed furtive glance from the woman next door, the servant girl, the movie star, and the hero's calamitous fate is sealed. But this is America, she insists. There is no place for feelings here! We are both a new breed, testing new feelings in new battle-grounds. We must give in to the old world's curb.

"Let's be civilized," she pleads, by which she means, let's be modern and Indian. "Take your cup, and let's sit in the patio. My husband will be here any minute and he'd be so disappointed if you left without seeing him. He thinks you're a brilliant boy." She's pleased at her own diplomacy. She has nipped passion before it can come to full fury, she has flattered his intelligence and she has elevated herself to the role of older sister or youngish aunt.

"Confess!" he demands. "I must mean something special to you. Otherwise you wouldn't have tolerated me this long. You'd have called Mr. Kumar or the police."

"I think you are unwell," she ventures. She hates him for considering her lascivious. She hates herself for not having thought of calling her husband.

But what could she have said over the phone to a dark-suited man in an office cubicle concentrating hard on a computer terminal? Please come home and protect me from that Khanna boy who fancies he's in love with me?

He lunges at her. Suddenly the kitchenette counter seems a frail barrier. Tea spurts into a pretty saucer and stains the butcher's block. She has no time to tear off squares of paper towel and wipe up the spill. His right arm snakes toward her, reaches up through the chiffon sari; the snake's jaws, closing on a breast, scratch her hand instead.

"Madman!" she screams. Her side, her breast, her hand, all burn with shame. The snake's jaws have found the breast. She is paralyzed.

"You have no right to play with my feelings, Vinita! Confess at once!"

The situation is absolutely preposterous. She has been taught by Mother Stella and by her parents how to deal with revolutions. She can disarm an emaciated Communist pointing a pipe-gun at her pet chihuahua. She can drive her father's new Hindustan Ambassador and she's beginning to drive on weekends to local shopping malls. But banal calamities, the mad passions of a maladjusted failed American make her shudder.

Rajiv lets go. He picks up his cup and saucer and flounces off to the patio. She watches him curl up on the wicker love seat, his New Balance shoes polluting the new cushions with street germs. He admires Sailen's careful grouping of rare orchids with all the confidence of an invited guest. All but one of the orchids are in their prime this afternoon, and their thick petals glow in the odd New Jersey light. Her breast tingles. It feels warm; it feels recently caressed. She leans her forehead against the fake Ionic column that marks the alcove for the refrigerator, and wonders if the torment that the madman in her atrium feels is the same torment she, too, would have suffered if she had the courage to fall in love.

At seven-twenty, Sailen comes home. Tonight he has brought Vinod Mehra and Kailash Kapoor with him. They go to the same fitness club after work. Rajiv Khanna left soon after finishing his cup of tea, so Vinita has had time to bathe at five-thirty as usual (she maintains the Indian habit of bathing twice a day), to put on a purple silk sari that she knows looks quite seductive on her, dress her long hair elaborately with silver pins and cook dinner. The dinner includes six courses, not counting the bottled pickles and the store-bought pie for dessert. Cooking a fancy meal has been her self-acknowledged expiation, though in her heart she is sure (why shouldn't she be sure?) that she has committed no transgression. Now seeing the unexpected guests, she is re-

VISITORS | 159

lieved that their visit coincides with the night of her extra effort. What if she had made nothing but *dal,* rice and a vegetable curry? Rumors about Sailen Kumar's bride starving Sailen Kumar would have started to swirl through highrises in Brooklyn and Rego Park.

The men congregate in the atrium. It is quite obviously Sailen's pride and joy; therefore, by extension, it is Vinita's pride and joy, too. She watches him show off his newest acquisitions in plants and flowers. In India, where the gardener and his grandson had taken care of such things, she had thought of blossoms only in terms of interior decoration, how they look against a background of new pink silk drapes, for instance. Now she has to view them differently, as though selecting them at the florist's, nursing them through the winter in overheated rooms and pruning them to look their most gorgeous is self-expression. In fact, she has heard Sailen justify his choice of buying a condominium in New Jersey instead of across the river where the action is by pointing at the atrium. You couldn't afford that in Manhattan, no sir. Unless you were a millionaire. Of course, she knows that Sailen intends to be a millionaire, as do his close friends, especially Vinod Mehra. Everybody in the Indian community knows that Vinod Mehra is likely to reach his goal before he is fifty. He plays the stock market better than most professional brokers. Everyone respects him for being a money wizard.

She reminds her husband to fix their guests drinks—"I am knowing so little about shaking cocktails and pouring jiggers, I'm afraid," she apologizes with her infectious laugh—and runs between kitchenette and patio with spiced cashews and deep-fried tidbits like vegetable pakoras. It is obvious that the men find her seductive, charming and inviolable. They alternate between being deferential and being flirtatious. They plague her with questions about local politics in India. They tease her about being a spoiled, rich girl and therefore a novice cook who makes pakoras and samosas. They beg her to sing them a Tagore song (but my harmonium hasn't arrived yet!) because it's already gotten around (from that nice Khanna boy who studies at Columbia, a bright boy, says Sailen) that she must be a talented singer. She is ecstatic; she serves the men and manipulates them with her youth and her beauty and her unmaskable charm. She has no idea that she is on the verge of hysteria. She has no idea.

That night in bed, for the first time since she has left Calcutta, she is bothered by insomnia. Within reach, but not touching her, Sailen sleeps on his stomach. He is breathing through his mouth. She imagines his fleshy lips; they flap like rubber tires. He is a good man, and one day he will be a millionaire. He has never, not once, by gesture or word, made her feel that she is anything but the queen of his heart.

Why, then, is she moved by an irresistible force to steal out of his bed in the haven of his expensive condominium, and run off into the alien American night where only shame and disaster can await her?

The Imaginary Assassin

I WAS BORN IN YUBA CITY, California, in July—the month of *Sravan* by my grandfather's calendar—of 1960. Grandfather had first come to the Valley at age thirteen to visit relatives. The plan had been for Grandfather to slip into the illegal aliens' underground at the end of the visit, make a fortune, then bring in the rest of his family. In those days work with Sikh farmers wasn't hard to find. Many had started out just that way, as robust illegals on the run, and made fortunes in the Valley. Some claimed that they had had to marry off daughters to rich, ugly men in big cities like Amritsar and Delhi in order to pay the one-way fare to Los Angeles. But all such sacrifices had paid off, and in time they'd been able to bring over these daughters, too, and *their* families.

California was paradise to starving men from dusty Ludhiana villages. But what good was access to paradise if you weren't happy? The first time around, California had made Grandfather homesick.

All the Sikhs in America, Grandfather'd complained, were knock-kneed and weakly. They'd lost their *dum*, their zest, as soon as they'd landed overseas.

This was not at all true, of course. Many of our people in the Valley got into scuffles with local youths and with the police. We gave more than we got, and Sikh pride remained intact. But Grandfather as a teenager must have been stubborn as well as lonely. He drove himself out of paradise by getting picked up for shoplifting and did not return to live here until November of 1948, a month after a madman shot Mahatma Gandhi, the bony man in loincloth who delivered India from the British.

Some scandal surrounded Grandfather's second coming to the Valley. In our ancestral village in Ludhiana, which Grandfather had left as a young man to find happiness in Sind, all the men seem to have been high-spirited. Grandfather's youngest uncle, younger than him by three years at least, had been jailed for spitting at a British soldier in 1926. My mother's older brother had fallen in love with a brigand's daughter and been slain by police bullets in a millet field. Incest, blasphemy, misadventure: in a small, dark guest room with papered walls, Grandfather sat cross-legged on the bed and initiated me into the family's marvelous prodigality.

THE IMAGINARY ASSASSIN | *161*

I came to hate my parents. The shabby diligence of our immigrant lives in Yuba City shamed the romantic in me.

I WAS A HEADACHY, bookish boy, a collector of foreign coins from visiting uncles who'd worked in Africa, Malaya, England and Germany. I was a gatherer and embellisher of nostalgic family gossip. Other California kids had their rock stars to make life bearable; I had my great-uncle the spitter and my uncle the foolhardy lover. My younger sister, Manorma, inherited all the Singh family's high spirits. She lives in Canada now, organizes farmworkers' unions in British Columbia and has twice been arrested by the Mounties. I was the good student, the one destined (Father hoped) to break with the Singh tradition of working the soil. He had dreams and schemes invested in my getting good grades and going on to Cal Tech for aerospace engineering. Father counted on good grades, initiative and a neat appearance more than I did. Father studied the names of scholarship winners. Yee, Wang, Yamamota: neat to a fault, I would have to agree. Why did I harbor a secret fascination with a different kind of immigrant, Sirhan B. Sirhan? Can madmen, tuned in to God, derail our ordinary destinies?

It was Grandfather, the teller of old-country tales at dusk, who asked such questions. His tales were full of spectacular coincidences and miracles. The death rattle of a dutiful son could deafen a mother five hundred miles away. Headless ghosts, eager to decapitate, could hide in trees along dark country lanes.

One night when I was about nine or ten, Grandfather told me a remarkable story. We had the little house nearly to ourselves. Mother was out that night. She was at the temple for a meeting of the temple's executive committee. Manorma was sleeping over at Amrita Duggal's, a slow girl with oily braids, with whom she would quarrel in another three weeks. Father was out with Uncle Pritam, having a bit of fun and forbidden whiskey. Father was dismissed by the Sikh community as a big-hearted man who'd never get rich. Money and manly honor: these were the only virtues for our people. Father dreamed of wealth and virility, too, and he had dozens of rags-to-riches schemes that got their start over scotch in Uncle Pritam's den. At heart Father was a merchant, an exporter and importer of other men's talents, not a farmer. His most recent project had been the printing of mail-order bride catalogs for Ludhiana women. We still had two hundred catalogs in our basement. I'm not against the bringing in of hardy, grateful peasant women. Manorma, with her high spirits and her shrill union-worker's voice, is no more likely to make a Yuba City Sikh happy than an illiterate, slow, Ludhiana girl. And the project might have made Fa-

162 | MIDCAREER STORIES (1985–1988)

ther some money. But Mother made him fold his "Mutual Happiness, Inc." firm when fifteen American males, one from as far away as Scottsdale, Arizona, mailed in their subscriptions.

"Have you no shame?" Mother screamed. "You want to sell girls to *them* now?" She threatened to call the Bureau of Immigration and Naturalization with an anonymous tip.

That night Father was at Uncle Pritam's to talk over a new scheme, something more in the line of showbiz. A new man from Varanasi was traveling from Valley town to Valley town and being put up by local Sikh and Hindu families. The man was charismatic, our people said. He was a holy man with special gifts. He would sleep on beds of nails in high school auditoria and church basements if the money from ticket sales were given to orphanages in India. The future of the world, the man believed, would be decided by embittered orphans. Father was eager to back the holy man and move Indian culture out of basketball courts and Unitarian basements. But this was in the late sixties when holy men from India were no longer a novelty.

Grandfather and I would have had the house all to ourselves if it hadn't been for a houseguest who slept on a cot in the basement. He was a slender young man in a cheap new suit. He must have been a progressive Sikh, because he wore no turban and his hair had a jagged, raw, freshly chopped-off look to it. He stayed in the basement all day, even ate his meals off a tray down there. Now and then we heard his ghostly footsteps as he paced the basement in new sturdy shoes with two-inch heels.

The night was warm and very windy. The winds came off the orchards with a mess of leaves and twigs. I could hear the cackle and swish of wind-blown headless ghosts. It was the kind of night when even a nine-year-old American boy with good grades can confess his fear of gods and unholy spirits.

Grandfather was in bed, sucking on a pinch of powdered tobacco leaf, when I came into the room. A forty-watt bulb in a broken wall fixture made the room seem dreary.

"Tell me a new ghost story," I begged.

He offered me the flat tin of powdered tobacco. I squeezed a large, gritty pinchful and dropped it on my tongue. He slipped the tin under his pillow and said, "Not a ghost story. I'll tell you a true story. I'll tell you why I had to come back to America to live."

"You *had* to? You mean someone forced you?"

"Yes," Grandfather said. "I killed a man in Delhi. I killed Mahatma Gandhi."

I didn't know what to do with this boastful confession. It wasn't true. Grandfather hadn't killed Mahatma Gandhi. A Hindu fanatic had, at a public prayer meeting on October 2, 1948. The fanatic had been caught and hanged. How could Grandfather lie to me about verifiable history?

But Grandfather had an odd, zealous look in his good eye—the other was creamy with cataracts—and asked me to sit on the bed. He said, "Gurcharan, I'm going to tell you what happened. This time it is not a story."

I said nothing. I pushed the quilt to one side, so I could stretch out my legs without getting the sheets dirty. Mother worked hard all day in a canning factory and I didn't want to upset her about extra laundry. Downstairs I could hear our unsocial houseguest pace the unfinished basement floor. The warm, moist winds had made us too restless.

This is the tale that Grandfather told me in a mixture of Punjabi and English.

"IN 1947, long before you, my little friend, were in your mother's belly, a tall Englishman named Lord Mountbatten and Mahatma Gandhi sat down to a lunch of dal-chapati. There were no knives or forks, and so Gandhi was teaching Mountbatten to eat Indian-style, with the fingers. Gandhi was flicking his tongue against the side of his fingers, against the fingertips, and saying, 'See, Your Excellency, this way, the lentil doesn't drip.' The Englishman was not liking to eat with the fingers and to get his nails messy. He was not liking Indian peasant food. He was probably thinking, Indian curries in silver bowls in the Nehru dining room, now that is quite another story! But being a diplomat and a gentleman, Mountbatten changed the subject from inedible food to politics. He said, 'Mr. Gandhi, how can you expect His Majesty to give you national independence when civil war is about to break out between you Hindus and the Muslims?' But Gandhi had his answer ready. He said, 'God will guide the King, don't worry. But if I don't show you how to eat without cutlery, Your Excellency, you will go today with hunger pains in your belly.' Then Gandhi did what we do with chapatis on our plates. He held his chapati down with the heel of his right hand and with a quick flick of the fingers, tore off a biteable piece. 'Here, Your Excellency,' Gandhi explained. 'This bit I'm holding for you to see is Pakistan for the Muslims. The rest of the chapati on my plate, that's India for us Hindus. You are seeing, milord, how simple the question of sovereignty is?' That's how we got rid of the Muslims and the British quick-quick. A coarse wheat chapati in a peasant's hand gave us liberty.

"But liberty became a sad and bloody gift to us Hindus and Sikhs who lived in the bit of land that His Majesty King George gave away to the Muslims. The Muslims snatched, torched, spoiled. It is the way of human nature; I am not blaming Muslims. But Gandhi, the spiritual leader, what did he un-

164 | MIDCAREER STORIES (1985-1988)

derstand about evil and sin? A man with his head in the clouds does not see the shit pile at his feet.

"Men in uniforms put us refugees on trains. I was put on a train for Delhi. Delhi was everybody's first choice. In my compartment refugees crouched on seats, bunks, floor spaces, even on luggage racks, like monkeys. A pretty city-woman in a muddy silk *kameez*[1] dozed on a cardboard suitcase so near me that I had to sit pigeon-toed all night. A wide red scar bled down her forehead. Dagger knicks marred the creamy brown skin of her arms and midriff. Oh, how heedless Mahatma Gandhi had been with our lives!

"Sometime deep in the night, the woman put both her hands on my thighs. I tautened my muscles. We were a trainful of insomniacs. Everybody could see everything. Refugees have no privacy. She laughed. She moved her fingers this way and that, and I twisted my knees out of her reach. She was quite demented, you see, thinking I was her husband who must have been killed. We were decent men and women thrown into indecent situations by a dal-chapati-eating Gandhi. I admired her boldness at the same time that I was embarrassed by it.

"The woman touched me again. She prodded me on the knee. This time her fingers were wifely, tender, provocative. In that train of misery, she wanted conjugal sex. I felt lust swell as I tucked my feet under me on the seat. Ill-bred men were watching and making encouraging noises.

"She got off at dawn at a village, but her scar, her cruel, sleepless eyes, her lecherous touch, she left these behind to disconcert me. My own wife was dead. This woman was no better off. Gandhi had hurt our women. The man who could sleep between virgins and feel no throb of virility had despoiled the women of our country. Gandhi was the enemy of women. And so, Gandhi, the Mahatma, the Great Soul, became my enemy.

"When I got to Delhi, right away I set about to assassinate that man. I could think of nothing else. My body was made of stone; it suffered no hunger, no sun and rain. I'd need a weapon, and I'd need safe passage after the event. I saw myself raiding police depots and armories. I hoarded soda bottles to hurl into Gandhi's face. I held a gardener's job for a whole week so I could steal a hatchet. I mailed an aerogram to your father. 'Sponsor my immigration,' I wrote him. 'I'll be in need of paradise any day.' Nights I dreamed of hacking the Mahatma to bits. Hindu saviors have dry, stringy bodies, the bodies of men who fast excessively. I was afraid the blunt blade of my hatchet wouldn't cut through Gandhi's armored flesh. He should have had the soft, lubricated flesh of politicians and businessmen. The purity of my vengeance made me

---

1. Long tunic worn by South Asian women.—Ed.

THE IMAGINARY ASSASSIN | *165*

delirious. I read signs in shooting stars. The stars were women with accusatory faces.

"Months passed. My delirium kept me from holding regular jobs. Other refugees from West Punjab, ex-farmers like me, made new lives for themselves in new, desperate cities. They became itinerant cooks with stoves on wheels, they became washermen, taxi drivers, bus conductors. I couldn't settle down until I had killed. In my mind, Gandhi the celibate was the biggest rapist in history. I slept on sidewalks. I begged. I dreamed of public execution if safe passage to California failed.

"On October 2, Gandhi was to lead a public prayer meeting. October is a fine, cool month in Delhi, so the organizers expected millions to come out and pray. Gandhi was a genuine hero, a stooped little peasant like us in loincloth, who had driven King George away. But this time there were nasty rumors. We heard that even Gandhi clapped his hands over his ears because widows moaned too loudly under his balcony. They said that Gandhi knew about assassins in alleys. They said even a savior has his bitter moments and his dreams of fasting to death.

"The day of the prayer meeting, I tied the stolen hatchet to my chest, slipped a loose *khadi kurta*[2] over it and followed the crowds. Worshipers choked the streets and lanes. Gandhians with 'volunteer' armbands guided us toward the garden where the prayer meeting was to be held. The Gandhians were ecstatic. They counted and recounted heads. But the policemen were sullen. They patroled the boulevards in sweaty boots and pinned Gandhians against tree trunks to give them random bodychecks.

"I didn't care. I wasn't afraid. Many in our family are subject to nervous disorders. Euphoria kept me from all anxiety and pain. How often in life is our duty made so clear? How often is a man given the opportunity to avenge mass murder and rape?

"The Gandhians were slack-muscled. I kept my head down and pushed forward toward the garden. The Gandhians gave way. The police were watchful. But no hand jerked me out of line—truly God protects the saint—no baton fell on my head.

"Gandhi made us wait a while in the garden. The more important Gandhians stood in straggly rows on a platform. They were mill owners and politicians, the true beneficiaries of national independence. The rest of us gathered on grassy stretches, or climbed weak-limbed trees. One lady-Gandhian fell off a low branch and two policemen carried her away.

---

2. A type of shirt for South Asian men.—Ed.

"Finally Gandhi came out of a building. Everyone started chanting, 'Raghupati Ravana'; it was Gandhi's special hymn. I did, too, and my voice sounded loud and passionate. Gandhi looked pleased. He was a small, skinny man in a clean white loincloth, and he looked very pleased with us as he made his way to the platform in his bowlegged gait. Two very plain-faced girls held him by his elbows. They were his virgin bodyguards. They forced him into a brisker pace. When Gandhians reached for their savior, the girls swatted them gently away.

"I put out my assassin's hand. My fingertips touched sun-wrinkled flesh. Gandhians pushed me from behind, the girls took fast, mincing steps, and I lost my grip on the Mahatma. But he turned around, and I swear he smiled. 'Raghupati Ravana Raja Ram,' Gandhi chanted. 'Patita Pavana Sita Ram,' I finished, elated. This time Gandhi stopped. He shrank from the delirium in my eyes. But I reached out. We touched. I grabbed his dark, coarse, peasant flesh. These hands held the Mahatma's body. I pressed the Mahatma against my chest.

"A howl came out of him when he felt the hatchet. He scraped my *kurta* with his nails. He struggled, he meant to push me away but it looked like a brotherly embrace. No Gandhian would have guessed that even a savior might be unready for violent death. But death came to him all right, death came while he was slumped in my embrace. Bullets tore up Gandhi's skinny body. The body collapsed in my arms, it was a sad bloody mess.

"'Ram, Ram,' we prayed for the Mahatma.

"A corpse, even a savior's corpse, jerks and stiffens in demeaning ways.

"Now comes the confusing part. The Mahatma died in my arms but it was not me the police arrested that day. I killed the Mahatma out of delirious hate, but it was a slim, fair Hindu fanatic from Maharashtra that they arrested instead.

"I left Delhi for Bombay that night. There was talk of accomplices, of extremist Hindu parties with terrorist cells. From Bombay I fled to Liverpool, signing on as a lascar[3] on a cargo boat. From Liverpool, I wrote your father and he sent me dollars for a boat ticket to New York and for a train to California. Who knows, if I had stayed in California the first time I came, I might have been a chartered accountant in a fancy tie and jacket. And poor Mahatma Gandhi like the rest of us might have lived out his life to embittered ripeness."

AT THE END OF THE STORY, Grandfather straightened up against the headboard of the bed and recited lines from an English poem:

---

3. An old word for sailors of color from countries colonized by European imperial powers.—Ed.

For the world, which seems
To lie before us like a land of dreams,
So various, so beautiful, so new,
Hath really neither joy, nor love, nor light,
Nor certitude, nor peace, nor help for pain;
And we are here as on a darkling plain
Swept with confused alarms of struggle and flight,
Where ignorant armies clash by night.

A nine-year-old Californian, I hadn't heard of Matthew Arnold. And I didn't know until much later that it was Grandfather, not the great-uncle, who had spat on the British captain in 1926 and had been forced to memorize *Dover Beach* in jail. I think now of the despair of that English soldier as he tried to subdue schoolboys on a subcontinent where night armies were already on the march. At nine I knew only that an illiterate and senile man reciting a foreign poem was a wondrous feat.

So that was how one summer night Grandfather told me the fantastic story of Mahatma Gandhi and himself. The Californian boys had their rock stars and their movie stars and their cute sexy girlfriends who went all the way. I had nothing. The family's prodigality expresses itself in slow, secretive ways. From that night began my hallucinations and nervous spells that kept me from that desired good and neat appearance and the aerospace scholarship to Pasadena.

Father's showbiz scheme came to nothing, again. In a school auditorium in San Diego, the holy man lost his concentration and tore his chest on a strip of nails. Father wasn't American enough to grasp the fact that blood is better showbiz than any yogic performance.

The slender houseguest with the raw, amateurish haircut was picked up by Yuba City police the only night he left our basement. They said he'd killed another Sikh in Toronto, Canada. I don't know how, or why, or when.

Courtly Vision

JAHANARA BEGUM STANDS behind a marble grille in her palace at Fatehpur-Sikri.

Count Barthelmy, an adventurer from beyond frozen oceans, crouches in a lust-darkened arbor. His chest—a tear-shaped fleck of rust—lifts away from

168 | MIDCAREER STORIES (1985–1988)

the gray, flat trunk of a mango tree. He is swathed in the coarse, quaint clothes of his cool-weather country. Jacket, pantaloons, shawl, swell and cave in ardent pleats. He holds a peacock's feather to his lips. His face is colored an admonitory pink. The feather is dusty aqua, broken-spined. His white-gloved hand pillows a likeness of the Begum, painted on a grain of rice by Basawan, the prized court artist. Two red-eyed parrots gouge the patina of grass at the adventurer's feet; their buoyant, fluffy breasts caricature the breasts of Moghul virgins. The Count is posed full-front; the self-worshipful body of a man who has tamed thirteen rivers and seven seas. Dainty thighs bulge with wayward expectancy. The head twists savagely upward at an angle unreckoned except in death, anywhere but here. In profile the lone prismatic eye betrays the madman and insomniac.

On the terrace of Jahanara Begum's palace, a slave girl kneels; her forearms starry with jewels strain toward the fluted handle of a decanter. Two bored eunuchs squat on their fleshy haunches, awaiting their wine. Her simple subservience hints at malevolent dreams, of snake venom rubbed into wine cups or daggers concealed between young breasts, and the eunuchs are menaced, their faces pendulous with premonition.

In her capacious chamber the Begum waits, perhaps for death from the serving-girl, for ravishing, or merely the curtain of fire from the setting sun. The chamber is open on two sides, the desert breeze stiffens her veil into a gauzy disc. A wild peacock, its fanned-out feathers beaten back by the same breeze, cringes on the bit of marble floor visible behind her head. Around the Begum, retainers conduct their inefficient chores. One, her pursed navel bare, slackens her grip on a *morchal*[1] of plumes; another stumbles, biceps clenched, under the burden of a gold hookah bowl studded with translucent rubies and emeralds; a third stoops, her back an eerie, writhing arc, to straighten a low table littered with cosmetics in jeweled pillboxes. The Begum is a tall, rigid figure as she stands behind a marble grille. From her fists, which she holds in front of her like tiny shields, sprouts a closed, upright lotus bloom. Her gaze slips upward, past the drunken gamblers on the roof-terraces, to the skyline where fugitive cranes pass behind a blue cloud.

Oh, beauteous and beguiling Begum, has your slave-girl apprised the Count of the consequences of a night of bliss?

Under Jahanara Begum's window, in a courtyard cooled with fountains into whose basin slaves have scattered rose petals, sit Fathers Aquaviva and Henriques, ingenuous Portuguese priests. They have dogged the emperor

---

1. Defined as "a fan, or a fly-whisk, made of peacock's feathers" by Henry Yule and Arthur Coke Burnell in *Hobson-Jobson* (1886).—Ed.

COURTLY VISION | *169*

through inclement scenery. Now they pause in the emperor's famed new capital, eyes closed, abstemious hands held like ledges over their brows to divert the sullen desert breeze. Their faces seem porous; the late afternoon has slipped through the skin and distended the chins and cheeks. Before their blank, radiant gazes, seven itinerant jugglers heap themselves into a shuddering pyramid. A courtier sits with the priests on a divan covered with brocaded silk. He, too, is blind to the courage of gymnasts. He is distracted by the wondrous paintings the priests have spread out on the arabesques of the rug at their feet. Mother and Child. Child and Mother. The Moghul courtier—child of Islam, ruler of Hindus—finds the motif repetitive. What comforting failure of the imagination these priests are offering. What precarious boundaries set on life's playful fecundity. He hears the Fathers murmur. They are devising stratagems on a minor scale. They want to trick the emperor into kissing Christ, who on each huge somber canvas is a bright, white, healthy baby. The giant figures seem to him simple and innocuous, not complicated and infuriating like the Hindu icons hidden in the hills. In the meantime his eyes draw comfort from the unclad angels who watch over the Madonna to protect her from heathens like him. Soft-fleshed, flying women. He will order the court artists to paint him a harem of winged women on a single poppy seed.

The emperor will not kiss Christ tonight. He is at the head of his army, riding a piebald horse out of his new walled city. He occupies the foreground of that agate-colored paper, a handsome young man in a sun-yellow *jama*.[2] Under the *jama* his shoulders pulsate to the canny violent rhythm of his mount. Behind him in a thick choking diagonal stream follow his soldiers. They scramble and spill on the sandy terrain; spiky desert grass slashes their jaunty uniforms of muslin. Tiny, exhilarated profiles crowd the battlements. In the women's palace, tinier figures flit from patterned window grille to grille. The citizens have begun to celebrate. Grandfathers leading children by the wrists are singing of the emperor's victories over invisible rebels. Shopkeepers, coy behind their taut paunches, give away their syrupy sweets. Even the mystics with their haggard, numinous faces have allowed themselves to be distracted by yet another parade.

So the confident emperor departs.

The Moghul evening into which he drags his men with the promise of unimaginable satisfactions is grayish gold with the late afternoon, winter light. It spills down the rims of stylized rocks that clog the high horizon. The light is charged with unusual excitement and it discovers the immense intimacy of darkness, the erotic shadowiness of the cave-deep arbor in which the Count

---

2. Opulent, long-sleeved outer garment worn by Mughal royalty.—Ed.

170 | MIDCAREER STORIES (1985–1988)

crouches and waits. The foliage of the mango tree yields sudden, bountiful shapes. Excessive, unruly life—monkeys, serpents, herons, thieves naked to the waist—bloom and burgeon on its branches. The thieves, their torsos pushing through clusters of leaves, run rapacious fingers on their dagger blades.

They do not discern the Count. The Count does not overhear the priests. Adventurers all, they guard from each other the common courtesy of their subterfuge. They sniff the desert air and the air seems full of portents. In the remote horizons three guards impale three calm, emaciated men. Behind the low wall of a *namaz*[3] platform, two courtiers quarrel, while a small boy sneaks up and unties their horses. A line of stealthy women prostrate themselves and pray at the doorway of a temple in a patch of browning foliage. Over all these details float three elegant whorls of cloud, whorls in the manner of Chinese painting, imitated diligently by men who long for rain.

The emperor leaves his capital, applauded by flatterers and loyal citizens. Just before riding off the tablet's edge into enemy territory, he twists back on his saddle and shouts a last-minute confidence to his favorite court-painter. He is caught in reflective profile, the quarter-arc of his mustache suggests a man who had permitted his second thoughts to confirm his spontaneous judgments.

Give me total vision, commands the emperor. His voice hisses above the hoarse calls of the camels. *You, Basawan, who can paint my Begum*[4] *on a grain of rice, see what you can do with the infinite vistas the size of my opened hand. Hide nothing from me, my co-wanderer. Tell me how my new capital will fail, will turn to dust and these marbled terraces be home to jackals and infidels. Tell me who to fear and who to kill but tell it to me in a way that makes me smile. Transport me through dense fort walls and stone grilles and into the hearts of men.*

"EMPEROR ON HORSEBACK LEAVES WALLED CITY"
PAINTING ON PAPER, 24 CMS X 25.8 CMS
PAINTER UNKNOWN. NO SUPERSCRIPTION
C. 1584 A.D.
LOT NO. SLM 4027-66
EST. PRICE $750

---

3. A Muslim prayer.—Ed.
4. Honorific traditionally used to describe an aristocratic Muslim woman.—Ed.

The Middleman and Other Stories (1988)

The Middleman

THERE ARE ONLY TWO SEASONS in this country, the dusty and the wet. I already know the dusty and I'll get to know the wet. I've seen worse. I've seen Baghdad, Bombay, Queens—and now this moldering spread deep in Mayan country. Aztecs, Toltecs, mestizos, even some bashful whites with German accents. All that and a lot of Texans. I'll learn the ropes.

Forget the extradition order, I'm not a sinful man. I've listened to bad advice. I've placed my faith in dubious associates. My first American wife said, in the dog-eat-dog, Alfred, you're a beagle. My name is Alfie Judah, of the once-illustrious Smyrna, Aleppo, Baghdad—and now Flushing, Queens—Judahs.

I intend to make it back.

This place is owned by one Clovis T. Ransome. He reached here from Waco with fifteen million in petty cash hours ahead of a posse from the SEC. That doesn't buy much down here, a few thousand acres, residency papers and the right to swim with the sharks a few feet off the bottom. Me? I make a living from things that fall. The big fat belly of Clovis T. Ransome bobs above me like whale shit at high tide.

The president's name is Gutiérrez. Like everyone else he has enemies, right and left. He's on retainer from men like Ransome, from the *contras*, maybe from the Sandinistas as well.

The woman's name is Maria. She came with the ranch, or with the protection, no one knows.

President Gutiérrez's country has definite possibilities. All day I sit by the lime green swimming pool, sunscreened so I won't turn black, going through my routine of isometrics while Ransome's *indios* hack away the virgin forests. Their hate is intoxicating. They hate gringos—from which my darkness exempts me—even more than Gutiérrez. They hate in order to keep up their intensity. I hear a litany of presidents' names, Hollywood names, Detroit names—Carter, *chop*, Reagan, *slash*, Buick, *thump*—bounce off the vines as machetes clear the jungle greenness. We spoke a form of Spanish in my old Baghdad home. I always understand more than I let on.

In this season the air's so dry it could scratch your lungs. Bright-feathered birds screech, snakeskins glitter, as the jungle peels away. Iguanas the size of wallabies leap from behind macheted bushes. The pool is greener than the

172 | MIDCAREER STORIES (1985–1988)

ocean waves, cloudy with chemicals that Ransome trucked over the mountains. When toads fall in, the water blisters their skin. I've heard their cries.

Possibilities, oh, yes.

I must confess my weakness. It's women.

In the old Baghdad when I was young, we had the hots for blonds. We'd stroll up to the diplomatic enclaves just to look at women. Solly Nathan, cross-eyed Itzie, Naim, and me. Pinkish flesh could turn our blood to boiling lust. British matrons with freckled calves, painted toenails through thin-strapped sandals, the onset of varicose, the brassiness of prewar bleach jobs—all of that could thrill us like cleavage. We were twelve and already visiting whores during those hot Levantine lunch hours when our French masters intoned the rules of food, rest, and good digestion. We'd roll up our fried flat bread smeared with spicy potatoes, pool our change, and bargain with the daughters of washerwomen while our lips and fingers still glistened with succulent grease. But the only girls cheap enough for boys our age with unspecified urgencies were swamp Arabs from Basra and black girls from Baluchistan, the broken toys discarded by our older brothers.

Thank God those European women couldn't see us. It's comforting at times just to be a native, invisible to our masters. *They* were worthy of our lust. Local girls were for amusement only, a dark place to spend some time, like a video arcade.

"You chose a real bad time to come, Al," he says. He may have been born on the wrong side of Waco, but he's spent his adult life in tropical paradises playing God. "The rains'll be here soon, a day or two at most." He makes a whooping noise and drinks Jack Daniels from a flask.

"My options were limited." A modest provident fund I'd been maintaining for New Jersey judges was discovered. My fresh new citizenship is always in jeopardy. My dealings can't stand too much investigation.

"Bud and I can keep you from getting bored."

Bud Wilkins should be over in his pickup anytime now. Meanwhile, Ransome rubs Cutter over his face and neck. They're supposed to go deep-sea fishing today, though it looks to me as if he's dressed for the jungle. A wetted-down hand towel is tucked firmly under the back of his baseball cap. He's a Braves man. Bud ships him cassettes of all the Braves games. There are aspects of American life I came too late for and will never understand. It isn't love of the game, he told me last week. It's love of Ted Turner, the man.

His teams. His stations. His America's cup, his yachts, his network.

If he could clone himself after anyone in the world, he'd choose Ted Turner. Then he leaned close and told me his wife, Maria—once the mistress of Gutiérrez himself, as if I could miss her charms, or underestimate their price in a seller's market—told him she'd put out all night if he looked like Ted Turner. "Christ, Al, here I've got this setup and I gotta beg her for it!" There *are* things I can relate to, and a man in such agony is one of them. That was last week, and he was drunk and I was new on the scene. Now he snorts more JD and lets out a whoop.

"Wanna come fishing? Won't cost you extra, Al."

"Thanks, no," I say. "Too hot."

The only thing I like about Clovis Ransome is that he doesn't snicker when I, an Arab to some, an Indian to others, complain of the heat. Even dry heat I despise.

"Suit yourself," he says.

Why do I suspect he wants me along as a witness? I don't want any part of their schemes. Bud Wilkins got here first. He's entrenched, doing little things for many people, building up a fleet of trucks, of planes, of buses. Like Ari Onassis, he started small. That's the legitimate side. The rest of it is no secret. A man with cash and private planes can clear a fortune in Latin America. The story is Bud was exposed as a CIA agent, forced into public life and made to go semipublic with his arms deals and transfer fees.

"I don't mind you staying back, you know. She wants Bud."

Maria.

I didn't notice Maria for the first days of my visit. She was *here*, but in the background. And she was dark, native, and I have my prejudices. But what can I say—is there deeper pleasure, a darker thrill than prejudice squarely faced, suppressed, fought against, and then slowly, secretively surrendered to?

Now I think a single word: adultery.

On cue, Maria floats toward us out of the green shadows. She's been swimming in the ocean, her hair is wet, her big-boned, dark-skinned body is streaked with sand. The talk is Maria was an aristocrat, a near-Miss World whom Ransome partially bought and partially seduced away from Gutiérrez, so he's never sure if the president owes him one, or wants to kill him. With her thick dark hair and smooth dark skin, she has to be mostly Indian. In her pink Lycra bikini she arouses new passion. Who wants pale, thin, pink flesh, who wants limp, curly blond hair, when you can have lustrous browns, purple-blacks?

Adultery and dark-eyed young women are forever entwined in my memory. It is a memory, even now, that fills me with chills and terror and terrible,

terrible desire. When I was a child, one of our servants took me to his village. He wanted me to see something special from the old Iraqi culture. Otherwise, he feared, my lenient Jewish upbringing would later betray me. A young woman, possibly adulterous but certainly bold and brave and beautiful enough to excite rumors of promiscuity, was stoned to death that day. What I remember now is the breathlessness of waiting as her husband encircled her, as she struggled against the rope, as the stake barely swayed to her writhing. I remember the dull thwock and the servant's strong fingers shaking my shoulders as the first stone struck.

I realize I am one of the very few Americans who knows the sound of rocks cutting through flesh and striking bone. One of the few to count the costs of adultery.

Maria drops her beach towel on the patio floor, close to my deck chair, and straightens the towel's edge with her toes. She has to have been a dancer before becoming Ransome's bride and before Gutiérrez plucked her out of convent school to become his mistress. Only ballerinas have such blunted, misshapen toes. But she knows, to the right eyes, even her toes are desirable.

"I want to hear about New York, Alfred." She lets herself fall like a dancer on the bright red towel. Her husband is helping Eduardo, the houseboy, load the jeep with the day's gear, and it's him she seems to be talking to. "My husband won't let me visit the States. He absolutely won't."

"She's putting you on, Al," Ransome shouts. He's just carried a case of beer out to the jeep. "She prefers St. Moritz."

"You ski?"

I can feel the heat rising from her, or from the towel. I can imagine as the water beads on her shoulders how cool her flesh will be for just a few more minutes.

"Do I look as though I ski?"

I don't want to get involved in domestic squabbles. The *indios* watch us. A solemn teenager hefts his machete. We are to have an uncomplicated view of the ocean from the citadel of this patio.

"My husband is referring to the fact that I met John Travolta in St. Moritz," she says, defiantly.

"Sweets," says Ransome. The way he says it, it's a threat.

"He has a body of one long muscle, like an eel," she says.

Ransome is closer now. "Make sure Eduardo doesn't forget the crates," he says.

"Okay, okay," she shouts back. "Excuse me." And I watch her corkscrew to her feet. I'm so close I can hear her ligaments pop.

SOON AFTER, Bud Wilkins roars into the cleared patch that serves as the main parking lot. He backs his pickup so hard against a shade tree that a bird wheels up from its perch. Bud lines it up with an imaginary pistol and curls his finger twice in its direction. I'm not saying he has no feeling for wildlife. He's in boots and camouflage pants, but his hair, what there is of it, is blow-dried.

He stalks my chair. "We could use you, buddy." He uncaps a beer bottle with, what else, his teeth. "You've seen some hot spots."

"He doesn't want to fish." Ransome is drinking beer, too. "We wouldn't want to leave Maria unprotected." He waits for a retort, but Bud's too much the gentleman. Ransome stares at me and winks, but he's angry. It could get ugly, wherever they're going.

They drink more beer. Finally Eduardo comes out with a crate. He carries it bowlegged, in mincing little half-running steps. The fishing tackle, of course. The crate is dumped into Bud's pickup. He comes out with a second and third, equally heavy, and drops them all in Bud's truck. I can guess what I'm watching. Low-grade arms transfer, rifles, ammo and maybe medicine.

"*Ciao, amigo*," says Bud in his heavy-duty Texas accent.

He and Ransome roar into the jungle in Ransome's jeep.

"I HOPE you're not too hungry, Alfie." It's Maria calling from the kitchen. Alfred to Alfie before the jeep can have made it off the property.

"I'm not a big eater." What I mean to say is I'm adaptable. What I'm hoping is, let us not waste time with food.

"Eduardo!" The houseboy, probably herniated by now, comes to her for instructions. "We just want a salad and fruit. But make it fast, I have to run into San Vicente today." That's the nearest market town. I've been there, it's not much.

She stands at the front door about to join me on the patio when Eduardo rushes us, broom in hand. "*Vaya!*" he screams.

But she is calm. "It must be behind the stove, stupid," she tells the servant. "It can't have made it out this far without us seeing it."

Eduardo wields his broom like a night stick and retreats into the kitchen. We follow. I can't see it. I can only hear desperate clawing and scraping on the tiles behind the stove.

Maria stomps the floor to scare it out. The houseboy shoves the broom handle in the dark space. I think first, being a child of the overheated deserts, giant scorpions. But there are two fugitives, not one, a pair of ocean crabs.

176 | MIDCAREER STORIES (1985–1988)

The crabs, their shiny purple backs dotted with yellow, try to get by us to the beach where they can hear the waves.

How do the mating ocean crabs scuttle their way past Clovis T. Ransome's kitchen? I feel for them.

The broom comes down, thwack, thwack, and bashes the shells in loud, succulent cracks. *Ransome, Gringo*, I hear.

He sticks his dagger into the burlap sacks of green chemicals. He rips, he cuts.

"Eduardo, it's all right. Everything's fine." She sounds stern, authoritative, the years in the presidential palace have served her well. She moves toward him, stops just short of taking his arm.

He spits out, "He kills everything." At least, that's the drift. The language of Cervantes does not stretch around the world without a few skips in transmission. Eduardo's litany includes crabs, the chemicals, the sulfurous pool, the dead birds and snakes and lizards.

"You have my promise," Maria says. "It's going to work out. Now I want you to go to your room, I want you to rest."

We hustle him into his room but he doesn't seem to notice his surroundings. His body has gone slack. I hear the word Santa Simona, a new saint for me. I maneuver him to the cot and keep him pinned down while Maria checks out a rusty medicine cabinet.

He looks up at me, "You drive *Doña* Maria where she goes?"

"If she wants me to, sure."

"Educardo, go to sleep. I'm giving you something to help." She has water and a blue pill ready.

While she hovers over him, I check out his room. It's automatic with me. There are crates under the bed. There's a table covered with oilcloth. The oilcloth is cracked and grimy. A chair by the table is a catchall for clothes, shorts, even a bowl of fruit. Guavas. Eduardo could have snuck in caviar, imported cheeses, Godiva candies, but it's guavas he's chosen to stash for siesta hour hunger pains. The walls are hung with icons of saints. Posters of stars I'd never have heard of if I hadn't been forced to drop out. Baby-faced men and women. The women are sensual in an old-fashioned, Latin way, with red curvy lips, big breasts and tiny waists. Like Maria. Quite a few are unconvincing blonds, in that brassy Latin way. The men have greater range. Some are young versions of Fernando Lamas, some are in fatigues and boots, striking Robin Hood poses. The handsomest is dressed as a guerilla with all the right accessories: beret, black boots, bandolier. Maybe he'd played Che Guevara in some B-budget Argentine melodrama.

"What's in the crates?" I ask Maria.

"I respect people's privacy," she says. "Even a servant's." She pushes me roughly toward the door. "So should you."

THE DAYLIGHT SEEMS TOO BRIGHT on the patio. The bashed shells are on the tiles. Ants have already discovered the flattened meat of ocean crabs, the blistered bodies of clumsy toads.

Maria tells me to set the table. Every day we use a lace cloth, heavy silverware, roses in a vase. Every day we drink champagne. Some mornings the Ransomes start on the champagne with breakfast. Bud owns an air-taxi service and flies in cases of Épernay, caviar, any damned thing his friends desire.

She comes out with a tray. Two plates, two fluted glasses, chèvre cheese on a bit of glossy banana leaf, water biscuits. "I'm afraid this will have to do. Anyway, you said you weren't hungry."

I spread a biscuit and hand it to her.

"If you feel all right, I was hoping you'd drive me to San Vicente." She gestures at Bud Wilkins' pickup truck. "I don't like to drive that thing."

"What if I didn't want to?"

"You won't. Say no to me, I mean. I'm a terrific judge of character." She shrugs, and her breasts are slower than her shoulders in coming down.

"The keys are on the kitchen counter. Do you mind if I use your w.c. instead of going back upstairs? Don't worry, I don't have horrible communicable diseases." She laughs.

This may be intimacy. "How could I mind? It's your house."

"Alfie, don't pretend innocence. It's Ransome's house. This isn't *my* house."

I get the key to Bud's pickup and wait for her by the bruised tree. I don't want to know the contents of the crates, though the stenciling says "fruits" and doubtless the top layer preserves the fiction. How easily I've been recruited, when a bystander is all I wanted to be. The Indians put down their machetes and make signs to me: *Hi, Mom, we're Number One.* They must have been watching Ransome's tapes. They're all wearing Braves caps.

The road to San Vicente is rough. Deep ruts have been cut into the surface by army trucks. Whole convoys must have passed this way during the last rainy season. I don't want to know whose trucks, I don't want to know why.

Forty minutes into the trip Maria says, "When you get to the T, take a left. I have to stop off near here to run an errand." It's a strange word for the middle of the jungle.

"Don't let it take you too long," I say. "We want to be back before hubby gets home." I'm feeling jaunty. She touches me when she talks.

"So Clovis scares you." Her hand finds its way to my shoulder.

178 | MIDCAREER STORIES (1985–1988)

"Shouldn't he?"

I make the left. I make it sharper than I intended. Bud Wilkins' pickup sputters up a dusty rise. A pond appears and around it shacks with vegetable gardens.

"Where are we?"

"In Santa Simona," Maria says. "I was born here, can you imagine?"

This isn't a village, it's a camp for guerrillas. I see some women here, and kids, roosters, dogs. What Santa Simona is is a rest stop for families on the run. I deny simple parallels. Ransome's ranch is just a ranch.

"You could park by the pond."

I step on the brake and glide to the rutted edge of the pond. Whole convoys must have parked here during the rainy season. The ruts hint at secrets. Now in the dry season what might be a lake has shrunk into a muddy pit. Ducks float on green scum.

Young men in khaki begin to close in on Bud's truck.

Maria motions me to get out. "I bet you could use a drink." We make our way up to the shacks. The way her bottom bounces inside those cutoffs could drive a man crazy. I don't turn back but I can hear the unloading of the truck.

So: Bud Wilkins' little shipment has been hijacked, and I'm the culprit. Some job for a middleman.

"*This* is my house, Alfie."

I should be upset. Maria's turned me into a chauffeur. You bet I could use a drink.

We pass by the first shack. There's a garage in the back where there would be the usual large, cement laundry tub. Three men come at me, twirling tire irons the way night sticks are fondled by Manhattan cops. "I'm with her."

Maria laughs at me. "It's not you they want."

And I wonder, *who* was she supposed to deliver? Bud, perhaps, if Clovis hadn't taken him out? Or Clovis himself?

We pass the second shack, and a third. Then a tall guerrilla in full battle-dress floats out of nowhere and blocks our path. Maria shrieks and throws herself on him and he holds her face in his hands, and in no time they're swaying and moaning like connubial visitors at a prison farm. She has her back to me. His big hands cup and squeeze her halter top. I've seen him somewhere. Eduardo's poster.

"Hey," I try. When that doesn't work, I start to cough.

"Sorry," Maria swings around still in his arms. "This is Al Judah. He's staying at the ranch."

THE MIDDLEMAN | *179*

The soldier is called Andreas something. He looks me over. "Yudah?" he asks Maria, frowning.

She shrugs. "You want to make something of it?"

He says something rapidly, locally, that I can't make out. She translates, "He says you need a drink," which I don't believe.

We go inside the command shack. It's a one-room affair, very clean, but dark and cluttered. I'm not sure I should sit on the narrow cot; it seems to be a catchall for the domestic details of revolution—sleeping bags, maps and charts, an empty canteen, two pairs of secondhand army boots. I need a comfortable place to deal with my traumas. There is a sofa of sorts, actually a car seat pushed tight against a wall and stabilized with bits of lumber. There are bullet holes through the fabric, and rusty stains that can only be blood. I reject the sofa. There are no tables, no chairs, no posters, no wall decorations of any kind, unless you count a crucifix. Above the cot, a sad, dark, plaster crucified Jesus recalls His time in the desert.

"Beer?" Maria doesn't wait for an answer. She walks behind a curtain and pulls a six-pack of Heinekens from a noisy refrigerator. I believe I am being offered one of Bud Wilkins' unwitting contributions to the guerrilla effort. I should know it's best not to ask how Dutch beer and refrigerators and '57 two-tone Plymouths with fins and chrome make their way to nowhere jungle clearings. Because of guys like me, in better times, that's how. There's just demand and supply running the universe.

"Take your time, Alfie." Maria is beaming so hard at me it's unreal. "We'll be back soon. You'll be cool and rested in here."

Andreas manages a contemptuous wave, then holding hands, he and Maria vault over the railing of the back porch and disappear.

She's given me beer, plenty of beer, but no church key. I look around the room. Ransome or Bud would have used his teeth. From His perch, Jesus stares at me out of huge, sad, Levantine eyes. In this alien jungle, we're fellow Arabs. You should see what's happened to the old stomping grounds, compadre.

I test my teeth against a moist, corrugated bottle cap. It's no good. I whack the bottle cap with the heel of my hand against the metal edge of the cot. It foams and hisses. The second time it opens. New World skill. Somewhere in the back of the shack, a parakeet begins to squawk. It's a sad, ugly sound. I go out to the back porch to give myself something to do, maybe snoop. By the communal laundry tub there's a cage and inside the cage a mean, molting bird. A kid of ten or twelve teases the bird with bits of lettuce. Its beak snaps open for the greens and scrapes the rusty sides of the bar. The kid looks defective, dull-eyed, thin but flabby.

180 | MIDCAREER STORIES (1985–1988)

"Gringo," he calls out to me. "Gringo, gum."

I check my pockets. No Dentyne, no Tums, just the plastic cover for spent traveler's checks. My life has changed. I don't have to worry about bad breath or gas pains turning off clients.

"Gringo, Chiclets."

The voice is husky.

I turn my palms outward. "Sorry, you're out of luck."

The kid leaps on me with moronic fury. I want to throw him down, toss him in the scummy vat of soaking clothes, but he's probably some sort of sacred mascot. "How about this pen?" It's a forty-nine cent disposable, the perfect thing for poking a bird. I go back inside.

I am sitting in the HQ of the Guerrilla Insurgency, drinking Heineken, nursing my indignation. A one-armed man opens the door. "Maria?" he calls. "*Prego.*" Which translates, indirectly, as "The truck is unloaded and the guns are ready and should I kill this guy?" I direct him to find Andreas.

She wakes me, maybe an hour later. I sleep as I rarely have, arm across my eyes like a bedouin, on top of mounds of boots and gear. She has worked her fingers around my buttons and pulls my hair, my nipples. I can't tell the degree of mockery, what spillover of passion she might still be feeling. Andreas and the idiot boy stand framed in the bleaching light of the door, the boy's huge head pushing the bandolier askew. Father and son, it suddenly dawns. Andreas holds the birdcage.

"They've finished," she explains. "Let's go."

Andreas lets us pass, smirking, I think, and follows us down the rutted trail to Bud's truck. He puts the birdcage in the driver's seat, and in case I miss it, points at the bird, then at me, and laughs. Very funny, I think. His boy finds it hilarious. I will *not* be mocked like this. The bird is so ill-fed, so cramped and tortured and clumsy it flutters wildly, losing more feathers merely to keep its perch.

"*Viva la revolución, eh?* A leetle gift for helping the people."

No, I think, a leetle sign to Clovis Ransome and all the pretenders to Maria's bed that we're just a bunch of scrawny blackbirds and he doesn't care who knows it. I have no feeling for revolution, only for outfitting the participants.

"Why?" I beg on the way back. The road is dark. "You hate your husband, so get a divorce. Why blow up the country?"

Maria smiles. "Clovis has nothing to do with this." She shifts her sandals on the birdcage. The bird is dizzy, flat on its back. Some of them die, just like that.

"Run off with Andreas, then."

"We were going to be married," she says. "Then Gutiérrez came to my school one day and took me away. I was fourteen and he was minister of education. Then Clovis took me away from him. Maybe you should take me away from Clovis. I like you, and you'd like it, too, wouldn't you?"

"Don't be crazy. Try Bud Wilkins."

"Bud Wilkins is, you say, dog meat." She smiles.

"Oh, sure," I say.

I concentrate on the road. I'm no hero, I calculate margins. I could not calculate the cost of a night with Maria, a month with Maria, though for the first time in my life it was a cost I might have borne.

Her voice is matter-of-fact. "Clovis wanted a cut of Bud's action. But Bud refused and that got Clovis mad. Clovis even offered money, but Bud said no way. Clovis pushed me on him, so he took but he still didn't budge. So—"

"You're serious, aren't you? Oh, God."

"Of course I am serious. Now Clovis can fly in his own champagne and baseball games."

She has unbuttoned more of the halter and I feel pressure on my chest, in my mouth, against my slacks, that I have never felt.

———

ALL THE LIGHTS ARE ON in the villa when I lurch Bud's pickup into the parking lot. We can see Clovis T. Ransome, very drunk, slack-postured, trying out wicker chairs on the porch. Maria is carrying the birdcage.

He's settled on the love seat. No preliminaries, no questions. He squints at the cage. "Buying presents for Maria already, Al?" He tries to laugh.

"What's that supposed to mean?" She swings the cage in giant arcs, like a bucket of water.

"Where's Bud?" I ask.

"They jumped him, old buddy. Gang of guerrillas not more'n half a mile down the road. Pumped twenty bullets in him. These are fierce little people, Al. I don't know how I got away." He's watching us for effect.

I suspect it helps when they're in your pay, I think, and you give them Ted Turner caps.

"Al, grab yourself a glass if you want some Scotch. Me, I'm stinking drunk already."

He's noticed Bud's truck now. The emptiness of Bud's truck.

"That's a crazy thing to do," Maria says. "I warned you." She sets the cage down on the patio table. "Bud's no good to anyone, dead or alive. You said it yourself, he's dog meat." She slips onto the love seat beside her husband. I watch her. I can't take my eyes off her. She snakes her strong, long torso until her lips touch the cage's rusted metal. "Kiss me," she coos. "Kiss me, kiss, kiss, sweetheart."

Ransome's eyes are on her, too. "Sweets, who gave you that filthy crow?"

Maria says, "Kiss me, loverboy."

"Sweetie, I asked you who gave you that filthy crow."

I back off to the kitchen. I could use a shot of Scotch. I can feel the damp, Bombay grittiness of the air. The rains will be here, maybe tonight.

When I get back, Ransome is snoring on the love seat. Maria is standing over him, and the birdcage is on his lap. Its door is open and Clovis' fat hand is half inside. The bird pecks, it's raised blood, but Clovis is out for the night.

"Why is it," she asks, "that I don't feel pride when men kill for me?"

But she does, deep down. She wants to believe that Clovis, mad jealous Clovis, has killed for her. I just hate to think of Maria's pretty face when Clovis wakes up and remembers the munitions are gone. It's all a family plot in countries like this; revolutions fought for a schoolgirl in white with blunted toes. I, too, would kill for her.

"Kill it, Alfie, please," she says. "I can't stand it. See, Clovis tried but his hand was too fat."

"I'll free it," I say.

"Don't be a fool—that boy broke its wings. Let it out, and the crabs will kill it."

Around eleven that night I have to carry Ransome up the stairs to the spare bedroom. He's a heavy man. I don't bother with the niceties of getting him out of his blue jeans and into his pajamas. The secrets of Clovis T. Ransome, whatever they are, are safe with me. I abandon him on top of the bedspread in his dusty cowboy boots. Maria won't want him tonight. She's already told me so.

But she isn't waiting for me on the patio. Maybe that's just as well. Tonight love will be hard to handle. The dirty glasses, the booze and soda bottles, the styrofoam-lidded bowl we used for ice cubes are still on the wicker-and-glass coffee table. Eduardo doesn't seem to be around. I bring the glasses into the kitchen. He must have disappeared hours ago. I've never seen the kitchen in this bad a mess. He's not in the villa. His door has swung open, but I can't hear the noises of sleeping servants in the tropics. So, Eduardo has vanished. I accept this as data. I dare not shout for Maria. If it's ever to be, it must be tonight. Tomorrow, I can tell, this cozy little hacienda will come to grief.

Someone should go from room to room and turn out the lights. But not me. I make it fast back to my room.

"You must shut doors quickly behind you in the tropics. Otherwise bugs get in."

THE MIDDLEMAN | *183*

Casually, she is unbuttoning her top, untying the bottom tabs. The cut-offs have to be tugged off, around her hips. There is a rush of passion I have never known, and my fingers tremble as I tug at my belt. She is in my giant bed, propped up, and her breasts keep the sheet from falling.

"Alfie, close the door."

Her long thighs press and squeeze. She tries to hold me, to contain me, and it is a moment I would die to prolong. In a frenzy, I conjugate crabs with toads and the squawking bird, and I hear the low moans of turtles on the beach. It is a moment I fear too much, a woman I fear too much, and I yield. I begin again, immediately, this time concentrating on blankness, on burnt-out objects whirling in space, and she pushes against me murmuring, "No," and pulls away.

Later, she says, "You don't understand hate, Alfie. You don't understand what hate can do." She tells stories; I moan to mount her again. "No," she says, and the stories pour out. Not just the beatings; the humiliations. Loaning her out, dangling her on a leash like a cheetah, then the beatings for what he suspects. It's the power game, I try to tell her. That's how power is played.

SOMETIME AROUND THREE, I wake to a scooter's thin roar. She has not been asleep. The rainy season must have started an hour or two before. It's like steam out there. I kneel on the pillows to look out the small bedroom windows. The parking lot is a mudslide. Uprooted shrubs, snakes, crabs, turtles are washed down to the shore.

Maria, object of my wildest ecstasy, lies inches from me. She doesn't ask what I see. The scooter's lights weave in the rain.

"Andreas," she says. "It's working out."

But it isn't Andreas who forces the door to my room. It is a tall, thin Indian with a calamitous face. The scooter's engine has been shut off, and rain slaps the patio in waves.

"*Americano.*" The Indian spits out the word. "Gringo."

Maria calmly ties her halter tabs, slowly buttons up. She says something rapidly and the Indian steps outside while she finds her cutoffs.

"Quickly," she says, and I reach for my pants. It's already cold.

When the Indian returns, I hear her say "Jew" and "Israel." He seems to lose interest. "*Americano?*" he asks again. "Gringo?"

Two more Indians invade my room. Maria runs out to the hall and I follow to the stairs. I point upward and try out my Spanish. "Gringo is sleeping, drunk."

The revolution has convened outside Clovis' bedroom. Eduardo is there, Andreas, more Indians in Ted Turner caps, the one-armed man from Santa Simona. Andreas opens the door.

"Gringo," he calls softly. "Wake up."

I am surprised, truly astonished, at the recuperative powers of Clovis T. Ransome. Not only does he wake, but he sits, boots on the floor, ignoring the intrusion. His Spanish, the first time I've heard him use it, is excellent, even respectful.

"I believe, sir, you have me at a disadvantage," he says. He scans the intruders, his eyes settling on me. "Button your fly, man," he says to me. He stares at Maria, up and down, his jaw working. He says, "Well, sweets? What now?"

Andreas holds a pistol against his thigh.

"Take her," Ransome says, "You want her? You got her. You want money, you got that, too. Dollars, marks, Swiss francs. Just take her—and him—" he says, pointing to me, "—out of here."

"I will take your dollars, of course."

"Eduardo—" Ransome jerks his head in the direction, perhaps, of a safe. The servant seems to know where it is.

"And I will take her, of course."

"Good riddance."

"But not him. He can rot."

Eduardo and three Indians lug out a metal trunk. They throw away the pillows and start stuffing pillow cases with bundles of dollars, more pure currency than I've ever seen. They stuff the rest inside their shirts. What must it feel like? I wonder.

"Well, *señor* Andreas, you've got the money and the woman. Now what's it to be—a little torture? A little fun with me before the sun comes up? Or what about him—I bet you'd have more fun with him. I don't scream, *señor* Andreas, I warn you now. You can kill me but you can't break me."

I hear the safety clicking off. So does Clovis.

I know I would scream. I know I am no hero. I know none of this is worth suffering for, let alone dying for.

Andreas looks at Maria as though to say, "you decide." She holds out her hand, and Andreas slips the pistol in it. This seems to amuse Clovis Ransome. He stands, presenting an enormous target. "Sweetie—" he starts, and she blasts away and when I open my eyes he is across the bed, sprawled in the far corner of the room.

She stands at the foot of their bed, limp and amused, like a woman disappointed in love. Smoke rises from the gun barrel, her breath condenses in little clouds, and there is a halo of condensation around her hair, her neck, her arms.

When she turns, I feel it could be any of us next. Andreas holds out his hand but she doesn't return the gun. She lines me up, low, genital-level, like Bud Wilkins with a bird, then sweeps around to Andreas, and smiles.

She has made love to me three times tonight. With Andreas today, doubtless more. Never has a truth been burned so deeply in me, what I owe my life to, how simple the rules of survival are. She passes the gun to Andreas who holsters it, and they leave.

In the next few days when I run out of food, I will walk down the muddy road to San Vicente, to the German bar with the pay phone: I'll wear Clovis' Braves cap and I'll salute the Indians. "Turtle eggs," I'll say. "Number One," they'll answer back. Bud's truck has been commandeered. Along with Clovis' finer cars. Someone in the capital will be happy to know about Santa Simona, about Bud, Clovis. There must be something worth trading in the troubles I have seen.

A Wife's Story

IMRE SAYS FORGET IT, but I'm going to write David Mamet. So Patels are hard to sell real estate to. You buy them a beer, whisper Glengarry Glen Ross, and they smell swamp instead of sun and surf. They work hard, eat cheap, live ten to a room, stash their savings under futons in Queens, and before you know it they own half of Hoboken. You say, where's the sweet gullibility that made this nation great?

Polish jokes, Patel jokes: that's not why I want to write Mamet.

Seen their women?

Everybody laughs. Imre laughs. The dozing fat man with the Barnes & Noble sack between his legs, the woman next to him, the usher, everybody. The theater isn't so dark that they can't see me. In my red silk sari I'm conspicuous. Plump, gold paisleys sparkle on my chest.

The actor is just warming up. *Seen their women?* He plays a salesman, he's had a bad day and now he's in a Chinese restaurant trying to loosen up. His face is pink. His wool-blend slacks are creased at the crotch. We bought our tickets at half-price, we're sitting in the front row, but at the edge, and we see things we shouldn't be seeing. At least I do, or think I do. Spittle, actors goosing each other, little winks, streaks of makeup.

Maybe they're improvising dialogue, too. Maybe Mamet's provided them with insult kits, Thursdays for Chinese, Wednesdays for Hispanics, today for Indians. Maybe they get together before curtain time, see an Indian woman settling in the front row off to the side, and say to each other: "Hey, forget Friday. Let's get *her* today. See if she cries. See if she walks out."

Maybe I shouldn't feel betrayed.

Their women, he goes again. *They look like they've just been fucked by a dead cat.*

The fat man hoots so hard he nudges my elbow off our shared armrest.

"Imre. I'm going home." But Imre's hunched so far forward he doesn't hear. English isn't his best language. A refugee from Budapest, he has to listen hard. "I didn't pay eighteen dollars to be insulted."

I don't hate Mamet. It's the tyranny of the American dream that scares me. First, you don't exist. Then you're invisible. Then you're funny. Then you're disgusting. Insult, my American friends will tell me, is a kind of acceptance. No instant dignity here. A play like this, back home, would cause riots. Communal, racist, and antisocial. The actors wouldn't make it off stage. This play, and all these awful feelings, would be safely locked up.

I long, at times, for clear-cut answers. Offer me instant dignity, today, and I'll take it.

"What?" Imre moves toward me without taking his eyes off the actor. "Come again?"

Tears come. I want to stand, scream, make an awful scene. I long for ugly, nasty rage.

The actor is ranting, flinging spittle. *Give me a chance. I'm not finished, I can get back on the board. I tell that asshole, give me a real lead. And what does that asshole give me? Patels. Nothing but Patels.*

This time Imre works an arm around my shoulders. "Panna, what is Patel? Why are you taking it all so personally?"

I shrink from his touch, but I don't walk out. Expensive girls' schools in Lausanne and Bombay have trained me to behave well. My manners are exquisite, my feelings are delicate, my gestures refined, my moods undetectable. They have seen me through riots, uprootings, separation, my son's death.

"I'm not taking it personally."

The fat man looks at us. The woman looks, too, and shushes.

I stare back at the two of them. Then I stare, mean and cool, at the man's elbow. Under the bright blue polyester Hawaiian shirt sleeve, the elbow looks soft and runny. "Excuse me," I say. My voice has the effortless meanness of well-bred displaced Third World women, though my rhetoric has been learned elsewhere. "You're exploiting my space."

Startled, the man snatches his arm away from me. He cradles it against his breast. By the time he's ready with comebacks, I've turned my back on him. I've probably ruined the first act for him. I know I've ruined it for Imre.

It's not my fault; it's the *situation*. Old colonies wear down. Patels—the new pioneers—have to be suspicious. Idi Amin's lesson is permanent. AT&T wires move good advice from continent to continent. Keep all assets liquid. Get into 7-Elevens, get out of condos and motels. I know how both sides feel, that's the trouble. The Patels sniffing out scams, the sad salesmen on the stage: postcolonialism has made me their referee. It's hate I long for; simple, brutish, partisan hate.

After the show Imre and I make our way toward Broadway. Sometimes he holds my hand; it doesn't mean anything more than that crazies and drunks are crouched in doorways. Imre's been here over two years, but he's stayed very old-world, very courtly, openly protective of women. I met him in a seminar on special ed. last semester. His wife is a nurse somewhere in the Hungarian countryside. There are two sons, and miles of petitions for their emigration. My husband manages a mill two hundred miles north of Bombay. There are no children.

"You make things tough on yourself," Imre says. He assumed Patel was a Jewish name or maybe Hispanic; everything makes equal sense to him. He found the play tasteless, he worried about the effect of vulgar language on my sensitive ears. "You have to let go a bit." And as though to show me how to let go, he breaks away from me, bounds ahead with his head ducked tight, then dances on amazingly jerky legs. He's a Magyar, he often tells me, and deep down, he's an Asian, too. I catch glimpses of it, knife-blade Attila cheekbones, despite the blondish hair. In his faded jeans and leather jacket, he's a rock video star. I watch MTV for hours in the apartment when Charity's working the evening shift at Macy's. I listen to WPLJ on Charity's earphones. Why should I be ashamed? Television in India is so uplifting.

Imre stops as suddenly as he'd started. People walk around us. The summer sidewalk is full of theatergoers in seersucker suits; Imre's year-round jacket is out of place. European. Cops in twos and threes huddle, lightly tap their thighs with night sticks and smile at me with benevolence. I want to wink at them, get us all in trouble, tell them the crazy dancing man is from the Warsaw Pact. I'm too shy to break into dance on Broadway. So I hug Imre instead.

The hug takes him by surprise. He wants to let me go, but he doesn't really expect me to let go. He staggers, though I weigh no more than 104 pounds, and with him, I pitch forward slightly. Then he catches me, and we walk arm in arm to the bus stop. My husband would never dance or hug a woman on Broadway. Nor would my brothers. They aren't stuffy people, but they went to Anglican boarding schools and they have a well-developed sense of what's silly.

"Imre." I squeeze his big, rough hand. "I'm sorry I ruined the evening for you."

188 | MIDCAREER STORIES (1985–1988)

"You did nothing of the kind." He sounds tired. "Let's not wait for the bus. Let's splurge and take a cab instead."

Imre always has unexpected funds. The Network, he calls it, Class of '56.

In the back of the cab, without even trying, I feel light, almost free. Memories of Indian destitutes mix with the hordes of New York street people, and they float free, like astronauts, inside my head. I've made it. I'm making something of my life. I've left home, my husband, to get a Ph.D. in special ed. I have a multiple-entry visa and a small scholarship for two years. After that, we'll see. My mother was beaten by her mother-in-law, my grandmother, when she'd registered for French lessons at the Alliance Française. My grandmother, the eldest daughter of a rich zamindar,[1] was illiterate.

Imre and the cabdriver talk away in Russian. I keep my eyes closed. That way I can feel the floaters better. I'll write Mamet tonight. I feel strong, reckless. Maybe I'll write Steven Spielberg, too; tell him that Indians don't eat monkey brains.

We've made it. Patels must have made it. Mamet, Spielberg: they're not condescending to us. Maybe they're a little afraid.

———

CHARITY CHIN, my roommate, is sitting on the floor drinking Chablis out of a plastic wineglass. She is five foot six, three inches taller than me, but weighs a kilo and a half less than I do. She is a "hands" model. Orientals are supposed to have a monopoly in the hands-modeling business, she says. She had her eyes fixed eight or nine months ago and out of gratitude sleeps with her plastic surgeon every third Wednesday.

"Oh, good," Charity says. "I'm glad you're back early. I need to talk."

She's been writing checks. MCI, Con Ed, Bonwit Teller. Envelopes, already stamped and sealed, form a pyramid between her shapely, knee-socked legs. The checkbook's cover is brown plastic, grained to look like cowhide. Each time Charity flips back the cover, white geese fly over sky-colored checks. She makes good money, but she's extravagant. The difference adds up to this shared, rent-controlled Chelsea one-bedroom.

"All right. Talk."

When I first moved in, she was seeing an analyst. Now she sees a nutritionist.

"Eric called. From Oregon."

"What did he want?"

---

1. Historical word for an Indian landowner.—Ed.

"He wants me to pay half the rent on his loft for last spring. He asked me to move back, remember? He *begged* me."

Eric is Charity's estranged husband.

"What does your nutritionist say?" Eric now wears a red jumpsuit and tills the soil in Rajneeshpuram.

"You think Phil's a creep, too, don't you? What else can he be when creeps are all I attract?"

Phil is a flutist with thinning hair. He's very touchy on the subject of *flautists* versus *flutists*. He's touchy on every subject, from music to books to foods to clothes. He teaches at a small college upstate, and Charity bought a used blue Datsun ("Nissan," Phil insists) last month so she could spend weekends with him. She returns every Sunday night, exhausted and exasperated. Phil and I don't have much to say to each other—he's the only musician I know; the men in my family are lawyers, engineers, or in business—but I like him. Around me, he loosens up. When he visits, he bakes us loaves of pumpernickel bread. He waxes our kitchen floor. Like many men in this country, he seems to me a displaced child, or even a woman, looking for something that passed him by, or for something that he can never have. If he thinks I'm not looking, he sneaks his hands under Charity's sweater, but there isn't too much there. Here, she's a model with high ambitions. In India, she'd be a flat-chested old maid.

I'm shy in front of the lovers. A darkness comes over me when I see them horsing around.

"It isn't the money," Charity says. Oh? I think. "He says he still loves me. Then he turns around and asks me for five hundred."

What's so strange about that, I want to ask. She still loves Eric, and Eric, red jumpsuit and all, is smart enough to know it. Love is a commodity, hoarded like any other. Mamet knows. But I say, "I'm not the person to ask about love." Charity knows that mine was a traditional Hindu marriage. My parents, with the help of a marriage broker, who was my mother's cousin, picked out a groom. All I had to do was get to know his taste in food.

It'll be a long evening, I'm afraid. Charity likes to confess. I unpleat my silk sari—it no longer looks too showy—wrap it in muslin cloth and put it away in a dresser drawer. Saris are hard to have laundered in Manhattan, though there's a good man in Jackson Heights. My next step will be to brew us a pot of chrysanthemum tea. It's a very special tea from the mainland. Charity's uncle gave it to us. I like him. He's a humpbacked, awkward, terrified man. He runs a gift store on Mott Street, and though he doesn't speak much English, he seems to have done well. Once upon a time he worked for the railways in Chengdu, Szechwan Province, and during the Wuchang Uprising, he was shot at. When

I'm down, when I'm lonely for my husband, when I think of our son, or when I need to be held, I think of Charity's uncle. If I hadn't left home, I'd never have heard of the Wuchang Uprising. I've broadened my horizons.

***

VERY LATE that night my husband calls me from Ahmadabad, a town of textile mills north of Bombay. My husband is a vice president at Lakshmi Cotton Mills. Lakshmi is the goddess of wealth, but LCM (Priv.), Ltd., is doing poorly. Lockouts, strikes, rock-throwings. My husband lives on digitalis, which he calls the food for our *yuga*[2] of discontent.

"We had a bad mishap at the mill today." Then he says nothing for seconds.

The operator comes on. "Do you have the right party, sir? We're trying to reach Mrs. Butt."

"Bhatt," I insist. "*B* for Bombay, *H* for Haryana, *A* for Ahmadabad, double *T* for Tamil Nadu." It's a litany. "This is she."

"One of our lorries was firebombed today. Resulting in three deaths. The driver, old Karamchand, and his two children."

I know how my husband's eyes look this minute, how the eye rims sag and the yellow corneas shine and bulge with pain. He is not an emotional man— the Ahmadabad Institute of Management has trained him to cut losses, to look on the bright side of economic catastrophes—but tonight he's feeling low. I try to remember a driver named Karamchand, but can't. That part of my life is over, the way *trucks* have replaced *lorries* in my vocabulary, the way Charity Chin and her lurid love life have replaced inherited notions of marital duty. Tomorrow he'll come out of it. Soon he'll be eating again. He'll sleep like a baby. He's been trained to believe in turnovers. Every morning he rubs his scalp with cantharidine oil so his hair will grow back again.

"It could be your car next." Affection, love. Who can tell the difference in a traditional marriage in which a wife still doesn't call her husband by his first name?

"No. They know I'm a flunky, just like them. Well paid, maybe. No need for undue anxiety, please."

Then his voice breaks. He says he needs me, he misses me, he wants me to come to him damp from my evening shower, smelling of sandalwood soap, my braid decorated with jasmines.

"I need you, too."

"Not to worry, please," he says. "I am coming in a fortnight's time. I have already made arrangements."

---

2. In Hinduism, a term used to mean an age of time.—Ed.

Outside my window, fire trucks whine, up Eighth Avenue. I wonder if he can hear them, what he thinks of a life like mine, led amid disorder.

"I am thinking it'll be like a honeymoon. More or less."

When I was in college, waiting to be married, I imagined honeymoons were only for the more fashionable girls, the girls who came from slightly racy families, smoked Sobranies in the dorm lavatories and put up posters of Kabir Bedi, who was supposed to have made it as a big star in the West. My husband wants us to go to Niagara. I'm not to worry about foreign exchange. He's arranged for extra dollars through the Gujarati Network, with a cousin in San Jose. And he's bought four hundred more on the black market. "Tell me you need me. Panna, please tell me again."

———

I CHANGE OUT of the cotton pants and shirt I've been wearing all day and put on a sari to meet my husband at JFK. I don't forget the jewelry; the marriage necklace of *mangalsutra*, gold drop earrings, heavy gold bangles. I don't wear them every day. In this borough of vice and greed, who knows when, or whom, desire will overwhelm.

My husband spots me in the crowd and waves. He has lost weight, and changed his glasses. The arm, uplifted in a cheery wave, is bony, frail, almost opalescent.

In the Carey Coach,[3] we hold hands. He strokes the fingers one by one. "How come you aren't wearing my mother's ring?"

"Because muggers know about Indian women," I say. They know with us it's 24-karat. His mother's ring is showy, in ghastly taste anywhere but India: a blood-red Burma ruby set in a gold frame of floral sprays. My mother-in-law got her guru to bless the ring before I left for the States.

He looks disconcerted. He's used to a different role. He's the knowing, suspicious one in the family. He seems to be sulking, and finally he comes out with it. "You've said nothing about my new glasses." I compliment him on the glasses, how chic and Western-executive they make him look. But I can't help the other things, necessities until he learns the ropes. I handle the money, buy the tickets. I don't know if this makes me unhappy.

———

CHARITY DRIVES her Nissan upstate, so for two weeks we are to have the apartment to ourselves. This is more privacy than we ever had in India. No parents, no servants, to keep us modest. We play at housekeeping. Imre has lent us a

---

3. Carey is a global executive transport firm.—Ed.

hibachi, and I grill saffron chicken breasts. My husband marvels at the size of the Perdue hens. "They're big like peacocks, no? These Americans, they're really something!" He tries out pizzas, burgers, McNuggets. He chews. He explores. He judges. He loves it all, fears nothing, feels at home in the summer odors, the clutter of Manhattan streets. Since he thinks that the American palate is bland, he carries a bottle of red peppers in his pocket. I wheel a shopping cart down the aisles of the neighborhood Grand Union, and he follows, swiftly, greedily. He picks up hair rinses and high-protein diet powders. There's so much I already take for granted.

One night, Imre stops by. He wants us to go with him to a movie. In his work shirt and red leather tie, he looks arty or strung out. It's only been a week, but I feel as though I am really seeing him for the first time. The yellow hair worn very short at the sides, the wide, narrow lips. He's a good-looking man, but self-conscious, almost arrogant. He's picked the movie we should see. He always tells me what to see, what to read. He buys the *Voice*. He's a natural avant-gardist. For tonight he's chosen *Numéro Deux*.

"Is it a musical?" my husband asks. The Radio City Music Hall is on his list of sights to see. He's read up on the history of the Rockettes. He doesn't catch Imre's sympathetic wink. Guilt, shame, loyalty. I long to be ungracious, not ingratiate myself with both men.

That night my husband calculates in rupees the money we've wasted on Godard. "That refugee fellow, Nagy, must have a screw loose in his head. I paid very steep price for dollars on the black market."

Some afternoons we go shopping. Back home we hated shopping, but now it is a lovers' project. My husband's shopping list startles me. I feel I am just getting to know him. Maybe, like Imre, freed from the dignities of old-world culture, he, too, could get drunk and squirt Cheez Whiz on a guest. I watch him dart into stores in his gleaming leather shoes. Jockey shorts on sale in outdoor bins on Broadway entrance him. White tube socks with different bands of color delight him. He looks for microcassettes, for anything small and electronic and smuggleable. He needs a garment bag. He calls it a "wardrobe," and I have to translate.

"All of New York is having sales, no?"

My heart speeds watching him this happy. It's the third week in August, almost the end of summer, and the city smells ripe, it cannot bear more heat, more money, more energy.

"This is so smashing! The prices are so excellent!" Recklessly, my prudent husband signs away traveler's checks. How he intends to smuggle it all back I don't dare ask. With a microwave, he calculates, we could get rid of our cook.

This has to be love, I think. Charity, Eric, Phil: they may be experts on sex. My husband doesn't chase me around the sofa, but he pushes me down on Charity's battered cushions, and the man who has never entered the kitchen of our Ahmadabad house now comes toward me with a dish tub of steamy water to massage away the pavement heat.

TEN DAYS INTO HIS VACATION my husband checks out brochures for sightseeing tours. Shortline, Grayline, Crossroads: his new vinyl briefcase is full of schedules and pamphlets. While I make pancakes out of a mix, he comparison-shops. Tour number one costs $10.95 and will give us the World Trade Center, Chinatown, and the United Nations. Tour number three would take us both uptown *and* downtown for $14.95, but my husband is absolutely sure he doesn't want to see Harlem. We settle for tour number four: Downtown and the Dame. It's offered by a new tour company with a small, dirty office at Eighth and Forty-eighth.

The sidewalk outside the office is colorful with tourists. My husband sends me in to buy the tickets because he has come to feel Americans don't understand his accent.

The dark man, Lebanese probably, behind the counter comes on too friendly. "Come on, doll, make my day!" He won't say which tour is his. "Number four? Honey, no! Look, you've wrecked me! Say you'll change your mind." He takes two twenties and gives back change. He holds the tickets, forcing me to pull. He leans closer. "I'm off after lunch."

My husband must have been watching me from the sidewalk. "What was the chap saying?" he demands. "I told you not to wear pants. He thinks you are Puerto Rican. He thinks he can treat you with disrespect."

This bus is crowded and we have to sit across the aisle from each other. The tour guide begins his patter on Forty-sixth. He looks like an actor, his hair bleached and blow-dried. Up close he must look middle-aged, but from where I sit his skin is smooth and his cheeks faintly red.

"Welcome to the Big Apple, folks." The guide uses a microphone. "Big Apple. That's what we native Manhattan degenerates call our city. Today we have guests from fifteen foreign countries and six states from this U.S. of A. That makes the Tourist Bureau real happy. And let me assure you that while we may be the richest city in the richest country in the world, it's okay to tip your charming and talented attendant." He laughs. Then he swings his hip out into the aisle and sings a song.

"And it's mighty fancy on old Delancey Street, you know . . ."

My husband looks irritable. The guide is, as expected, a good singer. "The bloody man should be giving us histories of buildings we are passing, no?" I pat his hand, the mood passes. He cranes his neck. Our window seats have both gone to Japanese. It's the tour of his life. Next to this, the quick business trips to Manchester and Glasgow pale.

"And tell me what street compares to Mott Street, in July . . ."

The guide wants applause. He manages a derisive laugh from the Americans up front. He's working the aisles now. "I coulda been somebody, right? I coulda been a star!" Two or three of us smile, those of us who recognize the parody. He catches my smile. The sun is on his harsh, bleached hair. "Right, your highness? Look, we gotta maharani with us! Couldn't I have been a star?"

"Right!" I say, my voice coming out a squeal. I've been trained to adapt; what else can I say?

We drive through traffic past landmark office buildings and churches. The guide flips his hands. "Art deco," he keeps saying. I hear him confide to one of the Americans: "Beats me. I went to a cheap guide's school." My husband wants to know more about this art deco, but the guide sings another song.

"We made a foolish choice," my husband grumbles. "We are sitting in the bus only. We're not going into famous buildings." He scrutinizes the pamphlets in his jacket pocket. I think, at least it's air-conditioned in here. I could sit here in the cool shadows of the city forever.

ONLY FIVE OF US appear to have opted for the "Downtown and the Dame" tour. The others will ride back uptown past the United Nations after we've been dropped off at the pier for the ferry to the Statue of Liberty.

An elderly European pulls a camera out of his wife's designer tote bag. He takes pictures of the boats in the harbor, the Japanese in kimonos eating popcorn, scavenging pigeons, me. Then, pushing his wife ahead of him, he climbs back on the bus and waves to us. For a second I feel terribly lost. I wish we were on the bus going back to the apartment. I know I'll not be able to describe any of this to Charity, or to Imre. I'm too proud to admit I went on a guided tour.

The view of the city from the Circle Line ferry is seductive, unreal. The skyline wavers out of reach, but never quite vanishes. The summer sun pushes through fluffy clouds and dapples the glass of office towers. My husband looks thrilled, even more than he had on the shopping trips down Broadway. Tourists and dreamers, we have spent our life's savings to see this skyline, this statue.

"Quick, take a picture of me!" my husband yells as he moves toward a gap of railings. A Japanese matron has given up her position in order to change film. "Before the Twin Towers disappear!"

I focus, I wait for a large Oriental family to walk out of my range. My husband holds his pose tight against the railing. He wants to look relaxed, an international businessman at home in all the financial markets.

A bearded man slides across the bench toward me. "Like this," he says and helps me get my husband in focus. "You want me to take the photo for you?" His name, he says, is Goran. He is Goran from Yugoslavia, as though that were enough for tracking him down. Imre from Hungary. Panna from India. He pulls the old Leica out of my hand, signaling the Orientals to beat it, and clicks away. "I'm a photographer," he says. He could have been a camera thief. That's what my husband would have assumed. Somehow, I trusted. "Get you a beer?" he asks.

"I don't. Drink, I mean. Thank you very much." I say those last words very loud, for everyone's benefit. The odd bottles of Soave with Imre don't count.

"Too bad." Goran gives back the camera.

"Take one more!" my husband shouts from the railing. "Just to be sure!"

THE ISLAND ITSELF DISAPPOINTS. The Lady has brutal scaffolding holding her in. The museum is closed. The snack bar is dirty and expensive. My husband reads out the prices to me. He orders two french fries and two Cokes. We sit at picnic tables and wait for the ferry to take us back.

"What was that hippie chap saying?"

As if I could say. A day-care center has brought its kids, at least forty of them, to the island for the day. The kids, all wearing name tags, run around us. I can't help noticing how many are Indian. Even a Patel, probably a Bhatt if I looked hard enough. They toss hamburger bits at pigeons. They kick styrofoam cups. The pigeons are slow, greedy, persistent. I have to shoo one off the table top. I don't think my husband thinks about our son.

"What hippie?"

"The one on the boat. With the beard and the hair."

My husband doesn't look at me. He shakes out his paper napkin and tries to protect his french fries from pigeon feathers.

"Oh, him. He said he was from Dubrovnik." It isn't true, but I don't want trouble.

"What did he say about Dubrovnik?"

I know enough about Dubrovnik to get by. Imre's told me about it. And about Mostar and Zagreb. In Mostar white Muslims sing the call to prayer.

I would like to see that before I die: white Muslims. Whole peoples have moved before me; they've adapted. The night Imre told me about Mostar was also the night I saw my first snow in Manhattan. We'd walked down to Chelsea from Columbia. We'd walked and talked and I hadn't felt tired at all.

"You're too innocent," my husband says. He reaches for my hand. "Panna," he cries with pain in his voice, and I am brought back from perfect, floating memories of snow, "I've come to take you back. I have seen how men watch you."

"What?"

"Come back, now. I have tickets. We have all the things we will ever need. I can't live without you."

A little girl with wiry braids kicks a bottle cap at his shoes. The pigeons wheel and scuttle around us. My husband covers his fries with spread-out fingers. "No kicking," he tells the girl. Her name, Beulah, is printed in green ink on a heart-shaped name tag. He forces a smile, and Beulah smiles back. Then she starts to flap her arms. She flaps, she hops. The pigeons go crazy for fries and scraps.

"Special ed. course is two years," I remind him. "I can't go back."

My husband picks up our trays and throws them into the garbage before I can stop him. He's carried disposability a little too far. "We've been taken," he says, moving toward the dock, though the ferry will not arrive for another twenty minutes. "The ferry costs only two dollars round-trip per person. We should have chosen tour number one for $10.95 instead of tour number four for $14.95."

With my Lebanese friend, I think. "But this way we don't have to worry about cabs. The bus will pick us up at the pier and take us back to midtown. Then we can walk home."

"New York is full of cheats and whatnot. Just like Bombay." He is not accusing me of infidelity. I feel dread all the same.

THAT NIGHT, after we've gone to bed, the phone rings. My husband listens, then hands the phone to me. "What is this woman saying?" He turns on the pink Macy's lamp by the bed. "I am not understanding these Negro people's accents."

The operator repeats the message. It's a cable from one of the directors of Lakshmi Cotton Mills. "Massive violent labor confrontation anticipated. Stop. Return posthaste. Stop. Cable flight details. Signed Kantilal Shah."

"It's not your factory," I say. "You're supposed to be on vacation."

"So, you are worrying about me? Yes? You reject my heartfelt wishes but you worry about me?" He pulls me close, slips the straps of my nightdress off my shoulder. "Wait a minute."

I wait, unclothed, for my husband to come back to me. The water is running in the bathroom. In the ten days he has been here he has learned American rites: deodorants, fragrances. Tomorrow morning he'll call Air India; tomorrow evening he'll be on his way back to Bombay. Tonight I should make up to him for my years away, the gutted trucks, the degree I'll never use in India. I want to pretend with him that nothing has changed.

In the mirror that hangs on the bathroom door, I watch my naked body turn, the breasts, the thighs glow. The body's beauty amazes. I stand here shameless, in ways he has never seen me. I am free, afloat, watching somebody else.

Loose Ends

SHE SENDS FOR THIS Goldilocks doll in April.

"See," she says. The magazine is pressed tight to her T-shirt. "It's porcelain."

I look. The ad calls Goldilocks "the first doll in an enchanting new suite of fairy tale dolls."

"*Bisque* porcelain," she says. She fills out the order form in purple ink. "Look at the pompoms on her shoes. Aren't they darling?"

"You want to blow sixty bucks?" Okay, so I yell that at Jonda. "You have any idea how much I got to work for sixty dollars?"

"Only twenty now," she says. Then she starts bitching. "What's with you and Velásquez these days? You shouldn't even be home in the afternoon."

It's between one and two and I have a right, don't I, to be in my Manufactured Home—as they call it—in LagunaVista Estates instead of in Mr. Vee's pastel office in the mall? A man's mobile home is his castle, at least in Florida. But I fix her her bourbon and ginger ale with the dash of ReaLemon just the way she likes it. She isn't a mail-order junky; this Goldilocks thing is more complicated.

"It makes me nervous," Jonda goes on. "To have you home, I mean."

I haven't been fired by Mr. Vee; the truth is I've been offered a raise, contingent, of course, on my delivering a forceful message to that greaser goon, Chavez. I don't get into that with Jonda. Jonda doesn't have much of a head for details.

"Learn to like it," I say. "Your boyfriend better learn, too."

She doesn't have anyone but me, but she seems to like the jealousy bit. Her face goes soft and dreamy like the old days. We've seen a lot together.

"Jonda," I start. I just don't get it. What does she want?

"Forget it, Jeb." She licks the stamp on the Goldilocks envelope so gooey it sticks on crooked. "There's no point in us talking. We don't communicate anymore."

I make myself a cocktail. Milk, two ice cubes crushed with a hammer between two squares of paper towel, and Maalox. Got the recipe from a Nam-Vets magazine.

"Look at you." She turns on the TV and gets in bed. "I hate to see you like this, at loose ends."

I get in bed with her. Usually afternoons are pure dynamite, when I can get them. I lie down with her for a while, but nothing happens. We're like that until Oprah comes on.

"It's okay," Jonda says. "I'm going to the mall. The guy who opened the new boutique, you know, the little guy with the turban, he said he might be hiring."

I drop a whole ice cube into my Maalox cocktail and watch her change. She shimmies out of khaki shorts—mementoes of my glory days—and pulls a flowery skirt over her head. I still don't feel any urge.

"Who let these guys in?" I say. She doesn't answer. He won't hire her— they come in with half a dozen kids and pay them nothing. We're coolie labor in our own country.

She pretends to look for her car keys which are hanging as usual from their nail. "Don't wait up for me."

"At least let me drive you." I'm not begging, yet.

"No, it's okay." She fixes her wickedly green eyes on me. And suddenly bile pours out in torrents. "Nine years, for God's sake! Nine years, and what do we have?"

"Don't let's get started."

Hey, what we have sounds like the Constitution of the United States. We have freedom and no strings attached. We have no debts. We come and go as we like. She wants a kid but I don't think I have the makings of a good father. That's part of what the Goldilocks thing is.

But I know what she means. By the time Goldilocks arrives in the mail, she'll have moved her stuff out of LagunaVista Estates.

I like Miami. I like the heat. You can smell the fecund rot of the jungle in every headline. You can park your car in the shopping mall and watch the dope change hands, the Goldilockses and Peter Pans go off with new daddies, the dishwashers and short-order cooks haggle over fake passports, the Mr. Vees in limos huddle over arms-shopping lists, all the while gull guano drops on your car with the soothing steadiness of rain.

Don't get me wrong. I liked the green spaces of Nam, too. In spite of the consequences. I was the Pit Bull—even the Marines backed off. I was Jesse James hunched tight in the gunship, trolling the jungle for hidden wonders.

"If you want to stay alive," Doc Healy cautioned me the first day, "just keep consuming and moving like a locust. Do that, Jeb m'boy, and you'll survive to die a natural death." Last winter a judge put a vet away for thirty-five years for sinking his teeth into sweet, succulent coed flesh. The judge said, *when gangrene sets in, the doctor has no choice but to amputate.* But I'm here to testify, Your Honor, the appetite remains, after the easy targets have all been eaten. The whirring of our locust jaws is what keeps you awake.

I TAKE CARE of Chavez for Mr. Vee and come home to stale tangled sheets. Jonda's been gone nine days.

I'm not whining. Last night in the parking lot of the mall a swami with blond dreadlocks treated us to a levitation. We spied him on the roof of a discount clothing store, nudging his flying mat into liftoff position. We were the usual tourists and weirdos and murderous cubanos. First he played his sinuses OM-OOM-OOMPAH-OOM, then he pushed off from the roof in the lotus position. His bare feet sprouted like orchids from his knees. We watched him wheel and flutter for maybe two or three minutes before the cops pulled up and caught him in a safety net.

They took him away in handcuffs. Who knows how many killers and felons and honest nut cases watched it and politely went back to their cars? I love Miami.

THIS MORNING I lean on Mr. Vee's doorbell. I need money. Auguste, the bouncer he picked up in the back streets of Montreal, squeezes my windbreaker before letting me in.

I suck in my gut and make the palm trees on my shirt ripple. "You're blonder than you were. Blond's definitely your color."

"Don't start with me, Marshall," he says. He helps himself to a mint from a fancy glass bowl on the coffee table.

Mr. Vee sidles into the room; he's one hundred and seventy-five pounds of jiggling paranoia.

"You look like hell, Marshall," is the first thing he says.

"I could say the same to you, Haysoos," I say.

His face turns mean. I scoop up a mint and flip it like a quarter.

"The last job caused me some embarrassment," he says.

My job, I try to remind him, is to show up at a time and place of his choosing and perform a simple operation. I'm the gunship Mr. Vee calls in. He pinpoints the target, I attempt to neutralize it. It's all a matter of instrumentation and precise coordinates. With more surveillance, a longer lead time, a neutral setting, mishaps can be minimized. But not on the money Mr. Vee pays. He's itchy and impulsive; he wants a quick hit, publicity, and some sort of ego boost. I served under second looies just like him, and sooner or later most of them got blown away, after losing half their men.

The story was, Chavez had been sampling too much of Mr. Vee's product line. He was, as a result, inoperative with women. He lived in a little green house in a postwar development on the fringes of Liberty City, a step up, in some minds, from a trailer park. By all indications, he should have been alone. I get a little sick when wives and kids are involved, old folks, neighbors, repairmen—I'm not a monster, except when I'm being careful.

I gained entry through a window—thank God for cheap air conditioners. First surprise: he wasn't alone. I could hear that drug-deep double-breathing. Even in the dark before I open a door, I can tell a woman from a man, middle age from adolescence, a sleeping Cuban from a sleeping American. They were entwined; it looked like at long last love for poor old Chavez. She might have been fourteen, brassy-haired with wide black roots, baby-fat-bodied with a pinched, Appalachian face. I did what I was paid for; I eliminated the primary target and left no traces. Doc Healy used to teach us: torch the whole hut and make sure you get the kids, the grannies, cringing on the sleeping mat—or else you'll meet them on the trail with fire in their eyes.

Truth be told, I was never much of a marksman. My game is getting close, working the body, where accuracy doesn't count for much. We're the guys who survived that war.

The carnage at Chavez's cost me, too. You get a reputation, especially if young women are involved. You don't look so good anymore to sweatier clients.

I lean over and flick an imaginary fruit fly off Haysoos Velásquez's shiny lapel. Auguste twitches.

"What did you do that for?" he shrieks.

"I could get you deported real easy." I smile. I want him to know that for all his flash and jangle and elocution lessons so he won't go around like an underworld Ricky Ricardo, to me he's just another boat person. "You got something good for me today?"

A laugh leaks out of him. "You're so burned out, Marshall, you couldn't fuck a whore." He extracts limp bills from a safe. Two thousand to blow town for a while, till it cools.

"*Gracias, amigo.*" At least this month the trailer's safe, if not the car. Which leaves me free to hotwire a newer model.

WHERE DID AMERICA GO? I want to know. Down the rabbit hole, Doc Healy used to say. Alice knows, but she took it with her. Hard to know which one's the Wonderland. Back when me and my buddies were barricading the front door, who left the back door open?

And just look at what Alice left behind.

She left behind a pastel house, lime-sherbet color, a little south and a little west of Miami, with sprinklers batting water across a yard the size of a badminton court. In the back bedroom there's a dripping old air conditioner. The window barely closes over it. It's an old development, they don't have outside security, wire fences, patrol dogs. It's a retirement bungalow like they used to advertise in the comic pages of the Sunday papers. No one around in those days to warn the old folks that the lots hadn't quite surfaced from the slime, and the soil was too salty to take a planting. And twenty years later there'd still be that odor—gamey, fishy, sour rot—of a tropical city on unrinsed water, where the blue air shimmers with diesel fumes and the gray water thickens like syrup from saturated waste.

Chavez, stewing in his juices.

And when your mammy and pappy die off and it's time to sell off the lime-sherbet bungalow, who's there to buy it? A nice big friendly greaser like Mr. Chavez.

Twenty years ago I missed the meaning of things around me. I was seventeen years old, in Heidelberg, Germany, about to be shipped out to Vietnam. We had guys on the base selling passages to Sweden. And I had a weekend pass and a free flight to London. Held them in my hand: Sweden forever, or a weekend pass. Wise up, kid, choose life, whispered the cook, a twenty-year lifer with a quarter million stashed in Arizona. Seventeen years old and guys are offering me life or death, only I didn't see it then.

When you're a teenage buckaroo from Ocala, Florida, in London for the first time, where do you go? I went to London Zoo. Okay, so I was a kid checking out the snakes and gators of my childhood. You learn to love a languid, ugly target.

I found myself in front of the reticulated python. This was one huge serpent. It squeezed out jaguars and crocodiles like dishrags. It was twenty-eight feet long and as thick as my waist, with a snout as long and wide as a croc's. The *scale* of the thing was beyond impressive, beyond incredible. If you ever want to feel helpless or see what the odds look like when they're stacked against you, imagine the embrace of the reticulated python. The tip of its tail at the far end of the concrete pool could have been in a different county. Its head was out of water, resting on the tub's front edge. The head is what got me, that broad, patient, intelligent face, those eyes brown and passionless as all of Vietnam.

Dead rabbits were plowed in a corner. I felt nothing for the bunnies.

Then I noticed the snakeshit. Python turds, dozens of turds, light as cork and thick as a tree, riding high in the water. Once you'd seen them, you couldn't help thinking you'd smelled them all along. *That's* what I mean about Florida, about all the hot-water ports like Bangkok, Manila and Bombay, living on water where the shit's so thick it's a kind of cash crop.

Behind me, one of those frosty British matrons whispered to her husband, "I didn't know they *did* such things!"

"Believe it, Queenie," I said.

That snakeshit—all that coiled power—stays with me, always. That's what happened to us in the paddyfields. We drowned in our shit. An inscrutable humanoid python sleeping on a bed of turds: that's what I never want to be.

So I keep two things in mind nowadays. First, Florida was built for your pappy and grammie. I remember them, I was a kid here, I remember the good Florida when only the pioneers came down and it was considered too hot and wet and buggy to ever come to much. I knew your pappy and grammie, I mowed their lawn, trimmed their hedges, washed their cars. I toted their golf bags. Nice people—they deserved a few years of golf, a garden to show off when their kids came down to visit, a white car that justified its extravagant air conditioning and never seemed to get dirty. That's the first thing about Florida; the nice thing. The second is this: Florida is run by locusts and behind them are sharks and even pythons and they've pretty well chewed up your mom and pop and all the other lawn bowlers and blue-haired ladies. On the outside, life goes on in Florida courtesy of middlemen who bring in things that people are willing to pay a premium to obtain.

Acapulco, Tijuana, Freeport, Miami—it doesn't matter where the pimping happens. Mr. Vee in his nostalgic moments tells me Havana used to be like that, a city of touts and pimps—the fat young men in sunglasses parked at a corner in an idling Buick, waiting for a payoff, a delivery, a contact. Havana has shifted its corporate headquarters. Beirut has come west. And now, it's Miami that gives me warm memories of always-Christmas Saigon.

It's life in the procurement belt, between those lines of tropical latitudes, where the world shops for its illicit goods and dumps its surplus parts, where it prefers to fight its wars, and once you've settled into its give and take, you find it's impossible to live anywhere else. It's the coke-and-caffeine jangle of being seventeen and readier to kill than be killed and to know that Job One is to secure your objective and after that it's unsupervised play till the next order comes down.

In this mood, and in a Civic newly liberated from a protesting coed, I am heading west out of Miami, thinking first of driving up to Pensacola when I am sideswiped off the highway. Two men get in the Civic. They sit on either side of me and light up cigarettes.

"Someone say something," I finally say.

They riffle through the papers in the glove compartment. They quickly surmise that my name is not Mindy Robles. "We know all about this morning. Assault. Grand theft auto."

"Let's talk," I say.

I wait for the rough stuff. When it comes, it's an armlock on the throat that cuts air supply. When they let me speak, I cut a deal. They spot me for a vet; we exchange some dates, names, firefights. Turns out they didn't like Mindy Robles, didn't appreciate the pressure her old man tried to put on the police department. They look at our names—Robles and Marshall—and I can read their minds. We're in some of these things together and no one's linked me to Chavez—these guys are small time, auto-detail. They keep the car. They filch a wad of Mr. Vee's bills, the wad I'd stuffed into my wallet. They don't know there's another wad of Mr. Vee's money in a secret place. And fifty bucks in my boots.

Instead of an air-conditioned nighttime run up the Gulf Coast, it's the thumb on the interstate. I pass up a roadside rest area, a happy hunting ground for new cars and ready cash. I hitch a ride to the farthest cheap motel.

THE FIRST AUTOMOBILE I crouch behind in the dark parking lot of the Dunes Motel is an Impala with Alabama license plates. The next one is Broward County. Two more out-of-staters: Live Free or Die and Land of Lincoln. The farther from Florida the better for me. I look in the windows of the Topaz from New Hampshire. There's a rug in the back seat, and under the rug I make out a shiny sliver of Samsonite. Maybe they're just eating. Clothes hang on one side: two sports jackets for a small man or an adolescent, and what looks to me like lengths of silk. On the rear-view mirror, where you or I might hang a kid's booties or a plastic Jesus and rosaries, is an alien deity with four arms or legs. I don't know about borrowing this little beauty. These people travel a little too heavy.

The Dunes isn't an absolute dump. The pool has water in it. The neon VACANCY sign above the door of the office has blown only one letter. The annex to the left of the office has its own separate entrance: SANDALWOOD RESTAURANT.

I stroke the highway dust out of my hair, so the office won't guess my present automobileless state, tuck my shirt into my Levis and walk in from the parking lot. The trouble is there's nobody behind the desk. It's 11:03; late but not late enough for even a junior high jailbait nightclerk to have taken to her cot.

Another guest might have rung the bell and waited, or rung the bell and banged his fist on the counter and done some swearing. What I do is count on the element of surprise. I vault into the staff area and kick open a door that says: STRICTLY PRIVATE.

Inside, in a room reeking with incense, are people eating. There are a lot of them. There are a lot of little brown people sitting cross-legged on the floor of a regular motel room and eating with their hands. Pappies with white beards, grammies swaddled in silk, men in dark suits, kids, and one luscious jailbait in blue jeans.

They look at me. A bunch of aliens and they stare like I'm the freak.

One of the aliens tries to uncross his legs, but all he manages is a backward flop. He holds his right hand stiff and away from his body so it won't drip gravy on his suit. "Are you wanting a room?"

I've never liked the high, whiny, Asian male voice. "Let's put it this way. Are you running a motel or what?"

The rest of the aliens look at me, look at each other, look down at their food. I stare at them, too. They seem to have been partying. I wouldn't mind a Jack Daniels and a plate of their rice and yellow stew stuff brought to me by room service in blue jeans.

"Some people here say we are running a 'po-tel.'" A greasy grin floats off his face. "Get it? My name is Patel, that's P-A-T-E-L. A Patel owning a motel, get it?"

"Rich," I say.

The jailbait springs up off the floor. With a gecko-fast tongue tip, she chases a gravy drop on her wrist. "I can go. I'm done." But she doesn't make a move. "You people enjoy the meal."

The women jabber but not in English. They flash gold bracelets. An organized raid could clean up in that room, right down to the rubies and diamonds in their noses. They're all wrapped in silk, like brightly-colored mummies. Pappy shakes his head, but doesn't rise. "She eats like a bird. Who'll marry her?" He says in English to one of his buddies.

"You should advertise," says the other man, probably the Living Free or Dying. They've forgotten me. I feel left out, left behind. While we were nailing up that big front door, these guys were sneaking in around back. They got their money, their family networks, and their secretive languages.

I verbalize a little seething, and when none of the aliens take notice, I dent the prefab wall with my fist. "Hey," I yell. "I need a room for the night. Don't any of your dummies speak American?"

Now she swings toward me apologetically. She has a braid that snakes all the way down to her knees. "Sorry for the inconvenience," she says. She rinses gravy off her hands. "It's our biggest family reunion to date. That's why things are so hectic." She says something about a brother getting married, leaving them short at the desk. I think of Jonda and the turbaned guy. He fired her when some new turbaned guy showed up.

"Let's just go," I say. "I don't give a damn about reunions." I don't know where Jonda ended up. The Goldilocks doll wasn't delivered to LagunaVista Estates, though I had a welcome planned for it.

This kid's got a ripe body. I follow the ripe body up a flight of outdoor stairs. Lizards scurry, big waterbugs drag across the landings.

"This is it," she says. She checks the air conditioning and the TV. She makes sure there are towels in the bathroom. If she feels a little uneasy being in a motel room with a guy like me who's dusty and scruffy and who kills for a living, she doesn't show it. Not till she looks back at the door and realizes I'm not carrying any bags.

She's a pro. "You'll have to pay in cash now," she says. "I'll make out a receipt."

"What if I were to pull out a knife instead," I joke. I turn slightly away from her and count the balance of Haysoos' bills. Not enough in there, after the shakedown. The fifty stays put, my new nest egg. "Where were you born, honey? Bombay? I been to Bombay."

"New Jersey," she says. "You can pay half tonight, and the rest before you check out tomorrow. I am not unreasonable."

"I'll just bet you're not. Neither am I. But who says I'm leaving tomorrow. You got some sort of policy?"

That's when I catch the look on her face. Disgust, isn't that what it is? Distaste for the likes of me.

"You can discuss that with my father and uncle tomorrow morning." She sashays just out of my reach. She's aiming to race back to the motel room not much different than this except that it's jammed with family.

206 | MIDCAREER STORIES (1985–1988)

I pounce on Alice before she can drop down below, and take America with her. The hardware comes in handy, especially the kris. Alice lays hot fingers on my eyes and nose, but it's no use and once she knows it, Alice submits.

———————

I CHOOSE ME the car with the Land of Lincoln plates. I make a double switch with Broward County. I drive the old Tamiami Trail across the remains of the Everglades. Used to be no cars, a narrow ridge of two-lane concrete with swamps on either side, gators sunning themselves by day, splattered by night. Black snakes and mocassins every few hundred yards. Clouds of mosquitoes.

This is what I've become. I want to squeeze this state dry and swallow it whole.

Orbiting

ON THANKSGIVING morning I'm still in my nightgown thinking of Vic when Dad raps on my apartment door. Who's he rolling joints for, who's he initiating now into the wonders of his inner space? What got me on Vic is remembering last Thanksgiving and his famous cranberry sauce with Grand Marnier, which Dad had interpreted as a sign of permanence in my life. A man who cooks like Vic is ready for other commitments. Dad cannot imagine cooking as self-expression. You cook *for* someone. Vic's sauce was a sign of his permanent isolation, if you really want to know.

Dad's come to drop off the turkey. It's a seventeen-pounder. Mr. Vitelli knows to reserve a biggish one for us every Thanksgiving and Christmas. But this November what with Danny in the Marines, Uncle Carmine having to be very careful after the bypass, and Vic taking off for outer space as well, we might as well have made do with one of those turkey rolls you pick out of the freezer. And in other years, Mr. Vitelli would not have given us a frozen bird. We were proud of that, our birds were fresh killed. I don't bring this up to Dad.

"Your mama took care of the thawing," Dad says. "She said you wouldn't have room in your Frigidaire."

"You mean Mom said Rindy shouldn't be living in a dump, right?" Mom has the simple, immigrant faith that children should do better than their parents, and her definition of better is comfortingly rigid. Fair enough—I believed it, too. But the fact is all I can afford is this third-floor studio with an art deco shower. The fridge fits under the kitchenette counter. The room has potential. I'm content with that. And I *like* my job even though it's selling, not designing, jewelry made out of seashells and semiprecious stones out of a boutique in Bellevue Plaza.

Dad shrugs. "You're an adult, Renata." He doesn't try to lower himself into one of my two deck chairs. He was a minor league catcher for a while and his knees went. The fake zebra-skin cushions piled as seats on the rug are out of the question for him. My futon bed folds up into a sofa, but the satin sheets are still lasciviously tangled. My father stands in a slat of sunlight, trying not to look embarrassed.

"Dad, I'd have come to the house and picked it up. You didn't have to make the extra trip out from Verona." A sixty-five-year-old man in wingtips and a Borsalino hugging a wet, heavy bird is so poignant I have to laugh.

"You wouldn't have gotten out of bed until noon, Renata." But Dad smiles. I know what he's saying. He's saying *he's* retired and *he* should be able to stay in bed till noon if he wants to, but he can't and he'd rather drive twenty miles with a soggy bird than read the *Ledger*[1] one more time.

Grumbling and scolding are how we deMarcos express love. It's the North Italian way, Dad used to tell Cindi, Danny, and me when we were kids. Sicilians and Calabrians are emotional; we're contained. Actually, *he's* contained, the way Vic was contained for the most part. Mom's a Calabrian and she was born and raised there. Dad's very American, so Italy's a safe source of pride for him. I once figured it out: *his* father, Arturo deMarco, was a fifteen-week-old fetus when his mother planted her feet on Ellis Island. Dad, a proud son of North Italy, had one big adventure in his life, besides fighting in the Pacific, and that was marrying a Calabrian peasant. He made it sound as though Mom was a Korean or something, and their marriage was a kind of taming of the West, and that everything about her could be explained as a cultural deficiency. Actually, Vic could talk beautifully about his feelings. He'd brew espresso, pour it into tiny blue pottery cups and analyze our relationship. I should have listened. I mean, really listened. I thought he was talking about us, but I know now that he was only talking incessantly about himself. I put too much faith in mail-order nightgowns and bras.

"Your mama wanted me out of the house," Dad goes on. "She didn't used to be like this, Renata."

Renata and Carla are what we were christened. We changed to Rindy and Cindi in junior high. Danny didn't have to make such leaps, unless you count dropping out of Montclair State and joining the Marines. He was always Danny, or Junior.

---

1. Likely to refer to *The Star-Ledger*, New Jersey's highest circulation newspaper.—Ed.

I lug the turkey to the kitchen sink where it can drip away at a crazy angle until I have time to deal with it.

"Your mama must have told you girls I've been acting funny since I retired."

"No, Dad, she hasn't said anything about you acting funny." What she *has* said is do we think she ought to call Doc Brunetti and have a chat about Dad? Dad wouldn't have to know. He and Doc Brunetti are, or were, on the same church league bowling team. So is, or was, Vic's dad, Vinny Riccio.

"Your mama thinks a man should have an office to drive to every day. I sat at a desk for thirty-eight years and what did I get? Ask Doc, I'm too embarrassed to say." Dad once told me Doc—his real name was Frankie, though no one ever called him that—had been called Doc since he was six years old and growing up with Dad in Little Italy. There was never a time in his life when Doc wasn't Doc, which made his professional decision very easy. Dad used to say, no one ever called me Adjuster when I was a kid. Why didn't they call me something like Sarge or Teach? Then I would have known better.

I wish I had something breakfasty in my kitchen cupboard to offer him. He wants to stay and talk about Mom, which is the way old married people have. Let's talk about me means: What do you think of Mom? I'll take the turkey over means: When will Rindy settle down? I wish this morning I had bought the Goodwill sofa for ten dollars instead of letting Vic haul off the fancy deck chairs from Fortunoff's. Vic had flash. He'd left Jersey a long time before he actually took off.

"I can make you tea."

"None of that herbal stuff."

We don't talk about Mom, but I know what he's going through. She's just started to find herself. He's not burned out, he's merely stuck. I remember when Mom refused to learn to drive, wouldn't leave the house even to mail a letter. Her litany those days was: when you've spent the first fifteen years of your life in a mountain village, when you remember candles and gaslight and carrying water from a well, not to mention holding in your water at night because of wolves and the unlit outdoor privy, you *like* being housebound. She used those wolves for all they were worth, as though imaginary wolves still nipped her heels in the Clifton Mall.

Before Mom began to find herself and signed up for a class at Paterson, she used to nag Cindi and me about finding the right men. "Men," she said; she wasn't coy, never. Unembarrassed, she'd tell me about her wedding night, about her first sighting of Dad's "thing" ("Land Ho!" Cindi giggled. "Thar she blows!" I chipped in) and she'd giggle at our word for it, the common word, and she'd use it around us, never around Dad. Mom's peasant, she's earthy but never coarse. If I could get that across to Dad, how I admire it in men or in women, I would feel somehow redeemed of all my little mistakes with them, with men, with myself. Cindi and Brent were married on a cruise ship by the ship's captain. Tony, Vic's older brother, made a play for me my senior year. Tony's solid now. He manages a funeral home but he's invested in crayfish ponds on the side.

"You don't even own a dining table." Dad sounds petulant. He uses "even" a lot around me. Not just a judgment, but a comparative judgment. Other people have dining tables. *Lots* of dining tables. He softens it a bit, not wanting to hurt me, wanting more for me to judge him a failure. "We've always had a sit-down dinner, hon."

Okay, so traditions change. This year dinner's potluck. So I don't have real furniture. I eat off stack-up plastic tables as I watch the evening news. I drink red wine and heat a pita bread on the gas burner and wrap it around alfalfa sprouts or green linguine. The Swedish knockdown dresser keeps popping its sides because Vic didn't glue it properly. Swedish engineering, he said, doesn't need glue. Think of Volvos, he said, and Ingmar Bergman. He isn't good with directions that come in four languages. At least he wasn't.

"Trust me, Dad." This isn't the time to spring new lovers on him. "A friend made me a table. It's in the basement."

"How about chairs?" Ah, my good father. He could have said, friend? What friend?

Marge, my landlady, has all kinds of junky stuff in the basement. "Jorge and I'll bring up what we need. You'd strain your back, Dad." Shot knees, bad back: daily pain but nothing fatal. Not like Carmine.

"Jorge? Is that the new boyfriend?"

Shocking him makes me feel good. It would serve him right if Jorge was my new boyfriend. But Jorge is Marge's other roomer. He gives Marge Spanish lessons, and does the heavy cleaning and the yard work. Jorge has family in El Salvador he's hoping to bring up. I haven't met Marge's husband yet. He works on an offshore oil rig in some emirate with a funny name.

"No, Dad." I explain about Jorge.

"El Salvador!" he repeats. "That means 'the Savior.'" He passes on the information with a kind of awe. It makes Jorge's homeland, which he's shown me pretty pictures of, seem messy and exotic, at the very rim of human comprehension.

After Dad leaves, I call Cindi, who lives fifteen minutes away on Upper Mountainside Road. She's eleven months younger and almost a natural blond, but we're close. Brent wasn't easy for me to take, not at first. He owns a discount camera and electronics stores on Fifty-fourth in Manhattan. Cindi met

210 | MIDCAREER STORIES (1985–1988)

him through Club Med. They sat on a gorgeous Caribbean beach and talked of hogs. His father is an Amish farmer in Kalona, Iowa. Brent, in spite of the obvious hairpiece and the gold chain, is a rebel. He was born Schwartzendruber, but changed his name to Schwartz. Now no one believes the Brent, either. They call him Bernie on the street and it makes everyone more comfortable. His father's never taken their buggy out of the county.

The first time Vic asked me out, he talked of feminism and holism and macrobiotics. Then he opened up on cinema and literature, and I was very impressed, as who wouldn't be? Ro, my current lover, is very different. He picked me up in an uptown singles bar that I and sometimes Cindi go to. He bought me a Cinzano and touched my breast in the dark. He was direct, and at the same time weirdly courtly. I took him home though usually I don't, at first. I learned in bed that night that the tall brown drink with the lemon twist he'd been drinking was Tab.

I went back on the singles circuit even though the break with Vic should have made me cautious. Cindi thinks Vic's a romantic. I've told her how it ended. One Sunday morning in March he kissed me awake as usual. He'd brought in the *Times* from the porch and was reading it. I made us some cinnamon rose tea. We had a ritual, starting with the real estate pages, passing remarks on the latest tacky towers. Not for us, we'd say, the view is terrible! No room for the servants, things like that. And our imaginary children's imaginary nanny. "Hi, gorgeous," I said. He is gorgeous, not strong, but showy. He said, "I'm leaving, babe. New Jersey doesn't do it for me anymore." I said, "Okay, so where're we going?" I had an awful job at the time, taking orders for MCI. Vic said, "I didn't say we, babe." So I asked, "You mean it's over? Just like that?" And he said, "Isn't that the best way? No fuss, no hang-ups." Then I got a little whiny. "But *why*?" I wanted to know. But he was macrobiotic in lots of things, including relationships. Yin and yang, hot and sour, green and yellow. "You know, Rindy, there are *places*. You don't fall off the earth when you leave Jersey, you know. Places you see pictures of and read about. Different weathers, different trees, different everything. Places that get the Cubs on cable instead of the Mets." He was into that. For all the sophisticated things he liked to talk about, he was a very local boy. "Vic," I pleaded, "you're crazy. You need help." "I need help because I want to get out of Jersey? You gotta be kidding!" He stood up and for a moment I thought he would do something crazy, like destroy something, or hurt me. "Don't ever call me crazy, got that? And give me the keys to the van."

He took the van. Danny had sold it to me when the Marines sent him overseas. I'd have given it to him anyway, even if he hadn't asked.

"Cindi, I need a turkey roaster," I tell my sister on the phone.

"I'll be right over," she says. "The brat's driving me crazy."

"Isn't Franny's visit working out?"

"I could kill her. I think up ways. How does that sound?"

"Why not send her home?" I'm joking. Franny is Brent's twelve-year-old and he's shelled out a lot of dough to lawyers in New Jersey and Florida to work out visitation rights.

"Poor Brent. He feels so *divided*," Cindi says. "He shouldn't have to take sides."

I want her to ask who my date is for this afternoon, but she doesn't. It's important to me that she like Ro, that Mom and Dad more than tolerate him.

All over the country, I tell myself, women are towing new lovers home to meet their families. Vic is simmering cranberries in somebody's kitchen and explaining yin and yang. I check out the stuffing recipe. The gravy calls for cream and freshly grated nutmeg. Ro brought me six whole nutmegs in a Ziplock bag from his friend, a Pakistani, who runs a spice store in SoHo. The nuts look hard and ugly. I take one out of the bag and sniff it. The aroma's so exotic my head swims. On an impulse I call Ro.

The phone rings and rings. He doesn't have his own place yet. He has to crash with friends. He's been in the States three months, maybe less. I let it ring fifteen, sixteen, seventeen times.

Finally someone answers. "Yes?" The voice is guarded, the accent obviously foreign even though all I'm hearing is a one-syllable word. Ro has fled here from Kabul. He wants to take classes at NJIT and become an electrical engineer. He says he's lucky his father got him out. A friend of Ro's father, a man called Mumtaz, runs a fried chicken restaurant in Brooklyn in a neighbourhood Ro calls "Little Kabul," though probably no one else has ever noticed. Mr. Mumtaz puts the legal immigrants to work as waiters out front. The illegals hide in a back room as pluckers and gutters.

"Ro? I miss you. We're eating at three, remember?"

"Who is speaking, please?"

So I fell for the accent, but it isn't a malicious error. I *can* tell one Afghan tribe from another now, even by looking at them or by their names. I can make out some Pashto words. "Tell Ro it's Rindy. Please? I'm a friend. He wanted me to call this number."

"No knowing any Ro."

212 | MIDCAREER STORIES (1985–1988)

"Hey, wait. Tell him it's Rindy deMarco."

The guy hangs up on me.

I'M CRUMBLING cornbread into a bowl for the stuffing when Cindi honks half of "King Cotton" from the parking apron in the back. Brent bought her the BMW on the gray market and saved a bundle—once discount, always discount—then spent three hundred dollars to put in a horn that beeps a Sousa march. I wave a potato masher at her from the back window. She doesn't get out of the car. Instead she points to the pan in the back seat. I come down, wiping my hands on a dish towel.

"I should stay and help." Cindi sounds ready to cry. But I don't want her with me when Ro calls back.

"You're doing too much already, kiddo." My voice at least sounds comforting. "You promised one veg and the salad."

"I ought to come up and help. That or get drunk." She shifts the stick. When Brent bought her the car, the dealer threw in driving gloves to match the upholstery.

"Get Franny to shred the greens," I call as Cindi backs up the car. "Get her involved."

THE PHONE IS RINGING in my apartment. I can hear it ring from the second-floor landing.

"Ro?"

"You're taking a chance, my treasure. It could have been any other admirer, then where would you be?"

"I don't have any other admirers." Ro is not a conventionally jealous man, not like the types I have known. He's totally unlike any man I have ever known. He wants men to come on to me. Lately when we go to a bar he makes me sit far enough from him so some poor lonely guy thinks I'm looking for action. Ro likes to swagger out of a dark booth as soon as someone buys me a drink. I go along. He comes from a macho culture.

"How else will I know you are as beautiful as I think you are? I would not want an unprized woman," he says. He is asking me for time, I know. In a few more months he'll know I'm something of a catch in my culture, or at least I've never had trouble finding boys. Even Brent Schwartzendruber has begged me to see him alone.

"I'm going to be a little late," Ro says. "I told you about my cousin, Abdul, no?"

Ro has three or four cousins that I know of in Manhattan. They're all named Abdul something. When I think of Abdul, I think of a giant black man with goggles on, running down a court. Abdul is the teenage cousin whom immigration officials nabbed as he was gutting chickens in Mumtaz's back room. Abdul doesn't have the right papers to live and work in this country, and now he's been locked up in a detention center on Varick Street. Ro's afraid Abdul will be deported back to Afghanistan. If that happens, he'll be tortured.

"I have to visit him before I take the DeCamp bus. He's talking nonsense. He's talking of starting a hunger fast."

"A hunger strike! God!" When I'm with Ro I feel I am looking at America through the wrong end of a telescope. He makes it sound like a police state, with sudden raids, papers, detention centers, deportations, and torture and death waiting in the wings. I'm not a political person. Last fall I wore the Ferraro button because she's a woman and Italian.

"Rindy, all night I've been up and awake. All night I think of your splendid breasts. Like clusters of grapes, I think. I am stroking and fondling your grapes this very minute. My talk gets you excited?"

I tell him to test me, please get here before three. I remind him he can't buy his ticket on the bus.

"WE GOT HERE too early, didn't we?" Dad stands just outside the door to my apartment, looking embarrassed. He's in his best dark suit, the one he wears every Thanksgiving and Christmas. This year he can't do up the top button of his jacket.

"Don't be so formal, Dad." I give him a showy hug and pull him indoors so Mom can come in.

"As if your papa ever listens to me!" Mom laughs. But she sits primly on the sofa bed in her velvet cloak, with her tote bag and evening purse in her lap. Before Dad started courting her, she worked as a seamstress. Dad rescued her from a sweatshop. He married down, she married well. That's the family story.

"She told me to rush."

Mom isn't in a mood to squabble. I think she's reached the point of knowing she won't have him forever. There was Carmine, at death's door just a month ago. Anything could happen to Dad. She says, "Renata, look what I made! Crostoli." She lifts a cake tin out of her tote bag. The pan still feels warm. And for dessert, I know, there'll be a jar of super-thick, super-rich Death by Chocolate.

The story about Grandma deMarco, Dad's mama, is that every Thanksgiving she served two full dinners, one American with the roast turkey,

214 | MIDCAREER STORIES (1985–1988)

candied yams, pumpkin pie, the works, and another with Grandpa's favorite pastas.

Dad relaxes. He appoints himself bartender. "Don't you have more ice cubes, sweetheart?"

I tell him it's good Glenlivet. He shouldn't ruin it with ice, just a touch of water if he must. Dad pours sherry in Vic's pottery espresso cups for his women. Vic made them himself, and I used to think they were perfect blue jewels. Now I see they're lumpy, uneven in color.

"Go change into something pretty before Carla and Brent come." Mom believes in dressing up. Beaded dresses lift her spirits. She's wearing a beaded green dress today.

I take the sherry and vanish behind a four-panel screen, the kind long-legged showgirls change behind in black-and-white movies while their mustached lovers keep talking. My head barely shows above the screen's top, since I'm no long-legged showgirl. My best points, as Ro has said, are my clusters of grapes. Vic found the screen at a country auction in the Adirondacks. It had filled the van. Now I use the panels as a bulletin board and I'm worried Dad'll spot the notice for the next meeting of Amnesty International, which will bother him. He will think the two words stand for draft dodger and Communist. I was going to drop my membership, a legacy of Vic, when Ro saw it and approved. Dad goes to the Sons of Italy Anti-Defamation dinners. He met Frank Sinatra at one. He voted for Reagan last time because the Democrats ran an Italian woman.

Instead of a thirties lover, it's my mustached papa talking to me from the other side of the screen. "So where's this dining table?"

"Ro's got the parts in the basement. He'll bring it up, Dad."

I hear them whispering. "Bo? Now she's messing with a Southerner?" and "Shh, it's her business."

I'm just smoothing on my pantyhose when Mom screams for the cops. Dad shouts, too, at Mom for her to shut up. It's my fault, I should have warned Ro not to use his key this afternoon.

I peek over the screen's top and see my lover the way my parents see him. He's a slight, pretty man with hazel eyes and a tufty mustache, so whom can he intimidate? I've seen Jews and Greeks, not to mention Sons of Italy, darker-skinned than Ro. Poor Ro resorts to his Kabuli prep-school manners.

"How do you do, madam! Sir! My name is Roashan."

Dad moves closer to Ro but doesn't hold out his hand. I can almost read his mind: *he speaks.* "Come again?" he says, baffled.

I cringe as he spells his name. My parents are so parochial. With each letter he does a graceful dip and bow. "Try it syllable by syllable, sir. Then it is not so hard."

Mom stares past him at me. The screen doesn't hide me because I've strayed too far in to watch the farce. "Renata, you're wearing only your camisole."

I pull my crew neck over my head, then kiss him. I make the kiss really sexy so they'll know I've slept with this man. Many times. And if he asks me, I'll marry him. I had not known that till now. I think my mother guesses.

He's brought flowers: four long-stemmed, stylish purple blossoms in a florist's paper cone. "For you, madam." He glides over the dirty broadloom to Mom who fills up more than half the sofa bed. "This is my first Thanksgiving dinner, for which I have much to give thanks, no?"

"He was born in Afghanistan," I explain. But Dad gets continents wrong. He says, "We saw your famine camps on TV. Well, you won't starve this afternoon."

"They smell good," Mom says. "Thank you very much but you shouldn't spend a fortune."

"No, no, madam. What you smell good is my cologne. Flowers in New York have no fragrance."

"His father had a garden estate outside Kabul." I don't want Mom to think he's putting down American flowers, though in fact he is. Along with American fruits, meats, and vegetables. "The Russians bulldozed it," I add.

Dad doesn't want to talk politics. He senses, looking at Ro, this is not the face of Ethiopian starvation. "Well, what'll it be, Roy? Scotch and soda?" I wince. It's not going well.

"Thank you but no. I do not imbibe alcoholic spirits, though I have no objection for you, sir." My lover goes to the fridge and reaches down. He knows just where to find his Tab. My father is quietly livid, staring down at his drink.

In my father's world, grown men bowl in leagues and drink the best whiskey they can afford. Dad whistles "My Way." He must be under stress. That's his usual self-therapy: how would Francis Albert handle this?

"Muslims have taboos, Dad." Cindi didn't marry a Catholic, so he has no right to be upset about Ro, about us.

"Jews," Dad mutters. "So do Jews." He knows because catty-corner from Vitelli's is a kosher butcher. This isn't the time to parade new words before him, like *halal*, the Muslim kosher. An Italian-American man should be able to live sixty-five years never having heard the word, I can go along with that. Ro, fortunately, is cosmopolitan. Outside of pork and booze, he eats anything else I fix.

BRENT AND CINDI TAKE forever to come. But finally we hear his MG squeal in the driveway. Ro glides to the front window; he seems to blend with the ficus tree and hanging ferns. Dad and I wait by the door.

216 | MIDCAREER STORIES (1985–1988)

"Party time!" Brent shouts as he maneuvers Cindi and Franny ahead of him up three flights of stairs. He looks very much the head of the family, a rich man steeply in debt to keep up appearances, to compete, to head off middle age. He's at that age—and Cindi's nowhere near that age—when people notice the difference and quietly judge it. I know these things from Cindi—I'd never guess it from looking at Brent. If he feels divided, as Cindi says he does, it doesn't show. Misery, anxiety, whatever, show on Cindi though; they bring her cheekbones out. When I'm depressed, my hair looks rough, my skin breaks out. Right now, I'm lustrous.

Brent does a lot of whooping and hugging at the door. He even hugs Dad who looks grave and funereal like an old-world Italian gentleman because of his outdated, pinched dark suit. Cindi makes straight for the fridge with her casserole of squash and browned marshmallow. Franny just stands in the middle of the room holding two biggish Baggies of salad greens and vinaigrette in an old Dijon mustard jar. Brent actually bought the mustard in Dijon, a story that Ro is bound to hear and not appreciate. Vic was mean enough last year to tell him that he could have gotten it for more or less the same price at the Italian specialty foods store down on Watchung Plaza. Franny doesn't seem to have her own winter clothes. She's wearing Cindi's car coat over a Dolphins sweatshirt. Her mother moved down to Florida the very day the divorce became final. She's got a Walkman tucked into the pocket of her cords.

"You could have trusted me to make the salad dressing at least," I scold my sister.

Franny gives up the Baggies and the jar of dressing to me. She scrutinizes us—Mom, Dad, me and Ro, especially Ro, as though she can detect something strange about him—but doesn't take off her earphones. A smirk starts twitching her tanned, feral features. I see what she is seeing. Asian men carry their bodies differently, even these famed warriors from the Khyber Pass. Ro doesn't stand like Brent or Dad. His hands hang kind of stiffly from the shoulder joints, and when he moves, his palms are tucked tight against his thighs, his stomach sticks out like a slightly pregnant woman's. Each culture establishes its own manly posture, different ways of claiming space. Ro, hiding among my plants, holds himself in a way that seems both too effeminate and too macho. I hate Franny for what she's doing to me. I am twenty-seven years old, I should be more mature. But I see how wrong Ro's clothes are. He shows too much white collar and cuff. His shirt and his wool-blend flare-leg pants were made to measure in Kabul. The jacket comes from a discount store on Canal Street, part of a discontinued line of two-trousered suits. I ought to know, I took him there. I want to shake Franny or smash the earphones.

Cindi catches my exasperated look. "Don't pay any attention to her. She's unsociable this weekend. We can't compete with the Depeche Mode."

I intend to compete.

Franny, her eyes very green and very hostile, turns on Brent. "How come she never gets it right, Dad?"

Brent hi-fives his daughter, which embarrasses her more than anyone else in the room. "It's a Howard Jones, hon," Brent tells Cindi.

Franny, close to tears, runs to the front window where Ro's been hanging back. She has an ungainly walk for a child whose support payments specify weekly ballet lessons. She bores in on Ro's hidey hole like Russian artillery. Ro moves back to the perimeter of family intimacy. I have no way of helping yet. I have to set out the dips and Tostitos. Brent and Dad are talking sports, Mom and Cindi are watching the turkey. Dad's going on about the Knicks. He's in despair, so early in the season. He's on his second Scotch. I see Brent try. "What do you think, Roy?" He's doing his best to get my lover involved. "Maybe we'll get lucky, huh? We can always hope for a top draft pick. End up with Patrick Ewing!" Dad brightens. "That guy'll change the game. Just wait and see. He'll fill the lane better than Russell." Brent gets angry, since for some strange Amish reason he's a Celtics fan. So was Vic. "Bird'll make a monkey out of him." He looks to Ro for support.

Ro nods. Even his headshake is foreign. "You are undoubtedly correct, Brent," he says. "I am deferring to your judgment because currently I have not familiarized myself with these practices."

Ro loves squash, but none of my relatives have ever picked up a racket. I want to tell Brent that Ro's skied in St. Moritz, lost a thousand dollars in a casino in Beirut, knows where to buy Havana cigars without getting hijacked. He's sophisticated, he could make monkeys out of us all, but they think he's a retard.

Brent drinks three Scotches to Dad's two; then all three men go down to the basement. Ro and Brent do the carrying, negotiating sharp turns in the stairwell. Dad supervises. There are two trestles and a wide, splintery plywood top. "Try not to take the wall down!" Dad yells.

When they make it back in, the men take off their jackets to assemble the table. Brent's wearing a red lamb's wool turtleneck under his camel hair blazer. Ro unfastens his cuff links—they are 24-karat gold and his father's told him to sell them if funds run low—and pushes up his very white shirt sleeves. There are scars on both arms, scars that bubble against his dark skin, scars like lightning flashes under his thick black hair. Scar tissue on Ro is the color of freshwater pearls. I want to kiss it.

MIDCAREER STORIES (1985–1988)

Cindi checks the turkey one more time. "You guys better hurry. We'll be ready to eat in fifteen minutes."

Ro, the future engineer, adjusts the trestles. He's at his best now. He's become quite chatty. From under the plywood top, he's holding forth on the Soviet menace in Kabul. Brent may actually have an idea where Afghanistan is, in a general way, but Dad is lost. He's talking of being arrested for handing out pro-American pamphlets on his campus. Dad stiffens at "arrest" and blanks out the rest. He talks of this "so-called leader," this "criminal" named Babrak Karmal and I hear other buzz-words like Kandahār and Pamir, words that might have been Polish to me a month ago, and I can see even Brent is slightly embarrassed. It's his first exposure to Third World passion. He thought only Americans had informed political opinion—other people staged coups out of spite and misery. It's an unwelcome revelation to him that a reasonably educated and rational man like Ro would die for things that he, Brent, has never heard of and would rather laugh about. Ro was tortured in jail. Franny has taken off her earphones. Electrodes, canes, freezing tanks. He leaves nothing out. Something's gotten into Ro.

Dad looks sick. The meaning of Thanksgiving should not be so explicit. But Ro's in a daze. He goes on about how—*inshallah*[2]—his father, once a rich landlord, had stashed away enough to bribe a guard, sneak him out of this cell and hide him for four months in a tunnel dug under a servant's adobe hut until a forged American visa could be bought. Franny's eyes are wide, Dad joins Mom on the sofa bed, shaking his head. Jail, bribes, forged, what is this? I can read his mind. "For six days I must orbit one international airport to another," Ro is saying. "The main trick is having a valid ticket, that way the airline has to carry you, even if the country won't take you in. Colombo, Seoul, Bombay, Geneva, Frankfurt, I know too too well the transit lounges of many airports. We travel the world with our gym bags and prayer rugs, unrolling them in the transit lounges. The better airports have special rooms."

Brent tries to ease Dad's pain. "Say, buddy," he jokes, "you wouldn't be ripping us off, would you?"

Ro snakes his slender body from under the makeshift table. He hasn't been watching the effect of his monologue. "I am a working man," he says stiffly. I have seen his special permit. He's one of the lucky ones, though it might not last. He's saving for NJIT. Meantime he's gutting chickens to pay for room and board in Little Kabul. He describes the gutting process. His face is trans-

---

2. Arabic for "God willing," usually employed to refer to an event that has not yet happened.—Ed.

formed as he sticks his fist into imaginary roasters and grabs for gizzards, pulls out the squishy stuff. He takes an Afghan dagger out of the pocket of his pants. You'd never guess, he looks like such a victim. "This," he says, eyes glinting. "This is all I need."

"Cool," Franny says.

"Time to eat," Mom shouts. "I made the gravy with the nutmeg as you said, Renata."

I lead Dad to the head of the table. "Everyone else sit where you want to."

Franny picks out the chair next to Ro before I can put Cindi there. I want Cindi to know him, I want her as an ally.

Dad tests the blade of the carving knife. Mom put the knife where Dad always sits when she set the table. He takes his thumb off the blade and pushes the switch. "That noise makes me feel good."

But I carry in the platter with the turkey and place it in front of Ro. "I want you to carve," I say.

He brings out his dagger all over again. Franny is practically licking his fingers. "You mean this is a professional job?"

We stare fascinated as my lover slashes and slices, swiftly, confidently, at the huge, browned, juicy breast. The dagger scoops out flesh.

Now I am the one in a daze. I am seeing Ro's naked body as though for the first time, his nicked, scarred, burned body. In his body, the blemishes seem embedded, more beautiful, like wood. I am seeing character made manifest. I am seeing Brent and Dad for the first time, too. They have their little scars, things they're proud of, football injuries and bowling elbows they brag about. Our scars are so innocent; they are invisible and come to us from rough-housing gone too far. Ro hates to talk about his scars. If I trace the puckered tissue on his left thigh and ask "How, Ro?" he becomes shy, dismissive: a pack of dogs attacked him when he was a boy. The skin on his back is speckled and lumpy from burns, but when I ask he laughs. A crazy villager whacked him with a burning stick for cheekiness, he explains. He's ashamed that he comes from a culture of pain.

The turkey is reduced to a drying, whitened skeleton. On our plates, the slices are symmetrical, elegant. I realize all in a rush how much I love this man with his blemished, tortured body. I will give him citizenship if he asks. Vic was beautiful, but Vic was self-sufficient. Ro's my chance to heal the world.

I shall teach him how to walk like an American, how to dress like Brent but better, how to fill up a room as Dad does instead of melting and blending but sticking out in the Afghan way. In spite of the funny way he holds himself and the funny way he moves his head from side to side when he wants to say yes,

220 | MIDCAREER STORIES (1985–1988)

Ro is Clint Eastwood, scarred hero and survivor. Dad and Brent are children. I realize Ro's the only circumcised man I've slept with.

Mom asks, "Why are you grinning like that, Renata?"

Fighting for the Rebound

I'M IN BED watching the Vanilla Gorilla stick it to the Abilene Christians on some really obscure cable channel when Blanquita comes through the door wearing lavender sweats, and over them a frilly see-through apron. It's a November Thursday, a chilly fifty-three, but she's hibachiing butterfly lamb on the balcony.

"Face it, Griff," Blanquita says, wielding the barbecue fork the way empresses wield scepters.

"Face what?"

"That's what I mean," she says. "You're so insensitive, it's awesome."

"Nobody says awesome anymore," I tease. Blanquita speaks six languages, her best being Tagalog, Spanish, and American.

"Why not?" she says. Back in Manila, she took a crash course in making nice to Americans, before her father sent her over. In her family they called her Baby. "Bite him, Marcos," she orders her cat. "Spit on him." But Marcos chooses to stay behind the harpsichord and leggy ficus. Marcos knows I am not a cat person; he's known me to sneak in a kick. He takes out his hostilities on the ficus. What he does is chew up a pale, new leaf. I get my greenery for free because the office I work in throws out all browning, scraggly plants and trees. I have an arboretum of rejects.

"Let's start this conversation over," I plead. I'm tentative at the start of relationships, but this time I'm not throwing it away.

"Let's," she says.

"You're beautiful," I say.

"Do you mean that?"

I hate it when she goes intense on me. She starts to lift off the Press-On Nails from her thumbs. Her own nails are roundish and ridged, which might be her only imperfection.

"Blanquita the Beautiful." I shoot it through with melody. If I were a songwriter I'd write her a million lyrics. About frangipani blooms and crescent moons. But what I am is a low-level money manager, a solid, decent guy in white shirt and maroon tie and thinning, sandy hair over which hangs the sword of Damocles. The Dow Jones crowds my chest like an implant. I unlist

FIGHTING FOR THE REBOUND | *221*

my telephone every six weeks, and still they find me, the widows and ortho-dontists into the money-market. I feel the sword's point every minute. Get me in futures! In Globals, in Aggressive Growth, in bonds! I try to tell them, for every loser there's a winner, somewhere. Someone's always profiting, just give me time and I'll find it, I'll lock you in it.

Blanquita scoops Marcos off the broadloom and holds him on her hip as she might a baby. "I should never have left Manila," she says. She does some very heavy, very effective sighing. "Pappy was right. The East is East and the West is West and never the twain shall meet."

I get these nuggets from Kipling at least once a week. "But, Baby," I ob-ject, "you did leave. Atlanta is halfway around the world from the Philippines."

"Poor Pappy," Blanquita moons. "Poor Joker."

She doesn't give me much on her family other than that Pappy—Joker Rosario—a one-time big-shot publisher tight with the Marcos crew, is stuck in California stocking shelves in a liquor store. Living like a peon, serving winos in some hotbox *barrio*. Mother runs a beauty shop out of her kitchen in West Hartford, Connecticut. His politics, and those of his daughter, are—to un-derstate it—vile. She'd gotten to America long before his fall, when he still had loot and power and loved to spread it around. She likes to act as though real life began for her at JFK when she got past the customs and immigration on the seventeenth of October, 1980. That's fine with me. The less I know about growing up in Manila, rich or any other way, the less foreign she feels. Dear old redneck Atlanta is a thing of the past, no need to feel foreign here. Just wheel your shopping cart through aisles of bok choy and twenty kinds of Ja-maican spices at the Farmers' Market, and you'll see that the US of A is still a pioneer country.

She relaxes, and Marcos leaps off the sexy, shallow shelf of her left hip. "You're a racist, patronizing jerk if you think I'm beautiful. I'm just different, that's all."

"Different from whom?"

"All your others."

It's in her interest, somehow, to imagine me as Buckhead's primo swinger, maybe because—I can't be sure—she needs the buzz of perpetual jealousy. She needs to feel herself a temp. For all the rotten things she says about the Philippines, or the mistiness she reserves for the Stars and Stripes, she's kept her old citizenship.

"Baby, Baby, don't do this to me. Please?"

I crank up the Kraftmatic. My knees, drawn up and tense, push against my forehead. Okay, so maybe what I meant was that she isn't a looker in the blondhair-smalltits-greatlegs way that Wendi was. Or Emilou, for that matter.

222 | MIDCAREER STORIES (1985–1988)

But beautiful is how she makes me feel. Wendi was slow-growth. Emilou was strictly Chapter Eleven.

I can't tell her that. I can't tell her that I've been trading on rumor, selling on news, for years. Your smart pinstriper aims for the short-term profit. My track record for pickin 'em is just a little better than blindfold darts. It's as hard to lose big these days as it is to make a killing. I understand those inside traders—it's not the money, it's the rush. I'm hanging in for the balance of the quarter.

But.

If there's a shot, I'll take it.

Meantime, the barbecue fork in Blanquita's hand describes circles of such inner distress that I have to take my eyes off the slaughter of the Abilene Christians.

"You don't love me, Griff."

It's hard to know where she learns her lines. They're all so tragically sincere. Maybe they go back to the instant-marriage emporiums in Manila. Or the magazines she reads. Or a series of married, misunderstood men that she must have introduced to emotional chaos. Her tastes in everything are, invariably, unspeakable. She rests a kneecap on the twisted Kraftmatic and weeps. Even her kneecaps . . . well, even the kneecaps get my attention. It's not fair. Behind her, the Vanilla Gorilla is going man-to-man. Marcos is about to strangle himself with orange wool[1] he's pawed out of a dusty wicker yarn basket. Wendi was a knitter. Love flees, but we're stuck with love's debris.

"I'm not saying you don't *like* me, Griff. I'm saying you don't love me, okay?"

Why do I think she's said it all before? Why do I hear "sailor" instead of my name? "Don't spoil what we have." I am begging.

She believes me. Her face goes radiant. "What do we have, Griff?" Then she backs away from my hug. She believes me not.

All I get to squeeze are hands adorned with the glamor-length Press-On Nails. She could make a fortune as a hands model if she wanted to. That skin of hers is an evolutionary leap. Holding hands on the bed, we listen for a bit to the lamb fat spit. Anyone can suffer a cold shooting spell. I'm thirty-three and a vet of Club Med vacations; I can still ballhandle, but one-to-one is a younger man's game.

"All right, we'll drop the subject," Blanquita says. "I can be a good sport."

"That's my girl," I say. But I can tell from the angle of her chin and the new stiffness of her posture that she's turning prim and well-brought-up on me. Then she lobs devastation. "I won't be seeing you this weekend."

---

1. British word for "yarn."—Ed.

"It's *ciao* because I haven't bought you a ring?"

"No," she says, haughtily. "The Chief's asked me out, that's why. We're going up to his cabin."

I don't believe her. She's not the Chief's type. She wants to goad me into confessing that I love her.

"You're a fast little worker." The Chief, a jowly fifty-five, is rumored to enjoy exotic tastes. But, Christ, there's a difference between exotic and *foreign*, isn't there? Exotic means you know how to use your foreignness, or you make yourself a little foreign in order to appear exotic. Real foreign is a little scary, believe me. The fact is, the Chief brought Blanquita and me together in his office. That was nearly six months ago. I was there to prep him, and she was hustled in, tools of the trade stuffed into a Lancôme tote sack, to make him look good on TV. Blanquita's a makeup artist on the way up and up, and Atlanta is Executives City, where every Chief wants to look terrific before he throws himself to the corporate lions. I watched her operate. She pumped him up a dozen ways. And I just sat there, stunned. The Chief still had moves.

"You sound jealous, Griff." She turns her wicked, bottomless blacks on me and I feel myself squirm.

"Go up to the cabin if you want to. I don't do jealousy, hon."

She starts trapping on defense herself now. "You don't do jealousy! Well, you don't have the right to be jealous! You don't have any rights, period! You can't change the ground rules!"

Maybe Wendi wasn't all that certifiable a disaster. Come to think of it, Wendi had her moments. She could be a warm, nurturing person. We talked, we did things together. The summer we were breaking up, I built her kid a treehouse, which might be the only unselfish good I've accomplished in my life. Blanquita's a Third World aristocrat, a hothouse orchid you worship but don't dare touch. I wouldn't dare ask her help me knock together a bookcase or scrub the grout around the bathroom tiles. But Wendi, alas, never made me feel this special, this loved.

"I'm serious, Griff." She closes her eyes and rams her fists in eyelids that are as delicately mauve as her sweatshirt. "You keep me in limbo. I need to know where I stand."

"I don't want you to go," I say. I'm not myself. I'm a romantic in red suspenders.

"What do you want me to do?"

"Whatever you want to do, hon."

Her body sags inside her oversized sweatshirt. She gets off the mattress, strokes Marcos with the toes of her Reeboks, checks a shredded ficus leaf, tosses the skein of orange wool from the balcony down to the parking lot.

"Hullo," I say. "Hey, Baby." I really want to reach her. "Hey, watch him!" Wendi was a big basketball fan, a refugee from Hoosierland, and she was the first and so far the only woman I've known who could sit through a Braves or Falcons game. If I could get Miss Bataan to watch the Gorilla stuff it, we'd be okay, but she doesn't even pretend to watch.

"I'm going to make myself a cup of tea," she says.

We say nothing while she brews herself a pot of cherry almond. Then she sits on the bed and drinks a slow cup, fiddling with the remote control and putting to flight all ten sweaty goons. F. Lee Bailey comes on and talks up the Bhopal tragedy. I can't believe it's been a year. I must have been seeing Emilou on the side when it happened. Yes, in fact Emilou cried, and Wendi had made a fuss about the mascara on my sixty-buck shirt. An auditorium packed with Herbalifers comes on the screen. The Herbalifers are very upbeat and very free enterprise. They perk her up.

"We don't need that," I plead.

"You don't know what you need," she snaps. "You're so narcissistic you don't need anyone. You don't know how to love."

Sailor, I think. It thrills me.

"That's not fair."

But Blanquita the Beautiful races on to bigger issues. "Not just you, Griff," she scolds in that eerily well-bred, Asian convent-schooled voice. "You're all emotional cripples. All you Americans. You just worry about your own measly little relationships. You don't care how much you hurt the world."

In changing gears, she's right up there with Mario Andretti. I envy her her freedom, her Green Card politics. It's love, not justice, that powers her. Emilou and Wendi would have died if I caught them in an inconsistency.

She jabs at more buttons on the remote control doodad. Herbalifers scuttle into permanent blackness, and a Soweto funeral procession comes on. Big guys in black boots come at pallbearers with whips and clubs. Blanquita lays her teacup on the top sheet. These are serious designer sheets, debris from my months with Emilou. When Joker Rosario went to South Africa back in the long, long ago, he was treated very, very white. He wrote pleasant things about South Africa in his paper. Yesterday's statesman is today's purveyor of Muscatel. South Africa is making her morose, and I dare not ask why. I suddenly remember that the neighborhood dry cleaner doesn't know how to take tea stains off but does a good job with Kahlúa. Blanquita flashes the black inscrutables one more time and says, "I can't stand it anymore, Griff. It's got to stop."

South Africa? I wonder, but dare not hope. I carefully remove her teacup and take hold of her fingertips, which are still warm from holding the cup, and pull them up to my beard. "We have each other," I say.

"Do we?"

It's time to take charge, to force the good times to roll. Some nations were built to take charge. It's okay for a nation of pioneers to bully the rest of the world as long as the cause is just. My heart is pure, my head is clear. I retrieve the doodad from Blanquita's perfect hand. I want to show her the funtimes of TV-land. I slice through a Mexican variety show on SIN. Any time of the day or night, those Mexicans are in tuxedos. All those blow-dried Mexican emcees in soccer stadiums, looking like Ricardo Montalbans who never made it.

I know she's a secret fan.

On cue, my trusty nineteen-incher serves up the right stuff. It's National Cheerleading Contest time. A squad in skimpy skirts, Oceanside High's cutest, synchronizes cartwheels and handstands, and starts to dust the competition. I feel godly powers surge through my body as Blanquita relaxes. Soon she relaxes enough to laugh.

"Did you ever try out as a cheerleader?" I ask. I can sense the imminence of terrific times.

Blanquita the Beautiful watches the kids on the screen with gratifying intensity. Then she thrusts a hesitant leg in the air. It's the fault of the French maid's apron that she's wearing over her baggy sweats; my saucy exotic's turned a schoolgirl routine into something alien and absurd. Oh, Blanquita, not so fast!

"I'm too good for you, Griff," she pants, twirling an invisible baton and high-stepping across the condo's wall-to-wall. "Pappy would call you illiterate scum."

"And so I am. But Joker's selling rotgut through a retractable grate and Mama's perming Koreans in her living room. Ferdie and Imelda they're not." If People Power hadn't cut them down, if Joker's own reporters hadn't locked him out, Blanquita was promised a place in the Miss Universe contest. That's why she kept her citizenship.

"That's needlessly cruel."

"Baby, you've got to stop living in the past."

"Okay." She stops the twirling and marching. She turns the TV off without the doodad though I've begged her not to many times. Without the light from the screen, the condo room seems as dull and impersonal as a room in a Holiday Inn.

Without Blanquita I'd be just another Joe Blow Buckhead yuppie in his Reeboks. It's she who brings me to bed each night and wakes me up each morning, big as a house and hard as a sidewalk.

"Okay," she goes again. "Who needs a crummy tropical past?"

We're out of the woods. I start to relax.

"Two cheers for cable sleaze," I shout. She plucks Marcos from his hidey hole behind the ficus and babies him. "I'm saying yes to the Chief, Griff. Hip, Hip!"

"What?"

"He says I make him look like a million dollars and make him feel like even more."

"Get it in writing. That's a low-rent come-on. He wouldn't dare try it on the office girls."

"Of course not."

She's not been getting my point.

"I have to get on with my life. And anyway, you said you weren't jealous so what's to hold me up?"

I check out her pulse rate with my lips. I'm not verbal. Maybe I don't love Blanquita. Because I don't know what love is. I'm not ready for one-on-one.

Baby Blanquita is too agitated to smell the charred lamb whooshing off the hibachi, so it's up to me, the narcissist, to rescue the rescue-worthy. The balcony that holds the smoking hibachi is eighteen floors up. Standing between the high gray sky and the pocket-sized pool, I feel omnipotent. Everything's in place.

While I poke the ruined meat with the barbecue fork, an uncommonly handsome blond woman in a ponytail and a cherry-red tracksuit comes out of the building's back door. She hurls a bashed pizza box, like a Frisbee, into the dumpster. Excess energy floats toward me, connecting us. She can't stand still. She tightens a shoelace. We're a community of toned, conditioned athletes. Use it or lose it. Hands pressed down on somebody's Firebird, she does warm-up routines. I've seen her run in the Lullwater Estate close by, but I've never felt connected enough to her to nod. I heave the meat from the rack to a platter. The woman's still hanging around in that hyper, fidgety way of hers. She's waiting. She's waiting for someone. When a man in a matching tracksuit jogs out the back door, I get depressed. She used to run alone.

Blanquita doesn't say anything about the state of our dinner. It's already stuffed away conveniently in the past. She's got the TV going again. The latest news, hot from Mexico City. "They had this news analyst chap on a minute ago," she says. "They were talking about Vitaly Yurchenko."

I put the butterfly lamb in the kitchen sink. "Why don't you watch about Vitaly Yurchenko on an American station?" I ask. Usually, that steams her. Mexican *is* American! she'll squeal. But instead she says, "He could have had it all if he'd stayed. What's so great about Moscow?"

"Sometimes you blow it for love. It can happen."

She runs to me, lavender arms going like wings. Her face—the skin so tight-pored that in the dark I feel like I'm stroking petals—glows with new hope. "What are you saying, Griff? Are you saying what I think you're saying?"

I know what I would say if I weren't the solid corporate guy in maroon tie and dark suit. I buy and sell with other people's money and skim enough to just get by. It's worked so far.

"Griff?"

Sailor?

"Let's go for a run, Blanquita."

The woman of many men's dreams doesn't wrench herself free from my kissing hold. I don't deserve her.

"Just a short run. To clear our heads. Please?"

Before I met her I used to pump iron. I was pumping so hard I could feel a vein nearly pop in the back of my head. I was a candidate for a stroke. Self-love may be too much like self-hate, who knows? Blanquita got me running. We started out real easy, staying inside the Lullwater Estate like that woman in the red tracksuit. We ran the Peachtree 10K. We could run a marathon if we wanted to. Our weightless feet beat perfect time through city streets and wooded ravines. The daily run is the second best thing we do together, I like to think.

"All right," she says. She gives me one of her demure, convent smiles. "But what'll we do with dinner?"

I point at the shriveled, carbonized thing in the stainless steel sink. "We could mail it to Africa."

"Biafra?" she asks.

"Baby, Baby . . . Ethiopia, Mozambique. Biafra was gone a long time ago," I tell her. She's very selective with her news. Emilou was a news hound, and I took to watching CNN for a solid winter.

Blanquita pins my condo key to her elasticized waistband and goes out the front foor ahead of me. The lawyer from 1403 is waiting by the elevator. I am far enough behind Blanquita to catch the quickie gleam in his eyes before he resumes his cool Duke demeanor and holds the elevator for us. In your face, Blue Devil.

THAT NIGHT BLANQUITA WHIPS UP some green nutritive complexion cream in the Cuisinart. She slaps the green sludge on her face with a rubber spatula. Her face is unequivocally mournful. The sludge in the Cuisinart fills the condo with smells I remember from nature trails of my childhood. Woodsy growths. Mosses. Ferns. I tracked game as a kid; I fished creeks. Atlanta wasn't always this archipelago of developments.

"Better make tonight memorable," she advises. The mask is starting to stiffen, especially around the lips. She has full, pouty, brownish lips. "It's our last night."

228 | MIDCAREER STORIES (1985–1988)

How many times has she said that? I've never said it, never had to. The women of my life always got the idea in plenty of time, they made it a mutual-consent, too-bad and so-long kind of thing. Wendi was really looking for a stepfather to her kids. Emilou was looking for full-time business advice to manage her settlement.

"What's that supposed to mean?"

The lips make a whistling noise from inside the mask's cut-out. "Anyway," she says, "it wasn't all cherry bombs and rockets for me either. Just sparklers."

Sex, intimacy, love. I can't keep any of it straight anymore.

"You're not going to the Chief's cabin in the north woods, period. He's Jack the Ripper."

"You think I can't handle the situation, right? You think I'm just a dumb, naive foreigner you have to protect, right?"

"Yeah."

Then she leaps on me, green face, glamor-length nails, Dior robe and all. I don't know about Baby, but for me those rockets explode.

ALL DAY SUNDAY IT RAINS. The raindrops are of the big, splashy variety, complete with whiffs of wild winds and churned seas. Our winter is starting. I don't do much; I stay in, play Bach on the earphones and vacuum the broadloom. Marcos seems here to stay because I can't bring myself to call the ASPCA.

When the hour for the daily run rolls around, I start out as usual in the doctors' wing of the VA Hospital parking lot, pick my way around Mazdas, Audis, Volvos—they don't have too many station wagons in this neighborhood—keep pace with fit groups in running shoes for as long as it feels good, then shoot ahead, past the serious runners who don't look back when they hear you coming, past the dogs with Frisbees in their jaws, past the pros who scorn designer tracksuits and the Emory runners with fraternity gizmos on their shirts, pick up more speed until the Reeboks sheathe feet as light as cotton. Then it's time to race. Really race. After Emilou and just before Baby I did wind sprints for a spring at the Atlanta Track Club, ran the three-minute half, ran four of them. I can let it out.

Today in the rain and the changing weather, colder tomorrow, I run longer, pushing harder, than any afternoon in my life. Running is here to stay, even if Baby is gone.

Today I run until a vein in the back of my head feels ready to pop. The stopgap remedy is Fiorinal, and so I pop one while I slump in the shower. It feels so good, the exhaustion, the pile of heavy, cold, sweaty clothes, the whole

FIGHTING FOR THE REBOUND | *229*

paraphernalia of deliberate self-depletion. At the track club they had a sign from William Butler Yeats: Torture Body to Pleasure Soul. I believe it.

What to do now? The rain is over, the Falcons are dying on the tube, the sun is staging a comeback. Already, my arms and legs are lightening, I'm resurging, I'm pink and healthy as a baby.

THE NEARBY MALL IS SO UPSCALE that even the Vendoland janitor is dressed in a bright red blazer. The mall's got the requisite atriums, tinted skylights, fountains, and indoor neo-sidewalk cafés. It's a world-within-the-world; perfect peace and humidity, totally phony, and I love it. The Fiorinal's done its job. My head is vacant and painless.

It must still be raining on the Chief's woodsy acres.

I walk into an art framer's. It's the only empty store and the woman behind the counter, a Buckhead version of Liv Ullmann, with a wide sympathetic face, doesn't seem to mind that I don't look like a serious shopper. I give her my toothiest.

"Just looking," I apologize.

"Why?"

"That's a very reasonable question," I say. She is neatly and expensively dressed; at least, everything looks color coordinated and natural fiberish. She seems many cuts above mall sales assistant.

Besides, Blanquita thinks she's too good for me.

"Don't tell me you have something to frame," she says, laughing. "And I know you wouldn't buy the junk on these walls." She's really a great saleslady. She's narrowed my choices in about ten seconds. She's flattered my tastes. Her eyes are the same greenish blue as her paisley sweater vest.

She's intuitive. It's closing time and it's Sunday, and she opens late on Monday. "But you knew that, didn't you?" she smiles. She helps me out in her amused, laid-back way. Her name is Maura. Thirty-four, divorced, no kids; she gets the statistics out of the way. She's established an easy groundwork. In an hour or two she'll ask those leading questions that are part, more and more, of doing love in the eighties. I check automatically for wedding and friendship rings. The flesh on her ring finger isn't blanched and fluted so I know she's been divorced a while. That's a definite plus. The newly single are to be avoided.

Maura came down from Portland, Oregon, three winters ago. "I don't know why I stay." We're having a pitcher of sangría, still in the mall. I like her voice; it's rueful and teasing. I think I even like her big, sensible hands, so unlike Blanquita's. I spot slivers, chewed nails, nothing glazed or pasted on. Hands

230 | MIDCAREER STORIES (1985–1988)

that frame the art of Atlanta, such as it is. "Let's see, there's Farmers' Market and the International Airport. What else?"

"The CDC," I protest. The doctors and researchers at the Centers for Disease Control may all be aliens but this is no time to diminish the city's glory. "I'm betting on AIDS to put us on the map." There, I've made it easy, no sweat.

She laughs. I feel witty. I malinger, making small talk. Hard to tell what real time it is, out there in the world, but it must be dark. She suggests we go on to Appleby's on the other side of the mall. Appleby's is perfect for what we have going: relaxed fun and zero sentiment. I've struck gold.

No, I've lost my claim.

We have to drive around to the back of the mall. Her car's a banged-up blue Subaru. Not her fault, she explains; an Oriental sideswiped her just outside Farmers' Market on her first week in Atlanta. She kept the dent and let it rust. Her anti-sunbelt statement.

We order ten-cent oysters for her and Buffalo wings for me and a dollar pitcher. We don't feed each other forkfuls as we might have in a prevenereal era. Afterwards we have to walk around some in the parking lot before finding our way back to her Subaru. I haven't oriented myself to her car yet. It's these little things, first moves, losing the first step, that become so tiring, make me feel I'm slowing down. We've had a pleasant time and what I really want is to let her go.

"Want to hear me play the harpsichord?"

She locates her key inside her pocketbook. "That's very original," she says. "Should I believe you?"

"Only one way to find out." The harpsichord was part of love's debris. Wendi was musically inclined.

"It's the best line to date," Maura says as she unlocks the door on the passenger side for me.

SUNDAY NIGHT EASES into the dark, cozy A.M. of Monday. Maura and I are having ourselves perfect times. The world's a vale of tears only if you keep peering six weeks into the future.

"You're good for me," she keeps whispering, and makes me believe it. "Griff and the Farmers' Market. You're a whole new reason for me to stay."

"We make a good team," I say, knowing I've said it before. I'm already slipping back. I never used a line on Baby, and she never got my jokes anyway. Maura's hair, silvery blond in the condo's dimness, falls over my face. "Partner."

"But we shouldn't talk about it," she says. "That's one of my superstitions."

THE TENANT | *231*

I feel a small, icy twinge around my heart. I've swallowed too many superstitions these past few months.

Then the phone rings. I lift the phone off the night table and shove it under the bed.

"Oh, Christ, I just knew it," Maura says. "It's too good to be true, isn't it?" I can feel her body tremble. It's the first panic she's displayed.

"Look, I'm ignoring it."

"No you're not."

The ringing stops, waits a while, and starts up again.

"I don't have to answer it." I squeeze her rough hand, then splay the palm flat over my beard. "Give me a smile, pardner."

"It's all right with me," she says in her frank, Northwest way. "You have a life. Your life doesn't begin and end with me." She's already out of bed, already fishing through clothes for the simple things she dropped. "But if you ever need anything framed, do me a big favor, okay?"

The phone keeps up its stop-and-start ringing. It's the Muzak of Purgatory. Maura's dressed in an instant.

"There's no reason why you shouldn't be involved with someone."

Because I can't bear to hear it ring anymore, I shout into the mouthpiece, "What's with you, anyway? You're the one who left!"

But Blanquita the Brave, the giver of two cheers for a new life in a new continent, the pineapple of Joker Rosario's eyes, his Baby, sounds hysterical. I make out phrases. The Chief's into games. The Chief doesn't love her. Oh, Blanquita, you're breaking my heart: don't you know, didn't anyone ever tell you about us? Under it all, you still trust us, you still love. She's calling me from a diner. She's babbling route numbers, gas stations, how to find her. Can't I hear the semis? I'm all she's got.

I hear my voice, loud and insistent. "*Amoco?*" I'm shouting. "There's a hundred Amocos between the perimeter and Chattanooga."

"I don't want to know," I hear Maura tell Marcos as I rush the front door, warm-ups pulled over my pajamas. "I don't want to start anything complicated."

The Tenant

MAYA SANYAL has been in Cedar Falls, Iowa, less than two weeks. She's come, books and clothes and one armchair rattling in the smallest truck that U-Haul would rent her, from New Jersey. Before that she was in North Carolina. Before that, Calcutta, India. Every place has something to give. She is sitting at the kitchen table with Fran drinking bourbon for the first time in her life. Fran Johnson found her the furnished apartment and helped her settle in. Now she's brought a bottle of bourbon which gives her the right to stay and talk for a bit. She's breaking up with someone called Vern, a pharmacist. Vern's father is also a pharmacist and owns a drugstore. Maya has seen Vern's father on TV twice already. The first time was on the local news when he spoke out against the selling of painkillers like Advil and Nuprin in supermarkets and gas stations. In the matter of painkillers, Maya is a universalist. The other time he was in a barbershop quartet. Vern gets along all right with his father. He likes the pharmacy business, as business goes, but he wants to go back to graduate school and learn to make films. Maya is drinking her first bourbon tonight because Vern left today for San Francisco State.

"I understand totally," Fran says. She teaches Utopian Fiction and a course in Women's Studies and worked hard to get Maya hired. Maya has a Ph.D. in Comparative Literature and will introduce writers like R. K. Narayan and Chinua Achebe to three sections of sophomores at the University of Northern Iowa. "A person has to leave home. Try out his wings."

Fran has to use the bathroom. "I don't feel abandoned." She pushes her chair away from the table. "Anyway, it was a sex thing totally. We were good together. It'd be different if I'd loved him."

Maya tries to remember what's in the refrigerator. They need food. She hasn't been to the supermarket in over a week. She doesn't have a car yet and so she relies on a corner store—a longish walk—for milk, cereal, and frozen dinners. Someday these exigencies will show up as bad skin and collapsed muscle tone. No folly is ever lost. Maya pictures history as a net, the kind of safety net traveling trapeze artists of her childhood fell into when they were inattentive, or clumsy. Going to circuses in Calcutta with her father is what she remembers vividly. It is a banal memory, for her father, the owner of a steel company, is a complicated man.

Fran is out in the kitchen long enough for Maya to worry. They need food. Her mother believed in food. What is love, anger, inner peace, etc., her mother used to say, but the brain's biochemistry. Maya doesn't want to get into that, but she is glad she has enough stuff in the refrigerator to make an omelette. She realizes Indian women are supposed to be inventive with food, whip up exotic delights to tickle an American's palate, and she knows she should be meeting Fran's generosity and candor with some sort of bizarre and effortless countermove. If there's an exotic spice store in Cedar Falls or in neighboring Waterloo, she hasn't found it. She's looked in the phone book for common Indian names, especially Bengali, but hasn't yet struck up culinary intimacies.

THE TENANT | *233*

That will come—it always does. There's a six-pack in the fridge that her land-lord, Ted Suminski, had put in because she'd be thirsty after unpacking. She was thirsty, but she doesn't drink beer. She probably should have asked him to come up and drink the beer. Except for Fran she hasn't had anyone over. Fran is more friendly and helpful than anyone Maya has known in the States since she came to North Carolina ten years ago, at nineteen. Fran is a Swede, and she is tall, with blue eyes. Her hair, however, is a dull, darkish brown.

"I don't think I can handle anything that heavy-duty," Fran says when she comes back to the room. She means the omelette. "I have to go home in any case." She lives with her mother and her aunt, two women in their mid-seventies, in a drafty farmhouse. The farmhouse now has a computer store catty-corner from it. Maya's been to the farm. She's been shown photographs of the way the corner used to be. If land values ever rebound, Fran will be worth millions.

Before Fran leaves she says, "Has Rab Chatterji called you yet?"

"No." She remembers the name, a good, reliable Bengali name, from the first night's study of the phone book. Dr. Rabindra Chatterji teaches Physics.

"He called the English office just before I left." She takes car keys out of her pocketbook. She reknots her scarf. "I bet Indian men are more sensitive than Americans. Rab's a Brahmin, that's what people say."

A Chatterji has to be a Bengali Brahmin—last names give ancestral se-crets away—but Brahminness seems to mean more to Fran than it does to Maya. She was born in 1954, six full years after India became independent. Her India was Nehru's India: a charged, progressive place.

"All Indian men are wife beaters," Maya says. She means it and doesn't mean it. "That's why I married an American." Fran knows about the divorce, but nothing else. Fran is on the Hiring, Tenure, and Reappointment Com-mittee.

Maya sees Fran down the stairs and to the car which is parked in the back in the spot reserved for Maya's car, if she had owned one. It will take her sev-eral months to save enough to buy one. She always pays cash, never borrows. She tells herself she's still recovering from the U-Haul drive halfway across the country. Ted Suminski is in his kitchen watching the women. Maya waves to him because waving to him, acknowledging him in that way, makes him seem less creepy. He seems to live alone though a sign, THE SUMINSKIS, hangs from a metal horse's head in the front yard. Maya hasn't seen Mrs. Suminski. She hasn't seen any children either. Ted always looks lonely. When she comes back from campus, he's nearly always in the back, throwing darts or shooting baskets.

"What's he like?" Fran gestures with her head as she starts up her car. "You hear these stories."

234 | MIDCAREER STORIES (1985–1988)

Maya doesn't want to know the stories. She has signed a year's lease. She doesn't want complications. "He's all right. I keep out of his way."

"You know what I'm thinking? Of all the people in Cedar Falls, you're the one who could understand Vern best. His wanting to try out his wings, run away, stuff like that."

"Not really." Maya is not being modest. Fran is being impulsively democratic, lumping her wayward lover and Indian friend together as headstrong adventurers. For Fran, a utopian and feminist, borders don't count. Maya's taken some big risks, made a break from her parents' ways. She's done things a woman from Ballygunge Park doesn't do, even in fantasies. She's not yet shared stories with Fran, apart from the divorce. She's told her nothing of men she picks up, the reputation she'd gained, before Cedar Falls, for "indiscretions." She has a job, equity, three friends she can count on for emergencies. She is an American citizen. But.

FRAN'S BRAHMIN CALLS her two nights later. On the phone he presents himself as Dr. Chatterji, not Rabindra or Rab. An old-fashioned Indian, she assumes. Her father still calls his closest friend, "Colonel." Dr. Chatterji asks her to tea on Sunday. She means to say no but hears herself saying, "Sunday? Fiveish? I'm not doing anything special this Sunday."

Outside, Ted Suminski is throwing darts into his garage door. The door has painted-on rings: orange, purple, pink. The bull's-eye is gray. He has to be fifty at least. He is a big, thick, lonely man about whom people tell stories. Maya pulls the phone cord as far as it'll go so she can look down more directly on her landlord's large, bald head. He has his back to her as he lines up a dart. He's in black running shoes, red shorts, he's naked to the waist. He hunches his right shoulder, he pulls his arm back; a big, lonely man shouldn't have so much grace. The dart is ready to cut through the September evening. But Ted Suminski doesn't let go. He swings on worn rubber soles, catches her eye in the window (she has to have imagined this), takes aim at her shadow. Could she have imagined the noise of the dart's metal tip on her windowpane?

Dr. Chatterji is still on the phone. "You are not having any mode of transportation, is that right?"

Ted Suminski has lost interest in her. Perhaps it isn't interest, at all; perhaps it's aggression. "I don't drive," she lies, knowing it sounds less shameful than not owning a car. She has said this so often she can get in the right degree of apology and Asian upper-class helplessness. "It's an awful nuisance."

"Not to worry, please." Then, "It's a great honor to be meeting Dr. Sanyal's daughter. In Calcutta business circles he is a legend."

THE TENANT | 235

ON SUNDAY she is ready by four-thirty. She doesn't know what the afternoon holds; there are surely no places for "high tea"—a colonial tradition—in Cedar Falls, Iowa. If he takes her back to his place, it will mean he has invited other guests. From his voice she can tell Dr. Chatterji likes to do things correctly. She has dressed herself in a peach-colored nylon georgette sari, jade drop earrings and a necklace. The color is good on dark skin. She is not pretty, but she does her best. Working at it is a part of self-respect. In the mid-seventies, when American women felt rather strongly about such things, Maya had been in trouble with her women's group at Duke. She was too feminine. She had tried to explain the world she came out of. Her grandmother had been married off at the age of five in a village now in Bangladesh. Her great-aunt had been burned to death over a dowry problem. She herself had been trained to speak softly, arrange flowers, sing, be pliant. If she were to seduce Ted Suminski, she thinks as she waits in the front yard for Dr. Chatterji, it would be minor heroism. She has broken with the past. But.

Dr. Chatterji drives up for her at about five ten. He is a hesitant driver. The car stalls, jumps ahead, finally slams to a stop. Maya has to tell him to back off a foot or so; it's hard to leap over two sacks of pruned branches in a sari. Ted Suminski is an obsessive pruner and gardener.

"My sincerest apologies, Mrs. Sanyal," Dr. Chatterji says. He leans across the wide front seat of his noisy, very old, very used car and unlocks the door for her. "I am late. But then, I am sure you're remembering that Indian Standard Time is not at all the same as time in the States." He laughs. He could be nervous—she often had that effect on Indian men. Or he could just be chatty. "These Americans are all the time rushing and rushing but where it gets them?" He moves his head laterally once, twice. It's the gesture made famous by Peter Sellers. When Peter Sellers did it, it had seemed hilarious. Now it suggests that Maya and Dr. Chatterji have three thousand years plus civilization, sophistication, moral virtue, over people born on this continent. Like her, Dr. Chatterji is a naturalized American.

"Call me Maya," she says. She fusses with the seat belt. She does so because she needs time to look him over. He seems quite harmless. She takes in the prominent teeth, the eyebrows that run together. He's in a blue shirt and a beige cardigan with the K-Mart logo that buttons tightly across the waist. It's hard to guess his age because he has dyed his hair and his mustache. Late thirties, early forties. Older than she had expected. "Not Mrs. Sanyal."

This isn't the time to tell about ex-husbands. She doesn't know where John is these days. He should have kept up at least. John had come into her life as a graduate student at Duke, and she, mistaking the brief breathlessness of sex for love, had married him. They had stayed together two years, maybe a little less. The pain that John had inflicted all those years ago by leaving her had subsided into a cozy feeling of loss. This isn't the time, but then she doesn't want to be a legend's daughter all evening. She's not necessarily on Dr. Chatterji's side is what she wants to get across early; she's not against America and Americans. She makes the story—of marriage against the Brahminic pale, the divorce—quick, dull. Her unsentimentality seems to shock him. His stomach sags inside his cardigan.

"We've each had our several griefs," the physicist says. "We're each required to pay our karmic debts."

"Where are we headed?"

"Mrs. Chatterji has made some Indian snacks. She is waiting to meet you because she is knowing your cousin-sister who studied in Scottish Church College. My home is okay, no?"

Fran would get a kick out of this. Maya has slept with married men, with nameless men, with men little more than boys, but never with an Indian man. Never.

THE CHATTERJIS LIVE in a small blue house on a gravelly street. There are at least five or six other houses on the street; the same size but in different colors and with different front yard treatments. More houses are going up. This is the cutting edge of suburbia.

Mrs. Chatterji stands in the driveway. She is throwing a large plastic ball to a child. The child looks about four, and is Korean or Cambodian. The child is not hers because she tells it, "Chung-Hee, ta-ta, bye-bye. Now I play with guest," as Maya gets out of the car.

Maya hasn't seen this part of town. The early September light softens the construction pits. In that light the houses too close together, the stout woman in a striped cotton sari, the child hugging a pink ball, the two plastic lawn chairs by a tender young tree, the sheets and saris on the clothesline in the back, all seem miraculously incandescent.

"Go home now, Chung-Hee. I am busy." Mrs. Chatterji points the child homeward, then turns to Maya, who has folded her hands in traditional Bengali greeting. "It is an honor. We feel very privileged." She leads Maya indoors to a front room that smells of moisture and paint.

In her new, deliquescent mood, Maya allows herself to be backed into the best armchair—a low-backed, boxy Goodwill item draped over with a Rajasthani bedspread—and asks after the cousin Mrs. Chatterji knows. She doesn't want to let go of Mrs. Chatterji. She doesn't want husband and wife to get into whispered conferences about their guest's misadventures in America, as they make tea in the kitchen.

The coffee table is already laid with platters of mutton croquettes, fish chops, onion pakoras, ghugni with puris, samosas, chutneys. Mrs. Chatterji has gone to too much trouble. Maya counts four kinds of sweetmeats in Corning casseroles on an end table. She looks into a see-through lid; spongy, white dumplings float in rosewater syrup. Planets contained, mysteries made visible.

"What are you waiting for, Santana?" Dr. Chatterji becomes imperious, though not unaffectionate. He pulls a dining chair up close to the coffee table. "Make some tea." He speaks in Bengali to his wife, in English to Maya. To Maya he says, grandly, "We are having real Indian Green Label Lipton. A nephew is bringing it just one month back."

His wife ignores him. "The kettle's already on," she says. She wants to know about the Sanyal family. Is it true her great-grandfather was a member of the Star Chamber[1] in England?

Nothing in Calcutta is ever lost. Just as her story is known to Bengalis all over America, so are the scandals of her family, the grandfather hauled up for tax evasion, the aunt who left her husband to act in films. This woman brings up the Star Chamber, the glories of the Sanyal family, her father's philanthropies, but it's a way of saying, *I know the dirt.*

The bedrooms are upstairs. In one of those bedrooms an unseen, tormented presence—Maya pictures it as a clumsy ghost that strains to shake off the body's shell—drops things on the floor. The things are heavy and they make the front room's chandelier shake. Light bulbs, shaped like tiny candle flames, flicker. The Chatterjis have said nothing about children. There are no tricycles in the hallway, no small sandals behind the doors. Maya is too polite to ask about the noise, and the Chatterjis don't explain. They talk just a little louder. They flip the embroidered cover off the stereo. What would Maya like to hear? Hemant Kumar? Manna Dey? Oh, that young chap, Manna Dey! What sincerity, what tenderness he can convey!

Upstairs the ghost doesn't hear the music of nostalgia. The ghost throws and thumps. The ghost makes its own vehement music. Maya hears in its voice madness, self-hate.

Finally the water in the kettle comes to a boil. The whistle cuts through all fantasy and pretense. Dr. Chatterji says, "I'll see to it," and rushes out of the room. But he doesn't go to the kitchen. He shouts up the stairwell. "Pol-

---

1. The Star Chamber, an English court for judges and privy councilors, was abolished in the seventeenth century, so Mukherjee may be thinking of another elite legal establishment in London here.—Ed.

too, kindly stop this nonsense straightaway! We're having a brilliant and cultured lady-guest and you're creating earthquakes?" The kettle is hysterical.

Mrs. Chatterji wipes her face. The face that had seemed plump and cheery at the start of the evening now is flabby. "My sister's boy," the woman says.

So this is the nephew who has brought with him the cartons of Green Label tea, one of which will be given to Maya.

Mrs. Chatterji speaks to Maya in English as though only the alien language can keep emotions in check. "Such an intelligent boy! His father is government servant. Very highly placed."

Maya is meant to visualize a smart, clean-cut young man from south Calcutta, but all she can see is a crazy, thwarted, lost graduate student. Intelligence, proper family guarantee nothing. Even Brahmins can do self-destructive things, feel unsavory urges. Maya herself had been an excellent student.

"He was First Class First in B. Sc. from Presidency College," the woman says. "Now he's getting Master's in Ag. Science at Iowa State."

The kitchen is silent. Dr. Chatterji comes back into the room with a tray. The teapot is under a tea cozy, a Kashmiri one embroidered with the usual chinar leaves, loops, and chains. "*Her* nephew," he says. The dyed hair and dyed mustache are no longer signs of a man wishing to fight the odds. He is a vain man, anxious to cut losses. "Very unfortunate business."

The nephew's story comes out slowly, over fish chops and mutton croquettes. He is in love with a student from Ghana.

"Everything was A-Okay until the Christmas break. Grades, assistantship for next semester, everything."

"I blame the college. The office for foreign students arranged a Christmas party. And now, *baapre baap!* Our poor Poltoo wants to marry a Negro Muslim."

Maya is known for her nasty, ironic one-liners. It has taken her friends weeks to overlook her malicious, un-American pleasure in others' misfortunes. Maya would like to finish Dr. Chatterji off quickly. He is pompous; he is reactionary; he wants to live and work in America but give back nothing except taxes. The confused world of the immigrant—the lostness that Maya and Poltoo feel—that's what Dr. Chatterji wants to avoid. She hates him. But.

Dr. Chatterji's horror is real. A good Brahmin boy in Iowa is in love with an African Muslim. It shouldn't be a big deal. But the more she watches the physicist, the more she realizes that "Brahmin" isn't a caste; it's a metaphor. You break one small rule, and the constellation collapses. She thinks suddenly that John Cheever—she is teaching him as a "world writer" in her classes, cheek-by-jowl with Africans and West Indians—would have understood Dr. Chatterji's dread. Cheever had been on her mind, ever since the late afternoon light slanted over Mrs. Chatterji's drying saris. She remembers now how full of a soft, Cheeverian light Durham had been the summer she had slept with John Hadwen; and how after that, her tidy graduate-student world became monstrous, lawless. All men became John Hadwen; John became all men. Outwardly, she retained her poise, her Brahminical breeding. She treated her crisis as a literary event; she lost her moral sense, her judgment, her power to distinguish. Her parents had behaved magnanimously. They had cabled from Calcutta: WHAT'S DONE IS DONE. WE ARE CONFIDENT YOU WILL HANDLE NEW SITUATIONS WELL. ALL LOVE. But she knows more than do her parents. Love is anarchy.

Poltoo is Mrs. Chatterji's favorite nephew. She looks as though it is her fault that the Sunday has turned unpleasant. She stacks the empty platters methodically. To Maya she says, "It is the goddess who pulls the strings. We are puppets. I know the goddess will fix it. Poltoo will not marry that African woman." Then she goes to the coat closet in the hall and staggers back with a harmonium, the kind sold in music stores in Calcutta, and sets it down on the carpeted floor. "We're nothing but puppets," she says again. She sits at Maya's feet, her pudgy hands on the harmonium's shiny, black bellows. She sings, beautifully, in a virgin's high voice, "Come, goddess, come, muse, come to us hapless people's rescue."

Maya is astonished. She has taken singing lessons at Dakshini Academy in Calcutta. She plays the sitar and the tanpur, well enough to please Bengalis, to astonish Americans. But stout Mrs. Chatterji is a devotee, talking to God.

A LITTLE AFTER EIGHT, Dr. Chatterji drops her off. It's been an odd evening and they are both subdued.

"I want to say one thing," he says. He stops her from undoing her seat belt. The plastic sacks of pruned branches are still at the corner.

"You don't have to get out," she says.

"Please. Give me one more minute of your time."

"Sure."

"Maya is my favorite name."

She says nothing. She turns away from him without making her embarrassment obvious.

"Truly speaking, it is my favorite. You are sometimes lonely, no? But you are lucky. Divorced women can date, they can go to bars and discos. They can see mens, many mens. But inside marriage there is so much loneliness." A groan, low, horrible, comes out of him.

She turns back toward him, to unlatch the seat belt and run out of the car. She sees that Dr. Chatterji's pants are unzipped. One hand works hard under his Jockey shorts; the other rests, limp, penitential, on the steering wheel.

"Dr. Chatterji—*really!*" she cries.

THE NEXT DAY, Monday, instead of getting a ride home with Fran—Fran says she *likes* to give rides, she needs the chance to talk, and she won't share gas expenses, absolutely not—Maya goes to the periodicals room of the library. There are newspapers from everywhere, even from Madagascar and New Caledonia. She thinks of the periodicals room as an asylum for homesick aliens. There are two aliens already in the room, both Orientals, both absorbed in the politics and gossip of their far off homes.

She goes straight to the newspapers from India. She bunches her raincoat like a bolster to make herself more comfortable. There's so much to catch up on. A village headman, a known Congress-Indira party worker, has been shot at by scooter-riding snipers. An Indian pugilist has won an international medal— in Nepal. A child drawing well water—the reporter calls the child "a neo-Buddhist, a convert from the now-outlawed untouchable caste"—has been stoned. An editorial explains that the story about stoning is not a story about caste but about failed idealism; a story about promises of green fields and clean, potable water broken, a story about bribes paid and wells not dug. But no, thinks Maya, it's about caste.

Out here, in the heartland of the new world, the India of serious newspapers unsettles. Maya longs again to feel what she had felt in the Chatterjis' living room: virtues made physical. It is a familiar feeling, a longing. Had a suitable man presented himself in the reading room at that instant, she would have seduced him. She goes on to the stack of *India Abroads*, reads through matrimonial columns, and steals an issue to take home.

INDIAN MEN WANT INDIAN BRIDES. Married Indian men want Indian mistresses. All over America, "handsome, tall, fair" engineers, doctors, data processors—the new pioneers—cry their eerie love calls.

Maya runs a finger down the first column; her fingertip, dark with newsprint, stops at random.

Hello! Hi! Yes, you *are* the one I'm looking for. You are the new emancipated Indo-American woman. You have a zest for life. You are at ease in USA and yet your ethics are rooted in Indian tradition. The man of your dreams has come. Yours truly is handsome, ear-nose-throat specialist, well-settled in Connecticut. Age is 41 but never married, physically fit, sportsmanly, and strong. I adore idealism, poetry, beauty. I abhor smugness, passivity, caste system. Write with recent photo. Better still, call!!!

Maya calls. Hullo, hullo, hullo! She hears immigrant lovers cry in crowded shopping malls. Yes, you who are at ease in both worlds, you are the one. She feels she has a fair chance.

A man answers. "Ashoke Mehta speaking."

She speaks quickly into the bright-red mouthpiece of her telephone. He will be in Chicago, in transit, passing through O'Hare. United counter, Saturday, two P.M. As easy as that.

"Good," Ashoke Mehta says. "For these encounters I, too, prefer a neutral zone."

ON SATURDAY at exactly two o'clock the man of Maya's dreams floats toward her as lovers used to in shampoo commercials. The United counter is a loud, harrassed place but passengers and piled-up luggage fall away from him. Full-cheeked and fleshy-lipped, he is handsome. He hasn't lied. He is serene, assured, a Hindu god touching down in Illinois.

She can't move. She feels ugly and unworthy. Her adult life no longer seems miraculously rebellious; it is grim, it is perverse. She has accomplished nothing. She has changed her citizenship but she hasn't broken through into the light, the vigor, the *hustle* of the New World. She is stuck in dead space.

"Hullo, Hullo!" Their fingers touch.

Oh, the excitement! Ashoke Mehta's palm feels so right in the small of her back. Hullo, hullo, hullo. He pushes her out of the reach of anti-Khomeini Iranians, Hare Krishnas, American Fascists, men with fierce wants, and guides her to an empty gate. They have less than an hour.

"What would you like, Maya?"

She knows he can read her mind, she knows her thoughts are open to him. *You*, she's almost giddy with the thought, with simple desire. "From the snack bar," he says, as though to clarify. "I'm afraid I'm starved."

Below them, where the light is strong and hurtful, a Boeing is being serviced. "Nothing," she says.

He leans forward. She can feel the nap of his scarf—she recognizes the Cambridge colors—she can smell the wool of his Icelandic sweater. She runs her hand along the scarf, then against the flesh of his neck. "Only the impulsive ones call," he says.

The immigrant courtship proceeds. It's easy, he's good with facts. He knows how to come across to a stranger who may end up a lover, a spouse. He makes over a hundred thousand. He owns a house in Hartford, and two income properties in Newark. He plays the market but he's cautious. He's good at badminton but plays handball to keep in shape. He watches all the sports on television. Last August he visited Copenhagen, Helsinki and Leningrad. Once upon a time he collected stamps but now he doesn't have hobbies, except for reading. He counts himself an intellectual, he spends too much on books. Ludlum, Forsyth, MacInnes; other names she doesn't catch. She suppresses a smile, she's told him only she's a graduate student. He's not without his vices. He's a spender, not a saver. He's a sensualist: good food—all foods, but easy on the Indian—good wine. Some temptations he doesn't try to resist.

And I, she wants to ask, do I tempt?

"Now tell me about yourself, Maya." He makes it easy for her. "Have you ever been in love?"

"No."

"But many have loved you, I can see that." He says it not unkindly. It is the fate of women like her, and men like him. Their karmic duty, to be loved. It is expected, not judged. She feels he can see them all, the sad parade of need and demand. This isn't the time to reveal all.

And so the courtship enters a second phase.

WHEN SHE GETS to Cedar Falls, Ted Suminski is standing on the front porch. It's late at night, chilly. He is wearing a down vest. She's never seen him on the porch. In fact there's no chair to sit on. He looks chilled through. He's waited around a while.

"Hi." She has her keys ready. This isn't the night to offer the six-pack in the fridge. He looks expectant, ready to pounce.

"Hi." He looks like a man who might have aimed the dart at her. What has he done to his wife, his kids? Why isn't there at least a dog? "Say, I left a note upstairs."

The note is written in Magic Marker and thumb-tacked to her apartment door. DUE TO PERSONAL REASONS, NAMELY REMARRIAGE, I REQUEST THAT YOU VACATE MY PLACE AT THE END OF THE SEMESTER.

Maya takes the note down and retacks it to the kitchen wall. The whole wall is like a bulletin board, made of some new, crumbly building material.

THE TENANT | *243*

Her kitchen, Ted Suminski had told her, was once a child's bedroom. Suminski in love: the idea stuns her. She has misread her landlord. The dart at her window speaks of no twisted fantasy. The landlord wants the tenant out.

She gets a glass out of the kitchen cabinet, gets out a tray of ice, pours herself a shot of Fran's bourbon. She is happy for Ted Suminski. She is. She wants to tell someone how moved she'd been by Mrs. Chatterji's singing. How she'd felt in O'Hare, even about Dr. Rab Chatterji in the car. But Fran is not the person. No one she's ever met is the person. She can't talk about the dead space she lives in. She wishes Ashoke Mehta would call. Right now.

Weeks pass. Then two months. She finds a new room, signs another lease. Her new landlord calls himself Fred. He has no arms, but he helps her move her things. He drives between Ted Suminski's place and his twice in his station wagon. He uses his toes the way Maya uses her fingers. He likes to do things. He pushes garbage sacks full of Maya's clothes up the stairs.

"IT'S ALL RIGHT TO STARE," Fred says. "Hell, I would."

That first afternoon in Fred's rooming house, they share a Chianti. Fred wants to cook her pork chops but he's a little shy about Indians and meat. Is it beef, or pork? Or any meat? She says it's okay, any meat, but not tonight. He has an ex-wife in Des Moines, two kids in Portland, Oregon. The kids are both normal; he's the only freak in the family. But he's self-reliant. He shops in the supermarket like anyone else, he carries out the garbage, shovels the snow off the sidewalk. He needs Maya's help with one thing. Just one thing. The box of Tide is a bit too heavy to manage. Could she get him the giant size every so often and leave it in the basement?

The dead space need not suffocate. Over the months, Fred and she will settle into companionship. She has never slept with a man without arms. Two wounded people, he will joke during their nightly contortions. It will shock her, this assumed equivalence with a man so strikingly deficient. She knows she is strange, and lonely, but being Indian is not the same, she would have thought, as being a freak.

ONE NIGHT IN SPRING, Fred's phone rings. "Ashoke Mehta speaking." None of this "do you remember me?" nonsense. The god has tracked her down. He hasn't forgotten. "Hullo," he says, in their special way. And because she doesn't answer back, "Hullo, hullo, hullo." She is aware of Fred in the back of the room. He is lighting a cigarette with his toes.

"Yes," she says, "I remember."

244 | MIDCAREER STORIES (1985–1988)

"I had to take care of a problem," Ashoke Mehta says. "You know that I have my vices. That time at O'Hare I was honest with you."

She is breathless.

"Who is it, May?" asks Fred.

"You also have a problem," says the voice. His laugh echoes. "You will come to Hartford, I know."

When she moves out, she tells herself, it will not be the end of Fred's world.

Fathering

ENG STANDS JUST INSIDE our bedroom door, her fidgety fist on the doorknob which Sharon, in a sulk, polished to a gleam yesterday afternoon.

"I'm starved," she says.

I know a sick little girl when I see one. I brought the twins up without much help ten years ago. Eng's got a high fever. Brownish stains stiffen the nap of her terry robe. Sour smells fill the bedroom.

"For God's sake leave us alone," Sharon mutters under the quilt. She turns away from me. We bought the quilt at a garage sale in Rock Springs the Sunday two years ago when she moved in. "Talk to her."

Sharon works on this near-marriage of ours. I'll hand it to her, she really does. I knead her shoulders, and I say, "Easy, easy," though I really hate it when she treats Eng like a deaf-mute. "My girl speaks English, remember?"

Eng can outcuss any freckle-faced kid on the block. Someone in the killing fields must have taught her. Maybe her mama, the honeyest-skinned bar girl with the tiniest feet in Saigon. I was an errand boy with the Combined Military Intelligence. I did the whole war on Dexedrine. Vietnam didn't happen, and I'd put it behind me in marriage and fatherhood and teaching high school. Ten years later came the screw-ups with the marriage, the job, women, the works. Until Eng popped up in my life, I really believed it didn't happen.

"Come here, sweetheart," I beg my daughter. I sidle closer to Sharon, so there'll be room under the quilt for Eng.

"I'm starved," she complains from the doorway. She doesn't budge. The robe and hair are smelling something fierce. She doesn't show any desire to cuddle. She must be sick. She must have thrown up all night. Sharon throws the quilt back. "Then go raid the refrigerator like a normal kid," she snaps.

Once upon a time Sharon used to be a cheerful, accommodating woman. It isn't as if Eng was dumped on us out of the blue. She knew I was tracking my kid. Coming to terms with the past was Sharon's idea. I don't know what happened to *that* Sharon. "For all you know, Jason," she'd said, "the baby died of malaria or something." She said, "Go on, find out and deal with it." She said she could handle being a stepmother—better a fresh chance with some orphan off the streets of Saigon than with my twins from Rochester. My twins are being raised in some organic-farming lesbo commune. Their mother breeds Nubian goats for a living. "Come get in bed with us, baby. Let Dad feel your forehead. You burning up with fever?"

"She isn't hungry, I think she's sick," I tell Sharon, but she's already tugging her sleeping mask back on. "I think she's just letting us know she hurts."

I hold my arms out wide for Eng to run into. If I could, I'd suck the virus right out of her. In the jungle, VC mamas used to do that. Some nights we'd steal right up to a hootch—just a few of us intense sons of bitches on some special mission—and the women would be at their mumbo jumbo. They'd be sticking coins and amulets into napalm burns.

"I'm hungry, Dad." It comes out as a moan. Okay, she doesn't run into my arms, but at least she's come as far as the foot of our bed. "Dad, let's go down to the kitchen. Just you and me."

I am about to let that pass though I can feel Sharon's body go into weird little jerks and twitches when my baby adds with emphatic viciousness, "Not her, Dad. We don't want her with us in the kitchen."

"She loves you," I protest. Love—not spite—makes Eng so territorial; that's what I want to explain to Sharon. She's a sick, frightened, foreign kid, for Chrissake. "Don't you, Sharon? Sharon's concerned about you."

But Sharon turns over on her stomach. "You know what's wrong with you, Jase? You can't admit you're being manipulated. You can't cut through the 'frightened-foreign-kid' shit."

Eng moves closer. She comes up to the side of my bed, but doesn't touch the hand I'm holding out. She's a fighter.

"I feel fire-hot, Dad. My bones feel pain."

"Sharon?" I want to deserve this woman. "Sharon, I'm so sorry." It isn't anybody's fault. You need uppers to get through peace times, too.

"Dad. Let's go. Chop-chop."

"You're too sick to keep food down, baby. Curl up in here. Just for a bit?"

"I'd throw up, Dad."

"I'll carry you back to your room. I'll read you a story, okay?"

Eng watches me real close as I pull the quilt off. "You got any scars you haven't shown me yet? My mom had a big scar on one leg. Shrapnel. Boom boom. I got scars. See? I got lots of bruises."

I scoop up my poor girl and rush her, terry robe flapping, to her room which Sharon fixed up with white girlish furniture in less complicated days.

Waiting for Eng was good. Sharon herself said it was good for our relationship. "Could you bring us some juice and aspirin?" I shout from the hallway.

"Aspirin isn't going to cure Eng," I hear Sharon yell. "I'm going to call Dr. Kearns."

DOWNSTAIRS I HEAR SHARON on the phone. She isn't talking flu viruses. She's talking social workers and shrinks. My girl isn't crazy; she's picked up a bug in school as might anyone else.

"The child's arms are covered with bruises," Sharon is saying. "Nothing major. They look like . . . well, they're sort of tiny circles and welts." There's nothing for a while. Then she says, "Christ! no, Jason can't do enough for her! That's not what I'm saying! What's happening to this country? You think we're perverts? What I'm saying is the girl's doing it to herself."

"Who are you talking to?" I ask from the top of the stairs. "What happened to the aspirin?"

I lean as far forward over the railing as I dare so I can see what Sharon's up to. She's getting into her coat and boots. She's having trouble with buttons and snaps. In the bluish light of the foyer's broken chandelier, she looks old, harrowed, depressed. What have I done to her?

"What's going on?" I plead. "You deserting me?"

"Don't be so fucking melodramatic. I'm going to the mall to buy some aspirin."

"How come we don't have any in the house?"

"Why are you always picking on me?"

"Who was that on the phone?"

"So now you want me to account for every call and every trip?" She ties an angry knot into her scarf. But she tells me. "I was talking to Meg Kearns. She says Dr. Kearns has gone hunting for the day."

"Great!"

"She says he has his beeper on him."

I hear the back door stick and Sharon swear. She's having trouble with the latch. "Jiggle it gently," I shout, taking the stairs two at a time. But before I can come down, her Nissan backs out of the parking apron.

BACK UPSTAIRS I CATCH Eng in the middle of a dream or delirium. "They got Grandma!" she screams. She goes very rigid in bed. It's a four-poster with canopy and ruffles and stuff that Sharon put on her MasterCard. The twins slept on bunk beds. With the twins it was different, totally different. Dr. Spock can't be point man for Eng, for us.

"She bring me food," Eng's screaming. "She bring me food from the forest. They shoot Grandma! Bastards!"

"Eng?" I don't dare touch her. I don't know how.

"You shoot my grandmother?" She whacks the air with her bony arms. Now I see the bruises, the small welts all along the insides of her arms. Some have to be weeks old, they're that yellow. The twins' scrapes and cuts never turned that ochre. I can't help wondering if maybe Asian skin bruises differently from ours, even though I want to say skin is skin; especially hers is skin like mine.

"I want to be with Grandma. Grandma loves me. I want to be ghost. I don't want to get better."

I READ TO HER. I read to her because good parents are supposed to read to their kids laid up sick in bed. I want to do it right. I want to be a good father. I read from a sci-fi novel that Sharon must have picked up. She works in a camera store in the mall, right next to a B. Dalton. I read three pages out loud, then I read four chapters to myself because Eng's stopped up her ears. Aliens have taken over small towns all over the country. Idaho, Nebraska: no state is safe from aliens.

Some time after two, the phone rings. Since Sharon doesn't answer it on the second ring, I know she isn't back. She carries a cordless phone everywhere around the house. In the movies, when cops have bad news to deliver, they lean on your doorbell; they don't call. Sharon will come back when she's ready. We'll make up. Things will get back to normal.

"Jason?"

I know Dr. Kearns' voice. He saw the twins through the usual immunizations.

"I have Sharon here. She'll need a ride home. Can you drive over?"

"God! What's happened?"

"Nothing to panic about. Nothing physical. She came for a consultation."

"Give me a half-hour. I have to wrap Eng real warm so I can drag her out in this miserable weather."

"Take your time. This way I can take a look at Eng, too."

"What's wrong with Sharon?"

"She's a little exercised about a situation. I gave her a sedative. See you in a half-hour."

I ease delirious Eng out of the overdecorated four-poster, prop her against my body while I wrap a blanket around her. She's a tiny thing, but she feels stiff and heavy, a sleepwalking mummy. Her eyes are dry-bright, strange.

It's a sunny winter day, and the evergreens in the front yard are glossy with frost. Where the gutter leaks, the steps feel spongy. The shrubs and bushes my ex-wife planted clog the front path. I've put twenty years into this house. The steps, the path, the house all have a right to fall apart.

I'm thirty-eight. I've let a lot of people down already.

The inside of the van is deadly cold. Mid-January ice mottles the windshield. I lay the bundled-up child on the long seat behind me and wait for the engine to warm up. It feels good with the radio going and the heat coming on. I don't want the ice on the windshield to melt. Eng and I are safest in the van.

In the rear-view mirror, Eng's wrinkled lips begin to move. "Dad, can I have a quarter?"

"May I, kiddo," I joke.

There's all sorts of junk in the pockets of my parka. Buckshot, dimes and quarters for the vending machine, a Blistex.

"What do you need it for, sweetheart?"

Eng's quick. Like the street kids in Saigon who dove for cigarettes and sticks of gum. She's loosened the blanket folds around her. I watch her tuck the quarter inside her wool mitt. She grins. "Thanks, soldier."

At Dr. Kearns', Sharon is lying unnaturally slack-bodied on the lone vinyl sofa. Her coat's neatly balled up under her neck, like a bolster. Right now she looks amiable, docile. I don't think she exactly recognizes me, although later she'll say she did. All that stuff about Kearns going hunting must have been a lie. Even the stuff about having to buy aspirins in the mall. She was planning all along to get here.

"What's wrong?"

"It's none of my business, Jason, but you and Sharon might try an honest-to-goodness heart-to-heart." Then he makes a sign to me to lay Eng on the examining table. "We don't look so bad," he says to my daughter. Then he excuses himself and goes into a glass-walled cubicle.

Sharon heaves herself into a sitting position of sorts on the sofa. "Everything was fine until she got here. Send her back, Jase. If you love me, send her back." She's slouched so far forward, her pointed, sweatered breasts nearly touch her corduroy pants. She looks helpless, pathetic. I've brought her to this state. Guilt, not love, is what I feel.

I want to comfort Sharon, but my daughter with the wild, grieving pygmy face won't let go of my hand. "She's bad, Dad. Send *her* back."

FATHERING | 249

Dr. Kearns comes out of the cubicle balancing a sample bottle of pills or caplets on a flattened palm. He has a boxer's tough, squarish hands. "Miraculous stuff, this," he laughs. "But first we'll stick our tongue out and say *ahh*. Come on, open wide."

Eng opens her mouth real wide, then brings her teeth together, hard, on Dr. Kearns' hand. She leaps erect on the examining table, tearing the disposable paper sheet with her toes. Her tiny, funny toes are doing a frantic dance. "Don't let him touch me, Grandma!"

"He's going to make you all better, baby." I can't pull my alien child down, I can't comfort her. The twins had diseases with easy names, diseases we knew what to do with. The thing is, I never felt for them what I feel for her.

"Don't let him touch me, Grandma!" Eng's screaming now. She's hopping on the table and screaming. "Kill him, Grandma! Get me out of here, Grandma!"

"Baby, it's all right."

But she looks through me and the country doctor as though we aren't here, as though we aren't pulling at her to make her lie down.

"Lie back like a good girl," Dr. Kearns commands.

But Eng is listening to other voices. She pulls her mitts off with her teeth, chucks the blanket, the robe, the pajamas to the floor; then, naked, hysterical, she presses the quarter I gave her into the soft flesh of her arm. She presses and presses that coin, turning it in nasty half-circles until blood starts to pool under the skin.

"Jason, grab her at the knees. Get her back down on the table."

From the sofa, Sharon moans. "See, I told you the child was crazy. She hates me. She's possessive about Jason."

The doctor comes at us with his syringe. He's sedated Sharon; now he wants to knock out my kid with his cures.

"Get the hell out, you bastard!" Eng yells. "*Vamos!* Bang bang!" She's pointing her arm like a semiautomatic, taking out Sharon, then the doctor. My Rambo. "Old way is good way. Money cure is good cure. When they shoot my grandma, you think pills do her any good? You Yankees, please go home." She looks straight at me. "Scram, Yankee bastard!"

Dr. Kearns has Eng by the wrist now. He has flung the quarter I gave her on the floor. Something incurable is happening to my women.

Then, as in fairy tales, I know what has to be done. "Coming, pardner!" I whisper. "I got no end of coins." I jiggle the change in my pocket. I jerk away from our enemies. My Saigon kid and me: we're a team. In five minutes we'll be safely away in the cold chariot of our van.

Jasmine

JASMINE CAME to Detroit from Port-of-Spain, Trinidad, by way of Canada. She crossed the border at Windsor in the back of a gray van loaded with mattresses and box springs. The plan was for her to hide in an empty mattress box if she heard the driver say, "All bad weather seems to come down from Canada, doesn't it?" to the customs man. But she didn't have to crawl into a box and hold her breath. The customs man didn't ask to look in.

The driver let her off at a scary intersection on Woodward Avenue and gave her instructions on how to get to the Plantations Motel in Southfield. The trick was to keep changing vehicles, he said. That threw off the immigration guys real quick.

Jasmine took money for cab fare out of the pocket of the great big raincoat that the van driver had given her. The raincoat looked like something that nuns in Port-of-Spain sold in church bazaars. Jasmine was glad to have a coat with wool lining, though; and anyway, who would know in Detroit that she was Dr. Vassanji's daughter?

All the bills in her hand looked the same. She would have to be careful when she paid the cabdriver. Money in Detroit wasn't pretty the way it was back home, or even in Canada, but she liked this money better. Why should money be pretty, like a picture? Pretty money is only good for putting on your walls maybe. The dollar bills felt businesslike, serious. Back home at work, she used to count out thousands of Trinidad dollars every day and not even think of them as real. Real money was worn and green, American dollars. Holding the bills in her fist on a street corner meant she had made it in okay. She'd outsmarted the guys at the border. Now it was up to her to use her wits to do something with her life. As her daddy kept saying, "Girl, is opportunity come only once." The girls she'd worked with at the bank in Port-of-Spain had gone green as bananas when she'd walked in with her ticket on Air Canada. Trinidad was too tiny. That was the trouble. Trinidad was an island stuck in the middle of nowhere. What kind of place was that for a girl with ambition?

The Plantations Motel was run by a family of Trinidad Indians who had come from the tuppenny-ha'penny country town Chaguanas. The Daboos were nobodies back home. They were lucky, that's all. They'd gotten here before the rush and bought up a motel and an ice cream parlor. Jasmine felt very superior when she saw Mr. Daboo in the motel's reception area. He was a pumpkin-shaped man with very black skin and Elvis Presley sideburns turning white. They looked like earmuffs. Mrs. Daboo was a bumpkin, too; short, fat, flapping around in house slippers. The Daboo daughters seemed very American, though. They didn't seem to know that they were nobodies, and kept looking at her and giggling.

She knew she would be short of cash for a great long while. Besides, she wasn't sure she wanted to wear bright leather boots and leotards like Viola and Loretta. The smartest move she could make would be to put a down payment on a husband. Her daddy had told her to talk to the Daboos first chance. The Daboos ran a service fixing up illegals with islanders who had made it in legally. Daddy had paid three thousand back in Trinidad, with the Daboos and the mattress man getting part of it. They should throw in a good-earning husband for that kind of money.

The Daboos asked her to keep books for them and to clean the rooms in the new wing, and she could stay in 16B as long as she liked. They showed her 16B. They said she could cook her own roti; Mr. Daboo would bring in a stove, two gas rings that you could fold up in a metal box. The room was quite grand, Jasmine thought. It had a double bed, a TV, a pink sink and matching bathtub. Mrs. Daboo said Jasmine wasn't the big-city Port-of-Spain type she'd expected. Mr. Daboo said that he wanted her to stay because it was nice to have a neat, cheerful person around. It wasn't a bad deal, better than stories she'd heard about Trinidad girls in the States.

All day every day except Sundays Jasmine worked. There wasn't just the bookkeeping and the cleaning up. Mr. Daboo had her working on the match-up marriage service. Jasmine's job was to check up on social security cards, call clients' bosses for references, and make sure credit information wasn't false. Dermatologists and engineers living in Bloomfield Hills, store owners on Canfield and Woodward: she treated them all as potential liars. One of the first things she learned was that Ann Arbor was a magic word. A boy goes to Ann Arbor and gets an education, and all the barriers come crashing down. So Ann Arbor was the place to be.

She didn't mind the work. She was learning about Detroit, every side of it. Sunday mornings she helped unload packing crates of Caribbean spices in a shop on the next block. For the first time in her life, she was working for a black man, an African. So what if the boss was black? This was a new life, and she wanted to learn everything. Her Sunday boss, Mr. Anthony, was a courtly, Christian, church-going man, and paid her the only wages she had in her pocket. Viola and Loretta, for all their fancy American ways, wouldn't go out with blacks.

One Friday afternoon she was writing up the credit info on a Guyanese Muslim who worked in an assembly plant when Loretta said that enough was enough and that there was no need for Jasmine to be her father's drudge.

"Is time to have fun," Viola said. "We're going to Ann Arbor."

Jasmine filed the sheet on the Guyanese man who probably now would never get a wife and got her raincoat. Loretta's boyfriend had a Cadillac parked out front. It was the longest car Jasmine had ever been in and louder than a country bus. Viola's boyfriend got out of the front seat. "Oh, oh, sweet things," he said to Jasmine. "Get in front." He was a talker. She'd learned that much from working on the matrimonial match-ups. She didn't believe him for a second when he said that there were dudes out there dying to ask her out.

Loretta's boyfriend said, "You have eyes I could leap into, girl."

Jasmine knew he was just talking. They sounded like Port-of-Spain boys of three years ago. It didn't surprise her that these Trinidad country boys in Detroit were still behind the times, even of Port-of-Spain. She sat very stiff between the two men, hands on her purse. The Daboo girls laughed in the back seat.

On the highway the girls told her about the reggae night in Ann Arbor. Kevin and the Krazee Islanders. Malcolm's Lovers. All the big reggae groups in the Midwest were converging for the West Indian Students Association fall bash. The ticket didn't come cheap but Jasmine wouldn't let the fellows pay. She wasn't that kind of girl.

The reggae and steel drums brought out the old Jasmine. The rum punch, the dancing, the dreadlocks, the whole combination. She hadn't heard real music since she got to Detroit, where music was supposed to be so famous. The Daboo girls kept turning on rock stuff in the motel lobby whenever their father left the area. She hadn't danced, really *danced*, since she'd left home. It felt so good to dance. She felt hot and sweaty and sexy. The boys at the dance were more than sweet talkers; they moved with assurance and spoke of their futures in America. The bartender gave her two free drinks and said, "Is ready when you are, girl." She ignored him but she felt all hot and good deep inside. She knew Ann Arbor was a special place.

When it was time to pile back into Loretta's boyfriend's Cadillac, she just couldn't face going back to the Plantations Motel and to the Daboos with their accounting books and messy files.

"I don't know what happen, girl," she said to Loretta. "I feel all crazy inside. Maybe is time for me to pursue higher studies in this town."

"This Ann Arbor, girl, they don't just take you off the street. It *cost* like hell."

She spent the night on a bashed-up sofa in the Student Union. She was a well-dressed, respectable girl, and she didn't expect anyone to question her right to sleep on the furniture. Many others were doing the same thing. In the morning, a boy in an army parka showed her the way to the Placement Office. He was a big, blond, clumsy boy, not bad-looking except for the blond eyelashes. He didn't scare her, as did most Americans. She let him buy her a Coke and a hot dog. That evening she had a job with the Moffitts.

Bill Moffitt taught molecular biology and Lara Hatch-Moffitt, his wife, was a performance artist. A performance artist, said Lara, was very different from being an actress, though Jasmine still didn't understand what the difference might be. The Moffitts had a little girl, Muffin, whom Jasmine was to look after, though for the first few months she might have to help out with the housework and the cooking because Lara said she was deep into performance rehearsals. That was all right with her, Jasmine said, maybe a little too quickly. She explained she came from a big family and was used to heavy-duty cooking and cleaning. This wasn't the time to say anything about Ram, the family servant. Americans like the Moffitts wouldn't understand about keeping servants. Ram and she weren't in similar situations. Here mother's helpers, which is what Lara had called her—Americans were good with words to cover their shame—seemed to be as good as anyone.

Lara showed her the room she would have all to herself in the finished basement. There was a big, old TV, not in color like the motel's and a portable typewriter on a desk which Lara said she would find handy when it came time to turn in her term papers. Jasmine didn't say anything about not being a student. She was a student of life, wasn't she? There was a scary moment after they'd discussed what she could expect as salary, which was three times more than anything Mr. Daboo was supposed to pay her but hadn't. She thought Bill Moffitt was going to ask her about her visa or her green card number and social security. But all Bill did was smile and smile at her—he had a wide, pink, baby face—and play with a button on his corduroy jacket. The button would need sewing back on, firmly.

Lara said, "I think I'm going to like you, Jasmine. You have a something about you. A something real special. I'll just bet you've acted, haven't you?" The idea amused her, but she merely smiled and accepted Lara's hug. The interview was over.

Then Bill opened a bottle of Soave and told stories about camping in northern Michigan. He'd been raised there. Jasmine didn't see the point in sleeping in tents; the woods sounded cold and wild and creepy. But she said, "Is exactly what I want to try out come summer, man. Campin and huntin."

Lara asked about Port-of-Spain. There was nothing to tell about her hometown that wouldn't shame her in front of nice white American folk like the Moffitts. The place was shabby, the people were grasping and cheating and lying and life was full of despair and drink and wanting. But by the time she finished, the island sounded romantic. Lara said, "It wouldn't surprise me one bit if you were a writer, Jasmine."

Ann Arbor was a huge small town. She couldn't imagine any kind of school the size of the University of Michigan. She meant to sign up for courses in the spring. Bill brought home a catalog bigger than the phone book for all of Trinidad. The university had courses in everything. It would be hard to choose; she'd have to get help from Bill. He wasn't like a professor, not the ones back home where even high school teachers called themselves professors and acted like little potentates. He wore blue jeans and thick sweaters with holes in the elbows and used phrases like "in vitro" as he watched her curry up fish. Dr. Parveen back home—he called himself "doctor" when everybody knew he didn't have even a Master's degree—was never seen without his cotton jacket which had gotten really ratty at the cuffs and lapel edges. She hadn't learned anything in the two years she'd put into college. She'd learned more from working in the bank for two months than she had at college. It was the assistant manager, Personal Loans Department, Mr. Singh, who had turned her on to the Daboos and to smooth, bargain-priced emigration.

Jasmine liked Lara. Lara was easygoing. She didn't spend the time she had between rehearsals telling Jasmine how to cook and clean American-style. Mrs. Daboo did that in 16B. Mrs. Daboo would barge in with a plate of stale samosas and snoop around giving free advice on how mainstream Americans did things. As if she were dumb or something! As if she couldn't keep her own eyes open and make her mind up for herself. Sunday mornings she had to share the butcher-block workspace in the kitchen with Bill. He made the Sunday brunch from new recipes in *Gourmet* and *Cuisine.* Jasmine hadn't seen a man cook who didn't have to or wasn't getting paid to do it. Things were topsy-turvy in the Moffitt house. Lara went on two- and three-day road trips and Bill stayed home. But even her daddy, who'd never poured himself a cup of tea, wouldn't put Bill down as a woman. The mornings Bill tried out something complicated, a Cajun shrimp, sausage, and beans dish, for instance, Jasmine skipped church services. The Moffitts didn't go to church, though they seemed to be good Christians. They just didn't talk church talk, which suited her fine.

Two months passed. Jasmine knew she was lucky to have found a small, clean, friendly family like the Moffitts to build her new life around. "Man!" she'd exclaim as she vacuumed the wide-plank wood floors or ironed (Lara wore pure silk or pure cotton). "In this country Jesus givin out good luck only!" By this time they knew she wasn't a student, but they didn't care and said they wouldn't report her. They never asked if she was illegal on top of it.

To savor her new sense of being a happy, lucky person, she would put herself through a series of "what ifs": what if Mr. Singh in Port-of-Spain hadn't turned her on to the Daboos and loaned her two thousand! What if she'd been ugly like the Mintoo girl and the manager hadn't even offered! What if the customs man had unlocked the door of the van! Her daddy liked to say, "You is a helluva girl, Jasmine."

"Thank you, Jesus," Jasmine said, as she carried on.

Christmas Day the Moffitts treated her just like family. They gave her a red cashmere sweater with a V neck so deep it made her blush. If Lara had worn it, her bosom wouldn't hang out like melons. For the holiday weekend Bill drove her to the Daboos in Detroit. "You work too hard," Bill said to her. "Learn to be more selfish. Come on, throw your weight around." She'd rather not have spent time with the Daboos, but that first afternoon of the interview she'd told Bill and Lara that Mr. Daboo was her mother's first cousin. She had thought it shameful in those days to have no papers, no family, no roots. Now Loretta and Viola in tight, bright pants seemed trashy like girls at Two-Johnny Bissoondath's Bar back home. She was stuck with the story of the Daboos being family. Village bumpkins, ha! She would break out. Soon.

Jasmine had Bill drop her off at the RenCen. The Plantations Motel, in fact, the whole Riverfront area, was too seamy. She'd managed to cut herself off mentally from anything too islandy. She loved her daddy and mummy, but she didn't think of them that often anymore. Mummy had expected her to be homesick and come flying right back home. "Is blowin sweat-of-brow money is what you doin, Pa," Mummy had scolded. She loved them, but she'd become her own person. That was something that Lara said: "I am my own person."

The Daboos acted thrilled to see her back. "What you drinkin, Jasmine girl?" Mr. Daboo kept asking. "You drinkin sherry or what?" Pouring her little glasses of sherry instead of rum was a sure sign he thought she had become whitefolk-fancy. The Daboo sisters were very friendly, but Jasmine considered them too wild. Both Loretta and Viola had changed boyfriends. Both were seeing black men they'd danced with in Ann Arbor. Each night at bedtime, Mr. Daboo cried. "In Trinidad we stayin we side, they stayin they side. Here, everything mixed up. Is helluva confusion, no?"

On New Year's Eve the Daboo girls and their black friends went to a dance. Mr. and Mrs. Daboo and Jasmine watched TV for a while. Then Mr. Daboo got out a brooch from his pocket and pinned it on Jasmine's red sweater. It was a Christmasy brooch, a miniature sleigh loaded down with snowed-on mistletoe. Before she could pull away, he kissed her on the lips. "Good luck for the New Year!" he said. She lifted her head and saw tears. "Is year for dreams comin true."

Jasmine started to cry, too. There was nothing wrong, but Mr. Daboo, Mrs. Daboo, she, everybody was crying.

What for? This is where she wanted to be. She'd spent some damned uncomfortable times with the assistant manager to get approval for her loan. She thought of Daddy. He would be playing poker and fanning himself with a magazine. Her married sisters would be rolling out the dough for stacks and stacks of roti, and Mummy would be steamed purple from stirring the big pot of goat curry on the stove. She missed them. But. It felt strange to think of anyone celebrating New Year's Eve in summery clothes.

In March Lara and her performing group went on the road. Jasmine knew that the group didn't work from scripts. The group didn't use a stage, either; instead, it took over supermarkets, senior citizens' centers, and school halls, without notice. Jasmine didn't understand the performance world. But she was glad that Lara said, "I'm not going to lay a guilt trip on myself. Muffie's in super hands," before she left.

Muffie didn't need much looking after. She played Trivial Pursuit all day, usually pretending to be two persons, sometimes Jasmine, whose accent she could imitate. Since Jasmine didn't know any of the answers, she couldn't help. Muffie was a quiet, precocious child with see-through blue eyes like her dad's, and red braids. In the early evenings Jasmine cooked supper, something special she hadn't forgotten from her island days. After supper she and Muffie watched some TV, and Bill read. When Muffie went to bed, Bill and she sat together for a bit with their glasses of Soave. Bill, Muffie, and she were a family, almost.

DOWN IN HER BASEMENT ROOM that late, dark winter, she had trouble sleeping. She wanted to stay awake and think of Bill. Even when she fell asleep it didn't feel like sleep because Bill came barging into her dreams in his funny, loose-jointed, clumsy way. It was mad to think of him all the time, and stupid and sinful; but she couldn't help it. Whenever she put back a book he'd taken off the shelf to read or whenever she put his clothes through the washer and dryer, she felt sick in a giddy, wonderful way. When Lara came back things would get back to normal. Meantime she wanted the performance group miles away.

Lara called in at least twice a week. She said things like, "We've finally obliterated the margin between realspace and performancespace." Jasmine filled her in on Muffie's doings and the mail. Bill always closed with "I love you. We miss you, hon."

One night after Lara had called—she was in Lincoln, Nebraska—Bill said to Jasmine, "Let's dance."

She hadn't danced since the reggae night she'd had too many rum punches. Her toes began to throb and clench. She untied her apron and the fraying, knotted-up laces of her running shoes.

Bill went around the downstairs rooms turning down lights. "We need atmosphere," he said. He got a small, tidy fire going in the living room grate

JASMINE | 257

and pulled the Turkish scatter rug closer to it. Lara didn't like anybody walking on the Turkish rug, but Bill meant to have his way. The hissing logs, the plants in the dimmed light, the thick patterned rug: everything was changed. This wasn't the room she cleaned every day.

He stood close to her. She smoothed her skirt down with both hands.

"I want you to choose the record," he said.

"I don't know your music."

She brought her hand high to his face. His skin was baby smooth.

"I want *you* to pick," he said. "You are your own person now."

"You got island music?"

He laughed, "What do you think?" The stereo was in a cabinet with albums packed tight alphabetically into the bottom three shelves. "Calypso has not been a force in my life."

She couldn't help laughing. "Calypso? Oh, man." She pulled dust jackets out at random. Lara's records. The Flying Lizards. The Violent Fems. There was so much still to pick up on!

"This one," she said, finally.

He took the record out of her hand. "God!" he laughed. "Lara must have found this in a garage sale!" He laid the old record on the turntable. It was "Music for Lovers," something the nuns had taught her to foxtrot to way back in Port-of-Spain.

They danced so close that she could feel his heart heaving and crashing against her head. She liked it, she liked it very much. She didn't care what happened.

"Come on," Bill whispered. "If it feels right, do it." He began to take her clothes off.

"Don't, Bill," she pleaded.

"Come on, baby," he whispered again. "You're a blossom, a flower."

He took off his fisherman's knit pullover, the corduroy pants, the blue shorts. She kept pace. She'd never had such an effect on a man. He nearly flung his socks and Adidas into the fire. "You feel so good," he said. "You smell so good. You're really something, flower of Trinidad."

"Flower of Ann Arbor," she said, "not Trinidad."

She felt so good she was dizzy. She'd never felt this good on the island where men did this all the time, and girls went along with it always for favors. You couldn't feel really good in a nothing place. She was thinking this as they made love on the Turkish carpet in front of the fire: she was a bright, pretty girl with no visa, no papers, and no birth certificate. No nothing other than what she wanted to invent and tell. She was a girl rushing wildly into the future.

MIDCAREER STORIES (1985–1988)

His hand moved up her throat and forced her lips apart and it felt so good, so right, that she forgot all the dreariness of her new life and gave herself up to it.

Danny's Girls

I WAS THIRTEEN when Danny Sahib moved into our building in Flushing. That was his street name, but my Aunt Lini still called him Dinesh, the name he'd landed with. He was about twenty, a Dogra boy from Simla with slicked-back hair and coppery skin. If he'd worked on his body language, he could have passed for Mexican, which might have been useful. Hispanics are taken more seriously, in certain lines of business, than Indians. But I don't want to give the wrong impression about Danny. He wasn't an enforcer, he was a charmer. No one was afraid of him; he was a merchant of opportunity. I got to know him because he was always into ghetto scams that needed junior high boys like me to pull them off.

He didn't have parents, at least none that he talked about, and he boasted he'd been on his own since he was six. I admired that, I wished I could escape my own family, such as it was. My parents had been bounced from Uganda by Idi Amin, and then barred from England by some parliamentary trickery. Mother's sister—Aunt Lini—sponsored us in the States. I don't remember Africa at all, but my father could never forget that we'd once had servants and two Mercedes-Benzes. He sat around Lini's house moaning about the good old days and grumbling about how hard life in America was until finally the women organized a coup and chucked him out. My mother sold papers in the subway kiosks, twelve hours a day, seven days a week. Last I heard, my father was living with a Trinidad woman in Philadelphia, but we haven't seen him or talked about him for years. So in Danny's mind I was an orphan, like him.

He wasn't into the big-money stuff like drugs. He was a hustler, nothing more. He used to boast that he knew some guys, Nepalese and Pakistanis, who could supply him with anything—but we figured that was just talk. He started out with bets and scalping tickets for Lata Mangeshkar or Mithun Chakraborty concerts at Madison Square Garden. Later he fixed beauty contests and then discovered the marriage racket.

Danny took out ads in papers in India promising "guaranteed Permanent Resident status in the U.S." to grooms willing to proxy-marry American girls of Indian origin. He arranged quite a few. The brides and grooms didn't have to live with each other, or even meet or see each other. Sometimes the "brides" were smooth-skinned boys from the neighborhood. He used to audition his brides in our apartment and coach them—especially the boys—on keeping their faces low, their saris high, and their arms as glazed and smooth as caramel. The immigration inspectors never suspected a thing. I never understood why young men would pay a lot of money—I think the going rate was fifty thousand rupees—to come here. Maybe if I remembered the old country I might feel different. I've never even visited India.

Flushing was full of greedy women. I never met one who would turn down gold or a fling with the money market. The streets were lousy with gold merchants, more gold emporia than pizza parlors. Melt down the hoarded gold of Jackson Heights and you could plate the Queensboro Bridge. My first job for Danny Sahib was to approach the daughters in my building for bride volunteers and a fifty buck fee, and then with my sweet, innocent face, sign a hundred dollar contract with their mothers.

Then Danny Sahib saw he was thinking small. The real money wasn't in rupees and bringing poor saps over. It was in selling docile Indian girls to hard-up Americans for real bucks. An Old World wife who knew her place and would breed like crazy was worth at least twenty thousand dollars. To sweeten the deal and get some good-looking girls for his catalogs, Danny promised to send part of the fee back to India. No one in India could even imagine *getting* money for the curse of having a daughter. So he expanded his marriage business to include mail-order brides, and he offered my smart Aunt Lini a partnership. My job was to put up posters in the laundromats and pass out flyers on the subways.

Aunt Lini was a shrewd businesswoman, a widow who'd built my uncle's small-time investor service for cautious Gujarati gentlemen into a full-scale loan-sharking operation that financed half the Indian-owned taxi medallions in Queens. Her rates were simple: double the prime, no questions asked. Triple the prime if she smelled a risk, which she usually did. She ran it out of her kitchen with a phone next to the stove. She could turn a thousand dollars while frying up a *bhaji*.[1]

Aunt Lini's role was to warehouse the merchandise, as she called the girls, that couldn't be delivered to its American destination (most of those American fiancés had faces a fly wouldn't buzz). Aunt Lini had spare rooms she could turn into an informal S.R.O. hotel. She called the rooms her "pet shop" and she thought of the girls as puppies in the window. In addition to the flat rate that Danny paid her, she billed the women separately for bringing gentlemen

---

1. Savory, fried Indian snack.—Ed.

260 | MIDCAREER STORIES (1985–1988)

guests, or shoppers, into the room. This encouraged a prompt turnover. The girls found it profitable to make an expeditious decision.

———————

THE SUMMER I WAS FIFTEEN, Aunt Lini had a paying guest, a Nepalese, a real looker. Her skin was white as whole milk, not the color of tree bark I was accustomed to. Her lips were a peachy orange and she had high Nepalese cheekbones. She called herself "Rosie" in the mail-order catalog and listed her age as sixteen. Danny wanted all his girls to be sixteen and most of them had names like Rosie and Dolly. I suppose when things didn't work out between her and her contract "fiancé" she saw no reason to go back to her real name. Or especially, back to some tubercular hut in Katmandu. Her parents certainly wouldn't take her back. They figured she was married and doing time in Toledo with a dude named Duane.

Rosie liked to have me around. In the middle of a sizzling afternoon she would send me to Mr. Chin's store for a pack of Kents, or to Ranjit's liquor store for gin. She was a good tipper, or maybe she couldn't admit to me that she couldn't add. The money came from Danny, part of her "dowry" that he didn't send back to Nepal. I knew she couldn't read or write, not even in her own language. That didn't bother me—guaranteed illiteracy is a big selling point in the mail-order bride racket—and there was nothing abject about her. I'd have to say she was a proud woman. The other girls Danny brought over were already broken in spirit; they'd marry just about any freak Danny brought around. Not Rosie—she'd throw some of them out, and threaten others with a cobra she said she kept in her suitcase if they even thought of touching her. After most of my errands, she'd ask me to sit on the bed and light me a cigarette and pour me a weak drink. I'd fan her for a while with the newspaper.

"What are you going to be when you finish school?" she'd ask me and blow rings, like kisses, that wobbled to my face and broke gently across it. I didn't know anyone who blew smoke rings. I thought they had gone out with black-and-white films. I became a staunch admirer of Nepal.

What I wanted to be in those days was someone important, which meant a freedom like Danny's but without the scams. Respectable freedom in the bigger world of America, that's what I wanted. Growing up in Queens gives a boy ambitions. But I didn't disclose them. I said to Rosie what my ma always said when other Indians dropped by. I said I would be going to Columbia University to the Engineering School. It was a story Ma believed because she'd told it so often, though I knew better. Only the Indian doctors' kids from New Jersey and Long Island went to Columbia. Out in Flushing we got a different message. Indian boys were placed on earth to become accountants and engineers. Even old *Idi Amin* was placed on earth to force Indians to come to America to become accountants and engineers. I went through high school scared, wondering what there was in my future if I hated numbers. I wondered if Pace and Adelphi had engineering. I didn't want to turn out like my Aunt Lini, a ghetto moneylender, and I didn't want to suffer like my mother, and I hated my father with a passion. No wonder Danny's world seemed so exciting. My mother was knocking herself out at a kiosk in Port Authority, earning the minimum wage from a guy who convinced her he was doing her a big favor, all for my mythical Columbia tuition. Lini told me that in America grades didn't count; it was all in the test scores. She bought me the SAT workbooks and told me to memorize the answers.

"Smashing," Rosie would say, and other times, "Jolly good," showing that even in the Himalayan foothills, the sun hadn't yet set on the British Empire.

Some afternoons Rosie would be doubled over in bed with leg pains. I know now she'd had rickets as a kid and spent her childhood swaying under hundred pound sacks of rice piled on her head. By thirty she'd be hobbling around like an old football player with blown knees. But at sixteen or whatever, she still had great, hard, though slightly bent legs, and she'd hike her velour dressing gown so I could tightly crisscross her legs and part of her thighs with pink satin hair ribbons. It was a home remedy, she said, it stopped circulation. I couldn't picture her in that home, Nepal. She was like a queen ("The Queen of Queens," I used to joke) to me that year. Even India, where both my parents were born, was a mystery.

Curing Rosie's leg pains led to some strong emotions, and soon I wanted to beat on the gentlemen callers who came, carrying cheap boxes of candy and looking her over like a slave girl on the auction block. She'd tell me about it, nonchalantly, making it funny. She'd catalog each of their faults, imitate their voices. They'd try to get a peek under the covers or even under the clothing, and Danny would be there to cool things down. I wasn't allowed to help, but by then I would have killed for her.

I was no stranger to the miseries of unrequited love. Rosie was the unavailable love in the room upstairs who talked to me unblushingly of sex and made the whole transaction seem base and grubby and funny. In my Saturday morning Gujarati class, on the other hand, there was a girl from Syosset who called herself "Pammy Patel," a genuine Hindu-American Princess of the sort I had never seen before, whose skin and voice and eyes were as soft as clouds. She wore expensive dresses and you could tell she'd spent hours making herself up just for the Gujarati classes in the Hindu Temple. Her father was a major surgeon, and he and Pammy's brothers would stand outside the class to protect her from any contact with boys like me. They would watch us filing out of the classroom, looking us up and down and smirking the way Danny's catalog brides were looked at by their American buyers.

I found the whole situation achingly romantic. In the Hindi films I'd see every Sunday, the hero was always a common man with a noble heart, in love with an unattainable beauty. Then she'd be kidnapped and he'd have to save her. Caste and class would be overcome and marriage would follow. To that background, I added a certain American equality. I grew up hating rich people, especially rich Indian immigrants who didn't have the problems of Uganda and a useless father, but otherwise were no better than I. I never gave them the deference that Aunt Lini and my mother did.

With all that behind me, I had assumed that real love *had* to be cheerless. I had assumed I wouldn't find a girl worth marrying, not that girls like Pammy could make me happy. Rosie was the kind of girl who could make me happy, but even I knew she was not the kind of girl I could marry. It was confusing. Thoughts of Rosie made me want to slash the throats of rivals. Thoughts of Pammy made me want to wipe out her whole family.

One very hot afternoon Rosie, as usual, leaned her elbows on the windowsill and shouted to me to fetch a six-pack of tonic and a lemon. I'd been sitting on the stoop, getting new tips from Danny on scalping for an upcoming dance recital—a big one, Lincoln Center—but I leaped to attention and shook the change in my pockets to make sure I had enough for Mr. Chin. Rosie kept records of her debts, and she'd pay them off, she said, just as soon as Danny arranged a green card to make her legit. She intended to make it here without getting married. She exaggerated Danny's power. To her, he was some kind of local bigwig who could pull off anything. None of Danny's girls had tried breaking a contract before, and I wondered if she'd actually taken it up with him.

Danny pushed me back so hard I scraped my knee on the stoop. "You put up the posters," he said. After taping them up, I was to circulate on the subway and press the pictures on every lonely guy I saw. "I'll take care of Rosie. You report back tomorrow."

"After I get her tonic and a lemon," I said.

It was the only time I ever saw the grown-up orphan in Danny, the survivor. If he'd had a knife or a gun on him, he might have used it. "I give the orders," he said, "you follow." Until that moment, I'd always had the implicit sense that Danny and I were partners in some exciting enterprise, that together we were putting something over on India, on Flushing, and even on America.

Then he smiled, but it wasn't Danny's radiant, conspiratorial, arm-on-the-shoulder smile that used to warm my day. "You're making her fat," he said. "You're making her drunk. You probably want to diddle her yourself, don't you? Fifteen years old and never been out of your Auntie's house and you want a real woman like Rosie. But she thinks you're her errand boy and you just love being her smiley little *chokra-boy*,[2] don't you?" Then the smile froze on his lips, and if he'd ever looked Mexican, this was the time. Then he said something in Hindi that I barely understood, and he laughed as he watched me repeat it, slowly. Something about eunuchs not knowing their place. "Don't ever go up there again, *hijra*-boy."

I was starting to take care of Danny's errands quickly and sloppily as always, and then, at the top of the subway stairs, I stopped. I'd never really thought what a strange, pimpish thing I was doing, putting up pictures of Danny's girls, or standing at the top of the subway stairs and passing them out to any lonely-looking American I saw—what kind of joke was this? How dare he do this, I thought, how dare he make me a part of this? I couldn't move. I had two hundred sheets of yellow paper in my hands, descriptions of Rosie and half a dozen others like her, and instead of passing them out, I threw them over my head and let them settle on the street and sidewalk and filter down the paper-strewn, garbage-littered steps of the subway. How dare he call me *hijra*, eunuch?

I got back to Aunt Lini's within the hour. She was in her kitchen charring an eggplant. "I'm making a special *bharta*[3] for you," she said, clapping a hand over the receiver. She was putting the screws on some poor Sikh, judging from the stream of coarse Punjabi I heard as I tore through the kitchen. She shouted after me, "Your ma'll be working late tonight." More guilt, more Columbia, more engineering.

I didn't thank Aunt Lini for being so thoughtful, and I didn't complain about Ma not being home for me. I was in a towering rage with Rosie and with everyone who ever slobbered over her picture.

"Take your shoes off in the hall," Lini shouted. "You know the rules."

I was in the mood to break rules. For the first time I could remember, I wasn't afraid of Danny Sahib. I wanted to liberate Rosie, and myself. From the hall stand I grabbed the biggest, sturdiest, wood-handled umbrella—gentlemen callers were always leaving behind souvenirs—and in my greasy hightops I clumped up the stairs two at a time and kicked open the door to Rosie's room.

Rosie lay in bed, smoking. She'd propped a new fan on her pillow, near her face. She sipped her gin and lime. *So*, I thought in my fit of mad jealousy, he's bought her a fan. And now suddenly she likes limes. Damn him, *damn* him. She won't want me and my newspapers, she won't want my lemons. I

---

2. Danny is dismissing the unnamed narrator-protagonist as merely Rosie's servant.—Ed.

3. North Indian spicy eggplant dish.—Ed.

264 | MIDCAREER STORIES (1985–1988)

wouldn't have cared if Danny and half the bachelors in Queens were huddled around that bed. I was so pumped up with the enormity of love that I beat the mattress in the absence of rivals. Whack! Whack! Whack! went the stolen umbrella, and Rosie bent her legs delicately to get them out of the way. The fan teetered off the pillow and lay there beside her on the wilted, flopping bed, blowing hot air at the ceiling. She held her drink up tight against her nose and lips and stared at me around the glass.

"So, you want me, do you?" she said.

Slowly, she moved the flimsy little fan, then let it drop. I knelt on the floor with my head on the pillow that had pressed into her body, smelling flowers I would never see in Flushing and feeling the tug on my shoulder that meant I should come up to bed and for the first time I felt my life was going to be A-Okay.

Buried Lives

ONE MARCH MIDAFTERNOON in Trincomalee, Sri Lanka, Mr. N.K.S. Venkatesan, a forty-nine-year-old schoolteacher who should have been inside a St. Joseph's Collegiate classroom explicating Arnold's "The Buried Life," found himself instead at a barricaded intersection, axe in hand and shouting rude slogans at a truckload of soldiers.

Mr. Venkatesan was not a political man. In his neighborhood he was the only householder who hadn't contributed, not even a rupee, to the Tamil Boys' Sporting Association, which everyone knew wasn't a cricket club so much as a recruiting center for the Liberation Tigers. And at St. Joe's, he hadn't signed the staff petition abhorring the arrest of a peaceful anti-Buddhist demonstration of Dr. Pillai, the mathematics teacher. Venkatesan had rather enjoyed talking about fractals with Dr. Pillai, but he disapproved of men with family responsibilities sticking their heads between billy clubs as though they were still fighting the British for independence.

Fractals claimed to predict, mathematically, chaos and apparent randomness. Such an endeavor, if possible, struck Mr. Venkatesan as a virtually holy quest, closer to the spirit of religion than of science. What had once been Ceylon was now Sri Lanka.

Mr. Venkatesan, like Dr. Pillai, had a large family to look after: he had one set of grandparents, an aunt who hadn't been quite right in the head since four of her five boys had signed up with the Tigers, and three much younger unmarried sisters. They lived with him in a three-room flat above a variety store. It was to protect his youngest sister (a large, docile girl who, before she got herself mixed up with the Sporting Association, used to embroider napkin-and-tablecloth sets and sell them to a middleman for export to fancy shops in Canada) that he was marching that afternoon with two hundred baby-faced protestors.

Axe under arm—he held the weapon as he might an umbrella—Mr. Venkatesan and his sister and a frail boy with a bushy mustache on whom his sister appeared to have a crush, drifted past looted stores and charred vehicles. In the center of the intersection, a middle-aged leader in camouflage fatigues and a black beret stood on the roof of a van without tires, and was about to set fire to the national flag with what looked to Mr. Venkatesan very much like a Zippo lighter.

"Sir, you have to get in the mood," said the sister's boyfriend. The mustache entirely covered his mouth. Mr. Venkatesan had the uncanny sensation of being addressed by a thatch of undulating bristles. "You have to let yourself go, sir."

This wasn't advice; this was admonition. Around Mr. Venkatesan swirled dozens of hyperkinetic boys in white shirts, holding bricks. Fat girls in summer frocks held placards aloft. His sister sucked on an ice cream bar. Every protester seemed to twinkle with fun. He didn't know how to have fun, that was the trouble. Even as an adolescent he'd battened down all passion; while other students had slipped love notes into expectant palms, he'd studied, he'd passed exams. Dutifulness had turned him into a pariah.

"Don't think you chaps invented civil disobedience!"

He lectured the boyfriend on how his generation—meaning that technically, he'd been alive though hardly self-conscious—had cowed the British Empire. The truth was that the one time the police had raided the Venkatesans' flat—he'd been four, but he'd been taught anti-British phrases like "the salt marsh" and "*satyagraha*" by a cousin ten years older—he had saluted the superintendant smartly even as constables squeezed his cousin's wrists into handcuffs. That cousin was now in San Jose, California, minting lakhs and lakhs of dollars in computer software.

The boyfriend, still smiling awkwardly, moved away from Mr. Venkatesan's sister. His buddies, Tigers in berets, were clustered around a vendor of spicy fritters.

"Wait!" the sister pleaded, her face puffy with held-back tears.

"What do you see in that callow, good-for-nothing bloke?" Mr. Venkatesan asked.

"Please, please leave me alone," his sister screamed. "Please let me do what I want."

266 | MIDCAREER STORIES (1985–1988)

What if *he* were to do what he wanted! Twenty years ago when he'd had the chance, he should have applied for a Commonwealth Scholarship. He should have immured himself in a leafy dormitory in Oxford. Now it was too late. He'd have studied law. Maybe he'd have married an English girl and loitered abroad. But both parents had died, his sisters were mere toddlers, and he was obliged to take the lowest, meanest teaching job in the city.

"I want to die," his sister sobbed beside him.

"Shut up, you foolish girl."

The ferocity of her passion for the worthless boy, who was, just then, biting into a greasy potato fritter, shocked him. He had patronized her when she had been a plain, pliant girl squinting at embroidered birds and flowers. But now something harsh and womanly seemed to be happening inside her.

"Forget those chaps. They're nothing but troublemakers." To impress her, he tapped a foot to the beat of a slogan bellowing out of loudspeakers.

Though soldiers were starting to hustle demonstrators into double parked paddy wagons, the intersection had taken on the gaudiness of a village fair. A white-haired vendor darted from police jeep to jeep hawking peanuts in paper cones. Boys who had drunk too much tea or soda relieved themselves freely into poster-clogged gutters. A dozen feet up the road a housewife with a baby on her hip lobbed stones into storefronts. A band of beggars staggered out of an electronics store with a radio and a television. No reason not to get into the mood.

"Blood for blood," he shouted, timidly at first. "Blood begets blood."

"Begets?" the man beside him asked. "What's that supposed to mean?" In his plastic sandals and cheap drawstring pajamas, the man looked like a coolie or laborer.

He turned to his sister for commiseration. What could she expect him to have in common with a mob of uneducated men like that? But she'd left him behind. He saw her, crouched for flight like a giant ornament on the hood of an old-fashioned car, the March wind stiffly splaying her sari and long hair behind her.

"Get down from that car!" he cried. But the crowd, swirling, separated him from her. He felt powerless; he could no longer watch over her, keep her out of reach of night sticks. From on top of the hood she taunted policemen, and not just policemen but everybody—shopgirls and beggars and ochre-robed monks—as though she wasn't just a girl with a crush on a Tiger but a monster out of one's most splenetic nightmares.

Months later, in a boardinghouse in Hamburg, Mr. Venkatesan couldn't help thinking about the flock of young monks pressed together behind a police barricade that eventful afternoon. He owed his freedom to the monks because, in spite of their tonsure scars and vows of stoicism, that afternoon they'd behaved like any other hot-headed Sri Lankan adolescents. If the monks hadn't chased his sister and knocked her off the pale blue hood of the car, Mr. Venkatesan would have stayed on in Sri Lanka, in Trinco, in St. Joe's teaching the same poems year after year, a permanent prisoner.

What the monks did was unforgivable. Robes plucked knee-high and celibate lips plumped up in vengeful chant, they pulled a girl by the hair, and they slapped and spat and kicked with vigor worthy of newly initiated Tigers.

It could have been another girl, somebody else's younger sister. Without thinking, Mr. Venkatesan rotated a shoulder, swung an arm, readied his mind to inflict serious harm.

It should never have happened. The axe looped clumsily over the heads of demonstrators and policemen and fell, like a captured kite, into the hands of a Home Guards officer. There was blood, thick and purplish, spreading in jagged stains on the man's white uniform. The crowd wheeled violently. The drivers of paddy wagons laid panicky fingers on their horns. Veils of tear gas blinded enemies and friends. Mr. Venkatesan, crying and choking, ducked into a store and listened to the thwack of batons. When his vision eased, he staggered, still on automatic pilot, down side streets and broke through garden hedges all the way to St. Joseph's unguarded back door.

In the men's room off the Teachers' Common Room he held his face, hot with guilt, under a rusty, hissing faucet until Father van der Haagen, the Latin and Scriptures teacher, came out of a stall.

"You don't look too well. Sleepless night, eh?" the Jesuit joked. "You need to get married, Venkatesan. Bad habits can't always satisfy you."

Mr. Venkatesan laughed dutifully. All of Father van der Haagen's jokes had to do with masturbation. He didn't say anything about having deserted his sister. He didn't say anything about having maimed, maybe murdered, a Home Guards officer. "Who can afford a wife on what the school pays?" he joked back. Then he hurried off to his classroom.

Though he was over a half-hour late, his students were still seated meekly at their desks.

"Good afternoon, sir." Boys in monogrammed shirts and rice-starched shorts shuffled to standing positions.

"Sit!" the schoolmaster commanded. Without taking his eyes off the students, he opened his desk and let his hand locate *A Treasury of the Most Dulcet Verses Written in the English Language*, which he had helped the headmaster to edit though only the headmaster's name appeared on the book.

Matthew Arnold was Venkatesan's favorite poet. Mr. Venkatesan had talked the Head into including four Arnold poems. The verses picked by the Head hadn't been "dulcet" at all, and one hundred and three pages of the total of

268 | MIDCAREER STORIES (1985–1988)

one hundred and seventy-four had been given over to upstart Trinco versifiers' martial ballads.

Mr. Venkatesan would have nursed a greater bitterness against the Head if the man hadn't vanished, mysteriously, soon after their acrimonious coediting job.

One winter Friday the headmaster had set out for his nightly after-dinner walk, and he hadn't come back. The Common Room gossip was that he had been kidnapped by a paramilitary group. But Miss Philomena, the female teacher who was by tradition permitted the use of the Head's private bathroom, claimed the man had drowned in the Atlantic Ocean trying to sneak into Canada in a boat that ferried, for a wicked fee, illegal aliens. Stashed in the bathroom's air vent (through which sparrows sometimes flew in and bothered her), she'd spotted, she said, an oilcloth pouch stuffed with foreign cash and fake passports.

In the Teachers' Common Room, where Miss Philomena was not popular, her story was discounted. But at the Pillais' home, the men teachers had gotten together and toasted the Head with hoarded bottles of whiskey and sung many rounds of "For He's a Jolly Good Fellow," sometimes substituting "smart" for "good." By the time Mr. Venkatesan had been dropped home by Father van der Haagen, who owned a motorcycle, night had bleached itself into rainy dawn. It had been the only all-nighter of Mr. Venkatesan's life and the only time he might have been accused of drunkenness.

The memory of how good the rain had felt came back to him now as he glanced at the first stanza of the assigned Arnold poem. What was the function of poetry if not to improve the petty, cautious minds of evasive children? What was the duty of the teacher if not to inspire?

He cleared his throat, and began to read aloud in a voice trained in elocution.

> Light flows our war of mocking words, and yet,
> Behold, with tears mine eyes are wet!
> I feel a nameless sadness o'er me roll.
> Yes, yes, we know that we can jest,
> We know, we know that we can smile!
> But there's a something in this breast,
> To which thy light words bring no rest,
> And thy gay smiles no anodyne.
> Give me thy hand, and hush awhile,
> And turn those limpid eyes on mine,
> And let me read there, love! thy inmost soul.

BURIED LIVES | *269*

"Sir," a plump boy in the front row whispered as Venkatesan finally stopped for breath.

"What is it now?" snapped Venkatesan. In his new mood Arnold had touched him with fresh intensity, and he hated the boy for deflating illusion. "If you are wanting to know a synonym for 'anodyne,' then look it up in the *Oxford Dictionary*. You are a lazy donkey wanting me to feed you with a silver spoon. All of you, you are all lazy donkeys."

"No, sir." The boy persisted in spoiling the mood.

It was then that Venkatesan took in the boy's sweaty face and hair. Even the eyes were fat and sweaty.

"Behold, sir," the boy said. He dabbed his eyelids with the limp tip of his school tie. "Mine eyes, too, are wet."

"You are a silly donkey," Venkatesan yelled. "You are a beast of burden. You deserve the abuse you get. It is you emotional types who are selling this country down the river."

The class snickered, unsure what Mr. Venkatesan wanted of them. The boy let go of his tie and wept openly. Mr. Venkatesan hated himself. Here was a kindred soul, a fellow lover of Matthew Arnold, and what had he done other than indulge in gratuitous cruelty? He blamed the times. He blamed Sri Lanka.

It was as much this classroom incident as the fear of arrest for his part in what turned out to be an out-of-control demonstration that made Mr. Venkatesan look into emigrating. At first, he explored legal channels. He wasted a month's salary bribing arrogant junior-level clerks in four consulates—he was willing to settle almost anywhere except in the Gulf Emirates—but every country he could see himself being happy and fulfilled in turned him down.

So all through the summer he consoled himself with reading novels. Adventure stories in which fearless young Britons—sailors, soldiers, missionaries—whacked wildernesses into submission. From lending libraries in the city, he checked out books that were so old that they had to be trussed with twine. On the flyleaf of each book, in fading ink, was an inscription by a dead or retired British tea planter. Like the blond heroes of the novels, the colonials must have come to Ceylon chasing dreams of perfect futures. He, too, must sail dark, stormy oceans.

In August, at the close of a staff meeting, Miss Philomena announced coyly that she was leaving the island. A friend in Kalamazoo, Michigan, had agreed to sponsor her as a "domestic."

"It is a ploy only, man," Miss Philomena explained. "In the autumn, I am signing up for postgraduate studies in a prestigious educational institution."

"You are cleaning toilets and whatnot just like a servant girl? Is the meaning of 'domestic' not the same as 'servant'?"

Mr. Venkatesan joined the others in teasing Miss Philomena, but late that night he wrote away to eight American universities for applications. He took great care with the cover letters, which always began with "Dear Respected Sir" and ended with "Humbly but eagerly awaiting your response." He tried to put down in the allotted blanks what it felt like to be born so heartbreakingly far from New York or London. *On this small dead-end island, I feel I am a shadow-man, a nothing. I feel I'm a stranger in my own room. What consoles me is reading. I sink my teeth into fiction by great Englishmen such as G. A. Henty and A. E. W. Mason. I live my life through their imagined lives. And when I put their works down at dawn I ask myself, Hath not a Tamil eyes, heart, ears, nose, throat, to adapt the works of the greatest Briton. Yes, I am a Tamil. If you prick me, do I not bleed? If you tickle me, do I not laugh? Then, if I dream, will you not give me a chance, respected Sir, as only you can?*

In a second paragraph he politely but firmly indicated the size of scholarship he would require, and indicated the size of apartment he (and his sisters) would require. He preferred close proximity to campus, since he did not intend to drive.

But sometime in late April, the school's porter brought him, rubber-banded together, eight letters of rejection.

"I am worthless," Mr. Venkatesan moaned in front of the porter. "I am a donkey."

The porter offered him aspirins. "You are unwell, *sahib.*"

The schoolteacher swallowed the tablets, but as soon as the servant left, he snatched a confiscated Zippo lighter from his desk and burned the rejections.

When he got home, his sister's suitor was on the balcony, painting placards, and though he meant to say nothing to the youth, meant to admit no flaw, no defeat, his body betrayed him with shudders and moans.

"Racism!" the youth spat as he painted over a spelling error that, even in his grief, Mr. Venkatesan couldn't help pointing out. "Racism is what's slamming the door in your face, man! You got to improvise your weapons!"

Perhaps the boy was not a totally unworthy suitor. He let the exclamations play in his head, and soon the rejections, and the anxiety that he might be stuck on the futureless island fired him up instead of depressing him. Most nights he lay in bed fully dressed—the police always raided at dawn—and thought up a hundred illegal but feasible ways to outwit immigration officials.

The least wild schemes he talked over with Father van der Haagen. Long ago and in another country, Father van der Haagen had surely given in to similar seductions. The Jesuit usually hooted, "So you want to rot in a freezing, foreign jail? You want your lovely sisters to walk the streets and come to harm?" But, always, the expatriate ended these chats with his boyhood memories of skating on frozen Belgian rivers and ponds. Mr. Venkatesan felt he could visualize snow, but not a whole river so iced up that it was as solid as a grand trunk highway. In his dreams, the Tamil schoolteacher crisscrossed national boundaries on skates that felt as soft and comforting as cushions.

In August his sister's suitor got himself stupidly involved in a prison break. The sister came to Mr. Venkatesan weeping. She had stuffed clothes and her sewing basket into a camouflage satchel. She was going into the northern hills, she said. The Tigers could count on the tea pickers.

"No way," Mr. Venkatesan exploded. When he was safely in America's heartland, with his own wife and car and all accoutrements of New World hearth and home, he wanted to think of his Trinco family (to whom he meant to remit generous monthly sums) as being happy under one roof, too. "You are not going to live with hooligan types in jungles."

"If you lock me in my room, I'll call the police. I'll tell them who threw the axe at the rally."

"Is that what they teach you in guerrilla camps? To turn on your family?" he demanded.

The sister wept loudly into her sari. It was a pretty lilac sari, and he remembered having bought it for her seventeenth birthday. On her feet were fragile lilac slippers. He couldn't picture her scrambling up terraced slopes of tea estates in that pretty get-up. "Nobody has to teach me," she retorted.

In her lilac sari, and with the white fragrant flower wreath in her hair, she didn't look like a blackmailer. It was the times. She, her boyfriend, he himself, were all fate's victims.

He gave in. He made her promise, though, that in the hills she would marry her suitor. She touched his feet with her forehead in the traditional farewell. He heard a scooter start up below. So the guerrilla had been waiting. She'd meant to leave home, with or without his permission. She'd freed herself of family duties and bonds.

Above the motor scooter's sputter, the grateful boyfriend shouted, "Sir, I will put you in touch with a man. Listen to him and he will deliver you." Then the dust cloud of destiny swallowed up the guerrilla bride-to-be and groom.

The go-between turned out to be a clubfooted and cauliflower-eared middle-aged man. The combination of deformities, no doubt congenital, had nevertheless earned him a reputation for ferocity and an indifference to inflicted suffering. He appeared on the front porch early one Saturday afternoon. He didn't come straight to the point. For the first half-hour he said very little and

272 | MIDCAREER STORIES (1985–1988)

concentrated instead on the sweet almond-stuffed turnovers that the Venkatesan family had shaped and fried all day for a religious festival they'd be attending later that afternoon.

"You have, perhaps, some news for me?" Mr. Venkatesan asked shyly as he watched the man help himself to a chilled glass of mango fool. "Some important information, no?"

"Excuse me, sir," the man protested. "I know that you are a teacher and that therefore you are in the business of improving the mind of man. But forthrightness is not always a virtue. Especially in these troubled times."

The man's furtiveness was infectious, and Mr. Venkatesan, without thinking, thinned his voice to a hiss. "You are going over my options with me, no?"

"Options!" the man sneered. Then he took out a foreign-looking newspaper from a shopping bag. On a back page of the paper was a picture of three dour *sahibs* fishing for lobster. "You get my meaning, sir? They have beautiful coves in Nova Scotia. They have beautiful people in the Canadian Maritimes."

On cushiony skates and with clean, cool winds buoying him from behind, Mr. Venkatesan glided all the way into Halifax, dodging posses of border police. He married a girl with red, dimpled cheeks, and all winter she made love to him under a goose-down quilt. Summers he set lobster traps. Editors of quarterlies begged to see his poetry.

"Beautiful people, Canadians," he agreed.

"Not like the damn Americans!" The go-between masticated sternly. "They are sending over soldiers of fortune and suchlike to crush us."

Mr. Venkatesan, wise in ways of middlemen, asked, "This means you're not having a pipeline to America?"

The agent dipped into a bowl of stale fried banana chips.

"No matter. The time has come for me to leave."

The next day, Sunday, the man came back to find out how much Mr. Venkatesan might be willing to pay for a fake passport / airline tickets / safe houses en route package deal. Mr. Venkatesan named a figure.

"So you are not really anxious to exit?" the man said.

Mr. Venkatesan revised his figure. He revised the figure three more times before the go-between would do anything more human than sigh at him.

He was being taken by a mean, mocking man who preyed on others' dreams. He was allowing himself to be cheated. But sometime that spring the wish to get away—to flee abroad and seize the good life as had his San Jose cousin— had deepened into sickness. So he was blowing his life's savings on this malady. So what?

The man made many more trips. And on each trip, as Mr. Venkatesan sat the man down on the best rattan chair on the balcony, through the half-open door that led into the hallway he saw the women in his family gather in jittery knots. They knew he was about to forsake them.

Every brave beginning, in these cramped little islands, masked a secret betrayal. To himself, Mr. Venkatesan would always be a sinner.

MR. VENKATESAN THREW himself into the planning. He didn't trust the man with the cauliflower ears. Routes, circuitous enough to fool border guards, had to be figured out. He could fly to Frankfurt via Malta, for instance, then hole up in a ship's cargo hold for the long, bouncy passage on Canadian seas. Or he could take the more predictable (and therefore, cheaper but with more surveillance) detours through the Gulf Emirates.

The go-between or travel agent took his time. Fake travel documents and work permits had to be printed up. Costs, commissions, bribes had to be calculated. On each visit, the man helped himself to a double peg of Mr. Venkatesan's whiskey.

In early September, three weeks after Mr. Venkatesan had paid in full for a roundabout one-way ticket to Hamburg and for a passport impressive with fake visas, the travel agent stowed him in the damp, smelly bottom of a fisherman's dinghy and had him ferried across the Palk Strait to Tuticorin in the palm-green tip of mainland India.

Tuticorin was the town Mr. Venkatesan's ancestors had left to find their fortunes in Ceylon's tea-covered northern hills. The irony struck him with such force that he rocked and tipped the dinghy, and had to be fished out of the sea.

THE FRIENDS OF THE TIGERS were waiting in a palm grove for him. He saw their flashlights and smelled their coffee. They gave him a dry change of clothes, and though both the shirt and the jacket were frayed, they were stylishly cut. His reputation as an intellectual and killer (he hoped it wasn't true) of a Buddhist policeman had preceded him. He let them talk; it was not Venkatesan the schoolmaster they were praising, but some mad invention. Where he was silent from confusion and fatigue, they read cunning and intensity. He was happy to put himself in their hands; he thought of them as fate's helpers, dispatched to see him through his malady. That night one of them made up a sleeping mat for him in the back room of his shuttered grocery store. After that they passed him from back room to back room. He spent pleasant afternoons with them drinking sweet, frothy coffee and listening to them plan to derail trains or blow up bus depots. They read his frown as skepticism and redoubled their vehemence. He himself had no interest in destruction, but he listened to them politely.

When it was safe to move on, the Friends wrote out useful addresses in Frankfurt, London, Toronto, Miami. "Stay out of refugee centers," they advised. But an old man with broken dentures who had been deported out of Hamburg the year before filled him in on which refugee centers in which cities had the cleanest beds, just in case he was caught by the wily German police. "I shan't forget any of you," Mr. Venkatesan said as two Friends saw him off at the train station. The train took him to Madras; in Madras he changed trains for Delhi where he boarded an Aeroflot flight for Tashkent. From Tashkent he flew to Moscow. He would like to have told the story of his life to his two seatmates—already the break from family and from St. Joe's seemed the stuff of adventure novels—but they were two huge and grim Uzbeks with bushels of apricots and pears wedged on the floor, under the seat, and on their laps. The cabin was noisier than the Jaffna local bus with squawking chickens and drunken farmers. He communed instead with Arnold and Keats. In Moscow the airport officials didn't bother to look too closely at his visa stamps, and he made it to Berlin feeling cocky.

At Schönefeld Airport, three rough-looking Tamil men he'd not have given the time of day to back home in Trinco grappled his bags away from him as soon as he'd cleared customs. "This is only a piss stop for you, you lucky bastard," one of them said. "You get to go on to real places while hard-working fuckers like us get stuck in this hellhole."

He had never heard such language. Up until a week ago, he would have denied the Tamil language even possessed such words. The man's coarseness shocked Mr. Venkatesan, but this was not the moment to walk away from accomplices.

The expatriate Tamils took him, by bus, to a tenement building—he saw only Asians and Africans in the lobby—and locked him from the outside in a one-room flat on the top floor. An Algerian they did business with, they said, would truck him over the border into Hamburg. He was not to look out the window. He was not to open the door, not even if someone yelled, "Fire!" They'd be back at night, and they'd bring him beer and rolls.

Mr. Venkatesan made a slow show of getting money out of his trouser pocket—he didn't have any East German money, only rupees and the Canadian dollars he'd bought on the black market from the travel agent in Trinco—but the Tamils stopped him. "Our treat," they said. "You can return the hospitality when *we* make it to Canada."

Late in the evening the three men, stumbling drunk and jolly, let themselves back into the room that smelled of stale, male smells. The Algerian had come through. They were celebrating. They had forgotten the bread but remembered the beer.

That night, which was his only night in East Germany, Mr. Venkatesan got giggly drunk. And so it was that he entered the free world with a hangover. In a narrow, green mountain pass, trying not to throw up, he said goodbye to his Algerian chauffeur and how-do-you-do to a Ghanaian-born Berliner who didn't cut the engine of his BMW during the furtive transfer.

He was in Europe. Finally. The hangover made him sentimental. Back in Trinco the day must have deepened into dusk. In the skid of tires, he heard the weeping of grandparents, aunts, sisters. He had looked after them as long as he could. He had done for himself what he should have ten years before. Now he wanted to walk where Shelley had walked. He wanted to lie down where consumptive Keats had lain and listened to his nightingale sing of truth and beauty. He stretched out in the back seat. When Mr. Venkatesan next opened his eyes, the BMW was parked in front of a refugee center in Hamburg.

"End of trip," the black Berliner announced in jerky English. *"Auf Wiedersehen."*

Mr. Venkatesan protested that he was not a refugee. "I am paid up in full to Canada. You are supposed to put me in touch with a ship's captain."

The black man snickered, then heaved Mr. Venkatesan's two shiny new bags out on the street. "Goodbye. *Danke.*"

Mr. Venkatesan got out of the private taxi.

"Need a cheap hotel? Need a lawyer to stay deportation orders?"

A very dark, pudgy man flashed a calling card in his face. The man looked Tamil, but not anxious like a refugee. His suit was too expensive. Even his shirt was made of some white-on-white fancy material, though his cuffs and collar were somewhat soiled.

Mr. Venkatesan felt exhilarated. Here was another of fate's angels come to minister him out of his malady.

"The name is Rammi G. Rammi, Esquire. One-time meanest goddamn solicitor[1] in Paramaribo, Suriname. I am putting myself at your service."

He allowed the angel to guide him into a *rijstafel* place and feed him for free.

MR. VENKATESAN ATE greedily while the angel, in a voice as uplifting as harp music, instructed him on the most prudent conduct for undocumented tran-

---

1. British word for a particular type of lawyer.—Ed.

sients. By the end of the meal, he'd agreed to pay Rammi's cousin, a widow, a flat fee for boarding him for as long as it took Rammi to locate a ship's captain whose business was ferrying furtive cargoes.

Rammi's cousin, Queenie, lived in a row house by the docks. Rammi had the cabdriver let them off a block and a half from Queenie's. He seemed to think cabdrivers were undercover immigration cops, and he didn't want a poor young widow bringing up a kid on dole getting in trouble for her charity.

Though Queenie had been telephoned ahead from a pay phone, she was dressed in nothing more formal than a kimono when she opened her slightly warped front door and let the men in. The kimono was the color of parrots in sunlight and reminded Mr. Venkatesan of his last carefree years, creeping up on and capturing parrots with his bare hands. In that glossy green kimono, Queenie the landlady shocked him with her beauty. Her sash was missing, and she clenched the garment together at the waist with a slender, nervous fist. Her smooth gold limbs, her high-bouncing bosom, even the stockingless arch of her instep had about them so tempting a careless sensuality that it made his head swim.

"I put your friend in Room 3A," Queenie said. "3B is less crowded but I had to put the sick Turk in it." She yelled something in German which Mr. Venkatesan didn't understand, and a girl of eight or nine came teetering out of the kitchen in adult-sized high heels. She asked the girl some urgent questions. The girl said no to all of them with shakes of her braided head.

"We don't want the fellow dying on us," Rammi said. Then they said something more in a Caribbean patois that Mr. Venkatesan didn't catch. "God knows we don't want complications." He picked up the two bags and started up the stairs.

3A was a smallish attic room blue with unventilated smoke, fitted with two sets of three-tier bunks. There were no closets, no cupboards, and on the bunk that Rammi pointed out as his, no bed linen. Four young men of indistinguishable nationality—Asia and Africa were their continents—were playing cards and drinking beer.

"Okay, 'bye," Rammi said. He was off to scout ship captains.

When Rammi left, despite the company, Mr. Venkatesan felt depressed, lonely. He didn't try to get to know where the men were from and where they were headed which was how he'd broken the ice in back room dormitories in Tuticorin. One man spat into a brass spittoon. What did he have in common with these transients except the waiting?

By using his bags as a stepladder, he was able to clamber up to his allotted top bunk. For a while he sat on the bed. The men angled their heads so they could still stare at him. He lay down on the mattress. The rough ticking material of the pillow chafed him. He sat up again. He took his jacket and pants off and hung them from the foot rail. He slipped his wallet, his passport, his cloth bag stuffed with foreign cash, his new watch—a farewell present from Father van der Haagen—between the pillow and the mattress. He was not about the trust his cellmates. A little after the noon hour all four men got dressed in gaudy clothes and went out in a group. Mr. Venkatesan finally closed his eyes. A parrot flew into his dream. Mr. Venkatesan thrilled to the feathery feel of its bosom. He woke up only when Queenie's little girl charged into the room and ordered him down for lunch. She didn't seem upset about his being in underwear. She leaped onto the middle bunk in the tier across the room and told him to hurry so the food wouldn't have to be rewarmed. He thought he saw the flash of a man's watch in her hand.

———————

QUEENIE HAD MADE him a simple lunch of lentil soup and potato croquettes, and by the time he got down to the kitchen it was no longer warm. Still he liked the spiciness of the croquettes and the ketchup was a tasty European brand and not the watery stuff served back home.

She said she'd already eaten, but she sat down with a lager and watched him eat. With her he had no trouble talking. He told her about St. Joe's and Father van der Haagen. He told her about his family, leaving out the part about his sister running wild in the hills with hooligans, and got her to talk about her family, too.

Queenie's grandfather had been born in a Sinhalese village the name of which he hadn't cared to pass on—he'd referred to it only as a "hellhole"— and from which he'd run away at age seventeen to come as an indentured laborer to the Caribbean. He'd worked sugar cane fields in British Guiana until he'd lost a thumb. Then he'd moved to Suriname and worked as an office boy in a coconut oil processing plant, and wooed and won the only daughter of the proprietor, an expatriate Tamil like him who, during the War, had made a fortune off the Americans.

He tried to find out about her husband, but she'd say nothing other than that he'd been, in her words, "a romantic moron," and that he'd hated the hot sun, the flat lands, the coconut palms, the bush, her family, her family's oil factory. He'd dreamed, she said, of living like a European.

"You make me remember things I thought I'd forgotten." She flicked her lips with her tongue until they shone.

"You make me think of doing things I've never done." He gripped the edge of the kitchen table. He had trouble breathing. "Until dinnertime," he said. Then he panted back up to his prison.

But Mr. Venkatesan didn't see Queenie for dinner. She sent word through the girl that she had a guest—a legitimate guest, a tourist from Lübeck, not an illegal transient—that evening. He felt no rage at being dumped. A man without papers accepts last-minute humiliations. He called Rammi from the pay phone in the hall.

That night Mr. Venkatesan had fun. Hamburg was not at all the staid city of burghers that Father van der Haagen had evoked for him in those last restless days of waiting in the Teachers' Common Room. Hamburg was a carnival. That night, with Rammi as his initiator into fun, he smoked his first joint and said, after much prodding, "*sehr schön*" to a skinny girl with a Mohawk haircut.

The tourist from Lübeck had been given the one nice room. Queenie's daughter had shown Mr. Venkatesan the room while the man was checking in. It was on the first floor and had a double bed with a duvet so thick you wanted to sink into it. The windows were covered with *two* sets of curtains. The room even had its own sink. He hadn't seen the man from Lübeck, only heard him on the stairs and in the hall on his way to and from the lavatory walking with an authoritative, native-born German tread. Queenie hadn't instructed him to stay out of sight. Secretiveness he'd learned from his bunkmates. They could move with great stealth. Mr. Venkatesan was beginning to feel like a character in Anne Frank's diary. The men in 3A stopped wearing shoes indoors so as not to be heard pacing by the tourist from Lübeck.

The tourist went out a lot. Sometimes a car came for him. From the Tourist Office, Mr. Venkatesan imagined. How nice it would be to tour the city, take a boat trip! Meantime he had to eat his meals upstairs. That was the sad part. Otherwise he felt he had never been so happy.

Every morning as soon as he got the chance he called Rammi, though he was no longer keen for Rammi to find a crooked captain. He called because he didn't want Rammi to catch on that he was feeling whatever it was that he was feeling for Queenie. Like Rammi, he didn't want complications. What he did was remind Rammi that he wouldn't go into the hold of a ship that dumped its cargo into the Atlantic. He told Rammi that both in Trinco and in Tuticorin he'd heard stories of drowned Tamils.

Mr. Venkatesan's roommates stopped going out for meals. They paid Queenie's girl to buy them cold meats and oranges from the corner store. The only thing they risked going out for was liquor. He gathered from fragments of conversation that they were all sailors, from Indonesia and Nigeria, who'd jumped ship in Hamburg harbor. Whenever they went out, he could count on the girl prowling the attic room. He let her prowl. It was almost like having Queenie in the room.

BURIED LIVES | *279*

There was only one worry. The girl lifted things—small things—from under pillows. Sometimes she played under the beds where he and the other men stored their suitcases, and he heard lids swish open or closed. He didn't think the things she stole were worth stealing. He'd seen her take a handful of pfennigs from a jacket pocket once, and another time envelopes with brilliant stamps from places like Turkey and Oman. What she seemed to like best to pilfer were lozenges, even the medicated kind for sore throat. It was as if covetousness came upon her, out of the blue, making her pupils twitch and glow.

He didn't mind the loss to his roommates. But he worried that they'd get her in trouble by sending her to the store. He would have to stop her. He would have to scold her as a father might or should without messing things up with Queenie.

ONE MORNING Queenie showed up in 3A herself. "I have good news," she whispered. Two of the four men were still in bed. Mr. Venkatesan could tell they hated having a grown woman in their room. "Rammi should have word for you tonight. I'm meeting him to find out more." The morning light, streaming in through a cracked stained-glass panel in the window, put such a heavenly sheen on her face that Mr. Venkatesan blurted out in front of his roommates, "I love you, I love you."

Queenie laughed. "Hush," she said. "You're not there yet. You don't want to wake up our Teuton. I need the legitimate business, too."

It seemed to Mr. Venkatesan like an invitation. He followed her down into the front hall in his night clothes. In Tamil movies heroes in his position would have been wearing brocade smoking jackets. It didn't matter. He had made his declaration. Now fate would have to sink the crooked captain and his boat.

Queenie fussed with a pink, plastic clip in her hair. She knotted and reknotted the wispy silk square around her throat. She tapped the longest fingernail he'd ever seen on the butterfly buckle of her belt. She was teasing him. She was promising he wouldn't really have to go. He wanted to stay, Anne Frank or not.

"Tonight should be a champagne night," she grinned. He saw the tensing of a dainty calf muscle as she straightened a stocking. "I'll see to coffee," she said.

Upstairs the man from Lübeck had hot water running in the bathroom sink. The pipes moaned. It was best to hide out in the kitchen until the man was back in his own room. Mr. Venkatesan joined Queenie's daughter at the dinette table. She had lozenges spread out on the tablecloth, like a sun spiked with long rays. She didn't look like a thief. She looked like a child he might have fathered if he'd married the bride his mother had picked for him in the days he'd still been considered a good catch. He hadn't married. Something dire had shown up in the conjunction of their horoscopes.

What if, just what if, what had seemed disastrous to the astrologer at the time had really been fate's way of reserving him for a better family with Queenie and this child in Hamburg?

"I'll sell you some," the child said. "I have English toffees, too."

"Where?" He wanted to see her whole loot.

She ducked and brought out an old milk bottle from under the table. He saw the toffees in their red and blue wrapping papers. He saw a Muslim's worry beads. Some things in the bottle were shiny—he made out two rings among the keys and coins and coat buttons. There were two ID cards in the bottle. She reached for the cards. She had to have stolen one of the cards from a man in Room 3A. In the ID picture, which was amateurishly doctored, the room-mate looked like a playboy sheikh, and not at all like a refugee without travel papers. He grabbed the roommate's card from her. It wouldn't hurt to have the fellow in his debt. The other card belonged to a very blond, very German man.

The child was shrewd. "I didn't steal anything," she snapped. "I don't know how the stuff got in that jar."

She tossed the blond man's ID to him to get rid of it, and he caught it as he had paper flowers, silk squares, and stunned rabbits hurled to front-row boys by magicians on fete days in his kindergarten. He had loved the magicians. They alone had given him what he'd wanted.

As in dreams, the burly blond man materialized out of thin air and blocked the doorway. The man had on a touristy shirt and short pants, but he didn't have the slack gait of a vacationer. He had to be the man who lived in the nice upstairs room, the man who slept under the cozy duvet, who brushed his teeth in a clean, pink sink he didn't have to share, the man from whom transients like Mr. Venkatesan himself had to hide out. This man yelled something nasty in German to Queenie's daughter. The child cowered.

The man yelled again. Mr. Venkatesan started to back away. Minute by minute the man ballooned with rage.

"No *deutsch*," Mr. Venkatesan mumbled.

"You filthy swine," the man shouted in English. "We don't want you mak-ing filthy our Germany." He threw five passports down on the kitchen table and spat on the top one. "The girl, she stole something from each of you scums," he hooted.

Mr. Venkatesan recognized his in the heap of travel documents. The child must have stolen it. The child must have filched it from under his pillow while he'd slept. She was a child possessed with covetousness. Now, because of her sick covetousness, he would rot in jail. He yanked the girl by her braids and shook her. The girl made her body go limp, taking away all pleasure in hate and revenge. The tourist from Lübeck ignored the screaming child. He got on the pay phone, the one Mr. Venkatesan called Rammi on every morning. Mr. Venkatesan heard the word "*Polizei*!" He was almost fifty. By fifty a man ought to stop running. Maybe what seemed accidental now—Queenie's daughter's kleptomania blowing away his plans for escape—wasn't accidental. He remembered what had consoled Dr. Pillai at the time of his arrest. Fractals. Nothing was random, the math teacher used to say. Nothing, not even the curliness of a coastline and the fluffiness of a cloud.

Mr. Venkatesan thought about the swoops and darts of his fate. He had started out as a teacher and a solid citizen and ended up as a lusty criminal. He visualized fate now as a buzzard. He could hear the whir of fleshy wings. It hopped off a burning car in the middle of a Trinco intersection.

Then, suddenly, Queenie the beauteous, the deliverer of radiant dreams, burst through the door of the kitchen. "Leave him alone!" she yelled to the man from Lübeck. "You're harassing my fiancé! He's a future German citizen. He will become my husband!"

The Management of Grief

A woman I don't know is boiling tea the Indian way in my kitchen. There are a lot of women I don't know in my kitchen, whispering and moving tactfully. They open doors, rummage through the pantry, and try not to ask me where things are kept. They remind me of when my sons were small, on Mother's Day or when Vikram and I were tired, and they would make big, sloppy omelets. I would lie in bed pretending I didn't hear them.

Dr. Sharma, the treasurer of the Indo-Canada Society, pulls me into the hallway. He wants to know if I am worried about money. His wife, who has just come up from the basement with a tray of empty cups and glasses, scolds him. "Don't bother Mrs. Bhave with mundane details." She looks so monstrously pregnant her baby must be days overdue. I tell her she shouldn't be carrying heavy things. "Shaila," she says, smiling, "this is the fifth." Then she grabs a teenager by his shirttails. He slips his Walkman off his head. He has to be one of her four children; they have the same domed and dented foreheads. "What's the official word now?" she demands. The boy slips the headphones back on. "They're acting evasive, Ma. They're saying it could be an accident or a terrorist bomb."

282 | MIDCAREER STORIES (1985–1988)

All morning, the boys have been muttering, Sikh bomb, Sikh bomb. The men, not using the word, bow their heads in agreement. Mrs. Sharma touches her forehead at such a word. At least they've stopped talking about space debris and Russian lasers.

Two radios are going in the dining room. They are tuned to different stations. Someone must have brought the radios down from my boys' bedrooms. I haven't gone into their rooms since Kusum came running across the front lawn in her bathrobe. She looked so funny, I was laughing when I opened the door.

The big TV in the den is being whizzed through American networks and cable channels.

"Damn!" some man swears bitterly. "How can these preachers carry on like nothing's happened?" I want to tell him we're not that important. You look at the audience, and at the preacher in his blue robe with his beautiful white hair, the potted palm trees under a blue sky, and you know they care about nothing.

The phone rings and rings. Dr. Sharma's taken charge. "We're with her," he keeps saying. "Yes, yes, the doctor has given calming pills. Yes, yes, pills are having necessary effect." I wonder if pills alone explain this calm. Not peace, just a deadening quiet. I was always controlled, but never repressed. Sound can reach me, but my body is tensed, ready to scream. I hear their voices all around me. I hear my boys and Vikram cry, "Mommy, Shaila!" and their screams insulate me, like headphones.

The woman boiling water tells her story again and again. "I got the news first. My cousin called from Halifax before six A.M., can you imagine? He'd gotten up for prayers and his son was studying for medical exams and he heard on a rock channel that something had happened to a plane. They said first it had disappeared from the radar, like a giant eraser just reached out. His father called me, so I said to him, what do you mean, 'something bad'? You mean a hijacking? And he said, *behn,* there is no confirmation of anything yet, but check with your neighbors because a lot of them must be on that plane. So I called poor Kusum straightaway. I knew Kusum's husband and daughter were booked to go yesterday."

Kusum lives across the street from me. She and Satish had moved in less than a month ago. They said they needed a bigger place. All these people, the Sharmas and friends from the Indo-Canada Society had been there for the housewarming. Satish and Kusum made homemade tandoori on their big gas grill and even the white neighbors piled their plates high with that luridly red, charred, juicy chicken. Their younger daughter had danced, and even our boys had broken away from the Stanley Cup telecast to put in a reluctant appearance. Everyone took pictures for their albums and for the community newspapers—another of our families had made it big in Toronto—and now I wonder how many of those happy faces are gone. "Why does God give us so much if all along He intends to take it away?" Kusum asks me.

I nod. We sit on the carpeted stairs, holding hands like children. "I never once told him that I loved him," I say. I was too much the well brought up woman. I was so well brought up I never felt comfortable calling my husband by his first name.

"It's all right," Kusum says. "He knew. My husband knew. They felt it. Modern young girls have to say it because what they feel is fake."

Kusum's daughter, Pam, runs in with an overnight case. Pam's in her McDonald's uniform. "Mummy! You have to get dressed!" Panic makes her cranky. "A reporter's on his way here."

"Why?"

"You want to talk to him in your bathrobe?" She starts to brush her mother's long hair. She's the daughter who's always in trouble. She dates Canadian boys and hangs out in the mall, shopping for tight sweaters. The younger one, the goody-goody one according to Pam, the one with a voice so sweet that when she sang *bhajans*[1] for Ethiopian relief even a frugal man like my husband wrote out a hundred dollar check, *she* was on that plane. *She* was going to spend July and August with grandparents because Pam wouldn't go. Pam said she'd rather waitress at McDonald's.[2] "If it's a choice between Bombay and Wonderland, I'm picking Wonderland," she'd said.

"Leave me alone," Kusum yells. "You know what I want to do? If I didn't have to look after you now, I'd hang myself."

Pam's young face goes blotchy with pain. "Thanks," she says, "don't let me stop you."

"Hush," pregnant Mrs. Sharma scolds Pam. "Leave your mother alone. Mr. Sharma will tackle the reporters and fill out the forms. He'll say what has to be said."

Pam stands her ground. "You think I don't know what Mummy's thinking? *Why her?* That's what. That's sick! Mummy wishes my little sister were alive and I were dead."

Kusum's hand in mine is trembly hot. We continue to sit on the stairs.

---

1. A *bhajan* is an Indian devotional song.—Ed.

2. Given that Pam is employed by a fast-food outlet, Mukherjee may mean "worker" rather than "waitress" here.—Ed.

284 | MIDCAREER STORIES (1985–1988)

SHE CALLS before she arrives, wondering if there's anything I need. Her name is Judith Templeton and she's an appointee of the provincial government. "Multiculturalism?" I ask, and she says "partially," but that her mandate is bigger. "I've been told you knew many of the people on the flight," she says. "Perhaps if you'd agree to help us reach the others . . . ?"

She gives me time at least to put on tea water and pick up the mess in the front room. I have a few samosas from Kusum's housewarming that I could fry up, but then I think, why prolong this visit?

Judith Templeton is much younger than she sounded. She wears a blue suit with a white blouse and a polka dot tie. Her blond hair is cut short, her only jewelry is pearl drop earrings. Her briefcase is new and expensive looking, a gleaming cordovan leather. She sits with it across her lap. When she looks out the front windows onto the street, her contact lenses seem to float in front of her light blue eyes.

"What sort of help do you want from me?" I ask. She has refused the tea, out of politeness, but I insist, along with some slightly stale biscuits.

"I have no experience," she admits. "That is, I have an MSW and I've worked in liaison with accident victims, but I mean I have no experience with a tragedy of this scale—"

"Who could?" I ask.

"—and with the complications of culture, language, and customs. Someone mentioned that Mrs. Bhave is a pillar—because you've taken it more calmly."

At this, perhaps, I frown, for she reaches forward, almost to take my hand. "I hope you understand my meaning, Mrs. Bhave. There are hundreds of people in Metro directly affected, like you, and some of them speak no English. There are some widows who've never handled money or gone on a bus, and there are old parents who still haven't eaten or gone outside their bedrooms. Some houses and apartments have been looted. Some wives are still hysterical. Some husbands are in shock and profound depression. We want to help, but our hands are tied in so many ways. We have to distribute money to some people, and there are legal documents—these things can be done. We have interpreters, but we don't always have the human touch, or maybe the right human touch. We don't want to make mistakes, Mrs. Bhave, and that's why we'd like to ask you to help us."

"More mistakes, you mean," I say.

"Police matters are not in my hands," she answers.

"Nothing I can do will make any difference," I say. "We must all grieve in our own way."

THE MANAGEMENT OF GRIEF | *285*

"But you are coping very well. All the people said, Mrs. Bhave is the strongest person of all. Perhaps if the others could see you, talk with you, it would help them."

"By the standards of the people you call hysterical, I am behaving very oddly and very badly, Miss Templeton." I want to say to her, *I wish I could scream, starve, walk into Lake Ontario, jump from a bridge.* "They would not see me as a model. I do not see myself as a model."

I am a freak. No one who has ever known me would think of me reacting this way. This terrible calm will not go away.

She asks me if she may call again, after I get back from a long trip that we all must make. "Of course," I say. "Feel free to call, anytime."

FOUR DAYS LATER, I find Kusum squatting on a rock overlooking a bay in Ireland. It isn't a big rock, but it juts sharply out over the water. This is as close as we'll ever get to them. June breezes balloon out her sari and unpin her knee-length hair. She has the bewildered look of a sea creature whom the tides have stranded.

It's been one hundred hours since Kusum came stumbling and screaming across my lawn. Waiting around the hospital, we've heard many stories. The police, the diplomats, they tell us things thinking that we're strong, that knowledge is helpful to the grieving, and maybe it is. Some, I know, prefer ignorance, or their own versions. The plane broke into two, they say. Unconsciousness was instantaneous. No one suffered. My boys must have just finished their breakfasts. They loved eating on planes, they loved the smallness of plates, knives, and forks. Last year they saved the airline salt and pepper shakers. Half an hour more and they would have made it to Heathrow.

Kusum says that we can't escape our fate. She says that all those people— our husbands, my boys, her girl with the nightingale voice, all those Hindus, Christians, Sikhs, Muslims, Parsis, and atheists on that plane—were fated to die together off this beautiful bay. She learned this from a swami in Toronto.

I have my Valium.

Six of us "relatives"—two widows and four widowers—choose to spend the day today by the waters instead of sitting in a hospital room and scanning photographs of the dead. That's what they call us now: relatives. I've looked through twenty-seven photos in two days. They're very kind to us, the Irish are very understanding. Sometimes understanding means freeing a tourist bus for this trip to the bay, so we can pretend to spy our loved ones through the glassiness of waves or in the sun-speckled cloud shapes.

I could die here, too, and be content.

286 | MIDCAREER STORIES (1985–1988)

"What is that, out there?" She's standing and flapping her hands and for a moment I see a head shape bobbing in the waves. She's standing in the water, I, on the boulder. The tide is low, and a round, black, head-sized rock has just risen from the waves. She returns, her sari end dripping and ruined and her face is a twisted remnant of hope, the way mine was a hundred hours ago, still laughing but inwardly knowing that nothing but the ultimate tragedy could bring two women together at six o'clock on a Sunday morning. I watch her face sag into blankness.

"That water felt warm, Shaila," she says at length.

"You can't," I say. "We have to wait for our turn to come."

I haven't eaten in four days, haven't brushed my teeth.

"I know," she says. "I tell myself I have no right to grieve. They are in a better place than we are. My swami says I should be thrilled for them. My swami says depression is a sign of selfishness."

Maybe I'm selfish. Selfishly I break away from Kusum and run, sandals slapping against stones, to the water's edge. What if my boys aren't lying pinned under the debris? What if they aren't stuck a mile below that innocent blue chop? What if, given the strong currents . . .

Now I've ruined my sari, one of my best. Kusum has joined me, knee-deep in water that feels to me like a swimming pool. I could settle in the water, and my husband would take my hand and the boys would slap water in my face just to see my scream.

"Do you remember what good swimmers my boys were, Kusum?"

"I saw the medals," she says.

One of the widowers, Dr. Ranganathan from Montreal, walks out to us, carrying his shoes in one hand. He's an electrical engineer. Someone at the hotel mentioned his work is famous around the world, something about the place where physics and electricity come together. He has lost a huge family, something indescribable. "With some luck," Dr. Ranganathan suggests to me, "a good swimmer could make it safely to some island. It is quite possible that there may be many, many microscopic islets scattered around."

"You're not just saying that?" I tell Dr. Ranganathan about Vinod, my elder son. Last year he took diving as well.

"It's a parent's duty to hope," he says. "It is foolish to rule out possibilities that have not been tested. I myself have not surrendered hope."

Kusum is sobbing once again. "Dear lady," he says, laying his free hand on her arm, and she calms down.

"Vinod is how old?" he asks me. He's very careful as we all are. *Is*, not was.

"Fourteen. Yesterday he was fourteen. His father and uncle were going to take him down to the Taj and give him a big birthday party. I couldn't go with them because I couldn't get two weeks off from my stupid job in June." I process bills for a travel agent. June is a big travel month.

Dr. Ranganathan whips the pockets of his suit jacket inside out. Squashed roses, in darkening shades of pink, float on the water. He tore the roses off creepers in somebody's garden. He didn't ask anyone if he could pluck the roses, but now there's been an article about it in the local papers. When you see an Indian person, it says, please give him or her flowers.

"A strong youth of fourteen," he says, "can very likely pull to safety a younger one."

My sons, though four years apart, were very close. Vinod wouldn't let Mithun drown. *Electrical engineering,* I think, foolishly perhaps: this man knows important secrets of the universe, things closed to me. Relief spins me lightheaded. No wonder my boys' photographs haven't turned up in the gallery of photos of the recovered dead. "Such pretty roses," I say.

"My wife loved pink roses. Every Friday I had to bring a bunch home. I used to say, why? After twenty odd years of marriage you're still needing proof positive of my love?" He has identified his wife and three of his children. Then others from Montreal, the lucky ones, intact families with no survivors. He chuckles as he wades back to shore. Then he swings around to ask me a question. "Mrs. Bhave, you are wanting to throw in some roses for your loved ones? I have two big ones left."

But I have other things to float: Vinod's pocket calculator; a half-painted model B-52 for my Mithun. They'd want them on their island. And for my husband? For him I let fall into the calm, glassy waters a poem I wrote in the hospital yesterday. Finally he'll know my feelings for him.

"Don't tumble, the rocks are slippery," Dr. Ranganathan cautions. He holds out a hand for me to grab.

Then it's time to get back on the bus, time to rush back to our waiting posts on the hospital benches.

KUSUM IS ONE OF THE LUCKY ones. The lucky ones flew here, identified in multiplicate their loved ones, then will fly to India with the bodies for proper ceremonies. Satish is one of the few males who surfaced. The photos of faces we saw on the walls in an office at Heathrow and here in the hospital are mostly of women. Women have more body fat, a nun said to me matter-of-factly. They float better.

Today I was stopped by a young sailor on the street. He had loaded bodies, he'd gone into the water when—he checks my face for signs of strength—when the sharks were first spotted. I don't blush, and he breaks down. "It's all right," I say. "Thank you." I had heard about the sharks from Dr. Ranganathan. In his orderly mind, science brings understanding, it holds no terror. It is the shark's duty. For every deer there is a hunter, for every fish a fisherman.

The Irish are not shy; they rush to me and give me hugs and some are crying. I cannot imagine reactions like that on the streets of Toronto. Just strangers, and I am touched. Some carry flowers with them and give them to any Indian they see.

After lunch, a policeman I have gotten to know quite well catches hold of me. He says he thinks he has a match for Vinod. I explain what a good swimmer Vinod is.

"You want me with you when you look at photos?" Dr. Ranganathan walks ahead of me into the picture gallery. In these matters, he is a scientist, and I am grateful. It is a new perspective. "They have performed miracles," he says. "We are indebted to them."

The first day or two the policemen showed us relatives only one picture at a time; now they're in a hurry, they're eager to lay out the possibles, and even the probables.

The face on the photo is of a boy much like Vinod; the same intelligent eyes, the same thick brows dipping into a V. But this boy's features, even his cheeks, are puffier, wider, mushier.

"No." My gaze is pulled by other pictures. There are five other boys who look like Vinod.

The nun assigned to console me rubs the first picture with a fingertip. "When they've been in the water for a while, love, they look a little heavier." The bones under the skin are broken, they said on the first day—try to adjust your memories. It's important.

"It's not him. I'm his mother. I'd know."

"I know this one!" Dr. Ranganathan cries out suddenly from the back of the gallery. "And this one!" I think he senses that I don't want to find my boys. "They are the Kutty brothers. They were also from Montreal." I don't mean to be crying. On the contrary, I am ecstatic. My suitcase in the hotel is packed heavy with dry clothes for my boys.

The policeman starts to cry. "I am so sorry, I am so sorry, ma'am. I really thought we had a match."

With the nun ahead of us and the policeman behind, we, the unlucky ones without our children's bodies, file out of the makeshift gallery.

FROM IRELAND most of us go on to India. Kusum and I take the same direct flight to Bombay, so I can help her clear customs quickly. But we have to argue with a man in uniform. He has large boils on his face. The boils swell and glow with sweat as we argue with him. He wants Kusum to wait in line and he refuses to take authority because his boss is on a tea break. But Kusum won't let her coffins out of sight, and I shan't desert her though I know that my parents, elderly and diabetic, must be waiting in a stuffy car in the scorching lot.

"You bastard!" I scream at the man with the popping boils. Other passengers press closer. "You think we're smuggling contraband in those coffins!"

Once upon a time we were well brought up women; we were dutiful wives who kept our heads veiled, our voices shy and sweet.

IN INDIA, I become, once again, an only child of rich, ailing parents. Old friends of the family come to pay their respects. Some are Sikh, and inwardly, involuntarily, I cringe. My parents are progressive people; they do not blame communities for a few individuals.

In Canada it is a different story now.

"Stay longer," my mother pleads. "Canada is a cold place. Why would you want to be all by yourself?" I stay.

Three months pass. Then another.

"Vikram wouldn't have wanted you to give up things!" they protest. They call my husband by the name he was born with. In Toronto he'd changed to Vik so the men he worked with at his office would find his name as easy as Rod or Chris. "You know, the dead aren't cut off from us!"

My grandmother, the spoiled daughter of a rich zamindar,[3] shaved her head with rusty razor blades when she was widowed at sixteen. My grandfather died of childhood diabetes when he was nineteen, and she saw herself as the harbinger of bad luck. My mother grew up without parents, raised indifferently by an uncle, while her true mother slept in a hut behind the main estate house and took her food with the servants. She grew up a rationalist. My parents abhor mindless mortification.

The zamindar's daughter kept stubborn faith in Vedic rituals; my parents rebelled. I am trapped between two modes of knowledge. At thirty-six, I am too old to start over and too young to give up. Like my husband's spirit, I flutter between worlds.

COURTING APHASIA, we travel. We travel with our phalanx of servants and poor relatives. To hill stations and to beach resorts. We play contract bridge

---

3. Historical term meaning an Indian landowner.—Ed.

in dusty gymkhana clubs. We ride stubby ponies up crumbly mountain trails. At tea dances, we let ourselves be twirled twice round the ballroom. We hit the holy spots we hadn't made time for before. In Varanasi, Kalighat, Rishikesh, Hardwar, astrologers and palmists seek me out and for a fee offer me cosmic consolations.

Already the widowers among us are being shown new bride candidates. They cannot resist the call of custom, the authority of their parents and older brothers. They must marry; it is the duty of a man to look after a wife. The new wives will be young widows with children, destitute but of good family. They will make loving wives, but the men will shun them. I've had calls from the men over crackling Indian telephone lines. "Save me," they say, these substantial, educated, successful men of forty. "My parents are arranging a marriage for me." In a month they will have buried one family and returned to Canada with a new bride and partial family.

I am comparatively lucky. No one here thinks of arranging a husband for an unlucky widow.

Then, on the third day of the sixth month into this odyssey, in an abandoned temple in a tiny Himalayan village, as I make my offering of flowers and sweetmeats to the god of a tribe of animists, my husband descends to me. He is squatting next to a scrawny *sadhu*[4] in moth-eaten robes. Vikram wears the vanilla suit he wore the last time I hugged him. The *sadhu* tosses petals on a butter-fed flame, reciting Sanskrit mantras and sweeps his face of flies. My husband takes my hands in his.

You're beautiful, he starts. Then, *What are you doing here?*

Shall I stay? I ask. He only smiles, but already the image is fading. *You must finish alone what we started together.* No seaweed wreathes his mouth. He speaks too fast just as he used to when we were an envied family in our pink split-level. He is gone.

In the windowless altar room, smoky with joss sticks and clarified butter lamps, a sweaty hand gropes for my blouse. I do not shriek. The *sadhu* arranges his robe. The lamps hiss and sputter out.

When we come out of the temple, my mother says, "Did you feel something weird in there?"

My mother has no patience with ghosts, prophetic dreams, holy men, and cults. "No," I lie. "Nothing."

But she knows that she's lost me. She knows that in days I shall be leaving.

---

4. An ascetic Indian holy person.—Ed.

Kusum's put her house up for sale. She wants to live in an ashram in Hardwar. Moving to Hardwar was her swami's idea. Her swami runs two ashrams, the one in Hardwar and another here in Toronto.

"Don't run away," I tell her.

"I'm not running way," she says. "I'm pursuing inner peace. You think you or that Ranganathan fellow are better off?"

Pam's left for California. She wants to do some modeling, she says. She says when she comes into her share of the insurance money she'll open a yoga-cum-aerobics studio in Hollywood. She sends me postcards so naughty I daren't leave them on the coffee table. Her mother has withdrawn from her and the world.

The rest of us don't lose touch, that's the point. Talk is all we have, says Dr. Ranganathan, who has also resisted his relatives and returned to Montreal and to his job, alone. He says, whom better to talk with than other relatives? We've been melted down and recast as a new tribe.

He calls me twice a week from Montreal. Every Wednesday night and every Saturday afternoon. He is changing jobs, going to Ottawa. But Ottawa is over a hundred miles away, and he is forced to drive two hundred and twenty miles a day. He can't bring himself to sell his house. The house is a temple, he says; the king-sized bed in the master bedroom is a shrine. He sleeps on a folding cot. A devotee.

There are still some hysterical relatives. Judith Templeton's list of those needing help and those who've "accepted" is in nearly perfect balance. Acceptance means you speak of your family in the past tense and you make active plans for moving ahead with your life. There are courses at Seneca and Ryerson we could be taking. Her gleaming leather briefcase is full of college catalogs and lists of cultural societies that need our help. She has done impressive work, I tell her.

"In the textbooks on grief management," she replies—I am her confidante, I realize, one of the few whose grief has not sprung bizarre obsessions—"there are stages to pass through: rejection, depression, acceptance, reconstruction." She has compiled a chart and finds that six months after the tragedy, none of us still reject reality, but only a handful are reconstructing. "Depressed Acceptance" is the plateau we've reached. Remarriage is a major step in reconstruction (though she's a little surprised, even shocked, over *how* quickly some of the men have taken on new families). Selling one's house and changing jobs and cities is healthy.

292 | MIDCAREER STORIES (1985–1988)

How to tell Judith Templeton that my family surrounds me, and that like creatures in epics, they've changed shapes? She sees me as calm and accepting but worries that I have no job, no career. My closest friends are worse off than I. I cannot tell her my days, even my nights, are thrilling.

She asks me to help with families she can't reach at all. An elderly couple in Agincourt whose sons were killed just weeks after they had brought their parents over from a village in Punjab. From their names, I know they are Sikh. Judith Templeton and a translator have visited them twice with offers of money for air fare to Ireland, with bank forms, power-of-attorney forms, but they have refused to sign, or to leave their tiny apartment. Their sons' money is frozen in the bank. Their sons' investment apartments have been trashed by tenants, the furnishings sold off. The parents fear that anything they sign or any money they receive will end the company's or the country's obligations to them. They fear they are selling their sons for two airline tickets to a place they've never seen.

The high-rise apartment is a tower of Indians and West Indians, with a sprinkling of Orientals. The nearest bus stop kiosk is lined with women in saris. Boys practice cricket in the parking lot. Inside the building, even I wince a bit from the ferocity of onion fumes, the distinctive and immediate Indian-ness of frying *ghee*, but Judith Templeton maintains a steady flow of information. These poor old people are in imminent danger of losing their place and all their services.

I say to her, "They are Sikh. They will not open up to a Hindu woman." And what I want to add is, as much as I try not to, I stiffen now at the sight of beards and turbans. I remember a time when we all trusted each other in this new country, it was only the new country we worried about.

The two rooms are dark and stuffy. The lights are off, and an oil lamp sputters on the coffee table. The bent old lady has let us in, and her husband is wrapping a white turban over his oiled, hip-length hair. She immediately goes to the kitchen, and I hear the most familiar sound of an Indian home, tap water hitting and filling a teapot.

They have not paid their utility bills, out of fear and the inability to write a check. The telephone is gone; electricity and gas and water are soon to follow. They have told Judith their sons will provide. They are good boys, and they have always earned and looked after their parents.

We converse a bit in Hindi. They do not ask about the crash and I wonder if I should bring it up. If they think I am here merely as a translator, then they may feel insulted. There are thousands of Punjabi-speakers, Sikhs, in Toronto to do a better job. And so I say to the old lady, "I, too, have lost my sons, and my husband, in the crash."

THE MANAGEMENT OF GRIEF | *293*

Her eyes immediately fill with tears. The man mutters a few words which sound like a blessing. "God provides and God takes away," he says.

I want to say, but only men destroy and give back nothing. "My boys and my husband are not coming back," I say. "We have to understand that."

Now the old woman responds. "But who is to say? Man alone does not decide these things." To this her husband adds his agreement.

Judith asks about the bank papers, the release forms. With a stroke of the pen, they will have a provincial trustee to pay their bills, invest their money, send them a monthly pension.

"Do you know this woman?" I ask them.

The man raises his hand from the table, turns it over and seems to regard each finger separately before he answers. "This young lady is always coming here, we make tea for her and she leaves papers for us to sign." His eyes scan a pile of papers in the corner of the room. "Soon we will be out of tea, then will she go away?"

The old lady adds, "I have asked my neighbors and no one else gets *angrezi*[5] visitors. What have we done?"

"It's her job," I try to explain. "The government is worried. Soon you will have no place to stay, no lights, no gas, no water."

"Government will get its money. Tell her not to worry, we are honorable people."

I try to explain the government wishes to give money, not take. He raises his hand. "Let them take," he says. "We are accustomed to that. That is no problem."

"We are strong people," says the wife. "Tell her that."

"Who needs all this machinery?" demands the husband. "It is unhealthy, the bright lights, the cold air on a hot day, the four gas rings. God will provide, not government."

"When our boys return," the mother says. Her husband sucks his teeth. "Enough talk," he says.

Judith breaks in. "Have you convinced them?" The snaps on her cordovan briefcase go off like firecrackers in that quiet apartment. She lays the sheaf of legal papers on the coffee table. "If they can't write their names, an X will do— I've told them that."

Now the old lady has shuffled to the kitchen and soon emerges with a pot of tea and two cups. "I think my bladder will go first on a job like this," Judith says to me, smiling. "If only there was some way of reaching them. Please thank her for the tea. Tell her she's very kind."

---

5. Hindi word meaning "English," presumably referring here to white anglophone Canadians such as Judith Templeton.—Ed.

I nod in Judith's direction and tell them in Hindi, "She thanks you for the tea. She thinks you are being very hospitable but she doesn't have the slightest idea what it means."

I want to say, humor her. I want to say, my boys and my husband are with me, too, more than ever. I look in the old man's eyes and I can read his stubborn, peasant's message: *I have protected this woman as best I can. She is the only person I have left. Give to me or take from me what you will, but I will not sign for it. I will not pretend that I accept.*

In the car, Judith says, "You see what I'm up against? I'm sure they're lovely people, but their stubbornness and ignorance are driving me crazy. They think signing a paper is signing their sons' death warrants, don't they?"

I am looking out the window. I want to say, *In our culture, it is a parent's duty to hope.*

"Now Shaila, this next woman is a real mess. She cries day and night, and she refuses all medical help. We may have to—"

"—Let me out at the subway," I say.

"I beg your pardon?" I can feel those blue eyes staring at me.

It would not be like her to disobey. She merely disapproves, and slows at a corner to let me out. Her voice is plaintive. "Is it anything I said? Anything I did?"

I could answer her suddenly in a dozen ways, but I choose not to. "Shaila? Let's talk about it," I hear, then slam the door.

A WIFE AND MOTHER begins her life in a new country, and that life is cut short. Yet her husband tells her: Complete what we have started. We, who stayed out of politics and came halfway around the world to avoid religious and political feuding, have been the first in the New World to die from it. I no longer know what we started, nor how to complete it. I write letters to the editors of local papers and to members of Parliament. Now at least they admit it was a bomb. One MP answers back, with sympathy, but with a challenge. You want to make a difference? Work on a campaign. Work on mine. Politicize the Indian voter.

My husband's old lawyer helps me set up a trust. Vikram was a saver and a careful investor. He had saved the boys' boarding school and college fees. I sell the pink house at four times what we paid for it and take a small apartment downtown. I am looking for a charity to support.

We are deep in the Toronto winter, gray skies, icy pavements. I stay indoors, watching television. I have tried to assess my situation, how best to live my life, to complete what we began so many years ago. Kusum has written me from Hardwar that her life is now serene. She has seen Satish and has heard her daughter sing again. Kusum was on a pilgrimage, passing through a village, when she heard a young girl's voice, singing one of her daughter's favorite *bhajans*. She followed the music through the squalor of a Himalayan village, to a hut where a young girl, an exact replica of her daughter, was fanning coals under the kitchen fire. When she appeared, the girl cried out, "Ma!" and ran away. What did I think of that?

I think I can only envy her.

Pam didn't make it to California, but writes me from Vancouver. She works in a department store, giving makeup hints to Indian and Oriental girls. Dr. Ranganathan has given up his commute, given up his house and job, and accepted an academic position in Texas where no one knows his story and he has vowed not to tell it. He calls me now once a week.

I wait, I listen, and I pray, but Vikram has not returned to me. The voices and the shapes and the nights filled with visions ended abruptly several weeks ago.

I take it as a sign.

One rare, beautiful, sunny day last week, returning from a small errand on Yonge Street, I was walking through the park from the subway to my apartment. I live equidistant from the Ontario Houses of Parliament and the University of Toronto. The day was not cold, but something in the bare trees caught my attention. I looked up from the gravel, into the branches and the clear blue sky beyond. I thought I heard the rustling of larger forms, and I waited a moment for voices. Nothing.

"What?" I asked.

Then as I stood in the path looking north to Queen's Park and west to the university, I heard the voices of my family one last time. *Your time has come,* they said. *Go, be brave.*

I do not know where this voyage I have begun will end. I do not know which direction I will take. I dropped the package on a park bench and started walking.

LATE STORIES

(1997–2012)

Happiness (1997)

MY FATHER WAS DYING of cancer, but he hung in long enough to select a groom for me out of Aunt Flower Garland's short list of three. The night before he passed away, he gave me his last advice and blessing. He said, "In the areas I can control, namely financial security and temperamental compatibility, I have hedged all bets. Happiness in marriage? That, even I can't guarantee."

He rejected the candidacy of a physics professor in Tulsa, Oklahoma, and a dentist in San Leandro, California, in favor of Arjun. The physics professor had a grandfather who had nearly won a Nobel Prize in quantum theory, and the dentist's family owned a profitable pharmaceutical company, but Arjun had a Ph.D. in electrical engineering from Columbia University. Columbia was where my father would like to have studied, if his father, so the story went, hadn't died of a ruptured appendix at (even by the local standards) the premature age of twenty-six. My grandmother, two aunts, and father owed their second start in life to the generosity of a maternal uncle, who, being a relative from the maternal side, of course was under no obligation to take them in. This uncle, who had five daughters and three sons of his own, paid for the weddings of my Aunts Flower Garland and Leafy Vine, and, when my father turned seventeen, arranged an apprentice job for him with an engineer friend at a hydroelectric plant an overnight's train ride from the city.

"And as the Calcutta Chamber of Commerce knows," my father was fond of saying, and he said it always in English, "the rest is very much history, isn't it?"

In his anecdotes, he gave his youth Dickensian twists and darkenings, not all of which I believed, probably because by the time I was born he'd made one fortune in lumber up in Assam, and another down in Andhra in steel. In a previous incarnation, Horatio Alger had to have been Bengali.

My father and I were very close, closer than most fathers and daughters in our traditional neighborhood, Mother having died of an overnight fever when I was three. I can't visualize Mother since there are no photographs of her, no likeness for me to have had framed and hung on the wall next to my late grandfather's and grandmother's portraits above the altar of gods in the room of worship, but her presence or absence persists in my brain as a faint stain of melancholy.

A week before my father died, Arjun, whose full name is Arjun Kumar Roy Chowdhury, flew in from New York on a two-week vacation from his job—he was a vice-president in charge of operations research at an electronics company—interviewed the women on the Roy Chowdhury family's short list of bridal candidates that he thought he might survive a lifetime with on the basis of photo, bio, and relatives' preliminary impressions, and picked me. I need to believe that his family's short list was longer than my father's.

Given the long lines for immigrant visas at the U.S. consulate, Arjun was impatient to get the legal formality of marriage over with before he returned to New York at the end of his two-week leave, but we, Ghoses, insisted on letting a respectable time lapse between celebration of funeral and wedding. I don't call it *my* wedding, or Arjun's and my wedding, because the bride and groom played the least assertive role during the lawyerly dowry negotiations, the by-fax-and-priority-mail transcontinental preparations, and the long, complicated, exhausting pre- and postnuptial ceremonies. We fasted when we were told to, we bathed with turmeric paste in Ganges water as prescribed, we played the laid-down games auguring connubial contentment, and when, toward the end of all the chants by the Brahmin priest and the vows in Sanskrit by Arjun and my maternal great-uncle, the dramatic moment came for the veiled bride to lift her head and look into the groom's eyes, we both managed I'm-ready-for-whatever-adventure smiles.

Two days after the wedding, the day known as *bou-bhat*, which I later translated into English for Karin Stein, my neighbor in Upper Montclair, New Jersey, as *the day the bride moves to her husband's house and cooks rice perfect enough for him to eat, because if the rice is too crunchy or too sticky she'll be sent back in disgrace to her parents' house*, Arjun and I boarded an Air India 747, and, strangers safety-belted into side-by-side seats, headed for instant intimacy.

Within a month of making my home in America, I learned how wise my father, the Cheetah of the Calcutta Chamber of Commerce, had been to hedge those bets that he could. At social gatherings, like the Tagore Society evenings in the Bannerjees' split-level in Chappaqua, New York, or at the organizational meetings of the Bengali Heritage Preservation Association in the Dases' condo in Queens, I sniffed out heartache and heard deceit. I picked up words and phrases that I hadn't been taught by Aunts Flower Garland and Leafy Vine: Creedmoor, Prozac, shelter for abused women, defenestration.

Comfortable living and decent conduct had been taken for granted by my family. I was grateful that the Ghoses hadn't been deceived by the Roy Chowdhurys. Arjun hadn't lied about his degrees, his salary, his stocks and bonds holdings. He owned the Tudor-style house in Montclair, and the black BMW we had been shown photos of. And he owned things I hadn't seen before: a refrigerator with an ice-water faucet set in its door, a convection oven, an outdoor gas barbecue grill.

The more personal habits and peeves revealed themselves enticingly to me. For instance, every night before coming to bed, he dropped two Alka-Seltzer tablets into a highball glass of water, said, "Plop, plop, fizz, fizz, bottoms up!

Prosit!" and gulped the noisy drink down while pinching his nose. I got to look forward to chasing the antacid grains off his lips with my tongue. It made me feel uninhibited. Who cares about long-term happiness when the tongue is tracing, teasing, tormenting, in fulfillment of its own, distinct destiny?

Arjun and I made our voluntary accommodations. At the dinner table, I learned to taste the difference between chardonnay and sauvignon blanc, and pretended preferences for merlots and pinot noirs and contempt for all California cabernets. He cut back on port and beef. I filled him in on Indian politics: he'd missed so much of which party leaders had defected and why, and which cabinet ministers had been arrested and on what charges among the usual frauds, graft, currency violations, embezzlements. He reciprocated by dictating which senators and Congress representatives I was to trust and explaining the glories and ghastlinesses of the American two-party system. Politics was bedtime story. It didn't matter that I didn't have a vote in this country, that I hadn't voted in any election in any country. I still think of politics as love's foreplay.

Give and take; take and give: that was the flow of our intimacy. Arjun liked to make money, and he liked me to spend it. I did. I drove the BMW— bigger, shinier than in the photos I'd been shown—to the malls, and displayed what money could buy when, late in the New Jersey night, he came through the front door, carrying a briefcaseful of work he had yet to get through. It wasn't about being pliant. My father taught me, through example, that self-worth based on cash-worth is the shortest cut to tragedy.

"Class and conscience," my father said, "go together like a washerman and his donkey. Class is the washerman, but he has to follow the path that his stubborn donkey takes, isn't it?"

My father's analogies were not for me to question. In his adolescent days as apprentice laborer, he'd composed a notebookful of morally uplifting couplets in Bengali, the point of all of which was, cultivate your conscience so that money and rank may not lead you astray.

I have followed his advice by never buying insurance. I wouldn't shed a tear if a burglar broke into the house while Arjun was in the Softron, Inc., offices in Manhattan and I at the cosmetics counter at Bendel's, and made off with a vanload of our belongings. But I have followed his advice for lascivious reasons. Penury neither alarms me nor goads me to covetous ambitiousness. Money, in my marriage to Arjun, was the consensual currency of intimacy. All around me in suburban New York and New Jersey, love was ending in sleeping pills, straitjackets, fatal automobile accidents. Not love, not loyalty, but steel-tipped intimacy, so sharp and thrilling that it has entered and exited before you have touched the wound, felt the pain: that intimacy was our strength.

302 | LATE STORIES (1997–2012)

Forget the prenuptial haggling between the Roy Chowdhurys and the Ghoses. To each other we made no promises. We gave and took freely, greedily. We demonstrated large-hearted poor sense instead of self-interest. There should have been time for me to let my father know that before intimacy, happiness in marriage pales.

This is the way that our most special night happened. What does it matter which year, which season? It was a weeknight like any other weeknight in our America life. Arjun came through the front door, which the previous owners, whom Karin Stein remembered as "a moody Middle East type, don't ask me from where exactly, except that he was definitely not from Israel," had fitted with chimes that tinkled out a bar or two of what Karin identified as "It's a Most Beautiful Day"; he dropped his umbrella in its ceramic stand, hung up his all-weather coat in the hall closet; he thrust a cold, heavy bottle of champagne instead of the usual chardonnay against my bosom, grabbed me in a bear hug, and whispered, "Tonight we celebrate!" into the Austrian crystal necklace, which was what I had bought from a just-opened boutique earlier in the day.

"Celebrate what?" I assumed a bonus or promotion, or, for Arjun, more pleasing still would be a stock market coup. My role in our partnership was to draw the answers out of him.

"Who cares what?" He popped the cork right there in the hall, and with the champagne foaming down the sides of the bottle and leaving sticky droplets on the wood floor, dragged me in a bear hug to the kitchen.

A finicky housemaker would have blotted clean the champagne trail while Arjun was reaching for the fluted glasses I'd stuck way in the back of the highest cabinet shelf. They were still in the manufacturer's box. I'd bought them at a going-out-of-business sale in Paramus Mall. Arjun was a Glenfiddich drinker. Wine collecting was a hobby with him. He'd made a wine cellar out of what had been the last owner's woodworking shop. "Forget carpentry," Karin scoffed when she came over for our first wine-tasting party, "the guy was making bombs. Don't you hear any funny ticking noises when you're in the basement?"

A woman with good sense would have first turned off the gas flames under the pots of Basmati rice and goat vindaloo, then attended to whatever adventure destiny had lassoed.

"Let me guess," I laughed. "I've never seen you this happy, so it has to be something special."

Arjun pulled two champagne flutes out of their box, and held them under the kitchen faucet. I'd forgotten they were etched with a cloudy circlet of leaves and rimmed with a bright, thin band of gold.

"So happy," Arjun retorted, "that I'm not complaining about having to rinse dishes."

"We aren't in Calcutta anymore." I tore off squares of paper towels and held them out to Arjun. Rolls of parch-tongued paper towels, packages of thick, crisp bond paper into which no insect bodies have been processed: those are the American marvels I prize.

"Try telling that to your Chappaqua friends. You think Prafulla Bose comes home at eight and does the dishes?"

He crumpled the dry paper squares and tossed them in the garbage. The track light aimed at the sink caught the bright slitheriness of water coating the inside of each flute.

"You've been nominated Most Valuable Functionary by your CEO."

"Don't even try," Arjun said. He poured the champagne carefully into a glass for me.

I had watched him pour wine before, but I hadn't noticed, really noticed, his wrists. I'd admired his fingers before, told him many times how movingly delicate I found them on a man who claimed to abhor painters and poets. The wrists that rotated with the bottle neck had the showy, arrogant sureness of wrists of the concert pianists I caught by chance on cable channels. "All right, you're a secret gambler, and you've just made a killing." I arced my body to kiss that confident wrist. So what that my head knocked the filled glass out of his surprised grasp.

"A gambler?"

I heard his shoes push aside broken glass. He was thinking of my feet, not his floor. I don't wear shoes or slippers at home. I didn't in Calcutta where our floors were of cool marble or stone mosaic, and I didn't in Upper Montclair with its oak, tile, lino, and wool-blend wall-to-wall.

"You don't mind drinking a toast to gambling?" He poured champagne into the second flute.

"Plop, plop, fizz, fizz!" I whispered. "Bottoms up!"

"Prosit!" he whispered back.

I took a gulp, he an assessor's sip. "How much, Arjun?" I was thinking how large a sum I would have to find creative ways for spending.

"Every asshole gambler should be so lucky to have you as a wife!"

Then he whirled me into the living room with strides that resembled waltzers' on colorized, afternoon movies on TV, humming tunes I didn't know and at the same time wriggling out of his suit jacket, stiffening his spine and outstretched arms, tightening his buttocks.

It wasn't natural clumsiness that kept me stepping on his champagne-dampened shoes. Like most young women on my block, I took years of weekend classes in Tagore-style singing and dancing. Aunt Leafy Vine keeps my certificates in the vault compartment of her most secure cabinet, which by the way is made of steel manufactured in one of my father's factories. I am no more and no less physically graceful than the other tristate Bengali wives who have volunteered for bit parts in Tagore's drama *Red Oleander*, which the Tagore Society intends to stage next October.

That night I tripped, I kept tripping, stumbling, apologizing, because I couldn't feel the beat to his hummed tune. He rose on the balls of his feet; I thumped with my heels as though I was wearing dance bells on my ankles. He covered the available floor space with wide swoops in circles; I concentrated my energies on the slightest movements of finger joints and neck muscles. I had danced duets as Radha the Milkmaid to a girl-cousin's Krishna the God Biding His Time as Amorous Goatherd in family theatricals. But in those duets, Radha and Krishna never touched. Nobody led, nobody followed. There wasn't any need to. Power was shared by god and mortal. We improvised the depths of the lovers' passion, but never the way their loves turned out. That was the trouble, I told myself. I had no way of telling when the humming and the prancing would come to their natural close. There were no scripted roles, no sage-revealed unalterable storyline, no faith that through dance I might discover the simple secret of cosmic chaos.

"It's no good," Arjun said.

He let go of me, suddenly, and I fell back into his favorite chair, a massive leather rocker, embarrassed at my own ungainliness, but thankful the ordeal was over while he hummed, whistled, twirled around the room solo.

"See how easy it is?"

I heard relief, not taunt, in Arjun's question. From the rocker, the posture and the footwork did seem easy. "I think my problem is I'm not hearing what you're hearing. I'm not *feeling* what you're feeling."

"What am I feeling?" He dipped his head back to ask his question, but by the time I answered, "You're feeling good, very good," he'd waltzed away to the farthest corner of the living room.

For another hour I watched, cowering at the unself-conscious celebration of . . . what was it that he was celebrating? What had he gambled on? How destructive could his winnings be? Was I a witness to bliss or lunacy?

When I went to bed that night, he was still dancing.

The next morning he left home at six-thirty as he always did to catch his commuter train. I haven't seen him since. I did find a note, an orange Post-It actually, stuck to the neck of the champagne bottle. It said: *There is another woman, but that's not the reason. Arranged marriages carry no risk. I know you'll react to my leaving, and to a gambler, certainty is boring. Ciao! Have a happy life.*

That was seven years ago. The changes in my life are mostly invisible. I still have the BMW and the house on North Fullerton Street. Karin Stein is still my friend, but she chucked her law practice for a bearded baker somewhere in the Northwest. She sends me postcards with grease stains. Last year I talked myself into starting law school. Night classes, not Harvard or Yale. All the same, it's exciting work, and I am a hardworking student. My father's failure to arrange a lasting marriage has alchemized into new strengths and excitements. Now, for instance, I stay awake nights arguing the legal rights of frozen sperm or defending UFO-borne alien scientists against charges of rape. Are UFO abductions and orifice penetrations punishable crimes in U.S. courts? For amendments to immigration bills, do "UFObacks" fall into the category of undocumenteds? Is Arjun physically as well as legally dead? In American English is self-esteem a synonym for happiness?

Homes (2008)

I AM WRITING this in a shingled cottage on a leafy three-block lane in the village of Southampton, New York. My writing desk is a Chinese antique I bought cheap on eBay as soon as I realized I needed to keep a journal. Ben and Hugh, who live across from me, hauled it up my narrow staircase to the smaller of two guest bedrooms. Ben's a real estate agent, and Hugh's a stager for Ben's clients. They're not just good neighbors; since Rahul drowned, they've morphed into dedicated caregivers.

I spotted the cottage quite accidentally on my first ever trip to the South Fork. We were being shown properties in the village by Traci Hollings, an agent who had been talked up by a Belgian hedge-fund analyst Rahul regularly beat at racquetball. Rahul had more faith in real estate than in the stock market, so we'd taken the jitney in from Manhattan just for the day, prepared to bid on one of seven houses in the two-million-dollar range that Traci had lined up for us. My husband was looking to invest; I was hoping to nest. In his loft in Soho, which had been his bachelor pad for years, I felt more a party guest than wife.

It was a Friday afternoon in mid-May, and Traci's SUV was zigzagging through heavy traffic on North Sea Road to get us to the fifth on Traci's to-show list: a four-bedroom, four-bath "steal" new on the market because of a divorce. Migrant workers, who still hadn't given up on being hired, loitered in listless clusters in the parking lot of a 7-Eleven and lined both sidewalks.

306 | LATE STORIES (1997–2012)

I couldn't hear the hecklers at street corners, but I counted one "Go Back to Mexico" and three "America for Americans" hand-made signs before we turned into a lane named after a deciduous tree, and passed the cottage. All I could see of it through a scruffy hedge were green-shuttered windows and brilliant purple domes of mature azalea bushes flanking a front porch. A For Sale sign from a realty company other than Traci's was stuck on the sliver of sandy soil between road and hedge.

Traci eased the SUV to a stop a couple of yards beyond the For Sale sign, but kept the engine running. Migrants rushed the SUV, then backed away scowling when they realized we were not potential employers. I sensed Traci sizing us up, too, and being disappointed: Rahul and I were the wrong kind of moneyed immigrants, clueless about the Hamptons, a waste of her time. She waved a manicured hand, ropy with veins, at the frame houses with sagging stoops on large, overgrown lots on the block. Teardowns, she announced in a hard voice, an "unstable" neighborhood. Once the old-timer residents died, their heirs would sell to developers who would subdivide the lots. Also, how did we feel about buying so close to train tracks? Then she glanced pointedly at her wafer-thin gold watch.

We viewed three more houses. All the properties, with their staged interiors, designer gardens, patios paved with tumbled travertine tiles, commodious hot tubs, Gunite infinity pools, were grander than any home I'd ever fantasized about owning. I tried to calculate what two million U.S. dollars came to in rupees, but gave up. Like Rahul, I had grown up in a rented flat in a once-genteel neighborhood of south Kolkata. But unlike Rahul, I was a diffident American consumer. When Traci dropped us off at The Omni for our jitney back to Manhattan, he let her know that she had wasted his day.

On the ride back, however, he complimented me for having brought the cottage off North Sea Road to his attention. A property on an iffy street but within the village of Southampton for under a million dollars and low property taxes was a smarter investment than Traci's pricey houses with better addresses. I didn't fool myself into thinking that he was asking for my input. He wasn't consulting me; he was informing me of a decision he had already made. All the same, I glowed all the way to Manhattan as I pictured us watching CNBC together on a flat screen in a living room I had not entered; making up a king-size bed we didn't yet own with color-coordinated sheets, duvets, pillows; cooking slow food dinners together on an old-fashioned stove in a rustic kitchen. I wanted the ride to last forever.

That night he emailed Ben Moretti, the agent listed on the For Sale sign for the cottage. The next weekend Ben took us through the cozy, two-story structure and its modest grounds. Ben described the neighborhood as "transitional," but he made "transitional" sound desirable. He had sold a TLC[1] on a parallel lane to a fortyish stockbroker with high alimony and child support payments, a teardown catty-corner from the LIRR station to two aromatherapist sisters, and he himself had just put in a bid for the older house directly across from the cottage. Rahul quizzed Ben on heating and cooling costs, financing options, summer rental potential. I left the two of them talking figures at the kitchen table, and settled into a deck chair on the front porch to savor the blinding radiance of azalea bushes in full bloom. Our azaleas. Our house.

As soon as the sale went through, Rahul hired a local contractor and a landscaper recommended by Ben. He had a showy master bedroom suite with champagne spa tub and walk-in closet built above the kitchen, the back and side yards landscaped, a new privet hedge planted, a heated pool put in. The contractor fell two weeks behind schedule, because one of his workers, an Ecuadoran, sliced his hand badly on site, and didn't complete the job until mid-May, leaving Rahul barely enough time to rent out the cottage for the Memorial Day to Labor Day summer season. I had visualized Rahul and me rather than tenants, soaking in scented, fizzy bathwater in candlelight, Tiffany flutes in hand, but I knew to hide my disappointment. The occasional winter and spring weekends we did spend in Southampton were as hosts (he relaxed, I harassed) to swarms of his relatives visiting from Kolkata or his South Asian business associates. It's only been a month that I've been living in it full-time; well, more drifting through life than living.

Rahul continues to dictate plans for me to follow. He barges into my dreams, orders me to sell the Southampton cottage, rent out the Soho loft, move back to Kolkata, buy a large luxury condo in a new high-rise apartment building with an elevator and shops, and make a home for myself and his widowed mother. His advice is, as always, shrewd as well as wise. I should go back to where I have family. I have parents as well as Rahul's mother to care for. Selflessness is a worthy goal. Besides, Rahul whispers, my dollar savings will stretch farther in Kolkata than in New York.

So why did I listen instead to Ben's partner, Hugh, and set up camp in Southampton? Hugh brings me homemade meals—fish stews, pappardelle with mascarpone sauce, pot-roasted guinea fowl—in microwaveable containers. He coaxes me out of the cottage for strolls on Main Street and buying trips for Haughty Haute, a home design store on Jobs Lane he owns. Most of the furniture in this room, the white wrought iron daybed, for instance, the candy-striped love seat, the white wicker bookcase, are from Hugh's store, as are the

---

1. Mukherjee may mean "Tender Loving Care," that is, a property that needs a lot of work.—Ed.

308 | LATE STORIES (1997–2012)

tastefully worn Aubusson rug, the pink, fringed Victorian shade on the floor lamp Rahul scavenged from the town dump, the pile of cushions that pick up the rug's faded colors just so, the watercolors with nautical themes, and the three-foot-long ceramic mermaid sunning on a ceramic rock. Only the sleek, silver MacBook Air that sits incompatibly on the ornate rosewood desk is mine. It had been Rahul's.

Ben tells me that if I decide to sell the cottage, I'd do all right even in these days of mortgage meltdown, but sooner is better than later. I'll need to ready the property for realtors' brochures. Extend the deck off the kitchen, Ben advises, spruce up the pool house, put up a pergola (he and Hugh went for a gazebo as well as a pergola), and voila! I know what Ben is really up to: he's trying to come up with a therapeutic project for me. Grief stagnates: he doesn't say that to my face, but that's what he's thinking. I need to progress from what Hugh's yoga instructor calls "the foothills of loss" to the "peak of solitude." The instructor has his own holistic fitness show on cable TV. Hugh has bought me a how-to DVD, but I haven't watched it yet. First, I have to figure out what I'm grieving. I'm thirty-seven; widowed by a freak accident; childless. My life is on PAUSE.

The journal project gives my days comforting focus. I know the project's goals: assess the past; imagine the future; suppress the present. I've set myself rules. I must be at my desk by 9:10 A.M., switch off my cell phone, skim news events on the Internet, read but not answer my email, report spam, light an incense stick in front of the shrine that holds a silver statue of Goddess Kali and a framed photograph of Rahul. I stay at the screen until 2:00 P.M. every day, weekends as well as weekdays. The UPS driver can ring the doorbell, the answering machine can blink away, the Sub-Zero may be empty except for mold-speckled cheeses: between 9:10 A.M. and 2:00 P.M. I permit myself no procrastination. If I concentrate hard enough, journal entries will birth themselves on the screen. The fingers on the keyboard are the midwife's. I believe that. I really do.

While I wait for new life to emerge, I experiment with fonts, margins and line spacing. Does form inhibit content? As a schoolgirl in Kolkata I wrote my weekly essays for Mother Paul in careful longhand in a lined notebook with my grandfather's Parker 51 fountain pen. Some feelings are too nuanced, some discoveries too intimate, to feed into a word processor.

This morning, as most mornings and early afternoons, I find myself distracted by the angled view of North Sea Road that the only window in this room offers. Migrant workers, mostly stocky men with morose faces under hooded sweatshirts, lounge on a grassy strip by a bus stop, waiting for drive-by contractors to pull up, or to at least slow down. Fast food wrappers sprout like blooms on hedges; empty pop bottles and coffee cups roll like skittles into gutters. Rahul didn't care that the cottage looks out on a year-round seafood store and a cantina instead of dune and ocean. I mouth Rahul's mantra: *Plan smart, buy low, trade up; think with your head not your heart; attachment ends in disappointment*. His only "home" was the rented ground-floor flat on Rash Behari Avenue, Kolkata, where he had been born, where his father had died, and where his mother still lives. I stare at the migrants and the lone placard-toting protester. I strain to hear *their* mantra for better lives.

Rahul and I grew up twenty minutes' bus ride apart, but met for the first time three and a half years ago in the Bloomfield, New Jersey, home of my father's first cousin. My uncle and aunt arranged the meeting. In another month my tourist visa was to expire, and they had promised my father when they sent a pre-paid Air India ticket for me that they would find him a suitable Bengali-American son-in-law. My father is a proud man on very limited income. He accepted the ticket on my behalf only after my uncle had explained that I would be doing him, his wife and married daughter a favor instead of the other way around. The daughter, an oncologist married to a dermatologist, was about to give birth to twins and would be grateful for help with baby care. Unlike my father, I didn't think accepting a rich relative's charity was at all humiliating. A thirty-four-year-old unmarried woman with a Bachelor of Arts degree (Third Class) from Calcutta University, aging by the hour: what did I have to lose?

What little I knew of my New Jersey relatives before arriving in their home was from family gossip and brief letters, enclosing photographs and dutiful inquiries about our health, my aunt wrote my mother in Bangla[2] every few months. The photographs disclosed a fuller biography than the letters. We understood that my aunt had become so Americanized that she wore pants, parka, boots, cleared snow off her front steps with a heavy shovel, and drove her very own Lexus. My uncle, too, had de-Indianized enough to pose without shame in a bright red apron like a woman or a servant and turn slabs of smoking meat on an outdoor grill. My father would never be caught in the kitchen, not even to boil water for his hourly cups of tea.

According to family lore (details of which changed, but never the outline), in the mid-1970s this uncle, a civil engineer, had resigned from pensionable government employment in a *mofussil*[3] town in West Bengal and emigrated to Trenton, New Jersey, sponsored by an engineering college classmate who had already settled there. My uncle had worked full-time in his sponsor's construction company, lived five to a room with fellow Indian immigrants, saved

---

2. Bengali.—Ed.

3. "Provincial" or "rural" in the Indian context.—Ed.

obsessively, invested smartly, and within five years had brought over his wife, toddler daughter, and all four of his younger brothers and their families. When I shared my uncle's success story with Rahul soon after we were married, he sneered, "That first wave of Indians here, they were pathetic!"

I should have corrected Rahul, should have described how loving and generous they were to me, and how I repaid them with diligence (my only currency in America) in the nursery and the kitchen, but I hadn't felt secure enough to contradict him. I was still feeling my way in our marriage. Rahul proposed after we had gone on six dates, the first two chaperoned by my uncle and aunt in their home, the next four just the two of us in Rahul's Soho loft. My uncle gave him top marks for decisiveness and efficiency. My aunt made grateful offerings to Lakshmi, the goddess of prosperity, and pronounced me exceptionally lucky. Oh, I'd had my teenaged fantasies about marrying well. My father would miraculously convince a good-hearted surgeon or solicitor[4] to marry me without dowry. We would own, not rent, a flat, or maybe a whole house in Alipur. For two weeks every summer we would vacation in a Five Star hotel in a hill station like Darjeeling or a seaside resort like Gopalpur. Rahul was a provider beyond my daydreams. I agreed with my aunt.

Rahul was practiced in the art of wooing. He couriered elaborate edible arrangements of fruits made to look like flowers to my aunt, electronic gadgets to my uncle, Belgian chocolates to my cousin and me. On the first date he arrived on our doorstep with plush animals for the twins and a small bottle of Chanel perfume for me. Chanel perfume, my aunt gloated, not cologne. On the second of our chaperoned dates in Bloomfield, he brought an out-of-print copy of a Bengali poet-freedom-fighter's book of poems for the house and a gold Rolex for me. But it was with tales of his devotion to his parents that he won me. On the four dates in his loft, after take-out meals from neighborhood restaurants, in mellow light, and with half-Bengali Norah Jones on Bose speakers, he laid out his life for me to examine. Whatever he had achieved— his obstinate ambition to be a "somebody," his dogged drive to make money, his risky dive into short selling on Wall Street rather than going into medicine or engineering—he owed to the faith his father had had in him. His parents had done without, so that they could give him, their only child, the best: eggs, fish and fowl; vitamins, digestives and brain-enhancing tonics; two custom-made, three-piece suits from a men's store on Park Street. His father had borrowed money at a usurious rate to pay for Rahul's adult orthodontics. "Dream big, plan smart" had been his father's mantra. I understand now that it wasn't

---

4. British word for a particular type of lawyer.—Ed.

greed that fueled Rahul's obsessive planning. What he hadn't planned on was dying at age forty-one. He hadn't planned on dying, period.

I have no plans, only the duty as Rahul's widow to return to Kolkata, care for the relatives who loved him, and my ailing parents who love me. Go home, Rahul pleads. Home is two wary widows bound together by Rahul.

What am I to do?

Hugh asks instead, "What do you *want* to do?"

Ben's suggestion: Take the small decisions first, like getting the walls painted; then make the big one about staying on or going back. He knows just the right house painter for me, a man who will round up guys from the corner and get the spackling and painting done fast, and cheap.

My laptop screen is dark, patient.

It is three o' clock on a crisp late May afternoon. "You need light and air," Hugh shouts up from the hallway. "You need to get out of the house." He has a key to my front door.

Hugh, Bonbon, his rescue Maltese, and I stroll aimlessly on Main Street. "Sell the loft," but the way he says it, I hear a question. "Get a dog. You need a dog. Everybody needs a dog. We'll go to the shelter together the week after Labor Day. You'd be amazed how many pure breeds people lose or abandon."

A balding young father walks his flaxen-haired daughter of three or four and a chocolate Lab with a limp just ahead of us. "Now when we get to the corner . . ." he begins.

"I want you to take me to Mummy's[5] house," the daughter shrieks.

The father pats her head with a tolerant hand. "When we get to the corner, we'll let Dexter decide which way we go, left or right." The daughter flops to a squat on the sidewalk. I don't want to be caught up in this family drama of desire, divorce and abandonment. I should cross the street. "We don't know what goes on in Dexter's head, do we? We don't know which way he'll lead us." The father grips the little girl's wrists and tugs her to her feet. She is wearing bright pink Crocs, one of which slips off a tiny foot as she tries to pull away from him. Hugh, Bonbon and I are now so close that I can see red stenciled stars on her tiny toenails.

Bonbon, off leash, darts toward the Lab, which is also off leash. The dogs nose each other, and Hugh and I stand around smiling.

"I want to go to Mummy's house. Now. I hate you."

---

5. "Mommy" seems more likely here but, perhaps reflecting the different cultural influences on Mukherjee (Indian, British, Canadian, American), she uses the British word "Mummy" instead.—Ed.

312 | LATE STORIES (1997–2012)

"No, you don't, Blakelee." He seems unaware of eavesdropping strangers. "We'll follow Dexter's lead. That would be making a random choice."

"I do so." The little girl is in tears. "Hate you. And Dexter hates you. I want us to turn left and get in the car." She hurls a pink Croc at Bonbon and Dexter, but misses. The Lab limps off to retrieve the Croc.

"I'm trying to teach you an important concept, Blakelee," the father says. "Randomness. We can't always control what happens."

I snatch Bonbon out of harm's way and cradle her.

I don't want to be taken to my mother's flat. I don't want to take myself to Rahul's mother's flat either. My life should not be in turmoil. Rahul had no right to go on a business trip with Keiko from his office, try parasailing on a dare, drown accidentally. I want to tell Hugh I shouldn't get myself a dog, because I don't know how to love or be loved. I want to tell Ben to go ahead, hire the house painter he has worked with before. I want the cottage invaded by the migrants I spy on, the muscular men with desperate faces on North Sea Road, I want them to wreck the cottage Rahul bought as investment and build a home. I want them to build my home slowly, very slowly, I want, oh I so want the absurdity of their hope for better lives to rub off on my walls.

A Summer Story (c. 2008)

LATE LAST THURSDAY NIGHT I was deep into *Tech Crunch* when my dear wife, to whose ambitious cooking I owe my nightly heartburn, invaded my study, cradling Tums in a cupped palm. "I hope you're happy," she sighed. There was no missing the bitterness in that sigh. "Leela has ruined her life, and what are you doing about it? Nothing. Not a thing!" She slapped the antacid down beside the water pitcher and highball glass on my desk. "Did I not advise you against renting a Manhattan apartment for Leela? Tell me, did I not beg you *not* to sign the lease? Whose idea was it to let an innocent girl live all by . . ." She stopped in midharangue because, in grabbling for the glass, I'd knocked it to the floor. Fortunately, the glass didn't break, because the floor is covered almost wall-to-wall by a Kashmiri wool carpet, a thank-you gift in rupees from a bachelor uncle of hers who had lived with us—and lived off us—for five months in this house in Montclair, New Jersey.

My wife blotted the spilled single malt with wadded tissues from the box on my desk. The tissue-box holder is made of sea-green velvet decorated with glued-on seashells, embroidered jellyfish, and sequin stars: a day-camp craft project from the summer our daughter was. . .I don't really remember how old she was that summer.

"I warned you this would happen. She'll ruin her life, those were my exact words, *she'll ruin her life*. Well, now she has, and I had to hear of it from, who else, Mrs. Dasgupta."

I do remember my wife's words. She hadn't said Leela would ruin her life; what she had actually said was that *I'll* ruin Leela's life if I let her move into a place of her own. Leela is twenty-three years old, and our only child. When she got into Barnard College, I persuaded my wife that we had no choice other than to let her move out of the family home and into a dorm room. How could I have predicted that one thing would lead to another, meaning, without consulting us, Leela would drop out of Barnard her junior year and enroll in FIT? We had had plans for Leela to eventually go to law school. On my side of the family there are two solicitors, three barristers,[1] and a High Court judge; on her mother's side, twin great-uncles were admitted to Lincoln's Inn in London.

It was our neighbor, Mrs. Dasgupta, an issueless widow, who'd first apprised us of Leela's pursuit of a career in fashion design; also that our Leela was now blue-haired and sharing a studio apartment in Soho with boys with pierced tongues. So I did the right fatherly thing: I rescued my daughter. I got her into an eight-hundred-square-foot one-bedroom in a clean new apartment complex on the Upper West Side, within sprinting distance of Barnard, just in case she decides to drop out of FIT, complete Barnard requirements, and cram for LSAT or MCAT: call me an optimist. A parent must hope, and it is surely the duty of a Bengali father with financial resources to do more than simply level the playing field.

"So what calumny is that vile woman spreading now?" In a theatrical gesture meant to convey my disgust for my wife's tolerance of gossipmongers, I popped the Tums in my mouth, meaning to dry-swallow them, a bad move, and instead gagged, eyes bulging, Adam's apple heaving. If my wife had been in my situation, I would have dialed 911. But she who, at various times in our two decades-plus married life, has acquired certificates in life-saving skills such as CPR and is currently taking a life coach training course online, performed her heavy-handed version of the Heimlich maneuver on me. Then she cleaned up the gooey mess I had spat out with more wadded tissues.

"Why do you accept calls from that woman?" I demanded in a hoarse, angry whisper. "Why do we have caller ID if not to avoid gloating meddlers like Mrs. Dasgupta?"

"Leela has ruined her life and you're giving me grief about caller ID?"

---

1. British terms for two different types of lawyer.—Ed.

314 | LATE STORIES (1997-2012)

"Ruining her life" is my wife's euphemism for young Bengali-American women engaging in imprudent romance. Though we make a point of having dinner with her in Manhattan one weeknight every week and home-cooked lunch every Sunday in Montclair, I'd had no intimation that Leela was being courted by a suitor judged dangerously inappropriate by Mrs. Dasgupta, the watchdog of Bengali respectability. Our Sunday lunches draw around twenty Bengali guests, a dozen of them invited, the rest our guests' houseguests, among whom, given my wife's reputation as the finest cook of East Bengali dishes in the tristate area, there are bound to be two or three hungry young bachelors in finance or medicine.

The only way to save Leela from herself, my wife informed me, was to pack her off right away to Kolkata to live with my wife's brother's family for a couple of months. Physical separation would wither infatuation. Added bonus: Leela'd be surrounded not only by her maternal grandmother, uncle, and aunt but, more importantly, by cousins preparing for solid professions. She had already checked available flights from JFK to Netaji Subhas Bose International Airport that week and made tentative reservations for Leela and herself. She wanted my permission to speed-dial Leela right then and lure her to Kolkata by informing her that her *didima*,[2] Leela's favorite among the many family elders, was ill (true) and declining fast (a fabrication).

In my professional life—I have occupied corner offices in leading financial institutions in New York, London, and Brussels—I am considered an aggressive leader. In domestic matters, however, I defer to my wife, whose hunches are infallible. Besides, I am not ignorant of passion's force; ours was a "love marriage," love having welled up in a classroom with rain-stained walls in a dilapidated building on the campus of Calcutta University. Our good fortune was that each of us, respectful of *our* traditional parents' sentiments about intercaste marriage, had scrupulously avoided caste-inappropriate targets of Cupid's arrows. Leela, I understood from the scale of my wife's agitation, had been recklessly impulsive or, should I say, is self-centered, *American*, in ways we would never be?

I didn't press for details—taking comfort instead in proverbs memorized in English courses of my boyhood—for instance, why rouse sleeping dogs?—but my wife disgorged them anyway. Between deep, croupy sobs, she informed me that Leela's suitor was a cabdriver; worse, a Muslim recently arrived from Bangladesh; even worse, that this fellow, Sattar Rahman, was known to stay overnight in Leela's apartment two to three times a week. We discharge our parental duties in very different ways: she by intuiting, snooping, and lying;

---

2. Bengali word for "maternal grandmother."—Ed.

I by applying my version of "Don't Ask, Don't Tell" to our father-daughter relations. Discourage confessions; distrust confidences.

"How do you know this fellow is a professional cabbie and not an impoverished Columbia student?" I didn't believe this, but I was desperate to comfort her.

She nestled her wet face against my brocade smoking jacket. Yes, I still own the smoking jacket my late mother had her verandah-tailor cut and sew for me in a single day when I got the acceptance letter from Wharton. I think Ma got her idea that successful businessmen relax in smoking jackets from the Bollywood movies of her girlhood. I managed to get in a tentative hug, "Don't you remember how I used to walk all the way from Bhabanipur to College Street and save the tram[3] fare to buy textbooks?" "It's our fault," my wife moaned into my lapels. "We're careless parents."

Leela will always be exotic and unfathomable to us because she was born an American in Philadelphia when I was getting my M.B.A.; we are naturalized U.S. citizens, born in and shaped by Kolkata and our traditional Hindu families. Don't get me wrong: we hold progressive views on social issues. I explain the ferocity of my wife's reaction to Leela's infatuation with this Muslim fellow by reminding myself that her great-grandparents were forced to flee their ancestral homes in eastern Bengal during the violent Hindu-Muslim riots of 1946. But I wonder whether her plans to end this courtship would have been less precipitous if Rahman had been a surgeon or a banker. The Indian-American community in New Jersey, of which we are "pillars," expects its sons and daughters to study hard, win national spelling bees and science competitions, ace the SATs, and get into Ivy League schools or MIT and CalTech. If our only child had been a son instead of a daughter, and if he had suddenly announced his ambition was to study fashion design . . . but why dwell on an averted tragedy?

"DON'T THINK I don't know how lonely you'll be," my wife said to me at JFK as she held up her passport and boarding pass for a TSA agent to inspect. Then she shocked me by bestowing a peck on my cheek, her first public gesture of affection in the twenty-five years we have been married, before taking her place behind Leela in the slow, shuffling line of international passengers.

I hung around on my side of the security barrier and watched Leela place her iPad, iPod, magazines, a paperback, and pocketbook in a plastic bin; next peel off her ballet-slipper-like footwear, her gauzy jacket, her jangly metal ear-

---

3. British word for "trolley" or "streetcar."—Ed.

316 | LATE STORIES (1997–2012)

rings, and the baggie of lotions and cosmetics and toss them in a second bin; then, finally, with one smooth, seductive movement, heave the Louis Vuitton (I know because I pay her credit card bills) carry-on onto the conveyor belt for screening. A smiling male TSA agent waved her toward the full-body scanner, and she stepped into it with the grace of an Odissi dancer. In some back room of the airport, agents I was powerless to confront were ogling unclothed images of my daughter's body. I was so disconcerted that I hurried away instead of waiting until my wife, too, had gone through.

Our home is on a hill. On clear summer evenings my wife and I like to sit side by side on the blue leather sectional sofa and savor the spectacular Manhattan skyline, because we started out in a first-floor, one-bedroom in Flushing, Queens. But the first thing I did that night when I got back to a house that felt too huge, too still without my wife's bold, booming voice echoing in the high-ceilinged rooms was pour myself a single malt, then another, and another, and probably several more because, when I came to at dawn, I was still wearing jacket and tie and sitting on a kitchen stool with my forehead pressed into the granite counter. I missed my wife, that's the simple truth. She had left instructions for me on Post-its on the refrigerator, on the microwave, on the pantry doors, and even the dishwasher. I read them as a rainbow of love notes. "I called in your Lipitor refill." "Please, no more than ¼ tsp. of Cascade!" "Heat Mutton Biriyani in Pyrex dish WITH LID for 3–4 mins." "Plenty sag paneer, kabuli chana, etc., in freezer." "4 silk shirts ready for pick up Wednesday; check blue shirt for successful removal of korma stain." "Samsonite suitcase in yellow guest-room closet, packed for upcoming Zurich trip."

I forced myself to drink two mugfuls of ice water so as to lubricate my scratchy throat and, holding on to the banister, staggered up the wide, curved staircase to the second floor where the master bedroom suite, Leela's bedroom, a guestroom that doubles as my wife's prayer-room, and my study are. There is a third floor, reached by a narrow staircase of steep, uncarpeted steps. The warren of dark, dusty rooms and the one tiny bathroom with a shower stall but no tub were probably intended to house live-in help, but my wife, being the suspicious type, has turned this floor into a warehouse for the ugly furniture, the bulky TV sets and music systems, and some small kitchen appliances from our Flushing era; garbage sacks of clothes that we no longer care to wear but that she cannot bear to donate; an old Singer sewing machine with pedal she had picked up in a pawn shop for converting fading Indian bedspreads into curtains during our frugal Wharton days; a couple of plastic-tented exercise bicycles and a treadmill; and rows of stacked file boxes containing tax data so old that they should no longer be of interest to the IRS. "Our rainy-day survival kit" is her excuse; nostalgia mine. We're not compulsive hoarders; it's just that we haven't yet needed to let go the lives we've already lived.

Out of consideration for her older brother, a successful cardiologist, who would meet them at the airport, my wife had arranged to arrive in Kolkata on Sunday, which meant they'd flown out of New York on Friday night. Given my condition, I was grateful that I had the weekend to pull myself together. To seal off daylight, I tugged the ill-fitting bedroom drapes together and pinned the edges of the two panels at intervals with safety pins from my wife's dressing table; undressed; tossed jacket, slacks, and tie on the floor and underwear in the laundry hamper; and fumbled into the pajamas my wife had handwashed and steam-smoothed before leaving. What can I say other than confess that the luxurious slipperiness of silk against my skin after a long, anxious day at work calms me? That's why I'd bought myself three identical pairs of silk pajamas, each printed all over with rows of tiny elephants—the store's signature—from the Jim Thompson flagship store on my last business trip to Bangkok. I have a fondness for elephants that I cannot muster for the family pets, the white rats, rabbits, gerbils, hamsters, and, for a short while, a couple of turtles that I have had to tolerate through Leela's childhood. My fiercely protective mother, widowed two months before my birth, viewed all animals, dogs, cats, rats, as fanged predators, and I grew up afraid of even the exhausted, bowlegged donkey burdened with loads of laundry and bleeding from raw scars that the dhobi tied to the tree at our front gate twice weekly, but especially of the German shepherd with mean eyes and alert ears that my mother's oldest brother, an inspector of police, brought with him on Sunday lunch visits in spite of her objections. My uncle had trouble changing roles, from inspector of police to loving close relative, and always countered my mother with "Dogs can sniff out villainy faster than humans." Who would have guessed that a joyride on the back of one of my maternal great-grandfather's work elephants in the Assam hills, where he owned a sawmill, would free me of my phobia? I can't remember how old a child I was then, except that it was before Maoist insurgency in the sawmill, before my great-grandfather's nervous breakdown and bankruptcy. It was on a dare from the mahout's son, a sturdy teenager filling in for his father as elephant driver. Not a spoken dare, of course; just a flash in his scornful eyes. I remember shouting a command to him in broken Assamese, the choking feel as the trunk curled around my chest, the terror at having broken my mother's rules, the slow lift through dusty air, the mahout's son making room for me, the whoosh of adrenaline that is liberty. Disobedience is deliverance.

Ma never mentioned that joyride and I never again consciously disobeyed her. I choose not to wonder whether I am a victim of uncontrollable love or

318 | LATE STORIES (1997–2012)

of all-encompassing paranoia. What puzzles me is why I conspired with my wife to exile Leela to Kolkata. If I had faith in psychotherapy, I suppose I would pay a stranger to pry free and pulverize jagged maladies of the mind. Instead, I accept their mysterious presence and seek not cures but damage-deflecting talismans. That afternoon, lonely, disoriented, queasy, I lay down under the duvet and trusted the rows of tiny pachyderms dancing frivolously across my silken chest to carry me into deep and healing sleep.

Insomnia is not one of my afflictions: chronic heartburn, sinusitis, high cholesterol, hypertension, but never insomnia. My wife scolds me for dozing off while we watch movies ON DEMAND that we have to pay for. But that day, in spite of my hangover, sleeping mask, muscle relaxant, and, in desperation, my ingestion of one and a half capfuls of nighttime Nyquil, I couldn't sleep. I knew why, of course. For me to fall asleep, my body needs to nestle against my wife's, which is of robust proportions. Every night she starts out on her back with her feet propped on a long, plump, old-fashioned bolster she had loved as a child and that her cardiologist brother had shipped to New Jersey as our fifteenth wedding anniversary gift; later in the night, her body, which seems to have comfort demands of its own, makes continual half-turns on our king-size Tempur-Pedic mattress without interfering with her or my sleep. This need, I suddenly realized, is a mature expression of love. Lust, which convulsed us in the classroom of Calcutta University—we were taking an introductory class in statistics—leaves paper cuts until blunted by conjugal habit. Love is need. I called out her name in my need. "Jharna." In our mother tongue, her name means "waterfall." "Jharna, Jharna, Jharna!" Suddenly she and I are on a narrow-gauge train, a relic of the British Raj, clawing its way up fog-wreathed mountain ranges to the picture-postcard pretty hill-station Darjeeling, for the honeymoon we've delayed for seven years. We've fled the grime and noise of Kolkata, escaped the hovering gangs of oversolicitous relatives, put our Queens lives of frugality and caution out of our minds. We're holding hands. Her fingers are long, big-knuckled, her wrists slender, encircled with the married Hindu Bengali woman's many bangles of gold, iron, conch, coral. I push the bangles up her forearm and stroke the soft skin of the underside of a wrist. My eyes are fastened on the slow-moving green, rocky landscape to hide from her the tenderness that is overwhelming me. "Look!" she shouts, startling me. She pulls her hand away and points at something out there. A skinny diamond-bright stream spurts out of a coal-black crevice. "A jharna," she whispers. We've visited Niagara Falls and Victoria Falls since, but spectacular as those falls remain in our family photographs, neither *feels* as miraculous as this trickle from an anonymous scar in the Lesser Himalayas.

My sleeping mask feels too tight, the silk pressing against my eyelids, the elastic bands digging into my temples. I'm anxious—and desolate on this vast, expensive mattress. From my wife's side of the bed, I pull her two pillows close to me, breathing in the tart fragrance of her favorite hair oil. I squeeze the unresisting down pillows as though they are my wife's soft, ample flesh. "Jharna, Jharna, Jharna." The love call lasts all night. Who knew insomnia could exhilarate rather than alarm?

The word "bed-tea" does not exist in American English, but for those of us who grew up in countries once upon a time ruled by Queen Victoria, being served a sleep-sloughing pot of tea in bed at dawn by a live-in servant who has already been up for hours is an institution. As immigrant homemaker, my wife has adapted the bed-tea rite to our Montclair circumstances. Every morning for as long as we have been married, she has woken me with a cup of tea and two biscuits—I mean, cookies—on the saucer. I'd been too wasted the first Saturday morning after she and Leela left for Kolkata to miss the jangling of gold bangles on her wrists as she lowers the tea tray on the nightstand, the sinus-clearing whiff of steaming gingered tea, and the anticipation of her caressing fingertips on my head. But in the predawn darkness of Sunday, I was startled awake by the hysterical barking of a neighborhood dog—a raccoon attacking the Jack Russell puppy next door? a skunk spraying Henry, Mrs. Kern's blind rescue pitbull?—and was overwhelmed with an aching loss for the conjugal love that until that moment I'd taken for granted.

There was no going back to sleep, so I shuffled down the stairs to the kitchen to brew myself a cup of tea in the microwave. Hot, sweet, milky tea restores equilibrium, especially when slurped Bengali-fashion to the accompaniment of joyous sucking noises. After two cups, I was up to checking my email for Jharna's messages. On the drive out to JFK, she had promised to send me daily bulletins on Leela's emotional health. If physically separating the lovers didn't dissipate our daughter's misplaced ardor, I was to fly into Kolkata, a one-man special forces team, and eradicate "our Sattar problem."

Sunday "nightcap time" in Kolkata is Sunday "bed-tea time" in Montclair. Jharna's reports on mercurial Leela would probably be inaccurate by the time I accessed them. Still, it was a way of staying connected.

The first bulletin read "L distraught & refusing food. Relatives highly distressed. Take care of yourself. Remember next week's dental appointment." A great-uncle on her father's side had died of an abscessed tooth at age thirty-three. Her solicitous reminder of my tartar-cleaning appointment with Dr. A. K. Das, D.D.S., sparked unintended dread. Fatality can result from the slightest self-neglect. I scrolled up to her second bulletin, ignoring other unread messages. "ALL relatives, i.e., your side/my side, highly agitated re L's mental state. All alert for danger signs. Shall keep you posted."

By Friday morning of that first wife-deprived week, I longed for mendacious palliatives instead of unvarnished accuracy. What I received, instead, was this vexing update: "Neighbors spreading malicious gossip re causes of L's untoward condition. Fortunately pragmatic solutions are available here for every kind of mishap. *Dada*'s[4] close chum from schooldays is prominent ob/gyn."

What's the point of long-distance venting at vicious lies? The neighbors I'd grown up among, in the hometown that, deep down, no longer felt like home, had the grayness and weightlessness of ghosts. Wrath heals only when its object is precisely targeted. I identified the enemy (who else but Sattar?) but not the way to avenge the shame he continued to heap. *Think creative; break with habit.* I reached for the electric coffeemaker Jharna stores on the top shelf of a kitchen cabinet and uses only when we have non-Bengali dinner guests. Do not interpret this switch to coffee as a gesture of rebellion.

Coffee, first thing in the morning, sharpens my emotional reactions to Jharna's bulletins, which now arrive two, sometimes three, a day. "L still dejected. Have yet to ascertain if L in secret communication with u-no-who." "L stubbornly rejecting all cheering-up ploys by cousin-sisters." "*Boudi*[5] fearful of consequences of prolonged sadness. *Boudi*'s fifth brother, as u no, committed fatal act while postgraduate student in Edinburgh. Any undisclosed mental disease, e.g., depression, in yr family?" "*Boudi* @ wit's end, so has consulted her swamiji for ultrablessed amulet. Only Ma sanguine about future happy outcome." "Have joined *boudi* in her weekly trips to Kali Temple, and to swamiji. Her optimism infecting me, but not L." "Am remorseful about my initial accusation that your overindulgence of L is primary cause of current crisis. Crying over spilt milk hurts us only, no?"

Midway through the third week, however, I detected a note of buoyancy in her bulletins. "Cousins planning surprise party for L. May prove to be game-changer, a/c[6] to *dada*." "Several boys at last night's party manifested interest in L. All top-grade students in IIT or IIM. In *dada*'s words, 'background compatibility' guaranteed. L displaying Sphynx-like indifference." On the weekend, my wife sounds almost joyous. "Two boys manifesting persistent & protracted interest. Instant messaging, etc., a/c to cousin-sisters but am not privy to contents of IM." "Persistence persisting! *Boudi* expressing strong preference for one of the 2 boys. *Dada,* predictably, conducting background check on both."

---

4. *Dada* is a Bengali term for "elder brother."—Ed.
5. "Elder brother's wife" in Bengali.—Ed.
6. The abbreviation means "according" here.—Ed.

A SUMMER STORY (c. 2008) | *321*

From Leela herself, there have been no personal emails. I could have but choose not to follow her Facebook postings. The lessons of my boyhood English-medium schooling are indelible: "a little knowledge is a dangerous thing" or was Pope's phrase "a little learning . . .?" Ah, the vast and increasing chasm between "learning" (ongoing, evolving) and "knowledge" (received, fixed)! I do not know and I do not want to learn the mystery that is Leela, my American offspring.

On the fifth Monday after my wife and daughter left for Kolkata, I stopped by Leela's apartment on a whim. I'd been scheduled to meet a client for lunch at the Four Seasons at 1:15 P.M. that day, but, just as I was stepping out of my office building for the lunch meeting, I got word that the client had been rushed to the ER at Mount Sinai Hospital. It was an unseasonably warm day in late March. Low-fenced flowerbeds on the sidewalk sprouted bright rows of daffodils, lilacs, and petunias. Sinuous women in heels cooed unheeded commands to yappy lapdogs. Garrulous nannies clustered in twos and threes in the middle of the sidewalk, forcing pedestrians to stride around bulky strollers. At the curb, a shirtless bicycle messenger sped by against the light, almost knocking me over. I felt overdressed in my dark suit, and suddenly lonely. The freed-up time unnerved me. Don't get me wrong, I have adequate leisure skills, such as tennis and golf, but *unscheduled* leisure is dangerous. Visions of Patrick Dent, the client, on a gurney wheeled into and out of an ambulance tortured me. I stood at the curb through several light changes. I saw Patrick Dent, an obese man in his mid- to late thirties, his chest hacked open for quadruple bypass. I saw his large inert body, hovered over by hospital staff, vultures in white lab coats. I felt Death's chill on that warm, windless spring afternoon. That's when I started running, not running back to my office or club or home, but running away, a stout, winded man in Gucci loafers, fleeing intimations of decay, and despair.

So **HERE I STAND**, seeking not relief but grace, in front of 20D, the one-bedroom apartment in a new glass-and-steel tower that has been the ruin of Leela's life; my palm is cupped like an alms bowl around the key chain with two keys and a fob that will let me into a stress-free, pre-Sattar Rahman past. The last time that I'd stopped by had been at the end of a particularly satisfying workday. My wife had tasked me with dropping off a stack of *Desh*, her favorite Bangla[7]-language magazine, and a bottle of green amla oil, which, my wife swears, guarantees thicker, glossier hair. "Got a bottle of champagne chill-

---

7. Bengali.—Ed.

322 | LATE STORIES (1997–2012)

ing?" I'd joked when I'd called from the lobby to announce my arrival. She'd opened her front door before I could ring the bell. "Sorry, Baba, no Dom Perignon in the fridge, no Blue Label, not even a beer." She'd held the door only partially open, but her smile had been so radiant that I'd felt like a suitor being told to await my turn. I remember the cut flowers bunched tight in one of her hands, the angled view of more flowers in the sink in the galley kitchen, the sound of a dripping faucet, a potbellied vase waiting to be filled on the counter, and most of all the nimbus of crisp mid-February light from a supersized window behind her. I sensed that I was witnessing an unfamiliar exuberant womanliness. She'd given me a boisterous hug, bruising fragrant petals into my overcoat, and a gentle push out the door. I hadn't wondered why she had sworn off booze but splurged on flowers. In my mood of earned cockiness of that evening, a liquor-averse Muslim lover had not been on my radar.

In the center of the 20th-floor hallway, an elevator door whirrs open. I hear a dog's low growl behind me; then a friendly "Hey, looking for Sattar? He's switched shifts." I turn around. "No, you must be family. Leela's family, I mean. How's she doing?" The voice belongs to a short-skirted woman with tattooed legs, a dog walker I assume, since she has three large dogs and a ratlike one on leashes of different lengths. "Please tell her the orchid's doing great. No problem, I'm on top of it. Come on Dexter, let's get you home."

I walk away without unlocking Leela's door. "Hey, looking for Sattar?" I can't get that out of my head. I should go back to the office. I believe in the moral weightiness of self-imposed routines. Submission to such routines engenders self-composure. The impulsive are gamblers. I *shall* stride crosstown to the safety of my corner office in a stolid building on a once-venerable block of Park Avenue. Instead, I make my way to a nearly empty bar on Broadway, two blocks from Leela's apartment. The tattooed woman is still singing in my head, "Hey, looking for Sattar?"

AFTER A CALMING round or two, I should have taken a cab to the garage where my car is parked, but, given Fate's partiality to irony, the cabbie I'd flag down would no doubt turn out to be Sattar, and what did the big, gloomy house in New Jersey have to offer a man coming to terms with his terror of solitude? I stayed on in that unfamiliar bar, savoring a new kind of buzz from cheap whiskey, and watched the tables and booths fill up. Later that evening, by which time the patrons had become boisterous, and the buzz in my head dangerous, I had just enough habitual prudence left in me to pay the bill with cash, slide my pleasantly limp body off the barstool, and shuffle the four blocks back to

A SUMMER STORY (c. 2008) | *323*

Leela's place, where I could count on a recuperative night on the Raymour & Flanigan sofa bed with an extra-thick mattress her mother had picked for her living-dining-kitchen without ever anticipating this stay-over emergency.

Already waiting for an up elevator at the bank of four elevators in the lobby were two fatigued, trolley-pushing Latino men from a catering service. Three elevators seemed to be stuck on PH5, and one on 3, the conviviality-enhancing floor with saltwater swimming pool, fitness center, community lounge, kids' playroom, and possibly other amenities I didn't bother to check out the day I signed the lease on Leela's apartment. I stood in line behind the caterer's employees and wondered about the well-heeled party beasts on PH5, who could afford to send for so many cases of champagne and trays of aromatic canapés. Overtestosteroned Wall Street guys? Louche, trust-fund Columbia and Barnard undergraduates slumming four per bedroom and subletting living-room space to couch surfers? My wife is right; she is always right. I have contributed to Leela's ruination by signing the lease agreement on her apartment in this temple of self-indulgence. The shorter of the two caterer's men broke into my guilt-ridden wonderings with a series of explosive sneezes, and I thought I spied a wet spray of mucus on the starched white cloth covering the topmost tray. Unaccustomed pity suddenly overwhelmed me, pity for ailing men with fatigued faces forced by circumstances to serve rather than be served. I began to torture myself with the blessings fate had bestowed on me: family, a paid-up primary home in Montclair, a vacation shack in Montauk, a rented-out retirement bungalow in Bangalore, Jharna's Lexus, Leela's Prius, and my Jaguar in the garage; two directorships . . . stop! Empathy is for the weak! I focused on the lights above each stalled elevator and felt joyful when one of the elevators zoomed down from PH5 to 25, then to 20, and next made a long stop on 14, finally arriving in the lobby and disgorging a half-dozen well-turned-out young party-hoppers and one thirty-something Bangladeshi man in a green windbreaker. An ethnic Bengali, Muslim or Hindu, citizen of India or of Bangladesh, can spot another; our facial bone structure is that distinct. I followed the green windbreaker out of the lobby into Columbus Avenue up to West 100th Street, where, halfway down the block between Columbus and Central Park West, its wearer unlocked a parked yellow cab, shot a noisy plume of phlegm into the gutter, and slid into the driver's seat. The engine started up. Adrenaline-fueled car chase fantasies swirled in my head. I had my smart key in my pants pocket, but my car was in a midtown East Side parking garage. The thief of Leela's heart eased into spotty traffic, then swung left into Manhattan Avenue. All I could do was memorize the disappearing license plate.

324 | LATE STORIES (1997–2012)

OUR SLIGHTEST GESTURES trigger inescapable consequences. One workday morning you leave your suburban home on landscaped grounds, a man of decent and sober impulses; that evening you return to the same spacious house, click your garage-door opener and tandem-park your car behind your wife's, unlock the kitchen door, disarm the security system, then, as a matter of habit, go into the powder room to flush away work-related stresses, and there, in the mirror above the designer sink your wife had installed in spite of your remonstrance, taunting you is a monster's cruel, malicious smiling face.

What-ifs are for cowards: what if Patrick Dent the client had kept his lunch-hour appointment instead of dying, as I was to learn the next morning, on a hospital bed in an ICU? What if I hadn't run into Dexter's dog walker in the hallway outside Leela's door? What if the up elevator I'd been waiting for in Leela's building late that night had arrived before the down elevator, carrying the Bangladeshi I've arbitrarily decided is Sattar because it had halted on Leela's floor?

I accept what I see in the mirror: self-knowledge, unsought and unearned, bestowed like grace by invisible forces.

BY DAY I REMAIN a respected private equity fund manager; at nightfall I morph into the obsessive avenger of my family's shame. There is no conflict between the daylight man of sedate probity and the nighttime stalker with relentless energy. When daylight dims into dusk, my suburban New Jersey concepts of right and wrong blur. Having grown up in a Hindu Bengali family that marks spiritual time on the lunar calendar, I *trust* the rhythm and fluidity of my heliocentric metamorphoses. Suns and moons, gods and demons, heroes and villains, expatriate Indian and naturalized U.S. citizen: we are shape-changers in a multiverse that is as insubstantial as a hologram.

Around noon yesterday, a Sunday, buoyed by Jharna's bulletin of the day ("Out of blue third potential groom has surfaced. *Dada* convinced this best match. L not indifferent to this candidate. Preliminary background inquiry in process. We will expedite negotiation if you give go-ahead"), I took my first coffee of the day out to the back deck instead of downing it at the kitchen counter. The rock garden was colorful with flowers I cannot name, and in the speckled noon-hour light even the steep, blackish hill just behind my property line seemed uncharacteristically verdant. I was composing email responses in my head, one to Jharna ("Light at end of tunnel?"), another to her older brother ("Permission to proceed poste-haste; total confidence in your judgment of new candidate . . ."), when Mrs. Kern, the elderly widow or divorced neighbor next door, sputtered into her driveway in her vintage Citroën. Mrs. Kern goes to two different farmers' markets on Sunday mornings, one for organic grains and legumes in bulk, the other for raw goat-milk cheeses and seasonal produce. I know this from Jharna, whom Mrs. Kern consults for tips on picking the best eggplants and the readiest-to-eat pineapples. I ambled over to the Citroën to offer help with carrying the grocery bags indoors. "Oh, thank you, Mr. H." Mrs. Kern shouted to me. "You are proof that old-world gallantry isn't dead. And how's Mrs. H? She's been gone so long." I murmured I was fine, Jharna was fine, and lied about her having asked after Mrs. Kern, but before I could haul the first bag off the front passenger seat, Mrs. Kern's blind pitbull, which had been dozing on a blanket on the kitchen porch, snarled and loped down the saggy wooden steps toward me. I backed off in instinctive self-defense. "Oh, Molly," Mrs. Kern scolded her dog in a fond voice, "you don't have to protect me from a nice man like Mr. H!" I set the bag down on the car's hood and kept backing away. "Molly, shame on you!" she exclaimed in the same sweetly forgiving voice. Molly softened her snarl to growls but didn't let down her guard. "You're not afraid of my Molly, are you, Mr. H? Don't they have family pets where you came from?"

I spent the afternoon watching pre-Bollywood classic romances starring the beautiful Madhubala and the dashing Raj Kapoor, lost in the tormenting intensity of their characters' emotions; microwaved the last of Jharna's frozen home-cooked chicken korma; scanned the address book Jharna keeps by the kitchen phone to call someone who would cheer me, and discovered that, while Jharna has "friends," I only have "business contacts"; so I retired to my study to web-surf information on New York City haunts of Bangladeshi cabbies. Sometime that night I found myself confiding my loneliness to easygoing Bob Farkas, the only colleague I sometimes hang with after work now that I have no Jharna to hurry home to. Over the third round of Belvedere vodka, his preferred drink, he misdiagnosed my condition as midlife crisis. Then he shared his own tale of midlife misery and his survival tip: his wife of eleven years (his second, and a former Brazilian beauty queen) recently ran off with their only child's soccer coach; he could have bought himself a red, sporty car or invested in therapy, but he had taken charge and got a good thing going twice a week with a Haitian paralegal in the law offices two floors below ours. *Stuff happens, so deal with it*, Bob Farkas counseled, except that he used a different word than *stuff*. Then I woke up and felt lonelier than before I'd fallen asleep researching Sattar's habitat.

Okay, I concede that narratives in some dreams provide neat closures that life—at least my life—does not. The bit about Bob Farkas having been dumped by his wife is water-cooler chatter; the paralegal is a frequent co-rider in the elevator. But "stuff" is happening to me, and I need to deal with it, to take charge and *thrive* because of it. Fate has sent me Sattar in midlife for a purpose. In the hope of decoding that purpose, I have started to shadow him. This has become my workday routine: I reclaim my Jaguar from the midtown Manhattan garage, drive cautiously back home to Montclair, down a can of Ensure muscle health, change dark suit for sweats, and slip into the driver's seat of Leela's Prius to stalk the license plate I'd memorized the night my sense of who I am imploded on a sidewalk. Leela's father, Leela's lover, Leela's Prius: I want my prey to *feel* the raw intimacy that binds us. A recklessness courses through me as the Prius makes its near-soundless way to a block of commodious houses in Jamaica, Queens, where three or four yellow cabs are sloppily parked, including the vehicle of my future redemption. A pumped-up predator, I take pleasure in watching its driver, a scrawny man with a morose face, arrive on foot, settle behind the steering wheel, snack on a fast-food taco or burger, adjust the rearview mirror. That this taxi driver works all-night shifts is a bonus.

The yellow cab prowls the boroughs, and Leela's Prius follows. Trendy strips in Long Island City, gentrifying blocks in Brooklyn, going-out-of-business minimalls in Queens, bleak projects in the Bronx: New York City is opening up to me. Spellbound, I swallow all that it offers. Unfamiliar nightscapes unleash unacknowledged feelings that both excite and shame me. I long to be confronted. So what that the quarry is quicker, younger, stronger?

Two weeks into my new life of nocturnal adventures, this is all I have learned about my prey: he rents bunk space in a Bangladeshi-run flophouse on Merrick Boulevard in South Jamaica, Queens; he has his preshift meal in a neighborhood Dunkin' Donuts; he suffers from severe back and/or neck pain, because twice in these two weeks he has switched on the "Off Duty" light and parked for forty minutes in front of Fatima's Relief-Guaranteed Yoga and Massage Center (Astoria branch); at the end of his shift, after leaving off the taxi on the block where he'd picked it up, he limps to Rashid's Roti-Kebab, a 24-hour diner, two streets from the flophouse.

I, too, am spent; I drive back to Montclair instead of waiting for Sattar to reemerge.

The House on Circular Street (c. 2008)

IT WAS PRABIR-UNCLE who gave me the news about my father's final day in our family home in Chappaqua. It was also Prabir-uncle who found me this rent-free room in Saratoga Springs in which to grieve his passing. Prabir-uncle wasn't really my uncle; he was one of a tight circle of my parents' Kolkata-born friends, and like my father a pulmonologist. My parents and their expatriate friends would have considered me a boorish American if I'd addressed him as Dr. Dutta instead of "uncle."

I'd always felt closer to Prabir-uncle than to the other "uncles," probably because, when I was a freshman in high school, at my mother's insistence he'd lived in our guest room for the many months it took his bride to get her green card. His marriage had been semiarranged by his parents, and he had flown back to Kolkata on a two-week vacation, accepted their choice of Sunita-auntie as his bride, married her and then returned to New York, a lonely husband resigned to the slow processing of immigrant visas. Mother, a formidably nosy woman, had ferreted out of him enough Dutta family anecdotes to know that he was the only son after five daughters and had grown up among women devoted to his welfare. That was probably why Mother hadn't wanted the new bridegroom to return to the squalid apartment in Queens he had shared with three other Indian bachelor doctors, none of whom had cooked or cleaned house before coming to America.

From the day he had moved in with us—his only belongings in a shiny new suitcase (one of many wedding gifts from his in-laws) and two cardboard boxes of files—I'd felt he really was a member of our family. All three of us had. Mother had pampered him as though he were my father's younger brother— in Bengali tradition, the bond between *boudi* and live-in young unmarried *bhasur*[1] is close, and in some households they are permitted to be playfully flirtatious. The *boudi* in her had got him to open up, to talk about not just schoolboy triumphs, prize books awarded and debate trophies won, but, on nights Father was away for conferences, about *feelings,* which is rare in middle-class families like ours. Dashing into the kitchen to grab a snack, I would hear him confess his boyhood anxiety that no matter how well he did in med school, in life he would disappoint his otolaryngologist father, who had made his reputation throughout South Asia and the Emirates for his unmatched skill with cochlear implants. From his stories about home, Mother had divined the Bengali dishes he missed most, and even though a nutritionist by profession, Mother had cooked him multicourse dinners that required frying ingredients in ghee and dousing with heavy cream. Father, usually a taciturn man, too, had been drawn to Prabir-uncle. Over single malts, he had engaged our young houseguest in impassioned debates about Indian politics, debates that had lasted late into weekend nights. He and I had bonded over sports: I'd taught him the rules of American football and baseball, and he'd tried to get me fired

---

1. In Bengali, *boudi* means "elder brother's wife," while *bhasur* is "brother-in-law."—Ed.

328 | LATE STORIES (1997–2012)

up about cricket, but, more important, he'd helped me with my math homework. We had been more of a family, a happy family, during the months he had lived with us. Come to think of it, Mother had seemed angry rather than relieved when Prabir-uncle's bride's immigration papers finally came through. Father and I chalked up her mood change to her recent diagnosis of stage 2 breast cancer. She went through lumpectomy, chemo, and radiation therapies. I had to take Prabir-uncle's anxious calls about her health, because she wouldn't. The newlyweds—though of course they had been married for almost a year before being reunited—had set up house in Albany. That was because, while she was in Kolkata waiting for her U.S. visa, Sunita-auntie, Prabir-uncle's bride, had successfully applied for admission to the Master of Social Work program at SUNY–Albany. Prabir-uncle had no trouble finding a job at Albany Medical Center, and we didn't see them more than once, at most twice, a year.

The last time Prabir-uncle and Sunita-auntie, hugely pregnant with her second child, visited us in Chappaqua was in mid-August a year ago. My parents always celebrated the anniversary of Indian independence with a boisterous Sunday buffet for their many friends. But last year the celebration went awry. I'm not prepared—not yet—to go over what exactly happened that afternoon, but a quarrel between Father and me, a quarrel that had started with my announcing that I was abandoning a nascent career in finance and enrolling in the Master of Fine Arts program in poetry at the University of Iowa, somehow escalated into my father disowning me in front of his friends in shockingly crude language. Imagine the scene: Mother ignores Father and leads the embarrassed guests into the dining room. The dining table is laid out with the feast she has prepared over two days. Prabir-uncle is raving over Mother's goat curry. "You're eating like a bird," Mother scolds and serves him a huge second helping. Sunita-auntie is heaping turmeric-dusted, deep-fried eggplant slices onto my plate, when Father rushes out of the living room and comes at me, arms outstretched and fists balled, looking for a physical confrontation. I am a head taller, and, thanks to the fierce hours I spent on squash courts battling "cubicle claustrophobia" during my Wall Street years, I am visibly in better shape. "Get out of my house!" he screams, landing a punch on my right bicep. I lose my grip and greasy eggplant slices slide off my plate onto the rug. Mother is sobbing. The guests are so mesmerized by our family drama that they don't want Father to stop. "Do something," Sunita-auntie implores Prabir-uncle. "Get out right now!" Father grabs my plate out of my hand and flings it on the floor. Mango pickle, *daal makhani* and *raita*[2] seep into the Kash-

---

2. These terms refer, respectively, to a creamy North Indian lentil dish and a savory yogurt sauce.—Ed.

THE HOUSE ON CIRCULAR STREET (c. 2008) | *329*

miri rug. "Okay, okay, not a problem," I say, "I'm out of here." That incenses him even more. He shakes off Prabir-uncle's restraining hands, grips me by my collar, pulls me out of the dining room and through the foyer, and thrusts me out the open front door, still screaming at me. "Get out, you traitor, get out! Get the hell out before I kill you! From today, we have no son."

I appeared in my landlady's life on an early August morning. Prabir-uncle had told me little about her other than her name, Uma Bose, and that she had been recently widowed and was, like me, grieving. In my parents' homeland, last names give away religion, caste, ethnicity, and mother tongue, and so I deduced that, like Prabir-uncle, Sunita-auntie, and me, she was a Hindu Bengali of the *kayastha*[3] caste, and from a traditional enough family to have been given Uma, an alternate name for Durga the Mother Goddess, as her first name. In lieu of rent, Prabir-uncle had arranged for me to be the widow's live-in chauffeur, handyman, gardener, and collector of rent from the three unreliable tenants in the carriage house behind her Victorian on Circular Street. Mr. Bose had inherited the tenants when he had purchased this investment property. His plan had apparently been to sell off the carriage house, and upgrade the main house for lucrative summer rental.

From the parking lot of Pizza Hut, I called the number Prabir-uncle had given me for Mrs. Bose—I was pretty sure that, as did Mother and her women friends, she would prefer to be addressed as Mrs., not Ms. Prabir-uncle had confided that she was still "bonkers with grief" and so paranoid about burglars and rapists breaking in now that Mr. Bose couldn't protect her that she might call 911 if a strange male, with luggage, suddenly showed up on her doorstep. I took his advice to phone ahead and to judge for myself from her voice on the phone how fragile my landlady's emotional health was. Unfortunately, I got the answering machine and a bland, computerized-white-male voice instructing me to leave a brief message after the beep. I left my name, Bikash Mitter, and my cell phone number, saying that I'd arrived in Saratoga and would soon be making my way to the address I had for her; then drove to a nearby downtown mall, which looked as though it had lost its patrons to a newer, larger, glitzier shopping complex on the outskirts of town and parked in front of its only liquor store. The liquor store, flanked on either side by two thrift shops selling children's clothes, was doing brisk business that hot early August afternoon, and I had to make my nimble way through thirsty throngs of racetrack workers and straw-hatted hedonists to buy myself a bottle of bourbon (a taste acquired in Iowa City from my Alabaman roommate who is also in the Poetry Workshop). When I made my call to Mrs. Bose, I hadn't figured

---

3. The name of a prominent Hindu caste in India.—Ed.

330 | LATE STORIES (1997–2012)

in that I was in Saratoga Springs at the start of the racing season, and that honking, cussing traffic clogged all the main roads in the center of town where I was. To put off the dreaded moment when I'd have to ease out of the mall's exit, I treated myself to a pint of cookie dough ice cream from the supermarket next to the liquor store and devoured the pint in the car with a plastic spoon I'd had the forethought to pick up from the deli counter.

I don't have a GPS in my car, but I easily located Circular Street, a busy thoroughfare, and Mrs. Bose's address. A slender woman with a sorrowful face was on the porch, just outside the heavy wooden front door, sizing me up as I parallel-parked on the street instead of in her driveway. She looked to me to be in her late forties, that is, not as obviously middle-aged as Mother but not as confidently youthful as Sunita-auntie. The sunlit oval panel of stained glass embedded in the front door framed her head like a nimbus. She made me think of Hindu goddesses in the posters I'd bought from sidewalk vendors on a boyhood vacation in Kolkata, all with faces serenely beautiful and bodies wet-dream voluptuous and warrior-strong. We were visiting Mother's mother, who was shocked at how little I knew of the deities on the posters I'd be taking home to Chappaqua. She filled my head with the dangerous missions carried out by these superheroes. In her stories, these ancient superheroes successfully used their superhero powers against shape-changing superdemons to rescue battle-weary gods and despairing mortals. This summer I am one among that legion of despairing mortals. When Prabir-uncle called me with news of Father's death, all notions of right and wrong, of duty and dependability I'd absorbed from my secular immigrant parents collapsed into rubble as though someone had taken a hammer to my transcontinental heritage.

I grabbed my computer bag, into which I'd shoved the bottle of bourbon, locked the rest of my stuff (a half-empty duffle bag, a backpack, two boxes of books) in the trunk, and climbed the sagging wooden steps of the stoop. The three-storied house, with its wide, wraparound porch, was the largest and must once have been the grandest on this block of Circular Street.

"Hi, I'm Bikash. I left a message." She acknowledged this with a slight nod. Then, sounding more emotional than I'd intended to, I blurted, "Mrs. Bose, thank you, thank you very much." I held out a grateful hand in greeting, but she joined her palms in the traditional Bengali *namaskar*[4] and said in our shared mother tongue as she ushered me into the high-ceilinged, oversize foyer, "You must be exhausted. Tea will be ready by the time you've washed up. There's a powder room behind the staircase."

---

4. A traditional Hindu greeting where one presses one's palms together in front of one's chest or face before bowing.—Ed.

THE HOUSE ON CIRCULAR STREET (c. 2008) | *331*

The staircase, wide and curving, too, was outsize, as were the two velvet-curtained windows. Having grown up in a contemporary home in Chappaqua, designed specifically to Mother's expectations of new-world comfort and convenience, from what I could see of Mrs. Bose's house from the hallway—the vast wood-paneled living room with an elaborate stone mantelpiece and rounded glass windows, the floral-shaped wood carvings on the ceiling, the parquet floor—the scale of this family home astonished me. Everything, except its owner, seemed oversize.

Mrs. Bose disappeared down a long hall, past the powder room and through a doorway into what I assumed was the kitchen. I didn't know whether I should follow her into the kitchen area after I'd washed up; I didn't want to be intrusive, a just-arrived freeloader barging in and making himself at home in her kitchen. I had a clear enough sense of the chores Prabir-uncle had signed me up for, but how was I, a prodigal son treading water, meant to survive the emotional riptide of this newly bereaved widow's household? How much of *my* situation had Prabir-uncle disclosed?

I heard the slap-slap of Mrs. Bose's sandals in the hallway while I was still toweling my face and shaved head, which I had wetted in the sink. In Hindu Bengali tradition, bereaved sons shave their heads and travel shoeless during the mourning period. I had on Vans.[5]

"Take your time," Mrs. Bose said in Bangla,[6] addressing me as "*tumi*" rather than the formal "*apni*"[7] to indicate our significant age difference. I had to listen hard to understand her, not because I'd spoken mostly English peppered with Bangla phrases at home, but because her Bangla accent was different from that of my Kolkata-born parents.

I relieved Mrs. Bose of the tarnished silver tray she was gripping with both hands as though she were afraid she might drop it and its load of two delicate-looking teacups, a teapot in the shape of a London bus, a tea-strainer, a small pitcher of steaming milk, a matching sugar bowl filled with snowy cubes, and a paper plate stacked with graham crackers. Nostalgia stabbed my heart when I saw the teapot, because Mother, who collected antique "biscuit" tins and teapots in amusing shapes, owned an identical one from Harrod's. Mrs. Bose led the way into the formal dining room; I followed, awed again by the scale of the public rooms. The furniture, all of it undistinguished "modern," however, made the room look more like a storage locker for pieces from when she and her late husband had lived in a suburban house, probably in New Jersey. New Jersey towns

---

5. The name of a footwear company that manufactures sneakers and other casual shoes.—Ed.

6. Bengali.—Ed.

7. Mukherjee is referring to different forms of second-person address in Bengali here.—Ed.

332 | LATE STORIES (1997–2012)

with single-family homes, large yards, two-car garages, and desirable public schools are a popular choice for South Asian immigrants who have done well.

Mrs. Bose pointed to the top of a nightstand as the place for me to set down the tea tray. I did so, but I had to first clear off the dusty pile of Bangla-language magazines and yellowed newspapers on it; then I pulled two metal folding chairs from a stack of half a dozen for us to sit on.

"Do you like light or dark?" she asked, without looking at me. It took me a couple of seconds to realize she was asking me about the tea liquor. I drink only coffee (as a passive-aggressive response to my tea-aesthete parents); in Iowa City, I evolved from coffee lover to coffee addict as I tried again and again, unsuccessfully, to word-process the poems in full bloom in my head. A failed poet addicted to coffee and bourbon. Poetry workshops had damaged rather than nurtured.

She lifted the lid of the teapot and gave the tea leaves a careful stir. A delicate fragrance escaped. "People here don't know a thing about tea."

I leaned forward, pretending to check the color of the brew. "Looks and smells just right to me."

She poured me a half-cup of pale amber liquid through the strainer. The dainty cup was so small that I could have finished the tea in it in a single gulp. She lifted the milk pitcher and angled the spout over my cup. "I myself like just a touch of milk. Don't worry, it's hot-hot, thanks to the ubiquitous microwave in American kitchens." She repeated her remark about Americans knowing nothing about fine tea, this time with more venom. The sugar tongs proved tricky, so she plucked two cubes of sugar with her fingers and crumbled them into her cup. "This isn't the right kind of sugar. Too white, too fine. Have you ever eaten our kind of sugar on slices of buttered bread?" A sudden memory of Didima's[8] live-in servant picking ants out of brownish, granular sugar seized me. My Poetry Workshop friends would, because they *could*, extract a lyric poem out of such a memory. She helped herself to a graham cracker and dipped it into her tea. "I miss Nice biscuits. Do you know Nice biscuits? Covered with crunchy sugar?"

I didn't, but I was loath to confess I didn't for fear of risking immediate distrust. Her hospitality was essential to my recuperation. The survivalist strategy would be to keep our small talk inconsequential. But before I could come up with a lie about Nice biscuits, she burst suddenly into soft, delicate sobs. "Why did it have to come to this?" she whispered, "Why?" At this point, a gentleman, Prabir-uncle or Father, for instance, would have offered the distressed woman a spotless handkerchief. I couldn't; I don't own any. I wasn't

---

8. In Bengali *didima* means "maternal grandmother."—Ed.

THE HOUSE ON CIRCULAR STREET (c. 2008) | *333*

carrying even a balled-up single sheet of Kleenex in the pockets of my cargo pants. My instinct was to comfort her with a hug, and I rose from my chair, arms outstretched, but didn't dare actually touch her in case a physical embrace from a male stranger offended her. She struck me as way more observant of homeland traditions than Mother and her women friends, most of whom were doctors or medical technicians.

"Dhaka wasn't easy." Did she mean for the Hindu minority? I'd read of fatal hacking of secular bloggers in the *New York Times* as well as in the few papers from India the U of Iowa libraries subscribed to. But I realized how wrong I was when she followed up with "We came as refugees," glancing up at the dining room ceiling with its opulent wooden carvings. There was no missing the penniless-immigrant-makes-good implication of her glance. Then harsh, remorseful sobs, each ending in a wheezing cough, convulsed her body. I made out a few rueful phrases. "Heart attack." "I was no help." "I didn't know what to . . ." I looked away so as not to intrude on her memory of the moments just before her late husband's heart attack. We sat that way, not looking at each other, each of us frozen in our separate miseries. Who knows for how long? Let's just say I snapped out of our tableau of grief and guilt and sidled back into my role of impecunious graduate student in need of a temporary roof over my head when I heard the front door bang shut with unnecessary violence and the staccato strike of impatient boots on the uneven parquet floor of the foyer. A youngish woman in shapely white jeans, a bicycle helmet rakishly tilted on her head, strode into the dining room.

"So you're the poet-houseboy sent us by Dr. Dutta." She pulled the bicycle helmet off and lobbed it across the room to land in a blanket-covered Lazy-Boy. Her hair was fiercely curly, glossy black streaked with purple. "I wouldn't have expected our starving poet to drive a Beamer."

"Preowned," I lied, singed by her scorn. It was a graduation gift from an overindulgent Bengali mom, paid for by my affluent dad, who'd regarded my Harvard and Wharton expenses as safe investments.

"I'm the daughter," she announced as she pulled off a bicycle clip, "in case you weren't warned that you'd be having to look after *two* crazy women. Am I scaring you? Doesn't matter. You get free room, and we get you. Didn't Dr. Dutta make you sign a contract? Baba would certainly have. He was litigious, boy, was he ever!" She let out an eerie, high-pitched giggle. "The man had no Achilles heel. And then, boom! Felled by choking on a chicken bone! And so here you are, a poet—*poet*—caretaking his nutcase dependents." She giggled again. "He despised the arts, did you know?"

Could I last what was left of the summer under the roof of this melancholy mother and querulous daughter? "Bikash," I said, "Hi!" Mrs. Bose chose

334 | LATE STORIES (1997–2012)

that moment for a formal introduction. Bikash; Purnima. Purnima; Bikash. Instead of a "Hi!" or a "Hey," Purnima pounced on my name. "Bet you're Ash to your friends? Make things easy for them, right? Well, in our house, you'll be Bic. Bic, like the pen. And Bic, you'll pen sonnets to two dark ladies stashed in this ghoulish place."

Purnima was clearly, mercilessly, on a roll, but Mrs. Bose came to my rescue. "Show our guest to his room," she scolded. "Can't you see how tired Prabir-*babu*'s[9] friend is?" In Bangla she muttered to me, "My daughter's become totally American, what more can I say?" I was not about to take sides in my first hour in their home. "No respect for other people's feelings."

Purnima strutted toward us on expensive-looking purple leather high-tops. She had small feet for her height, which was about 5'8". I had a flash memory of the women's shoes in our Chappaqua house. The Gangoolys have large feet. Mother used to say that that meant we had our feet planted firmly on the ground, so my head surfing clouds for poetic images would not, could not, destroy the Gangooly solidity I'd inherited.

"It's a climb, Bic." Purnima delivered this with a genuine smile. Her face was as malleable as actors'. "We have to take the back staircase to get to your room, the steep one that was built for indefatigable staff. Now you're our only staff." She gripped my left hand just above the wrist, which I had broken two years ago on a hiking trip on Mount Hood with a couple of friends from Wharton. I'm a mountain climber of moderate ambition and modest skill. I matched the new Purnima's smile with a grin. "Okay, lead the way to my man-cave."

She let go of my wrist, which hasn't fully come back, probably because I hadn't been diligent enough about rehab exercises. That was when I was still putting in insane hours in the private equity firm that had wooed me straight out of Wharton. "Where's your luggage?" She dashed into the foyer, and I followed. "No bags, no baggage." She patted her chest to make sure I understood she was referring to "emotional" baggage. "Interesting! A nomad wary of heartache."

"Come on, let's go." As soon as I said that, I realized how genuinely exhausted I was from the long drive. My bags and books were safe enough in the locked trunk. I'd carry them up to the attic after I'd rested.

Purnima led me up the servants' narrow staircase off the back-door landing. On the way up she asked, "Do you cook? I mean, are you a real cook? The poet-types usually are, and I'd love to get away from Ma even if it's for an hour. If your culinary talents are limited to microwaving frozen dinners,

---

9. In India, *babu* is used as a respectful form of address for a man.—Ed.

don't bother us. Eat with us tonight if you can stand Ma's . . . The fridge in the attic is totally empty, so what the hey!"

My bedroom is one of three in the attic that Purnima, sounding like a realtor's agent, said was spacious because it had originally had to accommodate live-in cooks, maids, a butler, and a "bat boy." Was I scared of bats? They fly in through the chimneys, and this huge Victorian has too many fireplaces. "You have two options for dealing with the bat problem, Bic. Use the Bat-Boy's butterfly net hanging from a hook in the attic, and fling the creatures into the night. Or use a baseball bat to smash their little brains. Guess which I prefer." By that time, we'd reached the door to the suite of rooms in the attic. She lifted an old-fashioned heavy iron key that hung on a hook on the wall and struggled to unlock the door. An offer of help would probably have been judged as sexist. She thrust, cussed, jiggled. Finally, the key turned in the rusty lock. "Voila!" She pushed the door open with a triumphant, purple-booted kick. "Claim any of the three bedrooms you want. They're all equally poky." She handed me the rusty key and scampered back down the servants' staircase.

The attic, low-ceilinged and sparsely windowed, has its own living room furnished with a settee, a round oak dining table, and two mismatched wooden chairs; bedrooms just big enough to accommodate a double bed with a lumpy mattress and a bought-at-a-flea-market chest of drawers; a galley kitchen; and a bathroom with a rusting sink, a toilet with a splintered wooden seat, and a deep, claw-footed bathtub. I've lucked into a pretty sumptuous garret.

Mrs. Bose didn't renege on Purnima's offhand dinner invitation. I showed up in their kitchen around eight o'clock that first evening after a long nap and a quick shower in rusty water. Like my mother, Mrs. Bose is a prideful cook, and she had a multicourse dinner simmering or bubbling on the stove. Shrimp in mustard sauce, chicken in spicy tomato *jhol*, *aloo dum* potatoes, deep-fried eggplant, and sweet, creamy *payesh*.[10] We ate in what Purnima described as "the morning room," a cozy place in spite of the gilt Adams-style sculpture on the walls and around the ornate fireplace. The room smelt of Indian incense, powerful enough to muffle supermarket-bought air-fresheners. On the mantelshelf, in the center of a row of silver and brass deities and dwarfing them, was a sandalwood-garlanded studio photograph of a fiftyish male, who I assumed was the late Mr. Bose. We Hindu Bengalis, even transplanted ones in Chappaqua, light incense to departed relatives as well as to representations of our godhead. Mr. Bose, posed erect beside a studio-prop pillar, his squat body tightly encased in a three-piece suit, his heavy jowls clean-shaven except for

---

10. *Jhol* means "stew," *aloo dum* potatoes are steam cooked in a spicy tomato sauce, and *payesh* is a type of rice pudding.—Ed.

a bristly line of mustache above a full upper lip, exuded self-confidence. This was not the social occasion to clarify whether Mr. Bose had choked to death on a chicken bone or suffered a fatal heart attack. But over dinner I learned from mother and daughter that the Boses had lived in Dhaka until Purnima was five years old; that, as part of a diminishing Hindu community in Bangladesh, they had felt menaced enough to emigrate and had been lucky enough to get "landed immigrant" visas from Canada; that they had spent five years in Montreal, where they'd been forced by Quebec law to learn French; that Purnima, like other immigrant children, had had to enroll in a French-medium school; that, for his realtor job, Mr. Bose had had to prove his proficiency in French even though most of his clients were South Asian immigrants; and that, once they'd made it to the U.S., Mr. Bose had done well for himself "in finance."

"He worked too hard," Mrs. Bose sighed as she picked up our dessert bowls. "He worked himself to death for us."

"Greed. Baba just couldn't stop." An eerie, joyless laugh accompanied the daughter's indictment: "G-r-e-e-d." This time she spelled out the word. "Greed's the immigrant's fatal affliction."

I am the son of immigrants. I didn't agree, but I didn't speak up.

Mrs. Bose finished clearing the table, with some help from me but none from Purnima. Just as her mother was about to remove the tablecloth, Purnima half-rose from her chair, gripped a fistful of the linen, and screamed, "Aren't you angry, Ma? *Why* aren't you furious?" Then she walked away from the table to the window overlooking the long driveway. My Beamer was directly outside the window; parked closer to the carriage house was a tenant's panel truck. I expected another taunt about my Beamer. What burst out of Purnima's mouth instead was "Why do you always do this, Ma? Why do you shut me out?"

The nail of the forefinger of Mrs. Bose's right hand picked away at a crusting curry stain on the white tablecloth. Had I been clumsy when I helped myself a second time to the chicken thighs in turmeric-yellow-chili-red gravy? My error, but a correctible error: I'd pay the dry cleaner's bill. But Mrs. Bose scoured the stain inconsolably. She didn't raise her eyes from the stain, not even when Purnima swiveled to confront her. "Why do you keep doing this to me? Don't I count? You don't give a damn about *my* feelings."

Mrs. Bose gave up on the stain and focused her maternal attention on me. "You must be dead-tired, Bikash." She slid into the chair next to mine. "I'm sorry we've kept you down here for so long. Very selfish of us." I didn't dare glance at Purnima for her reaction. Don't get drawn into their family melodrama. You are *not* family. "A cup of Assam tea?" Mrs. Bose asked, touching my elbow. I knew not to accept her offer, and she knew that I wouldn't. She spread her right hand, palm down, fingers splayed, on the table. It was a bony, neglected hand. Her nails looked almost transparent, corrugated with vertical ridges; the ridges were tinged with turmeric yellow. "All that he did, he did for us, Bikash."

"For *us*? Gee, thanks for the guilt trip, Ma."

I felt Mrs. Bose's cool palm on a cheek, smelled the lingering pungency of turmeric. "You write poems, don't you, Bikash?" she asked. "You find inspiration everywhere, right?" I stayed as still as I could in my chair.

"He's not about to waste his creativity on us, Ma," Purnima snapped. "Maybe a cautionary limerick, but not a real poem."

You're their temporary houseboy, not the referee of their pain. Plead fatigue, escape upstairs, and drain the bottle of bourbon. Let bats swarm down the chimneys and invade their lugubrious rooms. Some choose butterfly nets, some baseball bats; I choose bourbon.

My first week in the Bose house was pleasingly uneventful. Mrs. Bose had me drive her in my car to the fancy mall just outside city limits, push her shopping cart up and down aisles of a huge, overstocked supermarket—she was a careful, frugal shopper—and sit in the car while she made a long stop at a chain pharmacy. She didn't own a car, she said, because she had never learned to drive. Mr. Bose had not wanted her to. Purnima didn't seem to own a car either, but I didn't have to chauffeur her. She had her bike, and in any case she was out of town whitewater rafting with friends in Colorado. Only women friends, the mother had quickly added. How long would she be away? My question was prompted by self-interest. How long would this respite from Purnima's sharp tongue last? Who knows, Mrs. Bose said, she comes and goes as she pleases, she has too many friends, her friends are her family . . . her voice dwindled to a whimper . . . she hates me, what have I done to her to deserve . . . I interrupted her litany of complaints with *my* litany of household problems that needed immediate fixing: leaky faucets, warped window frames, jagged holes in the parquet floor of the foyer, and the wasps' nest under an eave in the attic.

WITHOUT PURNIMA AROUND, Mrs. Bose seems less immersed in nostalgia. Afternoons she sits on an Adirondack rocking chair on the front porch, a tall glass of homemade *nimbu pani*[11] at her feet, bemused by the spectacle of August in Saratoga Springs swirling by. Sometimes, to cool down after a vigorous ride on Purnima's bike, I join her on the porch, pulling up one of the many Adirondack chairs that came with the property. I thrive in these moments of mute

---

11. Indian-style lemonade.—Ed.

338 | LATE STORIES (1997–2012)

contentment. She isn't curious about my family, which is uncharacteristic of an immigrant Bengali mother her age. She doesn't ask me if I have fallback career plans for when poetry won't pay the rent, as the Chappaqua "uncles" would. Nor does she pester me with questions about the kind of bride I would prefer to marry, meaning one from India or an American-born one, as would the Chappaqua "aunties."

I HAVE EASED into my houseboy role faster than I'd expected. The morning after Purnima took off for Colorado, Mrs. Bose gave me a tour of the half-block-long landscaped garden that separates the rented-out carriage house and the Victorian. Flowering bushes, a shade tree, a couple of fruit trees, beds of wilting flowers and herbs. I couldn't name any of the flowers. Nor could she. I was to enlarge all four herb beds. *Dhaniya, methi, tulsi*: she uttered these words with reverence. Coriander, mint, basil: I wondered whether she meant at the expense of the neglected but still thriving rosemary, oregano, thyme, and sage.

During the day, I weed, enlarge plant beds, and border them with stones; hoe and aerate the soil; put in coriander, mint, and three kinds of basil and many pots of colorful, low-maintenance flowers that looked pretty enough in the nursery. I discover that I actually like this physical work, the sun, the sweat, even the backache. Back in Chappaqua, a contractor's crew tended Mother's ambitious, extensive garden and modest swimming pool summers and cleared snow winters. Before Labor Day when I mean to move on, I'll lay a fancy herringbone brick path between the Victorian and the carriage house: I am not an ingrate.

Mrs. Bose has encouraged me to visit with her every evening, and whenever I do, she brings out a bottle of Johnny Walker Blue Label. "He had them delivered by the case," she says, pouring me the first of two hefty shots over ice cubes. She herself drinks fruit juice diluted with water. After the second shot, she insists I stay on for dinner, which she serves in the cozy eat-in alcove of her huge, drafty kitchen. She eats slowly, with her fingers, as both my grandmothers did. Our small talk is of tristate weather and petty crimes that have made it onto local news channels. On family visits back to Kolkata, my *didima*, my mother's mother, tried to teach me finger-eating etiquette. Remember: only the right hand. Didima demonstrated: long, supple fingers broke off bits from the mound of rice and the thick piece of fish on her plate, mashed them into tiny rice balls and fish balls, and slipped them into her mouth in a graceful, fluid motion. Over dessert, which is always *suji halwa*[12] with almonds

---

12. A semolina-based Indian sweetmeat.—Ed.

and raisins, Mrs. Bose entreats me to stay on into the fall. I haven't chosen "entreat" carelessly. *If you aren't in this house, Bikash, who'll know if I've dropped dead?* So what, I want to snap back, we'll all drop dead, what's the point in malingering when quality of life becomes dismal? I've stepped on rubble from my Chappaqua adolescence. Father was obsessed with "quality of life." He carried his official DO NOT RESUSCITATE instruction in his wallet. Caring about a loved one is having the guts to pull the plug: he would say this to Mother after harrowing days at the hospital. They would be in the large, efficient kitchen she had codesigned with the architect, she fixing dinner on the new six-burner stove she was so proud of, Father taking morose sips of single malt, me a preteen eavesdropper finishing up extra-credit homework. Caring is a burden I can't handle right now, Father. I should politely opt out of this dinner ritual, pretend I have plans to meet friends for pizza and beer, but she is a decent cook, dedicated to replicating for me the late Mr. Bose's favorite Bangladeshi dishes; and like her I am lonely, bewildered.

IT'S NOT QUITE SEVEN O'CLOCK ON my eighth Purnima-less morning when I hear Mrs. Bose scream my name. "Bikash! Bikash!" floats up the servants' stairwell. I'm still in bed, watching last night's *Real Time with Bill Maher* on my smartphone. "Aren't you up yet? Bikash!" I leap out of bed and pull on jeans and yesterday's T-shirt, imagining medical emergencies. Don't waste time brushing teeth and showering, though like Mother I have a fetish about not seeing anyone before I've finished my morning rituals. Definitely don't dawdle over whipping up a smoothie. "Bikash? Where are you, Bikash?" Kitchen-knife sliced a distracted hand? Catastrophic fall? Heart attack? I grab my billfold and car keys and hurtle down two steps at a time. Mrs. Bose is gripping the splintered newel of the servants' backstairs, her voice shrill, her face distorted by panic. No bleeding, writhing, gasping body. Her wounds are invisible.

"They're *goondas*, thugs, hooligans," she shouts in this new hysterical voice. "They look in my windows. They laugh at me." Who? The tenants? I'd seen only one of them while gardening; a pale-eyed, bowlegged teenager who told me he was hoping to find work as a stable hand. "Tenants!" Mrs. Bose screams. "You call them tenants when they've paid no rent, ever. Never." I can readily believe they've skipped paying rent, but I'm skeptical about their menacing her. "They want to scare me out of my own house!" They shoot air guns or pellet guns, some kind of guns anyway, out their windows. More than once pedestrians on the side street have called 911; and once two policemen showed up at her front door and asked scary questions about firearms she owned, as though she, not the tenants, were the criminal. "Bikash, you don't believe me." She

340 | LATE STORIES (1997–2012)

grabs my elbow, her grip so strong that I wince. "Why don't you believe me, Bikash? They want to drive me crazy, they want to lock me up as they did . . ."

I use just enough force to make her let go of my elbow. "What's Purnima's cell?" In my parents' circle, emotional breakdowns are best kept as family secrets. Patient privacy is a myth; hospital records are indelible humiliations. Try soothing inanities or rush her to ER? This has to be the daughter's decision.

Mrs. Bose doesn't bother to answer, too preoccupied staring, fierce-eyed, out the glass panel of the servants' back door at one of the renters' panel trucks in the driveway, its tires sunk in hardened ruts. "He is the main *goonda*!" She spits out the words, literally. A gob hits the glass and cuts a white, foamy track through grime as it slides down. The Boses don't employ a cleaning person, though what this dusty, derelict mansion needs is a professional cleaning *crew*. I keep the attic germ-free, my finicky cleanliness a downside of having grown up the only child of a doctor, but the other floors in this Victorian are not my responsibility. My immediate task is to lead hysterical Mrs. Bose away to where she can't see the truck; seat her at the butcher-block counter in her kitchen; boil a slow pot of *masala* tea from scratch, giving both of us time to calm down. Tea is my mother's first-try remedy for all ailments.

Mrs. Bose ignores the cup I set in front of her. Instead, she wanders out to the small deck off the kitchen's side door. Her wild-eyed gaze fastens on the parked truck. "*Dacoits*, thieves," she shouts at me. "He must have stolen that truck. What have I done to deserve a *dacoit* as tenant?" I haven't run into this man yet. The truck pulls out of the driveway late at night and returns, lights low, tires swerving in and out of the ruts, around four in the morning. I've become a listless sleeper since I left home—was thrown out by Father— a year ago.

"The bastard!" Actually, she spits out a string of coarse vulgarities in Bangla. This is the first time I've heard a woman utter them. I'm witnessing inexplicable panic morph into inexplicable rage. Her heaving, panting body stiffens; her moans deepen into gravelly threats. "Thief! Stealing from a helpless widow. Just because I have no husband, no brother-in-law, no son to protect me!"

"Has Purnima tried to get this guy to pay up?" I wouldn't want to be on the receiving end of Purnima's caustic fury.

"Purnima? She wants bad things to happen to me. Do you know that she laughed in his face when the worst happened to him? She isn't our daughter, she is a *rakshasi*!" On brief visits to my paternal grandparents' tea estate in cool, green hills preyed on by local insurgents, my *thakuma*[13] would terrify me with lurid tales of *rakshasis*, she-giants, stalking slow-footed humans and shredding

---

13. Bengali word for "paternal grandmother."—Ed.

THE HOUSE ON CIRCULAR STREET (c. 2008) | *341*

living flesh with saw-sharp teeth. Both *thakuma* and *thakurda*[14] died of cholera within hours of each other when I was four. I hadn't worried about she-giants until this moment.

"Barrenness would have been a better fate than giving birth to this *rakshasi.*"

I go through all four drawers under the kitchen counter for an address book that might list Purnima's cell number, but all they contain are Ziploc bags full of expired supermarket coupons, utility and phone bills paid by mail, a glassine envelope of Forever stamps, bank and credit card statements, an unopened box of long matches, metal and bamboo skewers, a yellowing sheaf of warranties for kitchen appliances, a wall calendar for last year, and a stack of the long-defunct *Gourmet* magazine mailed to an Emily Goldfarb at this Circular Street address.

"You're a good boy, Bikash." She places her hand on the top of my head in traditional Hindu blessing. A two-week bristly growth of stubble now covers my scalp. "Your parents are lucky." Prabir-uncle must not have told her about my fallout with Father. "They have you now, and they'll have both you and grandsons when they get old." This prodigal son can't return home. She is an innocent fomenter of guilt. I leave her on the kitchen porch and stride to the carriage house.

THE CARRIAGE HOUSE is a two-story round building, with rooms—originally for chauffeur, gardener, caretaker?—on the second floor. I rap the horseshoe-shaped clapper on the front door several times, and, since the door isn't locked, I let myself in, shouting, "Hello! Hello!" as I climb the winding staircase. The inside walls are covered with narrow white bathroom-style tiles, which must have been easy to hose clean in the era of prosperous owners but are now a jaundice-yellow streaked with hardened grime. I am met—more accurately, confronted—at the landing by a short, stout older man with a pugilist's large hands, which he presses hard into my T-shirted chest. He isn't about to f—ing pay rent for a f— shithole to f—ing foreign scum. He catches me looking at the two supermarket paper sacks full of his stuff—clothes, coffeepot, electric razor, mean-looking hunting knives—at his feet. His lips curl into a mocking smile. So what's a jerk like you going to do? F—ing stop me? He scoops up the bags, pushes past me, and races down the stairs.

Fred is the second tenant I encounter; at least the lined note card thumbtacked to the door identifies the room's resident as FRED in blue Sharpie. I knock

---

14. "Paternal grandfather" in Bengali.—Ed.

with my left hand while my right fist rests on the doorknob. "Chill," a man's voice growls. I don't like being told to chill, so I rotate the doorknob and thrust myself into a sunny, semicircular room with curved windows—no curtains, no shades—a precariously put-together cooking island, flanked on either side by a stove and refrigerator, and next to the refrigerator a toilet and shower stall. Fred is on a lumpy love seat upholstered in stained denim. A young woman with darkening blond hair is wedged in the love seat next to him, a syringe still stuck in her tanned right arm. "So the landlady sent you," he says. He can make the word "landlady" sound toxic. "Nima told me you'd show. Sooner or later." He heaves himself half-up from the love seat and then drops back on the edge of the cushion to remove the syringe and drop both it and a tubing in a gallon-size Ziploc bag. No sharps container here. Father, a Type 1 diabetic, was meticulous about disposing of his needles. "You're new here, right? Dutiful, trusting midwesterner, Nima says. And she's quick at sizing up character." It takes me too many minutes to figure out that Fred's "Nima" is my Purnima. So the daughter keeps secrets. But Fred has moved on to other topics. "Been to the races yet?" He fills me in on the Saratoga racing scene and the night scene in side-street bars, especially the dive where he is a bouncer. The young woman stirs but doesn't open her eyes. I can tell she is in a happy place. She may be the happiest person I've happened into in Saratoga.

"Dude, I want to be upfront with you." He doesn't have the rent money, period, he says, and dude, forget the back rent. His voice and posture aren't threatening, his grip on my shoulder firm but friendly. How would the landlady feel about barter? He can leave off a rib roast over the weekend. He brags about his shoplifting expertise. I've failed Mrs. Bose. No point in telling Fred that the landlady, an observant Hindu, doesn't eat beef or pork. Dude, don't bother with "the sad kid" next door. This must be the polite, pale-eyed teenager who'd told me he was looking for work in the stables. He's too far gone, Fred explains. The night that Fred had found the kid comatose in the men's room of the dive where he works, he had brought him back to the carriage house and installed him in the one empty room. That was a month or so before the sale of the property to Mr. Bose had gone through. How can I hate Fred?

My response to my abject failure is foolish gallantry. I withdraw eight hundred dollars from my savings account at the ATM, go back to my attic and hunt for an envelope—who writes letters anymore?—to slip the bills into it and, when I do, leave the envelope on the console table in the front hall. Five hundred for Fred's large room, and three hundred for each of the two other rooms I didn't see. By my Iowa street experience, these rents are minimal. As an afterthought, I scrawl a note on the envelope to alert Mrs. Bose that as of this day, she will have two, not three, tenants to get mad at.

THE HOUSE ON CIRCULAR STREET (c. 2008) | *343*

IT'S LONG PAST MIDNIGHT, and I am memorizing Robert Frost desperate for inspiration. I haven't written any new poems since March, so why go back to the Iowa Workshop for humiliating feedback on poems I'd scribbled on Wall Street to inoculate myself against "cubicle depression"? The ones I'd submitted to the Admissions Committee got me in, but now I worry that was a fluke. "Road Not Taken" speaks to me tonight with a bitterness Frost didn't intend. I've tried both forks. Fred's truck roars into the driveway, radio blaring. He usually coasts in, headlights and music off so as not to disturb Mrs. Bose. He isn't entirely thoughtless: I have to give him that. The truck door opens and bangs shut right outside the servants' entrance, letting a passenger out; then the tires growl forward closer to the carriage house. Someone enters the Victorian through the back door, *my* door. Did I forget to lock it as I often did in Iowa City? You must be vigilant during the racing season in Saratoga, when its population bulges with horse owners, betting tourists and gambling addicts, racetrack professionals, predators and marks. Breaking-and-entering episodes, barroom brawls that spill onto the sidewalk and end in stabbings, mysterious nighttime injuries to horses, vanished stable hands, heroin overdoses, public urinating, pickpocketing: the police blotter in the local paper is entertaining until you hear an intruder stumbling up your staircase. The drunken tread on the steps is a woman's, but not Mrs. Bose's. She has shut me out since I left the envelope of cash on the console table. I hear her slipper-shod shuffle on the second floor—there are six bedrooms and three bathrooms on that floor, though only two are in usable condition—but I've received no requests to drive her to and from the supermarket, no advice to prune back the mint that's choking the coriander in the enlarged herb beds; most startlingly, no more entreaties to drink Mr. Bose's single malt.

"Hey, let me in, Bic. I'm no way near ready for bed." Imperative thumps and kicks on the attic's front door. "Come on, open up, I've brought us a midnight picnic. Who thought I'd have my very own starving poet in my garret?"

I struggle into pants. She's still pounding and wheedling. "Come on, poetguy, it's your lucky night. You're getting food. Plus, your very own muse. You can't be a poet if you don't have a muse."

Purnima, hugging a liquor-store plastic bag and a supermarket paper sack, collapses into me as soon as I unlock the door. I have to use both my arms to prop her against my chest, push her toward the living area. Once I've got her halfway on the settee, she offers up the two bags. "Booze," she says, about the contents of the heavier one. I can smell rum and whiskey. "Cops make trouble if they catch you driving with open bottles."

"Does Mrs. Bose know you're back?"

"You want me to scare Ma by showing up in this condition? I'm not that cruel."

"She must have seen you get out of the truck. She paces all night and into the morning. Loose floorboards. She's doing it right now."

"So?"

"Boy, that's profound hate!"

"No, Bic. That's your poetic inflation of feelings I don't have."

I drop down to the threadbare Persian area rug, my back against the settee, but careful for my exhausted head not to accidentally touch her long, sun-browned, enticing legs.

"Be a good host and bring out two glasses, then I'll tell you why you're wrong. Why I can't hate Ma, I mean."

"Where's your stuff?"

"Stuff? I expect more elegant diction from a poet."

"Don't play dumb. Like your camping and kayaking gear."

"All borrowed from friends. This was my first time whitewater rafting. Boy, so fun."

"No backpack? What about your pocketbook?"

"Why this third degree, Bic?" She shifts positions until she has made room for more of her strong, muscled legs on the settee. I retreat to one of the two rickety chairs by the dining table. She is wearing a white shirt and denim cut-offs, and, on her feet, which rest on an arm of the settee, are sandals with shiny metal heels so high they look incongruous on a woman just back from white-water rafting—okay, sexy incongruous. This is an image that should coalesce into a lyrical verse.

"They're in the truck. I'll haul them home tomorrow."

"The truck'll get broken into." I'm thinking of Fred as much as opportunistic prowlers off the street. Two of the Adirondack chairs were stolen from the porch my third night here.

"You're pathetic! I'm not into *things*, Bic. And I lied just now. This was my fifth summer on the river. We started out a gang of six, but we're down to four. I don't know if I'd rather die slowly of breast cancer or be pushed off a subway platform by a crazy and be pulped by a train. Do you ever indulge in such morbid speculations?"

"I'm going to pass on that. We hardly know each other." Purnima's not the only one to have struggled with this.

"Bring out the glasses, Bic, and let's get to know each other better. Dixie cups from the bathroom will do, I'm not fussy."

I look inside the paper bag. There's a crown roast of beef bleeding through its shrink-wrap; no butcher's paper, no total price sticker. Shoplifted, for sure.

THE HOUSE ON CIRCULAR STREET (c. 2008) | *345*

"From one of the tenants."

"From Fred? What's with you and this fellow? He calls you 'Nima,' cheats your Ma, runs a heroin joint on your property . . ." Bitterness I have no right to feel has crept into my voice. "You plan to give your Ma this stolen bloody hunk of beef? You're wrong, you *do* hate her."

———————

"HIS NAME ISN'T FRED. It's Winthrop."

"Winthrop?" I start to laugh, because the guy in the carriage house shooting up a blond coed didn't look like someone who was given a last name as a first.

"It's his mother's maiden name. He comes from that kind of family. He says Fred is his *nom de guerre*."

We get into the whiskey from Fred's bar, and soon she is blabbing family secrets. Mr. Bose isn't dead; she spits that out, though not literally, as her mother had. He's serving an eight-year sentence for insider trading. Low-hanging fruit for an ambitious prosecutor, she complains. Didn't I read about the trial and his conviction last year? It made the Boses pariahs in the tristate South Asian American community. Lawyers' fees and court-levied fines turned mother and daughter into paupers. Ma *needs* the rent money, can you believe, Bic? No, of course you can't. You drive a Beamer, you blow money on a stupid fine arts degree, and that's a Rolex on your wrist. You've never been desperately poor, not as abjectly poor as Baba and Ma were in Dhaka, so don't pretend to understand their constant terror of poverty.

Her drunken soliloquy delivers memories I should not be privy to. And who knows how accurate they are? Baba had surreptitiously watched his wife ladle her and the child Purnima's shares of fish curry onto his brass plate. He had slurped the delicacies in the little bowls Ma had set around his plate and belched his appreciation. But inside he must have beaten himself up for failing to be the provider and protector that is every Hindu householder's duty. Maybe the insider trading wasn't about uncontrollable greed after all. Moral values are fungible: that's what came to her in a zen moment on a Colorado river.

The whiskey and the brandy are dissolving the anger against her father I'd sat through my first night in the Victorian. I can't keep up with her new philosophical garrulity, but it helps deflect my grief over how my parents ended their lives, and why. They orphaned me, holding hands. Tea was Mother's go-to solution, and on Father's orders the final two cups she served were poison-bitter. That I learned first from Prabir-uncle, and later from the coroner. They weren't well: Father had been diagnosed with Lewy bodies disease a month after he had cast me out; and Mother's breast cancer had snuck up to stage 4. "Qual-

346 | LATE STORIES (1997–2012)

ity of life" had dictated their final decision. *Mother chose to die with Father.* That's just beginning to sink in. I am an orphan. Mother collaborated in my orphaning. Love drove them *not* to outlive each other. Love stopped them from burdening me with caregiving and hospice duties. They pulled the plug on my life as the prodigal son and, instead, gave me a new life; a life to muddle through on my own terms, not theirs. And they left me the sole heir of their hefty fortune. Father, like all the Chappaqua "uncles," was an astute investor and estate planner. I picture him in his lawyer's office, with Mother at his side, going meticulously over every word in the trust document he had had drawn up a month before Mother and he had carried out their final act of love, and chuckling that not all poets need to starve as they explore the metaphysical.

"Don't abandon me, Bic." She is so far gone that I bring out a plastic pail from the broom closet. Too late as it turns out. Vomit stains her shirtfront. She struggles with words. "Bic, Fate sent you to this madhouse. We're puppets of Fate. You, me, your Prabir-uncle . . ." I'm not a believer in Fate, I'm not a believer in anything, period. With a wetted dishcloth I start to scrape drying vomit off her face, but she resists. "It wasn't chance that your Prabir-uncle stuck you here. He knew Baba. To his misfortune, I should add."

The gagging stench of her vomit is getting to me. I want it to be morning, I want to buy myself a dashing Saratoga straw hat, I want to lose myself among well-heeled tourists and shifty transients on Broadway, I want a greasy breakfast in a diner. . . .

"Who knows how heavily Baba ripped him off?"

I need her to fall asleep or pass out. There are no extra blankets and pillows in the linen closet, and so I pull them off my bed. "They smell of you, Bic." The summer throw is easy to arrange over Purnima, but I have to give up on trying to wedge my two pillows under her head. "You own a car, Bic, so help me hitchhike out of my private hell. Tonight. Like Winthrop, I'll give myself a *nom de guerre.* That'll make ditching Ma easier. . . ." Her eyes, unsteady but intense, are on me as I hurl the foul washcloth on the floor. "You know why you'll never be a poet, Bic? You don't know love." She mangles a half-line from a song my roommate in Iowa City used to hum when drunk, "I want to know what love is. . . ."

In midline, her hummed words give way to snores, loud and unflattering. Purnima probably knows all there is to know about hangover cures, but I leave an almost full bottle of mega B-Complex capsules by the plastic pail at her feet. Prabir-uncle would pop a couple of them after nightly single malt sessions with Father. Once upon a time we were a happy family. Who knows, before shutting themselves in this dilapidated Saratoga Victorian, the Boses, too, were happy.

My backpack and laptop are in the passenger seat, and the car is heading me toward the paddocks. The light of this August dawn has the wounding sharpness of broken glass. Epicures are breakfasting on strawberries and cream as tense jockeys exercise magnificent beasts in the mist. I linger at the paddocks. An orphan travels with no roadmap and no calendar.

The Laws of Chance (2011)

I AM WRITING this in a shingled cottage on a leafy three-block lane in the village of Southampton, New York. My writing desk is a Chinese antique I bought on eBay as soon as I realized I needed to keep a journal. Ben and his partner Hugh, who live across from me, hauled it up my narrow staircase to the smaller of two guest bedrooms. Ben's the real estate agent who sold this cottage to Rahul and me. We had a different agent, Traci Hollings, when I first glimpsed the cottage. Rahul had been in touch with Traci by email about listings for a couple of weeks before he had time to take a day off to look at properties. Rahul was in investment banking at the time, and it was that time when Wall Street bankers in custom-made Italian suits were envied rather than detested. Rahul's end of year bonus had been more than decent, and he had more faith in real estate than in stocks. Because he could spare only one afternoon to buy a Hamptons property, we took the jitney from Manhattan, prepared to make a bid on one of the seven she had lined up, and be back in our Manhattan loft by evening. What he talked of as "investment property," I thought of as a refuge, where there would be just the two of us, a bride and her groom playing house, feeding each other candlelit morsels in an eat-in kitchen, relaxing in rockers and gazing up at stars from windy porches, a place for that sort of in-love tenderness rather than dutiful conjugal sex. We were no longer newly marrieds, but because of Rahul's relentless professional ambition, our honeymoon was still on hold.

Traci was driving us to the fifth on her to-show list, when we passed the cottage. All I could see of it through a scruffy hedge were green-shuttered windows and brilliant purple domes of mature azalea bushes flanking a front porch. A For Sale sign from a realty company other than Traci's was stuck on the strip of grass between road and hedge.

Traci eased the SUV to a stop a couple of yards beyond the For Sale sign when I asked her to, but didn't turn off the engine. I sensed her sizing us up: we were the wrong kind of moneyed immigrants, clueless about the Hamptons, a waste of her time. She waved a manicured hand at the flaking frame houses on the block with sagging stoops on large, untended lots. Mostly teardowns, she sniffed. The neighborhood was "unstable." Once the old-timer residents passed away, their heirs would sell to developers who would subdivide the lots. Also, how did we feel about buying so close to train tracks? We were aware, weren't we, that the train station was where the treed lane made a T with a noisy artery. "I took this shortcut only because we're running late for the next appointment." She glanced pointedly at her wafer-thin, gold watch. The wide watchband, I noticed, was made of genuine crocodile skin. "As I said," Traci continued. "Thanks to a nasty divorce, this one's a steal. Otherwise it'd never be on the market. The husband's anxious to dump it. For buyers and realtors nasty divorces are pure gold."

"Twenty-four carat gold or just eighteen carat?" Rahul joked, signaling her to drive on to our appointment. Traci didn't get the joke. She had no way of knowing that we Bengalis are purists when it comes to "pure gold," which to us means twenty-four carat, and that we are condescending toward Bombayites who are satisfied with twenty-two carat, and that we are downright scornful of Americans who don't know better than eighteen carat.

We viewed the former happy home of the now-acrimoniously divorcing sellers, then two more houses in the two million dollar range that Rahul had specified in his emails. All the properties, with their staged interiors, landscaped gardens, patios paved with tumbled travertine tiles, commodious hot tubs and tarp-covered Gunite pools, were grander than any home I'd ever fantasized owning. I tried to calculate what two million U.S. dollars came to in Indian rupees, but gave up. Like Rahul, I had grown up in a rented flat in a once-genteel part of Kolkata. But unlike Rahul, I was a diffident consumer. He had earned the right to a lavish lifestyle, he believed, because he was making and shrewdly multiplying his savings; he wasn't a lazy heir dissipating a family fortune. Even though Rahul had established a joint account for us the day after we were married, I wasn't comfortable spending money on anything other than groceries. Our savings and assets weren't really *ours*, I felt; I had happened upon a financially astute man, a gregarious, good-looking Bengali bachelor, with a ladies'-man reputation I should add, at a time when he was looking to settle down with a Bengali, *kayastha*-caste[1] virgin. When Rahul proposed marriage, I felt I'd won the lottery.

As Traci dropped us off at the Omni for our jitney back to Manhattan, Rahul let her know in a way that bordered on rudeness that he was underwhelmed by the tour she had put together, and that he was willing to raise his

---

1. A prominent Hindu caste in India.—Ed.

ceiling by a couple of hundred grand. On the ride back, however, he lectured me on how the cottage on an iffy street within the village of Southampton for under a million dollars and low property taxes was a smarter investment than the pricey houses with better addresses we'd wasted our day on. That night he emailed Ben Moretti, the agent listed on the For Sale sign for the cottage.

The next weekend Ben Moretti took us through the cozy, two-story structure and its modest grounds. Ben described the neighborhood as "transitional," but he made "transitional" sound desirable. He had sold a TLC[2] on a parallel lane to a fortyish stockbroker with high alimony and child support payments, a teardown catty-corner from the Long Island Rail Road (LIRR) station to two aromatherapist sisters, and he himself had just put in a bid for the older house directly across from the cottage. Rahul quizzed Ben on heating and cooling costs, financing options, summer rental potential. I left the two of them talking figures at the kitchen table, and settled into a deck chair on the front porch to savor the blinding radiance of azalea bushes in full bloom. Our azaleas. Our house. Our hide-out. In Rahul's Soho loft that I'd moved into after he married me, I felt more a housekeeper than wife.

My immediate dream of an intimate weekend in the modest cottage within walking distance of Main Street and easy bicycling distance from the beach remained just that. As soon as the sale went through, Rahul hired a local contractor recommended by Ben, and had a showy master bedroom suite built above the kitchen, the back and side yards landscaped, a new privet hedge planted, a heated pool put in. The contractor was a large blond affable man whose ancestors had settled in Southampton Village in 1670. The contractor let us know that fact about him in order to inspire confidence that he was well-connected and so there would be no problems getting building permits and passing inspection. He had a hand-picked crew of Ecuadorans, ready to start. Not the unskilled Mexican day-laborers, who loitered on North Sea Road and ran after every passing vehicle in the hope of jobs. Rahul was inspired, but did some comparative checking of costs and workmanship before hiring the man. We had chanced on this cottage in a neighborhood Traci, the first realtor, had intended to avoid. Once Rahul had calculated cost of mortgage payment, renovation and property tax versus potential post-renovation rental income, he had approached it as a lucrative investment property. The renovations were completed almost on deadline. The delay was caused by two tragic workplace accidents. One of the Ecuadorans had tumbled off the roof of the pool-house and broken his back; another had mishandled equipment and nearly severed

---

2. Probably used here to mean "Tender Loving Care" or a property that needs a lot of work.—Ed.

his right hand. The contractor had personally escorted the maimed employees back to Ecuador for medical care. He'd apologized to us in his affable way. "My men are skilled, but accidents happen, what can I say?" In spite of these ghastly accidents, by mid-April Rahul had the cottage rented out for the Memorial to Labor Day summer season. I would have preferred that we, not tenants, enjoy hot, lazy weekends in our Southampton home, but from the start of our married life I had to accept that Rahul made decisions on his own for the both of us. The occasional winter and spring weekends we did spend in Southampton were as hosts (he relaxed, I harassed) to swarms of his relatives visiting from Kolkata or his South Asian business associates. It's only been a month that I've been living in it full-time.

My subletting the Soho loft and moving into the cottage was Hugh's advice. Hugh is one of three owners of Haughty Haute, a home design boutique I can't afford to shop in on Jobs Lane. Most of the furniture in this room, the white wrought iron daybed, for instance, the candy-striped love seat, the white wicker bookcase, are from Ben and Hugh's basement, as are the tastefully worn Aubusson rug, the pink, fringed Victorian shade on the floor lamp I scavenged from the town dump, the pile of cushions that pick up the rug's faded colors just so, the watercolors with nautical themes, and the three-foot-long ceramic mermaid sunning on a ceramic rock. The sleek, silver MacBook Air that sits incompatibly on the ornate rosewood desk, too, is on loan from them. They aren't just good neighbors. Since Rahul drowned, they've morphed into dedicated caregivers.

Hugh wants me to stay put in the cottage until I am healed. Think of it as a retreat, he says. You'll know when you are ready to move on with your life, he says. Ben, the pragmatic one, tells me that even in these days of mortgage meltdown, I'll do all right if I sell. Extend the deck off the kitchen, Ben advises, spruce up the pool house, put up a pergola (he and Hugh went for a gazebo as well as a pergola), and voila! He knows local architects and contractors; he'll make sure I'm not taken advantage of. Both Hugh and Ben are trying to come up with therapeutic projects for me. Grief stagnates: they don't say it to my face, but that's what they're thinking. I need to progress from what Hugh's yoga instructor calls "the foothills of loss" to "the peak of serene solitude." The instructor has his own holistic fitness show on cable TV. Hugh has brought over a how-to DVD, but I haven't watched it yet. First I have to figure out what I'm grieving for. I'm thirty-seven; widowed by a freak accident; childless. My life is on PAUSE.

The journal project gives my days comforting focus. I know the project's goals: assess the past; imagine the future; suppress the present. I've set myself rules. I must be at my desk by 9:10 A.M., switch off my cell phone, skim news events on the Internet, read and answer my email, light an incense stick in front of the shrine that holds a silver statue of Goddess Kali and a framed photograph of Rahul. I stay at the screen until 2:00 P.M. every day, weekends as well as weekdays. The UPS driver can ring the doorbell, the answering machine can record an urgent message, the refrigerator may be empty except for mold-speckled fruits and cheeses: between 9:10 A.M. and 2:00 P.M. I permit myself no procrastination. If I concentrate hard enough, journal entries will birth themselves on the screen. The fingers on the keyboard are the midwife's. I believe that. I really do.

While I wait for new life to emerge, I experiment with fonts, margins and line spacing. Does form inhibit content? As a schoolgirl in Kolkata I wrote my weekly essays for Mother Paul in careful longhand in a lined notebook with my grandfather's Parker 51 fountain pen. Some feelings are too nuanced, some discoveries too intimate, to feed into a word processor.

This morning, as most mornings and afternoons, I find myself distracted by the angled view of North Sea Road that the only window in this room offers. Migrant workers, mostly stocky men with morose faces under hooded sweatshirts, line its sidewalks. Fast food wrappers sprout like blooms on hedges; empty pop bottles and coffee cups roll like skittles in short driveways. Rahul didn't care that the cottage looks out on a year-round seafood store and a cantina instead of dune and ocean. His mantra: Get a toe-hold; then trade up. Think investment, not nest. Attachment ends in disappointment. His only "home" was the rented ground-floor flat on Rash Behari Avenue, Kolkata, where he'd been born, where his father had died, and where his mother was still living.

We grew up twenty minutes' bus ride apart in South Kolkata, but met by accident for the first time three and a half years ago in the Bloomfield, New Jersey, home of my father's first cousin. My uncle and aunt had invited a young Bengali-American doctor they knew for dinner hoping that something would come of this doctor meeting me, and they had included the doctor's roommate, so that their matchmaking intention would be apparent but not embarrassing. In another month my tourist visa was to expire, and they had promised my father when they sent a pre-paid Air India ticket for me that they would find him a suitable Bengali-American son-in-law during my six-month stay with them. My father is a proud man on very limited income. He accepted the ticket on my behalf only after my uncle had explained that I would be doing *him* and his wife and married daughter a favor. The daughter, an oncologist married to a dermatologist, was about to give birth to twins and would be grateful for help with baby care. Unlike my father, I didn't think accepting a rich relative's charity was at all humiliating. A thirty-four-year-old unmarried woman with a Bachelor of Arts degree (Third Class) from Calcutta University, aging by the hour: what did I have to lose?

What little I knew of my New Jersey relatives before arriving in their home was from family gossip and brief letters, enclosing photographs and dutiful inquiries about our health, that my aunt wrote in Bangla[3] to my mother every few months. The photographs disclosed a fuller biography than the letters. We understood that my aunt had become so Americanized that she wore pants, parka, boots, cleared snow off her front steps with a heavy shovel, and drove my uncle to his office in her very own Lexus. My uncle, too, had de-Indianized enough to the extent that he could pose without shame for the camera, wearing a bright red apron like a woman and cooking thick slabs of meat on an outdoor grille. My father would never be caught in the kitchen, not even to boil water for tea.

According to family lore (details of which changed but never the outline), in the mid-1970s this uncle, a civil engineer, had resigned from pensionable government employment in a *mofussil*[4] town in West Bengal and migrated to Trenton, New Jersey, on a tourist visa on the promise of a job by an engineering college classmate already settled there. The job had fallen through, but my uncle had worked full-time in the former classmate's brother-in-law's construction company in Trenton, lived five to a room with fellow Indian immigrants, saved obsessively, invested smartly, and within five years had acquired an immigrant's green card, brought over his wife, toddler daughter and all four of his younger brothers and their wives. When I shared my uncle's success story with Rahul soon after we were married, he snickered. "That first wave of Indians here, they were pathetic."

He was wrong to be so contemptuous of my uncle who, unlike his cousin, my timid father, had taken such a big risk and dealt with the consequences. I should have corrected Rahul, should have described how loving and generous they were to me, and how I repaid them with diligence (my only currency in America) in the nursery and the kitchen, but I hadn't felt secure enough yet to contradict him. As Rahul might have put it, by accepting his marriage proposal I had traded up. Oh, I'd had my teenaged fantasies all right, but on a smaller, more local scale. My father would miraculously convince a good-hearted surgeon or solicitor[5] to marry me without dowry. I would own, not rent, a flat, or maybe a whole house in Alipur. A chauffeur would drive me in air-conditioned comfort to the city's brand new mall for a whole day of self-indulgent shopping.

---

3. Bengali.—Ed.

4. An Indian word meaning "provincial."—Ed.

5. British word used to mean a particular type of lawyer.—Ed.

THE LAWS OF CHANCE (2011) | *353*

The doctor, with whom my uncle was matchmaking me, came down with the flu that morning, and knowing that my aunt must have gone to great lengths cooking the dinner for a potential bridegroom, he insisted that at least Rahul, his roommate, show up, apologize to my uncle, and flatter my aunt's hospitality. Rahul charmed us all, and proposed after we had gone on four dates, the first two chaperoned by my New Jersey relatives, the next two in Rahul's Soho loft.

Rahul was practiced in the art of wooing. He couriered elaborate flower arrangements in odd-shaped vases to my aunt, fruit baskets to my uncle, Belgian chocolates for my cousin and me. On the first date he arrived on our doorstep with enormous plush animals for the twins, and Chanel perfume for me. On the second of our chaperoned dates in Bloomfield, he brought an out-of-print copy of a Bengali poet-freedom-fighter's book of poems for the house, and a gold Rolex for me. But it was with tales of his devotion to his parents that he wooed and won me. On the two dates in his loft, after take-out meals from neighborhood restaurants, in mellow light, and with Norah Jones on Bose speakers, he laid out his life for me to examine. Whatever he had achieved—his ambition to be a "somebody," his dogged drive to make money, his decision to dive into the hedge fund business instead of going into traditional professions such as medicine and engineering favored by the earlier wave of Indian immigrants—he owed to his father. His parents had done without, so that they could give him, their only child, the best: eggs and fish every day, vitamins, digestives and brain-enhancing tonics, visits to expensive preventive care specialists. His father had borrowed from a moneylender and bought him imported hardcover books on finance at exorbitant sums; he had even stolen copies of business magazines from the American Center Library. From the moment, as a school boy, Rahul had discovered the word "plutocrat" in a newspaper clipping on an Indian entrepreneurial family for a class assignment, he had resolved to become one before he turned fifty. "Dream big, plan smart, live large" had been his father's mantra. What Rahul hadn't planned on was dying at age forty-one. He hadn't planned on dying, period.

When my New Jersey uncle learned that I was going to marry Rahul, he gave Rahul top marks for efficiency and expediency. My aunt hugged me and kept repeating that I was exceptionally lucky to have hooked such a go-getter "boy" who also happened to be of the right caste. I agreed. I didn't meet the doctor she had originally targeted as my bridegroom, a shy man with dimpled cheeks and oversized ears, until my wedding reception in New Jersey.

I have no plans, only the duty as Rahul's widow to return to Kolkata and care physically for his aged, bedridden mother. He has left me comfortably off, very comfortably off, but with an unspoken understanding that I will live with his mother under one roof and financially support his large and needy extended family. His mother and his widow: two wary strangers bound together by Rahul's expectations and his money.

What am I to do?

Hugh asks instead, "What do you *want* to do?"

Ben's suggestion: Take the small decisions and graduate to the big one about staying on or going back. Get the house painted as a first step to selling it. The walls must sparkle when he shows it. He knows just the right house-painter for me. That man will bring in his team of migrants and get the spackling and painting done fast, and cheap.

My laptop screen is dark; I am patient.

Hugh, his rescue Chihuahua and I stroll aimlessly on Main Street. "Sell the loft," but the way he says it, I hear a question, not advice. "Get a dog. You need a dog. Everybody needs a dog. We'll go to the shelter together the week after Labor Day. You'd be amazed how many people lose or abandon their pure breeds. A dog loves unconditionally. And this is a cozy small town when the summer people leave."

A balding young father walks his flaxen-haired daughter of three or four and a large chocolate Lab just ahead of us. "Now, when we get to the corner . . ."

"I want you to take me to Mummy's[6] house," the child screams.

Hugh's Chihuahua, off-leash, darts toward the Lab, which is also off-leash. The young father smiles tolerantly at his hysterical daughter. "We'll let Dexter decide which way we turn when we get to the corner."

Dexter seems so reliable a name for a dog. Maybe only dogs can offer unconditional love.

"I want to go to Mummy's house," the child shrieks, pulling away from the father. "Now! Right now!" The father is staring at Dexter; Dexter is batting the hyper Chihuahua circling him with a large, benevolent paw. The child runs to the curb. "I want us to turn left and get in the car! I want Mummy! I *hate* you, Daddy!"

"I'm trying to teach you the concept of randomness," the father is saying as we catch up with Hugh's Chihuahua. "We'll follow Dexter. Let's see where Dexter takes us. What you have, Blakelee, is a plan . . ." but I pretend I've overheard nothing, pluck Hugh's dog off the sidewalk and stride on, with Hugh following.

---

6. Although "Mommy" seems more plausible here, Mukherjee instead uses the British word "Mummy." Arguably, this choice reveals her range of cultural and linguistic influences: Indian, British, Canadian, and American.—Ed.

And in my panic to get away from this serene, philosophical father, I stumble hard into a Latino day-laborer swaggering out of the Thrift Store run to benefit the Southampton Hospital. The day-laborer is wearing an expensive navy blazer, complete with a yacht club's crest on the breast pocket and anchors on its shiny brass buttons, an in near-mint condition garment donated by a Dune Lane or Gin Lane multimillionaire. I remember my confident contractor's excuse for his delay in meeting his contractual deadline for renovating our cottage: accidents happen. In other words, *Don't blame me. Don't feel sorry for my workers. I pay them well enough.*

The Latino man is upset with me. He brushes imaginary dog hairs off his blazer. I mumble my apologies, eyes down. It's then that I notice that instead of boating shoes on sockless feet, the pre-used blazer's new owner has on a day-laborer's sensible thick socks and paint-splattered work boots.

"Mummy! Come and get me, Mummy!" Now I'm running, not striding. I'm running away from the child's commands. I don't want to be taken to my mother's flat. I don't want to take myself to Rahul's mother's flat. I want to tell Hugh that my life should not be in turmoil, that Rahul had no business to go on a business trip to Mexico with Keiko from his office, try parasailing on a dare, he had no right to drown accidentally. I want to tell him I have accepted life's randomness but I have not learned the *lesson* of randomness that this divorced or estranged father is trying to teach his daughter, Blakelee. I don't know how to trust my next move in life to a Dexter as does this serene father with the screeching daughter. I shouldn't get myself a dog because I don't know how to love or be loved. I want to tell Ben to go ahead, hire the house-painter he has worked with before. I want the cottage invaded by the migrants I spy on, the muscular men with desperate faces at the street corner. I want them to wreck and rebuild my home, but to do it slowly, very slowly, so that the absurdity of their hope for better times and the reality of hacked-off arms and broken spines has time to birth on my borrowed MacBook Air screen in redemptive, illuminated fonts.

The Going-Back Party (2012)

THROWING A FAREWELL PARTY for the Dasgupta family of Fremont, who were going back for good to India, had been her husband's idea. Shefali had gone along with it, partly because she still felt grateful to Mrs. Dasgupta for having mothered her through her first homesick year as an immigrant bride, but mostly because she had discovered over the seven years she had been married to Amar that a happy home life depended on keeping him humored. Amar's mood had been souring since Mr. Dasgupta announced at the last monthly meeting of the Calcutta Heritage Society of Northern California that he had accepted a job offer in Bangalore; when crossed, Amar was given to long spells of sudden withdrawal.

Shefali's was a progressive version of the traditional "arranged" marriage, which meant that she and Amar Sinha had been allowed one unchaperoned meeting over coffee and pakoras in an under-lighted, over-airconditioned Park Street restaurant in Calcutta, but their Internet-savvy parents had done the scouting and culling of spousal candidates. The two sets of parents had drawn up their short lists after surreptitiously researching family histories and reputations, ferreting out hereditary illnesses, and checking out horoscopes for cosmic compatibility. Before the meeting with Amar, Shefali had drained three iced coffees with three potential husbands in the same Park Street restaurant. All four shortlisted bridegrooms were Calcutta-born ethnic Bengalis of the *kayastha*[1] caste, working as engineers abroad. Of the four, however, only Amar, like Shefali's brothers, was a graduate of St. Xavier's College and the Indian Institute of Technology at Kharagpur, but unlike her brothers, he had gone on to Stanford University for an M.B.A. degree, co-founded a social media start-up in Palo Alto, and become a U.S. citizen. He had taken a twenty-day "wedding leave" from work to choose a bride from his parents' short list of five and marry her before returning home to Palo Alto. Shefali had found each of the four contenders acceptable, but, when her parents announced Amar the winner, she'd been relieved that marriage would deposit her in California instead of Dubai or Saskatoon or Hamburg.

Pretty almost to the point of being vain about her looks, a French Honors graduate of an elite women's college run by a European order of nuns, and the great-granddaughter of a Calcutta High Court barrister[2] who had been knighted when the subcontinent was part of the British Empire, Shefali was confident she more than met the Sinha family's baseline requirement of pleasing looks, social poise, and respectable pedigree. But Mrs. Sinha wasted three precious days of Amar's leave airing her doubts that the only daughter of a rich family was capable of the selfless devotion required of the wife of "a genius" and "a future Nobel Prize winner." All tactics being fair in Calcutta's com-

---

1. The name of a prominent Hindu caste in India.—Ed.
2. British word for a particular type of lawyer.—Ed.

THE GOING-BACK PARTY (2012) | *357*

petitive matrimonial market, Shefali's mother had been ready to lie about the untested selflessness of her overindulged daughter, but she hadn't needed to, because to Mr. Sinha, Shefali's father's standing in the Calcutta Chamber of Commerce mattered more than imagined or real flaws in Shefali's character. For Shefali's relatives, Amar's U.S. citizenship and dollar salary (staggering when converted into rupees) trumped his asthma and the suicide death of a maternal aunt. Amar and Shefali became husband and wife exactly two weeks after their formal betrothal, and Shefali kept to herself her romantic daydreams of the Dubai-based runner-up bridegroom.

IT IS A COOL SUNDAY AFTERNOON in late May in Palo Alto, and the Sinhas' guests who had gathered over a buffet lunch to say goodbye to Mr. and Mrs. Dasgupta and their two daughters, have wandered off to the garden to admire Shefali's tidy flowerbeds and jasmine-covered pergola or settled into deck chairs by the heated pool. Shefali—exhausted from having cooked prawn cutlets, chicken chops, three different kinds of freshwater fish curry, mutton curry, egg curry, *aloo gobi*, vegetable *daalna*, crisp-fried slices of okra and bitter gourd, as well as Bengali banquet staples such as pilau with cashews and raisins, steamed Govinda *bhog* rice, *dal* with *barhi*, *loochi* and *payesh*[3]—stays back in the emptied kitchen. Amar insists she cook Bengali delicacies when they have Bengali friends over, so she starts marinating and prepping three days before any party. In her social circle, for a homemaker wife to hire a catering service is to admit to laziness. Shefali's secret vice is reading recipes for casserole dishes in American cookbooks she borrows from the library. A whole meal in one pot! It's more a revenge fantasy than vice, she admits. Only an audacious Bengali, like Rupa Roy the widow next door, would have the nerve to serve a simple casserole to guests. She could load the dishwasher. There are enough pots and skillets in the double sink and stacks of platters and bowls on the counters to warrant three loads. Her cleaning woman comes on Tuesdays and Thursdays, and this is Sunday. She should at least start rinsing the silverware. Amar had urged her to use paper plates and plastic glasses. What does she want to prove?

The older of the Dasgupta daughters saunters in on high heels to refill her water glass. She manages to make pre-stressed blue jeans and a crisp white shirt look expensively stylish. Her mother says she is thirteen, but because of her well-developed bosom and shapely hips, she looks older.

---

3. *Daalna* is a special kind of curry, *barhi* are a type of date, *loochi* are Bengali flatbreads, and *payesh* is a milky rice pudding.—Ed.

"Oh, Auntie," the girl exclaims, sweeping blue bangs off her prominent forehead, "Mummy's[4] going to miss you! She was saying that to Daddy just last night . . ." but stops abruptly to dart into the dining room and clear the cluttered tops of the dining table and the sideboard.

Shefali is suddenly seeing her state-of-the art hospitality through the girl's pitying eyes. "Oh, there isn't that much cleaning up to do. Really." But the girl ignores her and carries a stack of dirty dishes into the kitchen. "Really!" This time it's an admonition. Shefali has refused all offers of help from her guests. She plants herself in front of the dishwasher before the teenager can yank its door open.

"Are you sure, Auntie?" The teenager dries her hand on the monogrammed hand towel that Shefali holds out to her. "Looks like an awful lot to me. That's one of the many things Daddy says Mummy should be pleased about. He says, 'Consider yourself lucky. You'll never have to wash another dish. In Bangalore, you'll sit leg upon leg.' Daddy's job comes with a big company house in Dollar Colony and servants, a cook, chowkidar,[5] driver, can you believe? Daddy tells Mummy all she has to do is choose the furniture." The teenager can't seem to contain her excitement. She, her mother, and her eleven-year-old sister will fly to Bangalore next week, a full month ahead of her father, to set up house.

Mr. Dasgupta had grown up despairingly poor in a Shyambazar tenement, his schoolteacher father having been killed in his early thirties in a bus accident: this is common knowledge in the Bengali community. The girl with blue streaks in her hair was born in San Jose, when her father was a graduate student at San Jose State and supporting his mother and unmarried sisters in Calcutta as well as his wife and infant daughter on a research assistantship. He has done well enough since those early years of hardship, but it is also common knowledge that he has not done as well as the majority of the Calcutta Heritage Society trustees, certainly not as well as Amar. Shefali understands that the Dasgupta girl boasting of her father's new job perks has equated moving to Dollar Colony with moving into a gated class of glamor and wealth. What an absurd name for a housing complex! Shefali has never visited Bangalore or any town in South India. She visualizes Dollar Colony as a block of affluent mansions on a Bollywood lot. Bollywood delivers on its promises. Always. Romance, intrigue, swashbuckling adventure forever! She inserts herself in the Dasguptas' Bangalore home even as she guides the gushing girl to-

---

4. "Mommy," rather than this British usage, might have been a more obvious word choice. But "Mummy" aptly reflects the different cultural influences—Indian, British, Canadian, American—on Mukherjee's writing.—Ed.

5. An Indian gatekeeper or watchman.—Ed.

ward the kitchen's French doors that open on the poolside patio. "I'll join all of you in a minute. Oh, is it too nippy outdoors? Tell the ladies I'm making *masala chai*. That should hit the spot, don't you think? And just holler for shawls if anyone's chilly." She is thankful for the Bollywood fantasy the thirteen-year-old has sown in the parched heart of a thirty-nine-year-old housewife. Happiness isn't necessarily beyond reach.

Come to think of it, in the long cocktail hours that preceded his signaling her to lay the buffet table, Amar's face had expressed contentment, though at the time, she had confused the placid slackness of contentment with the onset of drunkenness. In the dining room when the Treasurer of the Calcutta Heritage Society had raised a glass of single malt—the Treasurer's third or was it his fourth?—and made a flowery speech about "our cherished hostess' cookery prowess," Amar had shouted the loudest "Hear! Hear!" She'd covered her ears, embarrassed at his tipsy behavior. What if, in the clumsy ways of a "genius," he had actually meant the praise? Guiltily she hauls down the huge aluminum *dekchi* she reserves for boiling *chai* when she has thirty or more tea connoisseurs as guests. All Calcuttans, especially the expatriate ones, are tea snobs.

Shefali has worked hard at acquiring traditional Bengali wifely virtues. She is a perfectionist: she recognizes this as a serious character flaw, especially serious because she has allowed her goals in life to be set by people who have authority over her, but she is remorseless in her pursuit of those goals. Back in the Calcutta convent school, she had gratified Mauritius-born Mother Véronique who had assigned her the role of Athalie in Racine's *Athalie* with the Parisian precision of her French accent. Even Amar's skeptical mother has had to admit that she has been a good daughter-in-law, except for . . . with Amar's mother there's always an "except for," but Amar and she are trying, and the ob-gynecologist at the second fertility clinic offers hope.

The sweet, milky tea she has boiled in the *dekchi* is ready, but Shefali shrinks from having to pour the tea into bone china cups, line them in neat rows on the two lacquer trays that Amar brought back from his last business trip to Vietnam, and carry them outdoors to guests. Instead, from behind gauzy white curtains of a small back window in the kitchen, she spies on her silk *kurta*[6]-pajama-clad husband, who sits barefoot and cross-legged on a wicker chaise in the shade of a young red-leaf Japanese maple. Of all the trees and shrubs in the backyard, this struggling tree, which she has nurtured back from windburn, is her favorite. Amar is in deep conversation with Mr. Dasgupta, whom she can only see in profile as he smokes a cigarette, his back pressed hard into

---

6. South Asian man's shirt.—Ed.

the scrawny trunk of the Japanese maple. No, more accurately, Amar is doing all the talking, and Mr. Dasgupta, a condescending smile on his fleshy face, careless fingers bruising vulnerable leaves, is pretending to listen. She stifles the impulse to rush outdoors and rescue her tree. And Amar. But Amar, deep into a monologue she can't hear, seems oblivious to insults. He hasn't looked this animated in weeks. To deflect pity for him, she reminds herself that Mr. Dasgupta, for all his show of indolent superiority, is a middle-aged professional who was pink-slipped five or more months ago by the San Jose construction company he worked for and whose home has been foreclosed upon. Word of calamity and sex scandal spreads fast within the expatriate Bengali community. He has to know that the bulletins about his misfortunes have made the rounds. That explains why all through the elaborate lunch, Mr. Dasgupta raved about India's current economic boom. "Mark my words," he had prophesied, "China's the hare that'll lose the race to India's tortoise!"

Of the two men she is spying on, she feels sorrier for Amar. He is too ready to believe Mr. Dasgupta's self-serving pronouncements about the world economy. Pity for one's spouse has no place in marriages like hers. She must distract herself with uplifting duties. The *chai* has been simmering too long, and a brown, silky film has already formed on its neglected surface. Is that a tiny smudge from her fingertip on the gold rim of a teacup? But the tableau of the two men, host and guest of honor, keeps her rooted. Amar the actor in the tableau seems more physically real than Amar the husband of nine years. His ears stick out like large, stiffly spread wings from either side of his head. The ruched long sleeves of his fancy silk *kurta* are too short to cover up the wiry pelt on his simian arms. Once upon a time she had been a romantic young bride-in-waiting.

Pity for Amar loses itself in a brackish pool of self-pity as she watches five teenagers in bright sweaters and skinny jeans approach Amar and Mr. Dasgupta with the purposefulness of young people going on to another party, a more fun party where they can drink, dance, flirt, out of the censorious sight of their elders. Do they do drugs at these parties? Shefali pities them; wait, she envies them more than she pities them. They cohabit contiguous worlds: the permissive world of Silicon Valley high-schoolers and the repressive, reputation-obsessed world of their immigrant parents. They thrive on secrets. The parents know not to ask, and the children know not to share all they think and do.

Amar doesn't hide his disappointment at being interrupted by the Indian-American teenagers, who have been brought up to recite effusive thank-yous to hosts, no matter how boring the social event. But Mr. Dasgupta is suddenly all charm and gallantry. He swivels sharply to face the smiling youngsters.

THE GOING-BACK PARTY (2012) | *361*

Oh, the cruelty of his casual abandonment of a needy host! Shefali doesn't miss Mr. Dasgupta's roguish smile as he focuses on the oldest of the five. Nor the young woman's shy pleasure at the flirtatious attention he is paying her. She recognizes the young woman as one of the crippled Mr. Chowdhury's three orphaned nieces, though until this afternoon Shefali had not noticed how pretty she is, especially when she stands, slim body tautly angled away from the middle-aged flatterer, and smoothes imaginary tangles out of her wavy, waist-long hair. In fact, until this moment, Shefali had dismissed this teenager and her sisters as dreary youngsters obsessed with winning Spelling Bees and Science Fair Prizes. Is she the Chowdhurys' niece that's headed for Princeton on a scholarship in the fall? Oh dear, the young woman's flushed acceptance of his compliment has emboldened Mr. Dasgupta. He glides closer to his prey. His outstretched hand accidentally touches her hip, but he doesn't spring back, embarrassed. His fingers skim the shiny locks falling around the girl's shoulders, and then, in a triumphant gesture, plucks something out of her hair—a dry leaf or wilted petal? No, it has to be a bug, because when he holds it out to her—a grotesque creature on a steady, heroic palm—he is rewarded with grateful shrieks of girlish fright. The teenagers, all five of them, relax only when Mr. Dasgupta flicks the bug off his palm into the dense groundcover. Amar, too, must have witnessed this charade of chivalry. Amar's initial disappointment has deepened into sullen bitterness. Shefali should run to his side, she should comfort him, should tell him Mr. Dasgupta didn't deserve his respect. Except that she is fascinated by the middle-aged Mr. Dasgupta's next gesture, fascinated because she is shocked. He pulls the shy girl out of the comforting knot of her girlfriends and presses her head and shoulders against his chest in a hug. It is simultaneously a congratulatory gesture and a fatherly farewell. After all, the Chowdhurys' niece is headed for Princeton, he permanently for India, and this is a going-back-home party in his honor. To interpret the embrace less innocently is to confess to a capacity for lewd fantasy.

The teenagers move off as a group toward parked cars. Amar swings his legs off the chaise and looks for his leather *chappals*[7] in the nearest flowerbed, where a guest's child or pet dog may have hidden them. By now his disappointment has deepened into bitterness. Mr. Dasgupta, too, ambles toward the house, probably to say goodbye to her before he herds his wife and daughters for the ride back to Fremont. There's a spring in his walk—he wears smart, tasseled loafers, not sloppy *chappals* like the other men at the party—and a cocky lift to his chin. And suddenly she gets it: he is a die-hard optimist. He may have lost his job; he is certainly about to lose his house; but he hasn't lost

---

7. Indian slippers or sandals.—Ed.

his belief in his right to romance. There's a lesson to be learned from what she is witnessing. She must not confuse "romance" with "love." Romance delivers flesh wounds; love kills, then self-destructs. She must become wise enough now to avoid love.

The tableau having dissolved outdoors, Shefali is free to turn away from the window, to skim the milky film off the *chai* and bring it back to a gentle boil; she is finally free to serve perfect tea as she'd promised to her remaining guests.

Late that night Amar surprises Shefali with a question. They are in bed, she watching an episode of "The Good Wife" ON DEMAND and he tracking his investments on his laptop, when he asks, "Are you jealous of Mrs. Dasgupta?" Shefali is so absorbed in the legal sleuthing tactics her favorite character, Kalindi, the leather-booted Indo-American investigator, has just employed to insinuate herself into a locked apartment, that she lets Amar repeat his question before turning on her side toward him, and asking, "What for?"

"I'm thinking of retiring."

Kalindi scrapes powdery dust of crucial evidence off an ineptly vacuumed rug and struts out of the front door of the apartment she had no right to enter.

"No matter what, no money worries for you, remember that. Not like for the Dasgupta women."

In the Sinha home, retirement is an unacknowledged synonym for repatriation to India. Amar is forty-four, but she guesses that he has already made up his mind. She wonders, though, what he means by "no matter what." Quitting his job? Being crippled by a stroke like Mr. Chowdhury? Dropping dead on the golf course like Rupa's husband, Dr. Roy, who had been their first fertility specialist? Unlike her, Amar has met all goals he set himself as an IIT student; maybe that's why now he is mysteriously, profoundly unhappy. No point in trying to argue him out of his decision. She is certain of this. What she can't figure out is how and for how long she can delay his abandoning this life they have made together, just the two of them, in Palo Alto. If she were to provoke or soothe him into opening up, there would be no going back to the neutral space that is domestic tranquility.

A week after the going-back party for the Dasgupta family, Amar leaves on a business trip that will take him to Malaysia, Thailand, Singapore and Indonesia. Every day he skypes Shefali. He is tired of all his business travels, he says, bland hotel décor framing his face. He worries that she is too depressed to cook healthy meals, or any meal, just for herself. Is Rupa Roy stopping by regularly as she'd promised? If not, call Rupa, he pleads, she is such a live wire, she's just the right person to drag a lonely neighbor to shopping malls and restaurants.

Rupa has certainly kept her promise, but in her own way. She has texted Shefali every day to ask if she needs anything. Rupa is big-hearted and because she is eager to give of herself to the needy, always busy; she is also an attractive, sought-after widow in her early forties. Her gold Lexus is in her driveway only on rare evenings. To appease Amar, who has gone on from Kuala Lumpur to Bangkok, Shefali leaves a message on Rupa's cell phone: Amar sends his regards. Let's get together for coffee. How about early next week?

An hour after she has made the call, Rupa shows up at her front door. Rupa's Lexus is in the Sinhas' driveway, which must mean she is dropping in on her way to somewhere else.

"Hey, you sounded lonely. Are you doing okay? When does Amar get back?" Rupa strides into the over-furnished foyer. In her suede leggings, crisp white shirt, asymmetrical suede vest and bright orange booties, she looks efficient. Not quite a Kalinda, but definitely a woman ready to take on difficult "projects." Oh dear, does Rupa consider her a "project"? She is about to invite the neighbor into her living room, and just to prove that she is doing more than okay, offer a glass of wine instead of the usual tea or coffee, when Rupa announces, "I've come to kidnap you for an hour or so. I'm delivering dinner to Mr. Dasgupta. That poor man is so lonely and helpless without his family. Feeding him is the least we can do. He'll enjoy the company. The Heritage Society members don't bother to visit him much anymore."

And that's how lust sneaks into the life of a woman like Shefali Sinha, who has been a gratifying daughter and attentive wife. One weekday afternoon you arrive in a do-good neighbor's Lexus at an ugly house with a "foreclosure" sign in the front yard and, carrying a care package of four casserole dinners in a four-tier stainless steel tiffin-carrier,[8] you walk up the weed-sprouting brick path to the porch, the door opens wide even before you ring the bell, and oh dear, oh dear, you are standing on the edge of a precipice, thrilled and ready for take-off.

This time Mr. Dasgupta's charm and gallantry are focused on *her*. She doesn't care if her face gives away the joy she feels as she hands over the heavy tiffin-carrier. Casserole cuisine by Rupa, special delivery by Shefali. Rupa's boots make clicking noises on the brick path as she follows with a basket of flowers from her garden, store-bought snacks and a thermos. Shefali is glad that there is someone to bear witness. There's no going back, even if she chooses not to go forward. She will learn Mr. Dasgupta's first name; she will coo that first name, maybe only in her fantasies, into Mr. Dasgupta's ear. Who would have thought that hairy ears could so excite her? To impress her, he will

---

8. "Tiffin" is the name for a light Indian meal.—Ed.

tell her about how good his life has been and how much better it's about to become, and this time he'll be a skilled storyteller and she a rapt listener.

Shefali sails into the kitchen ahead of Mr. Dasgupta and Rupa. The shelves are mostly empty, the appliances smudgy with grease marks. She pulls open the drawer under the stove for a pan in which she can heat up this night's dinner. This is not like being a housewife. She is playing at keeping house. She will be turning on the oven for a handsome man she hardly knows but who makes her feel special. There is a tender intimacy in this imagined relationship of Mr. Dasgupta and her as lovers. The tenderness gathers and swells, enveloping the ugly house. There is no longer need for evasive silences. No need for perfectionist striving, no need at all for repressive dutifulness. Her imaginary lover will—no, *shall*—usher her into that space within her where all doubts are stilled and bliss reigns.

AFTERWORD

Lysley Tenorio

In the second sentence of "A Weekend," the opening story of this volume, the narrator says, "I am here" and repeats herself, just one paragraph later: "Yes, I am here." The narrator is Tara, a young Indian woman newly arrived from Calcutta (now Kolkata), studying at a midwestern college. Bharati Mukherjee herself was a graduate student at the University of Iowa when she wrote this story for her M.F.A. thesis, still in her early twenties, also a recent arrival from Calcutta. Having grown up privileged and overprotected in a large Brahmin family (Mukherjee once said she wasn't allowed to walk down a street alone until she was twenty years old), one might imagine her reading these words aloud as she typed them on the page—*I am here, yes, I am here*—a statement of disbelief and wonder, tinged with uncertainty and hope.

Given the body of work to come—eight novels, two books of nonfiction, two short story collections, and now, finally, this book of her collected stories—I suspect that Mukherjee, if perhaps subconsciously, wrote these lines as a kind of insistence, a demand that her presence in America—a destiny of her own willful making—be acknowledged as vital and necessary, as integral to the American reality as any other American's, immigrant or otherwise. It's a familiar, frustrating, and powerful feeling, this yearning for recognition, to know with absolute certainty that you belong.

For a long time, I didn't know I'd felt this way myself.

I was a junior at UC Berkeley when I picked up a copy of Mukherjee's second story collection, *The Middleman and Other Stories*. She was my professor at the time (to fulfill a graduation requirement, I took her History of the

Short Story class), and one freezing night, sitting in the kitchen of my unheated Oakland apartment, I started reading "Fighting for the Rebound," the fifth story in the book. Barely half a page in, I read this: "Blanquita speaks six languages, her best being Tagalog, Spanish, and American. . . . Back in Manila, she took a crash course in making nice to Americans, before her father sent her over. In her family they called her Baby."

Two words jumped out at me: *Tagalog* and *Baby*. Tagalog, of course, is the most commonly spoken language in the Philippines, which my parents and older siblings spoke at home (raised in California, in English, I couldn't speak it myself). And I grew up around women who called themselves Baby, a common Filipino nickname.

I read to the end. Though Blanquita wasn't the protagonist (she was the girlfriend of the narrator, a money manager named Griff), she was vividly alive on the page, a hopeless romantic not above playing relationship mind games ("You don't love me, Griff"). She was brash, melodramatic, exasperating, memorable.

She was also the first Filipino character I'd seen in American fiction.

The realization was thrilling: to see a Filipino on the page, even one whose life was nothing like my own, felt like the best kind of familiarity; fiction had never felt so real. But I was deeply troubled, too. My whole life I'd been a reader, so why had it taken so long to see a Filipino in the pages of the stories and books I'd read and loved? That absence was palpable now, that sense of missingness suddenly—painfully—visible in books, TV, movies, politics—the means of my participation and investment in American culture, *my* culture.

I felt like screaming: *I'm here.*

I TOOK A FICTION workshop with Bharati Mukherjee the following semester. My stories read, as one student pointed out, like immigrant-tragedies-of-the-week, in which dark immigrant secrets were revealed on page nine, formulaically resolved by page twelve. In one particularly rough session, Mukherjee had one positive comment to say about my story, which was about a young immigrant woman forced to sell her baby sister while (for reasons I fortunately cannot recall) struggling for an A in her drama class. "I love the characters' names," Mukherjee said, a way of being honest without being brutal. If her teaching style was often diplomatic, she was always practical, pinpointing where a story succeeded, where it fell flat. Though it was a political rallying cry that inspired my stories—*We are immigrants! We are here!*—Mukherjee didn't overemphasize the political implications of our work or the authorial visions behind it. Instead, she brought our focus to the page, showing us how the right words, sentences, and scenes could transform mere text into something close to real-time experience.

She could be wonderfully blunt. Once, a classmate asked what it was like being a student at the famed Iowa Writers' Workshop. "You've got to have a hard ass," she said, and though I wasn't *exactly* sure what she meant (*be tough? be stubborn?*), I wrote it down anyway. When we learned that she was giving a reading for her new novel, *The Holder of the World*, at Cody's Books in Berkeley, we asked whether we should show up extra early to beat the crowds. "I'm not Anne Rice," she said, glasses low on her face, and left it at that. She shared stories about elevator run-ins with Billy Idol and John Ritter, about shopping trips for a punk rock leather outfit to play Princess Bubbles, a backup singer for the Stephen King/Amy Tan band, The Rock Bottom Remainders. For our final class, she invited us to her San Francisco flat. I'd never been inside the home of an actual *writer* before, much less a *flat*, and I'd imagined memorizing the titles of the books on her shelves, stealing glances of her notebooks and rough drafts, anything instructive for becoming a brilliant writer. Instead, I found myself lingering in the corner of her kitchen, watching her prepare an Indian meal for my seventeen classmates and me. I was still intimidated by her, too awkward and shy to make real conversation, but right before we sat down to eat, I pulled my camera from my backpack, worked up the courage to ask whether I could take her photo. "Of course," she said, then turned from the boiling pot and smiled, wooden spoon in hand. I still have that picture.

I WASN'T A GOOD WRITER, but, under Mukherjee's guidance, I was becoming a better one. I focused more on the craft, less on the art. I learned that real labor—the hard work of scenes, sentences, words—was more in my control than any grand authorial vision or political message.

I learned from her outside the classroom, too.

Of course, I read all her stories. *The Middleman* was already like a bible to me, and her first story collection, *Darkness*, was another masterclass in the short form, the stories sharp and spare, surprising in their emotional breadth (one story in the collection, "Saints," narrated by a teenaged boy, was a direct influence on "Superassassin," the first story I ever published). I spent days and nights at the Berkeley library, hunting down any article or essay she'd written, every interview she'd done. One evening, on a microfiche copy (yes, *microfiche*—this was pre-Internet, after all) of *The New York Times Book Review*, I found her essay, "Immigrant Writing: Give Us Your Maximalists!" in which she wrote, "All around me I see the face of America changing. So do you, if you live in cities, teach in universities, ride public transport. But where, in fic-

368 | AFTERWORD

tion, do you read of it? Who, in other words, speaks for us, the new Americans from nontraditional immigrant countries? Which is another way of saying, in this altered America, who speaks for you?"

Later, I learned she did an interview with Bill Moyers and that—*eureka!*—the library had a VHS copy (again, pre-Internet). I checked it out immediately, watched it again and again: at one point in the conversation, she rejects the myth of the melting pot, preferring to see America as a "fusion chamber," one in which "you and I are both radically changed by the presence of new immigrants." *Fusion chamber!* It made perfect sense: I imagined America as an enormous Plexiglas capsule, lights crackling and gamma rays firing, the whole population inside in mid-mutual-transformation, an idea she discussed in an interview with *Mother Jones*: "my literary agenda begins by acknowledging that America has transformed me. It does not end until I show that I (along with the hundreds of thousands of immigrants like me) am minute by minute transforming America."

Mukherjee's words, written or spoken, were like a mantra—a way to live, a reason to write. Looking back, you might even say that I was obsessed with Bharati Mukherjee. But *obsessed* isn't the right word; I admired but didn't idolize her—Berkeley in the 1990s kept me too cynical for that—nor was I a kind of literary fanboy. What might have been an obsession was, in its truest, uttermost form, *inspiration*, a word whose rampantly sentimental overuse has nearly rendered it meaningless. But if inspiration really is *the power of moving the intellect or emotions*, then that's what Mukherjee's work was for me. Her short stories, particularly those in *The Middleman*, jump-started my brain, helped me see the vitality and urgency of the contemporary immigrant story, and that my own fiction, about Filipinos and Filipino Americans in America, could have a place in the American literary mainstream and, if I was lucky, perhaps even change it, one story at a time.

A few years after graduating from Berkeley, I applied to M.F.A. programs in creative writing; Mukherjee kindly agreed to write me a letter of recommendation and even took the time to read my writing sample, a short story I'd written specifically for the application. "You are the heir," she told me after reading it. We were in her office at Berkeley, and for a millisecond I wanted to burst out of my chair from the thrill of validation and the belief that she was somehow passing along a baton to me, trusting me with the responsibility of carrying out her own literary vision. But I fell back to earth just as quickly, realizing that her statement was mostly a kindness, a bit of encouragement and wish of good luck. But perhaps it was acknowledgment, too, her understanding of how much she'd meant to me—as writer, teacher, immigrant, Ameri-

AFTERWORD | *369*

can—both inside the classroom and out, and from the kitchen corner in her flat in San Francisco.

———

I MIGHT NOT BE *THE HEIR*, but in the hopes that my students might be, I pass along Mukherjee's stories to them, too.

The immigrant's story, I tell them, possesses the tenets of character-driven narrative. There is the inherent before and after that comes with leaving one home and arriving in another, and with that, the possibility for change, for better or worse, however great or small. The immigrant's story often culminates in a measure of gain against loss and, just like life, can never truly be resolved. At best, it might linger with possibility, making us question everything that's come before and what might lie ahead.

"The Management of Grief." "Saints." "A Wife's Story." "The Tenant." "A Father." So many others. Mukherjee's stories are among the finest examples of the short form itself and enduring proof of the vitality and potency of the immigrant narrative. In a time when people are claiming singular definitions of what it means to be American, when the power of identity is being misused for separatist gains, we need her stories now, more than ever.

How lucky we are, then, to have them gathered in a single volume, to be with Mukherjee's characters, these vibrant, brilliant, foolish, gutsy, unforgettable individuals who cross over and say to the world, to themselves, *I am here, yes, I am here.*

And to the reader: *So are you.*

Bharati Mukherjee (1940–2017) was the first South Asian American writer to receive major popular and critical acclaim. In a career spanning fifty years, she published eight novels, two long works of nonfiction, two collections of short stories, and many essays and reviews, and won the National Book Critics Circle Award for Fiction in 1988 for *The Middleman and Other Stories*.

Ruth Maxey is Associate Professor of Modern American Literature at the University of Nottingham and the author of *South Asian Atlantic Literature, 1970–2010* and *Understanding Bharati Mukherjee*.

Also in the series *Asian American History and Culture*:

Marguerite Nguyen, *America's Vietnam: The* Longue Durée *of U.S. Literature and Empire*

Vanita Reddy, *Fashioning Diaspora: Beauty, Femininity, and South Asian American Culture*

Audrey Wu Clark, *The Asian American Avant-Garde: Universalist Aspirations in Modernist Literature and Art*

Eric Tang, *Unsettled: Cambodian Refugees in the New York City Hyperghetto*

Jeffrey Santa Ana, *Racial Feelings: Asian America in a Capitalist Culture of Emotion*

Jiemin Bao, *Creating a Buddhist Community: A Thai Temple in Silicon Valley*

Elda E. Tsou, *Unquiet Tropes: Form, Race, and Asian American Literature*

Tarry Hum, *Making a Global Immigrant Neighborhood: Brooklyn's Sunset Park*

Ruth Mayer, *Serial Fu Manchu: The Chinese Supervillain and the Spread of Yellow Peril Ideology*

Karen Kuo, *East Is West and West Is East: Gender, Culture, and Interwar Encounters between Asia and America*

Kieu-Linh Caroline Valverde, *Transnationalizing Viet Nam: Community, Culture, and Politics in the Diaspora*

Lan P. Duong, *Treacherous Subjects: Gender, Culture, and Trans-Vietnamese Feminism*

Kristi Brian, *Reframing Transracial Adoption: Adopted Koreans, White Parents, and the Politics of Kinship*

Belinda Kong, *Tiananmen Fictions outside the Square: The Chinese Literary Diaspora and the Politics of Global Culture*

Bindi V. Shah, *Laotian Daughters: Working toward Community, Belonging, and Environmental Justice*

Cherstin M. Lyon, *Prisons and Patriots: Japanese American Wartime Citizenship, Civil Disobedience, and Historical Memory*

Shelley Sang-Hee Lee, *Claiming the Oriental Gateway: Prewar Seattle and Japanese America*

Isabelle Thuy Pelaud, *This Is All I Choose to Tell: History and Hybridity in Vietnamese American Literature*

Christian Collet and Pei-te Lien, eds., *The Transnational Politics of Asian Americans*

Min Zhou, *Contemporary Chinese America: Immigration, Ethnicity, and Community Transformation*

Kathleen S. Yep, *Outside the Paint: When Basketball Ruled at the Chinese Playground*

Benito M. Vergara Jr., *Pinoy Capital: The Filipino Nation in Daly City*

Jonathan Y. Okamura, *Ethnicity and Inequality in Hawai'i*

Sucheng Chan and Madeline Y. Hsu, eds., *Chinese Americans and the Politics of Race and Culture*

K. Scott Wong, *Americans First: Chinese Americans and the Second World War*

Lisa Yun, *The Coolie Speaks: Chinese Indentured Laborers and African Slaves in Cuba*

Estella Habal, *San Francisco's International Hotel: Mobilizing the Filipino American Community in the Anti-eviction Movement*

Thomas P. Kim, *The Racial Logic of Politics: Asian Americans and Party Competition*

Sucheng Chan, ed., *The Vietnamese American 1.5 Generation: Stories of War, Revolution, Flight, and New Beginnings*

Antonio T. Tiongson Jr., Edgardo V. Gutierrez, and Ricardo V. Gutierrez, eds., *Positively No Filipinos Allowed: Building Communities and Discourse*

Sucheng Chan, ed., *Chinese American Transnationalism: The Flow of People, Resources, and Ideas between China and America during the Exclusion Era*

Rajini Srikanth, *The World Next Door: South Asian American Literature and the Idea of America*

Keith Lawrence and Floyd Cheung, eds., *Recovered Legacies: Authority and Identity in Early Asian American Literature*

Linda Trinh Võ, *Mobilizing an Asian American Community*

Franklin S. Odo, *No Sword to Bury: Japanese Americans in Hawai'i during World War II*

Josephine Lee, Imogene L. Lim, and Yuko Matsukawa, eds., *Re/collecting Early Asian America: Essays in Cultural History*

Linda Trinh Võ and Rick Bonus, eds., *Contemporary Asian American Communities: Intersections and Divergences*

Sunaina Marr Maira, *Desis in the House: Indian American Youth Culture in New York City*

Teresa Williams-León and Cynthia Nakashima, eds., *The Sum of Our Parts: Mixed-Heritage Asian Americans*

Tung Pok Chin with Winifred C. Chin, *Paper Son: One Man's Story*

Amy Ling, ed., *Yellow Light: The Flowering of Asian American Arts*

Rick Bonus, *Locating Filipino Americans: Ethnicity and the Cultural Politics of Space*

Darrell Y. Hamamoto and Sandra Liu, eds., *Countervisions: Asian American Film Criticism*

Martin F. Manalansan IV, ed., *Cultural Compass: Ethnographic Explorations of Asian America*

Ko-lin Chin, *Smuggled Chinese: Clandestine Immigration to the United States*

Evelyn Hu-DeHart, ed., *Across the Pacific: Asian Americans and Globalization*

Soo-Young Chin, *Doing What Had to Be Done: The Life Narrative of Dora Yum Kim*

Robert G. Lee, *Orientals: Asian Americans in Popular Culture*

David L. Eng and Alice Y. Hom, eds., *Q & A: Queer in Asian America*

K. Scott Wong and Sucheng Chan, eds., *Claiming America: Constructing Chinese American Identities during the Exclusion Era*

Lavina Dhingra Shankar and Rajini Srikanth, eds., *A Part, Yet Apart: South Asians in Asian America*

Jere Takahashi, *Nisei/Sansei: Shifting Japanese American Identities and Politics*

Velina Hasu Houston, ed., *But Still, Like Air, I'll Rise: New Asian American Plays*

Josephine Lee, *Performing Asian America: Race and Ethnicity on the Contemporary Stage*

Deepika Bahri and Mary Vasudeva, eds., *Between the Lines: South Asians and Postcoloniality*

E. San Juan Jr., *The Philippine Temptation: Dialectics of Philippines–U.S. Literary Relations*

Carlos Bulosan and E. San Juan Jr., eds., *The Cry and the Dedication*

Carlos Bulosan and E. San Juan Jr., eds., *On Becoming Filipino: Selected Writings of Carlos Bulosan*

Vicente L. Rafael, ed., *Discrepant Histories: Translocal Essays on Filipino Cultures*

Yen Le Espiritu, *Filipino American Lives*

Paul Ong, Edna Bonacich, and Lucie Cheng, eds., *The New Asian Immigration in Los Angeles and Global Restructuring*

Chris Friday, *Organizing Asian American Labor: The Pacific Coast Canned-Salmon Industry, 1870–1942*

Sucheng Chan, ed., *Hmong Means Free: Life in Laos and America*

Timothy P. Fong, *The First Suburban Chinatown: The Remaking of Monterey Park, California*

William Wei, *The Asian American Movement*

Yen Le Espiritu, *Asian American Panethnicity*

Velina Hasu Houston, ed., *The Politics of Life*

Renqiu Yu, *To Save China, To Save Ourselves: The Chinese Hand Laundry Alliance of New York*

Shirley Geok-lin Lim and Amy Ling, eds., *Reading the Literatures of Asian America*

Karen Isaksen Leonard, *Making Ethnic Choices: California's Punjabi Mexican Americans*

Gary Y. Okihiro, *Cane Fires: The Anti-Japanese Movement in Hawaii, 1865–1945*

Sucheng Chan, *Entry Denied: Exclusion and the Chinese Community in America, 1882–1943*